South Carolina

*Four Distinct Novels Set
in the Palmetto State*

Yvonne Lehman

BARBOUR BOOKS
An Imprint of Barbour Publishing, Inc.

After the Storm © 1999 by Barbour Publishing, Inc.
Catch of a Lifetime © 2000 by Barbour Publishing, Inc.
Somewhere a Rainbow © 1999 by Barbour Publishing, Inc.
Southern Gentleman © 1994 by Yvonne Lehman.

ISBN 1-58660-398-1

Cover photo: © PhotoDisc, Inc.

All Scripture quotations, unless otherwise noted, are taken from the King James Version of the Bible.

Published by Barbour Books, an imprint of Barbour Publishing, Inc., P.O. Box 719, Uhrichsville, Ohio 44683, www.barbourbooks.com

Member of the
Evangelical Christian
Publishers Association

Printed in the United States of America.
5 4 3

YVONNE LEHMAN

As an award-winning novelist from Black Mountain in the heart of North Carolina's Smoky Mountains, Yvonne has written several novels for Barbour Publishing's **Heartsong Presents** line. Her titles include *Southern Gentleman, Mountain Man,* which won a National Reader's Choice Award sponsored by a chapter of Romance Writers of America, *Secret Ballot,* and *The Stranger's Kiss.* Yvonne has published more than two dozen novels, including books in the Bethany House "White Dove" series for young adults. In addition to being an inspirational romance writer, she is also the founder of the Blue Ridge Christian Writers' Conference. She and her husband are the parents of four grown children and grandparents to several dear children.

After the Storm

To Lisa, Lori, Cindy, and Howard

Acknowledgment
"To Remember Me" reprinted courtesy of
The Living Bank, P.O. Box 6725, Houston, Texas 77265
Written by Robert N. Test, printed in the *Cincinnati Post*,
reprinted in *Reader's Digest*, appeared in "Dear Abby's"
syndicated column, December 1977.

Chapter 1

When the phone rang that evening in her mother's living room, Sharon pushed the remote control button to turn down the TV. She picked up the receiver on the second ring. "Earline Johnson's residence."

"Ma'am, this is the South Carolina State Police. We're trying to locate a Sharon Martin."

Something in his voice made her fingers tighten on the phone. "I'm Sharon Martin." Why would the state police be calling? "Is something wrong?"

"We're on our way to Mount Pleasant, Ms. Martin. Could you tell us which house?"

From U.S. Highway 17, coming from Charleston, there was only one main road into Mount Pleasant, and that was Coleman Boulevard. She gave directions from there. "The third driveway on the right," she said, "but what—"

"We need to talk to you, Ms. Martin. Is anyone with you?"

"Yes," she said instinctively, thinking that this was someone pretending to be the police so that they could find out if she were alone. But her mother lived here alone. Who in the area would know Sharon Martin? "I mean, no."

"We'll be right there, Ma'am."

After hearing the click, then a dial tone, Sharon mechanically hung up the phone. She picked up the remote and turned up the volume on *Wheel of Fortune* to try to convince herself everything was all right. Why hadn't the caller said what was wrong?

How did he know to ask for her? *The next of kin* leapt into her mind. Did her mother have a heart attack or something? Or was there an accident? If so, what about Robert? And Karen? And little Bobby? Oh, please, not little Bobby. They had taken him to the petting zoo that afternoon and were going to stop at McDonald's for supper. *Did. . .someone choke. . .or something?*

Sharon went to the bathroom to brush her hair, as if that mattered should she have to go somewhere. Her soft cotton shirt and matching beige wrap-around skirt were presentable. She put on lipstick. Her light blue eyes stared into the mirror at the woman whose face was starkly ashen. Mechanically, she brushed her short brown hair into its usual style—away from her face on one side and falling softly alongside her face on the other.

You're forty-three years old, Sharon Martin, her mind lectured. *You've lost a husband and survived that. But don't think negative thoughts. Just pray that all is well.*

Her shaky hand put down the brush. The officer hadn't mentioned her mother. He hadn't mentioned anyone. What did that mean? Why couldn't her mother—or Robert—or Karen—call? Why the police? She got her purse from the bedroom.

Her sandaled feet automatically returned her to the living room. The players on TV were smiling. The audience was applauding. Sharon walked to the front screen and held onto the door casing. A line of distant clouds over the horizon formed sleepy eyelids, fast closing over the evening sun. Her knees grew weak, so she stepped outside to sit on the porch swing.

The heady scent of magnolias, azaleas, and camellias filled her senses. The chill began to settle on her skin and shiver along her spine. She attributed it to the cooler air that followed the storm that had appeared so suddenly that afternoon. And her mother's home was nearer the ocean than Sharon's home in Los Angeles.

She kept swinging. She kept hugging her arms, even as the sky grayed and twilight fell. Lights appeared in windows of the white clapboard houses set in irregular patterns in this older section of a quiet residential area. A few houses were new, but most had been here for generations. Sharon's grandparents and now her mother had owned this house.

As Sharon pushed with her foot, the swing swayed, making its usually calming creak. However, an invading uneasiness threatened to permeate her body and mind.

She became acutely aware of the calls of children playing, dogs barking, insects beginning to sing. They always sang louder after a rain. Now they reminded her of the hum of an airplane when she was thousands of miles in the sky, knowing she might as well relax because everything was out of her control. That never stopped her from praying, though.

She hardly noticed when night fell.

Finally, car lights appeared. They flashed against trees far down the road, dipped, and were lost as they rose and fell at the bottom of the long driveway. Sharon and her friends used to play as though the car lights were eyes of monsters. They'd shoot with clothespin guns and the monster would disappear. Then another would come and meet the same fate.

This one kept coming. It made its way up the drive, then stopped on the gravel beside the house. Their shoes crunched on the gravel path leading to the front steps. She could see the two uniformed officers clearly until they stepped from the night that had at some point brightened, onto the porch, shadowed by the overhanging roof.

"Looks like nobody's here," said one of them in a deep voice. It must have been the heavyset one. The thinner, taller man touched his arm and turned his head toward Sharon.

"Sorry, Ma'am. I didn't see you there," said the first one. The police officer walked closer, took off his cap, and held it with both hands in front of him, his head bowed. "Sharon Martin?" he asked.

"Yes." She would volunteer what information she could. "My mother lives here. She's Earline Johnson."

He looked sad. His voice was even and sympathetic. "There's been an accident."

Sharon nodded, dreamlike, in that state somewhere between disbelief and reality. She'd been there before—several times. She'd known then too, but it still had to be confirmed. She was older now. Better able to deal with life's blows—perhaps. She drew in a breath. "How bad?"

"Your mother was killed. Also, Robert and Karen Martin."

Just. . .words, she told herself. *My mother. Robert. . .son of my flesh. . .my young, beautiful, precious son. His wife. No!* She tried to shake her head, but it wouldn't move. Her unblinking eyes stared at her fingers, clenched into fists.

Suddenly, heavy thick air seared her paralyzed throat and settled like hot lead across her chest. Her head came up. *Please, God, leave me something.* Her luminous eyes searched the shadowed figures. "Bobby?" she whispered.

"He's in the hospital. We can take you there."

"Yes," Sharon breathed. "Thank you." She stood, lost her balance, but the officer's hand came out to steady her.

"I'm sorry," she said.

"It's all right."

They went inside with her. Sharon picked up the remote, but the buttons looked blurry, so she walked over to the TV where everyone was still smiling and applauding and the wheel was still turning. It had seemed like an eternity for Sharon since that phone call. She pushed the off button.

The officer picked up her purse from the couch. "Is this yours?"

She took it.

"Can we lock up for you or anything?"

A sound came from Sharon's throat. *Lock up? Why? What was there that mattered? Things!* "The door locks when it closes."

She hurried outside, trying not to look. Her disobedient glance saw the door close. She heard the lock click.

She swayed. The anticipating officer grasped her elbow. *Focus on the window,* she told herself. Somewhere she'd heard that when a door closes, a window opens.

She feared the answer but had to ask, "Is Bobby badly hurt?"

Chapter 2

After reviewing all the information, Helen Gamble, a tall, thin woman wearing white, unlocked the door to the small room in one corner of the emergency room. Perspiration formed on her brow, despite the cold chills running up her spine.

Officer Leland had called from Mount Pleasant, saying he was bringing in Sharon Martin. During the fifteen years she'd been nursing supervisor, Helen had never faced the almost impossible task of confronting someone who had just lost not one, not two, but three—three loved ones. No amount of training or experience could prepare her for this.

Helen had lost her father when she was twenty-three and later felt she could empathize with the grieving and bereaved. But no way could she empathize with Sharon Martin. And how was she going to give the woman hope, yet be honest about that small boy whose chances were so slim? She prayed the little boy would not die before she went off duty at eleven. She'd quit her job before telling that woman she had nobody left alive.

Helen flipped the switch that flooded the small room with recessed fluorescent light. Her eyes swept over the muted brown-toned carpet, the lighter couch that looked like stiff, brushed tweed, its matching armchairs, the arrangement of faded paper flowers on the low wooden table, the two watercolor prints of pastel blooms without stems on the wall above the couch. The intent was to provide comfort, peace, stability, and easy cleaning.

The bereaved woman wouldn't really see it, Helen told herself—nor would she care. That was soon confirmed by the dazed look on Sharon Martin's face when she hurried through the door, flanked by two officers Helen recognized as Leland and Burris. Helen's professionalism clicked in, and she walked toward Sharon, a woman about her own age.

"This is Sharon Martin," Leland said.

Helen nodded. "I am Helen Gamble, the nursing supervisor."

"Can I see Bobby?" asked the distraught woman.

"Not just yet, Mrs. Martin. Let's go in here and sit down." Helen gestured toward the small room. "We can talk in there."

Swiftly, Sharon headed for the room.

"Is there anything else we can do?" asked Leland.

"No, thank you," Helen replied, seeing both regret and relief in the officers' eyes before they walked away. She knew they were sorry about this terrible tragedy yet relieved to be free of its burden. They could go now, relive it and talk about it for awhile, tell their families, and eventually put it away in the back of their minds where it belonged. Helen would have to live with it awhile longer. Sharon would have to live with it forever.

Sharon sat on the edge of the couch as the nursing supervisor—had she said her name was Helen?—said a few words with the officers. She braced herself as she watched Helen cross the room and sit beside her on the couch. Her mind barely registered the gentle pressure of the woman's hands when she reached to clasp Sharon's. Sharon blinked, trying to keep her hot tears from spilling down her face. She had to hold herself together for Bobby's sake.

"What did the police officers tell you?" Helen asked.

"Not very much," Sharon answered, lowering her head. *Not much? Only that Robert, and Karen, and Mother. . . What did the officer say? Something about the storm. Blinding rain. High winds. Maybe the car, or the tractor-trailer, hydroplaned on the rain-soaked highway. They didn't know details.*

Sharon looked up into the caring gray eyes, the kindly mature face of Helen Gamble. "They said. . .that Bobby is alive."

"Bobby is in surgery now," Helen said softly. "I can't tell you much more than that. He's in the best of hands," she said, trying to console. "Dr. Paul Thomas is one of our finest pediatric surgeons. Three other members of his team are assisting. Everything possible is being done."

Sharon nodded. "He has to be all right," she choked.

Helen nodded too and brushed at the wetness rolling down her cheeks. "I'm sorry," she said, letting go of Sharon's hands. She stood and reached into her pocket for a package of tissue.

"Don't apologize," Sharon replied with a trembly smile, taking the tissue Helen held out to her. "Thank you. . .for being here."

Helen gently placed her hand on Sharon's shoulder. "Sharon, do you happen to have type AB-negative blood?"

"I don't," Sharon replied fearfully. "That's Bobby's type! Surely you have it or can get it."

"Oh, yes. That's no problem," Helen quickly assured her, returning to the couch. "I just thought you might prefer to donate if you had his type."

"You'll let me know if you don't get a donor?" Sharon pled. She grabbed Helen's hand. "Promise me Bobby will have the needed blood. You won't let the supply get too low. Promise me."

"Yes, Sharon, yes, I promise," Helen said before Sharon could even finish her plea. She paused, and Sharon braced herself for more bad news.

"Sharon, there's another matter that I have to bring up."

"Another matter?"

Helen took a deep breath. "It's about organ donation, Sharon."

Sharon stared blankly in front of her. Organ donation? Did Bobby need an organ? "If I have anything he needs. . ."

"No, I mean. . ." Helen swallowed hard. "Your other family members. Robert's driver's license indicates he is a donor. However, we consult family members about this."

Sharon continued to stare. A look of horror crossed her face. She understood. She rose from the couch and gazed at the flowers without stems. After a long moment her head slowly turned and looked down at Helen. She tried to think of anything—but that. Then the head moved, and Helen's eyes met hers.

"We have to know soon," said the pale woman in white.

So others can live, Sharon was thinking. No, she wasn't really thinking. Inadvertently, thoughts of Robert, Karen, and her mother tripped across her mind. She sat down again.

"My mother mentioned it one time. When her driver's license was renewed they asked her if she wanted to be a donor. She laughed and said she was too old."

"She isn't," Helen said quietly. "What can't be used on patients can be used in research in medical schools."

Sharon's mind leaped back to high school days. Some students had laughed and others had vomited when they dissected frogs. She felt, now, like she might do one or the other. "Robert and Karen are so young. But it's the kind of thing they would want to do when they were older. . . . They were such good kids."

"I'm sure they were," Helen responded.

"I don't know," Sharon said distantly. "I don't know if they should be donors. I know it would help others, but. . .they're. . .my family."

Helen nodded, and Sharon noticed that the woman didn't push her one way or the other. "Is there anyone I can call for you?" Helen asked. "Relatives?"

"My mother has a sister in Wisconsin who's in a nursing home. She has Alzheimer's. I'm the only other relative that Robert has."

"And Robert's wife?" Helen asked.

Sharon's mouth fell open. She felt a wave of shock. "Karen's parents," she said in a whisper. "I have not thought. . .they have to be told."

"Where do they live, Sharon?"

"California. Los Angeles."

"There's a time difference. Would anyone be home?"

Sharon looked at her watch. James Davis owned a small accounting firm. He usually got home around six o'clock. Occasionally his wife, Mary, helped out in the office. School was out, and their teenagers could be anywhere. "Mary might be home," she said. "But I wouldn't want to tell her this if she's alone."

"It might be wise to wait," Helen agreed.

Sharon had mixed emotions. She didn't want to be the bearer of such tragic news. But it had to be done. And she was the only one who could do it. There were arrangements to make. She turned a pallid face to Helen. "Where. . .are they?" she asked.

Helen took a deep breath before answering. "They're in the ER on life support to keep the organs alive," she said with difficulty. "Would you like to see them?"

"No!" Sharon said immediately, then just as quickly said, "Yes!" She shook her head. "I don't know."

"That's all right. You don't have to decide now. Think about it." Helen paused, adding softly, "When you can. There's a waiting room outside Pediatric ICU. That's where Bobby will be taken after surgery. Or you could go to the chapel."

Sharon didn't want any of that. She wanted her family. She wanted to see Bobby. She didn't want to be making these decisions. Her options were limited. "Where is the chapel?"

Helen led her down the hall to a door with a cross on it. "I'll stay with you, if you like."

"I'd like to be alone for awhile," Sharon told her.

Helen handed her the package of tissues. "I'll be back later," she promised. "We also have a chaplain who will come by as soon as he can."

"Thank you," Sharon said. She stepped inside and closed the door.

She wanted to escape—escape from Helen's words. *"They're in the ER,"* *she'd said. All this talk about organs. . .being cut apart. . .my dear Robert. . .sweet* *Karen. . .my own mother. . .and yet. . .and yet. . .someone needs to donate blood for* *Bobby. What would happen if they didn't?*

And. . .and. . .do I never see them again? Do I remember them as they were? *Or. . .see them. . .mangled? I don't know! I don't know!*

Her eyes squeezed shut. Her fingers came up and grabbed bunches of hair from each side of her head. Her hands pulled—pulled as if trying to force out some answers from her mind. No answers came. Only pain. Slowly her grip loosened. Her hands fell limply to her sides. Her eyes opened.

For an instant, while her eyes adjusted to the different surroundings, she saw only the far wall where light radiated from behind a huge cross that reached to where crossbeams met at the apex of the ceiling. Facing that symbol of omniscient power, she felt afraid and uncertain. When Mitchell died, she'd found comfort, peace, acceptance. But this. . .this was too much. Darkness and despair threatened to overwhelm her.

As the room came into focus, she walked unsteadily down the narrow carpeted aisle that separated several rows of rich mahogany pews. About halfway down, she slid into one.

With her eyes fixed on the cross, she remembered when she'd been a young, single, frightened girl and had prayed that she wouldn't be pregnant. But she had been. Robert had been born. She'd been blessed with him for twenty-two years. She wanted him longer. But he was gone.

"Gone," she whispered in the awesome silence. "How can I stand it?"

Then, like a voice speaking in the dreadful silence, she saw the words inscribed in gold. The wooden strip along the wall below the cross read, "Come unto me, all ye that labour and are heavy laden, and I will give you rest. Matthew 11:28."

The realization was as clear as if the words had been spoken: If there was no help here, then there was none—anywhere.

Trembling, Sharon grasped the back of the pew in front of her and stood. With unsteady steps, she moved to the kneeling pad below the raised dais. She fell to her knees and looked up at the cross for a timeless moment.

With a cry, her hands clenched, her forearms reached out onto the dais, and her forehead touched the carpet between them.

"Please, help Bobby. Help. . .me," she implored weakly. And she sobbed—like a helpless child who needed to be cradled in her Father's arms.

Chapter 3

After her desolate wails subsided, Sharon lay drained. With her face turned away from the door and feeling an incredible sense of help-lessness, she allowed blessed blackness to overtake her.

A long time later, she heard a voice calling her out of the enveloping dark-ness, but her mind and body rebelled against it. Finally, sensing the urgency in the voice, Sharon tried to open her eyes, tried to move her limbs, but felt void of the ability to react.

Slowly, sensations began to come. Her eyes could move beneath closed lids. They did not want to open—did not want to see. Her hair felt wet and matted against the side of her face that lay against the carpet. She heard a raspy sound, then realized her mouth was open, taking in air down a dry and parched throat.

Why couldn't she move? Or feel anything? How long had she lain in that contorted position—half sitting, half lying? She willed her arms to move, but they lay lifeless against the nubby surface of the carpet. Her fingers tightly clutched a wet tissue.

She felt hands on her back, gently shaking, while a masculine voice demanded, "Mrs. Martin. Wake up. Wake up, Mrs. Martin."

Her eyes slowly opened. She saw the paneled wall. The cross. She felt cold. The hands felt warm. Then as the blood began to course through her veins like pinpricks, the flood of memory ripped through her heart.

Flinching, she closed her eyes again. But the insistent voice kept saying her name and the hands tried to move her arms. Had she fallen asleep? Or lost consciousness? What time was it? There was something she had to do. . . .

And who was this person, forcing her awake? She moaned softly, and the hands moved away. She missed their warmth, their strength. She managed to lift her head and turn her face toward the intruder.

Kneeling beside her was a dark-haired man with a pleasant face and kind, sympathetic eyes. He wore a light green smock and had a face mask around his neck. "I'm Dr. Paul Thomas," he said gently.

The doctor? "Bobby?" she whimpered. If Bobby wasn't all right, she would have no reason to move from this spot. No reason to go on.

"He came through the surgery well," the doctor said, his eyes avoiding hers.

Sharon saw the gentle pain in the man's averted face. Something was wrong. But he said Bobby came through. . . . "He's going to be all right?"

"Here, let me help you," he said, as Sharon managed to rise to a sitting position. She welcomed his assistance as she stood up on shaky legs. He helped her to the first pew. Sharon brushed back the strands of damp hair that had stuck to her face. She must look a fright. But that didn't matter.

"May I see him?" she asked.

"After he's taken to ICU," Dr. Thomas said. "Someone will let you know."

"He'll need me," she said.

Dr. Thomas nodded, but his moment of hesitation told Sharon there was more. Then he explained. "He hasn't regained consciousness."

"You mean, he's in a coma?"

He nodded. "We're doing everything we can for him, Mrs. Martin. But it's basically out of our hands now."

She looked at him with frightened eyes. "But he will. . .recover. Won't he?"

She noticed the doctor pause, as if he were choosing his words with great care. "His being young and healthy is in his favor, Mrs. Martin. But being young and having so much trauma is against him too. We can only wait. And pray."

"How badly is he hurt?"

Before he could answer, the overhead page sounded. "Dr. Thomas, 5534, Stat!"

"Excuse me," he said, "I'll get back with you." He jumped up and ran up the aisle as the page was repeated.

Sharon followed. When she reached the door, she heard the page again. "Bobby," she said weakly, standing in the doorway with the door pressed against her. The doctor disappeared around a corner, just as a man and woman appeared.

The man introduced himself as John Cameron, hospital chaplain, and the woman as Beth Frame, hospital social worker.

"It's Bobby, isn't it?" Sharon asked, desperation in her voice.

"I can't say, Mrs. Martin," the chaplain replied gently. "But it's my understanding the pediatric surgeon is in with Bobby and will speak with you soon."

Beth put her arms around Sharon's shoulders. "Come on, you need a cup of coffee."

Sharon welcomed any diversion. They led her to a room behind a nurses' station, and she accepted the coffee. Why she said it, she wasn't sure—maybe because she had to keep her mind and body busy with something—but as soon as she sat on the couch, she lifted her eyes to Beth.

"Could you tell me more about organ donation?" Maybe it was a deep inner feeling that her loved ones had to live. . .somehow.

Beth handed Sharon some material.

She read.

To Remember Me

The day will come when. . .at a certain moment a doctor will determine that. . .for all intents and purposes, my life has stopped. When that happens, do not attempt to instill artificial life into my body by the use of a machine. And don't call this my deathbed. Let it be called the Bed of Life, and let my body be taken from it to help others lead fuller lives.

Give my sight to the man who has never seen a sunrise, a baby's face, or love in the eyes of a woman.

Give my heart to a person whose own heart has caused nothing but endless days of pain.

Give my blood to the teenager who was pulled from the wreckage of his car, so that he might live to see his grandchildren play.

Give my kidneys to one who depends on a machine to exist from week to week.

Take my bones, every muscle, every fiber and nerve in my body and find a way to make a crippled child walk.

Explore every corner of my brain. Take my cells, if necessary, and let them grow so that, someday, a speechless boy will shout at the crack of a bat and a deaf girl will hear the sound of rain against her window.

Burn what is left of me and scatter the ashes to the winds to help the flowers grow.

If you must bury something, let it be my faults, my weaknesses, and all prejudice against my fellow man. . . .

Give my soul to God.

If, by chance, you wish to remember me, do it with a kind deed or word to someone who needs you. . . .

Sharon lifted her tear-filled eyes. "Do I need to sign something?"

"Yes, for your mother and Robert," John replied, "but Karen's parents will need to make the decision about her."

Sharon realized that's why time had meant something to her earlier. They would probably be home now. "I must call them."

"Here," Beth said kindly. "Sit at my desk."

Sharon went over and sat in the swivel armchair. She reached for the phone, tried to press the buttons, but her hand was shaking so much she couldn't touch the right buttons. She looked up at John with a stark face, about to crumble.

"I'll do it," Beth offered.

Sharon automatically recalled the numbers like one who had been accustomed to calling them often. When the phone rang, Beth handed the receiver to Sharon.

"Hello," sounded the bright, cheerful voice of fifteen-year-old Kim.

"Kim, Honey, let me speak to your mother."

"Is this Sharon?"

"Yes, Honey. Get your mother, please."

"Mom!" she yelled. "It's Sharon. Hurry, it's long distance. She'll be right here. How's it going?"

Sharon inhaled sharply. "Not well, Honey."

"What's wrong?" Her voice faded. "Mom, something's wrong."

"Sharon?"

"Mary," Sharon began, and her voice caught in her throat.

"Sharon, what is it? Is something wrong?"

"Yes, Mary. Maybe you'd better get James."

"He's right here. We were eating dinner."

Sharon could hear James's voice in the background asking, "What is it?"

Sharon didn't know any other way. She had to say it. "I'm at the hospital, Mary. Bobby's hurt bad."

"Oh, no," Mary moaned. "What happened?"

"There was an accident. Robert and Karen and. . .Mother. They were all in the car, Mary."

"Are they hurt?" she asked.

"Yes. No. Oh, Mary. They're. . .gone."

"Gone? No! Sharon, no! James!" Mary screamed as she dropped the phone. She wouldn't stop screaming. Sharon moved the phone away from her ear and put her head on the desk and sobbed aloud.

Beth took the phone. James Davis got on, and Beth told him what details she could. He asked to speak with Sharon.

It was distressful, but comforting, talking with James. His voice was strained, but he talked of things that had to be done, giving Sharon a sense of direction. "Yes, I'll call as soon as I know anything more about Bobby," she promised.

She told him she had decided to donate Robert's and her mother's organs. James said to fax the donor information to his office. Sharon sighed with relief at that. Yes, that was a way for instant communication. She was not quite so alone anymore.

"I have to go to Mary now, Sharon. Just be strong for Bobby, and we'll be in touch."

As she hung up the receiver, a longing for Mitchell surged through Sharon with an intensity she'd never felt before. He'd been a stabilizing factor in her life since she'd married him when Robert was five years old. He'd been her strength while she grieved for her father. He'd given his blessing to Robert's marrying so young, while she had been reluctant. Now she was glad, so glad, that Robert had those few years of happiness with Karen and Bobby.

Oh, Robert, Robert, my son. Mitchell, why can't I be strong like you? Oh, God, how can I do this alone?

Suddenly a knock sounded, and the door opened. Dr. Thomas stepped into the room, and Sharon's first thought was that he'd come to report on Bobby. It hadn't been long since he'd been called away for the emergency that must surely have involved her grandson.

Then a younger man stepped in behind Dr. Thomas. He, too, wore a green smock, and a face mask hung around his neck. Her eyes riveted to the younger man's face. Dr. Thomas was making introductions, saying something about blood, even mentioning Bobby. But Sharon couldn't make out the words, couldn't hear above the hammering of her heart and the churning of her emotions.

She could not take her eyes from the young man. He wouldn't know her—but she knew him. And just what was this? Some cruel twist of fate to sever the last thin threads of her emotional stability?

For an instant, even thoughts of Bobby receded to the back of her mind. All she could think of was this young man to whom she needed no introduction, a man she had never expected to face, a man who by walking into this room became a part of her living nightmare—a man she knew was Dr. Luke Sinclair.

Sharon hadn't thought her distress could be any greater. But now, in addition to her concern about Bobby, a reminder of her past sins had walked into the room in the form of Dr. Luke Sinclair, the son of Marcus Sinclair.

Oh, God, is this punishment or blessing?

Forcing her thoughts away from the past, Sharon reminded herself that God had forgiven her. Past sins—or even someone learning about them—were not the most important factor here. Bobby was!

She felt Beth's hands on her shoulders, gently leading her to sit on the couch beside Chaplain John. The kind woman handed her a small cup of water. Sharon took a sip, then forced herself to listen as Dr. Thomas took a chair near the couch and Luke Sinclair sat on the edge of the couch near her.

Dr. Thomas described Bobby's injuries, most of which were common in extensive trauma such as automobile accidents. "The spleen developed a hematoma that ruptured. Bleeding became profuse. We removed his spleen and stopped the bleeding."

"He has a rare blood type," Sharon said, concerned.

"Members of my own family have the same type," Luke said. "Rest assured, there is plenty available."

"The surgery was successful, Mrs. Martin," Dr. Thomas added. "And Bobby is getting the best of care."

"When can I see him?" Sharon asked.

Dr. Thomas explained that Bobby was in recovery. "After he's taken to ICU, you may see him for a few minutes. But you can't stay. His heart rate, blood pressure, and cerebral pressure will be monitored constantly. He will have IVs and a catheter for draining urine. But children are resilient, Mrs. Martin. We expect that within three to five days he will move to a semiprivate room, and you may stay with him then if you wish."

Sharon nodded. "I need to let him know I'm with him."

She could tell by the distressed expression Dr. Thomas couldn't hide that something was wrong. She looked at Luke.

"Mrs. Martin," he began, and she dreaded what was to follow, hearing sympathy in his voice. "We suspect head trauma. We can't be sure when he will regain consciousness. It's too soon to know the extent of the damage. That's why the swelling and pressure in the brain is being monitored, so we will know immediately if it gets too high."

"And if it does?" Sharon asked, frightened.

"Then we would go to surgery and put in a shunt to relieve the fluid and blood pressure."

Sharon went numb. Her mind and emotions were battling each other. A part of her wanted to see Bobby, hug him, tell him she loved him, see for herself that he was all right. Another part was glad he was oblivious to all of this and that she didn't have to tell him that his world was shattered. How could she ever do that?

"Is there anything we can do for you, Mrs. Martin?" Dr. Thomas was asking. "I mean personally. Someone we can call?"

Before Sharon could answer, Beth said that Earline Johnson's pastor had called. He and his wife were on their way to the hospital.

"I'm also available," Chaplain John said, with a kind smile.

Sharon was grateful. But what could they do? What could anyone do? Then she remembered. "He has a favorite toy—a stuffed Barney dinosaur. He took it with him everywhere. Do you know if. . .if that is. . .somewhere? When he wakes up, he will need that. . .to hug."

"I'll find out," Dr. Luke Sinclair replied immediately. "I'll personally see that he gets a dinosaur."

Sharon's eyes closed on the pain. Bobby would never see his mom or dad again. He would never see his great-grandmother again.

When Bobby woke up, all he would see was a stuffed dinosaur.

Less than an hour later, with the Rev. John and Nancy Clark at her side, Beth told Sharon that Bobby was settled in ICU, and she could see him for a few minutes. Beth led her to the unit, where Luke Sinclair and a young woman he introduced as his assistant, Julie, awaited her.

"Has there been any change?"

"No, but that's a good sign," Luke assured her. "His system needs time to recover from the shock it's had."

Sharon nodded. Her eyes swept around the circle of rooms, most of which had curtains pushed aside so the children could be observed at all times from the circular nurses' station. Julie took Sharon by the arm and led her into a small room. "May I talk to him?" Sharon asked.

"For a moment," Julie replied and drew up a chair for Sharon, who sat and rubbed her hands together until her fingers felt warm, then reached through the high railing to touch a spot on Bobby's arm that was not bruised or near where the IV's were stuck in. She didn't know if he could hear her but felt he would sense her presence.

His hair appeared darker than usual, surrounding his face that appeared so ghostly white on the bed without a pillow. His little lips that hadn't been still since he learned to communicate in his own special language now lay motionless, parted slightly, but she could not tell if he breathed. She could not see the white blanket move. The place on his arm felt cold to her touch.

Sharon cleared her throat and tried to speak calmly, softly. "Grandmother is here with you, Bobby. I love you more than anything in the whole world. I know you're not feeling well right now, but there are a lot of people who will help you get better. Everything's going to be all right."

In a soft, low voice, while letting him feel the warmth of her touch, Sharon reminded Bobby of the special love that had existed between them from the time he was born. His parents had lived with Sharon while Karen worked and Robert was completing his education. It had been Sharon who heard Bobby's first word, encouraged him in taking his first step, taught him his first swimming strokes in the pool. She'd kissed his hurts and bandaged them with cartoon character Band-Aids.

She'd discovered anew the wonder and mystery of the world—the purpose of rain, the joy of sunshine, the beauty of a yellow moon, the excitement of finding tiny ants and miniature flowers usually so far away from an adult's eyes. She'd taught him the most simple, most profound answers to life's mysteries: God made them. He loves us.

"And I know, Bobby, why I'm called a grandmother. The grandest time of my life has been spent mothering you. My darling, I love you, and I'll take care of you."

She didn't know how long she'd been talking, perhaps to herself as much as to Bobby, when she felt strong, gentle fingers curl over one shoulder. She looked up to see the kind face, the caring eyes, that resembled her Robert, and she moved her hand away from Bobby, fearing he might feel the tremor of emotion that spread through her.

"We have to ask you to leave now, Mrs. Martin," Luke Sinclair said gently. "You may see him again in the morning. But tonight he will be monitored and watched constantly."

"Yes," Julie said, coming farther into the room. "I will be with him for several hours, and I'm on call. You might try and get some rest."

Reluctantly, Sharon left the room. Beth was still waiting for her.

"Beth, I can't leave the hospital tonight."

"I know," Beth replied, taking Sharon's arm and steering her toward the elevator.

Chapter 4

Seeing lights flash against the drapes as a car came up the drive late that evening, Trish Sinclair walked into the foyer. Luke was unlocking the front door to let himself in.

Except for Beethoven's Fifth playing softly in the background, all was quiet. "I'm beat," Luke groaned, setting his bag down and loosening his tie.

"Story of your life, huh?" Trish said with a smile, coming over to him in her cream silk robe that he used to love to touch, saying her skin was even more delectable to his caress. Her face tilted toward his, and her blond hair fell below her shoulders as she began to help unbutton his shirt.

He didn't quite meet her eyes. "Let me get a shower, then we'll talk," he said and hurried from the room.

"Story of my life," Trish muttered under her breath, her eyes clouding like a blue sky turning gray. He didn't even notice that her hair was not in its usual ponytail. Or that she wasn't wearing jeans, a T-shirt, and tennis shoes.

She was in the kitchen, taking dishes out of the dishwasher, when he returned from his shower, fully clad in pajamas and towel-drying his dark waves into mussed curls that accentuated his rugged handsomeness.

Trish determined not to argue. The children were asleep. It was just the two of them—alone. "Had dinner?"

"No, but all I want right now is to unwind a little."

Trish followed him into his study and sat on the couch, drawing her legs underneath her, while he tossed the towel onto his leather desk chair, sank into his recliner, and leaned his head back, closing his eyes.

"It was rough, Trish," he said, sighing heavily. "We had to operate on a little two-year-old boy."

"Was Julie there?"

He detected the edge to her voice.

A muscle tightened in his jaw.

"She's my assistant, Trish," he said blandly, opening his eyes.

Trish shrugged. "Even doctors get a day off now and then! Don't they? Seems I remember when you and I had a life."

He glanced toward the ceiling, his brow wrinkling. "That's not fair, Trish.

You didn't come into this marriage with your eyes closed. Your own dad was a doctor."

"I know, Luke," she said defensively. "I know your work is important and necessary. But I need something for myself."

His heavy brows formed a straight line as he scowled. "I don't understand you, Trish. I've given you this nice home—two wonderful boys—I don't make any unreasonable demands of you." He spread his hands. "I don't want this kind of thing when I come home worn-out from the hospital."

"Well, what about me?" Her voice rose, and she jumped from the couch. "You think I'm not worn-out? Day after day running after two nonstop boys? At least you get to sit down once in awhile!"

At his exasperated expression, she stalked over to the chair and grabbed the damp towel. "I pick up after the boys all day long. Then you come home, and I have to pick up after you too." She threw it on the floor. "Well, I won't! And I won't be ignored. You never ask about my day, or the boys'. All you want to talk about is yourself and the hospital."

"Trish, I need to be able to relax and unwind before I can go to sleep."

Her lip trembled. "You used to call me your sleeping pill."

He could not meet her eyes. Finally, he mumbled, "You've changed, Trish. I guess maybe you're tired. I've told you over and over you can hire somebody to help out around here."

"I don't need somebody to help," she shot back. "I need. . .to be appreciated. I mean, I spent all week cleaning this house and planning for this evening, cooking a special dinner for you and Marcus."

His head came up. "Was Dad upset?"

Trish snorted. "Your dad is never upset, Luke. He's a rock. He and the boys frolicked all over the backyard this afternoon while I cooked. It was really relaxing for me."

"Then why are you so tired? Do you need vitamins or something?"

"A doctor should recognize the signs, Luke. Maybe I'm depressed. Maybe I think a father should be home once in awhile to do those things with his children, instead of a grandfather having to always do them. Maybe I think I should be eating dinner with my husband, not with his dad."

"I'm sorry," Luke said and reached over to his desk for the remote control. "Let's catch the news. Maybe then you'll understand why I had to stay and why I'm tired."

Trish returned to the couch and sat stiffly. As the newscaster reported the horrible tragedy, the dead people, the little boy hanging by a slim thread of hope, she felt a stab of guilt.

"You operated on that little boy?" Trish whispered when the report ended.

"I assisted Paul," he said. "Then I talked with Sharon Martin. All of it, Trish—it just took everything out of me."

"I'm sorry," she said repentantly, tears in her eyes for what her husband had gone through. Tears because she hadn't been helpful. Tears for the family's tragedy, for the little boy, and for her own husband, who after a trying day tried to ease the mind of a suffering woman. Luke was a good man. She should not be so hard on him.

"I'm sorry too, Trish," he said. "I'll try to be a better husband and father."

"You're okay," she said contritely. *But why this tension between us? Why aren't we able to communicate anymore? Why couldn't it be like it used to be?* "I'll check on the boys, then I'd better hit the hay."

"Be there in a little while," he said. "I'll call Dad and apologize for missing dinner."

"You don't think it's too late?"

"He always watches the late news."

Trish nodded and left the room.

Luke sat on the edge of the chair, fingering the remote control. He grimaced. He tried to leave his work at the hospital—wanted to have the kind of camaraderie he and Trish used to have—but things changed. People changed.

Turning off the television, he forced his thoughts to the matter at hand, went to his desk chair, and reached for the telephone.

～

Fifty-one-year-old Criminal Court Judge Marcus Sinclair sat in his den at the back of his historic Charleston home, watching the late news and having a snack of skim milk and a piece of Trish's famous low-cal banana nut bread she'd sent home with him. It had been a good evening with her and his grandchildren. Would have been better had Luke joined them.

Then the report of the Martin family caught his complete attention. *Terrible tragedy* crossed his mind. The same phrase had run through his mind many times, including that very afternoon as he reviewed the files of a murder case.

Just before the sportscast, the phone rang.

Running his hand through his still-dark hair, Marcus smiled when he heard Luke's voice, apologizing for not being able to make it for dinner.

"We had an emergency, Dad." Luke told him about Bobby. "I donated blood. Bobby has the rare type that you and I have."

Marcus frowned. "Is the supply low, Son? I could—"

"No, no. There's ample supply for the time being. Of course, when you have a chance, it would be helpful in case of need later on."

Marcus heard the strain in Luke's voice. "I'll donate soon, Son."

"Dad. There is something you might do. Your being a judge carries a little clout."

"Does it?" Marcus said in a light tone. "With my own children?"

"Well," Luke retracted with a small laugh, "at least in a courtroom."

"Okay, what can I do?"

Luke told him about the Barney dinosaur. "You suppose you could find out if the police picked it up or if it's in the car? It was Bobby's favorite toy, and his grandmother thinks it might help."

Marcus grimaced at the sadness in Luke's voice. He did sound drained. "I can do better than that, Son. I'll go to the station and find that dinosaur, if possible. If it's not in good shape, I'll try and get one like it."

"Thanks, Dad. Again, I'm sorry I missed dinner tonight. I'm sure Trish and the children enjoyed your being there."

"Trish cooked a great meal, Luke. The kids and I had fun. But I think Trish is worried about your working too hard. Says you don't get enough rest."

"Dad, that's the life of a doctor. She knows that."

"Yeah, well. Try and take a little time for yourselves, Luke. That's important."

"Sure, Dad."

After they hung up, Marcus stared blankly at the TV. He'd noticed Trish's pain that afternoon. How could he miss it? It echoed so strongly the look he'd seen in his dear wife's eyes so many years ago. Would his own silence lead Luke to repeat those mistakes of the past?

Chapter 5

After the Rev. John Clark and his wife, Nancy, left, the nursing supervisor, Helen, reappeared. She told Sharon that she could stay in the room behind her office and lie on the couch. The night-shift head nurse would let her know the moment there was any change and when she could see Bobby. Helen got a pillow and blanket. "Lie down," she insisted.

Too distraught to do anything but obey, Sharon lay on the couch with her knees drawn up. Helen placed the blanket over her. "Try and rest," she said. "Could I go to your home and get anything for you?"

"No," Sharon said. "The preacher's wife said she would come in the morning and take me home. There will be so much to do."

"Don't think about it right now, Sharon. Just rest, and be ready for Bobby."

"Yes," Sharon said. "Thank you."

Helen touched her shoulder, then walked out of the room and to the desk. Sharon could hear her giving instructions to the head nurse.

Sharon prayed. That always helped, to know that God was near, that He cared, that He could take the mess people made out of things and bring some good from it. Oh, how wonderfully well He'd done that twenty-three years ago when the girl inside her died, and a woman began to emerge. Her thoughts drifted back in time.

~

Sharon had been nineteen years old. Her parents had presented her with the news that her father was divorcing her mother and transferring to California with his secretary, fifteen years his junior, who would become his new wife.

There'd be no money for her second year of college, and it was too late for her to take advantage of any scholarships or apply for financial aid. Her boyfriend found the situation deplorable. It didn't fit in with the plans he had for his future. A girl with divorced parents seemed flawed to him, as if it were somehow her fault. Sharon wondered if it were. Had her dreams, her plans, her hopes for college been too much for her parents to deal with?

Her boyfriend looked different then—as did her dad. She lost trust in men and had to face the fact that she didn't really know her parents. What she thought was a stable family was not. What she thought was a secure future with her boyfriend was not. Life was cruel, unfair.

She'd decided to ignore her feelings and instead had accepted an invitation to a friend's beach party. For the first time in her life, she accepted an alcoholic drink. But the party wasn't fun. Instead of feeling elated, Sharon felt only more depressed. Unable to join in the festivities, she wandered down the sandy shore until she came to an outcropping of rock in front of a darkened cottage. She climbed up onto the rocks and looked out over the billowing waves of the ocean, oblivious to the gathering storm clouds in the night sky and the cool breeze that stirred her hair, as if giving flight to the long strands.

The sea became rough, the night dark and stormy. The warm wetness on her face turned cold. She climbed down and walked toward the ocean, oblivious to the falling rain, stopping only when the waves splashed against her knees and she could feel the cold and the pull of the unstable sandy floor as it encouraged her to become part of that vast ocean.

The rain beat harder. A thunderclap was followed by a streak of light far out over the water. She turned away from the beckoning waves, stumbled, and felt strong arms helping her to rise.

"Come on," he said gently, and she leaned against him as he held onto her shoulders and told her to put her arm around his waist since her feet were unsteady. The thunder and lightning came closer, and he made her run to the beach house. He handed her a towel for her wet hair and demanded that she dry off and change into a terry cloth robe while her clothes dried.

When she returned to the front room, a fire was burning in the fireplace. He took an afghan from the back of the couch and put it around her shoulders, then gently motioned toward the couch, opposite the fireplace, where she snuggled into its corner against a cushion. He brought a rack from somewhere and arranged her clothes on it to dry near the fire.

The man sat in a chair where the firelight was not directly on his face. He asked what had brought her out on such a stormy night, and she poured out the story of her family, her boyfriend, and the reasons she left the party. Slowly, she became aware of him as a person, as a man, as one who was older than the college boys she knew.

"What's. . .your name?" she asked hesitantly.

He didn't answer immediately, instead rising to poke the fire. He threw on another log, then glanced at her and said his name. He looked at her expectantly, as if waiting for her name in turn.

She didn't want to be herself—Sharon Ann Johnson. She didn't want him to know she was only nineteen, so she said she was in college, her age was twenty-one. "My name," she said, feeling like the different person she wanted to be, "is Angela."

She took the glass of wine he offered and welcomed the escape from her troubles. While the rain beat against the windowpanes and blotted out the world, she focused her attention only on the handsome man who seemed to care about what was happening to her. He seemed to understand. Concern deepened his dark eyes. To avoid her growing awareness of him, she looked around and noticed a cupcake with a candle stuck in the middle of it on the coffee table. "What is that?" she asked.

A scoff accompanied his laugh. "A friend's idea of cheering me up. That's my birthday present."

"This is your birthday?"

He looked at his watch. "For at least another hour."

"How old are you?"

"Twenty-eight."

Now she was glad she'd said she was twenty-one. Why, she wasn't sure. Maybe she felt he wouldn't have given her the numbing glass of wine if he knew she was only nineteen. Maybe he would consider her just a child. She'd never be a child again—her daddy's little girl. She felt the tears about to come, but she wouldn't allow them. "Why are you alone on your birthday?" she asked.

"The same as you," he answered. "People problems. My wife threw me out of the house two days ago and is filing for divorce. This is not the time for celebrating a birthday." He studied his glass for awhile, then drank the remaining drop and looked at the fire. "She had every right to do that. I haven't been a very attentive husband. I've spent every spare moment studying for the bar exam."

He got up and went over to the table, picked up the cupcake, then threw it into the fire. "So much for birthdays," he said. "So much for marriage." He looked at her then. "Maybe your boyfriend did you a favor."

She thought of his marriage—her mom and dad's—over! Suddenly another thought struck her. "You saved my life."

He shook his head. "You'd already turned when I got there." He paused. "Maybe you saved my life." He smiled. The first smile she'd seen since she came into the cottage. They stared at each other.

"My clothes might be dry," she said.

"I'll walk you back when the storm dies down," he said. "Or you're welcome to stay the night. You can take the bedroom. I don't sleep well these nights. Too much on my mind. But that's enough of my troubles."

Sharon stepped out of the afghan and stood as he turned to move away from the fire. His eyes swept over her, and he looked away. Sharon reached out and touched his arm. "I'm so sorry to burden you with my troubles. You have—"

"No," he interrupted. "Strangely, it's been good for me, thinking about someone else's problems besides my own. I suppose it's kind of like your leaving the party. Sometimes you don't want to be around laughing, carefree people."

She never wanted to go back to that life awaiting her—a life without her family intact, without the security of the boyfriend she'd had for over a year.

"Happy birthday," she said and lifted her hands to touch his face. She drew his head close to hers. Her lips touched his in a gentle kiss.

Who, or why, or how had nothing to do with it, but she was lost in his kiss, in his arms that came around her in such swift, fierce intensity.

He pushed her away. "Angela," he said, "you don't know what you're doing."

"I do," she lied.

What followed had been wrong, of course, and desperately foolish. She'd slipped out the front door later that night after she was sure he was asleep and made her way down the beach, in the light rain.

She knew she couldn't go home right away. Her mom would suspect. So she'd gone to her grandmother's house, a few blocks from the beach. Her grandmother was surprised but accepted her explanation that she had left a dull party.

During that night of fitful sleep, Sharon remembered that she'd vowed never to speak to her father again. She'd said she hated his secretary. But now she herself had slept with an older man. She didn't even know the man. He might have been lying about getting a divorce, but even if he wasn't, how different was he from her own dad? *And I,* she thought shivering, *how different am I from my dad's secretary?*

~

Twenty-three years later, Sharon had forgiven herself and him. But she would never forget. That night in the beach house, her son, Robert, had been fathered by Marcus Sinclair.

Chapter 6

Two days after Luke had called him, Marcus sat in his office with his mind wandering. He glanced at his watch at a little before three o'clock in the afternoon. Unable to concentrate on the murder-case files he'd been reading, he impatiently closed them, buzzed Ellen, his secretary, and said he was calling it a day.

Ellen had picked up an exact replica of the blood-soaked toy the previous day but had said that if it had been the little boy's favorite toy, it shouldn't look new, so she took it home to wash it. She was insightful like that. That was one thing that made her such a good secretary. A couple years earlier, the idea of settling down with Ellen, a comfortable widow in her late forties, had crossed Marcus's mind.

As he washed his hands in a courthouse bathroom, he realized those thoughts of settling down had gone down the drain, just like soapy water.

His reflection didn't even seem to mind. The man in the mirror was a happy man. After drying his hands, he ran his fingers through his thick, dark hair that had silvered just enough to lend an air of distinction, so Ellen said.

Now Ellen was seeing someone else, and Marcus was enjoying his freedom. *Freedom?* As a judge, a father, a man, he well knew the implication of such a word—not only from the U.S. Constitution, which gave the right not of happiness, but of the "pursuit" of it, but also from the realization that the Lord Himself offered not happiness but "abundant" life. *Ah, well, no time for philosophizing at the moment.*

Inhaling deeply, he choked on the thick, odorous air, hurried from the small room, and continued on through the courthouse, toward the parking lot, smiling, speaking to colleagues with whom he'd had an enjoyable camaraderie for many years.

Once on the main road, he switched on his little red Thunderbird's radio, catching the three o'clock news. The same as last night—with an update on two-year-old Bobby Martin's condition. Still critical. The accident had been the talk of the courthouse yesterday and today.

Marcus didn't like hospitals. When his wife, Bev, died of cancer eight years ago, he'd gotten his fill of them. But he hadn't been able to shake Luke's entreaty for blood a couple of nights ago. And with his awareness that a little boy with the same blood type as one of his own grandsons needed his blood, he pulled into the hospital parking garage.

Oblivious to the warmth of the spring air and the rolling white clouds across an azure sky, Marcus chided himself that he, a grown man, should be apprehensive about giving blood. Yet he felt definitely squeamish by the time he reached Luke's office.

"You're white as a sheet, Dad," Luke said the moment he stepped inside the office. "Better sit down. Giving blood can make you light-headed."

So much for appearing macho in front of Luke's pretty young assistant. "Hi, Julie."

Her radiant smile lit up her face like the light reflecting from her luxurious mane of medium-brown hair that was caught back in a twist. One errant strand accented the appealing flush of youth on her cheek. "Good to see you again, Judge Sinclair." Her voice softened. "Luke said you might be a donor."

Marcus knew the color he felt flush his own cheeks had nothing to do with youth. Reluctantly he admitted, "I haven't given blood yet."

"Mmm," Luke mumbled, with a knowing look in his eyes that he turned mischievously toward Julie.

Julie bent her head and looked condescendingly at Marcus, as one might a senile old man.

Acquiescing, Marcus lifted his hand. "I'm going to, pass out or not." Then he noticed the abundance of flowers and bags on the floors and on every flat surface. "What's all this?"

"For Bobby." Julie's eyes turned sympathetic. "The public is responding, but we can't have these in ICU."

Luke stood, his face serious. "He's still in a coma. Julie and I were just getting ready to check Bobby's vital signs. Would you like to see him?"

He wouldn't, but Marcus knew that Luke was taking a particularly personal interest in this case—as was the entire city, according to newspaper and TV reports.

Marcus looked at the little boy in a coma. That might be Luke's blood flowing from that IV into the little boy, keeping him alive. The boy was bruised, cut. Dark circles appeared beneath his closed eyes, where long, dark lashes lay against his pale cheeks. On the white pillow lay a mop of reddish-golden brown hair, reminding him of the sun-touched hair of his own children when they were little, before their hair turned dark like his and Bev's.

Standing, watching Luke and Julie's quiet, professional teamwork, Marcus knew the little boy's life would mark them—had already. Trying to shake the depressing feeling of so young a life so near death, he walked out into the hallway.

When Luke and Julie joined him, Luke said there was no change. Bobby was barely holding on.

Marcus held out the bag containing the dinosaur. "What shall I do with this?"

"Mrs. Martin went home to finalize arrangements for her mother's funeral that's scheduled for tomorrow morning. We plan to meet her in the cafeteria for an update after Julie and I finish our rounds. Why don't you join us and give it to her?"

Marcus wanted to get out of there but knew Luke and Julie couldn't very well make their rounds with a purple dinosaur.

Later, feeling better at having given his blood and praying it might be helpful to Bobby or another needy person, Marcus walked down the long corridor to the cafeteria. He did not go in, however, for he saw Luke and Julie at a table with a woman who lifted a tissue and wiped her eyes. But she also smiled and reached over to squeeze Luke's hand.

Feeling squeamish at the thought of hospital food, the giving of blood, the woman's losses, and the memory of the injured boy, Marcus decided this was no time for a social gathering. He left the hospital. Trying to assuage a stab of guilt, he told himself tomorrow would be a better time. He knew, from experience, that facing reality was more difficult after a funeral.

∽

The following day, a warm spring morning, Sharon sat in the swing on her mother's front porch, waiting for one of the kind neighbor couples who had offered to give her a ride to the church for her mother's funeral. She tried to assimilate all that had happened. However, she felt dazed, going through the motions like a zombie.

She needed to thank the Lord for Helen Gamble—for her help in arranging organ donations, and for her kind sympathy that extended beyond professionalism. And Beth had been a true friend.

Her mother's neighbors must have watched for the moment Sharon came home for something. They came bringing food, expressing their admiration and love for her mother, and showing their readiness to do anything necessary. They insisted Sharon eat and created pleasant memories of how helpful Earline Johnson had been in their times of need. Sharon was never alone during the day. At night she drifted in and out of sleep.

∽

"It was instant," Pastor Clark was saying as he delivered the eulogy.

Instant? Sharon thought. Maybe that's what made it so difficult to believe. They were there one instant—gone another. At times, she thought this was only a nightmare. She would awaken and her family would be there. But

33

Pastor Clark was confirming they were in a better place.

Although the funeral was for Earline Johnson, he talked about Robert and Karen and how that as Christians they were with the Lord. Now the living must concentrate on and pray for Bobby—who had not yet awakened from his coma.

If I should die before I wake, settled upon Sharon's weary brain. Robert was only twenty-two. How awake was he? Little more than a child himself. And now Bobby—only two!

If I should die before I wake. . .

When Sharon had buried her husband five years before, she still had her son. She could expect her dad, who lived in Hawaii, to die someday, and her mother to die as well, because that was the natural order of things. "We begin to die the day we're born," she'd heard all her life. But it was no comfort. . .no comfort.

Even when she had to make the decision that her son and his wife would be flown to California to await decisions about their burial, even as she sat at her mother's funeral, the primary thought, the one reason to be not strong, not courageous, not brave—she was none of that—but just to hang on, was Bobby.

The prayer she prayed as a child kept echoing in her mind, even as the preacher extolled the attributes of her mother:

> *If I should die before I wake*
> *I pray the Lord my soul to take.*

Children weren't taught that prayer anymore. Parents thought it was too scary, too morbid. She had never thought of the morbidity of the prayer, only that she should have her heart right with God, should death happen. Now the thought touched her heart like an abscessed tooth, or a fingernail chewed to the quick.

Oh, God, don't let Bobby die before he wakes.

In her bereft, shocked world there was no longer reality. Instead, she stood in a place of waiting, as if she were on the shore waiting for the storm to come. She'd seen it. The storm clouds gather, hover, press down, the winds blow the palm fronds. She'd felt it on her face.

If I should die before I wake. Don't take him. He's all I've got. Oh, Lord, don't take him. I need him. My son is in him. I would be left with nothing—just. . .bereft. Yes, I know I will have my memories, my years of blessings. I've had a good life. Some people never do. I am grateful. I have thanked You. But Bobby is only two. He has not begun to live. No, that's not why. I want him for myself. I want that grandchild. For me. To give me a reason to live.

If he should die before he wakes then my life would be empty—like a motel with a flashing neon sign: VACANCY. . .VACANCY. . .VACANCY.

~

Later that day, Nancy Clark drove Sharon to the hospital. Sharon would be staying there as much as possible now that her mother was buried. She needed to be near Bobby, and even near Dr. Luke, the half-brother her son had never known he had.

She could not allow herself to break down. Later, she could cry, she could grieve. She could feel that vacancy sign hitting against her ribs, thudding against her chest. The heat of it burned her stomach. The tears constricted her throat. But it mustn't come yet.

Sharon had not been in Charleston several years before when Hurricane Hugo hit the coastline with gale force winds of 150 miles per hour, unleashing its fury, wreaking havoc, destroying homes, ruining businesses, taking lives. But she had seen the devastation on TV, had read the accounts in the newspaper. She remembered the nationally televised comments: "It's unbelievable. I've lost everything. I don't know what to do. I've been in hurricanes before, but never anything like this."

That's how Sharon felt. Three days before, her personal hurricane had struck. On a rain-slick highway, a tractor-trailer lost control and slammed into the car carrying her mother, her son, his wife, and her two-year-old grandson. She'd known tragedy, disaster, personal loss. But never anything like this.

But she had one chance for survival. Little Bobby was her lifeboat. She was clinging to the side—knowing all the while that in a storm like this, even a ship could sink.

She'd handled it well after her husband died five years before. But this was different. Robert was her son—her only son, her child, her baby who had grown inside her. He had been her reason for living. All that was gone. . .gone.

Spurred by sheer determination, Sharon strode purposefully down the somber hospital corridor, willing the walls not to close in on her. Bobby mustn't die. He was all she had. Head set, shoulders squared, emotions suppressed, she kept her mind's eye focused on her mission, and her light blue gaze on the door at the far end.

She pressed a button on the wall, and the doors to ICU opened. An unusual amount of movement stirred at Bobby's doorway, and she saw cleaning ladies with their carts. Hurrying to his room, she had to grasp the glass door to keep from falling. She couldn't speak, couldn't feel, was afraid to think.

Her breath came in short spurts.

The room was empty.

Bobby was gone.

Chapter 7

The corridor of the pediatric ward looked like a fantasyland with pink and blue castles, trees with tender green and yellow leaves, and a profusion of wildflowers in various shapes, sizes, and colors through which animals of every sort ran freely. Little people, nymphs, and elves roamed the forest, crossed bridges over sparkling streams, and danced in circles while holding hands. All of that beneath a blue sky dotted with fluffy white clouds and a big, smiling, yellow sun.

Passing rooms with open doors, Sharon saw that children were in rooms that had walls painted different colors. Smiling, happy nurses wore pink, purple, and light blue outfits, on which were boldly printed figures of animals.

Sesame Street characters ran across the bottom of the nurses' station. Sharon couldn't help but smile. Everything in this ward was so upbeat, so colorful, and would appeal to children.

Helen Gamble led Sharon into a room where Luke and Julie stood on each side of Bobby's bed, raising the rails, giving the appearance of a crib. That was good. They thought he was well enough that he might roll. Sharon looked from Luke to Julie, both smiling.

"He's coming out of the coma," Luke explained. "His eyes have fluttered open, and he's made faint sounds. He could awaken at any time."

"It's best that he awaken in a room like this," Julie added.

Sharon had not been able to take her eyes off Bobby. He was still hooked up to IVs and a catheter to drain his bladder.

"The soft restraints on his wrists," Julie explained, "are so he won't inadvertently pull out his IVs when he wakes up."

Sharon nodded. That meant they expected him to be well and active before long. He did look better. More color in his face. His bruises were darker, surrounded by a sickly yellow cast, but that was part of healing. Much of the swelling had gone down. After a moment, Julie's remark registered. Sharon looked around, seeing that colorful fish swam on a border around the middle of the light blue walls. There was another bed in the room—for her.

"Yes," she said. "It's a wonderful room."

Her eyes returned to Bobby. "Can he hear us?"

"That seems to be an individual thing," Luke said. "Many have claimed to know what was going on while they were unconscious or coming out of it. Others have known nothing. But we are keeping him sedated to alleviate any pain." Luke motioned for Sharon to come closer.

The urge to grasp Bobby in her arms and hold him close, never let him go, was overpowering. But Sharon had to merely reach out and let her fingers gently touch a place on his little face that wasn't bruised. Her finger traced a pattern around one ear. Her hand lay gently over his little heart, that beat steadily—with life.

She drew back, lest he feel her emotion. Since the accident, her tears had been drops of grief. She could not, would not, hold back these tears of relief. Bobby would recover.

Helen handed her a tissue. Sharon wiped her eyes and smiled.

Luke put his arm around her shoulders—like her son would have done, had he lived. How right it seemed, having her son's half-brother comfort her.

A smiling nurse came in, wearing an outfit with colorful teddy bears all over it. She introduced herself as Meg, Bobby's nurse until eleven P.M. Luke asked Sharon to step out into the hallway with him.

"We have every reason to believe Bobby will recover physically. But we can't know just yet what problems may have been caused by the head trauma. It's out of our hands now. But we can pray."

"Oh, yes," Sharon said, returning his smile. She was grateful for all these wonderful people who had been lifesavers for her—and Bobby.

She glanced down the hall as Luke and Julie walked away. His hand touched the small of Julie's back. The way his young assistant looked up at him gave Sharon the impression Julie greatly admired Dr. Luke. They obviously made a great team.

Helen Gamble walked from the nurses' station with a huge teddy bear. Beside her was an LPN bearing a pot of coffee and cups.

"You're so thoughtful, Helen," Sharon said.

"Well, I knew you wouldn't budge from this room anytime soon. Besides, I need to discuss this with you."

Sharon stared. She wasn't surprised that Helen might bring Bobby a bear, but this one was old and worn, with a missing eye. And the look in Helen's eye indicated something serious was afoot.

~

Luke and Julie walked to the nurses' station and went into a back office where they could discuss their cases. It was Luke's responsibility to train Julie. She was into her first year of the three years of residency required and was glad to have him as her supervisor. He had the reputation of sending out his residents as highly equipped MDs. On more than one occasion, he'd recommended a resident train for longer than three years. Lives hung in the balance. Working with him was an inspiration. Besides that, they had wonderful conversations about art and music.

Julie came from a family of doctors and strove to be as good as they had been. Lately, however, she felt like a tightrope about to snap. She'd been on the floor before 6:30 that morning, made rounds with Luke, then met with the attending physicians in the conference room on the pediatrics floor. They'd discussed patients' status, treatment plans, and expected the attending physicians' input.

She knew she wasn't the only one on such a schedule. The other residents were as exhausted as she, and they understood the doctors had all gone through the same thing. Julie was determined to make it. The morning wore on, and she wrote orders and progress notes, checked lab work, and talked with nurses and the families of patients.

At lunchtime, Julie went up to the suite of rooms set aside for the attending physicians. They shared a kitchen and bathroom, but each had a private bedroom. Julie went into her room and locked the door. She opened the top drawer of her bedside table and took out the bottle of pills. She sat on the bed, resisting the urge to crawl under the covers and sleep for hours. For a moment, she considered the little pill bottle bearing the name of Amy Smith. It contained a prescription of Prozac from Dr. Julie Dalton.

Her family doctor had prescribed the antidepressant Prozac while Julie was in medical school. She certainly wasn't the only med student who needed medication. There had been many reasons then to be depressed, not only with the demands of med school but with the loss of her boyfriend who couldn't wait for her.

Now she needed an occasional stimulant, and this was one of those times. She had had two hours of sleep last night, at the most. Bobby's case was taking up so much time. Another child with respiratory distress had to be incubated and placed on a ventilator.

These are not excuses, Julie reminded herself, forcing herself to rise from the bed and pour water from the pitcher on the dresser. She had reasons to get through this trying time. Luke was one of them. She couldn't chance making a bad impression on him. She quickly took the pill and rejoined life on the floor.

By the end of the afternoon, Julie desperately needed sleep but felt so wired she knew it wouldn't come. This was more difficult than med school. The hours were so long. She had decisions to make and had to be alert.

She was about to head for her room when an RN approached her with a chart. "Late last night Kaitlain woke up, complaining that her leg hurt. Then she didn't wake up again until noon. I'm concerned that her pain medication may be too strong."

"Let me see," Julie said and pondered over the chart. "Kaitlain had a longer physical therapy session yesterday than usual. That could have caused soreness in the muscles. I'll take a look at her. Here," she said, holding out her hands. "Let me take the medication in."

Walking toward the room, she heard the RN telling one of the other nurses, "Julie is so sweet and more dedicated than any doctor I know."

How could I be less dedicated? My entire family has been in some field of medicine. These little children need me. She realized, however, that Bobby's situation had taken its toll on her—emotionally and physically. But she would not be able to rest tonight if she didn't see Kaitlain.

Eleven-year-old Kaitlain was sitting up in bed, laughing while watching the Disney Channel. She glanced and groaned upon seeing Julie. Julie laughed. "Don't mind me. I just want to take a look at that leg." She set the tray on the bedside table.

Kaitlain paid little attention to Julie's probing hands and gentle massage of her calf that had been pulled severely in a skating accident when she'd fallen and another skater had fallen on top of her. At one point Kaitlain said, "Ouch!"

At Julie's questioning, Kaitlain revealed the leg felt better than it had previously. Today's therapy had seemed to take some of the soreness away.

"I understand you woke up with pain last night," Julie said.

"Yeah, but it feels better now than it has before."

"Great! That's how it's supposed to be."

Kaitlain returned her smile, then again focused on the TV.

Julie stepped over to the medication, turned the little cup upside down in her hand, and looked at the two pills. One was a children's Tylenol. The other, a stronger pain medication. She returned the Tylenol to the cup and slipped the other pill into her pocket.

"Take your medication," Julie gently instructed, holding out the cup and water. Kaitlain didn't ask why her medication had changed from two pills to one. She downed the Tylenol and returned her attention to the TV.

Julie returned the water cup to the table. "Glad you're feeling better. Keep on like this, and you'll be out of here before you know it."

Kaitlain grimaced. "No way! I'd have to go back to school."

They laughed, just as the supper tray was brought in.

"There'd better be ice cream on that tray," the girl said.

"Sorry," the woman said.

Julie patted Kaitlain's shoulder. "I'll see that you get ice cream."

Kaitlain smiled up at her. The woman smiled too, with a sidelong look that said Julie would spoil these children.

At the nurses' station, Julie dropped off the chart, ordered ice cream for Kaitlain, and said she was going to her room. They would call her if they needed her.

Just this once, Julie told herself. And it wasn't as if she were taking anything away from Kaitlain that she needed. This was a mild pain medication for an adult, just enough to take the edge off and help her sleep.

Her hand was in her pocket and a smile was on her face as she rode the elevator up to her room. She felt better already, knowing that sleep was ahead of her—in the form of a little pill.

Chapter 8

The following morning, Sharon was kneeling on the carpeted floor of the children's recreation room, loading a miniature school bus with little block people, counting as she loaded, which was a type of therapy for the little girl who'd had a head injury and had to relearn everything. Professionals were in charge, but Sharon had volunteered to help, at least for an hour or so each day. She was so grateful to all who were helping Bobby. She had to try to reciprocate in some way.

She had slept several hours last night, having lain in the bed just a few feet away from Bobby. During the evening she had talked to him, touched him, even turned the TV on for a brief period, coming to the realization that there was a world outside this hospital. She had been aware of nurses coming in through the night to check on Bobby and heard them whisper softly, "He's doing just fine."

Then early this morning, Julie had come in, with her bright, sparkling smile and exuberant spirit. She confirmed that Bobby was resting well while his little body healed. "A breakfast tray is being brought up for you, Sharon," Julie said. "My orders are that you eat it."

Sharon promised. She couldn't help but respond to such a lovely, caring young woman.

"Mrs. Martin?" came the soft voice of Suzie, a young LPN who appeared in the doorway of the recreation room. Suzie seemed to attend to Sharon's needs almost as much as she did the children's. Sharon felt a particular fondness for the young girl who believed her nursing career was God's mission for her life. "There's a man here to see you."

"A man?" Suzie would have named a doctor. Perhaps someone from an insurance company—business as usual, even if the losses had not completely struck her yet. Then Suzie's words caught her completely off guard.

"Not just any man," Suzie said, smiling. "It's Judge Sinclair. Dr. Luke's dad."

Never had Sharon been more grateful for a child's wail than when Suzie bent down to load the bus for Maria. Sharon felt paralyzed—more helpless than the children in wheelchairs. The emotional paralysis prevented her moving, prevented her breathing. She wasn't ready for this. She would never be ready for this. Was he. . .outside, looking through the window at her? Would

41

he wonder why she was on her knees even now when no child was near her?

Willing herself to move, Sharon rose to her feet and brushed at the knees of her pants as if the carpet had left some sort of stain on them. She stared at the closed door. *Ready!* Was she really ready? She told her heart to be reasonable and forced her mind to think calmly.

Robotlike, she opened the door and stepped out into the waiting area. He was not there, but beyond, in the hallway, conversing with a nurse at the station. Her eyes moved to the corner of the waiting room and studied the table on which a glass coffeepot sat, half empty. Near it was a stack of foam cups, plastic spoons, napkins, and a small bowl of pink-and-white paper packages. She wouldn't be able to hold a cup of coffee without spilling it. She must sit before she collapsed. But when he walked in, she'd have to stand out of politeness. Would she be able to? Maybe she could walk out to the nurses' station and lean against the partition.

She tried. But a nurse glanced in her direction, and he turned.

Sharon was bone-weary and mind-numb. She'd done some hard things in her life, but this was among the hardest.

She knew she had to be the first to speak. Just the thought of hearing his voice sent her emotions spiraling into the past. *This is the father of my beloved son—the grandfather of little Bobby.*

She hoped she was prepared to hear his voice, but when he questioned, "Mrs. Martin?" she felt as if someone had jabbed her in the sides. She started, swayed slightly, stopped, and held onto the door casing for balance. She drew in her breath. She would know him anywhere.

She had subscribed to the *Charleston Times* and saved newspaper articles and announcements about Marcus in case Robert ever wanted to know about his birth father. She learned that Marcus had not divorced when she read his wife had her third child, a boy now in college. She knew when Luke married, when Marcus's only daughter, Kathleen, married, when Luke got a scholarship to college. She knew when Marcus and his wife went on a trip to the Holy Land with a church group, and Sharon believed he had found peace within himself since that night so long ago when he was as troubled as she. She knew when he was appointed to the bench and when his wife died of cancer eight years ago. She'd seen him on TV, in the newspapers, in the face of her son— the son who had lived, and died, without Marcus ever knowing of his existence.

Sharon was sure he wouldn't remember her. She had changed since she was nineteen. Her hair was short now, a softer shade of brown. She was twenty pounds heavier and had replaced her Southern accent with a California brogue. Why would he remember her from one night in all of his fifty-one years? *He wouldn't want to remember.*

He was looking at her like he had twenty-three years ago, with that same expression of inquisitive kindness. She mustn't call him Marcus. She mustn't extend her hand for him to touch. She mustn't say, "Let's talk about our son, Robert, and grieve together."

His face began to swim before her eyes, and she took a deep breath, reminding herself that life was now about Bobby—only Bobby.

"Judge Sinclair," she said, repeating his words after he introduced himself. But still she did not extend her hand. She must not let go of the door casing, the only thing allowing her to stay on her feet.

What was he seeing as he looked at her? Her soft brown hair was swept back on one side and fell along her face on the other to just below her jawline. She wore casual yet stylish gray slacks with matching jacket over a cream-colored silk blouse. She knew her blue eyes would reveal her grief, but she tried to mask any emotion.

It seemed an eternity to Sharon before he said in the voice she remembered, "Could we sit and talk for a moment?"

That meant she'd have to let go of the door casing. She'd have to turn. But at least she could sit. His hand was outstretched in a gesture toward the waiting room. Automatically, she followed his motion, physically let go of the door casing, turned, and found a chair. He was a blur as he came into the room and she barely registered his dark blue suit. She was seeing him at that other time, before his hair turned to silver at the temples, when he was leaner, at a time when he wondered what life had in store for him. He'd done well. So well.

His quick steps across the multicolored carpet took him to the couch across from her. Spry, for a man of fifty-one. She knew his age. She knew his birthday. She wanted to say, "You've done well, Marcus." But she couldn't—mustn't.

He started to sit, then paused. His look was curious. "Would you like to sit, Mrs. Martin?"

She sat.

"Luke, my son, the doctor," he began, and Sharon nodded, still unable to meet his eyes. "He told me about the accident and has taken a personal interest in Bobby."

Sharon's smile was faint. She must concentrate on Bobby. Only Bobby. She nodded.

The judge took a Barney dinosaur from a bag that hadn't really registered with Sharon until now.

"Oh, it's Bobby's. Or like it."

"My secretary washed it to give it a worn look."

Sharon reached for it. "This is so good of you to do this. It will mean a lot to Bobby." She looked it over. There had been a worn patch on the left ear where the dog had roughed it up. But it was like the one Bobby had. Marcus must have seen it. It must have been in bad shape.

Bobby's grandfather was bringing him a toy—just like his favorite animal. It seemed so right. And yet, Marcus didn't know—must never know. Her eyes closed against the thought.

"I have donated my blood, Mrs. Martin," he was saying. "I have the same type as Bobby."

She looked down at the dinosaur and was grateful for something to hold on to. She willed her fingers not to squeeze so fiercely. "Thank you," she whispered. "So much."

"If there's anything I can do. . . ," he began.

She shrank back into the back of the chair when he leaned forward, his elbows resting on his thighs. "In the meantime," he said, "I'll. . .pray."

Pray? Her eyes met his and held for a long moment, before hers began to swim, and she closed them as the liquid bathed her cheeks.

"You do know the Lord will give you strength for this?" he questioned.

"Oh, yes," she replied. "Please pray."

He bowed his head and began to pray—for her, for Bobby, for God's will. Sharon was so surprised she did not even close her eyes. She simply stared at the man who did not wait until some more convenient, more private time to pray. He prayed openly, sincerely.

When he said, "Amen," Sharon echoed the word, then asked, "Would you like to see Bobby?"

～

Marcus's heart went out to the tiny, gaunt figure against the white sheets as Sharon told him how Bobby had awakened last evening and appeared to recognize her, and had even smiled before drifting off again into that realm where his little body was in the process of healing itself. She repeated what Luke had told Marcus, that the body would heal, but they didn't know yet about the little boy's swollen brain.

Trying to shake the depressing feeling of seeing a life so young lie so near death, Marcus looked around the room. His gaze fell upon a big stuffed brown bear on a side table. It looked almost as big as the child and about as abused, with worn spots, a missing eye, and an ear that had been hand-stitched back on. "The bear must be another of the little fellow's toys," Marcus commented.

"No," Sharon replied, as she took the dinosaur over and set it beside the bear. "It belonged to the teenage boy who received an organ donation from Bobby's dad. It was his favorite, and he'd kept it through the years. He wanted Bobby to have it."

Marcus stared blurry-eyed at the bear, absorbing this new information. What an exchange—and yet, it was the best the teenager had to offer. The bear sat staring expressionless with that one beady eye, as if watching over the child.

But what could a bear do? A memory flashed. Marcus saw his grandmother's wall. A faded picture of Jesus watching over a boy and a girl on a dilapidated old foot bridge. *Surely, Lord, You'll watch over this little guy? What is best? I can't know. Your will be done. But look down on this little one.*

Marcus's eyes then fell upon a picture in a small frame sitting beside the bear. He walked over and picked it up. A young man and woman were sitting, and a little boy was perched on the man's knee. So much like the studio pictures Luke's family had made once a year. This must be little Bobby. The inverted-bowl haircut, with bangs straight across the forehead, was like that of so many little boys, including his own grandsons.

If the little boy regained consciousness, he'd awaken to a picture—not parents. They were gone. His great-grandmother was gone. At least he had a grandmother. But what would all this do to the lifeless figure lying in that bed? And to this grandmother?

Marcus shuddered, and lest it be noticed by Sharon, he sat down in a nearby chair, even before Sharon sat on the edge of the extra bed in the room. She gestured to the many boxes stacked against the wall. "From the public," she said in awe. "I never knew strangers could be so caring."

"Strangers are caring. And here, I'm the attending physician's dad. How can I leave here with having only made that general remark of letting me know if I can do anything? Do you need transportation?" he asked. Luke had said she'd stayed at her mother's home until Bobby left ICU. "I'm free to drive you anywhere you need to go or pick up anything for you."

"I'm fine, thank you," Sharon answered. Helen had become a friend Sharon wouldn't mind asking a favor of when she wasn't working. Also, the pastor and his wife were available, as well as neighbors. Then there were always taxicabs.

Marcus stood. "When you're ready, Mrs. Martin, I can give legal advice, help with any decisions. Please feel free to call on me. I mean it." He reached inside his suit coat and drew out a business card.

Sharon took it, although she didn't need it to know how to reach him. She rose from the bed. "My mother's attorney has already been in touch with me. I think that will be sufficient, Judge Sinclair."

"Marcus," he corrected, and she looked down from his smile, his caring eyes, the warmth in his voice.

"Thank you," she murmured.

When he left the room, Sharon stood motionless. Only for an instant could she allow herself to admire the man Marcus had become—a man of God, a family man who had reared successful children and with whom Luke obviously had a close relationship. A man more personally appealing than that troubled young man of twenty-three years ago.

Sharon pictured Marcus walking down the hall, into the elevator with the doors slowly closing, until he disappeared altogether.

Like the elevator door, her mind must close on the past. She would have no further contact with Marcus Sinclair.

Chapter 9

Two days later, Marcus appeared at the doorway of Bobby's room. Luke had kept him posted on Bobby's condition and on Sharon, who had become like a member of the pediatric-floor family and insisted upon being called by her first name.

Luke said she was responding to every piece of mail that had a return address and that the money sent to her—a considerable amount—was being donated to the pediatric ward. Besides helping with the care of Bobby, she volunteered a couple hours a day in the play room.

Luke apparently considered her an exceptional woman, one to be greatly admired. Marcus himself had been drawn to her. It was not just sympathy because she had lost three loved ones in an instant. Nor the fact that she was an attractive woman. He had prayed aloud in her presence, for her and Bobby. Something about praying for a person formed a bond—made it personal—and he thought of her not as Mrs. Martin but as Sharon.

He stepped inside the room, holding a stack of books. When Sharon looked up, surprised, her face paled. Then he became aware that a couple sat on the edge of her bed.

He held out the books. "My grandchildren wanted to give these to Bobby. Three-year-old Mark said if you read this one to Bobby, he will wake up and laugh."

"Thank you, Judge Sinclair," she said, and her eyes flew to his and held a moment. "I mean. . .Marcus," she corrected. His dark eyes gleamed with pleasure.

"I won't intrude," he said, taking a step backward after Sharon took the books.

"Wait." Sharon laid the books on the table by Bobby's bed. "I'd like to introduce you to Bobby's maternal grandparents. They flew in this morning from California."

The couple stood. "Mary and James Davis. Judge Marcus Sinclair."

Marcus extended his hand to James. "I'm so sorry about your losses," he said, looking from James to Mary. He tried to convey his empathy with their situation. "If there is any way I can be of assistance to you, please don't hesitate to ask."

Seeing the questioning look in Mary's and James's eyes, Sharon said quickly, as if having to explain, "You met Dr. Luke Sinclair. Judge Sinclair is his father. They both have been so kind." She turned to look at the children's books.

"A judge?" James questioned.

"Municipal court," Marcus replied, feeling uncomfortable. At a time like this, Sharon Martin shouldn't have to explain him. She had enough problems. He, too, saw the inquisitive look in the couple's eyes and the way Sharon had turned to look at the books as if she were embarrassed.

"Nice to meet you," he said. "My prayers are with you. Is there anything I can do? Bring something for you? Take you out to dinner?"

"Thanks," James said, "but we're on California time and had a bite not long ago."

"We've been trying to get Sharon to at least go to the cafeteria," Mary added. "It's my understanding she hasn't left here in days."

"At least come down and have a cup of coffee, Sharon," Marcus offered.

She concentrated on inspecting the books. Finally, she turned, looking at the couple. "I've learned where all the coffee stations are. And my supper is always sent up to me, as if I were a patient." Her smile softened her face. "But I could run home for a few items."

"I'll be glad to drive you," Marcus offered.

"No, that's all right," Sharon said.

"You have a ride?" he asked.

"Not really," she hedged. "Perhaps I could take the rental car?" She looked from Mary to James.

"I believe that's against the law," Marcus said seriously, but a grin played about his mouth.

James laughed. "The insurance only covers Mary and me. And with a judge standing here, I'd say you might get arrested if you drove it."

"I'm on the verge of reading her Miranda Rights," Marcus said, and they all laughed lightly.

Sharon smiled.

"Please," Marcus said.

Sharon nodded her agreement.

Marcus sensed that she felt they'd ganged up on her, and she mustn't make a scene.

Mary added, "You can sleep at home tonight, Sharon, if you want. I can stay here. James can stay here or with you, whatever you like."

"No, no," Sharon said quickly. "I'll come right back. I. . .I need to stay here."

"All right, Sharon," Mary replied. "Whatever you want. Now, you scoot.

48

Everything will be fine here."

Sharon nodded. "I'll be back soon, sweet baby." She kissed her fingers, laid them gently on Bobby's cheek, then walked out into the hallway with Marcus Sinclair.

Marcus smiled to himself. A small victory had just been won.

~

"Oh, I'd better give you directions to Mount Pleasant," Sharon said when Marcus pulled out of the parking garage onto a main road.

"Mount Pleasant," he repeated. "I believe I can find it without any trouble."

Of course he could, she told herself. It was a suburb of Charleston. He had lived in the area all of his life. He would know it better than she.

Maybe it was simply saying the name of the quiet section, "Mount Pleasant," aloud, but she felt more relaxed than she had since the accident. It was so reassuring to not have to go through all this alone. Strangers cared, friends helped, Bobby's maternal grandparents were here, and her fear of Marcus recognizing her had been unfounded. This drive would become a part of her memories—the better ones.

Her eyes lifted. The sun had disappeared, leaving behind a serene, cloudless sky. If only it had been clear last week. If only the spring storm hadn't come on so suddenly or so violently. If only they had planned their annual trip for later in the year.

"Relatives," Marcus was saying, drawing her back to the present. "Do you have any close by? To be with you?"

"No," she said quietly and looked at her hands clutching her purse. "But Mother has neighbors who are willing to do anything."

She looked over at him helplessly. "It's just that there's not much anyone can do."

Marcus nodded with understanding.

"For several years now, I've come to Charleston during the Spoleto Festival and sometimes for holidays. This is the first year Robert, Karen, and Bobby flew down with me." She took a deep breath. "Mitchell used to come with me."

"Mitchell?" he questioned.

A forlorn smile touched Sharon's lips. "My husband." She liked talking about Mitchell, the man she had married when Robert was five years old. Mitchell had raised him, loved him as if he were his own son. "He treated me like a queen," she said. "He died of a heart attack five years ago."

Marcus frowned. "That must have been a shock."

Sharon nodded. "His family had a history of heart disease. But he took care of himself and had shown no signs of trouble. He lived longer than many members of his family with the same problem. He was sixty-one."

"Sixty-one?" Marcus questioned, wondering if he'd heard correctly.

"He was older than I."

Marcus smiled. "I would never have believed you were sixty-one anyway."

"I'm forty-three," she said. *No longer a naive nineteen year old.*

Marcus turned on the car lights. Others were being turned on, one by one, like yellow eyes, glowing in the twilight. Like the years of her life, they came close, then whizzed by, only to be followed by another. Life was like that. Yesterday she was nineteen—today she was forty-three. It came—and went—so swiftly. All the chances worth taking came only once.

A ray of late afternoon sun penetrated the windshield and sparked Marcus's dark brown eyes with golden flecks. It touched his hair, not tousled brown anymore, but laced with silver and cut conservatively short. He was as handsome now if not more so, with a fuller, more mature face. The lines around his mouth and at his eyes were deeper, giving character.

She knew he could empathize with her, having experienced personal loss himself. And at times like this, there really wasn't anything else to talk about. "You've lost someone," she said, rather than asked.

He turned onto a main street, leaving the sunshine behind them. "My wife died of cancer eight years ago," he said. "She lived only four months after it was discovered. We were glad she didn't have to suffer long."

"It's always hard on children," Sharon said, wondering how Bobby would deal with this. Her eyes closed, and her head felt like lead on her shoulders.

"They're more resilient than we often give them credit for," Marcus continued, as if knowing she thought of Bobby. "One of our sons was a teenager. Luke and our daughter were already married when Bev died. That helps, I think."

"When Mitchell died of a heart attack, Robert was in college. Robert. . ." Her voice broke. "Robert is my son. The only child I could ever have."

My son, my son! her mind screamed, and it made her throat and head ache. *Our son, Marcus.* She took a tissue from her purse and turned her head toward the window.

"You have Bobby. You have your memories." He added desolately, "That doesn't help, does it?"

"It does help. My world has ended several times during my forty-three years of life. But I've had many wonderful beginnings too. I have been greatly blessed, and I know this is the darkest time of my life. It's something I have to go through. There are no shortcuts through my grief. I know there is pain before there is healing. Although I may seem unable to cope. . ." She drew in a breath. "I am an optimist."

She lifted her shimmering blue eyes and met his sympathetic gaze.

"You'll make it, Sharon," he said with confidence. "You're a strong woman."

"Oh," she said suddenly, "You missed the turn-off."

"I know a different way. Just sit still and leave the driving to me," he said, and the sound of his voice held a playful intimacy that fluttered over her like a butterfly over flowers, fanning possibility. The thought both thrilled and frightened her.

Her eyes shut tightly against the intrusion of the thought of a man in her life. She had reconciled herself to the fact that there would never be another one after Mitchell.

"They lived with me," she said quickly, too quickly, but felt it imperative to dispel her mind's foolish ramblings. "Robert, Karen, and Bobby. Robert was studying architecture. Mitchell was a builder."

"I suppose his dad influenced that decision," Marcus said, watching the traffic carefully.

"Robert respected him so much." She did not reveal that she had been the receptionist in Mitchell's company until they married. "Karen—that's Robert's wife—she worked as an executive secretary for a businessman. Very efficient young woman."

She smiled over at Marcus. "Later on, I became Bobby's full-time baby-sitting grandmother." She laughed lightly. "Except there wasn't much sitting involved."

Marcus gave a short laugh. "I understand. I have three grandchildren of my own."

There was a pause as Marcus turned onto a road leading to the Cooper River Bridge. "Since your husband died, you've had no life of your own?"

"My family was my life."

He gave her a long look as his head turned toward the right, the direction in which the car turned.

Sharon felt she had not answered his question.

Marcus knew she had.

~

The first thing Sharon did when she and Marcus arrived at her mother's house was to call the hospital, letting Mary know they had arrived. Mary reported that all was fine.

As soon as Sharon hung up, a neighbor called, asking if she'd had supper.

"No, but—"

"How many are there?"

"Two, but we—"

51

"I'll be right over."

Several minutes later, an elderly woman and man parked behind Marcus's car, and each brought in a plate covered with foil. "Earline and I often exchanged recipes," she said. "This is her favorite meat loaf. I hope you'll like it."

Sharon couldn't refuse this kind offer. They left after repeating, "Let us know if we can do anything."

"I planned to take you out to a restaurant," Marcus began, but Sharon was shaking her head.

"That takes too long. I need to get back to the hospital soon." She removed the foil to see two plates filled with meat loaf, mashed potatoes, and broccoli. She didn't know if she could sit and have small talk with Marcus. After getting silverware, she said, "Tell me about your children."

He proudly spoke of his daughter Kathleen, expecting her first child, and living on the other side of Charleston. His son Grant was a senior at the Citadel.

The informal meal was soon over, and Marcus suggested he review Earline Johnson's legal papers while Sharon arranged the house for Mary and James's stay that night.

On the ride back to the hospital, Marcus explained that her mother's will left everything to Sharon, which she already knew. The house was paid for, and there was a small insurance policy. Her mother's car was new, since her mother preferred to trade every two years to prevent having to deal with repairs.

"You'll need to notify the Social Security Administration and Medicare of her death," Marcus advised.

Sharon was so grateful for Marcus's help. She'd had to do many of the things he advised after Mitchell died. But she'd had Robert with her then. They had helped each other get through it.

"Luke said Bobby will take several months to return to health, so I'll turn mother's bedroom into a room for him."

"I may be able to help out with some things," Marcus said. "Mark has only recently outgrown his high chair, and it's in Luke's basement. Seems like there's a youth bed. I'll check."

"I can't let you keep helping me like this, Marcus," Sharon protested.

"Why not?" he asked, with a sidelong glance and a grin.

Of course, she couldn't tell him.

Just then, they reached the front of the hospital, where Marcus dropped her off. Sharon hurried to Bobby's hospital room, but she felt as if the short time spent with Marcus had been a bright spot in this tragic situation. Sitting in the passenger seat, having a man drive her somewhere, was something she now realized she'd missed since Mitchell's death. She liked being independent, but she also liked having a man do things for her—with her.

She had faith that some good always came from the worst of things. She'd seen it happen time and again in her own life. And now, good was happening again. Bobby's relatives were near him, caring about him. Her mother, her son, and his wife were in heaven. Sharon would raise Bobby. She'd already had a good start, having been his primary caregiver from the time he was born. He would recover. They'd be a family.

Yes, she had much to look forward to. She was eager to tell Mary and James her plans for Bobby.

Shortly after going into Bobby's room and seeing that he was asleep, Sharon sat on her bed beside Mary and looked over at James in the chair.

"I've been making plans for Bobby," she said with the first trace of excitement she'd felt in a long time. "I want to get legal custody of him," she said, knowing he belonged to her in every way that mattered except as his legal parent.

"Sharon," James said seriously, while Mary looked down at the floor. "Mary and I have been discussing that very thing."

Mary looked up. Although her eyes were sad, her words were clear. "We think it best if James and I have custody of Bobby."

Chapter 10

Kaitlain's pain pill helped Julie through a rough time—and with no apparent adverse effects. After her first decent few hours of sleep in days, she'd checked the records. Kaitlain had slept, so Julie discussed the dosage with Luke and they reduced the level of the pain medication.

While Luke complimented Julie on her sensitivity to Kaitlain's needs, Julie rationalized that what she'd done had turned out even better for Kaitlain and herself. However, she felt so guilty, she vowed never, ever again to chance putting a child in jeopardy. Luke's trust in her must not be harmed, nor the children's, nor, for that matter, her own trust in herself.

She sailed through the morning like a new person, while Luke's face bore a perpetual smile. They exchanged a few jokes, lunched together, and he even asked her opinion about a particularly difficult case.

Julie stopped by Luke's office before leaving for the day. Several of the residents on the day shift for the weekend had decided to eat out and take in a movie.

"Want to join us?" Julie asked. She was wearing a sunny yellow dress that matched both her personality and the bright spring day.

Luke laughed and lifted his hand in a farewell gesture to the spirited young woman.

～

After two days of eight-hour shifts, Julie went on twenty-four-hour call. She felt ready for it. Until the school bus accident. She'd never been so shaken as when she saw those small, mangled children. But the little girl that Dr. Thomas, Luke, and she worked on all evening and into the night was going to be all right. She had to be.

They worked for hours, unaware of fatigue, only of having to save the child's life. After hours and hours of surgery and working with the child, the heart stopped. Julie administered resuscitation, but it didn't work. She willed the child to breathe, demanded the little girl's heart start beating.

The heart remained stubbornly still.

The child didn't take another breath.

The little girl was dead.

Luke held Julie while she cried. "I've never lost a patient before," she wailed.

"That's the worse part," Luke said. The two took comfort from each other. They had shared the most dreaded experience in medicine.

"Now, we have to tell the parents," he said.

Julie looked up at him. "Oh, I can't possibly." That was the hardest. One never learned to be totally objective. Saving lives was their top priority. In this case, they had been helpless. Their best had simply not been good enough.

"All right," he said. "Paul and I will do it. You try and get some rest."

Rest? How could she rest after such an ordeal? There was a way. The only way. Yesterday, after a day shift, Julie had written a prescription for Amy Smith and signed it Julie Dalton, MD. *It is only for emergency,* she told herself. At a drug store, far from the hospital, she'd gone to the pharmacy and looked around while the prescription was being filled. When the pharmacist called "Amy Smith," she paid no attention at first.

That's supposed to be me, she reminded herself after a moment and hurried over. She listened patiently as the pharmacist told her of possible side effects. Julie paid for the prescription and slipped the sleeping pills into her purse.

It's not as if I have to have these, she now told herself. But a child had died. Julie had not been able to save that little life. Sure, Dr. Thomas and Luke were more experienced and in charge, but she was part of the team. It was not anyone's fault. They had done everything within their power. But that didn't make it easy. She could still see that lifeless body in her mind. The little girl would never run and play and be a part of her family's life.

With shaking hands, Julie removed the cap from the bottle of pills. She would need two tonight. If ever there were a reason for a sleeping pill, it was now, and she refused to feel guilty about it. Whether for Amy Smith or Julie Dalton, surely this treatment would be highly recommended by any doctor.

There had been no changes in Bobby's condition. Luke knew he was dwelling on that fact too much. He tried to be objective, but that little boy had touched his heartstrings more than he would have imagined. Then another emergency occurred, requiring his total attention.

Late Friday night, Luke fell into an exhausted sleep, then awoke refreshed and spent the entire morning with his boys. The temperature was in the mid-seventies—a perfect day for splashing around in the pool. Trish joined them for almost an hour before going in to prepare a picnic lunch, which they enjoyed under the shade of an umbrella over a round table. It was almost like old times.

"I'm so glad you're home, Dad," five-year-old Caleb remarked.

Mark chirped, "Me too."

"So am I," Luke said, smiling at his boys. Couldn't Trish see that this was quality time—more important than how many times he was home for dinner or whether he tucked them in at night? "But you guys get to play like this everyday, don't you?"

"Rearing children is life's most important job," Trish said. "At least, that's what you said when you wanted me to stay home and start a family." She looked at the boys. "You guys go rinse off and get changed."

"Oh, Mom. . . ," Caleb began.

"You know you don't stay out in the hot sun too long," she said. They gave her a disappointed look and sent a helpless glance toward their dad. After they went inside, Trish took up the conversation where it had left off.

"It's not all play, Luke. You see, being with them all the time makes me the disciplinarian, which means I'm the villain and you're the good guy."

"I could have told them to go inside, Trish," he remarked.

"It's not that. It's just that I feel like you think every day is just play and no work."

Hearing the edge in her voice rankled him. "I know it's important to play with your children, Trish. But where's the work in that?"

Trish took a deep breath. "Who do you think will go into the bathroom and pick up wet bathing suits? Clean up the watery mess? Comb their hair? Pick up out here? Straighten up the kitchen?"

"Is that so hard, Trish?"

"No. I love taking care of my family. I just don't feel like you see it as important as. . .as saving lives."

He looked down, shaking his head. "I didn't save a life last night. The child died."

"Oh, Luke, I'm so sorry." Guilt washed over her. Her problems couldn't begin to compare with Luke's. Her everyday life was a breeze compared with the life-and-death situations he faced daily. *It's just that I love him so much,* she was thinking. *I want him to appreciate me.* She was about to tell him so when his next words stopped her cold.

"It was really hard on Julie," he said. "It was her first experience of losing a patient."

Trish blurted out, "She didn't do the surgery, did she?"

"She assisted, Trish. Just as I did when I was a resident. Remember?" His voice sounded as cold as Trish felt. "You used to want details. You empathized with me. That's what I'm doing with Julie. You know she's my responsibility for two more years."

Rankled, Trish retorted sharply, "Well, I happen to be your responsibility for life! So are the children! But do we ever see you? No! And when I do, what do you talk about? Julie!"

She jumped up and began clearing the table.

"Come on, Trish. Don't tell me you're jealous of Julie."

"Should I be?"

Luke snorted but didn't bother to answer. Trish strode toward the house with the tray of paper plates and cups. His eyes followed his wife. Trish was a beautiful woman, no doubt about that. But she'd turned into a nag. And her question kept turning around in his mind.

Should you be jealous of Julie, a good-natured, spirited, happy young woman who handles life with courage and purpose? Should you be jealous of a woman who can converse on topics that interest me and makes me feel like I'm doing something worthwhile with my life? Trish, you make me feel inadequate. I don't come up to your standards. I'm not a good husband and father. Should you be jealous?

You bet!

Trish and Luke were cordial for the rest of the day. The family went out for pizza and then took in a movie. The boys had a good time, and Luke realized it would protect his sons from hearing their parents argue. Whatever their troubles, he and Trish had the best interests of the boys at heart and wanted to give the appearance of a stable, happy family.

~

Since Luke had duty on Sunday, he couldn't go to church with his family the next day, so Trish invited Marcus home for lunch. She cleaned up while Marcus and the boys played games. Later, while the boys were resting, watching a video, she and Marcus sat in the shade of the patio roof.

As the afternoon progressed, Marcus realized his daughter-in-law was trying to hide a great unhappiness. While he didn't want to push a confidence, he also knew how isolated she could feel. She certainly couldn't confide to the wives of Luke's colleagues about her problems. Maybe he could be of some help.

"Trish," he asked quietly, "what's troubling you?"

"I wish Luke were more like you, Marcus. You're so good with the children, so patient, put them ahead of your own self. You work, but you're never too busy for us. You spend more time with the boys than their own father does."

"His work is more demanding, Trish. I have more time. And I need these kids. I don't have a wife, you know, and no one to really share my life with."

Trish bit on her lip to keep back the tears. "Neither does Luke—anymore." She shook her head. "He doesn't want me anymore, Marcus. He doesn't love me anymore."

"Now, Trish—" Marcus began.

"No, it's true. People fall out of love. And, he has."

"You want me to talk to him?"

"No," Trish said abruptly. "That would just give him another reason to dislike me. He hates me, Marcus."

"Trish, you know that's not true."

"You know the saying, hate is very close to love. This is love in reverse. We can't talk; we argue. He thinks I don't understand him. Well, I understand him quite well. Too well—and that's his problem. It's not me who's on his mind, Marcus. It's Julie."

"Julie? His assistant?"

"She's all he talks about."

Marcus's mind leaped into the past to that time when his own marriage had been so troubled. He hadn't liked his wife. It was as if the commitment to her had grown null and void. His feelings had been hostile toward her. He'd thought she didn't understand what it took to pass his bar exam or how important it was to him. She'd even said if he didn't pass it the first time, and many didn't, he could take it again, as if failure to pass or waiting to begin his career was of no consequence.

That had infuriated him. He'd thought she didn't care. Only years later did he come to realize she was right. It wouldn't have been the end of the world if he'd had to take it over. It would only have wounded his pride.

But it could have been the end of the world for his children if he and his wife had separated—if he had not remained and been a father to them, if he had not realized that he needed the Lord's help to be the kind of man he should be.

Marcus listened with a sense of familiarity as Trish poured out her doubts. "They seem trivial when I say them, don't they, Marcus? We don't have any big problems like the families affected by the school bus accident. I don't know; maybe it's just me."

"I can't say, Trish. But I know you two were in love when you married. And obviously, you still love Luke."

She nodded. "I just feel like I'm losing him."

"Marriages go through a lot of changes, Trish. People grow and change. It's not easy. Since you don't want me to talk to Luke, I can't speak for him. But let me give you a little advice. Although it may seem unfair and contrary to your natural reactions, don't lash out at him. Make him believe you understand the burden of his work."

"I really do," she admitted.

"Then remind him of your love. When he comes home, don't tell him he doesn't appreciate you. Just share your good experiences of the day. I don't know if a man can ever truly understand the effort it takes to be a good homemaker. I knew a little along the way, but not completely until after Bev died. I now know it takes up a lot of time just in daily living, shopping, cooking, laundry, keeping things straight. And I'm just one person. That's why I hired a housekeeper."

She smiled, and her eyes filled with tears. She laid her hand on his arm. "I wish you could find someone, Marcus."

"I'm all right," he said, but an unusual thought crossed his mind. He had been satisfied as a widower for years. But suddenly the idea of having a wife seemed appealing, and he didn't really want to admit why.

Chapter 11

Marcus wondered how he could approach Sharon—or if he should. This was such a difficult time in her life, trying to cope with her losses. She wouldn't be thinking of any kind of relationship with a man—not with every moment spent concentrating on her grandson's recovery.

It wasn't the kind of situation where he could just invite her out to dinner. No doubt, she wouldn't go any farther than the hospital cafeteria. He couldn't think of any way he might be of assistance to her, other than through what he'd already done. But that had been minor. The legal papers he'd looked over had been easy. Her mother left her everything—period!

Maybe he should remember what he'd said to Trish. He didn't have a woman in his life, and that meant he had time for his grandchildren. He'd been content with that for several years, even though he had enjoyed an occasional companionable dinner with a woman. He shouldn't be thinking of anything more serious.

But he was. Even when he responded to the buzzer indicating he had a call on line two.

"Marcus?"

"Speaking."

"This is Sharon Martin. I don't want to impose, but you did say to call if I needed—"

"I meant it," he interrupted, elation being replaced by concern. "Is Bobby all right?"

"Oh, he's improving by leaps and bounds," she said. "But I need some legal advice."

"Do you want me to come to the hospital?"

"When it's convenient."

Marcus pushed aside the file folders on his desk. "What about lunch?" He added quickly, "In the hospital cafeteria."

~

After her initial shock wore off, Sharon could not feel anger at Mary and James for wanting custody of Bobby. She knew they loved him. He was their deceased daughter's child—their first and only grandchild—but her home in California was the only home Bobby had ever known.

Sharon wanted what was best for Bobby. But how could she stand it if the best wasn't herself? She knew she had to put aside her resolve not to be involved with Marcus and instead follow through on his offer to give legal advice. Marcus had seemed eager to meet her. She was glad he suggested the cafeteria. She didn't want to be away from Bobby for too long now that Mary and James had returned to California.

Her heart skipped a beat, seeing that Marcus was waiting for her at a small table near a window. She chose a salad and skim milk, then sat opposite him.

"Shall we say grace?" he asked.

Sharon could have cried listening to Marcus's words while he offered a prayer of thanks and asked for wisdom to deal with life's difficulties. How different from her encounter with him twenty-three years ago. This is how a relationship should develop. But that was not possible in this instance.

After the prayer, before taking a bite of his veggie-burger, he asked, "How can I help you, Sharon?"

She told him about Mary and James wanting custody of Bobby. "I don't want Bobby to feel the tension of his grandparents fighting a battle in court," Sharon said. "But what choice do I have?"

"Tell me about Mary and James," Marcus urged.

Sharon told about their characters, their son and daughter, their lifestyle, their past involvement with Bobby. She feared this conflict would permanently damage her relationship with Mary and James. How could it ever be reconciled?

"Surely," she added after giving him the information, "a judge would take into account that I have been the mother figure for Bobby."

"We know that was your role, Sharon," Marcus said. "But a judge might see it differently. Many children are taken to baby-sitters or day-care workers until their parents get off work, but a judge wouldn't give custody to those persons."

"If Bobby could choose, he would choose me. He and his parents lived in my home in California. I was with him every moment."

"Yes, and if I were the judge, I'd choose you, but a judge has to try to be impartial and act according to the law. There is no doubt you have been like a mother to Bobby. However, the maternal grandparents, being of high moral character as you indicate and with two teenagers in the home, have an edge. It's a family, Sharon, with a male authority figure in the home.

"My suggestion is to continue as you have in the past. Give Bobby the best of care, and stay on good terms with Mary and James. They may think differently after some time has passed. Right now, they're trying to hold onto a part of their daughter."

Sharon closed her eyes for a moment. "How could I manage without him?"

"You have him right now," Marcus said. "Just take it a day at a time."

Her warm gaze met his eyes. A slight turn of her lips indicated she would try that. "I know you're right. God has a way of bringing so much good from a situation that looks hopeless."

He smiled, nodding, knowing what she meant.

For the next few weeks, Sharon did as Marcus suggested and as she had done many times in the past: She took things one day at a time. The IVs were removed from Bobby's arms, but he still had to be medicated for pain and to keep him from becoming so active that he'd risk damage to his internal organs while they healed. He had settled into a routine of long morning and afternoon naps as well as sleeping through the night.

He called for his mommy and daddy a time or two but seemed content when Sharon told him they couldn't come right now and she would tell him all about it later. She had been with Bobby almost every moment of his life. His parents had worked days, had even taken vacations without him. But Sharon had always been there for him, making sure he felt loved and secure.

There had not been a need for additional surgery. It was still uncertain what damage the head trauma might have done, but the swelling on the brain was receding, and Bobby was slowly coming out of his coma. His eyes had begun to flutter open, alight on Sharon, then close. She continued to spend nights in his room and most of her time during the day there as well so he would feel secure whenever he opened his eyes.

On Monday morning after the nurse had bathed him and he'd seemed to be breathing deeply as he slept, Sharon was answering mail that continued to come in with encouraging words. She looked over at his face. Something looked different. His face seemed more peaceful. Then she saw his eyelids quiver.

"Bobby?" Sharon whispered, hurrying over to the chair next to the bed, where she often sat and stroked his arm and talked or prayed aloud. She touched his forehead.

His eyes slowly opened but appeared glazed, and he didn't seem to recognize her before they closed again. Was there brain damage? She pressed a button, and a nurse's voice over the intercom immediately asked, "Do you need something?"

"I think Bobby's waking up," Sharon said in a soft, hopeful voice.

"I'll send someone in," the nurse said.

Sharon kept talking, telling Bobby she was with him, touching his face, his arm, his hand. His lips moved, but no sound came. Oh, how she wanted to see his eyes open, to hear his voice, to know he would be whole and healthy again. "So many people love you, Darling. Can you please wake up?"

His eyes moved beneath his lids, and they slowly opened again. This time his gaze held hers a little longer, in spite of the drowsy look.

By that time, the nurse came in. She was taking his temperature when Julie appeared and began to listen to his heart. Luke wasn't far behind. "The monitors indicate the swelling has almost completely receded," Luke said. "He probably is coming out of his coma." He watched as Julie checked Bobby's eyes.

Bobby tried to move away from the light. Julie stepped back and looked at Luke, then Sharon, with a huge smile on her face. She nodded.

Luke was obviously delighted that Bobby was regaining consciousness. "He's a little fighter."

"Yes, yes, he is," Sharon agreed. "Bobby, this is Grandmother, Honey."

His head turned toward her. His eyes focused for a short time, but long enough that Sharon knew he recognized her. A sound came from his throat. Luke said that was good. He was trying to talk, but it might take awhile.

Sharon would not leave the room now for anything. Her lunch was brought in to her. It was afternoon when it happened again. This time Bobby's eyes looked tired, but he muttered, "Granmudder." Then she watched as his eyes tried to focus as they looked around the room. They lit upon the dinosaur.

"Di-sor," he said in a tiny, weak voice.

"Yes, Darling," Sharon said and put the stuffed animal next to him so his cheek could brush against its plush fur. He tried to move his arms, but they were fastened down so he wouldn't be able to thrash around or pull out the IVs.

Sharon explained that he'd been hurt in an accident but was going to be fine. He drifted away again, and an hour later he awoke. "Granmudder," he said.

Sharon asked if he remembered that she told him he had been in an accident and was in the hospital, and he said yes. She thought that was a sign that his little mind was working just fine. "Mommy," he said.

"I'll tell you about Mommy and Daddy later, Darling. Right now, just rest and get well, so I can take you home." She told him about his grandparents having come to visit.

During visiting hours, Marcus came. He brought one of Caleb and Mark's videos and a monkey holding a plastic balloon that read "Get well soon."

"Luke told me the wonderful news," he said excitedly, coming into the room, then went right over to Bobby, whose eyes were closed. Marcus told him what he'd brought. Bobby opened his eyes and stared at Marcus. His little eyes lit up when he looked at the monkey, and his lips tried to smile.

Sharon felt her heart would burst. This was the first look that had passed between Bobby and his grandfather. Neither knew. Would they ever?

Chapter 12

Sharon thought that when Dickens wrote, "It was the best of times, it was the worst of times," he must have had her situation in mind. It was that way with Bobby and with Marcus.

She couldn't be happier that Bobby's complete recovery appeared imminent. She hired a private nurse for when Bobby would leave the hospital. The nurse, a very competent young woman named Lisa, was recommended by Luke. She was a good nurse but didn't want to work full-time and had been looking for the kind of private duty that suited her. She worked on the pediatric floor and had already fallen in love with Bobby, as had the entire city, so it seemed.

Lisa gave the hospital notice that she would leave the hospital at the end of the month and began to come into Bobby's room whenever she could. Finally, she was assigned to duty as his day nurse.

Along with the expectations of taking Bobby home in a few weeks, Sharon felt a terrible dread as the time grew closer when his maternal grandparents would seek custody. She couldn't possibly let that child go without a fight. At the same time, she wondered if she had enough courage to enter into a court battle against people she'd come to love and respect. However, she would do what she thought best for Bobby.

A couple of days after Bobby awoke, he'd asked for his mommy. Sharon had waited until he asked, then explained there had been a car wreck. His mommy and daddy were now in heaven with Jesus.

"Want Mommy 'n' Daddy," he protested.

"I know, Darling. So do I. But they are with Jesus in heaven. He wanted you to stay here with me and others who love you so much, like Grandma Mary, Grandpa James, Aunt Kim, Uncle Brad."

"And dem," he said. Sharon looked around to see that Luke and Julie were coming into the room. He must instinctively know how these doctors had cared about him, gently examined and talked to him.

"What's this all about?" Luke asked playfully.

Bobby giggled.

"We were talking about all the people who love him," Sharon said, moving back so the doctors could examine Bobby.

"I'd better be on that list," Luke said as Bobby looked trustingly at Luke, not just his doctor, but his uncle.

Sharon looked out the window for a long moment, thinking that Mitchell died before Bobby was born. None of Mitchell's relatives had even visited after he died.

How wonderful if Bobby could know his daddy's relatives—Uncle Luke in this room and others not very far away: Grandfather Marcus, Aunt Trish, Aunt Kathleen, Uncle Brian, Cousin Caleb, and Cousin Mark. These were his paternal relatives. Must he never know?

"One day at a time," Marcus had said.

Yes, she thought, *I will not worry but do whatever I think is best for my only relative in the world—my precious Bobby.*

She could capture picture memories for Bobby on film. She could get a video camera and film Luke with Bobby. She could tape Marcus stopping in to visit, bringing books and videos, as he had insisted his grandsons wanted him to do. She would keep the tape, along with the newspaper clippings she had in California about Marcus and his family. Someday, when Bobby grew up, he would want to know about his background. She could give him more than a verbal description. He could be proud of his dad's relatives.

When Marcus called to say that he wouldn't be able to get away from court to visit Bobby that day and asked if he could do anything, Sharon told him about wanting to get a video camera.

Marcus had a better idea. She could use his. It was rarely used anymore. Luke had his own that was used for family gatherings and capturing events involving Caleb and Mark.

He brought it the next day and took turns filming Bobby with his grandmother, with Lisa, and with the children in the playroom where Bobby was allowed to watch for the first time.

Later, when Luke and Julie came in to check on Bobby, Luke gave his dad and the video camera a mock annoyed look. "I guess you know, Dad, I wouldn't allow just anybody to do that."

Marcus laughed. "That's an advantage of being a father," he said.

"But in this hospital, the doctor's word is law, not the judge's," Luke retorted.

Julie and Sharon laughed, and so did Bobby, although Sharon didn't think he understood the light bantering. But he could understand the feeling of camaraderie that passed between Marcus and Luke. She was glad the conversation, too, was captured for Bobby to hear at some later time.

Oddly, it was the video camera that seemed to break down any barriers between her and Marcus. It was always there to turn to, to use, to focus attention upon. Bobby was becoming a regular little actor, saving his best performances for Marcus and the camera. Bobby was excited when Sharon told him she would fix up her mother's bedroom for him and would find some wallpaper to make it just right for when he'd go home in a few weeks.

Sharon rather regretted when Marcus asked, "What kind of pictures do you want on your wallpaper?" She knew it could be some impossible request but hoped it might be "Di-sor."

"Booey Beese," he said.

"What's that again?" Marcus questioned, glancing at Sharon, who grinned.

"Dis!" His finger stabbed the book that Mark had said he'd like—*Beauty and the Beast*.

"Oh, I think we can handle that," Marcus said confidently.

"Can we?" Sharon wasn't so sure. Especially about the "we" part.

However, when Lisa came in after Bobby's supper to sit and read to him, Marcus insisted that Sharon allow him to help her find "Booey-Beese" wallpaper.

~

Marcus could hardly believe how much he'd changed in the short time he'd known Sharon. Driving her to a home-decorating store and looking for *Beauty and the Beast* wallpaper had suddenly become the most important moment of his day. During the past few years, he'd enjoyed going out to dinner or a special function with a woman but was always glad to be going home alone, to his comfortable home where he liked his own space, his own peace and quiet. Lately, however, that peace and quiet had turned to loneliness. And he'd found himself thinking how nice it would be to share that home with someone, and invariably Sharon was on his mind.

"You don't need to go in, Marcus," Sharon said. "I know a lot of men hate to shop."

He'd never particularly liked it. But he wanted to do this. His smile was broad. "I'm looking forward to this," he said.

As it turned out, that pattern was popular in a couple of designs, and they decided to accentuate the cartoon characters and downplay the Beast without overdoing the Beauty. After getting the wallpaper, Marcus delighted in Sharon's appreciation of his reminding her they'd need paste, brushes, a cutter, and other tools.

"I thought you just wet it and hung it," she said.

Marcus laughed. "Have you never hung wallpaper before?"

"Like I mentioned before," she said, as if redeeming herself for not being an expert wallpaper hanger, "Mitchell was a builder. Our house is very modern, mainly white, and no wallpaper."

At last, he thought on the way to her house, *I've found a way to spend time with her. And whether or not she knows it, she will need me with this project.*

After unloading the materials in the kitchen, they went into her mother's bedroom that was to be remodeled for Bobby. Marcus sighed and shook his head, pretending chagrin. "I may be taking my life in my hands, but I'm willing to help you."

"Taking your life in your hands?" she questioned.

"Hanging wallpaper together leads to violence," he said, "as does teaching someone to drive a car."

Sharon laughed. "Oh, I've heard things like that, but I suspect it's grossly exaggerated. My dad taught me to drive when I was fifteen. We had no problems. Really, I think we can handle it. After all, we're both adults."

His glance was skeptical, but he said, "First thing is to get this furniture out of here."

"Really, Marcus. I can hire someone to do this."

He gazed at her thoughtfully, then grinned, "Let's try it together. I haven't had a good fight in a long time."

~

Sharon had liked Marcus's playfulness about their possibly fighting while hanging wallpaper, but she certainly had no intention of their project coming close to blows. She appreciated his willingness to help. Two nights later, however, after her mother's furniture had been stored away in the basement and they'd begun to cut, measure, paste, and hang, she did find a few things slightly irritating.

"You've got to let go if I'm going to match this up," Marcus said, standing on the ladder.

"You just told me to push the seams together and hold them."

"Right, after I get things lined up at the top."

"You didn't say that, Marcus."

"I expected you to know."

"Are you calling me stupid?" she asked and pulled the paper away from the wall.

"Now you've torn it," he said, letting go. The entire sheet tumbled down.

"Me? I'm not the one pulling and tugging and telling me to line up the seams, then saying let go. You have the easy part."

He came down. "Okay, we'll cut another piece, and you get up there."

She felt like lashing out at him, or crying, or something, but refused to let him see she was upset. He was helping. But she should have hired it out. Her hands trembled as she tried to cut along the metal square. Her eyes became blurry.

"Here, let me," Marcus said gently. "I'm sorry."

She sniffed. "So am I."

He cut the paper. She helped him turn it over on the kitchen table, and they were very careful to fold at the right places as he brushed on the paste.

He carried the folded piece into the bedroom, and Sharon climbed the ladder. She caught hold of the edges and matched it at the top, feeling she had redeemed herself. However, as he began to unfold the piece, her fingers relaxed. The weight of the paper pulled it off the wall and right down on his head.

"Get this stuff off me!" he yelled.

Sharon gasped, then began to laugh. "Don't move. You just hold it right there." Marcus stood stiff as a board while she hurried to get the video camera. "Oh, this is great," she said, still laughing while the camera began to grind.

"I'm sorry, Marcus," she said, "But this is priceless."

After filming for awhile from various angles, she put the camera down and went over to pick the wallpaper off him. "I shouldn't have done that, should I?"

He acted gruff. "People have gotten divorced over things like this."

She stared into his eyes and watched as they began to dance. "Of course," he added, "they have to get married first."

Sharon stopped her laughing and would not look into his eyes again. "Your hair is full of paste. Let's go back to the way we started."

Her eyes met his again, and she knew he thought what she did. They should go back, not just to his climbing the ladder, but to subjects that did not get too personal.

He climbed the ladder, and they continued with precision, each more careful than before.

"It's beautiful," Sharon exclaimed when they'd finished with the long pieces and cleaned up the mess.

Marcus nodded. "Looks pretty good," he said. "Even though you did throw wet wallpaper at me."

Sharon laughed. "You'd better get that paste out of your hair. There's shampoo in the bathroom."

While Marcus was shampooing his hair, Sharon called Mary and James, having figured that with the time difference the couple should be home from work and have finished supper. She wanted to keep them informed about Bobby's progress.

They were delighted that Bobby might soon be going home.

"I hope you're taking some time for yourself, Sharon," Mary said.

"Yes, I leave the hospital occasionally, usually after supper when Lisa comes in and reads to him. He goes to sleep right after that and doesn't awaken until morning."

"You go out alone?"

"Not always. You remember Marcus?"

"The judge?" James put in from another phone.

"Yes, he has been very helpful with things like legal matters." She also told them about his helping with the wallpaper.

"It would be wonderful if you had a man in your life, Sharon," Mary said.

"Oh, no. It's not like that. I'll be returning to California as soon as Bobby is well. We'll talk then, Mary, James."

"Are you angry with us, Sharon?" Mary asked gently.

Sharon took a deep breath. "Not angry. Oh, Mary, you and James please pray about this. I want what is best for Bobby. I. . .we'll talk about it when I return. Okay?"

"Sharon, we're not trying to hurt you, and this is not against you."

"Yes, I know, Mary. Like me, you want what is best for Bobby."

She stared at the phone for a long moment after they said their good-byes. What would a judge think was best for Bobby?

Just then, she heard Marcus coming out of the bathroom. When she turned and saw him, towel-drying his hair, she smiled. "Would you like a sandwich?"

While they ate in the kitchen, Marcus said they could paste the border on the following day.

"I don't know if that's a good idea," she replied, and laughed. "After today's fiasco."

He smiled. "Haven't you heard? A couple who survives wallpapering together can handle anything."

"Oh?" she quipped. "I thought the saying was about praying together."

The smile left his lips, and he looked across at her seriously. "We've done that too."

Sharon swallowed a bite too large and quickly took a sip of tea. Her heart leaped at the implication. But at the same time, she knew there could never be a close relationship between her and Marcus, because to tell him the truth would destroy their relationship.

"I will have to return to California as soon as Bobby is well enough," she reminded him.

"Would you consider returning to Mount Pleasant? If not permanently, then visits throughout the year. Where there's a will, there's a way, you know."

Oh, if things were different. If there were not that one night of indiscretion twenty-three years ago, she would be willing to discuss that and pursue a serious relationship with this wonderful man. Although the past could be forgiven, it could not be erased.

She shook her head. "I believe Bobby needs me, Marcus. If I don't get custody, I will still have to be nearby. Although he loves Mary and James, I know he would be devastated without me. If I do get custody, how could I take him from Mary and James?"

"It is a dilemma," Marcus admitted. "In the meantime, Sharon, I want to say that my time spent with you means a lot to me. I hope it can continue as long as you are here."

Sharon looked away. She couldn't see how there might be a future together for the two of them. But if the most there could be were memories, she would treasure them forever.

Chapter 13

Intent on helping Sharon get her mother's house ready for Bobby's release from the hospital, Marcus talked to Luke and Trish about their baby furniture. Both were eager to allow Sharon to borrow a youth bed that was stored in their basement. There was also a high chair that might be useful in helping confine Bobby instead of letting him run around too much before his body was ready.

When the day came to pick up the furniture, for a moment Sharon felt like she couldn't possibly go to the house where Marcus and Bev had lived, where they had reared their children. Then she told herself that was exactly what she should do to keep her own resolve in perspective. She must face reality and entertain no thoughts about a serious relationship between her and Marcus.

Sharon was soon put at ease by Trish's obvious delight in meeting her. Luke came home early for a change. He and Trish insisted Sharon and Marcus have dinner with them. Trish had beef roast, potatoes, onions, and carrots smothered in cream of mushroom soup warming in the oven, ready for the table.

Sharon's resistance to their dinner invitation didn't last long with Luke, Trish, and Marcus laying out the reasons why this was more practical and would get her back to the hospital more quickly than if she went home and prepared something for herself.

After dinner, they all settled on the patio with cool lemonade while the boys rode their bikes on the concrete around the pool. Sharon spoke of it reminding her of her own home in California.

When Sharon mentioned that she would return to California when Bobby was well, she didn't notice the darkening of Marcus's face. Trish did, however, and after the older couple left, she mentioned to Luke how it might be nice for his father to have a woman like Sharon in his life permanently. For the first time in a long time, they actually agreed on something. Luke even agreed that Trish and the boys might take a birthday gift to Bobby. He had told Sharon she could have a small gathering and even a cake. A big party or too much excitement wouldn't be good for him at this time, but Bobby had come to rely on Luke to care for him and upon Marcus to visit with him almost every day.

"I think it would be a nice gesture," Luke said to Trish, "if you and the boys were there as well."

Remembering Marcus's advice, Trish bit her tongue to keep from asking if Julie would be there. Of course she would. She was the resident physician, Luke's trainee. That's what Luke would have said had she asked.

~

It started out as a lovely day. At two in the afternoon, Trish, Caleb, and Mark arrived for the party. Marcus, Sharon, and Lisa were already in the room. A cake with blue frosting, a small car, and three candles sat on the portable eating tray. On the dresser were clown-decorated paper plates, napkins, cups, and apple juice.

Sharon was videotaping all the happenings.

Bobby got to sit in a chair for this occasion. As soon as Luke came in, they all sang "Happy Birthday" to Bobby. Almost immediately, Luke left because he had to see other patients.

Marcus took the camera while Sharon lit the candles and rolled the table over to Bobby.

"Make a wish," Caleb said.

"I wish. . .I wish—"

"No, it won't come true if you say it out loud," Caleb warned. "Make a wish and blow out the candles."

Bobby blew, and all three candles were out on the second try. Sharon noticed how much weaker his breaths had been than before the accident. She was thankful her grandson was healing, but obviously he was still very weak.

Bobby appeared stronger, however, when he tore into the presents. Luke and Trish gave him a doctor's kit.

"I got one like that," Mark told him.

Marcus got him a picture book that made sounds when he pressed certain buttons. "You're gonna like this," Mark said when Bobby began to open his present. It was a black dragon with orange wings that could be clipped off and on and flapped up and down.

Caleb gave him a video of the popular children's series of *Cupcakes,* acting out Christian principles. "That one's adorable," Trish said. "It's based on a true story of a child who fell off a cliff in North Carolina and was saved by the creator of these videos. He used his cupcake voices to keep her calm until rescuers could get to her."

"I haven't heard of these," Sharon said.

"They haven't been on the market very long," Trish explained.

"I can vouch for them too," Marcus said. "They're great baby-sitters and teachers at the same time."

"Oh, so that's what you guys do at your house, Marcus?" Trish quipped.

"At least one hour out of the entire day." He laughed. "Those grandsons of mine wouldn't sit still longer than that."

Lisa brought him a book of Bible stories. There was a gift from Julie—a bank in the shape of a clown that reached out to grab the coins and put them in the top of his head.

Sharon got Bobby a small farm with animals that might keep him occupied. It wouldn't be easy to keep a three-year-old boy down once he felt better, and he was showing every sign of that.

"Oh, neat," Caleb said. "I like that horse."

"Maybe you and Mark can come and play with Bobby sometime," Sharon said. She was operating the camera again.

"I wish I could play now," Bobby said, starting to get down from the chair.

"Hold it, Buddy," said a voice from the doorway. Luke had returned. "You have to rest now, so you'll feel like playing later."

"Can I eat some cake?"

"One piece, then to bed for a nap. Your toys will be waiting for you."

~

Trish knew she should have known better than to broach the subject of Julie again. And yet, the past few days' camaraderie with Luke had given her a false sense of security, as if things were back to the way they used to be. So that evening she brought the subject up.

"I thought Julie would be at Bobby's party."

"She had the day off," Luke said shortly.

Trish felt dismayed that Luke acted defensively if she even said Julie's name. "Right, but Bobby was your top priority for so long, I still thought she would have at least dropped by. I mean, you talked about how concerned she was about him, how much you two had to consult on his condition."

Seeing the cloud cover Luke's face, Trish knew she was treading in deep water. But she should be able to mention Julie without it becoming some kind of issue.

"She needed time away from her work, Trish. She asked me to take Bobby's present to him."

"It just seemed strange, that's all."

"No, Trish. The unusual part is that doctors get presents for patients in the first place."

"Not a patient like Bobby," Trish contradicted. "He has attracted the attention of the entire city, if not the nation."

"Then you might ask Julie why she wasn't at the party, if it's that important to you, Trish. She will be among our guests for the cookout."

Last year, the annual early summer cookout was at Paul Thomas's home. This year, it was Luke's turn. And Julie would be here. Trish dreaded seeing the woman she'd like to sue for alienation of her husband's affection. Maybe it would prove the opposite, however—that her fears were based on an overactive imagination. Maybe she was unnecessarily jealous because Julie had a closeness with Luke in a way she did not.

Trish knew how closely residents and physicians worked together, how much they collaborated and depended upon each other, and how each valued the other's expertise. She also knew that Luke considered Julie the brightest, prettiest, most valuable resident he'd ever trained.

"Are you up to it, Trish?" Luke asked, bringing her back to the issue at hand.

"I'm looking forward to it, Luke," she said and knew that pleased him. It was important to him to entertain his colleagues. And he needed a little relaxation. She was determined to make a good impression on Luke and their friends and was determined to stop imagining things that were probably only in her own mind. Luke was her husband. He came home to her every night, even if it was usually late and even if his conversation centered on Julie more than on her.

Actually, Trish hadn't realized that the cookout would be upon them in little over a week. Her days were fuller than usual, now that Caleb was out of school. She would ask Luke's sister, Kathleen, to keep the boys overnight. Marcus would be happy to help, but she wanted him at the cookout. He knew all the doctors anyway and was friends with a couple of them.

To be honest, she wanted Marcus there. He gave her confidence, but she also wanted his opinion about Luke and Julie after seeing them together in this informal setting. Maybe he would convince her that her imagination had run away with her or that any suspicions were totally unfounded. No, Trish decided, she'd ask for her mom's help and would borrow Marcus's housekeeper.

If she did it well enough, maybe she and Luke could have a romantic evening afterward. Guests would be arriving around four to take advantage of the pool, lounge on the patio, and play games in the basement rec room. Generally at these gathering, they ate around six, and guests began to leave by eight o'clock. Trish and Luke had always left as soon as politely able, eager to return home and spend the evening together—that is, before they began to drift apart after she became so busy with the children.

Maybe if she worked it right, Luke would appreciate her efforts and maybe see her, not just as his wife and the mother of his children, but as an attractive, appealing woman. They'd have the entire night alone, and the boys wouldn't come home the next day until she called Kathleen. Yes, maybe this would be the perfect time for her and Luke to get back on track.

And maybe Julie would make an excuse not to come.

That thought frightened Trish. She wanted Luke to tell her that his feelings for Julie were strictly on a business level. She wanted Julie to bring a boyfriend. The last thing she wanted was confirmation that her suspicions were true. Before now, she had not allowed herself to think what could happen to her marriage, to her family.

While continuing to make plans, Trish began to dread the reality of what she might discover at the cookout.

~

Marcus looked forward to the cookout and asked Sharon to join him. She gave several excuses why she shouldn't. She didn't want to infringe on his family's gatherings. She didn't want to leave Bobby for very long. Then she laughed and asked if he were so desperate for a date.

He smiled. "No, I've dated several women. And my friends manage to let me know they've invited a spare woman at couples' parties. This one doesn't require a date. But I'm asking you, Sharon."

She didn't consent until after Luke invited her. After examining Bobby, he had given her the good news. Bobby could go home on Sunday.

"Oh, Luke, thank you. Thank you so much." She couldn't resist hugging him. Feeling his strong young arms around her, for a moment she reveled in the thought that this was her son's half brother. Grief and joy threatened to overwhelm her. She stepped back and wiped her eyes with a tissue.

He smiled warmly. "Now, you are to take some time out for yourself," he said. "Doctor's orders. And on the agenda is a cookout at my house next Saturday."

"Oh, I wouldn't know anyone," she said.

"You know me. Trish. Caleb. Mark. Marcus. Julie. Paul Thomas. And you've met several others who'll be there. Also, my sister, Kathleen, and her husband, Bo, want to meet you."

Bobby had received a card from Kathleen and Bo, wishing him a speedy recovery. Sharon reminded herself that the past was past, and there was no real reason why she should refuse. Besides, she wanted to meet this daughter of Marcus's. She could file that memory along with others to tell Bobby about someday. Until now, she'd almost forgotten how she'd enjoyed such gatherings when Mitchell was alive.

Trish calling to invite Sharon clinched her decision. And it wasn't as if she or Marcus thought there was anything between them other than friendship. Now with Bobby's release scheduled to take place in a couple of days, the time was drawing closer when she would return to California.

When Marcus called that afternoon, Sharon told him she couldn't be away from Bobby for an entire afternoon and evening but would drop in for awhile if all was well with Bobby.

"Trish told me you accepted," Marcus said. "How did she manage to convince you?"

"She agreed to let me bring a batch of cookies from my mother's secret recipe."

"I'll let you bring cookies this evening if you'll have dinner with me, at my house."

"I haven't made the cookies yet, so I'll bring a special one for you to the cookout. But seriously, Marcus, I do want to talk to you about something."

"That's what I was about to say to you," he replied. "I'll pick you up at seven."

Chapter 14

Later that evening, Marcus picked Sharon up in his town car. She liked riding through the streets of historic Charleston. She'd taken this area for granted when she was a young girl and had preferred the more modern neighborhoods.

"Although I lived here when I was young," she said, "I never saw the inside of any historic homes until a few years ago when Mitchell came with me in the spring and we took the historic tour."

"My home is in the historic district, though not on the tour list," Marcus said. "But there's something exciting about seeing crowds of people throng the sidewalks and appreciate the beauty and history of these homes."

He mentioned several they passed, such as the Calhoun Mansion. "If anyone had told me when I was young that I'd return to the house I grew up in, I would have thought they'd lost their minds." He laughed. "I guess one appreciates history and memories more as one grows older."

"Oh, I think you're definitely right," Sharon said as Marcus pulled into a narrow driveway between two houses very close together as historic homes typically were built. She liked the smell of the sea and the looks of the cobblestone streets, the decorative wrought-iron railings that bordered the sidewalks, and the various designs of homes—Federal, Georgian, Early Victorian. "I particularly like the gardens."

"Be my guest," he said, gesturing straight ahead toward the high iron gate. They got out of the car, and he held open the gate for her to pass through, then fastened it. "It's more colorful when the azaleas are in bloom."

"Oh, but this is lovely," she said, always amazed at how much Charlestonians could pack into a garden. High wooden walls blocked out any sight of the nearby neighbors, giving complete privacy to the benches and tables surrounded by tall and short bushes, trimmed boxwood, beautiful pink, red, and white anemones, and myriads of plants, now lushly green.

"I admit I don't spend much time gardening," he said.

Sharon noticed, but the possibilities of the space abounded. With a little pruning here, a little weeding there. . . "I like it," she said.

"Since we're right at the back door, do you mind going in this way?"

"I've heard back doors mean the epitome of acceptance," she said and ascended the steps to the back door.

Marcus explained that he'd had some renovations done, such as modernizing the kitchen, while some of the other rooms had been restored to their eighteenth-century designs. "I've even kept some of my parents' furniture, now antiques."

Sharon was anxious to see this two-story, typically narrow home that exhibited so much character. But first she paused for introductions to a short, stout woman who was turning away from the kitchen sink. The woman wiped her hands on a dish towel and smiled at them while Marcus made the introductions.

Her name was Melba, and she said dinner was ready anytime. "You can go right on in to the dining room."

"I'll show you the house later," Marcus said, after he led Sharon into the long, narrow, paneled dining room, dominated by a long table that could seat at least ten people. On it were two place settings of fine china, opposite each other at one end. A crystal chandelier hung from the ceiling.

Old photographs Sharon assumed were of ancestors hung in antique frames on three walls. One wall was dominated by glass windows. The fading light indicated that dusk wasn't far behind. Marcus flipped on the chandelier, giving a cozy glow to the polished mahogany table and the centerpiece of fruit in a silver bowl. Everything was beautiful, but Sharon noted that a woman's touch could brighten and enhance such a lovely home.

She forced that thought away as Marcus held out a chair for her. Sharon hesitated. "Marcus, this is lovely. But I wouldn't mind being less formal."

"Frankly," he admitted, "I never eat here unless there's company. Even Luke and Trish and the boys prefer the kitchen or the serving bar."

"I'd like that," she said and, following his suggestion, moved the place setting to the serving counter that separated the dining area from another room, while Marcus switched on other lights.

"My den," he said, gesturing toward the cozy room that had a definite masculine look to it, with its paneled walls, oversized couch, heavy coffee table, and end tables. A desk was along one wall, flanked by bookshelves from floor to ceiling. A deep-green recliner faced a TV that dominated one corner.

When Melba rolled in a cart from the kitchen, Marcus told her that he and Sharon would eat at the counter. Melba set out gourmet salads with a choice of dressings. She uncovered a steaming seafood platter and placed before them hot, buttered, crusty bread. The aroma was fantastic, the food looked better than what any restaurant could serve, and Sharon could hardly wait for Marcus to finish saying grace so she could dig into it.

Melba joined in the "Amen" when Marcus finished saying grace, then gave them iced tea. Sharon felt the woman was waiting to see if everything was all right.

"This is delicious," Sharon said, even before swallowing the bite of tasty catfish, and looking longingly at the crab. "Mmm, I've never tasted better."

"I agree, Melba. It's perfect."

Melba smiled broadly. "You need anything, just let me know."

Marcus and Sharon talked about the house as they ate. It was after the banana pudding that they settled on the couch in the den, with coffee. Sharon nestled in a corner against several cushions, while Marcus sat near the other end. He set his cup on the coffee table.

The subdued colors of the room and the faint lighting seemed conducive to conversation. She could imagine Marcus sitting at the desk, poring over case studies, or napping on the couch, or reclining in the chair. This room seemed to invite intimacy and warm camaraderie.

"Now," she said, "what did you want to talk to me about?" She sipped her coffee and looked over the rim of the cup at him. *Maybe this is a little too intimate,* she decided, seeing the warmth in his eyes. Then his expression changed, as if he were reluctant to speak.

"Ladies first," he said and moved farther back on the couch.

"I called Mary and James today and told them about Bobby's being released from the hospital this coming Sunday."

Marcus nodded for her to continue.

She leaned forward to set her cup down on the table. "I had thought they might change their mind about custody. I told them I would stay in California, but they're more determined than ever. Mary is even willing to quit her job. Her teenagers are excited about the prospect of Bobby coming to live with them. How can I face my home with all my family gone? With Bobby gone?"

"Mary and James don't consider your feelings?"

"Yes, yes, they do. But they think this is best for Bobby. And. . .maybe they're right. He would miss me terribly. I've been his stability, the one always there for him. But he's young. He would adjust. But he's like my own child, Marcus. Am I being selfish?"

"Sharon," he said, "I don't think you're being selfish. Your having been his primary caregiver since his birth would hold a lot of weight in court."

Sharon felt a stronger ray of hope. "A judge wouldn't think I'm too old to raise this child?"

"Mary and James are around your age, so that would not be a consideration."

"I have no financial problems, Marcus. The house in California is paid for. Mother's house also. Mitchell's insurance—"

Marcus halted her words with an uplifted hand. "But could Mary and

James provide a comfortable living for Bobby?"

"Yes," Sharon admitted.

"Then the financial status would be no consideration." He took a deep breath as if deciding to plunge in. "As I see it, Sharon, you have the advantage of having been Bobby's primary caregiver and having been with him during his recuperation. However, Mary and James have an advantage. They are a married couple. Your chances are good, but they would be better if you were married or planning to be married."

Sharon was shocked into silence. Their eyes held for a long moment, then Sharon swallowed hard and leaned forward to set her cup on the coffee table, lest she drop it. Surely she was misinterpreting. She tried to jest. "I have no such plans. Since Mitchell, there's been no one."

"Sharon, I've known all along that I could fall in love with you. That feeling grows stronger day by day. With all you've been through and your concern for Bobby, I wouldn't expect that you've thought seriously about marriage to anyone. But the matter of custody isn't far off. Do you think you could find it in your heart to consider marriage with me?"

"Marcus, I could not treat you so unfairly by marrying you to get custody of Bobby."

"If you could love me enough, Sharon, for us to build a life together, and if you feel I could be the right father figure for Bobby, then it would be the right thing to do. But even if you say yes, that doesn't guarantee that you would get custody. It could improve your chances."

When she got up from the couch and walked over to the window and stared out into the darkness, Marcus came up beside her.

"I'm sorry, Sharon," he said, "if it's too soon for me to mention this."

No, her mind screamed. *It's too late—twenty-three years too late!*

"There's no problem with loving you, Marcus," Sharon said. She had begun to love him that night on the beach, had loved him in her son, her grandson. Now, she was more strongly drawn to him and found her need for him was even greater in her maturity than in her youth. However, she knew she had to withdraw. It would be disastrous to let him know she bore his child. She wanted and needed his presence with her—he was the father of her only son, grandfather of Bobby. But she could not consider marriage to him without telling him the truth. She could not tell him the truth without bringing up the past, and she knew that would only lead to complete alienation from him.

"Then?" he questioned as he placed his hands on her shoulders and turned her to face him.

She tried to speak, but no words came. Moisture filled her eyes.

"Sharon, I do love you," he said and moved his hands to her face where his thumbs gently wiped away the wetness spilling down her cheeks. "I need you," he whispered against her lips.

Sharon felt herself yielding to his kiss, to his closeness, but she knew she had to resist. Had she learned nothing through the years? For a moment, she felt as giddy as that nineteen-year-old girl. But at least now, she would not act on impulse. She had learned the hard way about runaway emotions. *I am older. I am wiser,* she kept repeating while reveling in this closeness to Marcus.

She forced herself to move away. "Under the circumstances, there's no way it would work, Marcus. Marriage takes more than just love."

"I'm well aware of that, Sharon. But you and I are compatible, don't you think?"

She nodded and smiled.

"And I know you can't live here. But Bobby will grow up, you know. In two more years, he'll start kindergarten. I could handle a long-distance relationship for that long. I've been a widow for eight years, I think I could handle a couple more, although it would be difficult, now that I know you."

"But that's just it, Marcus." Her eyes pleaded with him, and she hoped she would not say the wrong things. He was saying a permanent relationship was possible, but she knew it was impossible. "There are things you don't know about me, Marcus. Things in the past. . . ," she began and returned to sit on the edge of the couch.

"I know what I need to know, Sharon. You're a lovely, caring Christian woman. We all have our weaknesses, our failings, our pasts."

She looked up at him. "Its not that I've done something so horrible, Marcus. But it's something you would have to know if I were to consider anything beyond friendship."

"And we can't go back to just that," he said flatly.

Sharon shook her head, knowing he was right and feeling the loss already.

He sat beside her and took her hands in his. "Then, by all means, tell me about the past," he prompted.

Sharon looked at their hands, then lifted her eyes to his. "I'm not sure it's the right thing to do, Marcus. I will have to give it some thought."

Chapter 15

Saturday, the day of the cookout, was a lovely day. Trish told herself she shouldn't be nervous. Normally, she wouldn't be. After all, it was only an informal cookout. Her dad and Marcus were the grill chefs. Both had come to the house for several evenings and made sure the grills were in place and in working order. Besides the patio tables, they'd brought up the folding tables that Marcus had left with the house since he had no need or room for them in his house.

Trish's mom and Melba made sure Trish purchased everything she'd need from the supermarket. On Saturday, her mom brought extra help, and it looked like everything should go like clockwork. The cookout had been about the only subject Trish and Luke had discussed all week, and it had been a refreshing change that Julie hadn't been the center of their conversations.

Even the boys were helpful. Kathleen came around two o'clock. She and Bo would take the boys to the zoo right after they finished eating, which pleased Caleb and Mark.

"Bobby's not in the hospital anymore. Mom took us to see him at his home. Can he go with us?" Mark asked.

"He's not strong enough yet," Marcus said. "Why don't you get out the croquet set? Some of the guests might like to play, and they'll start coming before long."

Marcus walked over to Trish, who was setting out plates on the long tables. "Sharon's cookies will make a good addition, Trish. You'll be pleased."

"Oh, I'm sure I will," she said. "How are things with you two?"

"Now that Bobby's been released from the hospital, Sharon's busier than ever, even though she does have Lisa helping."

"I mean personally, Marcus."

Marcus nodded. "I suppose you could say we're at a crossroads, Trish." He stood thoughtfully for a moment, then said nothing more. He shrugged.

Trish felt she knew what he meant. She and Luke seemed to be at a crossroads, and she wasn't always sure what step to take or what direction to turn. She gave her father-in-law an encouraging squeeze on the arm. "Well, I'd better get changed before the guests arrive," she said, turning back toward the house.

"Trish!" her mom exclaimed a few minutes later when Trish walked into the kitchen. "How chic. You could have stepped out of the pages of *Vogue*."

"Yes," Melba agreed. "You're so pretty."

"What? In this old rag?" she joked, uncomfortable with the compliments which made her realize she must run around looking like a hag most of the time. No wonder Luke's eyes wandered. *Watch it,* she warned herself. *There's no real evidence of that. He sees me quite well, as a matter of fact. He just doesn't like what he sees.*

Actually, the outfit was new. White linen pants paired with a short-sleeved sailor-cut top with a wide collar. A thin strip of red binding bordered the collar and the gold buttons down the front. Chunky white sandals were the perfect accessory. Her figure was still great, thanks to swimming and running after the boys.

Her honey-blond hair fell in soft natural waves to below her shoulders and tucked behind her ear on one side. She'd enhanced her sea green eyes with mascara, applied peach-colored lip gloss, and added small gold earrings. Of course, she knew it was the inside that counted, but it was the outside that made first impressions. She admitted that her inner self hadn't been too attractive for awhile, and she hoped to impress Luke in some way.

"Who is this beautiful creature?" Marcus said when Trish stepped back out onto the patio. Trish felt a blush as Luke's head turned. He gazed at her curiously. Then he smiled.

"You look great, Trish. Really good."

"Thank you, gentlemen," she said brightly and turned toward the tables. Her heart sang. Luke hadn't complimented her in a long time. Maybe tonight they could recapture some of the romance that had gone out of their marriage.

Paul and Jan Thomas were the first guests to arrive. Soon after, others came, including Julie and a couple of other residents. Julie was very pretty with her shoulder-length medium brown hair framing a classic oval face. Her light brown eyes weren't outstanding. Neither was her conservative denim skirt or white short-sleeved cotton shirt. But everything about Julie was attractive, especially her bubbly personality.

Everyone seemed to like her. And, of course, she and Luke engaged in conversation. It would have seemed strange if they hadn't. Trish refused to watch, as if she would catch a suspicious look or a gesture.

Before long, the house, patio, pool, and yard were filled with people having fun. While Luke made sure he went around and talked to everyone, Marcus and Trish's dad were busy at the grills. Soon Sharon appeared with a huge tray of cookies. Trish smiled, seeing that the look passing between Marcus and Sharon was special. She saw how Sharon lowered her eyelids and a becoming blush colored her cheeks.

"Try a bite and see if you approve," Sharon prompted when Trish walked over.

Trish broke off a bite of a cookie. "These are not good, Sharon, they're superb. You made them?"

"My mom's secret recipe," Sharon said, happy to share something of her mother with someone else. "I've changed it a little to reduce the fat."

"Oh, well. I'll have more than a bite," Trish said, taking the rest of the cookie. She touched her stomach. "I forgot to eat lunch."

"From the looks of this spread," Sharon complimented, "I have a feeling we'll all stuff ourselves."

After everyone was settled in their choice of eating places, Trish tried to make sure everything was running smoothly. She was seated at an end spot next to Jan. Luke was farther down between a couple of colleagues. Julie and the two residents sat together at the other end of the table. Noticing that some iced tea and lemonade glasses needed refilling and everyone was engrossed in conversation, Trish got up for the pitchers.

She noticed that Julie's hand seemed to shake as she held up her glass for a refill. Trish poured, Julie put the glass to her lips, and Trish walked on by.

She stopped, hearing Julie say, "Oh, I'm so clumsy." A huge spot of tea was spreading over her white shirt.

"I had the glass too full," Trish said, trying to be the perfect hostess. "I'm sorry."

"I would like to wash it off, if I might," Julie said.

"The bathroom is right inside the sliding glass doors, to the left of the game room," Trish said.

"Thanks, I'll find it."

The incident bothered Trish. A pediatric surgeon's assistant, who must have steady hands, spills her tea? Had shaky hands? It just didn't fit. *Something* had caused Julie to be unsteady! *Being at Luke's house? Or. . .being around Luke's wife?*

After returning the pitcher to the table, Trish went into the house and knocked on the bathroom door. "Did you find everything you need, Julie?"

"Oh, yes, yes, thanks. I'll be right out."

"No hurry," Trish replied.

Soon the door opened and the smiling assistant emerged, looking sweet and calm and guilty as sin. *Guilty,* Trish thought. *Of what? Of wanting my husband? I mustn't do that—get all worked up over nothing. She's just embarrassed over spilling her tea. Everyone does such things. Let's just hope a pediatric surgeon isn't that clumsy in the operating room.*

Marcus wanted Sharon to feel welcome and at home during the cookout. He needn't have been concerned. As he took her around to introduce her, he discovered that all the guests had either met her or knew about her from the extensive news coverage about Bobby and the accident.

They all wanted to know how Bobby was adjusting, now that he'd gone home. Sharon graciously repeated the answer over and over, saying his adjustment was remarkably good. He'd already adjusted to his nurse, Lisa, in the hospital and was happy to have her helping care for him.

Marcus needn't have worried about Sharon's feeling comfortable. Almost before he knew it, she was walking around the pool with Trish's mom and Jan Thomas, conversing as if she'd known them for a long time. She apparently made friends easily. That didn't surprise him. He'd wanted to be her friend from the very beginning. Now he didn't want it to stop there.

When Luke summoned the crowd to the food, Sharon walked toward Marcus. His heart skipped a beat as if he were a teenager again. She looked up at him with a sparkle in her blue eyes and warmth in her smile.

"Thank you for inviting me, Marcus," she said. "This is so nice. I think it's just what the doctor would have ordered."

"What the judge ordered," he returned, and they both laughed.

He gestured for her to go ahead of him for a plate. His thoughts, however, went beyond this evening. Now that he'd found her, he couldn't imagine being content without her. For an instant, another thought crossed his mind. What could possibly have been so awful in her past?

Chapter 16

As each day passed, Sharon could detect rapid improvement in Bobby. Soon Luke would say he was able to travel. What should she do about Marcus? What could she do? Simply say she could not marry him, offering no explanation, and go to California? If they married, they could have a good life together, but not unless they faced the truth of their pasts. The truth might drive him away, but she could not keep something like this from him.

What to do? *Dear Lord,* she prayed, *guide me.*

If she married Marcus, she would still have to be near Bobby until he was old enough to accept Mary and James as his caregivers, assuming they got custody. Would Marcus move to California? Or would they have a long-distance marriage with infrequent visits until Bobby started school?

Sharon sighed. It all seemed too complicated.

Marcus had called a couple of times since the cookout, but he hadn't come over. Near the end of the week, he telephoned. "Sharon, I need to see you."

"Marcus, I haven't decided—"

"I'm not pressuring you, Sharon. I'd like for us to go for a short drive and a walk on the beach. There's something I have to tell you before this can go any further."

Sharon stared at the phone after hanging up. He sounded distressed. Perhaps he'd decided it was all too complicated. Suddenly her heart began to pound. Suppose, after she'd mentioned her past, he had delved into it. A judge would probably know how to do those things. Had he discovered this secret she had kept from him?

It was late afternoon, and Marcus was on his way. Bobby and Lisa were playing in the backyard. Lisa said she could stay as long as needed. Sharon didn't bother to change from her jeans, T-shirt, and sandals. She sat in the porch swing, waiting, as she had several months ago. Was this going to be another disaster?

Sharon didn't wait for Marcus to come to the porch, meeting him in the driveway instead. She got in the car. He smiled and greeted her, but the smile didn't reach his eyes. She had not seen him so concerned before. Marcus was one of those happy people with a ready smile. Not today.

His appearance was casual—he wore walking shorts, knit shirt, and sandals.

But his manner was far from casual. He did ask about Bobby, and she gave a progress report. He nodded, but she felt his mind was miles away. Sure enough, he turned toward the beach a few blocks away, then took a side road that wound around in the direction of the fateful cottage.

Marcus parked at the side of the beach cottage that had the windows and doors boarded up. Pieces of roof were missing, and the banister had broken away from the corner of the house.

"This was my parents' cottage years ago," he said. "I haven't kept it up. It holds unpleasant memories for me."

Sharon knew he must be speaking of that night, twenty-three years ago. She looked away from the cottage and from him. He led her down to the outcropping of rock, where they both could lean against the rocks and stare out over the foam-tipped waves of the ocean, licking at the sandy beach, then retreating.

"You spoke of the past, Sharon," he began distantly. "There is nothing in your past that could be worse than what I did."

Sharon's head turned to stare at him, opening her mouth to say that if he were speaking of twenty-three years ago, then it was a mistake they both shared—not just him. But Marcus stilled any words she might say with an uplifted hand and a sorrowful countenance.

He told her then about the night a troubled young girl appeared on the beach, and he invited her into the cottage. How it had started innocently, progressed to sharing of their problems, and resulted in intimacy. "I have never felt comfortable at the beach cottage since then."

Sharon felt it was because he regretted that night with her, but his next words left her cold. "When I awoke early in the morning, she was gone. Although I asked around, no one knew an Angela. I never found a trace of her." He took a deep breath, cleared his throat, and said in a strained voice, "I fear she walked into the ocean that night and never returned."

After a long moment he said, "I had the opportunity to help that girl, but I took advantage of her instead. I know the Lord has forgiven me, but I've never been able to completely forgive myself."

He turned toward her, and she saw his pain. "I've never told anyone about this. It would have hurt more than helped. But I wanted you to know that nothing in your past could be worse than this."

"Oh, Marcus," she said, feeling so touched that he confided in her. She knew instantly how cruel it would be not to tell him the truth. He should not be burdened with believing a young girl might have drowned because of him. She stood in front of him. "I know about that night, Marcus. Angela did not drown. That was not her real name. You see, I. . .am Angela."

He was shaking his head. "What are you talking about?"

"That night, I wanted to be anyone but myself, and chose the name Angela. I didn't want you to know I was only nineteen."

Sharon's eyes misted over. "You see, Marcus, we share the same guilt."

He stared at her, dumbfounded. "You're not surprised, Sharon. Then you have known, all along, who I was."

"Yes. It wasn't difficult finding out that the Sinclairs owned the cottage. The phone book listed a Marcus Sinclair. A few weeks after that night, I drove by the address given in the phone book. I saw you in the front yard with a pregnant woman and two small children."

"I'm so sorry you had to go through that, Sharon. I can say good came from it. That night changed my life. It caused me to make responsible decisions concerning my wife, my children, and my relationship with God. It seems your life has gone well too."

"It was hard at first. You see, I married Mitchell when Robert was five years old. I couldn't have asked for a better father or husband than Mitchell. The Lord has blessed me too, after I realized I needed Him so desperately in my life."

"So, Mitchell was your second husband?"

"No. I never married Robert's father."

"What happened? Did he not want to be a part of his son's life?"

Sharon swallowed hard. She began to shake her head. Her eyes clouded, and she bit on her lip. She would have fallen had Marcus not grasped her shoulders. She barely managed to utter the words: "I never wanted you to know."

"Know what?" he demanded. His hands dug into her shoulders.

"Marcus," she said pleadingly, "I got pregnant that night."

"What?" he rasped. He could only stare at her.

"I never intended to say anything, Marcus. I never expected to see you again or be involved with your family. I decided that years ago. But the accident changed all that. I haven't known what to do. I wanted Bobby to know you and your family. But I—"

He seemed to have turned to stone. Even his eyes didn't blink. He looked as if he were living a nightmare.

Sharon wrenched away from his hands. "I'll walk home. It's not far." She hurried around the rocks. She could feel his eyes following her, uncomprehending, unblinking. She began to run along the sand like she had so many years ago. She'd made another mistake, only this time she didn't have the excuse of innocence or youth.

Would that be her final memory of Marcus? How could she ever forget his eyes staring at her with a look of. . .what? Incredulity? Or loathing?

Marcus could not think clearly. A judge was supposed to be levelheaded, make difficult life-or-death decisions, but now his thoughts were a jumble, his emotions swirling like cardboard in a hurricane.

Marcus walked across the sand and down to the ocean's edge, thinking about that night so long ago. He had stayed at the cottage for two more days, wondering if Angela would return, asking others in the area if they knew her. No one did. He'd looked out at the ocean, wondering if she'd walked into the ocean and perhaps never walked out again.

Guilt had assailed him. He'd been unfaithful to Bev, to his own sense of morality, to his claim of being a Christian. When it came to the testing time, he'd failed miserably. He had gotten on his knees and poured out his heart to God, asking forgiveness. Believing it best not to burden Bev with his guilt, he returned home and asked her to forgive him for putting his studies ahead of everything else. She promised to be more supportive of him. Both promised to try and be more understanding of the other.

For a long time fear remained in his heart. What happened to Angela? He'd searched the papers for an Angela, wondering if she'd washed up on the beach. At times, he hoped he had only imagined her.

Now, turning to stare at the rocks and the beach house, he knew he had not imagined that night, nor had he imagined what the consequences might have been for her. *A troubled girl came to me, and I took advantage of her,* he admitted to himself. *As a man, a married man and father, as a Christian, I should have given her hope, a place to turn. Instead, I thought of myself, pitied myself for having a wife who didn't understand my needs while she was saying I didn't understand hers. I drank, which lowered my inhibitions, and I was tempted. I yielded to a girl looking for answers, and instead I gave her more trouble.*

How much damage had he caused that young girl? No, he couldn't blame her for not telling him she was pregnant. Of course she wouldn't want him to know. What could she have expected of him? A married man who walked away from his wife and children when the going got tough. When Bev had ordered him out and said she was going to get a divorce, he should have told her no, that this was his home, she was his wife, those were his children. He had sworn before God to love and cherish, and that's what he should have done.

Instead, he'd taken a young girl's word that she was twenty-one. Would it have made any difference if he'd known she was only nineteen? Or would that only have enticed him further? He might make all kinds of excuses for his behavior. That happened in his courtroom every day.

Numb from the revelations, Marcus made his way up to the cottage. He pulled the boards from the front door quite easily. No doubt someone else had done so and made use of the cottage. He turned the knob and discovered he didn't need a key to get inside. Someone had broken the lock. The afternoon light shining through the doorway revealed the couch pushed closer to the fireplace than he had left it. Someone had left ashes in the fireplace. Otherwise everything seemed to be intact. It didn't matter.

He reached for the poker and stirred the lifeless ashes. Sharon was Angela? This woman he'd come to respect and even love had lied to him. Twenty-three years ago she had lied about her name, her age. And these past months, she'd kept the truth from him. *Why? Why?*

He shuddered, feeling a trembling through his body like chills of the flu. His hand shook so he missed the hook when trying to replace the poker. It clattered to the hearth like the realization clanging in his brain. Sinking into the chair where he'd sat twenty-three years ago, with his elbows on his thighs, he covered his face with his hands.

Not only had Sharon lied to him, but she had denied him the knowledge of his own son for all these years. Her son, his son, had recently been killed, and he hadn't even known he had that son. It was not easy to absorb these facts.

Marcus stayed at the darkened cottage for hours, long after the light at the doorway turned to darkness. He grieved for the son he never knew, his own flesh and blood who was killed in that accident. He never got to see him, touch him, love him. *My son that I never knew is dead.*

And Sharon. She must have gone through much humiliation and suffering bearing a child out of wedlock, then rearing him for many years without a husband.

Another thought broke through. All the concern about Bobby's rare blood type. *Bobby,* he realized, *is my grandson.*

How could she help but harbor deep resentment toward him? And he could not blame her. Had she accepted his recent help because she felt he owed her and Bobby something? And of course—he did.

As the hours passed, Marcus could do nothing but face the truth, the facts. Then he wondered what he would do with the information. Was this some kind of second chance to make up for the hurt he had caused Sharon? Should he try and earn her forgiveness?

He thought of her rearing his child for five years without a father. Surely she must harbor some resentment toward him. That would explain her reluctance to respond to his admission of love. Now he could understand why she would not even consider a relationship with him. And who could blame her? Not Marcus!

Later at home, far into the night, completely awake after a restless sleep, Marcus stared through the darkness toward the ceiling. Like dawn breaking through the dark, he understood Sharon's reluctance to tell him about Bobby. Now he was faced with a dilemma. Was he going to share this knowledge or keep this secret from his own family?

Chapter 17

Deep inside, Marcus felt he knew what he should do but, dreading it, he procrastinated, telling himself he would wait until the Lord gave him a definite sign. No such sign came during the following days, and he threw himself into his work with renewed fervor.

On Sunday afternoon, he lounged on the patio after lunch with Luke, Trish, and the boys. Each of them were subdued after they asked about Sharon and Bobby. Marcus said he hadn't seen them or talked with them for days, but he didn't elaborate.

Luke and Trish were quiet, lost in their own thoughts. Marcus watched the boys frolic in the pool, thinking about his grandchildren. What would it do to them, knowing he had another grandchild? He glanced over at Luke and noticed the strain on his son's face. How would it change Luke's estimation of him? And Trish? She respected him so much. Would that change?

Suddenly, Luke's beeper sounded. He reached for it. "Hospital," he said, picking up the cell phone and punching in the number.

"Julie?" he exclaimed, swinging his legs around and rising to a sitting position. Abruptly he stood and paced. "I'll be right there."

He faced Trish and Marcus with a look of disbelief on his face. "Julie's overdosed. I have to go." He left Trish and Marcus in stunned silence.

～

Julie's attending physician talked to Luke as soon as he could but didn't think it wise for her to have visitors just yet. "We pumped her stomach and are trying to get it all out of her system."

Luke could hardly believe it. Paul Thomas was on duty, and the older doctor pulled him aside, discussing what had happened as best they could piece it together.

Julie hadn't come down to begin her shift at seven A.M. No one thought anything about it for awhile. She was on twenty-four-hour call and hadn't been able to go to her room until around two A.M.

Finally, she was called on the phone, then beeped. There was no response. Paul Thomas had the pediatric head nurse go up to Julie's room. When there was no response, they had the cleaning lady unlock the door. Julie was still in bed, and the head nurse was unable to wake her. After seeing a pill on the floor beside the bed, the nurse's eyes lit upon two bottles on the bedside table. She picked them up. One was a no-doze prescription for Julie. The other was a sleeping prescription for Amy Smith, prescribed by Julie Dalton, MD. The nurse knew immediately that Julie had either OD'd, or a mixture of the pills had poisoned her system.

"Why would she do it, Paul?" Luke questioned, but they both knew. Going through med school was tough. Being a resident under constant scrutiny and on call for twenty-four- and thirty-six-hour shifts demanded all one could give. It wasn't easy, but those who couldn't handle it shouldn't be in medicine. It was a demanding profession that didn't end at five o'clock in the afternoon.

"Apparently she just couldn't handle it, physically or emotionally," Paul said.

"She had such great potential," Luke countered. "Why would she chance throwing it all away?"

"You know the answer, Luke. An intelligent woman like her wouldn't do this deliberately. Like others in the past, she thought she could handle it. But she got hooked."

Luke returned home after supper, and Trish warmed his meal up in the microwave. "Julie has a problem," he said, "but I don't know the details yet."

"I hope she'll be all right," Trish said.

Luke flashed a skeptical look in Trish's direction. He hadn't expected such a mild response from her. But she had simply turned and was pouring herself a cup of coffee.

"Marcus is calling a family conference," she said, sitting across from him.

"Those are rare. What's up?"

"He didn't say, but it sounds serious. When's a good time for you?"

Luke sighed. Tomorrow was going to be a trying day at the hospital. His brightest star had ceased to shine. "Now?"

"I'll see if Kathleen and Bo can come. Marcus didn't want the children around, so I'll send them next door if it's okay with Marge."

~

Marcus knew Luke had a good heart and could never be totally objective about his patients, coworkers, family, or friends. He could understand having a colleague with whom you could relate about your profession in a way that you couldn't with those outside the profession. It formed a bond. That could easily have happened between Luke and Julie. And it would be easy for it to get out of perspective.

That was the deciding factor for Marcus as he had debated what to tell his family about his earlier relationship with Sharon. Maybe if he could explain some of what had happened in his own marriage, it would help Luke with his. And too, the situation was not just a private matter between him and

Sharon. He must do what he could for the woman who bore his child, who was caring for his and her grandson. He wanted no more secrets.

His family liked Sharon. Their acceptance and approval of her made Marcus feel it was safe to confess his one night of infidelity and his recently learning that Bobby was his grandson. Surely he could be forthright with his own grown children.

Kathleen and Bo had dropped everything to come right over. The boys were already at the neighbors by the time Marcus arrived. The six adults gathered at the round kitchen table, where important matters in the past had been discussed. Marcus accepted only a glass of water, and the others, sensing something serious, did the same.

Marcus took a sip of water. It went down the wrong way, and he had to cough and clear his throat.

Trying to make it easier, Luke asked, "Are you ill, Dad?"

Marcus gave a short, ironic laugh. "Ill at ease, Son."

Brian looked at his watch, and Marcus thought he'd better get on with it before Brian left for one of his numerous activities.

Marcus began. "This happened twenty-three years ago."

"Sure you don't want to talk to a priest instead of us?" Brian quipped with a grin.

"No, Son. It touches your lives too. It's not something I can keep to myself."

Hesitantly at first, and then with a stronger voice, Marcus told about the early years of his marriage to Bev. Perhaps they'd married too young, right out of high school, but they'd felt their love would see them through anything. They hadn't planned to have children right away. Bev would work while Marcus went to law school.

"We never considered you a mistake, Luke," Marcus said. "But you didn't conform to our well-thought-out plans."

Luke nodded and smiled. He'd never doubted his parents' love and devotion for him.

"For several years, things were great. We even had another child." Marcus smiled at Kathleen, and his daughter returned the smile. "But later, when I was in law school, things got tough. Mom and Dad helped out with my schooling, and things were fine until about a year before I was to take the bar exam."

Marcus knew he could have blamed the problems on about anything that all married couples faced. After the wedding came a marriage. After the honeymoon came daily living. All those factors played a role. But he had to be honest.

"The biggest problem was that I put my career, my needs, my wants, ahead of all else. My reasoning was that I had to pass that bar exam for my family. That was true. But mainly it was for me."

He told about frequent arguments over nothing in particular. "Accusations were made. Bev was pregnant with Brian," he said. "That pregnancy was particularly difficult, and for months she suffered from morning sickness."

"So I was the mistake," Brian quipped, trying to lighten the mood.

Kathleen punched him on the arm. "Don't be silly, Brian. You're no mistake." She made a playful face at him and kidded, "You just make everybody else sick."

Everybody laughed nervously. Apparently, the worst was yet to come. Marcus took another sip of water.

He set the glass down and continued. "Finally, Bev threw me out. She literally tossed some of my clothes out the door. Said she was going to file for divorce the next morning and she did not want me to show up on her doorstep, or she'd shoot me. She made a believer out of me," Marcus said.

"At the time, I was happy to go. My whole life seemed like a mistake, and the only thing that could fix it was passing that bar exam." He shook his head. "What I did then is inexcusable."

Marcus stared at his folded hands on the table, rather than look into the eyes of his family. He didn't want to see any disgust, disappointment, disapproval from these people he so dearly loved.

He told them then about the night at the beach house, as stormy as his emotions. About Angela. About fearing she had drowned and blaming himself for his irresponsibility. About turning his life over to the Lord and starting over. Not even Brian attempted to crack a joke.

Marcus was quiet for so long, Trish said softly, "Dad." She only called him that when she was particularly fond of him. He smiled faintly.

"Everybody makes mistakes," she said.

He took a deep breath. "That's not all."

After another pause, he said, "Only a few days ago I found out that. . . Sharon is Angela. She was that girl." He told of how she had reared her child alone for five years and had never wanted him to find out because of how it could affect him and his family. He looked around at them all now. "Do you understand what this means?"

He saw instant comprehension in Luke's eyes. "Bobby's rare blood type," he said.

Kathleen gasped.

Marcus nodded. "Sharon's son, who was killed." His voice broke. Tears stung his eyes. "He was my son that I never knew. Bobby is my grandson. He took a handkerchief from his back pocket, wiped his eyes, and blew his nose. "I'm sorry. I didn't think I'd get emotional."

"Are you and Sharon getting serious, Dad?" Brian asked.

"I thought we were, Brian. Now I think she wanted Bobby to be acquainted with me, with us. I couldn't blame her if she wants nothing to do with me personally."

"I have confidence in you, Dad," Brian said, using the words Marcus had said to him many times. "You'll work things out the right way."

Marcus looked around. Tears were streaming down Kathleen's cheeks. She looked over at Bo. "I guess we should go." She came over and hugged Marcus, but not with that special little squeeze she usually had for him.

Luke said nothing, nor did he look at Marcus. He simply got up from his chair and walked out of the room without a word.

Marcus strongly suspected he had accomplished nothing except to disillusion his daughter and alienate his older son.

Chapter 18

Several days later, Marcus called Sharon and asked if he could stop by after leaving the courthouse. She didn't ask if he would stay for dinner, instead telling him that Lisa could keep Bobby occupied while she and Marcus talked.

When he arrived, Sharon offered him a cup of coffee. They sat at the kitchen table where they could see Bobby and Lisa playing with a plastic horseshoe set.

"Sharon," he began, believing she must have resentment in her heart for him. "I can't say that I'm altogether sorry for that night years ago. It brought me into a renewed relationship with God and my family. It forced me to grow up and take responsibility like a man. It taught me about God's forgiveness and grace. I hope you can forgive me."

Sharon looked stunned. "I was just as much at fault as you, Marcus," she said, but he shook his head.

"You were a teenager. I was a twenty-eight-year-old married man."

"I knew right from wrong," she insisted. "I wanted revenge on my boyfriend and my dad. It was as if I were a different person that night. I didn't want to be myself with my problems."

"Was your family supportive during those years when you were unmarried?"

"Very," she said. "In a way it brought them closer to each other and to me. The damage had already been done to their marriage, but we all sat down and discussed the situation like reasonable adults. For a long time, all I had heard from them was bitter arguments. That changed. They assumed my boyfriend, Jimmy, was the father. I never told them differently, only that marriage to Jimmy was out of the question."

"I remember," he said, "how hurt you were about your father and the impending divorce."

"I suppose I never really got over my parents' separation. But I learned a lot, Marcus. My parents could make mistakes too and sin. I went to California and lived with my dad. He found a duplex apartment house so that I could live in one side with the baby. After his divorce was final, he and Barbara lived in the other side. Later, Barbara kept Robert while I worked.

"After I married Mitchell, my dad and Barbara moved to Hawaii. He died of a heart attack several years ago." She took a deep breath. "I thought it best to live in California. The last thing I wanted to do was cause any trouble for you or your family."

"They know now," Marcus replied, his brow furrowing.

"You told them?" When he nodded, she asked, "How did they take it?"

"Brian seems to separate himself from it, as if it's my business and not his. Kathleen is disappointed because I'm not perfect. Luke has become distant. He's cordial, polite, but it's like the closeness has gone from our relationship."

"I'm so sorry." Sharon laid her hand on his arm. "That is what I wanted to avoid all these years."

"But this is my doing, Sharon. Not yours. I have a responsibility to Bobby, and I will be as much of a grandfather to him as you will allow."

~

Two days later when Sharon and Lisa took Bobby for his checkup, Luke said the little boy had healed sufficiently to go to California. Bobby should still be kept from any vigorous activity, Luke warned, but there was no reason he couldn't be allowed to run and play like any other healthy little boy.

Luke tried to be kind, considerate, efficient, and professional as always, but he knew he was treating Sharon differently. His suspicion that she had noticed the change was confirmed when she asked, "Could I speak with you privately, Luke?"

"Certainly," he said, after a long pause.

Lisa said she would take Bobby to see the nurses and some of the little patients he had met while hospitalized.

Sharon and Luke went into his office. He motioned for Sharon to take a seat, but she remained standing, saying this wouldn't take long. "Bobby and I will be leaving for California as soon as I can take care of a few things and book a flight."

"I see," Luke said, walking around his desk. His fingers touched the edge of the desk, and he looked up at her coldly.

"Again, I want to thank you for what you've done for Bobby," Sharon said. "And for your kindness. I also want you to know I've always wanted to avoid causing any problem for Marcus and his family."

Luke looked down, deeply distressed.

"I'm sorry," Sharon said softly.

"I'm sorry too," he managed to say as she left the room. "I wish you and Bobby well."

Luke walked over to the window and stared out beyond the rooftops of hospital wings. He hadn't been very cordial to Sharon, but he was trying to cope with the implications of his father's confession—trying to absorb the fact that he'd had a half brother he never knew, that Bobby was a blood relative. Caleb, Mark, and Bobby were all Marcus's grandsons.

Luke saw traffic far below, going forward while his thoughts traveled back in time. He'd had a good childhood, with memories of fun activities and loving parents. Now, for the first time, he allowed himself to think about that troubled time in his parents' lives. He'd heard some arguments but accepted that as a normal part of life. He sometimes got angry with his little sister who swiped his toys and tore his books.

But one night he'd awoken from a deep sleep and the sound was different. He heard his parents yelling at each other. He thought they hated each other, and he was scared. He'd heard his mom tell his dad to go away and never come back. Luke jumped out of bed to tell his dad not to go away, but when he got to the living room, he saw his mom throwing clothes out the door. His dad was driving away.

Afterward, his mom fell against the slammed door and sobbed. Luke had gone over and tugged at her clothes until she noticed him. She turned and fell on her knees and put her arms around him. He tried to comfort her while she cried. He didn't know how, so he cried too.

When she put him back to bed, she told him it was just a bad argument and everything would be all right. He didn't think she believed that. He closed his eyes and she left the room, but he couldn't sleep. Later on, he kept remembering his dad's clothes lying outside in the rain. For a long time in his mind, he saw the red taillights of the car that finally disappeared into the darkness.

Luke had thought his dad didn't love them anymore, and the days that followed were the worst days in his life. When he asked where his dad was, his mom said she didn't know. Then Dad came back. Things were different for awhile, like everybody was scared to talk too much and nobody argued. Then things got better than they had been before. There were more hugs and more fun, and Dad was home a lot more.

After that, Luke had never doubted his parents' love for each other or for him. His had been a good life. Now he realized he had blocked out that unpleasant time, never to deal with it. He must deal with it now.

Another factor he must deal with was that Sharon, the woman he had come to respect and admire, was the one with whom his father cheated on his mother. How would he deal with that?

"Luke?" came a voice behind him. He turned. There stood Paul Thomas. "Is everything all right? Your door was open, and—"

"Sure, come on in, Paul. I was just. . .thinking."

"Yeah, this problem with Julie has us all concerned. I just heard her license has been revoked for writing the illegal prescriptions. And she's to be in treatment for a year."

That was something else Luke had to deal with. He was torn with disappointment in her and in himself. Accompanying that was a strong desire to help Julie, a bright, lovely woman who had taken herself along the road to self-destruction.

Is anyone who they appear to be? Sharon? My dad? Julie? And, he added reluctantly, *even myself?*

~

Sharon knew this was not the time to make any decisions about her mother's house and car. Lisa was glad to accept the responsibility of the house and see that the grass was cut, hoping that Sharon and Bobby would return.

At almost the last moment, Sharon realized she hadn't returned Marcus's video camera. She called Trish, asking if she could drop it by since she would be leaving later in the day and wouldn't see Marcus.

Trish asked her to come early enough for them to talk and bring Bobby. She said the boys had been asking about him. Lisa offered to drive them since Sharon had already notified the police that she was leaving and the car would be parked beside the house.

Caleb and Mark were overjoyed to see Bobby. Lisa took the three boys out back to the patio. Sharon and Trish sat in the rec room, watching the boys play. Bobby had adjusted to his situation. How satisfying it was to see him play with his little relatives—something Robert had never had the opportunity to do. Sharon tried not to think how satisfying it would be if these grandsons of Marcus could grow up together. Pushing aside the thought, she handed Trish a sheet of paper.

"This is Lisa's address and phone number," she said. "Lisa has a key to the house. Anytime you want the bed and high chair, just let her know."

"Oh, Sharon," Trish said, moving to the edge of her chair, opposite where Sharon sat on the couch. "You will come back, won't you?"

Sharon shook her head. "I think I've done irreparable damage, Trish. I told myself I was doing what was best for Bobby. But it seems I've only brought difficulties to Marcus's family. I'm so sorry."

"Sharon, none of us hold against you and Marcus something that happened so many years ago. We were shocked. But that's because Kathleen and I both thought Marcus was perfect. I still respect him more than anyone I know. And so does Kathleen. She and Bo were over here the other night and agreed that Marcus has not been as alive in years as he is around you. We all like you, Sharon. Believe it or not, some of *us* haven't always been perfect."

They laughed lightly. "But that's not the point, Trish," Sharon argued.

"It's not just a matter of a mistake years ago. The matter has been brought into the present. And from what I hear, Luke isn't accepting this very well."

Trish sighed. "Things at the hospital are occupying his mind right now, Sharon." Trish felt she would like to confide in Sharon, but reconsidered. Luke hadn't yet given Trish all the details about Julie. He'd told her not to talk about it. A hospital's reputation was at stake.

"He seemed distressed, and Marcus said he was distant toward him."

"Don't blame yourself, Sharon. Marcus is not upset with you. He's upset with himself and sorry he didn't know about your son. He's an honorable man and doesn't take his responsibilities lightly."

"I know," Sharon said, standing. "But I'm afraid I've hurt him personally. It was wrong of me to let things go so far."

A short while later, Lisa drove Sharon and Bobby to the airport. Sharon kept wondering if Trish might have called Marcus and perhaps he would show up at the airport to see them off.

One last glance before boarding the plane indicated that hadn't happened. She busied herself with explaining everything to inquisitive, excited Bobby, who kept calling the plane a big bird that ate people. Sharon laughed with him, enjoying the game and his wonderful healthy imagination.

Behind her laughter, however, was a nagging feeling. While they rose high in the air over Charleston, already Sharon missed the gentle people and soft southern skies of the area that deep in her heart was home.

~

Marcus had been in court all day. This was a difficult case, and he had to struggle to keep his mind off personal matters. He'd had files to read, matters to consider, and he'd hoped he could get a few hours' sleep before beginning another day of trial.

When Trish called, he was surprised. His family didn't bother him during a trial unless it was an emergency. "What's wrong, Trish?"

"I just wanted to let you know Sharon dropped your video camera off at my house."

He felt like a dark cloud hovered over him. "I guess that means she doesn't want me going to her house."

"Marcus, she's gone."

"Gone?"

"Yes. She and Bobby left this afternoon for California."

Her words hit him like a bolt of lightning. Gone. Sharon and Bobby were gone. He had to do something, say something. For the life of him he couldn't remember her ever saying what part of California she lived in. "Trish, did she give you her address or telephone number?"

"No. And I didn't think to ask. I assumed you would know. Maybe Luke has it."

Marcus called.

"There was no reason for me to ask for it, Dad," Luke said.

"Do you remember the names of Bobby's maternal grandparents? Mary and James something."

Luke thought. "I was introduced to them, but sorry, I don't remember. If I think of it, I'll let you know. But she'll be in touch with you, won't she, Dad?"

"I don't think so, Son. She wouldn't impose herself on people who don't seem to want her around."

"Dad," Luke said after a moment, "I'm about ready to leave here. Would you stop by the house before you go home?"

"Sure," Marcus said blandly. He felt as if all the life had gone out of him. He'd pick up his video camera and go home. Sharon would have taken the tape. Someday she might show it to Bobby and tell him that man was his grandfather. A man who was very busy—judging others.

A short while later, Marcus pulled into the driveway right behind Luke. At Luke's bidding they walked around the house and out onto the patio, near the pool.

"I want to apologize, Dad," Luke said. "Looking back, I realize I've probably given the wrong impression to both you and Sharon. Frankly, I expected you two to continue your relationship whether or not I approved." He walked over to a chair and sat down. "Some things aren't easy to admit, especially to one's father."

Marcus sat opposite him. "It's just as difficult for a father to confess to his son. But family members are the ones we should confide in."

Luke nodded, took a deep breath, and plunged in. "My attitude toward you and Sharon wasn't because of you at all, but because I could see so much of myself in your story about the past. I remembered seeing Mom unhappy during those days. I remember the arguments and how they made me feel."

"I'm so sorry," Marcus said.

"I know. I'm not saying this as a condemnation. I'm trying to confess."

They smiled at each other. "Sorry," Marcus said again.

"I, uh, got things out of perspective for awhile. My work, my time, my life became top priority. I haven't given the kind of thought to Trish and the boys like I should. So I want to thank you for telling us about your past. I'm going to get myself back on track." He stood, and Marcus joined him.

"Dad," Luke added, "I'm in total agreement that you have an obligation to Sharon and Bobby. In case it means anything, you have my blessing on whatever decision you make."

"It means everything, Son," Marcus said. "But I don't know how I can ever find a Sharon Martin who might be anywhere in the entire state of California."

~

Trish saw Marcus and Luke embrace, and it thrilled her heart. The two men she loved most in the world should not be at odds. As soon as they came through the door, she gave Marcus a slip of paper.

"I remembered that Sharon gave me Lisa's phone number. She has Sharon's address and phone number."

Marcus looked at it like it was his long-lost friend.

"You staying for dinner?" she asked.

"Dinner?" He was studying the address and phone number. "No, I have a lot to do this evening at home. Big trial going on, you know."

"Well, you have three extra hours," Trish said, ignoring the remark about the trial. "We're on a different time zone than California."

Chapter 19

Mary and James met Sharon and Bobby at the airport and drove them home. Their teens, Steve and Kim, were waiting at Sharon's home with a big "Welcome Home" sign outside in the yard. Attached to the sign, huge helium balloons danced in the breeze, displaying bright colors of red and yellow, white and green, blue and orange.

After hugs and kisses and words of welcome, they went into the kitchen to be greeted by crepe paper streamers, a stack of presents, Barney tablecloth, plates, cups, and a birthday cake for Bobby. The teens had also stocked Sharon's cabinets and refrigerator with groceries.

Before long, Bobby was interacting with these relatives he hadn't seen in months as if there had been no separation. After the party, Kim bathed Bobby and got him ready for bed. With the time difference, it was past his bedtime. Steve offered to clean up the kitchen.

Sharon filled Mary and James in about Bobby's recovery and how well he had adjusted to his environment. The other couple didn't even offer for Bobby to spend the night with them. Sharon wondered if that was because they thought his time with her would soon end. Sharon knew they would try to make a smooth transition if they gained custody, and Sharon knew that would only prolong her distress.

These were good, loving people and the only thing hanging over this wonderful reunion was the impending custody case, which no one mentioned.

The matter of custody, however, was uppermost in Sharon's mind. Later that night, after Bobby was asleep and Sharon stood in the doorway of Robert and Karen's room, the ring of the telephone shattered the silence.

Sharon hadn't informed any of her friends about her return to California, so she wasn't expecting any calls. Perhaps Mary had forgotten to tell her something. Or worse, maybe she and James expected Bobby to be asleep by now, and they wanted to talk about the custody case after all.

Trembling, Sharon picked up the phone. A man's voice answered. "Marcus?" she questioned when he said her name. His voice sounded strained as he apologized for not contacting her before she and Bobby left. He would be tied up with a court case for at least a week longer.

"I'm so grateful to you, Marcus," Sharon said, trying to put him at ease, "for being there when I so desperately needed someone."

"Sharon, I will come to California for the custody hearing, testify on your behalf, and relate my own personal desires and obligations to be involved in Bobby's life."

Sharon was touched by that and hardly knew how to respond. Her heart ached to think that his affection for her had waned. Yet she had to keep Bobby uppermost in her mind.

"Thank you, Marcus. I will consult with my attorney and see what he thinks best. How is your family?"

"I truly believe our relationships are growing stronger, Sharon. It seems they had set me up as some superdad. They're beginning to see me as a human being who needs them as much as they need me."

"And Luke?"

"It seems Luke wasn't upset with our situation at all. His concerns were both personal and work-related."

Sharon was glad to hear that the deep love and respect Marcus and Luke had for each other had prevailed. That was doubly confirmed a few days later when she got a letter from Luke.

"I regret," he wrote, "due to my own personal preoccupation that I did not communicate better with you in that my attitude was misconstrued as belligerence toward you and Dad. If you can accept us, with all our faults and failings, my siblings and I would feel honored if you will allow us, Bobby's relatives, to be involved with the two of you."

Sharon cried at this wonderful show of acceptance. Bobby should be allowed to grow up knowing his relatives. But how difficult it would be to see Marcus, now that she had foolishly allowed herself to fall in love with him. However, she must push her own feelings aside and do what was best for her grandson. Too many people would suffer if she didn't allow Marcus and his family to be involved with Bobby.

A couple of days later, after dinner with Mary and James, the teens took Bobby outside so the adults could talk privately.

Sharon knew this was the time. She had prayed about it. She knew facts would come out in court, that her past would be revealed, and that such information could well damage Mary and James's opinion of her. She wanted them to hear it firsthand.

She told them about that night twenty-three years ago, about Mitchell not being Robert's birth father, and about how she had married him when Robert was five years old.

Mary and James sat as if enthralled or perhaps stunned, like watching some kind of soap opera unfold before their eyes. Sharon told them that Marcus had asked her to marry him, but she couldn't do that just to improve her chances of getting custody of Bobby. She ended by saying that Marcus had called and was willing to come to California to help her.

"Regardless of what happens with the custody," Sharon said, "Bobby should be allowed to know his daddy's relatives. But I want you to know I intend to stay in California. I know Bobby needs us all."

"Was it serious between you and the judge?" James asked.

"It might have been," she admitted. "But I couldn't expect him to give up his job and come here, away from his grandchildren, in order to be with me and mine. And I can't leave Bobby."

"Oh, Sharon," Mary said, "you always put everyone else first and yourself last." Whatever else they might have said was halted when the children came in from outside.

~

The following day, Mary and James stopped in. Kim was with them and took Bobby out for ice cream.

"We've given this a lot of thought, Sharon," James began.

"And what you told us yesterday has brought us to a definite decision," Mary added.

Great dread washed over Sharon. Her confession had probably damaged her character in their eyes. Perhaps they had even talked with their attorney, and he had told them their chances were better than ever.

"We talked of getting custody of Bobby primarily because we wanted you to feel free to make a life for yourself, Sharon," Mary said. "You selflessly devoted your life to Robert and Karen. They lived with you. You became their housekeeper, cook, and baby-sitter. You were more like a parent to our daughter than we were."

Mary wiped her eyes, and James took up the conversation. "The thought of custody came to us that first night we saw you with the judge."

Mary sniffed. "You two seemed to belong together. We wanted to give you every chance of making a life with someone. We doubted that a middle-aged man would want to take on a little boy."

"But you said the judge is going to take on the responsibility, regardless?" James asked.

Sharon nodded, looking from one to the other. Was she dreaming?

"We want you to know that we weren't trying to hurt you, Sharon. We were trying to help you," Mary said.

James added quickly, "We are willing to take care of Bobby. But honestly, we would never put you through something like a court case."

"It's not easy for me to be as loving and giving as you, Sharon," Mary confessed. "But James and I want to try. We love Bobby, and his being Karen's child and part of us is something we can't ignore. But he is yours in every sense of the word."

Sharon looked from one to the other as they took turns talking. It was James's turn.

"We haven't bonded with Bobby the way you have, Sharon," he said. "And if you can find happiness in the South, if you want to take Bobby back there, then you have our blessing. I think he has forgotten much of his life here already. Go back if you want. We can visit back and forth. Just know we're behind you, whatever you decide to do."

A flood of tears washed Sharon's cheeks. She'd always known Mary and James were wonderful people. Now she knew they also had hearts of gold.

Two weeks later, Sharon did what she felt was right. She put her house up for sale and called Lisa.

"Can you meet us at the airport? Bobby and I are coming home."

Chapter 20

L uke had done a lot of soul-searching over the past few weeks. It was time he acted on what he knew was right. He hadn't seen Julie since the day she lay in the hospital bed, looking so pale and lifeless. She had refused to meet his eyes or offer an explanation. She was in rehab now.

He had often compared her to Trish. He had found it refreshing to see lovely Julie, neat, never disheveled. She never complained and was always efficient, bright, happy. But he hadn't gotten past the surface appearance. He'd missed the signs that one of his own residents was under too much stress, choosing instead to indulge in a fantasy.

He and Trish were having a lot of discussions these days. They were praying about their marriage instead of arguing. One early morning, before the boys were up, they slipped out on the patio with coffee.

"I've been thinking about Julie a lot," Luke said. "Maybe God put her in my path so I could help her. As a doctor, and having been an intern myself, I should have recognized some of the signs of her problem. No one can go through those long hours without sleep and always be efficient, bright, cheerful." He shook his head at his own lack of insight. "In spite of the drugs, she has great potential, Trish. I would like to help her."

"Have you been to see her in rehab?" Trish asked.

"No."

"Then do, Luke. Let her explain to you how she got into that mess. You need to get all this settled in your mind. And if you don't mind, I'd like to visit her. Maybe I can help somehow. At least I can pray with her. When she's clean, maybe a letter of recommendation from you will help reinstate her license."

Luke blinked his eyes against the emotion. His wife was a wonderful woman. "Have I told you lately," he said in a low voice, "that I love you?"

Trish rose from her chair and went over and bent down until her face was close to his. "And I love you," she said, her voice, soft as her lips, came against his. After a long moment, she moved away. "Would you like to go for a swim?"

"I'd rather watch you," he said.

Trish threw off her robe, revealing a swimsuit underneath. She ran to the edge of the pool and dove in.

Luke watched his beautiful, graceful wife swim several laps before climbing out of the pool, laughing as she leaned to the side and wrung the water from her hair. The water drops on her tanned skin gleamed in the early morning sunshine. "Gives me energy for the day," she said.

Luke stared at her, as if he hadn't seen her in a very long time. Perhaps he hadn't. But standing there, she was full of life, exuberant, ready to face the day and two active boys. She was tired at night, just as he was, just as most human beings were, but she was honest about her feelings and her limitations.

How could he have been so blind? He stood as she walked closer. "I love you, Trish."

Her eyes studied his for a moment. Then he saw that mischievous gleam in hers that hadn't been there in a long time. "Of course," she teased, "why wouldn't you?"

His arms came around her. "You'll get wet," she warned.

"Who cares?" he said, pulling her closer.

"Mom, what's for breakfast?" they heard from the doorway.

Trish laughed. "They care."

"They, my dear, can wait. Their parents are busy at the moment."

Their lips met in another lingering kiss, making up for a long dry spell.

～

Sharon had called to let Marcus know she had returned. He said he would stop by as soon as the trial ended. Another week passed before there was a guilty verdict. Marcus came after supper and played with Bobby in the backyard, while Sharon made a batch of the cookies that the two guys liked so much.

After cookies and milk, Marcus helped with Bobby's bath and read him a bedtime story. "He's sound asleep," Marcus said, coming into the kitchen.

"Trish took me to the Christian preschool today. She's considering enrolling Mark for this fall. Do you think I should consider that for Bobby?"

Marcus pulled out a chair and reached for a cookie. "It was good for Caleb. The teachers are all Christians, and they teach in fun ways. Every minute is scheduled, and children learn how to share and how to relate to each other."

"Yes, I saw the schedule, and it looks wonderful. I just wonder if Bobby is too young."

"It's only three hours in the mornings," Marcus said. "Why not enroll him, and if you aren't pleased, you can keep him at home."

"Now that's sensible," Sharon said and laughed.

"I'm glad you came back to Mount Pleasant, Sharon," Marcus said.

She nodded. "So am I. Bobby's happy here. And I'm glad he can know you and your family. You're a wonderful grandfather."

"It's not difficult, with a lad like Bobby. It's obvious he's had a good up-bringing. Could I take some of these?"

"That's why I baked them," she said.

"In that case. . ." He picked up the platter stacked with cookies.

Sharon playfully hit his arm. "Put those down. I'll get a bag for them."

Marcus laughed. "Reminds me of wallpapering days."

Sharon quickly turned, afraid she might let her feelings show. For an instant, she had felt so comfortable with Marcus that she almost forgot there would be no connection between them except as the grandparents of Bobby. After Sharon put cookies in a sandwich bag, Marcus took them, thanked her, and said good night.

Sharon felt lonely after he left. There had been no talk of love or marriage since her confession to him about the past. But she mustn't have regrets. Instead, she must count her numerous blessings.

Sharon couldn't have expected the additional blessing that occurred the following day. Marcus called during the morning. "Luke wants the two of us to meet him in his office around noon," he said.

Fear struck her heart. "Is something wrong? Has something come up about Bobby?" Why else would Luke want to see them together?

"No, nothing like that. You know Bobby's last examination showed a healthy little boy who has recovered completely." Marcus paused for a deep breath. "The boy who received Robert's corneas wants to meet you."

"Oh," Sharon said. "I didn't expect—"

"I know. I'll pick you up."

"Yes, I don't think I could drive. I'll call Lisa to stay with Bobby."

Sharon didn't think she had ever been so nervous. Marcus held onto her arm as they walked down the hospital corridor and stopped at Luke's door. "Just a moment," she said and closed her eyes a moment for a prayer and a deep breath. "Okay."

Marcus opened the door and let her pass in front of him. Luke stood from where he sat behind his desk. Three people rose from the couch—a middle-aged couple and a young man. All three began to cry as Luke introduced them as the Edwards and their son, Tim.

"We promised each other we wouldn't cry," Mrs. Edwards said. "We couldn't come before now. We just weren't able to emotionally."

Mr. Edwards pulled a handkerchief from his pocket and blew his nose. "Nobody could have given our son a greater gift than. . ." He paused, cleared his throat, then spoke brokenly, "Than your son did, Mrs. Martin."

Sharon trembled with emotion, and Marcus put his arm around her shoulders and led her to one of the additional chairs Luke had brought in earlier. Marcus sat in a chair next to her. Luke handed her a tissue. Marcus

110

reached for the box, and Sharon saw that tears had bathed his face.

They all sat except Tim. Sharon was afraid he might fall, for he looked as trembly as his voice. That didn't matter. His words of gratitude came from his heart. "I practiced what I would say," he began, "but I don't remember it now. I just know I was blind, and now I can see."

His breath came in short gasps. "That's from the Bible. And it's how I feel. I don't know why I got to live and your son. . ." He chewed on his lower lip and looked at the floor where his teardrops fell.

"I don't know either," Sharon said. "It wasn't God who caused the accident, any more than He caused your blindness. God could have prevented both, but He didn't. Sometimes we are the cause of our troubles; sometimes we are victims. But I know, for those who love God and have faith in Him, He works in all these circumstances. I'm glad you have Robert's eyes. Robert would be glad. Let me see. . .your eyes."

The young man slowly lifted his head and looked at Sharon. She smiled through her tears. "Robert would be pleased."

"I hope so. And I want you to be. And his little boy. If I can be a big brother to him, then I want to."

"I might take you up on that," Sharon said and saw a light appear in Tim's eyes—her son's eyes.

"I may seem young to you," Tim said, "but this changed my life. I was a Christian before the accident, but in a way it was like my life was dark too. I didn't live like a Christian. I thought life should be a party and someday I'd change."

He shook his head. "This changed me. The accident made things worse. I hated everybody, and God, and life. Now, I can see and. . .God has called me to tell other people about this. I hope your son would be pleased."

"Oh, he would," Sharon said. "I know he must be looking down and smiling on you right now. And I'm so pleased that a part of my son is still alive in you. Robert always wanted to make a difference in the world. Now he's doing that in such a unique way."

Tim finally sat down on the couch between his parents. "I won't have much free time, but if you would let me, I'd like to be kind of like a big brother to Bobby. Did he like the teddy bear?"

"Oh, yes, but I've told him it's from a very special friend, and he keeps it in a special place. Someday, I will explain the significance to him. Thank you for that."

"That bear has been his best friend since Tim was a wee lad," his dad said.

"Not anymore," Tim said. "Jesus said there's no greater friend than one who lays down his life for another." His voice broke, and his eyes misted over again.

"We know," Sharon said, nodding.

The group exchanged hugs, addresses, phone numbers, and expressions of gratitude for the meeting. Luke closed the door behind the Edwards family, then turned to Marcus and Sharon.

"As tragic as it is, Sharon—and I know your loss is great—I want to say that your son. . ." He looked at them both. "And my brother Robert has made a positive difference in the Edwards family, in those other donor recipients, in my family, and in myself. I am grateful for that. This is an example of God taking a tragedy and bringing good from it. I don't have a mother, and I wonder, could I have a motherly hug?"

Sharon fell into his outstretched arms, and it was as if she embraced her son. Particularly when Luke said, "I can't replace Robert, but I am here for you. Please know that."

Sharon moved away and looked into his eyes. Yes, Robert's brother was sincere. And he was right. So much good had come from that tragic mistake years ago and again from this recent tragedy. Physical life could be devastating. Spiritual life could be rejuvenating. She shared those thoughts with Marcus on the way home.

"I agree," he said. "And Luke expressed it well. Sharon, I'm proud of my son Robert. And I thank you and Mitchell for giving him a good life. I couldn't have done better."

"We shouldn't make comparisons, Marcus. Your children are fine."

"Yes, they are," he said and smiled. "But someday, I'd like for you to tell me all about Robert."

"I would love to do that. Most people are afraid to mention him, lest they make me sad. But I want to talk about him, remember him."

"Would you read that flyer to me again, Sharon? I want to be a donor too."

Sharon read and Marcus, thinking of Robert and Tim, found a couple of sections particularly significant.

> *Give my sight to the man who has never seen a sunrise, a baby's face, or love in the eyes of a woman. Give. . .to the teenager who was pulled from the wreckage of his car, so that he might live to see his grandchildren play.*

~

Later that week, Marcus went with Sharon to the courthouse, and they sat in a judge's private chambers. With the written consent of the maternal grandparents, Sharon was given permanent custody of Bobby. Marcus didn't mention legal visitation rights for himself, knowing he had no rights in this matter—only obligations.

The next Saturday, Luke and Trish took Bobby to the zoo with their boys and wanted him to stay overnight.

"That's asking a lot," Sharon said. "Three wild boys."

"I think I can handle it," Trish said, laughing.

"And I'm here to help," Luke reminded them. "Besides, there's a method to my madness. We will need you to reciprocate when I take Trish off on a second honeymoon cruise."

"Why haven't I heard anything about this?" Trish said.

"It was a surprise," Luke said. "What about the middle of next month?" His arm came around her and pulled her close to his side.

Trish looked up at him with loving eyes. "Anytime," she said, "would be perfect."

~

Marcus awoke to a stormy Sunday morning. Lightning streaked the sky, and he heard a clap of thunder. It was a good day for covering up one's head, rolling over, and going back to sleep. However, it was the Lord's Day, and he should be in church.

After church, Trish invited Marcus over for lunch. "Sharon and Bobby will be there. He spent the night with the boys."

Marcus was eager to accept. During lunch, the boys talked about the zoo. Bobby's eyes were big as he talked about a snake big enough to swallow him. But he liked all the animals, especially the big, colorful tropical birds.

Marcus thought how much like a big, happy family they seemed to be. Grandparents, children, grandchildren. Only one thing would make it perfect. But would Sharon think so?

"You must rest, Bobby," Sharon told him when he protested about going home. He wasn't ready to leave his energetic, fun-loving cousins. Reluctantly, he said thank you and good-bye.

Marcus walked them to the car. The rain had stopped, but the sky was still overcast. After buckling Bobby in the car seat in back, he leaned down at Sharon's window before she started the engine. "Maybe the three of us could drive down to the beach after Bobby's rest period. There's something I'd like to show you."

"Yeah, yeah," Bobby whooped, and the two adults couldn't help but smile at each other.

"That sounded very much like an answer to your question, Marcus." She looked up. "But that sky looks ominous."

He was thinking her eyes were bluer than any sky, and he often wished he could read what lay behind them. They did tell him a lot. She was a warm, caring, wonderful woman who made him feel alive.

"The weatherman said it will clear."

"Oh, then, no problem," she teased, starting the engine.

Marcus moved back, laughing. "See you around five-thirty?" He knew she had supper around five.

"After such a great lunch, we'll have sandwiches. Want to join us?"

"Yes," he said, feeling as if the clouds had disappeared even though he could feel a few drops of rain splattering down. Holding out his hand, he saw the drops. Yes, there was such a thing as liquid sunshine.

Chapter 21

Sharon was glad the sky was clearing. But she was uncertain about the direction Marcus was taking after their sandwich supper. She remembered how difficult things had become the other time they had gone to the cottage. She remained silent, however, as he continued driving toward the beach. Bobby was busy in the backseat with a bucket-shovel set Marcus had given him.

When the cottage came into view, Sharon could hardly believe it. It had a new roof, a new railing around the porch, and new steps. The broken windowpanes had been replaced, and it had a fresh coat of paint. "You've fixed it up!" she exclaimed.

Marcus pulled up beside the cottage. "I've had it renovated. And many of my evenings have been spent getting rid of the old furniture and cleaning up the inside. I had to do something with my lonely evenings while you two were away."

He was making it sound like he missed her as much as he missed Bobby. But she must be careful not to assume anything. "Maybe," he was saying, "you could give me some advice on furnishings."

Sharon didn't respond. She kept staring at the cottage. Just like so many lives lately, the cottage was being made new.

Marcus got out and took Bobby to a sandy spot in front of the cottage, and Bobby immediately began to dig. Sharon sat in the new swing on the porch. Marcus came up and sat beside her.

They both watched Bobby, seemingly trying to dig to China and finally reaching wet sand that he had flying all over himself. He was having such fun that they didn't have the heart to stop him.

Then Marcus began to speak of Cypress Gardens. "Several years ago it was destroyed by Hurricane Hugo. How devastating that seemed to be. But then something miraculous began to happen. New, exciting, unexpected growth began to appear. Sharon, although the gardens will be different than before, they will have just as great appeal."

His words seemed to have some kind of appeal in them. She turned and saw that his face had turned serious. "I wish, Sharon, that might happen with our relationship. I know you have experienced the effects of the past in a different way than I. But perhaps someday you can forgive me, even—" He stopped and looked up toward the scattered clouds.

"Love you, Marcus?" Sharon said in awe.

He looked at her again. "Yes. I don't want to ruin this wonderful relationship the three of us have. I don't want to pressure you. But Sharon, I love you."

"Marcus, I love you too. I love you for the fine man that you are. And I love you because. . .I just can't help it."

Joy spread over his face and disbelief filled his eyes. His hands grasped her arms. "Sharon," he said, "will you marry me?"

"Yes. Oh, yes." Her eyes filled with tears.

He took her in his arms and their lips sealed the promise of commitment. Their lips parted, and Marcus held her head to his chest. They allowed themselves the flow of love that had no age or limits. Finally, Marcus spoke again.

"I've never been to Scotland, my ancestral home. Does that sound like a good place for a honeymoon?"

Sharon straightened and held his hand. "I'd love to go to Scotland. But to begin our new life together, Marcus, I can't think of a better place than right here in this cottage. I can look back upon it as proof that God can turn a mistake into two of the finest blessings I've ever had—my son and my grandson." She paused. "Three blessings," she corrected. "I include you, Marcus. I do love you."

"I thought of that too, Sharon, but I was reluctant to suggest it." He drew her into his arms again, his chin touching the softness of her hair. A great burden had lifted from his shoulders—a burden of past irresponsibility. God had given him a second chance, and he felt the joy of loving Sharon and that precious child who was so intent on digging in the sand.

"Bobby," Marcus said suddenly, moving back. "I need to ask that young man's permission to marry you."

"Suppose he says no?"

"Where's your faith in me, woman?" Marcus jested and rushed down the steps like a young man.

Sharon watched as he knelt in front of Bobby. She couldn't hear what Marcus was saying, but she recognized the gesture when Bobby's mouth fell open in a huge "O" and his eyes widened. Then Marcus spread his arms, and Bobby fell into them, giving Marcus a big hug.

There was a glow about them. Sharon walked over to the railing and held onto it. Her eyes lifted toward the heavens. She caught her breath at the spectacular sight. Marcus and Bobby were silhouetted against an orange sun setting into the ocean. The clouds were gone. The storm was over. And shining down like a blessing from heaven was a golden sky.

Catch of a Lifetime

To Lori, Howard, and the one who gave me the inspiration for this novel by saying, "I married him for his money, why can't I love him for it?"

Prologue

I f you want to catch shrimp," Adella Spelding had heard her daddy say more than once, "you have to use the right bait or know where to cast your net."

That was the theme song of Clem Spelding's life. Every morning except Sundays, he went out on his shrimp boat, rain or shine, rough waters or calm, and spent his days casting his net. He'd come in at night, permeated with the rank odor of smelly fish, singing, "Shrimp Boats Are A-Coming."

"Daddy's home," Adella's mama would say, as if some special guest had arrived. She'd stop whatever she was doing and meet him at the door for a big hug, a kiss, and a laughing rendition of what the day had held for him out on the sea. The three girls imitated their mama's actions.

The girls also learned to mirror their parents' love of God. Each night, the family prayed together. They talked about God's love for them and the ways He provided for their needs. On Sunday mornings, smelling fresh and clean, they all went to church and sang, "When we all get to heaven, what a day of rejoicing that will be."

It didn't happen that way.

The day Mama died, trying to give birth to a stillborn baby, everybody cried. The doctors had done everything they could, but even with all modern medicine had to offer, there were no guarantees. Daddy sat staring into space, saying nothing. Neighbor ladies and church members came around for awhile, bringing food, saying how sorry they were.

Adella kept waiting for the rejoicing the song talked about.

It didn't come.

Daddy dragged home at night without even humming. Nobody met him at the door. Finances were tighter than ever. He'd say, "How'd things go today?" to Mandy, the black woman he could barely afford to pay to watch the children and teach Adella how to cook.

Adella's daddy still took the girls to church on Sunday. A couple of years after Mama died, Adella finally asked him, "Why? Why did Mama have to die?"

"The Lord gives and the Lord takes away" was his answer.

It didn't satisfy.

"Why did the Lord want my mama?" she asked Mandy.

"Your mama had a hard life, and she was frail. The Lord wanted to give

119

her a better life," Mandy said. Then she'd gather Adella onto her ample lap, hold her to her soft, warm breasts, and sing about a mansion over the hilltop where they'd never grow old.

"Why couldn't she have it here?" Adella sobbed.

"Now, don't you go talking like that," Mandy reprimanded. "You just trust the Lord. He knows best."

Adella tried. She drew comfort from Mandy's belief that the Lord was going to make everything all right. She learned a lot from Mandy. She began to rely on her.

Then one day when Adella was fifteen, her daddy married again. Another woman took Mama's place in Daddy's life—a woman who had been one of Mama's best friends at church. Mandy went away.

Adella tried to be the real mama to her younger sisters. But little Brittany was so lonesome for a mama, she took to Leona right away. Thirteen-year-old Peggy decided she didn't need a mama, stepmama, or big sister telling her what to do.

Adella had learned much during the five years since her mama had died. That she couldn't count on her loved ones living to a ripe old age. Her mother hadn't. That she couldn't count on the Lord to give her financial security. She remembered vividly the times when the shrimp catch wasn't very good and one of the girls needed a new pair of shoes but had to keep wearing the ones with holes in them that were too small anyway.

Much as she wanted to trust God, Adella knew she would have to rely on herself. And the one thing that remained steadfast in her mind was that she would be a success. She would do whatever was necessary to make her life secure. She knew that she was attractive and intelligent. That was the bait she was determined to use to make a catch much bigger than anything her daddy had ever brought home.

Chapter 1

Shortly after eleven P.M., Adella pulled into her parking place at the back of the antebellum mansion, entered through the back door, strode down the hallway between the dining room and kitchen, then ascended the grand staircase to her second-floor apartment. She liked living in the historic mansion, feeling that it was preparation for the day when she'd have her own. But she wouldn't be like Flora, the owner and landlady, who had resorted to converting the great house into apartments. Adella would make sure when she married that her future was secure.

Only for a second did a twinge of apprehension pass through her mind, reminding her that she was twenty-five years old and still single. *There's plenty of time,* she reminded herself, unlocking the door. The kind of man who would have the means to support her in the manner in which she wished would be no spring chicken. And she hoped he wouldn't want one.

She smiled, thinking of spring, as she closed and locked the door behind her. After switching on a lamp and stepping out of her heels, she reveled in the feeling of soft carpet beneath her feet. She passed by her hope chest, which lifted her spirits, thinking of the fine things she had managed to buy on sale and stash away for her future.

Opening the windows, she paused to enjoy the cool April breeze as it gently rippled the lacy curtains and began to freshen the air in the stuffy apartment. For a moment, Adella peered out at the other grand homes on the quiet street. This morning she'd been acutely conscious of the azalea blossoms that brilliantly arrayed the historic town of Beaufort, South Carolina. They had drunk from the rains that had drenched the area, then opened their blossoms to soft, warm sunshine.

Turning from the window, Adella noticed the red blinking light on the answering machine that sat on the countertop separating the compact kitchen area from the living room. Adella punched the button and listened to the easily recognizable sound of Mandy's throaty voice. "Got somethin' to tell you, Honey." Mandy had a way of getting right to the point.

Adella went about changing from her dress with its simple lines that spelled elegance and good taste into a nightgown that would feel comfortably warm as she slept beneath a single blanket, enjoying the cool night air. That was something she liked about living on the second floor. She could leave the windows open without worrying about an intruder.

Going through her nightly ritual of facial cleansing and applying an elastin refining crème, Adella thought of Mandy and how she had become her only real friend. In a way, Adella had lost her daddy when he lost his first wife, and she'd lost him again when he'd married Leona. Adella's middle sister, Peggy, married right out of high school and had a girl and boy and no ambition further than their mother had had when she lived her life only for her husband and her children. Peggy's husband, Paul, now worked with Clem Spelding on the shrimp boat, making only enough money to get by from paycheck to paycheck.

Adella's stepmother, Leona, worked as a checker in a supermarket, and a lot of her money went to help Peggy and Paul when something inevitably came up they couldn't pay for.

Adella's younger sister, Brittany, was eighteen and about to finish high school. Adella talked to her about going to college and making something of her life, and she replied her life was just like she wanted it. As soon as she graduated, she would be through with school. All she wanted was to marry, live a simple life like Peggy, and have children soon enough that they could grow up with their cousins.

Adella could not understand that kind of attitude. Perhaps it was because Brittany had been the baby of the family. It was different, being the oldest when the mama of the family died. It had been Adella who'd taken on the responsibility of demanding the girls do their homework right after school. It had been she who was expected to help put meals on the table, see that her sisters' clothes were clean, help with the housework, then work in the summers at a fast-food place and bring her money home for the family.

And Adella had been too big to run crying to her daddy and sit on his lap with his arms around her. She'd become the woman of the house before she'd ever become a teenager. And if that's what it took to have goals and ambition, then that was one good thing that came from the whole tragic mess.

But it hadn't all been tragic. From the very beginning, she'd had a sympathetic listener and ready hugs from Mandy. Mandy was the one person who listened to her goals without condemning, even though she did quote Scripture a lot and sing her gospel hymns that Adella knew were supposed to be some kind of lesson for her. A couple times, Adella had even overheard Mandy praying that Adella would learn to trust God again.

As she drifted off to sleep, Adella thought of Mandy's phone message. What news had so excited her older friend?

～

"I've found you a man, Honey," Mandy said the next morning, after she released Adella from a big hug.

"A man," Adella said blandly, following Mandy from the back door of the Cottingtons' house into the kitchen, where the Cottingtons didn't mind if Mandy received company, as long as she kept up with her work. "One who fits my criteria. . .and yours?" she asked skeptically.

Wearing a sly grin, Mandy poured them both cups of coffee and began to set a huge brunch on the table. "Now you know I wouldn't settle for nothing but the best for my girl."

Adella was still skeptical. Mandy knew she intended to marry rich, but Mandy had her own ideas of other qualities a man had to have before he would be good enough for Adella.

"Well, tell me."

"The blessing first," Mandy said, and when she prayed she also prayed for the man she thought would interest Adella, adding, "Lord, if it ain't right, don't let it be."

But the Lord didn't seem to mind if a man was rich or not, Adella added in her own thoughts. *Let him be.* If Mandy approved of him, he must be really something.

"You know the Goodsons," Mandy began after stirring cream into her coffee and taking a big gulp.

Adella nodded. Mr. and Mrs. Goodson lived in one of the antebellum homes right off Bay Street. They owned several marinas, including the one with fifty slips for big boats at Goodson Island, beyond Fripp. Their shipping supply warehouse was in Beaufort, not far from the marina there. She'd seen the Goodsons many times. They were friendly, of course, when Adella led them to a table in the Marina Club Restaurant where she worked as hostess.

"What about the Goodsons?" Adella asked, then poked into her mouth a small stuffed mushroom that probably was an hors d'oeuvre left over from the previous evening.

"They were dinner guests last night," Mandy explained. "Well, they're going to Florida," she added pointedly, "where they have another home. They're going to be at the business down there for awhile and let their son handle the business here."

Adella's eyes widened. That sounded interesting. "You've met him?"

"Oh, yes. His name's Derek. He was here at the dinner party too. It seems they've had him work at the other marinas, and now they want him to handle the businesses here for awhile. He will live in the Goodson home." Mandy gestured with her hand, indicating a house nearby.

Adella thought about the Goodsons. They were an average-looking, middle-aged couple. They dressed nicely, but there wasn't anything about them to attract particular attention. She had learned that wealthier people tended to be discreet about clothing when out in public. At least they were when they ate at the Marina Club Restaurant.

"Well, come on, Mandy. Give me the details. How old is he? What's he like?"

"I found out he's not married or engaged or anything. And I tell you this much," Mandy said, shaking her drumstick at Adella. "A man like him wouldn't be hard to love."

"Now, Mandy, you know I'm not going to get caught in that trap. Love has nothing to do with it. Most of the people I know who married for love are either unhappy, so busy with children they don't know which end is up, or divorced. You can't depend on emotion." Her finger tapped the side of her head. "You have to use your common sense if you want a good marriage and want it to last."

"And you think money is the answer?" Mandy said blandly.

"Definitely," Adella said.

"Hmmph!" Mandy snorted. "It takes more than money. It takes sharing faith in the Lord and living that faith every day. If my husband would've had more money, he would've just got into more trouble. Wouldn't have helped him none. Except he would have got drunker quicker and had that accident sooner that killed him."

"Maybe," Adella agreed. "But if he'd had money, you wouldn't have to clean other people's houses and cook for them. You'd have your own help."

Mandy was shaking her head. "I don't mind cleaning and cooking. Whatever you do, you do for the Lord, Honey. Then you won't go around wanting more than you should have."

"Well, once I marry I don't intend to clean any house. Not even my own. And you can bet I'll end up with something more than a house full of kids to raise alone, living on food stamps."

"There just might be an in-between, Adella."

"Not for me," Adella said staunchly. Then her voice softened. "Do you remember when I used to say when I got rich you could come and live with me?"

"And do you remember I told you it was more important to have a decent husband to live with?" Mandy shot back.

"But you will come and work for me, won't you?" Adella pressed.

"When you get rich?" Mandy's eyebrows rose along with her voice. "Sure, Baby. You know I would."

Adella grinned and sipped her coffee. Mandy shook her head as if she never would understand Adella. But she did understand. She knew how Adella felt about things and how her worst fear in life was ending up with nothing.

"Now come on," Adella urged. "You haven't told me about the Goodson man yet."

"Well, I've known you to pass up better-looking men than him, but I don't think any of them could be any nicer. I like him. He mostly listened while the families talked about the boat business and what he could expect here. They talked about the house he'd live in and what they'd be doing in Florida."

"What did he look like?"

"His hair was kind of golden, you know, like he's been out in the sun a lot. He had interesting eyes that moved from one person to another and had a little sparkle in them. He smiled a lot and had a dimple right about here."

Mandy poked her finger in her right cheek, making Adella laugh.

"You know I'm treated kind of like family here at the Cottingtons," Mandy added, "but he got up after dinner and helped clear the table. We talked awhile. That's when I noticed he has eyes the color of a fresh green meadow with dew sparkling on it early in the morning."

"Gold hair and green eyes," Adella droned. "Sounds like the color of money."

Mandy huffed. "Don't you let anybody else hear you talk like that, Della child. They might believe you. You might even believe it yourself, but I know money's not all you're looking for. You've had chances."

Adella smiled. She knew what she wanted. And from the moment Mandy started talking about Derek Goodson, Adella knew he was a prize catch.

～

"Bye, Honey. I'll be praying for you," Mandy said when she and Adella went out the back way. After a parting hug, Mandy watched the girl she loved with all her heart stroll through the garden and down the sidewalk in her jeans and T-shirt, with her dark hair flowing behind her, walking like she was free as the breeze.

Mandy knew that part of Adella's being all bound up about money wasn't just because she'd been brought up in a poor family. Adella had watched how Mandy had struggled too. There were times when she could have used a lot more. When her first husband drank up every drop he could get his hands on. Then after the accident, Mandy had had to raise two children without a man and with very little money. But she'd managed, and her children were already in high school when she went to work for the Speldings. Mr. Spelding hadn't minded that they came to his house after school and stayed until he got home from work.

She'd made them all sit down at the dining-room table and do their homework first thing. Then the younger children had played in the backyard together, or on rainy days they'd sat in the living room, reading books or playing games. Mandy didn't believe in watching much TV. She made Adella come in the kitchen, like her daddy wanted, and learn how to cook.

That girl mastered Southern cuisine, Lowcountry cooking, and jambalaya. It had been hard, leaving that girl after her daddy married again. She'd tried being a mama to Adella, made her promise to come to her house so she could keep teaching her how to cook. Adella came. It got to be a regular thing for her to come on Saturdays after she finished with her own chores at home.

As Mandy had expected, things changed when Adella started college. A lot of things happened that year. Mandy's children moved away, and then Mandy married her second husband, a long-distance truck driver. Mandy liked Hebert being away for long periods of time. She'd call Adella and say, "Come on down and see me, Girl," and Adella did. They would sit in Mandy's little kitchen or out on her back porch and talk about real things, like what was on both their minds. It was good. It wasn't exactly like mother and daughter. Mandy's own daughter never confided in her so much, and Mandy could tell Adella about feelings that she wouldn't tell her own child. The relationship was special.

Mandy sighed as she relived those conversations. Adella had always known she was a beautiful girl with that dark hair and deep blue eyes and soft, smooth, cream-colored skin. She'd held every beauty-queen title offered in the area from the time she was a little girl, even being elected homecoming queen in high school. But Mandy had always stressed the need for inner beauty, the qualities that make a person attractive to others throughout life.

Mandy knew Adella paid attention to her words. She'd told Mandy repeatedly that, for a man who had everything, she'd have to be able to offer something special. She had no worldly goods, but she had herself. She wanted to marry a rich man, and in exchange she would offer her beauty and her purity. The kind of man she had in mind would want a woman of principle with Christian values like the ones Mandy encouraged.

In high school and college Adella went to parties and proms, but she confided in Mandy that she was never even tempted to get serious with any fellow. Poor boys didn't appeal to her. They were not in her plan. And she defined a poor boy as anybody who couldn't give her all she wanted—the good life.

She wouldn't settle for less than her goal—which was to be worthy of a man with whom she could spend a comfortable life and have no financial struggles. She knew where a lot of the wealthy people were located—at the marina, where they came in by boat and yacht. After working her way through college as a waitress, she now served as hostess at the exclusive Marina Club Restaurant.

Mandy had watched over the years as Adella kept herself in shape by walking, swimming, and playing tennis. She bought her clothes at the finest shops, usually after season so she could get them on sale. Knowing what she wanted and keeping focused on her goal gave her a confident air.

But Mandy also loved Adella too much to tell her about a man simply because he was rich. Mandy knew that as a child, before her mother died, Adella had accepted Jesus as her Savior. But the hard times she had encountered and the losses she had faced had made it very hard for Adella to trust God for her security.

For years Mandy had prayed that God would bring a man into Adella's life who might help her once again understand how much her heavenly Father loved her. And one of the things about Derek Goodson that Mandy hadn't mentioned to Adella was how he'd made it clear at that dinner party that his top priority was not riches—it was a love for the Lord. Adella might think she needed money. But Mandy knew if there were anything that girl really needed, it was a good man who loved the Lord.

Chapter 2

Derek worked with his dad all week, getting the hang of how things operated in the supply store on the waterfront in Beaufort and at the marina on Goodson Island. It was similar to the marina in Florida, except on a smaller scale. At their Florida marina, there were one hundred and twenty slips where boats could come in; here there were fifty-two. In Florida, although he was the owner's son, he worked as an assistant. Here, he would be the top boss, with a manager underneath him.

"You think I'm ready to handle this, Dad?" he asked on Friday afternoon.

"I think you could have years ago," Judd Goodson said, his gaze warm and serious behind his eyeglasses. "I just felt like you should have experience on all levels."

Derek grinned. "I'll do everything in my power to live up to that confidence, Dad."

"Just give it your best, Son. That'll be good enough for me," his dad replied.

As the afternoon wore on, Derek thought about his dinner plans. His parents had plans that evening, so his mom wouldn't be preparing a meal at home. Next week, he'd be working without his dad, unless he needed him, and he wanted to be more than a boss to Jerry, the manager, and Bob, the assistant. He wanted to be their friend. "I'd like to take you two out to eat after work," he said. "That is, if you don't have plans. I wouldn't want to take you away from your families."

Jerry said he'd call and check with his wife. "She's been talking about having you over to our house for a home-cooked meal."

Bob's situation was entirely different. He said his wife would be happy to have one less mouth to feed at suppertime. He glanced at Jerry, making his call. "We'd like to have you over, but I'm afraid you'd have to fight the mongrels for the hot dogs."

"Are you talking about kids or dogs?" Derek asked.

"Both," Bob said with a wry grin. "Three kids and a stray that stayed."

Derek laughed. "I'm an only child who had no siblings to fight with and a trained dog who stopped wrestling upon command, so I'd like to take you up on that challenge one of these days."

Bob nodded.

Just then Jerry rejoined them. "Okay for tonight," he said. "Betty wanted to go visit her mother anyway."

Derek smiled. "Great! Where would you guys like to eat?"

"The Marina Club Restaurant," the two men answered in unison.

~

"Good evening, Sirs."

Derek's intended response died in his throat when his eyes met those of the hostess. He felt something like an electric shock rock his senses. Directly in front of him stood the most strikingly beautiful woman he'd ever seen. She could easily have stepped from the pages of a fashion magazine or onto the runway of a Miss Universe Pageant.

She didn't flinch or appear embarrassed by his stare. Instead, she smiled and asked, "How many in your party, please?" He couldn't immediately find his voice. His impulse was to send his employees away and say there was only a party of one—unless she cared to join him.

But Jerry replied, "Three."

She smiled, looking from one to another as if unaware of Derek's discomfort. He was grateful for the dim lighting, hoping it hid the shade of embarrassment he must have on his face from staring, as if he'd never before seen a beautiful woman.

He had, however, seen many of them. Some had their own yachts and docked at the slips in Florida. He'd even dated a beautiful actress who had been in Orlando filming a picture. For the fun of it, Derek had agreed to be a silent extra standing along the side of a street in the pouring rain.

The hostess gathered three menus from beneath the counter, stepped ahead of them, and spoke again. "We have a table in the corner if you'd like privacy for conducting business, or you might like to sit by the window that has a view of the marina."

"The view of the marina will be fine," Derek said.

He was not one to ogle, but his eyes seemed to have a mind of their own. After he sat, they noticed the soft fullness of her lovely lips turned into a smile over perfect white teeth. They noticed the simplicity of her dress that spoke of style and elegance. They looked at her hands when she placed a menu in front of them and noticed that she was not wearing wedding rings, nor any ring at all. Why did he do that? Had he lost his senses?

"Your waitress will be with you shortly," she said. He felt sure she looked straight at him and held his gaze. He said, "Thank you," as if she had done him some great favor.

Forcing his eyes not to follow her, Derek picked up his menu, hardly seeing it. *What's wrong with me? I've heard of spring fever when a young man's fancy turns to love, but I'm thirty-two years old, beyond all that. This has never happened to me before. It's not like I've never seen a beautiful woman.*

He'd never felt like this before either. Not even when he was a high school boy on a first date. And he certainly hadn't in college when he'd strayed from the Lord. Then he'd thought every pretty girl had been made only for him and had a couple of flings that neither his parents nor the Lord would approve of. He'd even imagined himself in love a few times. Fortunately, he'd come to his senses before doing any irreparable harm to himself or the girls. He'd seen the error of his ways and committed his life to the Lord one night at a meeting of Christian athletes.

Besides, he was well aware beauty went only skin deep. But this attraction had to do with something other than just beauty. What was it? Something in her eyes, the most arresting eyes he'd ever seen, as if he could look into them and become lost. They seemed to welcome him, challenge him, invite him—as if something were inevitable.

～

Veni, Vidi, Vici—I came, I saw, I conquered. That famous motto of Julius Caesar's kept running through Adella's mind from the moment Derek Goodson walked into the restaurant. She supplied her own paraphrase, however, and that was *He came, I saw, I conquered.*

It hadn't been difficult at all, gaining his interest. Increasing it, then keeping it, would be the challenge. Keeping a cool head had not been easy. This was it. Her big moment. What she had planned for and waited for all her life. Derek Goodson was even more than she could have hoped for. In addition to being very wealthy, or at least the heir to considerable wealth, he wasn't bad to look at. She'd drawn that conclusion not only from his parents' good looks and Mandy's description. She'd seen the golden-haired man leave the supply store a couple of times that week in a Bentley that she'd never noticed before.

She could now understand why Mandy had liked him upon first meeting. She'd decided long ago that she could live with an ugly man if he were rich enough. But how much better it would be if her husband could be attractive. Derek Goodson certainly was that. His rugged good looks were accompanied by a wholesomeness she didn't expect. She liked his wide mouth that smiled over strong white teeth. That dimple in his right cheek that Mandy had mentioned lent a certain charm.

Yes, the bait had been waiting for years. She had a strong feeling that all she needed to do for the moment was sit patiently on the shore and wait for the fish to bite. Then the challenge would begin. Could she reel him in?

～

With effort, Derek refrained from returning to the restaurant alone later Friday evening. The next morning while having breakfast, he asked his mother if she knew the hostess at the restaurant.

"That beautiful girl, I assume you mean," she said with a grin and gleam in her eyes.

"She is that," Derek agreed. He sipped his coffee and tried to look unconcerned.

"Her name is Adella. I don't know her last name, but she visits with Mandy quite often."

His brow wrinkled. "Mandy?"

"You met her last week at the Cottingtons'. Mandy is their cook and housekeeper."

"Oh, yes. An excellent cook, as I recall." Upon seeing his mother's eyebrows lift, he added quickly, "But not as good as you, of course."

"Of course," she said and grinned. "Anyway, I think Mandy was Adella's nanny years ago."

Derek nodded, knowing from experience that household staff became almost like family. His mother kept trying to read his expression, and he kept trying not to let his feelings show. Nevertheless, she pulled out a chair, faced him, and smiled. "You found her pretty, I suspect."

"Not bad," he said with a shrug. "But she is a little old for me. She wore a wedding band too."

His mother swatted at him. "Derek. You know perfectly well I wasn't referring to Mandy."

"Oh, I see. And you think Adella's *pretty?*"

His mother laughed lightly. "I suppose that's an understatement. There's not a more beautiful girl around. I only know what Vera Cottington has said, which isn't much, and then from seeing Adella at the restaurant. I get the impression she's as nice as she is beautiful."

Derek thought that quite complimentary, coming from his mother, who was a woman of very high standards.

She laid her hand on his arm, looking into his face with concerned eyes. "Derek, you know beauty is only skin deep."

"Yes, Mother. I do."

With that thought in mind, Derek felt compelled to find out if Adella were a temptation disguised as an angel of light. Or was she the one God had chosen for him, who would light up his life?

~

Dressed in a sport coat over a casual shirt and slacks and sunglasses, Derek entered the Marina Club Restaurant shortly after six o'clock that evening. He removed the glasses after stepping inside the door, quite pleased with himself that they did the trick. His eyes adjusted quickly to the dim room. She was just returning from having seated customers at a table. She was as beautiful, if not more so, than he had remembered. Tonight she wore a chic two-piece cream-colored pants suit. Her eyes met his, and she smiled, coming closer. "Good evening," she said pleasantly. "May I show you to a table?"

"Yes, thank you." He took a deep breath. "A corner table, please." Perhaps that would clue her in that he meant business. After she led the way to the table, Derek pulled out the chair nearest the corner that would give him a view of the entire room. . .and of her.

She laid the menu in front of him. He looked up. "Since I seem to be a regular customer since last night, may I introduce myself? I'm Derek Goodson."

"Adella Spelding," she said, extending her hand.

Derek felt the impact of her touch even before his hand reached hers. Her soft, warm, slender hand fit into his like it belonged there. In the background, music played—something about "I want to hold you." Never before in his life had his emotions overruled his mind. In those wild college days, his mind knew exactly what he was doing. Right now, he wasn't sure. Feeling the slight withdrawal of her hand, he managed to say, "I believe we have a mutual acquaintance."

"And who might that be?" she asked playfully.

"Mandy," he said.

He saw that Adella was not surprised. "Yes," she said. "Mandy told me she met you." She smiled. "Will anyone be joining you?"

"Not unless you'd like to."

"Mr. Goodson," she said in a slightly reprimanding tone, and he figured she'd heard that line only several hundred times. But she was still smiling. "Would you like something to drink?"

"Call me Derek," he said.

"Call me Adella," she returned.

"Adella," he said, "I would like coffee, thank you."

"Derek," she said, a small light dancing in her eyes, "your waitress will be right with you."

He watched as she walked away, then his gaze followed her as she led a couple to another table. She looked at him and smiled again. Was she flirting back? Or was he making a fool of himself? He turned to look at whatever view might be on his right and was confronted by a dark mahogany wall.

Glancing up, his eyes met hers again. He realized he'd have to order soon. Picking up the menu was no easy chore, considering the way his hand shook. Maybe he'd been bitten by a rabid sand flea, if there was such a thing. He definitely had some kind of strange fever. He stared unseeing at the menu. What should he order? What did he want?

What did he want? He wanted Adella to like him. His thoughts stopped when a cup of coffee was set before him. He looked up into the face of a wait-ress. "Thank you," he said. "Is there a specialty of the house tonight?" he asked.

"Other than our fresh seafood," she said, "I'd recommend our fresh cut black Angus steak."

"I'll have the steak," he said, handing her the menu. "Medium-rare. And an antipasto salad with the house dressing."

Derek had prided himself on being honest, upright, and aboveboard for the past several years. And he'd never considered himself an actor. But sitting there in the restaurant, eating the steak as if he tasted it, and never directly looking at the woman he saw stroll back and forth throughout the room, he felt he should get an Oscar for the best performance of a man who could sur-vive if a particular woman rejected him when he summoned up enough nerve to ask her out. He would still have to perform, leave a tip, pay the bill, and walk out the door without stumbling.

A thought entered his mind that perhaps he shouldn't ask her out the first time he talked with her. But if she wasn't interested, he needed to know right away. Why prolong the agony? Why wait for another day or another week? He knew exactly how he felt about her the moment he saw her. She might as well know, so that if she rejected him, he could leave and get on with his life—perhaps.

He'd almost finished his meal when Adella seated a couple at the table in front of him. Then she stepped over to him.

"Derek, I hope your meal was satisfactory," she said.

He chewed fast, swallowed quickly. "Excellent," he replied. "Good steak."

"I can recommend the perfect dessert. A triple fudge melt-in-the-mouth cake." She smiled, and he detected a trace of mischief in her eyes as she leaned forward slightly, saying in a soft tone, "It's very sinful."

He grinned. "No dessert," he said. "But I would like to know if you will accompany me to church in the morning."

Chapter 3

Church!

Adella rarely went to services on Sunday anymore. The restaurant closed at eleven Saturday nights. She often got to bed after midnight, then slept late on Sunday morning. After awakening, she lolled around, reading the Sunday papers—particularly the society pages—and catching up on world news, fashions, and what was taking place in the world of tennis, soccer, art, and literature. She liked working the cryptogram and jumble while eating brunch. Later she might watch an old movie while endulging in a light supper. She read the latest best-sellers. Sometimes she went to her family's church and ate lunch with them. She always went on Easter and Christmas. Occasionally, she went to Mandy's church, the only service that really entertained her, with its lively music and the rhythm created between the preacher's words and the church members' responses of "Amen" and "Praise the Lord" and "Preach it, brother." Then late in the afternoon, she'd be back at the restaurant to greet diners.

But here was an opportunity not to be missed. Telling Derek that she'd have to first speak with her boss, Adella found her boss in the office and told him something had come up and she wouldn't be able to work Sunday evening. Since she rarely missed a day, and he often said she was an asset to the restaurant, he accepted her excuse without question. She didn't want to have to rush back to work, in case Derek had some plans for the two of them after church.

She thought back to the night before, when he'd walked into the restaurant with his two friends. Immediately she recognized that he was interested. She knew the game and how to play it: the lighthearted bantering, the mild flirtation, the smiles, the glances. It reminded her of something she'd heard Mandy say upon occasion: "He chased her until she caught him."

She had "hooked" Derek Goodson.

Tonight, she had fully expected him to ask her out when she walked up to the table and mentioned the dessert. She was prepared to accept his invitation, expecting him to invite her out to dinner somewhere, away from the Marina Club Restaurant.

But he had thrown her for a loop—caught her quite off guard. Right after she mentioned the dessert being very sinful, he'd invited her to church, of all places.

What was his angle?

This definitely was going to be challenging.

Church?

~

To Adella's surprise the next morning, after leading her down the church aisle, Derek seated her beside Mrs. Goodson, whose husband sat on the other side of her. It even appeared she might have been saving the seat for them.

"Mom and Dad," Derek said, "this is Adella Spelding."

Mr. Goodson leaned forward and nodded.

"Hello, Dear," Mrs. Goodson said, moving her Bible and purse from the pew. "How good of you to join us this morning."

"Thank you," Adella replied. Her quick glance at Derek revealed his face, reminding her of the cat that swallowed the canary. She was pleased. What better respect could a man show for a woman than to have her meet his parents on the first date? Or. . .was he wanting to know if they approved of her? Would that make a difference to him?

Derek leaned over so that his lips were close to her ear. "I don't know most of these people anymore," he whispered. "Otherwise I would introduce you."

"That's all right," Adella assured him. Apparently, he, too, was aware of glances their way, followed by whispers.

The choir filed in and an organist began to play. Adella appreciated the beauty of the music. When the congregation stood to sing, Derek found the page and shared the hymnal with her. Adella glanced up at him. His green eyes met hers, and she watched his cheek dimple. The introduction to the hymn ended, and they joined the congregation in singing the familiar tune. As she'd expected from his speaking voice, Adella liked Derek's rich baritone voice. It blended perfectly with her velvety soprano.

During the sermon, similar to many she'd heard, her thoughts drifted back to earlier in the morning. At 9:30 on the dot, she had closed her apartment door, walked down the grand staircase, and waited in the foyer at the door with glass panels that allowed her to peer out but prevented anyone outside from looking in. She hadn't told Derek which apartment she lived in and didn't want him to knock on the wrong door.

The moment she reached the door, his silver-gray Bentley pulled up to the curb. Her heartbeat quickened as she watched Derek Goodson, wearing a navy blue suit, light blue shirt, and conservative tie, stride up the few steps to the door as if he were in a hurry. His golden hair shone in the morning sunlight.

Before he could ring the bell, she opened the door.

"Have you waited long?" he asked.

"Not at all," she said.

He smiled. "Your eyes are blue. I couldn't tell in the restaurant. You look lovely."

"Thank you," she replied with a smile and thought how right it felt after he closed the front door, then took her arm as they walked to the Bentley. She'd worn her cerulean spring suit that enhanced the deep blue of her eyes, a color that she'd always been told was a striking shade and rare for a brunette. Her hair was back in a neat French twist. Small sterling silver earrings were her only jewelry. During the days of winning beauty contests, she'd been told never to allow jewelry to compete with her natural beauty.

She had felt particularly special when Derek opened the car door for her, then closed it. She'd never before ridden in a Bentley. How comfortable it was. How smoothly it rode. How elegant its interior. How right it felt.

When he drove up to the church, she was glad to be able to tell him she had attended services there one Christmas. "I think it's beautiful," she had said.

He'd agreed, adding that he had grown up in the church. He thought it was built in the mid-1800s.

"There was a time," Adella could tell him, "when about two hundred whites and more than three thousand slaves attended this church. Later, it was used as a Union Army hospital."

He had been pleased that she could relate a little of its history. She was pleased to be sitting in the old historic church where the elite of the area attended.

It seemed almost as soon as the service started, the benediction was given. The service had ended. Numerous people gathered to welcome her, introduce themselves, and be introduced. No doubt they were quite curious about who she was, sitting between Derek Goodson and his mother.

As they exited the building, having stopped to exchange a few brief words with the pastor, Adella expected Derek to ask her out to lunch and then perhaps walk along the waterfront, talking about the rich history of the area.

Instead, he asked, "Would you like to go sailing?"

Surprised and delighted, she quickly agreed. "I would need to change," she added.

"I'll drop you off, go home and change, then pick you up," he said. "We could stop somewhere and get a bite to eat."

"I could whip us up a quick lunch," she offered.

"Don't bother with that," he said. "I'll change, then I'll go pick us up a bucket of chicken." He dropped her off and left.

What is this? Some kind of test? she wondered, while changing into shorts and a tank top. He was quickly becoming the surprise catch of the day. *A man with all that money goes to a fried chicken place?*

By the time he returned, she'd made iced tea and set their glasses on the table. She led him to the table and seated herself opposite him. He reached out his hands, but it wasn't to open up the sack of food.

"Shall we say grace?" he asked.

Adella put her hands in his and felt his warm grip as they bowed their heads and he thanked God for the food, the day, and their meeting and asked God's blessings on it all. "Amen," he said, and Adella looked over into his warm gaze, then quickly averted hers to the tea glass.

He was not as predictable as other men had been, but she knew he was interested in her. And he just might be the person who could offer her what she wanted in life. This was not only a day of testing on his part, but hers as well.

"How did you come to live with Flora?" he asked.

Adella told him truthfully about the woman whose finances had fallen upon hard times after her husband passed away. "She turned the house into four apartments and lives in one downstairs."

That was something Adella never intended to have happen to her. When she married money, she would ensure that she would never lose it.

A short while later, they drove to the dock. One glance at Derek's luxury sloop caused Adella's mind to swirl into the past. A mental picture of her daddy's shrimp boat came to mind. It was a toy compared to this. A toy about to fall apart. It was creaky, smelly, slow, and always breaking down. Her dad had put in a lot of hard work for what seemed like nothing in return. He'd made a meager living, going out in all kinds of weather, and developing arthritis in his hands that worsened as the years passed by.

"It's beautiful," she said with genuine pleasure as she stepped onto the sleek, shining vessel. This was a real boat. This is what a person should have, not some old weather-beaten tub.

If this excursion today is some kind of test by Derek Goodson, she was thinking, *it is one I don't mind taking.*

~

Derek had been as excited about his luxury sloop when he first got it as he had been about getting his first car when he was sixteen. After a few years, however, he took for granted that the vessel was part of his life. Now, seeing Adella's excitement and appreciation, his own enthusiasm resurfaced.

Derek was not selfish. He made a point of using his life, his time, and his money to help make the world a better place for those less fortunate than he. This boat had been used for many sunset excursions out on the water with groups of believers who studied the Bible and felt the joy of being part of God's creation. He was very much aware of the Scripture that said, "To whom much is given, much is required."

Now, someone had come along and caused him to see all his blessings anew. He needed that. It made him feel even closer to the Lord. *Thank You, Lord,* he prayed silently, *for letting me see my blessings through the eyes of one viewing them for the first time. Thank You that I have something to share with others. I recommit my blessings, and myself, to You. May my life and my belongings be used for Your glory.*

"I want to see it all," Adella said, relieving Derek's concern that she might think him egotistical. As she admired the hand-rubbed teak of the interior and the exquisite fabrics in the master stateroom and queen-sized berth, he realized she was not overwhelmed. She simply appreciated its beauty and quality. Obviously, she knew that things were not the measure of a person's worth. She was confident in herself. She'd already shown him that she had beauty, intelligence, a knowledge of God, and a desire for moral living. He knew he wasn't perfect, and he certainly didn't expect perfection of another human being. But Adella certainly had some very desirable qualities.

"Even a tub and a shower," she exclaimed, examining every nook and cranny, obviously impressed.

While exploring the U-shaped galley with its refrigerator, freezer, Corian counters, and portholes, she openly expressed her delight. *Yes,* he told himself, *a person should be appreciative of fine things. After all, doesn't God live among many mansions and streets of gold?*

She liked the salon area and crew quarters, although no crew was present this day. Derek did not intend to sail out on the open sea, planning on cruising around the islands instead. She asked about the electronics, which he explained, although not as well as his captain could have.

"It's absolutely fantastic!" she exclaimed, spreading her hands as if to encompass his world.

Derek smiled, pleased. He wouldn't tell her just yet that she should see his dad's yacht if she thought this sloop was impressive.

"Shall we go topside and cruise the islands?" he asked.

"Yes, let's," she said with enthusiasm. They ascended the companionway.

Derek wanted to see her reaction when he asked, "Can you help me with sails?"

"Well," she retorted saucily, knowing he was baiting her, "since there doesn't seem to be a crew around, I don't see that I have an option." She lifted her chin and shrugged as if this would be a piece of cake. "I know a little about rigging." She turned toward the mast.

Derek watched her for a moment. He was aware of the water splashing softly, caressing the boats bobbing in their slips. The warm sunshine and cool breeze made for perfect conditions. He took in a deep breath of the fragrant air. The day couldn't be more glorious.

He could have told her he was kidding with her. He had the latest equipment that allowed him to manipulate the boat without having to take along a crew. His recently installed push-button system included electric winches, hydraulic furling jib and main, and bow thruster. But seeing the look in her eyes that met his challenge, he walked over to her. "Okay, mate, let's see what kind of sea legs you have."

Adella knew she wasn't seaworthy at all. But she'd helped with the sails on her daddy's shrimp boat enough that she knew the basics of how they operated and enough of the language to intrigue Derek with it. She was quite impressed with his adeptness, his strength, and his muscular physique, which was quite in evidence as he manipulated the rigging.

Derek did most of the work, but she felt she was doing just fine as a first mate. Her sea legs were at times wobbly, and they both laughed when she landed on her seat while holding onto the rope. They yelled back and forth and ducked when the sails seemed to want to swat them off the boat.

He then showed her the controls that could have done the job for them. "What!" she exclaimed, holding out the palms of her hands for him to see. "You mangled my hands needlessly?"

"I'm sorry," he said seriously.

Then she laughed. "Don't be. I enjoyed that as much as you did."

"I do like working the boat manually," he admitted.

Again, Adella was aware that Derek wasn't a stereotypical wealthy man. It disturbed her slightly that she found him to be quite appealing and not at all. . .stuffy.

Derek could hardly believe that Adella had willingly helped him with the sails. He expected and would have accepted her refusal, using any excuse from not being adept at it, to she'd break a fingernail, or maybe even saying no because she'd get hot and sweaty. But she'd accepted his challenge, she'd liked it, and they'd worked well together.

Now, he was equally pleased with her relaxing and looking at home on the sunpad. She leaned against the cushioned padding at the curve of the flybridge, facing him, with her lovely legs bent at the knees and resting on the white seat. Derek sat at the ergonomic helm, glancing occasionally at the instruments. He liked being able to look at her against the background of blue water, its foam tips golden in the bright sunlight as they cruised along the Beaufort River, past Lady's Island, Gibbes, Cane, Cat, and Parris Island. Soon they sailed out into Port Royal Sound, toward Hilton Head Island.

They talked about the boat, the islands, the history of Beaufort, and its being the second oldest city in South Carolina.

"Can't you just imagine what it was like during the American Revolution," Adella said with a sense of awe, "when palmetto logs protected South Carolina from British warships?"

Derek smiled, gazing toward the stately trees standing like proud sentinels, even now guarding the islands. "Yes," he said fondly, appreciating his hometown more than ever. "If this couldn't be called the tomato state, I suppose palmetto is the next best thing."

Adella's laugh was spontaneous. "Oh, don't tell me you were raised on tomato sandwiches too?"

Derek nodded. "What true son of Beaufort wouldn't be?"

Adella conceded. "You're right. Beaufort is famous for them. When I was growing up, that was Mandy's lunch special."

"There's only one way to make a true Beaufort tomato sandwich," he said seriously.

"Of course. You have to have two pieces of white bread, slathered with a generous amount of mayonnaise, and salt and pepper."

"Ohhh," Derek moaned. "My mouth is watering."

They laughed together. Derek felt no tension, no strain between him and Adella. He liked everything about her. He'd thought that maybe someday the Lord would bring a woman into his life. But he hadn't been looking for one. He'd expected to know it when it happened. And it had happened. Derek wanted to know everything about her.

He used the controls to drop the sails and the anchor.

"I assume Mandy was your nanny," Derek said, moving away from the helm and sitting on a padded seat adjacent to her.

He expected an immediate reply, but she hesitated for an instant, running a finger along the hem of her shorts, then looked over at him. "Mandy was like a mother to me. Maybe more than a mother. She became my closest friend."

Again she surprised him with her forthrightness and honesty. He listened attentively, sympathetically, as she related the story of the loss of her mother. A happy family became like a ship without a sail, all sense of direction gone. A grieving dad with children who couldn't understand, and Adella having to try to become a substitute mom at age ten.

"I'm so sorry," Derek said. "And I thought I was deprived because I had no siblings." His voice held a touch of irony.

"I think you were blessed. Oh," she added quickly, "I don't mean to imply I don't like my sisters. It's just that. . .times were difficult."

"What line of work is your dad in?"

Again she hesitated before saying, "He has his own shrimp boat."

"Ah," Derek said, "I have your dad to thank for all those good meals I've eaten."

Her eyebrows lifted, giving him the impression that she didn't care much for her dad's profession. As they dallied over cups of cappuccino, she told him more about her family. About her dad's remarriage. As he asked questions and she answered in detail, he felt he saw her heart. As a child she'd been devastated by her mother's death, her dad's remarriage, and Mandy's departure. But he admired her ambition and determination to get her education. She had worked her way through college.

How different his own life had been. Although his parents had taught him responsibility and the importance of keeping God as top priority, he'd never had to give a second thought to where the next meal would come from or if there'd be enough money for any college he might wish to attend. He'd never given serious thought about his having traveled abroad with his parents, vacationed in exotic places. Adella had never gone farther than a few of the islands around Beaufort.

However, he discovered she had gone to many places in her dreams, in her mind, and she had educated herself in art, music, and sports. She even had sensible opinions about politics, which surprised him. Soon, he realized he shouldn't be surprised. She was a woman of incredible intelligence. She cared about important things in life. She'd gone to church with him, she valued her reputation, and in their conversation, he realized she had not used her college years in reckless behavior as he had. She had worked full time to put herself through college. She had remained faithful to her goals, had studied hard, had graduated with honors.

He was glad he knew more about her, but something inside him wanted to tell her leave all that behind her now and look to the future. He couldn't know what the future held, but he could do his best to make the present a pleasant experience.

"Have you seen Goodson Island?" he asked.

"No," she said, her eyes a deeper blue than the midafternoon sky, "but I'd love to."

That was the response Derek had hoped for. Before long, he cruised into one of the reserved slips at Goodson Island.

Chapter 4

Derek laughed at the way Adella exclaimed, "You own the island!"

"Well, my parents do. At least they own the land and the marina." He'd always taken that for granted. "But," he added, "I look at it this way. God is the One who really owns everything. We sort of rent it from Him."

"I suppose that's an attempt at modesty," she replied, her gaze scanning the plush Yacht Club, the resort hotels, and the many businesses lining the waterfront.

He nodded. Perhaps it looked like modesty. But it was a fact, nevertheless.

The sun was showering the land and sea with brilliant rays of gold when they returned to the boat. Derek sat near her on the sunpad. "May I ask you a personal question?"

Her light laugh was quick. "What could be more personal than all I've already told you?"

"I wonder," he said, "what a beautiful, intelligent, educated girl like you is doing working in a restaurant." Seeing her bristle slightly, he wished he hadn't asked.

"What's wrong with working in a restaurant?"

"Nothing," he said quickly. "You certainly give it class. But I would think with your education, you'd be doing something else. Perhaps something where your beauty could be an advantage in your work. Like modeling or acting. I think of beauty being like talent—something special God has given a person to be used as a gift."

"Interesting concept," she said. "A lot of people think it's something that should be hidden."

"Any asset can be used in good or bad ways," Derek said, his cheek dimpling.

She smiled. "I don't have a talent for acting. And I doubt that acting is a secure profession."

"I don't mean this as a put-down," Derek replied, "but it seems to me that being a hostess in a restaurant is not all that secure."

"Could you tell me what professions are that secure for women?" she asked.

Derek stared for a moment, thoughtful, gazing into her sunglasses and seeing the reflection of his distorted self. No, he could not. Perhaps there were a few, like physicians, which would require years of training as well as an aptitude for the work.

"Come to think of it, Adella, there is no lasting security in this life. That's why the Bible tells us not to lay up treasures on earth that dust and moth can corrupt. Our security lies in the hereafter."

Her face tilted downward, as if she were looking at her hands clasped against her legs. Her voice was soft. "That's easier to accept when you're rich than when you're poor."

Derek nodded. "I'm sure it is. That's why we have to be concerned about the physical needs of people as well as the spiritual." He thought of all the hungry children in the world and felt a pang of concern. He wondered, *Did Adella ever go hungry when she was a child?* The thought made him shudder. He recalled their conversation about tomato sandwiches. For him, it was something fun and different. Perhaps Mandy had made those for her and her sisters because that's all they could afford.

He wanted to escape that unpleasant thought and tried to speak casually. "You know," he said, "I would have thought some man would have snatched you up by now."

Adella's chin came up. He could not see her eyes behind the sunglasses, but he heard the confidence in her voice. "I'm not one to be easily snatched up."

He felt reprimanded. He must remember not to say such trite things to her. "Are you looking for any kind of man in particular?"

"Yes, I am," came her instant reply. "Perhaps, if we get to know each other better, I will tell you why I'm working at the restaurant and what kind of man is right for me."

If, she'd said. *If we get to know each other better.* Derek moved over to the helm. He'd never met a woman who so challenged or intrigued him. Never met one that made his pulse race like this just thinking about her.

They were both contemplative as they cruised back to the marina at Beaufort. The sun was setting. The sky and water were becoming one, and the horizon was vanishing. A pink hue from the faint streaks in the sky was fading. A quiet, calm, peaceful twilight was descending.

Derek didn't want their time together to end. On the short drive from the marina to her rooms at the Carder House, he remembered what she had said: *Perhaps. . .if. . .we get to know each other better.*

～

Derek wasn't the only person who surprised Adella that day. She surprised herself.

After he brought her back to the apartment, she unlocked the door and turned to him. He started to say something, and fearing it would only be "good night," she told him she had the next day off.

"Would you like to come for dinner and find out what kind of cook I am?" she asked, with a teasing smile.

"I would indeed," he said, "if you let me bring dessert. I have the perfect one in mind."

The mischief in his eyes implied he was thinking of that "very sinful" triple fudge cake.

"Seven?" she asked.

"Seven it is," he said. He looked at her very seriously. "I really enjoyed being with you today, Adella."

"I enjoyed it too, Derek." She smiled. "Good night."

She was still smiling when she opened the apartment door and closed it behind her. This time, she wasn't surprised that he didn't take her in his arms and try to kiss her. That was too stereotypical for Derek Goodson. Some of his unpredictability must have rubbed off on her.

She was surprised at herself for inviting him to dinner. But a big fish that might get away was more challenging than a predictable one, easy to reel in.

For a long time, Adella sat on her couch and looked through her notebook. For years, after Mandy went to work for the Cottingtons, she talked and Adella took notes on who attended the parties, how they dressed, what they ate, how Mandy prepared the food, what kind of dishes they ate from, on which side she set the drinking glasses, how many forks she placed beside the plates, what kind of centerpieces adorned the tables, and what the rich people talked about. The "social events" notebook would now be useful. Particularly the recipes.

The next morning, Adella visited her daddy and returned home with fresh-off-the-boat shrimp. She'd make the tastiest down-home Southern cooking Derek had ever eaten, including her famous jambalaya. She called Mandy later in the day to make sure she was doing everything right. She even got into her hope chest for an elegant tablecloth and matching napkins.

Later that evening, as she watched Derek enjoy dinner, she knew that if it were true that the way to a man's heart was through his stomach, she'd definitely used the right bait. After dinner, they walked along quiet streets beneath Spanish moss hanging from live oaks and commented on the myriad azaleas in full bloom. They strolled to the waterfront and sat on one of the wooden swings that hung on chains fastened to great wooden beams. They looked out across the marina and watched the yellow sun turn the sky and water to orange, pink, and gold and then fade into darkness.

Lights came on and a street dance began. They watched for awhile, then returned to her apartment for dessert and coffee. He talked about his growing-up years, which were in line with what she had expected from a boy growing up in a wealthy family. "I enjoyed life," he said, "but I never really knew how to appreciate this area back then."

They were washing dishes together when he said, "Tomorrow's my treat, if you're not busy."

"No, I have tomorrow off," she said.

"Great," he said, his green eyes dancing. "Wear something comfortable and I'll pick you up, say, around noon. Don't eat lunch."

Her eyebrows lifted slightly, but she agreed. She had known he could be serious about her the first time he came into the restaurant. But what his intentions were, and what he wanted from her, would take a little time to find out.

She thought she knew, right before he left, when again he didn't try to kiss her but asked like a little boy asking for candy, "Could I have a doggie bag of jambalaya? My mom and dad just have to taste that."

She burst out laughing, imagining his parents eating her jambalaya. She didn't believe a word of it, but found a plastic container and ladled it out of the pot. He was a funny guy.

The next day she discovered he was somewhat of a romantic too. He came for her in a horse-drawn buggy. He had rented one, along with its driver, and had an itinerary all laid out. The driver took them to a small waterfront restaurant for lunch, then gave them a guided tour of the historical district, and they discussed the history of the area. They didn't return until after dark.

For the next few weeks, on her days off, they spent time together. His mother called and invited her and Derek out to a restaurant for dinner. They had indeed tasted her jambalaya and raved about it. The evening passed pleasantly, and Adella felt accepted by the Goodsons.

One day Derek took her to a private spot on Goodson Island for a picnic. They often went sailing or motor cruising in his boat. When she worked, he came to the restaurant for dinner.

One night, he said, "We get along great, don't we, Adella?"

"Yes, we do, Derek," she said honestly, constantly surprised at how well they related and how much fun they had.

"There's only one thing that would make it better," he said.

Her heart skipped a beat. She felt reasonably sure he was the man she had waited for. Since she was a child, she'd been sure that having enough money brought happiness. These past few weeks he had proved that to her. And his gentlemanly behavior indicated he was serious about her.

"I wish you could go to church with me on Sundays," he said.

Lowering her gaze, she nodded. "Yes, it would be good not to have to work on Sundays." And she wouldn't, once she married into money like she'd always planned. She wouldn't work on Sundays or any other days.

There was still one other thing to be concerned about. He had often asked about her family. How they were getting along. It was time he met them.

~

At first, Adella was surprised by how Derek reacted to her family. Then she realized this would be a lark to him—not a lifestyle. Anyone could enjoy going onto a shrimp boat and having her daddy tell him and show him about shrimping for several hours and find it fascinating. This was, no doubt, like Derek's going to some Third World country and getting an education on how the unfortunate people lived.

But her family loved him for his attitude. He fit in better than she did, but he was a visitor, an observer. She had lived this life. A life of sometimes counting pennies to see if there was enough for school lunch money, of always being told to turn off the lights because that cost money, of lathering herself up then turning the shower water back on to rinse off because water cost money. After moving into the apartment on Carder Street, Adella had luxuriated beneath the spray of her first shower until the hot water ran cold.

Now, Adella had to admit Leona had given the small three-bedroom house a woman's touch. New living-room furniture replaced the old battered settee and even her daddy's favorite recliner. He and Leona presented the picture of a happy couple. Adella felt slightly embarrassed that Peggy behaved as if she'd reached her zenith in life by having two raucous children and that Brittany couldn't keep her eyes off her boyfriend, Freddie. They both behaved like lovesick teenagers.

However, Adella wanted Derek to know her background. She was not trying to fool him, any more than she had fooled herself. He would know what she wanted and why. She did not intend to go into a marriage and end up divorced because a man hadn't understood her intentions.

When she'd called her family to arrange the meeting, she hadn't been sure everyone would show up. After all, she'd only invited them to come and see her rooms at the Carder House, and she'd never invited them for dinner. Leona and Clem had come. Peggy and her family had. Brittany had stopped by only once after the initial visit. Adella hadn't invited them. They had ceased to invite her to their homes except on special occasions.

To ensure the entire family would gather at her daddy's, Adella had asked Mandy to come along and make her famous Lowcountry Boil. None of them would turn that down. Even Leona had a fondness for Mandy, who'd stopped by many times to help Leona out with whatever problems the girls might have. Leona had appreciated that, not being sure how to relate to Adella, who took care of herself; Peggy, who claimed she didn't need anyone; and Brittany, who clung to Leona like glue.

This night, after they stood around the long table in the big kitchen, holding hands for Clem's blessing, Leona and Mandy dipped out the stew into soup bowls, then took their seats at the table. "It's not that we don't have napkins," Leona explained. "But Mandy said we have to use paper towels like the people in Frogmore do."

"Why Frogmore?" Derek asked, feigning ignorance.

"Because it's Frogmore Stew," Peggy said.

"No way," he jested, poking around in his bowl of steaming shrimp, sausage, corn on the cob, potatoes, and onions. "This is Beaufort Stew, if ever I saw it."

"Really, Derek," Adella chimed in. "Take it from a restaurant expert. This is definitely Lowcountry Boil."

They all laughed, knowing quite well the stew was called by any of those three names and that Beaufort was famous for the delicious combination.

"It's Frogmore," said Peggy's oldest.

"Yes," Peggy agreed. "But it can be called the other names. However, a stew is a stew is a stew."

"Mmm," Derek said, talking with food in his mouth. "This is undoubtedly the best Frogmore, Beaufort, Lowcountry Stew I've ever tasted."

Adella could tell the family loved him.

"Where did that name come from anyway?" Brittany asked.

"A place called Frogmore on St. Helena Island," Adella answered.

"That crossroads along Highway 21," said Clem.

"That cotton plantation named after a royal palace in England," Mandy said.

They all three gave their explanations at the same time. By then, they'd all forgotten their manners, laughing and talking, not caring whether or not their mouths were full. Adella had to admit to herself that the stew was delicious. Everyone agreed. Then the accolades began all over again when she and Leona brought out sweet potato pies.

Mandy kept giving Adella glances, smiles, and little nods that meant, "I told you so, about Derek Goodson. He's the one for you."

Adella suspected she just might be right.

~

"Now you know my background and something of my family," Adella said later after she and Derek returned to Beaufort and strolled along the waterfront, then sat on a swing beneath live oaks draped with Spanish moss, looking out at the water as the moonlight began to turn the frothy tips to silver. "I have determined my life would be different."

Derek glanced at her quickly, thoughtfully, puzzled. Had it been so bad? Her family members seemed happy. Clem and Leona adored each other. Brittany and Freddie were obviously in love. Peggy and Paul ran laughing after their children and seemed to be a happy family.

"You can readily see why I wanted to escape that kind of life," Adella said.

Derek tried. He thought he could enjoy going out on a shrimp boat each day, the challenge of the catch. He'd like to come home to a house full of kids and pig out on good, down-home cooking. But he supposed he'd feel differently if the day's catch had been low, if there wasn't enough money to feed the children or buy what they needed, or if he couldn't provide what his wife wanted. He imagined it would be even worse for a woman who had no control over the finances but had to make do with whatever meager paycheck her husband could bring home. Maybe Adella's sisters weren't as happy as they appeared. Maybe Clem and Leona weren't as content as they seemed. Had it been a show, just for him?

"You asked me once," Adella said point-blank, "why I work at the restaurant."

Instant joy swept over Derek. She had said that when she knew him better, she would confide in him about why she worked at the restaurant and the kind of man she wanted. Did this mean she had come to know him and liked him well enough to go ahead and confide in him?

There was no hesitation in her voice. "I've worked there to meet the kind of men who could offer me financial security."

Derek felt mixed emotions. Despite his elation, something deep inside him recoiled at the idea that she would deliberately seek out men with money. Then again, his own mother had said many times, "Derek, you'll never meet a woman and settle down if you stay around that dock or on your boat all the time." Others, even in his singles' group at church, had said they needed to go to retreats or singles' conferences where they could meet a prospective mate. Would a farmer who wanted a wife seek one in New York City? Would a big-time city lawyer go to the country to find a spouse?

Was it any different, wanting your spouse to have money, than if you wanted her or him to have a sense of humor? Or responsible characteristics? What about himself? He enjoyed sailing. Was it wrong for him to want a mate who enjoyed it too?

Was Adella's desire any different than his wanting financial security in his business? He wanted to be successful. If his dad hadn't made possible his financial security, perhaps he would be the skipper on a shrimp boat. He hoped he would have been as good a one as Clem Spelding.

As he thought about it, Derek admired Adella for her honesty and for

148

pursuing her dreams. She wanted more than her family had. She wanted financial security.

Didn't the Bible indicate there was nothing wrong with money? How could you obey the Lord's command to share and help others if you had nothing? The Bible made it clear that it was "the love of money" that was harmful. Not money itself.

Adella was smart enough to know that.

So, he nodded. "And I want a woman," he said, "who appreciates my faith and serves the Lord with me."

Chapter 5

Mandy thought Adella might be too busy with Derek to attend the Gullah Festival with her as they had done near the end of May for the past several years. Nevertheless, she called her.

"Oh, I'm so glad to hear your voice," Adella said. "I was going to call you. Derek's gone to Florida to pick up more of his personal belongings. So let's go to the festival."

They met at the waterfront and talked while listening to the festivities, the African-American music, and the stories told in the Gullah language.

Mandy was proud of the way the festival presented the language—not as if Gullah were an assassination of the English language, but for what it was. The language contained grammar and vocabulary combined from various African languages. The rhythmic sound was as colorful as the beautiful dancers and musicians portraying the rich African and Sea Islands heritage. She knew her value before God and that she had a mansion in that fair land of heaven, but this festival gave her the feeling of being important here on earth too. These were her days, when white folks and black alike learned and appreciated the contribution the blacks had made both to the local area and to the world.

When she had taken care of the Spelding children, she had read the Bible to them in the Gullah language. They always listened, liking the dialect that almost sounded like a different language. Mandy had learned it early, along with the white language, from the time she was just a baby. Her mama and daddy had given her a pride of their ancestors, who'd come from Sierra Leone on the West Coast of Africa. They were freed more than a hundred years ago, during the earliest days of the Civil War. Since then, they'd been a poor, but proud, family. This was her beloved quaint Southern city, just as much as it was anybody's.

"You miss your Mr. Derek, don't you, Honey?" she said to Adella, having wanted to say that from the moment they'd met on the waterfront.

"Sure I do, Mandy," Adella said. "For the past month we've explored all of Beaufort and the islands together, as if neither of us had ever seen them. And would you believe it—we even rode around the area in a horse-drawn carriage."

"My, that's romantic," Mandy said.

"Now, Mandy. This is not about romance and those fantasy words you use. This is about compatibility. I think the word applies to me and Derek."

"I think that man is in love with you," Mandy said and felt sorry that Adella looked concerned at that statement.

"Mandy, I've been completely honest with Derek. He knows that I want a secure lifestyle. The rest is up to him. If he wants me on those terms, fine. If not. . ."

Mandy saw her shrug as if it didn't matter. But she thought it did. When Adella set her mind on something, she went after it. Derek Goodson could give her what she wanted. If she hadn't already, Adella would fall in love with him.

How could she not fall in love with such a fine Christian man?

~

Derek was gone almost a week. He'd taken one of the company's vans along with some of the items his parents hadn't taken when they moved to the house in Florida. He'd stayed over the weekend and gone to the church there, needing the support of longtime friends to assure himself that he did belong in Beaufort. He had the singles' group pray for him. He needed that. He needed to know what to do about Adella, who seemed to be with him, although her physical presence was hundreds of miles away. She was constantly on his mind and in his heart.

He achieved his purpose. He became even more convinced that he was not complete without Adella. It was as if he'd become half a person, and he thought of the Scriptures that say God made a helpmate for man and saw that it was good, that two should leave their father and mother and become one. If this were not God's will, how could he feel such a great love for this woman? He'd known, from the moment he looked at her, wanted her as a part of his life. If God said no, giving her up would be the hardest thing he'd ever done. God did not seem to be saying no. Everything pointed to the fact that Adella was the woman God had prepared for him. He could not imagine that there could ever be a woman who appealed to him more than Adella, or one with whom he could be more compatible. She shared his faith and his interests.

On Tuesday, Derek loaded up some of his own personal belongings and drove back to the Goodson house at Beaufort. He called the supply store, and after work, Jerry came over and helped him take in his recliner, replacing his dad's favorite one, which now sat in Florida. That, along with his stereo system, made the study seem more like his own. It was after midnight before he had his clothes hung in the closets and realized Adella was most likely in bed. He would probably be awake all night, regretting that he hadn't called her. But he'd tried to stay busy, tried to keep her off his mind, tried to keep things in perspective, knowing he was too emotionally involved now that he knew, without a doubt, he wanted to spend the rest of his life with her.

He roamed the house. He was alone. Jerry had left around eight o'clock and the housekeeper/cook had left shortly after that. He looked at the staircase and imagined watching Adella descend. He ate a snack and wanted Adella sitting across the table from him. He would like to fill the house with children—his and Adella's.

I love her. But does she love me?

He remembered every word she'd said. He knew what she wanted from a man—security. He could give her a secure life. He understood that about her and why she felt the way she did. Maybe that's why God brought them together. He needed a woman like her, and she wanted a man like him. Then what was he waiting for? How much more certain could he be? He loved her. He wanted her to be his wife. The mother of his children. The person he would grow old with.

The following morning Derek went to the store for part of the day. That evening he went to the Marina Club Restaurant. He felt that was the best way to see her after a week's absence. Otherwise, he might take her in his arms and scare her away with his feelings of never wanting to let her go.

When he walked in and feasted his eyes on her, he felt as stable as a fish out of water.

"Derek," she said in a slightly breathless tone, uncharacteristic of her usually controlled demeanor. Did that mean she thought he might not return? He'd tried to be cautious, but hadn't he made it clear how much she meant to him? Everything and everyone faded into the background as if nothing or no one else existed but her. From somewhere he had the presence of mind to stuff his hands in his pockets rather than take her in his arms.

Her eyes began to dance, and her smile lit up her beautiful face. "How many in your party, Sir?" she said, but the tone of her voice was not business as usual. He heard the teasing tone, the lower pitch, the softness that he took to mean she was as glad to see him as he was to see her.

Knowing that a line was forming behind him, he replied, "One...tonight."

A thought was forming in his mind. *If I have my way, then soon I won't be eating alone anymore.*

~

The next morning, Adella left her apartment and walked casually down the street toward the Goodson home. After his dinner at the restaurant, Derek had asked if she would like a tour of his house, and she'd said she would walk down there midmorning. The Goodson in-town plantation house was well known to her. She had walked past such houses in the historic district many times.

But today was different. She was going inside. The house was slightly larger than the Carder House where she lived, and its sprawling veranda could be accessed by ascending steps from either side of the house. With a smile on her lips, she thought of how she always went in the back way when visiting the Cottington House. Not wanting to appear too eager, she waited until around ten o'clock to reach the house. As she ascended the steps, she saw a movement and looked up. Derek rose from the rocking chair and stood facing her, ready to welcome her to his world.

It was all and more than she expected. Having seen the Cottington House and lived in the Carder House, she was not surprised by its impressive architectural details. However, to be seeing it by invitation of the man she'd been waiting for for so many years caused her heart to leap. The elegant foyer with its twelve-foot-high ceiling, from which hung a Baccarat chandelier, was the perfect welcome. Wanting to feel the grandeur she had known was waiting for her, she hadn't worn jeans or slacks. Instead, she wore a lightweight silk dress with a skirt that flowed with her movements, perfect for ascending the sweeping staircase that led to the suites on the second floor. Fireplaces, antiques, and private balconies completed this fairy-tale mansion.

Adella could not be more pleased with a house. She smiled at Derek with genuine approval.

"I'm not trying to impress you," he said. "After all, this isn't mine, but my parents'."

Right, she was thinking, *but you're heir to all this*. She expressed her genuine appreciation for the elegance and beauty of the Old South combined with all the modern conveniences one could want. She particularly liked the downstairs, the formal living room, dining room, Federal-style parlor, and the cypress-paneled library. She could well imagine being mistress of such a house.

He led her into a glass-surrounded eating area where they seemed to be part of the lovely gardens right outside the windows. Fresh flowers from the garden graced the small, round, glass-topped table. A middle-aged woman served them lunch.

It was then Adella looked across at him and said sincerely, "Derek, I love your house."

~

I love you, Derek could have said in instant reply, but he was trying with all his might to think before speaking. He'd never felt so ill at ease with himself. So he bit his tongue and waited until they'd finished lunch and were at the back door, ready to walk out into the gardens. They'd known each other for a couple months now. He was sure. Why wait? "Adella," he asked, "you don't plan to work after you marry, do you?"

"Not at the restaurant," she replied. "I expect to do charitable work."

He'd thought about how to propose to her. Should he do it at some special place? Like where? Have her sit on the living-room couch while he got on his knees? Take her out on the sailboat so if she said no, he could jump into the ocean and hope to be shark bait? Should he think of something unique?

Before he could catch them, the words slipped out. "Will you marry me, Adella?"

He saw her stiffen, her chin went up, her eyes met his, and they looked uncertain. He'd done it wrong. She was standing at the back door, and he was hanging onto the door casing. It was holding him up.

"You're sure this is what you want, Derek?" she asked.

"Positive, Adella. I love you. I've never felt this way about anyone and never could again. I know this is a once-in-a-lifetime situation. I want to share my life, all I have, with you." He thought he couldn't stand it any longer. Was this a beginning or an ending? What would he do if she said no? What would he do if she said yes? They'd never even kissed. Oh, he wanted to, but he was so afraid he would never be able to let her go. And he wanted her to know that his feelings for her were based on more than physical attraction. "I love you," he said again.

～

Adella looked out over the backyard, the patio, the winding path through the gardens, the pool, and the tennis courts beyond that. This was what she'd wanted all her life. She'd just toured one of the old historic houses that had a heritage of wealth. Wealthy people had lived here. She could live here until his parents returned, if they ever did. She would be one of the elite. She would never have to be concerned about being left with nothing. She could have a wonderful life without financial worries. And at the same time, she could enjoy it all with a man who loved her. That hadn't been a requisite, and that's what disturbed her. She'd rather this be a sensible, responsible, business agreement than a relationship with emotional ties.

But his words pulled at her heartstrings. Who wouldn't be pleased to hear they were loved?

She'd always heard that it was as easy to love a rich man as a poor one. She thought it would be easier. But she had never been and did not want to be in that state of "love" that so obscured the right thinking of otherwise reasonable people. Love had killed her mother. It imprisoned her middle sister. It blinded her youngest sister to her own potential. It got Mandy an alcoholic husband who ran into a tree and died. Love didn't make good sense. Two people who were compatible and got from each other what they wanted was much more sensible.

Slowly, her face turned toward him. She saw the tears in his eyes, as if he couldn't bear to be without her. That hurt. She didn't want to be vulnerable to those feelings herself. But she would be a loyal wife. She would be all he wanted. She would be fair and responsible and entertain his friends and go to his church. In exchange, she would be mistress of this house, have access to the finest places, the finest shops, and she wouldn't have to wait for sales.

She nodded. "Derek, if you're sure this is what you want, I'll marry you."

He blinked, but an errant teardrop streaked his cheek anyway. He moistened his lips as if they were dry. His shoulders rose, and he inhaled a deep breath. Then his hands were on her shoulders, gently pulling her close. His arms came around her. He'd held her before. She reminded herself to keep her emotions in check. She felt concern. Then his fingers gently lifted her face to his, and his lips touched hers in a sweet, gentle kiss.

It was not at all unpleasant.

Derek had never seen her look so shy, so lacking in confidence. That endeared her to him even more. His wife-to-be had never been in love before. How that delighted him. He would love to hear her say she loved him. *But,* he told himself, *words are cheap. Love is action.*

Adella let him kiss her. She let him hold her. She said she would marry him. How could he be more blessed? He silently thanked God for Adella and her willingness to share the rest of her life with him.

Tenderly, he held her from him. "I didn't get a ring. I was not so confident that you would accept. Well, frankly, I didn't intend to ask you this way. I wanted it to be special."

"It is special, Derek."

He smiled. "I wanted it to be romantic."

"What is more romantic than a proposal, regardless of where it takes place?"

He grinned. "You have a point there, I guess. Anyway, I wanted you to pick out your ring. I know you have very definite ideas, and you're the one who will be wearing it for the rest of your life."

Adella felt a slight reservation. "Will your parents be pleased?"

"Oh yes," he said. "They've always said my life's partner is my choice. But I could tell that my mom liked you the moment I mentioned you. And my dad is very taken with you."

She smiled.

"Let's call them," he said.

He did. His mother answered. "Mom," he said and paused. "No, nothing's wrong. In fact, things couldn't be better. No, Mom. Don't guess. I want to tell you. She said yes. To what? To marrying me, of course. How would you like to have a daughter?" He laughed. "Just a minute." He held out the phone. "She wants to talk to you."

Adella felt shaky. Without the blessing of Derek's parents, it would be difficult to be accepted into society. "Hello, Irene," she said. Then she began to laugh while listening to Irene's words and looking at Derek, nodding and grinning. Irene had said she'd told Derek she'd love to have a daughter as long as she didn't have to give birth to her.

"Seriously, Adella. I am so pleased. Judd will be too. We think you and Derek are just made for each other. Oh, we'll have so many plans to make. Have you set a wedding date?"

"No, he just asked me a few moments ago. Here's Derek. He's trying to take the phone away from me."

Derek took the receiver. "We'll talk later, Mom. Tell Dad. We'll be in touch."

He hung up the phone and opened his arms to her. Adella moved close and rested her head against his chest while his arms tenderly enfolded her. They stayed that way a long time. Adella was surprised at how right it felt, being close to him. She'd never expected, in all her years of planning, that she would feel so close to the man who would make her dreams come true. She knew she would be appreciative, but somehow her feelings were. . .she wasn't sure how to define them. Perhaps they were just more than she had expected.

Chapter 6

"Could we see those, please?" Derek asked.

"Yes, Sir, Mr. Goodson," the clerk said, looking like a penguin except for the bow tie and knowing smile.

Adella had a strong feeling that Derek had been in the shop recently—probably the day before while she was working.

The clerk unlocked the glass section beneath where Derek stood and brought out a square of rings on a black velvet background. There were no price tags on the rings, and Adella knew this was one of those times that if you had to ask the price, you couldn't afford it.

They both greatly admired two rings in particular. Finally, Adella handed the round ring back to the clerk. Since the other one was a perfect fit, she chose the yellow gold marquise diamond solitaire.

"Oh, Derek, it's so beautiful." She started to take it off, but her fingers didn't want to do the chore. With questioning eyes, she gazed at Derek.

He laughed. "It's yours," he said and placed his hand over hers for a moment.

She blinked away the moisture forming in her eyes. A diamond ring, far greater than she had envisioned, circled her finger. Yes, it was true. If you worked toward something and believed it would happen, then your dreams could come true.

"Now, for the wedding bands," Derek said to the most cooperative clerk.

~

Leona squealed. "Oh, Adella, is it what I think?"

Adella laughed. "I'm not telling this over the phone. That's why I asked when the family could get together."

"Well, it sounds important," Leona said. "I'll have them here tonight."

When Adella and Derek walked in, all the family members were crowded in the living room, looking like they were anticipating Christmas. When she held out her hand, words weren't necessary, but her family had plenty of heart-felt congratulatory words. She had a moment of regret that she hadn't been as excited when her dad married Leona or when Peggy married Paul. But she was too realistic to think they could have a happy life when she could see the financial struggles they would have.

Dismissing such thoughts, she welcomed their hugs for her and for Derek.

"I suppose I should have asked you for her hand in marriage," Derek said when Clem shook his hand and clapped him on the shoulder.

"And suppose I said no?" Clem Spelding jested.

Derek just laughed, and Adella replied, "I think you know the answer to that, Daddy."

They all hugged.

"You want to tell Mandy now?" Derek asked, after they left.

"Oh, yes," Adella said, laughing delightedly that Derek was enjoying this so. She was glad he wasn't stuffy. They would get along just fine, she was sure. "But she's working today."

Derek shrugged. "No problem."

A short while later, he pulled into the Cottingtons' driveway and marched Adella to the front door. Mandy answered. "Oh," she said, surprised, seeing them at the front door, obviously uncertain if she should let them in or ask them to come in the back way. "The Cottingtons are here," she said.

"Good," Derek said. "Would you let them know we stopped by, please?"

After a quizzical glance at Adella, a sparkle appeared in Mandy's eyes. She opened the door wider. "Yes, come on in."

When she returned with the Cottingtons, Derek introduced Adella.

"Oh, we know her," Mrs. Cottington said, smiling.

Mr. Cottington was equally congenial. He gestured toward the living room. "Come in and sit down."

"We can't stay," Derek said, as Mandy turned to leave the foyer. "We really needed to speak with Mandy."

Mandy stopped and looked over her shoulder, then slowly turned toward them again, her eyes wide. Adella bit on her lip to keep from laughing and looked toward the floor. She held her hands behind her back.

"Oh, well, go right ahead," Mrs. Cottington said. She put her hand on her husband's arm. "Would you like to go into the living room?"

"No, right here will be fine. And you two stay, by all means," Derek said. Adella couldn't help but think of all the times she'd come in the back door and stayed with Mandy in the kitchen. She knew the Cottingtons were neither rude nor snobbish, but here they were, because of Derek, even offering to let him use their home as if it were his own. She could foresee no problems with being accepted into society. She would be one of the Goodsons, friends of the Cottingtons and their set.

"I can say this in public. As a matter of fact, I wouldn't mind shouting this to the world. But first," he said, smiling at Mandy. "We wanted you to be among the first to know."

Adella stuck out her hand, and the diamond sparkled like the evening star.

Mandy took hold of Adella's hand. "Oh, my," she gasped, while the Cottingtons looked on with pleased expressions.

"Derek has asked for my hand in marriage," Adella said.

"Well now," Mandy scoffed, with a scowl on her face. "There's no halfway about something like this, Derek Goodson. If you want my baby's hand, you've got to take all of her."

"No problem," came Derek's vigorous response.

They all laughed, and then the hugs and congratulations began.

Later that afternoon, Adella went to work and gave her notice at the restaurant, and for the next two weeks she reveled in the attention and good wishes of workers and customers alike. She held the menus in a way to show off the ring and took a second longer than necessary to hand them out after seating people at their tables.

She wore her trophy well on her finger, proving that she had snagged, not some old useless tire, but the catch of a lifetime.

～

When her future mother-in-law came to Beaufort for a visit, she called Adella and asked if she could come over to the Carder House and talk with her. Adella assumed she wanted to discuss wedding plans; however, a shadow crept over Adella's elation when she saw the serious look in Irene's eyes and the tentative polite smile.

Were Irene and Judd Goodson not as accepting of her as she had thought?

Adella invited her in and asked if she'd like tea. She had just made a pot.

Irene accepted and followed Adella into the kitchen area and sat at the table. Adella had not seen Irene many times, but she had never known her to appear so concerned. Neither said anything until Adella served the tea. Mandy had told Adella that Irene took her tea with honey and lemon. The woman smiled faintly when Adella took the sliced lemon from the refrigerator and set it on the table next to the small honey pot.

Irene took a sip of the herbal tea and said it was good. "Now, let me see that ring," she said, then examined it. "It is as beautiful as Derek said." She smiled, then uncertainty again touched her eyes. Adella took her seat opposite Irene, with her hands on her lap, her right hand covering the diamond ring she never intended to part with. She waited, knowing Irene had something particular on her mind. She had not come to see a ring that was no more impressive than the ones she wore on several of her own fingers.

"I wanted to be the one to tell you about one of Judd's and my wedding presents to you and Derek," Irene began. "We want to give you the Goodson House. Only Goodsons have lived in it since it was built in 1852."

Adella's thoughts stopped on the idea that the Goodson House was to be only one of their presents. Was Irene reluctant to let the house go? "Oh, if you don't want to part with it," Adella hurriedly assured her, "I understand. Derek and I can build our own."

"Oh, no, my dear," Irene corrected immediately. "I'm only too happy to part with it. I'm a Florida girl from way back. Oh, I love Beaufort, but my family is in Florida. It's home to me. And anyway, Judd and I want to travel. He's about to turn the business over. . . . Oh, my goodness, I'm talking too much. Judd wants to tell you that. But let me get back to the matter of the house."

"That is such an extravagant present, Irene," Adella could honestly say. She'd never even had a bedroom of her own until she moved into Carder House. And strictly speaking, that wasn't hers. It was only rented. Here a woman was talking about giving her a house? But something was obviously disturbing Irene. Adella remained silent, waiting for the axe to fall.

Then Irene exhibited that habit of Derek's and drew in a deep breath that raised her shoulders. She lifted her chin bravely. "Now, I don't want you to think this is some kind of prenuptial agreement."

So that was it! They thought she was after Derek's money. They would ensure that she wouldn't get any money if she and Derek didn't remain married. Well, the outcome would depend upon what kind of agreement had been arranged. Did Derek know about it? She could not imagine Derek even considering a prenuptial agreement.

"There is a stipulation to you and Derek being given the house," Irene explained.

Adella listened carefully to the details. It was not, as Irene said, a prenuptial agreement. There would be a stipulation that the house someday be passed down to their children. In the case of the deaths of Derek and Adella, ownership would revert to Derek's parents if either or both of them were still living. If the younger couple survived the older couple and had no children, then upon their deaths, the Goodson House would become a historic home open to public tours. It was never to be sold or rented out.

Irene finished her explanation quickly. "This is how it's been for more than two hundred years, Adella. I had to agree to these stipulations when I married Judd. It did not set well with me at first."

Adella stared for a moment. Was that what concerned Irene? She began to shake her head. "Oh, I quite understand that, Irene. The history and heritage of such a house should be protected. A Goodson house it has always been, and a Goodson house it should remain."

Relief spread over Irene's face. She sighed as if she had been holding her breath for quite awhile. "You're so much more understanding than I was when this was told to me," she admitted. "But then, I was younger than you. Not nearly as mature. I argued that the gifts my parents were giving us were of equal value."

Before she could continue, Adella interrupted. "I'm afraid my family won't be able to give gifts of any great value."

"We won't even discuss such a thing," Irene said with a small swoop of her hand, indicating the subject was closed. Then she laid her hand on Adella's. "I've never had a daughter, so please let me pay for whatever kind of wedding you have in mind."

For the remainder of the morning, they made wedding plans like a mother and daughter. Adella wanted to please Irene and Derek. She would go traditional. It would be a church wedding—a society wedding—and Adella would proudly wear a white wedding dress, accurately symbolizing her purity. Her sisters would be matron of honor and bridesmaid. Peggy's little girl would be flower girl.

Derek would of course choose his groomsmen.

It was decided. Adella would pay for the wedding, but she would allow Irene to pay for the reception. Adella had saved for her wedding since she had completed college and begun working full time at the restaurant. A tidy sum, along with many nice items in that hope chest of hers, had been accumulated during that time. She would even buy her dad a new suit and Leona the kind of dress she wanted her to wear. There would be other occasions to which they would be invited probably, so it wouldn't be a waste. She would pay for the matron-of-honor and bridesmaid dresses. She had enough. It no longer mattered that her meager savings would be depleted.

Already, she had a ring worth thousands, and a deed was being made up to sign over one of the most valuable homes in the area. . .to Derek. . .and to her—Adella Spelding, who would very soon become the wealthy Mrs. Derek Goodson.

~

Adella carefully handled the high-quality fine paper and ran her fingers lightly over the gold embossed lettering and the imprint of the family seal. This was only the dinner-party invitation.

The Goodsons were giving a dinner party at the Goodson House to announce the engagement of their son and Adella. They'd asked Mandy to help with the cooking. All of the couples, except for one elderly man who was a well-known attorney, were middle-aged. For the first time, Adella met Keitha Keane, an elegant woman in her late fifties, whose influence and charitable work were widely known. The area wouldn't soon forget the terrible airplane crash that had taken the life of her husband, Martin Keane, the internationally known stock broker and financial consultant who had made his wife one of the richest women in the world.

"I'm delighted to meet you," Keitha Keane said in her cultured, polite voice, but Adella felt her shrewd eyes were appraising her every move and word. Instinctively, she knew this woman wouldn't be as accepting as the Goodsons and Cottingtons. She'd have to prove herself worthy of her approval. Marrying Derek Goodson wouldn't be enough.

"Nice to meet you, Mrs. Keane," Adella said.

The older woman smiled, without asking Adella to call her by her first name. Mrs. Keane turned slightly to graciously accept an hors d'oeuvre. Adella selected one of the same, but had a stomach-turning feeling that if Keitha Keane didn't like or accept her, irreparable damage would be done to Adella's prospective social life. She wanted to fit in, not just with the Goodsons, but with all the elite of the area. If she failed the test tonight, she doubted that she'd get another chance.

Mandy came into the room to tell Mrs. Goodson that dinner could be served at any time. "My daughter should be here soon," Mrs. Cottington said, looking toward the doorway, when suddenly it burst open and in walked a younger couple.

Derek introduced them as Sarah and Broc McKay.

Adella liked Sarah upon sight. She looked to be her own age. She was the kind of woman who looked naturally attractive. Wearing little or no makeup, she wouldn't be called pretty, but appealing. She was as tall as Broc, and her wheat-colored hair was brushed to the back of her head and fastened with a single clasp. Sarah looked lean and agile, without frills.

"So, you're going to tie the knot, huh?" Broc asked, the big redheaded man slapping Derek on the back.

"Looks that way," Derek conceded, his cheek dimpling and his eyes glinting with pleasure.

"Well, I'm so glad somebody is finally getting Derek to the altar," Sarah said, giving Adella a friendly smile. Adella liked her warmth and forthrightness.

"She didn't even have to try," Derek said. "I was hooked the moment I saw her."

"Oh, how romantic," Sarah gushed. "Was it love at first sight for you too, Adella?"

"Actually, it was my former nanny who fell in love with Derek at first sight. However, she was already married."

They laughed, and Derek's arm came around Adella's waist.

"You're referring to Mandy?" Sarah asked. "Mom said she used to be your nanny."

"Yes," Adella said and looked down a moment. She'd never before referred to Mandy as her nanny, although both Irene and Derek had. Mandy was like a mother and a friend. But saying "nanny" was the only word that put it all into perspective without explanations. Although poor people didn't have nannies, Mandy certainly filled that role, and others, for her. And too, it sounded like a step up from "hired hand" or "maid."

When she glanced up, her gaze collided with Keitha Keane's, whose eyes seemed to know exactly what Adella was thinking. Adella felt color rising to her face.

Irene saved the moment by suggesting, "Shall we go in to dinner now?"

At the dinner table, Derek sat on one side of Adella and Broc on the other. After Judd asked the blessing on the food, polite questions were asked about Adella's family, and Sarah wanted to know all about how she and Derek met.

Derek did most of the talking, making Clem Spelding's profession sound like the most fun and adventurous in the world. His stories of Adella's niece and nephew made them laugh. At one point, when Mandy was serving, Adella's eyes met hers, and the approval Adella saw there made her feel more comfortable, reminding her of what Mandy had said many times: "You don't ever need to be ashamed of your family. They were good, hard-working people."

But it wasn't that Adella was ashamed of her family. She just didn't want to live like them.

She breathed easier when the conversation turned to Sarah and Broc, who were athletes. Broc had been a pro tennis player in Europe, and Sarah had played in numerous tournaments, winning some. They had met at an international tournament in Europe and had lived in Scotland for the past few years. They'd returned to the area for the Christmas holidays and decided to settle in Beaufort. They were now coaching local tennis players, one Olympic hopeful, and were involved in some of the tournaments held on Hilton Head Island.

Soon the conversation turned to the activities of the other couples, and Adella was relieved. She no longer felt the speculative eyes of Keitha Keane evaluating her.

After dessert, when they all stood to retire to the living room, Sarah stopped Adella by placing her hand gently on her arm. "We've recently finished building a house overlooking the Beaufort River," Sarah said. "You'll have to come and see it."

"Thanks," Adella said. "I'd love to." Then she decided to absolve her conscience. Turning to Derek, she said, "I'll be with you in a moment. I want to speak to Mandy." Seeing that several were looking at her when she began to speak, she wanted to be perfectly honest. They already knew she came from a poor section of town, worked at a restaurant, and lived in a rented apartment. If any of these people wanted to hold that against her, then the sooner she knew it, the better off they would all be.

"Actually," Adella decided to say, honestly, "Mandy is like a mother to me. Mine died when I was ten, and I don't know how I could have gotten past that time without her. She's the closest thing I have to a mother, and she's my friend."

"I understand," Sarah said, and Adella saw Keitha's head turn toward her. Their eyes met for a second before the older woman turned away again. Adella wondered if that declaration would clinch her as being unacceptable in Keitha Keane's mind. It wouldn't be proper protocol to bring up such a morbid subject at such a celebratory social occasion.

"We'll be in the living room, Dear," Irene said. "Join us when you're ready."

Adella was not surprised that Derek was right beside her when she went into the kitchen to speak to Mandy and tell the cooks what a wonderful success the dinner had been.

"I'm proud of you," Derek said, after Mandy shooed them away to join the other guests.

After a brief time in the living room, guests began to leave. Keitha and the elderly attorney were among the last to go. Keitha made a point to come up to Adella. She took her hand and looked into Adella's eyes.

"My dear, loss of a loved one is hard at any age. But so much more devastating for a child. I'm so sorry you lost your mother at such a tender age."

"Thank you, Mrs. Keane," Adella said, surprised at this rather stiff-looking woman's sympathy. "It was a long time ago."

The woman's head lifted slightly and sadness appeared in her eyes. "Time helps, but I'm not sure it ever heals," she said. "If you ever need to talk, just let me know. And too, why don't you call me Keitha?" She patted Adella's hand and turned to go.

"Thank you, Keitha," Adella said softly, and the woman looked over her shoulder and smiled. *Yes,* Adella realized, *Mandy had been right when she instilled in me the principle "Honesty is the best policy."*

～

The next two months were like a fairy tale. It was more than Adella could have envisioned. Derek and Broc struck up a great friendship, having liked each other throughout the years when their paths had crossed. Derek had grown up with Sarah, and they were neighborhood friends.

Two weeks after the dinner party, Sarah gave a lingerie shower at her new riverside home, giving Adella the opportunity to meet some of the younger women she'd seen at church. She liked Sarah, and since Derek had asked Broc to be his best man, Adella asked Sarah to be one of her wedding attendants, and she readily agreed. Two friends of Derek's from Florida would also serve as groomsmen.

Irene stayed at the Goodson House for the express purpose of making sure all plans went right. Judd came up from Florida on weekends. His wedding present was turning over half the business to Derek, making him a full partner, with the assurance that he would become sole owner when Judd retired. Adella was aware that she would be Derek's beneficiary.

She hadn't realized how alone she had been for so many years. It seemed she had been alone, closed up inside herself, since her mother died. Now she had people doting on her. Derek had flowers delivered to her every Monday morning. Daily they saw each other and discussed wedding plans or what each had done. Derek insisted they go out alone at least one evening a week. The days were filled with making plans, but Adella didn't have to worry about it.

Adella did not have any close friends. She had not kept in touch with those in college. They would not be in her circle of friends when she married the man of her dreams. Now, she could see the wisdom in that decision. She had to include her sisters, because they were family and showed Adella the kind of respect they never had before. They were enchanted with Derek and in awe of her ring, the house, and what lay in store for her future.

Mandy kept trying to convince her that money wasn't everything, but Adella only laughed at that. *Oh, no?* Statements like that went in one ear and out the other. She was having the time of her life, watching her dreams come true, unfold like a magic carpet on which she could ride. On Sunday, after attending church together and hearing endless congratulations, she and Derek went sailing.

That was the only time she felt slightly uncomfortable. Yes, this was what she wanted. But the night always ended with his taking her in his arms and expressing his love for her. She could not say those three little words. She didn't want to feel the kind of devotion she saw in his eyes, in his words, in his actions. To love like that would only set her up for disappointment and hurt. She'd already experienced that with her mother. Why couldn't two people just enjoy life together without getting all mushy? But she could say, "Derek, you've made me so happy," and he would hold her close to his chest and she'd feel his heart beating fast and hers beat fast too, only because she felt so ill at ease with expressions about undying love. It could die! Things died! People died! And she didn't want to be reminded of all that.

To avoid the intimacy, she asked if her family could come and see the boat and go out with them the following Sunday. He answered the way she knew he would, saying he wanted to be alone with her, but they would have a lifetime together. Yes, it was all right for her family to come.

Despite that, her unease lingered when she was alone in her apartment. But on Monday morning, flowers arrived, and the wedding plans continued.

Chapter 7

No words could have described how Derek felt, standing at the front of the church, seeing his beloved walk down the aisle toward him. Somewhere in the back of his mind he knew that Broc and two friends from Florida stood near him. Now he understood why a groom might need groomsmen. They might have to help him stand. Never had his knees felt so weak, nor his breath so shallow. Vaguely, he'd been aware of Sarah and Adella's pretty sisters coming down the aisle. But when the wedding march sounded from the organ and the most beautiful woman in the world made her incredibly slow journey down the aisle, he almost lost it.

Now he knew how couples could pledge themselves to each other forever. He knew what it meant to leave one's parents and cleave unto one's wife. He knew what it meant for two to become one, and it was so much more than a physical act. In a few minutes, Adella would be his, to have and to hold until death did them part. He felt himself an unfit vessel to be in possession of such bliss.

But after she reached him, he reacted automatically, like they'd practiced. They stood side by side, their backs to the congregation, facing the rugged cross on the wall while the choir stood and sang the "Hallelujah Chorus" from Handel's *Messiah*. He felt the rise of the audience and the power and presence as the words "forever. . .and ever. . .and ever. . ." reverberated through his being.

I am the Lord's and He is mine. I shall serve Him forever. And He has given me the perfect mate. Forever. . .and ever. . .and ever.

Derek had to take a deep breath, swallow hard, and blink to keep the tears in his eyes from overflowing down his face. He dared not turn his head to look at Adella; he would surely bawl like a baby, take her in his arms, and never let her go.

He'd thought a ceremony short when he'd watched them from the audience. Now, this one seemed endless. But he reveled in the words to the song "True Love" performed by a couple as he and Adella faced each other.

He and Adella exchanged identical wedding bands. He meant every promise the minister asked him to make. He meant his vows. They were forever. He and Adella would merge their lives. He'd never felt so blessed.

"I now pronounce you husband and wife," the pastor said. "Derek

Goodson, you may kiss your bride."

Derek felt a trembling all the way to his toes. He dared not do more than let his lips touch hers lightly in a tender kiss. She was his wife now. His life's mate. So great a joy had never before engulfed him. After the brief kiss, they knelt together at the altar while an operatic soloist offered a moving rendition of "The Lord's Prayer."

The next thing he knew, he and his wife were making their way together down the aisle, beginning their life as husband and wife, walking fast, smiling, seeing only each other and the doorway leading them out into a new way of life.

How he endured the seemingly endless reception he never knew. He was anxious to be alone with his wife. But he could smile and be glad Adella seemed to be enjoying every minute of meeting new acquaintances and some people she'd never met. In addition to being beautiful, she was gracious, never seeming to tire of handshakes, hugs, and conversation. They did not bother with posed photographs. The videotaping at the wedding and at the reception should provide ample reproduction of the event.

Finally, all the traditions had been observed, the bouquet thrown into the lifted hands of Brittany, and the rice thrown at them as they raced for the back seat of the waiting car.

As Broc, with Sarah by his side, drove from the parking lot, Derek and Adella both turned to look out the back window to determine the source of the commotion. A pile of tin cans trailed behind them. "I can't believe you did this!" Derek exclaimed.

Broc laughed.

Sarah glanced over her shoulder. "What are friends for?" she asked, and Broc began tooting his horn to attract attention. Fortunately, the drive to the Goodson House was only a few blocks.

Adella had brought her traveling clothes to his. . .their. . .home to change. Derek grinned to himself as he changed in his bedroom. In another bedroom, Sarah was helping his wife change out of her wedding gown.

"Separate rooms already?" Broc kidded.

Derek grinned. "This married life is going to take some adjusting to."

But that was the purpose of a honeymoon, wasn't it? Getting to know each other intimately.

~

Derek didn't want a crew with them on the honeymoon, nor did he feel competent to cross the Gulf Stream where no horizon would be in sight and the open sea could become dangerous. And although this was mid-July, the season when the Bahamas Tourist Office planned a series of boating flings and could get them safely to the islands, he didn't want to travel in a group either. This was not just a fun excursion. This was the time for him and Adella to focus on each other, without worries or responsibilities.

There was no way possible they could explore all seven hundred islands. Derek suggested they fly in to Marsh Harbor, charter a yacht, and cruise to several of the Bahama islands. He wanted them to dress in casual attire and walk up the dusty street at Alice Town, claiming to be about the same as when Hemingway lived there. He wanted to tell her about the pirates' stronghold at New Providence in the seventeenth and eighteenth centuries. They could dock at Paradise Island and stay at a resort at Bimini. They would dress in their finery, and he would present her with the bracelet that matched the diamond earrings he'd given her as a wedding present. Then they would go to dinner, and he would be aware of all those who envied him having such a beautiful wife. He wanted her to taste the fantastic Abaco cuisine. He'd take her to Eleuthera, the first democracy in the New World, founded by pilgrims seeking religious freedom in the 1600s. She would like the pink sand beaches.

"If at any time you don't like the islands, then we will take off to the place of your choice." He shrugged. "We can do that anyway."

She'd smiled at him and laid her soft hand on top of his. "It sounds lovely, Derek. I've never been to the Bahamas."

"Good," he said. "I want to show you as much of the world as I can. If the world were mine, I'd give it to you."

"You're giving me all I've ever wanted, Derek. Thank you, so much."

He'd turned his hand over and grasped hers. "I love you, Adella. More than I ever thought possible."

On their wedding night, Derek never felt more insecure as he stood on the balcony of the resort, looking out over the private beach and to the ocean that melted into the night sky. He heard the soft sound of her approaching him, and he was almost afraid to turn. She walked up to him, and he took in a deep breath before facing her. She wore a robe of white satin, with long flowing sleeves and tiny buttons from the waist to the rounded neckline. Her dark hair was brushed down to her shoulders. Her smoky blue eyes held uncertainty.

Derek knew she couldn't be more uncertain than he. But she lowered her eyes, and a blush formed on her pale cheeks. He realized, *My wife is shy*. He knew Adella to be a strong-willed, purposeful, independent-minded woman. But in addition, she was shy. At least, on her wedding night. That endeared her to him all the more.

~

Derek hadn't considered they would be in Abaco at Regatta time, but the speedboat racing turned out to be Adella's favorite event. She picked out a boat because of its sleek lines and red color and joined the crowd in cheering for the race driver she didn't even know. She loved the speed and excitement. Derek loved watching her more than watching the race.

Adella talked about it long after the race had ended and her driver hadn't won. She hadn't cared. It was the speed and excitement that appealed to her. "I always go to the water festival at the Beaufort Marina," she said. "I love the races."

"For years Dad has thrown a big party in August for the workers and residents on Goodson Island. Any boaters are welcome to join the festivities."

Adella looked up at him. "I've heard something like that but never gave it much thought. I never had the right ticket to get onto the Goodson private island," she quipped.

Derek pulled her close. "You have the right ticket now," he said pointedly. "You are a Goodson. And I don't see any reason why we couldn't continue that tradition. Do you?"

"It sounds like fun," Adella admitted, and Derek could tell by the spark in her eyes that it appealed to her. His next words should change that spark into a flame.

"And I see no reason why we couldn't have a race there," he said.

Adella faced him. Yes, he was right. The flame was there. The excitement of a race on their island appealed to her. "Oh, could we?" she said.

"Sure. Why not a sloop regatta? Then you and I can enter the race."

"Oh, Derek. That would be fabulous."

As he walked on the beach in Abaco's pink sand with his arm around her waist, Derek was glad he could bring a special glow into his wife's face—that he was able to offer her things that delighted her.

~

Adella knew she was behaving like a child with a new toy, but Derek liked being the one who gave her the toys, although they were grown-up ones—surprise gifts, affection, flowers, words of endearment. She loved the Bahamas and knew this was only the beginning of a wonderful world she'd never seen. Derek said he would show her the world and give her as much of it as he could.

She pleased him. There was only one time she ever saw a shadow cross his eyes and that was when he said "I love you" and she didn't reply with the same words. She could only say, "And I need that love."

He would smile again, the light would come into his eyes, and they'd plan to go somewhere different or do something else. Being married turned out to be much more beautiful than she had ever imagined.

But it was good too, returning to Beaufort a month later, tanned, happy, and especially glad to see Mandy, who met them at the front door of the

Goodson House—Adella Goodson's house.

"Oh, Mandy, it's so good to see you," she said, falling into her arms.

"Here, let me look at you," Mandy said after a tearful embrace. She held Adella at arms' length and looked her over. "Yes, Ma'am. I do believe marriage agrees with you."

"At least the Bahamas do," Derek said, coming closer to give Mandy a big hug. "She took you away from the Cottingtons, huh?" he asked.

Mandy's smile was wide. "I can't refuse my baby anything."

He nodded and cast Adella an affectionate glance. "I know the feeling," he said.

Adella's eyes locked with Mandy's as if they were thinking the same thing. Mandy had promised to work for Adella—when she got rich.

After Derek went upstairs with their bags, Mandy said she'd moved all of Adella's things out of the Carder House and put them where she thought they should be in the master bedroom, the dressing room, and in the closets.

"I was thinking," Adella said, "why let all these bedrooms go to waste? Maybe I should have my own and Derek have—"

"No way, Missy," Mandy spoke up quickly, a warning fire in her eyes. "Don't you start none of that separate bedroom business. You do that and he might as well have married a pillow. Now, get that nonsense out of your mind or you'll be sleeping in another bedroom all right. You'll be right out on your pretty little bottom."

Adella couldn't help but laugh at Mandy's tirade. She hadn't really meant it that way. She had just been aware, stepping into the house as the mistress of it, how many rooms were in the house. In reality, she felt good in Derek's arms. She liked the intimacy of being loved. But she would never give her whole heart, soul, mind, and body to anyone. No way!

She would retain her own identity. She would not allow herself to fall under the spell of any man, to be dominated by him. Submitting oneself to one's husband physically was a natural act and a pleasurable one. But she would never abandon herself to any emotion. The closest she'd ever come to doing that was from the moment Derek placed that solitary diamond ring on her finger. She felt the power, the strength, the force of wealth. She wanted what his money could buy. He wanted her—her looks, her affection, her caring for others. She would give him that. But no amount of money could buy her heart, soul, mind, or body. She could trade one thing for another, but she could not be bought.

~

When Derek returned downstairs, he heard voices from the kitchen and stopped in the hallway when he heard Adella saying that she now had everything she'd ever wanted.

He hadn't meant to eavesdrop, but stood for a moment, reveling in the compliment. Then he heard Mandy say, "Your husband is one of the finest men I know."

Now why would he want to interrupt when these two women were praising him?

"That's the surprise of it all, Mandy," Adella said. "I never expected that. Oh, I knew my husband would have to be decent, but he's really good. And he loves me, Mandy. It's wonderful to be loved."

"Haven't you heard, it's more blessed to give than to receive?" Mandy said in a reprimanding tone.

"Maybe that's why he considers himself so blessed," Adella said, as if joking, and laughed lightly.

Derek forced negative thoughts from his mind. He mustn't let any doubts creep in because of his eavesdropping. He refused to allow suspicions to develop just because Adella didn't express herself the way he would like.

Every moment spent with her was a delight. She was perfect. Perfect but not. . .spontaneous. She never ran to him and threw her arms around him. She was never first to lift her face for a kiss. But she always responded to his kiss, to his arms around her. He must not let an overheard conversation cause him concern. What was there to be concerned about anyway? She'd been honest about what she wanted in life.

He could give her what she wanted.

And so far, he couldn't ask for a better wife. There was no other woman he ever wanted by his side. This was his wife. They had pledged themselves to each other, before God and witnesses. And anyway, he hadn't heard the context of the conversation he'd just overheard.

His wife had never allowed herself to be emotionally involved with any man. Perhaps that is why she never spontaneously said, "I love you." Maybe that's why she only said, "I'm glad," or "You make me happy, Derek," after he expressed his love. Words were cheap. He knew the biblical description of love was action.

He knew she reserved a part of herself. He felt there was something deep inside her he hadn't touched. Was her hurt over the loss of her mother so deep she couldn't trust herself to love unreservedly? With time, he told himself, she would trust him, confide in him, love him as he loved her. This emotional, verbal side of life and love was new to Adella. He could appreciate that.

He stepped into the kitchen. "Did I hear someone say I'm blessed?"

"Oh," Adella said, looking slightly startled.

Derek went over to her, smiling, and put his arms around her. She came

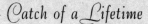

into his arms and laid her head against his chest.

Did Mandy turn away because she didn't want to intrude upon this embrace between him and his wife? Or was that some kind of concern he had seen in her eyes when she turned away? No, he mustn't speculate. *Thank You, Lord, for this blessing, this wonderful woman who is my wife.*

Chapter 8

A s soon as she saw it, Adella wanted it!

It struck her fancy more than anything had all evening. In fact, she was more excited about this than she had been the month before when they'd held their first sloop regatta on Goodson Island. She and Derek hadn't won, but the challenge had been in the trying. Sarah and Broc had come in a good second, although they'd rented their sloop from the marina since their motorboat was too small for such a race.

That had been a wonderfully fun time. But this was different.

This was a time when out-of-town guests—by invitation only—began arriving at the resort hotels early in the week by boat or car. On Saturday, they, joined by the elite of the area dressed in their finery, dined at the Yacht Club, then retired to the ballroom for their annual donations that went to help East Coast victims of the inevitable fall hurricanes.

Adella had planned only to observe on this important social occasion. Derek had already bid thousands of dollars, the amount they had discussed and agreed upon, for a stuffed bear from Boombears, Beaufort's famous toy emporium, where cast members took their children during the filming of *Forrest Gump*. However, she had her own bank account now, and she didn't care if it were depleted.

She had to have the item being auctioned.

When Judd started the bidding, she touched the tip of her nose, which was Derek's signal. He looked over. "Did you mean to do that?" he asked.

Determined, Adella nodded.

He shrugged slightly, but grinned.

Adella touched her nose again. After all, the bidding on this started only with one hundred dollars. Her second bid was three hundred dollars. That was nothing compared with what items had brought earlier in the evening.

Before the ball, Derek had explained what went on at this event. Judd Goodson had started it years before, after Hurricane Hugo had wreaked such havoc. It was held annually on Goodson Island, with Judd and Irene officiating. The Keanes, both of whom had been financial advisors, managed the money. After Dr. Keane died, Keitha had continued handling the financial part of the transactions for the charity.

Judd enjoyed it. To hold people's interest from year to year, he always came up with a theme and involved the participants in ways other than just donating money. Although Adella failed to see how it was possible, Judd indicated it was boring just to write a check. He wanted to motivate everyone and make it the kind of occasion that all the participants looked forward to attending and giving to generously.

One year was "Yachts," and another had been "Local Artists." This year the theme was "Movies Filmed in Beaufort." Just listening to the explanations was an education on movies made in the area. One person auctioned off an autographed copy of Pat Conroy's novel that was turned into the movie *The Great Santini*.

Another brought a collection of the Motown songs used in *The Big Chill*. An autographed picture of Nick Nolte, Barbra Streisand, and Blythe Danner, stars in *The Prince of Tides*, brought a huge sum.

Many other items were auctioned, including a fishing pole used by Robert Duvall, a golf ball hit by director Lasse Hallstrom, an item from the "castle," where Demi Moore had lived during the filming of *G. I. Jane*, and a fork supposedly used by Julia Roberts at an elegant dinner when she stayed at the Beaufort Inn while filming *Something to Talk About*.

Adella was amazed as she watched books and videos one could buy elsewhere for twenty to thirty dollars being auctioned off for thousands. And dinner for two at 11th Street Dockside in Port Royal brought many thousands of dollars. At the restaurant, one could look out at boats featured in scenes for *Bubba Gump Shrimp Company*. Everyone attending understood that the point of the evening was to make donations to help hurricane victims, not to get a good buy on something. The money poured in. At the same time, the evening was educational and fun. Many owned the businesses stars had frequented and owned the inns where they had stayed.

Then came the white elephant items. Keitha brought a picture of her veranda, where many scenes had been shot.

"Are you auctioning off your veranda?" Judd asked, as if serious.

She gave him her look, and he said, "I guess not," and began the bidding for the picture at one hundred dollars.

But it was Judd's own white elephant item that so intrigued Adella. He brought a jar half full of sand that he had scooped up just for the occasion when he knew he would use the movies theme.

"These are authentic footprints made in the sand on my stretch of beach where Tom Hanks trod," he explained.

Everyone laughed. And when Adella touched her nose to indicate five hundred dollars, Derek leaned over and whispered, "Are you sure you want that? Dad could be lying, you know."

She knew. But she wanted it. Derek had said his money was hers, and she knew that to be true, but she hadn't been foolish about it in the short time they'd been married. Although she had feared she'd been extravagant in buying one or more pairs of shoes for every new outfit, Derek never hinted that this was a problem. He simply complimented her on her taste and told her how beautiful she was.

But this? What would everyone think if she insisted?

But, she realized, she was being bid against.

She had to chance it. Her pulse raced at the thought. "Can you imagine what a conversation piece that is?" she said to Derek, watching Judd as the price continued to rise.

"Where would you put it?" Derek asked.

"In the antique vase on the mantle in the living room," she replied as the price rapidly rose, quickly passing seven hundred dollars.

"Mandy would clean it out," Derek said, as the price rose to eight hundred dollars.

"Not if we kept it in that little jar and put a 'Do not open' label on it and set it in the vase."

His lips pursed. "I guess you're right," he said and shrugged. "If you want it, then bid," he said just as Judd was saying, "Going, going—"

"One thousand dollars," Adella shouted, then quickly bit on her lip, having forgotten to touch her nose instead of shouting out the price. Everyone seemed to be chuckling good-naturedly. And she was too pleased to be embarrassed. Making a large donation to charity was one thing. But buying something so trivial as a half-pint jar of sand for one thousand dollars was mind boggling.

One in her position of being married to a wealthy Goodson could justify spending a great deal of money on clothes, household items, items for the boat, or on outings and trips. But she liked the feeling of bidding on this white elephant—more than when she went into the most expensive shops and spent whatever she wished on clothing.

Only a woman of means could spend one thousand dollars on something as meaningless as a half-jar of sand.

~

When and why the nudge of concern crept into her mind about her and Derek's relationship, Adella wasn't sure. Perhaps it was after the newness wore off. She'd cruised around the islands. She'd gone to the Bahamas. She'd helped plan the Goodson Island annual sloop regatta and party, enjoying that immensely. On their first anniversary, they'd flown to Hawaii. On their second anniversary, they'd taken a trip to Europe. She saw Windsor Castle and the changing of the guard, Buckingham Palace; she visited the Louvre, the Eiffel Tower, and the Leaning Tower of Pisa.

If she had her way, they would sail around the world or spend months in different countries. Derek had said he wanted to show her the world, and he'd made a good start. But once in awhile she saw something in his eyes that was not complete adoration. That mainly came when she said he worked too hard. His managers knew how to run the business. She certainly approved of the supply warehouse being a drop-off point for items and using the company vans to help the unfortunate, but he didn't have to do manual labor. Her main point was that he didn't have to be the one who drove a van, filled with supplies, into areas where hurricanes and flood disasters had hit.

"You could pay your employees to drop off supplies," she said.

Perhaps it was the look of surprise in his eyes before he replied blandly, "I need to be personally involved, Adella. And too, the Lord expects me to do something tangible."

The Lord again! Already they'd had discussions about her getting involved in Sunday school. She didn't see the need for that. She still believed in God and that Jesus had died on the cross for her sins. But after what she'd experienced as a child, nothing could convince her that God could be trusted. Sunday school classes involved sharing, and Adella didn't think people would be comfortable hearing what she really thought about God's promises to take care of His children. What did these people, who had been wealthy from birth, know about hardships, anyway? God's care for them was a theoretical belief— nothing that had ever been tested. So Adella simply told Derek that she wasn't comfortable sharing her thoughts with people she didn't know well. Derek seemed to understand. He went to Sunday school, and she met him at church afterward for the morning service.

Adella didn't like these little confrontations, and Mandy warned her not to complain about Derek's doing good things like helping other people and going to church. She supposed Mandy had a point. Although none of these issues became huge problems and Derek always apologized after any disagreement, she knew she mustn't chance losing him.

She knew he liked quiet evenings at home. But he seemed almost too quiet lately and didn't seem to enjoy her enthusiasm over travel and dinners out. He even said once, "Shopping again?"

"Is that not all right?" she'd asked quickly, surprised.

"Yes, darling. It's all right. If that makes you happy, do it." He took her in his arms and said he didn't mean to imply anything by his question. But she'd felt his outward sigh.

She would have to do something to cause him to look at her with the kind of adoration he'd had from the beginning. They'd been married almost three years. Maybe this was what others referred to as the honeymoon being over and settling down to old married life. She couldn't stand the thought.

Then an idea occurred to her. Maybe it was time she gave something to Derek. Sarah and Broc seemed even closer now that Sarah was expecting a baby. Most of their conversations centered around the upcoming event. Still holding onto Derek, Adella looked up into his face. "Would you like to consider our starting a family?"

Derek's eyes grew wide, and his mouth fell open. "You mean it? Oh, Adella, that would please me so. A little girl or a little boy who looks just like you."

"Well, I wouldn't mind if the boy looks like you," she said with a laugh, delighted that she had ignited a spark in him that was turning into a full-fledged blaze. Yes, she'd done the right thing. The unwavering adoration was in his eyes again.

～

Mandy watched it all happening again. After the announcement of her pregnancy, Adella began soaking up the attention like a sponge soaking up water. The Goodsons were ecstatic over the prospect of having a grandchild. They all began planning the nursery. Then came the baby showers. Mandy was happy to see Adella relating to Sarah on a more personal level. It was good for her to have a friend. And it made Derek appear to walk on cloud nine when Adella would say, "Derek and I are pregnant."

But to Mandy she said, "I'm starting to look like a watermelon with legs."

"No, you don't. You look like you're pregnant, carrying one of God's greatest miracles."

"You sound more like Derek every day."

"I've always sounded this way," Mandy retorted. "You just never listened." Adella laughed it off.

"And you're going to have to stop all that gallivanting all over the world when that little baby comes," Mandy warned.

Adella shrugged. "Well, you'll be here to take care of it, just like you did with me, won't you, Mandy? I wouldn't know where to begin. You're going to be here. Right?"

Mandy's heart softened looking at the genuine concern in Adella's eyes, hearing the uncertainty in her voice. Adella wasn't all that confident in herself. Always afraid of messing up, afraid of losing what she had.

Regardless of the reason, all during the pregnancy, Derek couldn't do enough for Adella. Time and again, Mandy heard Adella talk about losing her figure, so afraid Derek wouldn't find her beautiful anymore.

"The most beautiful woman in the world is the one carrying my child," he'd say. "There is nothing I have, nothing I could give you, that comes close to comparing with your giving me a child."

Mandy didn't know if Adella cried at that, but Mandy had to hurry away and swipe at her own tears and blow her nose. She wondered if Adella knew how fortunate she was to have a good man like Derek—not his money, but his heart.

Adella was a smart girl, and Mandy hoped to goodness that she hadn't decided to have a baby just to gain an extra hold on Derek Goodson—thinking of that baby as some kind of insurance policy. Relationships had to be built on love, and Mandy wondered if Adella would ever be able to trust both God's and Derek's love for her. Until she did, Mandy didn't think Adella would really be able to love either of them. Sighing, Mandy turned her worries over to her Lord.

Chapter 9

Adella was shocked at how she felt about the baby. All the discomfort, looking like she was carrying a watermelon, the pain of childbirth, were all forgotten when that beautiful, perfect, naked little baby was laid on her own body right after the birth cry. Adella cried. Derek cried. She felt more complete than she had in her entire life—she had fulfilled her role as a woman. Nothing could be more satisfying.

Derek put his hand on the baby's back and kissed Adella's sweaty forehead. "I love you so. I love you both," he said brokenly.

The nurse wrapped the baby in a blanket and laid her in Derek's arms. He looked as if either the baby would break or perhaps he himself might break. "She's an angel," Derek choked out in a whisper.

He too, had apparently forgotten that during the birth, when she said she'd never do this again, he'd said he didn't want her to. He couldn't stand to see her in such pain.

"My little miracle. My little angel," he said.

"We could name her Angela," Adella said. "And call her Angel."

They had picked out several names in advance. Family names on both sides of the family. They'd considered naming her after Adella's mother, but she wouldn't be comfortable calling her baby by her mother's name. Right away, Adella said the middle name would be Amanda, and Mandy would be her baby's godmother. Derek hadn't resisted at all, knowing how much Mandy meant to his wife. And Mandy had become so emotional over it, she hadn't been able to talk for days without bawling.

"Angela Amanda Goodson," Derek said. "Perfect! A perfect name for our perfect baby."

Everybody was enchanted by the tiny baby—six pounds, eight ounces—with a full head of black hair and dark purple eyes. Many referred to her as a little angel before they were told her name. She had no blemishes, just a little birthmark on her left thigh. Each nurse, and even Mandy, tried to wipe it away every time they changed her, forgetting that it was a birthmark.

The Goodsons, the Speldings, and Mandy took pictures. "She'll grow up thinking there's something wrong if she's not seeing flashbulbs," Judd said.

"She's beautiful enough to be in pictures," Derek said, then his voice softened even more, "like my wife." He reached out to touch Adella. He couldn't seem to express his joy and appreciation enough. It was as if Adella had given him the world. While Derek looked lovingly at Adella, they all stared at the baby. So precious. Barely a handful. Even Judd had tears in his eyes when he held the infant, as if she were more fragile than a piece of fine china. Then Angel yawned and cried in protest.

"Did I do something wrong?" he asked quickly, fear in his eyes.

"No, she just resents having to yawn," Mandy told them. "She's a sweet baby." Her eyes rolled toward Adella. "But already, she has a mind of her own. Wants everything her own way."

Adella refused to take Angel to the church nursery. "I hear the other mothers talking," she explained. "Parents will bring children to church with the croup and colds. I will not expose Angel to those germs. And, Derek, I know they are well-meaning people, but how can we entrust our daughter to strangers?"

Derek couldn't argue with that.

But from the time Angel was born, an idea had stuck in his mind. In Old Testament times, men of faith built rock altars as an acknowledgment to the Lord, and they made sacrifices. In New Testament times, Jesus said God didn't want stone and burnt offerings, but a contrite heart. Derek had never felt so close to the Lord, nor so grateful as he was to have Adella and Angel. He hadn't thought his heart could hold any more love than what he felt for Adella. But now, although he didn't love his baby more than his wife, he discovered his heart had room for both of them.

He wanted to do something more for the Lord than he already was doing, a tangible sign of his gratefulness to God.

"Any suggestions?" he asked Adella.

She shook her head. "You give so much already, Derek. I really don't know what you could do."

Then one summer day, when he had gone to Goodson Island, he'd stood at the marina and watched all the people get off their boats and yachts, looking for happiness in many ways. The marina provided resorts, entertainment, great food, and almost anything a person could want. All that was obvious. It was printed in magazines and brochures.

One thing was missing.

There was no place for worshiping the Lord.

That was it! He would do it. He talked over his idea with Adella, who said that if that's what he wanted to do, then by all means do it.

Broc was enthusiastic, offering his help.

They prayed about it.

Soon afterward, one of the small shops on the island decided to go out of business. Derek knew that would be the ideal place for his idea—a mission house, a church for those coming into the marina during the peak tourist months. During the rainy and hurricane seasons, the building could be used as another drop-off point for needed supplies and a place of refuge for anyone who might need clothing or help in any way. He would hire someone to work there five days a week, and there could be an answering service for any particular needs that might occur during off hours.

In the peak seasons, various church members could lead a service. It could be a time of praise and worship, with people offering testimonies to what God had been doing for them. There might even be a retired minister or a young preacher who would like to handle the services on a more permanent basis.

He would make the main room look like a chapel. Some church might even want to use it for special meetings.

Adella had been right when she'd said he could trust his managers to run the supply store. Derek began to spend most of his days on Goodson Island, at the marina, and helping with the work on the mission house. It gave him great joy. Each evening when he went home, he felt he was showing his appreciation to the Lord in that small way. He loved being home with his family, watching Adella with Angel, and seeing his little girl grow and learn new things almost daily.

After several months of both Adella and Angel staying home on Sunday, Mandy announced that she would watch Angel at home so that Adella could meet Derek for the worship service.

Mandy taught Angel to lift her little index finger when she asked, "Where's your little light?" Then Mandy would sing "This little light of mine." Angel would feel the rhythm of the music and move her little body and feet. They would all laugh.

The one cloud on Derek's horizon was his questions about Adella's insistence that Angel stay home from church, long after all the other children her age had begun attending regularly. Maybe he was just being jealous, or selfish, seeing other babies at church—even Broc and Sarah's—but not his own. Adella had always been a conscientious mother. Maybe she was just being overly cautious. After all, more than anyone Derek had ever known, Adella had reasons to worry about losing those she loved.

But when Angel became a toddler, he insisted it was past time for his daughter to be going to church. "She will go to Sunday school and stay in the toddler class while we're in the worship service," he announced. Adella didn't say anything, but the next Sunday, they all went.

When Angel turned three, Derek decided she should go to the church's preschool three weekday mornings a week. "She's a bright child and needs to learn to interact socially with other children," he told Adella.

"But I want her home with me," Adella protested. She loved the time spent with her daughter, playing with her, watching her blue eyes grow big at the zoo. Watching her dark hair blow in the wind when they took the boat out and seeing how obvious was her love for the water.

When the Goodson grandparents took Angel for a weekend or out on their yacht, Adella missed her terribly. She needed the child to make her life complete. And how could she explain to Derek that she was terrified that something would harm Angel if she wasn't there to protect her only daughter?

Derek was insistent that Angel should go to preschool. Adella cried, "She's only three years old. Why would you want to separate her from me?"

"It's not something against you, Adella. It's for Angel. She doesn't relate well to the children in church. She doesn't know how to share. She is eager to learn, and she will need this to be prepared for kindergarten."

"She's too little, too young," Adella protested.

"Let's try it," he said. "If we see that it serves no purpose, we can take her out."

Adella agreed to talk with the director. She planned to go alone and return with an adverse opinion. However, Derek insisted upon going with her and taking Angel so that they could see how the toddler reacted to the situation.

The director was pleased that Angel might join their group. While the adults talked, Angel walked around the room, looking at the gerbil in a glass container. She explored the bookshelf and selected a book, then sat at a table and pretended to read while looking at the pictures.

Adella could tell her child was fascinated with the paintings on the walls, the colorful furniture, the sectioned play areas that represented various rooms in a house. There was a play kitchen where Angel pretended to cook. Adella had to admit that Angel liked what she saw. She was an eager little girl, with boundless energy and a natural love for people. Adella knew her daughter would like it. She could tell by the look on Derek's face that he thought it would be good for Angel.

On the way home, Angel responded positively to Derek's questioning. Yes, she liked the gerbil and the rabbit. She liked the books. She would like to play with children.

"You enjoy playing with Meagan, don't you?" Adella asked, as a reminder to Derek that Angel wasn't without friends. She played with Sarah and Broc's daughter. Meagan's nanny and Mandy often walked the girls to the waterfront, where something fascinating was almost always going on—either a sidewalk art show, water sports, shrimp festival, music, or storytelling. Adella did not think being cooped up in a classroom was right for her daughter.

When she reminded Derek that Angel was receiving an education daily, he agreed. "But she also needs that structured environment," he insisted. "The preschool is Bible-based, so she will be getting her religious education along with learning to relate to other children and adults."

"But I would miss her so," Adella said later that night as they lay in bed after Angel was asleep.

"Have you thought about having another child?" Derek asked expectantly.

"No," she said. "I haven't."

"I'm going to be away for awhile. Would you think about it while I'm gone?" he asked.

"Of course," she said.

As she said it, she thought about the impossible problems having another child would bring. It was hard enough living with the constant fears she faced about Angel and her safety. How could she deal with the responsibility of caring for two children?

And although she could barely admit it to herself, much less to Derek, one of the reasons she resisted the idea of the preschool was that she wanted to protect Angel from trusting God too much. Of course she wanted Angel to know about Jesus. She even told Angel Bible stories about Jesus' birth and life and death. Trusting God for salvation was important, Adella understood. But she never wanted Angel to trust God for help in this life. She'd only end up being disappointed as her mother had been so long ago.

Chapter 10

Adella didn't know how to explain it to herself. She couldn't say exactly when, how, or why it happened. At first she made excuses, telling herself that Derek neglected her by running off to do "God's work" instead of taking care of his family first. But she knew that was only an excuse and not really true.

Derek was home every evening that they didn't have a social engagement or he wasn't tied up with hurricane relief work. The reality was that she just plain didn't join in his enthusiasm for doing good for the needy. Oh, she didn't resent any amount of money they donated, and it gave her a good feeling to know she had a part in helping the needy. She simply didn't see the point of doing everything. Some people were blessed with money, so they should give it. Shouldn't Derek leave some of the hands-on work for those who weren't blessed with money to give? She thought he had become overly enthusiastic—renovating that empty building and turning it into a chapel at the marina. That was not the kind of activity for their family that she'd had in mind when she married him.

Another excuse she made for her feelings was that her beautiful three-year-old daughter was getting an education from other women three mornings a week instead of being with her own mother, where she belonged. That reasoning didn't hold up very long. Angel came home from school, delighted with what she'd learned and eager to return. Adella had to admit that Angel would like to go to preschool every morning.

Always having prided herself in facing facts, no matter how unpleasant, Adella finally admitted the truth to herself. She was bored. Three mornings a week she filled the time with going for coffee with Sarah, shopping, having her hair or nails done, or planning what to wear to some event.

Judd had asked her to come up with a theme for the charity ball. She'd thought of "Gullah" and had just come down the stairs with that on her mind, planning to go into the kitchen and ask Mandy for ideas. She stopped in the foyer. Her gaze was riveted on the antique vase on the mantle. The half-full jar of sand was still there. It had been there for over five years.

She waited for some sense of accomplishment or excitement to wash over her. It didn't. She realized it hadn't in a long, long time. The sand was now. . .simply sand in a jar. Where was her joy? She had everything she'd set out to get—a wealthy husband, acceptance into society, and relationships with the wealthiest and most influential people in the area.

Maybe that's what her dissatisfaction was about. Perhaps she'd set her sights too low. It wasn't often that she became so contemplative. Most of the time she kept busy. From the moment Angel came home from school, her hours were filled with joy until the child went to bed. Then there were the activities required of her as a wealthy Goodson woman. Sometimes, though, she wondered if she was settling down to the kind of feelings Derek had often expressed. He enjoyed his friends, and he had a responsibility to be a part of charity drives and dinners. But he said none of that gave him satisfaction like reaching out personally to a needy person. But that was him. Reaching out to the needy was not her cup of tea. If she'd wanted to hobnob with the less fortunate, then she wouldn't have left the shrimp boat community, nor would she have set her sights on marrying a wealthy man.

She wasn't really seeking or looking for an answer, for she didn't allow negative or depressing thoughts to linger in her mind too long. It was just a vague awareness. A growing dissatisfaction she couldn't exactly put her finger on. She understood that she wouldn't have the same challenge and excitement of landing a wealthy husband once she'd accomplished that mission. Of course, she wasn't as excited about him now that they were married. However, she hadn't expected that the titillation of shopping in exclusive shops wherever they visited would wear thin. Derek continued to tell her she was beautiful. Her acquaintances complimented her, and she did the same with them. They too, shopped wherever they wanted. She was no different. Even the thrill of writing a huge check at a charity ball had grown thin. Others around her could write one of an equal amount, or bigger.

Maybe it would take a psychologist or a psychiatrist to figure it all out. She tried talking with Mandy, but the older woman always took Derek's side of things. "You have everything you ever wanted," Mandy would say. "Count your blessings, Honey. You've got a fine man, the sweetest daughter a body could have, and just thank the Lord for all His blessings."

Adella could agree with Mandy to a point. But she wasn't convinced that the Lord had much to do with all her blessings, and besides, recognizing what she had didn't alleviate her growing sense of dissatisfaction. She sensed that there was more out there she hadn't yet attained. Maybe she'd reached her goals too young. But if she'd waited, she might not have been able to reach them at all.

She'd never thought in terms of another man being the answer to anything. Frankly, she wasn't even sure what the question was that caused her vague sense of dissatisfaction. She wasn't so foolish as to think some other man held the key to her happiness. Besides, there wasn't any man she liked better than Derek. And if she wouldn't give herself over to her husband unequivocally, she certainly wasn't about to do so with some other man.

Maybe that's why she was so surprised at her reaction when Ramon Bartoli appeared on the scene. She'd had men pay her particular attention all her life. She still received compliments from men about her looks, always done in a respectful manner.

But from the moment she saw Ramon, something stirred inside her, like something was inevitable, reminding her of how she felt the moment Mandy had first mentioned Derek. Adella didn't welcome that feeling and even resisted Sarah's suggestion that they meet him.

It happened one morning after Adella had picked up Sarah and Meagan. They took the girls into the preschool, then drove out to Goodson Island to the Yacht Club until time to pick up the children at noon.

A few golfers went in ahead of them, laughing and talking and heading for the lounge. Sarah and Adella moved to a table at the glass side of the room where they could look out over the marina.

They both decided on cappuccinos. While waiting for them, Adella looked out and saw the largest yacht she'd ever seen at the marina. "Where did that come from?" she asked, not having to explain what she was talking about when Sarah followed her gaze.

"Oh, Broc said that some Spanish nobleman cruised in on it a couple of days ago. He didn't know any details except it dwarfs everything else in the marina."

That was obvious. Derek hadn't mentioned it, but then he never seemed to be impressed by signs of wealth, having been raised around the finer things money could buy. But even Judd and Irene Goodson's yacht was not in the same class as this one. Adella dismissed any thought of it as the waiter brought their cappuccinos.

"Uh-oh. Don't look now," Sarah said in a low tone, glancing toward the entry. "You won't believe who just walked in."

Adella couldn't resist turning her face toward the doorway. Just then, the man's eyes collided with hers. If ever there was a stereotypical Spanish nobleman, he was it. Tall, dark, and handsome were the words that came to mind, but that description seemed trite. She was accustomed to good-looking men, her husband included, but this one would cause any woman to take a second look.

Then she felt warmth coming into her cheeks as the man's wide, full lips turned into the slightest of smiles. His nod was slight, almost imperceptible, before he looked away, reminding her of how she used to react to stares at herself, knowing she was a beautiful woman. This man could not help but know he was handsome. It wasn't until after he and the woman with him had sat down at a table in a secluded corner that Adella registered who the woman with him was: Keitha Keane.

Adella faced Sarah. "Well!" was all she could find to say.

Sarah grinned. "I warned you not to look."

Adella laughed lightly. "I should have listened."

"He must be related to Keitha," Sarah speculated. "We really should go and speak to her."

Adella shook her head and picked up her cup. "Let's not," she said, turning her head to glance at the man and Keitha as a waiter went to their table. Again, the man glanced at Adella. She felt embarrassed that at their first glance, the man had looked away first. That had never happened to her before.

"It would not be polite to pretend we don't know Keitha," Sarah said.

Adella knew that to be true. If she wanted to stay in the good graces of anyone, it was Keitha Keane. And there was no reason to hesitate. Hadn't she always been eager to make new acquaintances?

They left their cappuccinos and walked over to the table. The man stood. Adella smiled, barely glancing at the man, and focused on Keitha, who seemed delighted to see them. "Ramon," the older woman quickly said, "I'd like to introduce two of my dear friends." She then introduced him as Ramon Bartoli, a friend of her distant cousin in Savannah. He was living on his yacht.

"Very good to meet you ladies," he said with a slight Spanish accent. Then he looked directly at Adella. "Mrs. Goodson?" he asked. "That is the name of this island, is it not?"

"Yes," she said, glancing at the other two smiling women.

"There's a definite connection," Keitha said, and they all laughed lightly.

Adella thought the slight nod of his handsome face was appealing. So was his charming smile. "Would you ladies join us?" he asked.

"Yes, do," Keitha said, so Adella and Sarah sat opposite each other at the table and the waiter brought over their cappuccinos and took the order for two more coffees.

"You're from Savannah?" Adella asked, before taking a sip of her cappuccino and glancing at Ramon over the rim of her cup.

She was sure his dark velvety-brown eyes held her gaze a moment longer than necessary before he glanced down and his long black lashes, the color of his curly hair, touched his bronzed cheeks. "My primary residence is in Spain," he said, as if almost reluctant to reveal such information, "but I have been up and down the East Coast for awhile on business."

"Business?" Sarah said, and cast a quick glance at Adella, which seemed to say she was having difficulty being polite about what she wanted to know of this handsome stranger.

"He's in the yachting business," Keitha volunteered.

Ramon's full lips spread over perfectly formed white teeth, and his heavy brows rose slightly. "I'm sure you lovely ladies do not wish to discuss business. Tell me more about this regatta."

"You do the honors, Adella," Keitha said, with a smile. "It's a Goodson tradition."

Adella spoke of the grand gala, complete with music, food, races, and ultimately the private charity ball.

"What sort of races?" Ramon asked. "Speedboats?"

"Afraid not," Adella said, with a sigh in her voice. "Sloop racing."

"Ah, I'm sure that is nice," Ramon said. "Speedboat racing is my sport."

"More than that," Keitha offered. "He is a racer."

"Oh, ever since I saw the Abaco Regatta, I've loved the sport." Adella did not look down this time as his gaze held hers. *Sloop racing is nice,* she was thinking. He was so right. For a moment, gazing into the eyes of a speedboat racer, she relived the excitement she had felt in Abaco, when on her honeymoon, watching the races. She had loved the feeling of their speeding over the water, competing and winning. What a life that must be for a racer.

It must be something akin to the challenge she had felt after meeting Derek. Could she or could she not win him? The thrill lay in the effort. How thrilling it must be for a racer to experience that challenge over and over again.

A long moment passed before Adella realized the conversation had moved on, but she was still the center of it.

"Most likely," Keitha was saying, "Adella's husband's company is supplying that part you needed for the yacht. He owns the supply company here."

"Then I shall definitely tell the mechanic about that," Ramon said.

"Do you have a family in Spain or in Savannah?" Sarah asked.

Ramon's countenance fell as abruptly as his eyelids covered his expressive eyes. The silence lasted long enough for Adella and Sarah to glance at each other speculatively and Keitha to wear a sad smile of compassion as she gazed at Ramon.

"My mother passed away several months ago after having been an invalid for many years," he said. "She could not bear for me to leave her side for long." He drew in a deep breath, then sighed. "I'm afraid I was confined to being much of what you call a recluse, I believe. Oh, I've had many friends, but the situation did not allow for serious relationships. So, for me, although I do not regret caring for my mother, I do regret I have no wife, no children. Ah, yes, please, a refill," he said to the waiter who stopped with a pot of hot coffee.

After the waiter left, Ramon spread his hands expressively and smiled with his lips, although his dark eyes looked sad. "Please forgive me. I did not intend to spoil this delightful morning with morbid talk. I left Spain to get away from the sadness." He leaned forward with his elbows on the table and his fingers entwined beneath his chin. "Let's talk about your happy lives. You have children?" He looked from one to the other.

After talking about their daughters, Sarah looked at her watch. "Speaking of children, we need to pick them up before noon." She rose from her chair. Adella did the same.

Ramon glanced at his Rolex, stood, and smiled at them. "It's been a pleasure. Perhaps we will meet again."

"Bye-bye, Dears," Keitha said.

After they were outside, Sarah commented, "He couldn't be a day over thirty-five. Having a yacht like that and traveling around at his leisure—he must be heir to something."

"Spain?" Adella jested, and they laughed.

On the short drive to Beaufort, Adella was thinking that she had never been to Spain. There were many places she hadn't been. She was thirty-one now, not getting any younger, and what lay ahead for her? More Beaufort parties, more charity drives, more waiting for Derek to come home only to feel the growing tension between them?

~

Two mornings later, after dropping Angel off at preschool, Adella again drove out to Goodson Island. For awhile she stood on the waterfront, looking at the boats, at her and Derek's sloop, all dwarfed by the magnificent yacht.

She walked farther away, took off her sandals, and felt the warm sand beneath her bare feet and the cool breeze blow her hair away from her face. Her eyes drifted out over the ocean and she thought of her daddy and his life's work. His life had been spent on a shrimp boat. How was hers to be spent? Growing old in the Goodson House in historic Beaufort? She tried to conjure up a feeling of pride and joy in that. It didn't come. Maybe she should see a doctor. Her depressed moods were becoming more frequent.

Suddenly she was shaken from her reverie when she sensed approaching footsteps, then heard, "Good morning. Mrs. Goodson, is it not?"

Adella recognized the accent before she looked around. She was not surprised. Had she come here this morning for this reason? Had she wanted something, someone new or different to give a lift to her life? A few feet from her stood the handsome Ramon Bartoli, dressed in walking shorts and knit shirt. She smiled. "Yes," she said. "I am Adella."

"A lovely name," he said and looked away. "A lovely day, is it not?"

"Yes, a touch of fall is in the air. But it is lovely."

"May Ramon," he said, stressing his given name, "intrude upon your solitude and walk with you?"

"Please do," she said, and they began to walk along the beach. On their left, the softly churning white foamy waves caressed the shore. On their right, the gentle breeze caused the palm fronds and palmettos to sway and wave a welcome to the solitary figures casting long shadows on the sand.

They spoke of racing, and Ramon described the thrill of it that Adella could feel in her innermost depths. "I wanted to win at something," he said. "Prove to my father that I could accomplish something of importance. He once called me a worthless philanderer."

He laughed, so Adella asked, "Were you?"

"Perhaps," he admitted with a gleam in his dark eyes. "I will admit I liked the girls. And I was not overly concerned with politics. But I was not entirely to blame for my lack of purpose. My father gave me everything. When you've walked through palaces, eaten with kings—I'm sorry. I did not mean to divulge that. Something about you, Adella, makes me feel you will understand without condemning me."

"I do understand about losing those you love and how it can make you feel so alone, like a boat without a sail, so to speak."

"Yes, I felt you would understand. I'm afraid mine is a sad story. My father divorced my mother and married a younger woman who could further his career and gain him entrance into the political scene, which he had coveted for many years. My mother's health began to fail. She was a dear, sweet woman. She was never bitter, just suffered silently with a broken heart."

"That must have been terribly sad for you," Adella sympathized.

"I think it woke me up to the fact that I did not want to be a worthless philanderer." He grinned, casting her a sideways glance. He quickly changed the subject by asking, "Have you been to Spain?"

"No," Adella admitted, "but it sounds fascinating." *Strolled through palaces? Eaten with kings?*

"Ah, it is. From my mother's villa," he paused, then said in a melancholy tone, "my villa now. Anyway, from the villa, atop a mountain. . ."

His deep, resonant voice seemed to lull her into seeing the scene as he spread his hands and spoke of the place he loved. Ramon stopped walking, looking out across the ocean. Adella looked too. It was as if she saw herself, standing on the veranda, holding onto a white banister. In the morning or midday, she could see the city spread out far below, looking like it must have been in medieval times when the serfs lived below a castle. At night, sitting on the veranda, she could see the city lights below or reach up and almost touch the stars. The sky spread out before her for glorious sunrises or spectacular sunsets. There was no other dwelling on the entire mountain.

"Other than the guest houses and servants' lodgings, of course," Ramon added, now looking down into her rapt face.

Looking up, lost in her imagination and the depths of his eyes, Adella nodded. "Of course."

Chapter 11

Derek was anxious to return to Beaufort, his home, his wife, his child, his many blessings. The devastation he'd come from was heartbreaking. The latest hurricane to hit the Southeast had caused so many people to lose their homes, all their belongings, their businesses. And worse, some had lost their loved ones.

Lord, forgive me, he prayed, *for thinking I had troubles. The little tensions and small disagreements with Adella are nothing compared with what many people go through. I don't have any problems compared with most. Please help me show my love to my wife and daughter and be a kinder, more loving person.*

When he arrived home, Mandy was just putting Angel to bed. He knew it would take her awhile to get to sleep, but he had to go in to see her after taking a hot shower. He needed to hold his little girl and tell her how much he loved her.

After showering and changing, he sat on her bed while she told about her adventures the day before with her mother at the regatta. "We went on a biiiiiiig yacht," she said, spreading her hands as far apart as they could go, her eyes widening with excitement. "And I know Spanish."

"Spanish?" Derek said. "Noooo."

She nodded her head up and down. *"Si."*

"See what?" Derek said, looking around.

Angel laughed and shook her head. "No. It's *si*. That means *yes* in Spanish."

"Very good," he complimented. "Do you know that your name is Spanish? It's Angela, but we call you Angel."

She nodded. "Mommy told me."

"Now, shall I read you a good night story?"

"In Spanish," she said.

"I don't know that much Spanish," he said. "I studied French in college."

"Speak it," Angel said.

"Oui," he said.

"We," she mimicked and giggled.

"That means *yes* in French."

"Okay. Read my story in Gullah."

"Oh, no," he said, and she began to giggle. "You'd be awake all night if I start that. Anyway, I'm not good at it like Mommy."

"She's going to tell a Gullah story at the party."

"She is?" He hadn't heard Adella's final decision about that. But then, he'd been gone awhile. He knew the theme of tonight's ball was Gullah. He hoped he'd make it in time to hear her tell such a story.

⁓

He made it just in time. He stepped inside the ballroom, and his first glance at her made his heart beat wildly with love and joy and happiness and blessedness. It seemed impossible that she could grow more beautiful with each passing day, for she had already been perfect to him. But she stood there, in a long, shimmering gold lamé dress that accentuated her mature figure and complemented her dark hair pulled back into an elegant twist and adorned with a gold and diamond comb he had given her. Her lovely coral-colored lips smiled, and her eyes were full of excitement he could detect from across the crowded room.

Only one thing spoiled the picture, causing his heart to skip a beat, causing all his good intentions to drain from him like he felt the blood draining from his face. Only one thing could cause his pulse to race with a fever quite new to him and make his blood boil.

Only one thing marred the picture, and that was her telling a delightful story in the Gullah language while a tall, dark man looked at her like she was the grandest prize he'd ever seen. Derek did not like that man's eyes on her. He knew what this meant. He'd even heard Adella mention that the item she might auction off was to tell a story to someone who bid for it.

Apparently, that man had bid the highest. Had his dad been standing there, he would be proud. Had Broc been standing there, he would smile and nod and enjoy the performance like the audience was doing. But somehow, this felt different. Maybe it was because Adella's eyes held an excitement he hadn't seen in a long time. He had seen it when he courted her, when he put the diamond ring on her finger, when she first began to buy the kind of clothes she'd never worn before. When she arrived in France, and London, and Switzerland. When she'd attended speedboat races. When she looked at her little Angel. When she bought a jar half full of beach sand.

And now, her dark eyes sparkled as her beautiful face lifted toward the dark stranger, and Derek felt a kind of rage he'd never felt before. He was shocked at the intensity of it. Fortunately, before he could make a fool of himself and cause a scene, someone touched his arm and motioned to a seat at the back. Like a robot, he sat. He wanted to look away, but his eyes were glued to the scene.

His mind was trying to lecture his heart, but it wasn't listening. And to make it worse—if things could get any worse—his dad laughed and asked the stranger if he understood the musical, rhythmic language from South Africa.

"Every word," the man said in an accent and seemed to be repeating it in a foreign language as the audience began to murmur and laugh appreciatively. The man knew how to work a crowd. Although he'd never studied it, Derek had no doubt that language was Spanish.

Sí!

He saw. All too well.

No one else seemed to. This was just another fun-filled charity ball, and that man was the highest bidder and had won the privilege of standing before Adella Goodson while she told a Gullah story. That's all. A man he hardly saw but had known for years turned toward him and said, "You're a lucky man. Your wife can sure liven up a dull party."

Derek thought he smiled. Yes, she could. She was the light of his life. But he couldn't take his eyes off his wife, who now walked to her seat in the front row.

Then Derek stared at the man who now stood at the table Keitha manned, where he was signing his pledge. How much had he bid to hear Adella tell a story in the Gullah language? Did it matter?

Don't I hear them for free? As soon as he asked, his mind, unbidden, asked another question. *Were the stories free? Was the excitement in her eyes really free? Has she ever given those things freely, Derek? Or did you buy them?*

Derek labeled his feelings pure jealousy. As soon as the festivities ended, he stood. His dad saw him and invited him to come up front and give a report on the flooded areas he had just returned from. Passing Adella, he gave her a special smile. He thought her expressive eyes looked startled for an instant. Perhaps she had given up on his returning in time for this event.

He reported on the great needs, how the supplies and donations made a great difference, particularly to the morale of the people who needed to know that others were concerned, helping, and praying for them.

"Please know how much your generosity means to them," Derek said, "and remember them in your prayers."

As soon as he stepped down from the podium, he walked over to Adella, who stood along with the other participants. She lifted her face and turned her cheek for him to plant a light kiss on it. He put his hand at the small of her back, then felt her slip aside to respond to another woman about the events of the evening. Others began to gather around her, commenting on her remarkable ability to speak Gullah.

Several men came up to him, asking when he got back and wanting a more detailed account of the flooded areas. Then he heard Keitha's voice calling his name, and the men stood aside to allow her to approach him.

"We've all been concerned, Derek," she said, "about the flooded areas and your driving up there. But I'm happy to report tonight's donations will help considerably." The total had already been announced to the group, and it was indeed considerable. As Keitha held the notebook for him to take another look, he saw the name he didn't recognize: Ramon Bartoli. His donation was by far the greatest amount donated. That's what made tonight's gifts so large.

"That's wonderful," Derek commented and tried to excuse his lack of joy as being tired and heavy-hearted for those living in the devastated areas. However, when Keitha said, "You must meet Ramon," he felt like replying, "Must I?"

Keitha introduced them, lavishly praising the generous man whose handshake was firm and gaze direct. He was a likeable fellow, impressive really. Normally, Derek didn't consider whether a man was good-looking. A few simply were. A few stood out in a crowd. Like Cary Grant, Mel Gibson, Sean Connery, Ramon Bartoli.

"May I congratulate you on your lovely, talented wife," Bartoli said. "She is most kind."

Kind? Si, señor. How kind? And have you been kind, señor? "Thank you," Derek said, reminding himself to be cordial. He had no reason to dislike this man. His handshake was firm. His gaze direct. His manner impressive. What about him was so disturbing?

Then it hit him. The man possessed something Derek hadn't felt about many facets of his life in some time. Ramon Bartoli exuded confidence.

～

Adella was ready to leave shortly after Ramon and Keitha left. "I'll be along shortly," Derek said. He hadn't seen his friends in almost a week. During the conversations, he asked about Ramon. Several agreed he was a friend of Keitha's. One said he'd heard Ramon was a nephew or cousin of Keitha's. Another said he'd heard that Ramon was descended from royalty or else his dad was very high in politics. Somebody said he owned a fleet of yachts, like the one parked in the marina. Broc said he heard Ramon was a nationally acclaimed speedboat racer. The general consensus was straightforward: Ramon Bartoli was a man people liked to know and be around.

Adella was slipping into a cream-colored satin robe over her nightgown when Derek walked into the bedroom. She sat at the dresser and began to take the pins from her hair. Derek went over and tilted her face toward his and planted a kiss on her lips. "It's good to be home," he said.

"Yes," she said. "You arrived just in time to upstage me."

Derek felt as if she'd knocked the breath from him. He stared at her, but she didn't look at him. She just resumed taking the pins from her hair. *Upstage her? But the object of the charity ball is for the audience to donate to help the needy. The entertainment is secondary.*

That fear, that thought which so often invaded his heart and mind was there again. *She doesn't love the Lord the way I thought she did.* But he always pushed it aside. He must never accuse anyone of such a thing. Works or words were not what made one a Christian.

She didn't have his enthusiasm about the Lord, but enthusiasm isn't what made one a Christian. She agreed they should tithe. She never resented any amount of money they gave to charity. She was right alongside him in everything he did and believed in. She simply wasn't vocal about it. She didn't help load up vans. She didn't drive into devastated areas. But he certainly didn't want her to do any of that.

She had gone to the charity ball without him and brought in the largest donation of the evening. Feeling guilty, he stepped over and laid his hand on her shoulder. "I'm sorry," he said.

Lowering her gaze, she picked up her hairbrush.

Derek walked over to sit on the bed and take off his shoes, then he propped up against the headboard to watch her brush her hair.

"I should have been the one to bid and let you tell me the Gullah story," Derek said, watching her in the mirror.

Her reflection's eyes met his. "You may be right," she answered, somewhat stiffly.

Derek lowered his gaze to his toes, far down the bed. What had he meant? What had she meant? If he'd been home, she wouldn't have been interested in taking Spanish lessons from Ramon? If he'd been there to bid on her story, then the two of them would have been up front, gazing into each other's eyes, laughing together?

Should he have sent someone else into the flooded areas? Was he neglecting his wife? He had to remind himself she hadn't been reared as he was. He took for granted his position in society. Adella had feared she wouldn't be accepted. She would consider it important for her to be accepted by Keitha's Spanish nobleman relative.

"I'm sorry if I have neglected you. Let's take a trip. We'll go anywhere you'd like to go."

"Anywhere?" she asked, turning her head slowly to look at him over her shoulder.

He wanted to see a light in her eyes. "If at all possible," he promised.

The light did come into her eyes when she said, "Let's go to Spain."

Chapter 12

I married Derek for his money. Why can't I love him for it? Adella asked herself as she stood on the veranda, her white robe flowing softly behind her, teased by the early-morning South Carolina breeze. Her gaze, as dark as her sable brown hair reaching to her shoulders, drifted beyond the marina to the vast Atlantic Ocean, gray in the morning light with a hint of silver lining the horizon.

Her glance fell to the sidewalk. How true it was that she could almost reach out and touch a passerby. How would it feel to own a villa on a mountain, with the countryside and the city spread out below as far as the eye could see? What an exhilaration that must be for Ramon.

Ramon. Why must her thoughts go constantly to him? But she knew. Deep inside, she knew. It was not the man himself, nor his extraordinary looks. It was what he represented—an entire world of new and exciting adventures.

Her thoughts vacillated between Ramon and Derek. She couldn't blame her dissatisfaction on the appearance of Ramon in the area. She'd begun to feel it long ago, and then more strongly from the moment Derek mentioned having another child. Now that Ramon had appeared, her discontent grew daily.

It didn't help that she could finally answer her mind's question about why she could not, must not, love Derek without reservation, unconditionally. Those words brought fear to her heart. Love meant abandoning her desire for control. It meant trusting a man with everything she was. It meant giving up her freedom. It meant relying on someone other than Adella Goodson to get her through life. She could not trust God that way, and if she couldn't place herself in God's hands, how could she ever totally rely on a man, no matter how good and caring he was?

Last night, things had gone from bad to worse. Derek had never denied her anything she wanted. But he had refused to take her to Spain. Then he began talking about having another child again. That always brought to mind the scene of her having to try and act like a mother to her younger sisters when she had been only a child herself. She knew her circumstances were entirely different now, but the difficulty of that experience still resided in her heart.

She didn't want anything to take away from the time and attention she gave to Angel.

"Mommy!" came an exuberant cry, breaking Adella's reverie.

Adella turned. Angel ran to her, tiny toes visible beneath her long gown, rubbing her sleepy eyes while Mandy looked on with a big smile on her velvety brown face.

Adella picked up Angel and hugged her tightly. But Angel was more interested in wanting to catch a bird that twittered from a nearby oak draped with Spanish moss.

Laughing, Adella set Angel's bare feet on the banister that enveloped three sides of the palatial mansion and held on around her little darling's midsection. Her smile was for the wonderful warmth of her daughter, but a sadness invaded her that she hoped the child did not detect.

If nothing changed between her and Derek, could she take this child from her father? The thought startled Adella, and she hugged her daughter more closely. When she'd married Derek, she'd intended to stay married for the rest of her life. Now, she wondered, had she set her goals too low? Or was it just that Derek's goals were different from hers? He was content with home and family and being actively involved in mission work. She liked those things too, but she'd always wanted to be a part of the larger picture of life, more into society, seeing the world, having new and different adventures.

She laughed deliciously, picturing herself gliding over the water, not in a sloop, but in a speedboat racer. Just the thought of it was exhilarating. Derek should not be so narrow-minded as to prevent her from enjoying life. Why couldn't he do his thing and let her do hers? Actually, this should not be a situation of his "letting" her do anything at all. He was his own person. She was her own person. She would make her own decisions.

~

Derek had resisted the urge to lay down ultimatums to Adella last night. But he'd made it perfectly clear that he didn't connect with Ramon Bartoli and had no intention of visiting him in Spain, and he'd agreed with her accusation that he was jealous.

"Yes," he'd said. "I'm jealous. I could come up with a few other adjectives about coming home from a mission trip and discovering that my daughter is speaking Spanish and that my wife has become friends with some Spanish prince or something and wants to go to Spain."

After that, when he'd said they should forget about Bartoli, concentrate on their own lives, and consider having another child, she'd shrugged away from any attempt he made to discuss it rationally or to touch her.

He'd spent a restless night, slept in that morning, and then gone in to work after ten o'clock. To his chagrin, the discussion there centered around Ramon Bartoli as well.

"One of his crew picked up the part for that mega-yacht first thing this morning," Jerry said. "Paid in cash. And that's an expensive part."

"A person doesn't normally carry around that much cash," Derek said. *Unless he's with the Mafia or a drug pusher* came an errant thought. Whenever he and Adella traveled abroad, he had certified checks and credit cards that would be acceptable in the countries they visited. "Just to be on the safe side, you'd better check it out, Jerry."

Jerry came back all smiles. "Checked out. He even chartered the yacht from his own line of International Yachts owned by Ramon Bartoli."

Derek knew that no one would have said anything if Bartoli had simply cruised out on one of the yachts from his own fleet. However, Bartoli had done the ethical thing—chartered the yacht as if he were a paying customer. That's what Derek did when he needed a part for his boat. He bought it from his own company, paid the workers to install it, and it was all a matter of record.

He told himself to put his jealousy behind him and concentrate on his family. Adella said Bartoli would be returning to Spain after the Charleston speedboat regatta coming up soon.

But he resented it that evening at suppertime when Angel talked about having gone to the beach and about that nice man who helped her and Mommy build a sand castle. Derek had no doubt who that "nice man" was. Then, Angel went on to say, she and her mommy had gone on the biggest boat she had ever seen. It was even bigger than a dinosaur.

"That sounds exciting, Honey," Derek said in a tone that he tried to keep under control, while Adella pretended nothing was out of the ordinary. One glance at Mandy showed disapproving eyes and a firm set of lips as if she didn't like what she was hearing.

"You did that this morning?" he asked lightly, feeling like his supper was coming up into his chest.

"No," Angel said, "it was another day." She sighed. "I went to school this day."

Derek smiled, telling himself that Adella had obviously come around to his way of thinking and stayed away from Bartoli. He encouraged Angel to tell him about her day at school and she exuberantly complied. He forced his thoughts away from anything unpleasant and concentrated them on his family, where they belonged.

Very soon, everything would get back to normal.

The following afternoon when he came home from work, Derek's heart swelled with joy at the sight. Walking into the playroom where he heard cheerful voices, he saw Adella on her knees beside Angel, who was drawing pictures on a chalkboard easel. There were the two people dearest to him in the world, all of them behaving like a happy family.

"Ahem," he said, standing in the doorway. Angel looked over her shoulder, squealed "Daddy," ran to him, and threw her arms around him.

"I love you, my little Angel," he said.

"I love you too," she said, then leaned back. "Come see what I drew."

Derek put her down and went over to Adella, who turned her cheek for him to kiss. She neither said nor did anything to indicate a problem, but he detected her coolness.

"And what did you do all day since you didn't have school?" he asked. Adella rose to her feet, picked up a couple books, and replaced them on a shelf.

"We worked in the garden," Angel said. Her beautiful blue eyes sparkled when she added, "I picked some flowers for you. Come see. They're on the dining-room table."

He cast Adella a grateful look, but she didn't acknowledge it. Neither did she go with them to the dining room. Later, after Angel was in bed, he couldn't resist saying, in a tone he hoped was appreciative, "You apparently didn't go to the island this morning." Of course, she would know he was really asking if she had seen Ramon that morning. There was some reason for her continued coolness toward him.

Her chin lifted. "No, I didn't. But it's not because you demanded it of me, Derek. You cannot make demands of me. I did not go walking with Ramon because he took Keitha Keane on a cruise around the islands on his yacht. It's such a fabulous craft, and he felt it the least he could do since she had so graciously introduced him to her circle of friends."

Derek regretted the feeling he had, the turn of the conversation, but how could he just sit back and do nothing, say nothing? "Did Keitha call and tell you that?" he asked bitingly.

Her chin lifted farther. "No."

Derek nodded. That left only one person. "Then how did you know?"

"He called me," she said blandly.

Derek began to see red. "I don't want him calling here."

Her mouth flew open. "I can't believe you said that."

"Well, I said it," he blared. "And I meant it."

"Are you saying I can't have friends that aren't yours?" she asked icily.

"Not men friends," he said. "I have no women friends that I run around with. You would not stand for that, Adella, and you know it."

"I'm not running around with him," Adella defended herself. "And besides, you spend more time with strangers than I ever have with Ramon."

"That's my Christian duty, Adella. You know that."

"But it's not my Christian duty to befriend a lonely person?"

Derek heard her words. They sounded right. There was nothing wrong with befriending a needy person, male or female, stranger or friend. But he knew how his wife could be blinded by money. He knew that's what had attracted her to him in the first place. He'd thought she'd learn to love him with the same kind of passion he felt for her. Facing facts, he knew that hadn't happened. When he'd seen the love light in her eyes it was during a trip to some exotic place, it was looking at a piece of jewelry he gave her, it was trying on a new dress and expressing her gratitude for what his money could buy.

How long—how long could he live with this ache in his heart?

Feeling miserable, he bent his head.

"This marriage isn't working," she mumbled.

Derek's head came up, and he stared at her. He'd known it was coming. He thought he was prepared.

He wasn't.

He closed his eyes against the words, against the feeling of having some giant hand take hold of his heart and squeeze the life out of it.

"Have you nothing to say?" she reproached. "Are you praying? You care more about God than you do about me anyway."

"I love you, Adella," he said desperately.

She apparently didn't want to hear that. She stated flatly, "You can buy yourself another woman."

"As I did you?" he snapped back, his hurt sounding like anger.

"Yes," she admitted. "I wanted security, Derek."

"I know that," he said, looking her full in the face. "And I understood the reasons why. I gave it to you. But it hasn't made you happy. It hasn't made you love me."

Her face looked almost as pained as he felt. "I have been happy, Derek. You've given me so much. We share a daughter. But. . ."

"But," he said, standing, "I can't give you as much as Ramon can? Adella Goodson is sold to the highest bidder? Is that it?"

"How dare you!" She stood to face him.

Adella felt her head spin and leaned against a nearby chair. The fight seemed to go out of her. But she couldn't let him make such accusations. "Ramon and I have done nothing wrong. I have not been unfaithful."

She watched the spirit go out of him, and his lips turned into a sad smile. "I don't doubt that, Adella. You're more decent than you think. But for now, you're my wife. I expect you to act like it. I will not sit by while the two of you flaunt your so-called friendship for all the world to see. And I don't want my daughter around him either. Is that clear?"

She'd never heard him use such an ominous tone with her. She hadn't intended it to come to this. But Derek's words were confirming that the marriage wasn't working. Then, making her feel guiltier, tears came into his eyes. "You don't need to fight me, Adella. I can't hold you against your will. But I do love you and want you here. I need you. Angel needs you."

Those words struck her like a slap in the face, and she stiffened, then drew back. She spoke slowly. "Angel. . .has me."

He shook his head. "Not if you leave me for Ramon."

"You're a hypocrite, Derek. You say you won't force me to stay. Yet you threaten me with my own child!"

"It's not because you've found another man, Adella. It's because you're not the best parent for her."

"How can you say that? I love her more than anything. More than anyone. You know I wouldn't do anything to hurt her."

"You do the worst thing, Adella," he said sadly.

"Worst? Oh, Derek, isn't it worse for a child to grow up in a loveless home?" She regretted the anguish she was putting them both through. But this had been building for a long time. It had to come out into the open.

"Perhaps, if you call our home a loveless one," he said. "But that's not what I'm talking about. I'm talking about something deeper, more important. Even though you claim an allegiance to God—"

"Oh, Derek," she interrupted. "Only a fool wouldn't believe in God. Of course I believe in Him."

"But you don't have a vital relationship with Jesus Christ, Adella. You don't trust Him in your daily life. That is something I will instill in my daughter— with or without you."

She couldn't believe what he was implying. Derek had always been kind and good and generous. No way, would he— "You'd try to take her from me?"

He did not raise his voice, and he did not take his gaze from her. He spoke with quiet certainty. "Not just try, Adella. I would accomplish it."

Chapter 13

I have a headache," Adella complained the next morning.

"Very well," Derek said, throwing off the covers and sitting on the side of the bed, feeling around with his feet for his slippers. "I'll get Angel to school. You can pick her up at noon."

Adella turned away from him onto her side—the way she'd gone to sleep after tossing and turning for half the night. She thought he hadn't moved at all but had kept to his side of the bed. She had told him to sleep in a guest room, and he'd retorted, "I most certainly will not. And neither will you. We're husband and wife, and we will sleep in the same bed and set the right example for our little girl. Understood?"

Adella hadn't replied. In fact, she hadn't said another word to him. But she'd tossed a pillow between them, turned on her side away from him, and felt the hot tears soak her pillow. After he turned out the light, he said, "Adella, I love you."

She hadn't answered. It was like she was living with a stranger. He wanted her to be something she had never been and could never be. This is not what her life was to be about. Love was not the answer to anything.

She respected Derek. She liked the fact that he was fighting for her. She hadn't really planned to leave him. She hadn't wanted things to go that far. Had she forced Derek to say the things he said, talk about her leaving him and his taking Angel? He couldn't. He wouldn't. Did he think by threatening to take Angel he would be able to force her to deal with the problems she had with trusting God, with trusting him?

Adella sighed. It wasn't that easy. The only way she would be able to trust God would be for God to show her in a very personal way that she could trust Him. If God did care about the hairs on her head, He would have to find a way to let her see that.

~

Once Adella was certain Derek had left with Angel, she got up, got dressed, and drove to the island where Ramon was already on the beach. After they greeted each other, she told him that Derek didn't think it wise for the two of them to see so much of each other. It could cause talk.

Ramon stopped and turned to her. "Oh, my dear, sweet Adella," he said,

204

grasping her hands in his and letting go quickly. "I am so sorry. I try to be a gentleman. But your loveliness, your friendship, your filling the empty space in my heart at this difficult time made me lose my senses. Please pardon me."

"We're friends, Ramon," she said softly. But from the way he looked into her eyes, Adella knew he wanted to be more than friends. And she could not keep from her mind the image of a Spanish villa high above the lights of a city and stars so close you could almost reach up and touch them.

Ramon reached for her to draw her into his arms, but she pulled away. "No, we mustn't," she insisted.

"Then it is to be farewell, after all," he sighed, shaking his head in regret. "Could we not, Adella, go out on the water one last time before I leave you? Please give me one last boat ride to remember you by."

Adella found it hard to tear her eyes away from his pleading face. She could not go now, but what if she and Angel took Ramon on their own boat after Angel got out from preschool? Then she and Ramon would not really be alone, and because it was her boat, she'd be in better control of the situation. She paused and then looked up at him. "Would you like to join Angel and me on our boat this afternoon?" she asked.

The light that appeared in his eyes revealed all sorts of possibilities. The kind that she hadn't seen in her husband's eyes for a long time. The kind that made her wonder about the wisdom of spending more time with this man, even with her daughter present.

~

When Adella got home, the house was empty. Mandy had apparently gone grocery shopping, so Adella left her a note, explaining that she and Angel would be taking Ramon on a short farewell cruise that afternoon. Then she took bread, lunch meat, tomatoes, and a few items she knew weren't on the Goodson boat so that they would have an enjoyable lunch.

She picked up Angel, who was excited about their going out on the boat. She didn't expect them to be gone more than a couple of hours at the most.

Ramon was waiting when she and Angel arrived. He too, was carrying a bag, and the look in his eyes made her once again feel nervous about whether they should be taking this trip.

"You do know how to operate the boat?" she questioned.

"Oh, yes," he replied. "The controls are automatic. Although my crew operates my yacht, I am familiar with all the controls there too. I do not think one's safety should be left entirely to one's crew."

She liked his answer. She welcomed the coolness of the wind that seemed to wipe away the heat from her face and clear some of the confusion and frustration from her mind.

As soon as they were on the boat, Ramon handed Angel the bag he was carrying. "For you," he said.

She pulled out a stuffed dog. He knelt in front of her. "Here, let me show you." He wound the key, then set the dog down to travel, bark, and turn in circles.

Delighted, Angel laughed and clapped her hands.

"There's something else in the bag," Ramon said.

The little girl reached in and pulled out several coloring books and crayons.

"You can get us started, Ramon," Adella said. "Angel and I will go down to the master cabin so she can play with the dog and color." She looked over at Ramon and lifted her bag. "I'll make us all some lunch."

She felt the warmth of his smile set in such a handsome face. She appreciated his thoughtfulness toward Angel. He obviously had a good heart.

Soon, she had Angel safely settled in the cabin, feeling a sense of relief that the boat was moving out into the water, away from the island. She prepared lunch, while having to go to the doorway every few seconds when Angel called, "Mommy, look at the doggie." Before long, she was calling, "Mommy, come look at Barky."

"Oh, you've named him?" Adella asked.

Angel nodded. "He barks, so I named him Barky."

"That's a good name for him. Hey, that's a fine tail you're trying to catch there, Barky." They laughed together at the little puppy's antics.

Soon, Adella put Angel's lunch in front of her. "Eat your lunch, Honey. Then you can play with the dog or color. I'll be back down in just a little while. If you need anything, all you need to do is come up the steps or call for me."

"Yes, Mommy," Angel said, already turning the pages of the coloring books to find a picture she wanted to color.

When Adella returned to the flybridge with lunch for her and Ramon, he had sailed away from the South Carolina Sea Islands and was out into the Atlantic Intracoastal Waterway. The wind had picked up considerably, catching the sails and sweeping them along at a good cruising speed. Adella didn't like the looks of the darkening sky, but Ramon knew what he was doing. After all, he had the mega-yacht and said he knew how to take over from his captain and steer it if he wished, for the fun of it.

And he was a speedboat racer. He would certainly know how to handle this boat in a little wind. They ate their sandwiches and washed them down with the canned soda. A sudden gust caught Adella's paper napkin, and she barely managed to grab it back. The wind seemed to rock the boat. The water was definitely more choppy than when they'd left. Surely they were still in the waterway.

"That wind's getting strong," she said, trying to sound casual. "I thought I felt a drop of rain. Did you get a weather report before we left?"

"No, I didn't think about it," he said.

"Neither did I," Adella said, realizing she'd never had to worry about it. Derek was very safety conscious, and he always handled such details.

"You're right, it's starting to rain," he said, and she thought there was a trace of worry in his expression. "The wind is working against us now. Let's take the sails down and go back."

"I'm not the greatest of sailors," she said, with a small laugh. But she and Derek had worked together well, when she had followed his careful instructions.

"Sails are not my forte either," Ramon admitted. "But we have to do it." The wind was beginning to play havoc with the sails and the water. The boat was rocking. They began to work with the sails. Ramon was strong, but he didn't know as much as she about taking down the sails.

"Mommy," Adella heard.

"It's okay, Baby," she yelled back. "Go back down and keep the door closed. We're just taking down the sails."

The water was no longer just choppy. The waves were now growing higher moment by moment. But it was nothing to fear. She'd been in choppy waters on a smaller boat than this when she'd been on the shrimp boat with her dad. He'd known how to handle the boat. She'd been with Derek on occasions when the boat leaned from one side to the other and they had laughingly worked with the sails and he had assured her the waves hadn't been big enough to capsize the boat. She had believed him.

Now, however, things were growing worse by the moment. The dark clouds hung above them, and the rain began to pound. Finally, they got the sails in place, but they got drenched in the process.

"I need to get down to the pilothouse," Ramon said, out of breath. "Don't worry. We'll be out of this soon."

Another quick glance at the sky revealed pouring rain from boiling clouds. No islands, no land was in sight at all, not even a buoy—only an angry sea.

Adella hurried down below with Ramon right behind her. He went into the pilothouse. Angel was crouched in a corner of the L-shaped couch in the salon, holding the stuffed dog close to her chest. Adella rushed to her and put her arms around her. "It's just wind and rain, Darlin'. We're headed back toward home now." She smiled and her little girl looked up at her, with her concerned eyes now turning to trust.

"Let's put our life jackets on. The boat's rocking a little." She put Angel's on, then her own. The engine was running, but the boat felt like it was moving from side to side instead of forward. Surely they'd be out of it soon. Or at least back on land. Ramon would know how to read the instruments.

She realized that he didn't have on a life jacket. "Stay right here," she instructed Angel. "I'll take Ramon a life jacket and be right back."

"Stay with me, Mommy," Angel pleaded.

Adella knew she was scared. "We want him to be safe, don't we?"

Angel nodded.

"Okay, you take good care of Barky and tell him to be brave. We'll be out of this storm and back home in no time."

Angel nodded and pressed herself back into the corner. "I'll pray to Jesus," Adella heard as she headed out of the room.

She hurried into the pilothouse with a life jacket. Ramon glanced at her. "I can't see a thing," he said. The wipers were flapping furiously, but the driving rain and the darkened sky obscured visibility.

"Did you call for help?" Adella asked.

"I don't think I got through," he said.

Adella immediately went to the controls. She pushed the VHF/DSC radio button that would transmit to the Coast Guard their location and identification number. She then stared at Ramon. "Don't you have one of these on your yacht?" she asked, surprised that he wouldn't have the latest equipment and know how to operate the emergency equipment, consisting of a single button, if nothing else.

"This is no time for discussion," he said curtly. "I'm just trying to get us out of this."

She looked out and could see only a few feet ahead. He was steering into the waves as best he could with the water churning from all directions. As if knowing what she was thinking, he glanced at her momentarily. "I know we're near the islands. I'm moving slowly because I can't see a buoy until I'm almost on one. But I'll get us back safely."

"Mommy," she heard.

"I have to go to Angel. Do you need me to come back and help?"

"No," he said. "I just need to be able to see where I'm going."

Adella had to hold onto anything she could grab to stabilize herself as she worked her way to the steps. The boat rocked precariously, worse than she'd ever felt on any craft before. She remembered a time when they were caught in a squall on her daddy's shrimp boat when she was a little girl. "I'll just head this thing into the wave, just meet it head on, and it doesn't stand a chance. Now watch me," he'd said.

She had watched as the huge wave came toward them. He steered the shrimp boat right into it and split it in two, leaving the two of them laughing, as they conquered the sea. Until now, she'd forgotten that she'd had fun with her dad on many occasions. When the two of them had been out in that boat, it was like he owned the sea and the boat and was master of all he surveyed.

When she'd been out with Derek, it was like that too. The two of them had conquered the waves, and nothing could touch them. Now, however, she was fearful. Ramon should have known about the radio button. He should have been more adept with the sails.

Coming to the salon, she saw Angel was facing the corner, holding onto the padding of the couch while her little body swayed with the movement of the boat. Adella went right to her and enfolded her in her arms. Angel began to sob.

Adella picked her up and carefully made her way into the master suite and put her on the queen-sized bed. She placed pillows around her and lay down beside her. Suddenly, in addition to the violent sound of the storm, she heard a scraping sound. Then she felt a strange sensation, reminding her of how she felt when a plane landed, going forward very fast while seeming to press her against the back of the seat. She felt it now, and then it stopped with a jolt. By this time, Adella was shielding Angel with her body, trying to keep them both on the bed, having no idea what had happened. Then she heard the engine revving, the angry wind howling and rocking the boat. Then the engine quit. The lights went out, plunging them into total darkness.

Chapter 14

Adella couldn't keep a spontaneous scream from escaping her throat. Angel began to wail, "Mommy, Mommy."

She feared she knew what had happened. "I need to get the flashlight, Honey, so we can have some light."

"I need to go too," Angel insisted. With Angel holding on tightly, Adella struggled off the bed and felt around for the compartment where the flashlight was kept. She switched it on and returned to the bed with Angel.

Ramon came to the door and confirmed what she suspected. "We've apparently run aground," he reported.

"The radio should have switched to battery," Adella told him. "Did you signal for help again?"

"I pushed that button several times," he said.

"Well, good," she said, trying to say what might calm her child. "Then the Coast Guard should be here any time to help us. Ramon, you'd better check to see if everything's all right. That there's no door or porthole open."

"You want to give me your flashlight?" he asked.

"There's one right beside the wheel in the pilothouse," Adella said, irritated as well as scared of the way the boat was being battered by the storm and the effect all of this was having on her little girl. Had he not thought to look for something as basic as a flashlight? Biting back her frustration, she asked, "Can you find your way back in there?"

"I think so," he said.

He seemed hesitant, and Adella wondered if he even knew what kind of damage to look for on the boat or if he was simply afraid of what he might find.

She tried to make excuses. But in her heart, she knew she was the one who should have made sure he knew about the weather, the emergency equipment, the safety features. After all, the safety of two adults was not the primary point here, but the safety of a helpless little four-year-old girl. A girl whose safety was Adella's responsibility.

Adella kept the flashlight on and propped herself and Angel up against pillows, trying to be as calm as possible. "Just pretend we're in a big cradle and. . ." She hesitated. She didn't want to say a giant was rocking them. That might frighten Angel even more. "And God is rocking us. He knows how to take care of us. And we're stuck on land," she said, hoping she was right. A grounding on land was better than being stuck on some sunken craft that could do irreparable damage to the hull. Holding Angel, she swayed with the boat, as if she, rather than the wind and waves, were rocking it.

"Do you remember that song 'Rock-A-Bye-Baby'?" she asked.

Angel shrugged against her.

Adella sang softly, about the baby being rocked in the treetop. She did the contemporary version where baby falls safely asleep. But she remembered Mandy telling her there had been another version that wasn't very comforting to a child. "When the bough breaks, the baby will fall. And down will come baby, cradle and all."

Oh, God. Don't let my baby fall. Don't let my baby go down.

Just as she thought the words, the boat began rocking more violently. It had apparently come loose from whatever had held it. If they had been on a reef, they were no longer. The rocking became more intense. It was all she could do to keep herself and Angel on the bed. The wind howled. The rain pounded. The elements were trying to push the boat over.

She stopped singing. She felt Angel trying to become part of her own flesh as the child clung more tightly. Adella tried to hold her with one hand and hold onto the flashlight with the other.

Light flashed at the doorway, and Ramon appeared. "There's a rip in the hull," he said. "Water's coming in. Slowly, but—"

He didn't need to say more. He wouldn't be able to estimate the extent of the damage. A steel hull couldn't withstand even a tiny hole with water coming in. Or the hole might be above the steel. It didn't matter what or how. She wished she had not seen the movie about the unsinkable *Titanic*.

If the Coast Guard couldn't get to them in time, Adella could see only two options: Either sink or have the storm rip the boat apart piece by piece. "We'd better consider the dinghy," she said to Ramon, now sitting at the bottom of the bed, holding on for dear life.

Before she knew what was happening, Ramon had climbed the steps to go topside. "I'll try and see if they're coming," he said, and before Adella could scream, "No, don't open the door," he did. A flood of water rushed down the steps like a waterfall, covering the floor. Rain blew in, dousing Ramon and spattering her and Angel. He was clinging desperately to the railing, trying to keep from being washed or blown back down. A horrible splintering sounded, and Adella knew that would be the door being ripped from its hinges.

They had no choice but to go for the dinghy. Water was coming in through the hole in the hull. Without power, the pumps couldn't get it out. The boat was tipping over on one side, then the other, and waves washed up over the deck and poured down the steps. The boat would sink. Derek's boat! The boat he'd loved. The boat they'd courted in. The boat he'd said was hers as much as his.

The boat?

No, her only thought must be for her child. Derek's daughter.

By this time, Angel was grabbing for her, reaching for her, not wanting to move away an inch and crying almost uncontrollably. "Mommy, Mommy. I wanna go home. I want Daddy. Please."

Adella wasn't sure what to do. Try and get to the dinghy? Stay where they were and hope the Coast Guard found them before the boat sank? She didn't even know if the distress signal had gotten through to them. And where was Ramon?

She had no idea how to console Angel, who clearly knew they were in trouble. "Just pray, Darlin'. Just pray," Adella said.

"I did," Angel moaned and began to wail louder, her little mouth open, her eyes red, and her cheeks soaked.

"Angel," she spoke sternly. "You have to do what I tell you. Put your legs around my waist and hold on. Keep your head on my chest so I can see over you. And don't let go. Can you do that?"

"I want Barky and my coloring books and—"

"We'll replace them. You have to do as I say now."

The girl began to wail louder.

"Angel, Honey," Adella said, desperate to distract her daughter from the terror that surrounded them, "why don't you sing for Mommy?"

Angel stopped crying long enough to ask, "What do you want me to sing?"

"I don't know," Adella said, running her mind over the songs that she knew Angel had memorized. "How about 'Jesus Loves Me.'"

Angel seemed satisfied with the choice, and as she began singing, Adella could feel her daughter relax. It wasn't easy, with the boat rocking wildly, to move through the room, but they managed, and Adella held the flashlight and began to slowly splash through the flooded floor and make her way toward the salon where even more water and rain were coming down the open doorway. Where was Ramon? Was he at the dingy with it ready, waiting?

Then she saw the light. She shone her light that way and the beam fell upon his face. She felt her rocking this time was not the sea. It was the look in his eyes before his hand came up to shield them from the bright light. She knew he was as frightened as she.

Now would be an ideal time for Derek to be there, saying something comforting like God was with them and would take care of them. But Derek

212

wasn't here. And she didn't have the kind of faith he had.

Ramon came to them. "Hold her," he said. "My flashlight will give enough light. I'll try and shield the two of you the best I can."

"Hold tight now, Baby," Adella said as she climbed the steps with Angel's head buried against her chest and hanging on around her neck. She sat in the water and scooted toward the dinghy with Ramon right beside them, hanging onto anything he could find.

Suddenly, a strong gust of wind and a huge wave tipped the boat until it seemed it would capsize completely. Adella, Angel, and Ramon were pressed up against the bridge, then the boat was thrown back onto the raging sea and pushed toward the other side so quickly and so violently, Adella had nothing to hold onto but flung her arms out to catch hold of the railing around the bridge. Angel was jerked away from her, just as Adella was sure she would go over the side. But the boat righted momentarily, long enough for Angel to be rolling and twisting and screaming over the deck, headed for the dinghy. Ramon was grabbing for her, unsuccessfully, and Adella was screaming at the top of her lungs and trying to get to her.

Ramon caught Angel's hand about the same time that she was thrown up against the dinghy. Even with the roar of the storm, Adella heard the sound as her daughter's head hit and saw the terror in her baby's eyes before they rolled back and went limp.

"Oh, God, let her be all right. Oh, please." They managed to get her into the dinghy. Since there was no power, they had to release the craft manually. Soon they were floating free, while the boat, low in the water, was being tossed to and fro at the will of the wind and waves.

Adella did the best she could to discover how badly Angel was hurt, while Ramon was trying to empty out the water as each wave splashed over the side. The storm seemed to have abated some. But between the murky gray and the falling rain, Adella couldn't tell the extent of Angel's wound, only that a knot had formed on top of her head and that the rain mingled with her blood and ran down her face, across Adella's hand, down her legs, and into the bottom of the dinghy.

Her blood is on my hands, came to Adella's mind. *Have I killed my own child?* No, no, she mustn't think that. Angel would be all right. She had to be.

Adella looked out at the scene of a murky gray sea meeting a gray sky. She couldn't tell where the one ended and the other began. The movement of the dinghy with the sea reminded Adella of having watched a balloon, filled with helium, drift with the wind, high and low, until it disappeared from view.

Is that what they would do? Be tossed and turned, one with the sea, until they disappeared—forever?

The dinghy had a motor, but they had no idea which direction pointed toward land.

Oh, God. What can I do?

God?

She hadn't really talked to God since she was a child and her mother had died. Oh, she had bowed her head in church. She had bowed it at the table when Derek or Mandy said the blessing. And she didn't mind that people prayed. But she'd had nothing in particular to pray for. She didn't believe God answered prayers about life on earth, so why bother praying? Instead, she'd relied on herself for her well-being and the safety of her loved ones.

But what should she do now? Angel, for whom she'd be willing to die, was injured, and there was nothing Adella could do for her. She had no control over where the dinghy was going, no control over whether the Coast Guard would arrive, no control over whether her baby would live. She hadn't prayed in years. Would it be right to pray now?

She could almost hear Mandy singing, "Where could I go? Oh, where could I go but to the Lord?"

If Mandy were with them, she'd feel better. Mandy had been her strength since she was a child. And come to think of it, Mandy still trusted God, even though her life had not been any easier than Adella's—in fact, a case could easily be made that Mandy's life had carried much more heartache. Then she remembered another song that Mandy had sung. Something about "in times like these, you need an anchor." Something about the anchor holding onto the solid rock. And the rock was Jesus.

She'd heard that song sung at church when she was just a child. But in the ensuing years, she'd intentionally closed herself off from such things. These songs reminded her of the pain of her childhood, and she'd tried to anesthetize that pain with things, thrill, excitement, a hectic schedule.

Ever honest with herself, Adella knew that if she were to turn to God now, she would have to have the courage to face her pain and deal with it. No more hiding. No more pretending. She looked at her unconscious daughter and knew that some things were more important than pride.

Taking a deep breath, she prayed silently. *"Lord, I know we can't make deals with You. But I want You to know that nothing I possess is worth the life of my daughter."* Tears mixed with the rain that soaked her face. *"Do You know,"* Adella asked with a heart-wrenching cry, *"can You understand what it is like to stand by and watch Your only child in great danger? Likely to die?"*

I stood by as My Son died for you.

"I know that. But how does that change the pain we go through every day on

Earth? Angel is hurt. Mandy's first husband was no good for her. And. . .and my mother died."

I never said that following Me would protect you from pain. As long as you live in a world where there is sin, you will experience pain. But you will not grieve as those who have no hope.

"So we have the promise of heaven. That's in the future. How does faith in You make a difference during this life?"

Lo, I am with you always, even unto the end of the world. Nothing can separate you from My love. Even when you run from Me, My love for you continues.

Adella stroked Angel's face and thought about God's love. She knew the Bible said that God's love for her was greater than a mother's love for her child. And nothing Angel could do would make Adella stop loving her. She thought of Mandy and how the older woman's love had provided a shelter for her after her mother died and so many times later as an adult. She thought of Derek and the love he had poured over her even when he couldn't help but sense that her love for him was not the same. Had God been showing her His love through these people? Had she been like a stubborn child, refusing to see God's love surrounding her because she was hurt and angry? She had deliberately cut herself off from her family and other people who offered her love. And she knew there were times when she had deliberately ignored God's still, small voice speaking to her in the quiet of her heart. Was she afraid of the power of God's love? Was she afraid of losing control?

Adella shook her head. Control had always been an illusion anyway. Look at the situation she was in right now. If she had so much control over her life, she and Angel wouldn't be bobbing in a dinghy in the middle of a storm without a clue of where to go. Come to think of it, Angel had taught her so much about love. She turned her thoughts to prayer.

Lord, I've been afraid of Your love because I thought love would bring pain. But when I think of all the joy I've experienced during the four years I've shared with Angel, I wouldn't trade it for anything—even being able to remove the anguish I feel now about how bad her injuries may be. I'm sorry I was so stubborn. I'm sorry I tried to make money and things and my own abilities take the place of my need for You. Please forgive me.

The storm had lessened. That's why it was such a surprise. She wasn't prepared for it. A huge wave caught the dinghy and lifted it high in the air. Adella screamed, trying to hold onto Angel. Ramon grabbed for the child and held, while holding the ropes. Adella felt herself being catapulted through the air. Then she was floundering in the sea, trying to reach the dinghy. She couldn't. It was being swept away from her. But Angel was still there, with Ramon. He was yelling for her, but she could do nothing. She was helpless.

With her last remembered breath, she said, "Lord, I'm sorry I didn't reach out to You with my pain and trust You to heal my shattered heart."

In that watery grave, she thought she heard Mandy singing, and she joined in with her last bit of strength. "All to Jesus I surrender, I surrender all."

Suddenly she felt herself growing numb from the cold water. Her eyes closed as she tasted salty water in her mouth.

Chapter 15

Derek stood at a window in the Yacht Club, looking out to sea. He was furious with his wife for going out on the boat with Ramon Bartoli. Incensed with her for taking their daughter. And he was frantic with worry. He saw no sign of the boat—no sign of the Coast Guard.

The heavy dark clouds had blown farther away and had seemed to disappear into a choppy sea. Lighter clouds that had sprinkled the area with nothing more than a light rain were disappearing. Dusk was settling in. If they weren't found while there was still some light, how could they be found when day turned to night?

It had been close to three that afternoon when Mandy had called the supply store to see if he was there and said she would be right there. He knew then that something was wrong, but he never could have imagined what she felt was so terrible that she couldn't tell him on the telephone.

Someone had called the house to say that a distress call had come in from the boat registered to him. Mandy told him Adella had left a note saying that she had taken Angel and Ramon sailing on what was intended to be a two-hour farewell lunch/cruise. "They wouldn't tell me what the problem was," she added, referring to the phone call. "Maybe it's nothing serious."

"I'll call," he said. That's when it was revealed to him that the Coast Guard didn't know the problem. Only that the distress call came in several times. That latest equipment on Derek's boat enabled the Coast Guard to pinpoint the boat's exact location. But there had been a sudden squall, a terrible storm in that vicinity.

"We can wait at the Yacht Club," Derek told Mandy, and they drove out there. From the club he called his parents, who said they would fly up as soon as possible. He also reached Adella's dad, who said he would contact the other family members.

Not more than an hour later, reporters were swarming the club with cameras, flashbulbs, and questions. Derek knew that silence on his part would only lead to speculation. Nor could he say anything that might lead them to think that Ramon was only his wife's friend. "My wife, daughter, and a friend of ours went sailing and were apparently caught in an unexpected storm," Derek said. "That's all I know."

"How old is your daughter?"

"What is your friend's name?"

"Was a crew with them?"

Hating the invasion of privacy, he directed them to the Coast Guard information officer, saying he was too concerned about his family and friend's safe return to be able to casually discuss the situation.

Soon the local TV station began airing the news about Derek Goodson's wife, daughter, and family friend, a Spanish nobleman named Ramon Bartoli, who were caught in a storm out at sea and how the Coast Guard was conducting a search-and-rescue operation. Mr. Goodson was waiting at dockside. They had no details, the reporter said, but added graphic speculations about what could be happening to them. The report only added to Derek's distress. He was trying to keep faith and keep praying, but it was so difficult. He felt like his entire life was lost out on that sea somewhere.

A short while later, Keitha Keane came into the club and hurried over to Derek and Mandy, both of whom were nursing cups of black coffee. "I just heard," Keitha said, placing her hand on Derek's arm in a consoling gesture before nodding at Mandy, then pulling out a chair to sit down. "Oh, Derek, I can't believe this. Those storms can be so unpredictable. But they'll be fine. You have a good boat. Ramon is a first-class seaman. He'll take good care of them."

A wave of nausea washed over Derek. He was too upset to respond. *My wife is out there. My daughter is out there. I am the one who's supposed to be taking good care of them. But I'm sitting here, helpless.*

One look at Mandy revealed she felt as distressed as he and Keitha. Most of the time she closed her eyes, and her lips were moving in prayer while she kept her fingers tightly clasped together. He realized that no, he wasn't entirely helpless. There was always prayer. There was a power greater than any stormy sea.

"Derek, what's going on?" Clem Spelding shouted, rushing up to him, followed by Leona, who said the others would be there soon.

Derek repeated what little he knew. Just as Adella's sisters were coming up, someone called, "They found them. The Coast Guard's bringing them in."

At the same time, Derek heard sirens and jumped to his feet. Everyone looked in the same direction as two ambulances pulled up.

Two? Why not three? How badly were the two persons hurt? Or—*No!* He wouldn't let his mind go there. Just keep praying. How could he stand it? Then he saw a Coast Guard rescue boat coming. An eternity of watching passed, during which he didn't dare to breathe.

He hardly noticed when a couple members of the Coast Guard crew helped Ramon off the boat and Keitha hurried up to him. His eyes were on the two long stretchers on which the two people he loved most in the world were strapped. He hurried to them, and it seemed his heart ceased to beat when he saw the pale, lifeless-looking faces of his wife and child. Neither opened her eyes, nor spoke a word, nor appeared to even be breathing.

~

The midmorning sun was streaming through a window, shining on a small table with a pitcher of water and a glass on it when Adella slowly opened her eyes. They felt like rocks. A painful survey revealed a white room, TV high in a corner, and an empty chair. She finally realized she was lying on her side in a bed in a hospital room.

She felt like she had the flu. A vague memory flitted through her mind. Someone was bending over her, pushing on her stomach, breathing in her mouth, and later the awful vomiting, followed by stomach spasms and dry heaves. Her head had felt like a thousand hammers were pounding nails into it. And worst of all, no one would tell her anything about her little girl. She'd screamed, despite the fire in her throat. She'd fought and had to be held down. Then she felt a needle in her arm. And slowly, the word "Angel" died on her tongue, which now felt and tasted like a dirty sock.

Despite her aching body, she rolled onto her back. Just then a middle-aged woman in a white uniform stood beside her bed. "Good morning, Mrs. Goodson. I see you finally woke up," the nurse said gently.

But Adella had only one thing on her mind. "My daughter?" she asked, as the nurse began to take her vital signs.

While pumping up the blood pressure cuff, the nurse said, "Your husband is in her room in the pediatric ward. We'll let him know you're awake."

"She's all right?" Adella asked fearfully.

"I just came on duty this morning," the nurse replied, silent for a moment while watching the red arrow indicate the blood pressure. After she removed the cuff, Adella tried to prop herself up in bed and moaned at the effort. The nurse put a pillow behind her back, and Adella sank back against it.

Adella didn't ask what her vital signs were. It didn't matter. At the moment she only needed to know that her daughter was going to be all right. She was in the pediatric ward. Derek was with her. He would see that she got the best care. He was that way. He was so good.

But I'm not. Hot tears filled her eyes as she thought of all the people she'd hurt while locked in her own pain and denial.

Then Derek rushed in, looking like he hadn't slept in a week, his eyes full of worry and his hair tousled like he'd run his fingers through it instead of a comb. Angel must be in bad shape.

"Angel?" she asked immediately, her eyes questioning.

"She had a nasty cut on her head," he said, pulling a chair up close to the bed. "She has a concussion and—"

"And?" she said, sitting up straighter, seeing the pain in his eyes, hearing the distress in his voice. "I have to know."

He took her hand in his. His tone was lower when he said, "She's in a coma. But her signs are good. She has the best doctors. They keep saying she could regain consciousness at any time."

Adella nodded. She knew Derek would see to that.

"As soon as you're able," he said, "you can go up and see her. The families have been here all night. And Mandy, of course. She went home and brought clothes for you. From what I hear, you had a rough time of it out there, Adella."

Her eyes flew to his. From what he heard? Who could he have heard it from? Only one person could have told him. She didn't know what to say. Should she ask about Ramon? Was he dead or alive? She needed to say so much to Derek. But this was not the time. Hot tears flowed down her cheeks.

Derek moved away and got a box of tissues for her. He walked over to the window. Then he turned, and with the sun behind him, she couldn't see his expression. But she heard his voice, heard the weariness in it. "Ramon was examined and released. He had minor scratches, rope burns on his hands, and bruises. Other than that, he's all right. He apologized. Keitha took him back to her house."

Adella nodded, wishing the light were not on her face. Wishing Derek were not looking at her. She felt so ashamed. She had destroyed the love of the finest man in the world. He had given so much. She had only taken.

Suddenly, she could stand it no longer. "I'm so sorry," she wailed. She was sorry for what she'd done to her husband for five years. Oh, she'd given him her wifely duty with her body and the one good thing—great thing—she'd given him was their little girl. But she hadn't really done it for him. She'd given herself a little girl. Derek just happened to supply the house, the food, the hired help, the cars, the trips, the boat—

"Your boat," she managed to rasp. "It's gone."

"Boats can be replaced," he said simply.

And so can I, she thought. That would be easy. Everyone knew what a wonderful man she had. She had been blinded by her love of money and the security she thought it could bring. She thought of the slanted rays of the sunset at certain times of the year. The golden glow was beautiful, but it held danger when it blinded you to your surroundings. That's what money had done to her. And where would it ever end? If she had left Derek for Ramon, would someone richer have come along later on? How many yachts would there be? How many rich husbands would there be? None of them would have filled the void in her heart that only a relationship with God could fill.

She closed her eyes on her inner pain. She couldn't bear to see herself as she really was. And this was not the time. She had responsibilities to her child. "I need to see Angel," she said.

~

After the doctor came in and examined Adella, he said she was fine and could be released before noon. But she would not be allowed to walk to the pediatric ward. She must ride in a wheelchair. After she had a warm shower, which stung her skin but diminished the aching of her muscles, she dressed in the comfortable slacks and shirt Mandy had brought for her. She didn't bother with make-up and simply combed her hair back into a wet ponytail.

"Is that the pediatric ward?" she asked the nurse, while waiting for the wheelchair. She was holding onto the windowsill and looking out at the building across from her.

"No," the nurse answered. "That's the cancer ward—for terminally ill children."

Terminally ill children?

How many parents, how many families, must be burdened with grief and worry. How could they stand it? Watching their children die? *Oh, God. Give them strength. Give us all strength.*

That prayer had just slipped out. It surprised Adella. Strange how she had thought more about God in her difficulty than she ever had in all the years of plenty. Why couldn't she have loved Him and thanked Him for her blessings? Why did it have to come to this?

"Are you ready to go?" the nurse asked.

"Oh—I," Adella stammered. "Yes. I'm ready." For an instant, she had the strange feeling she was being asked if she were ready to leave this world, ready to go and meet her Maker. *Was she?* Then she realized the wheelchair had arrived. "Yes, I want to see my little girl."

"Angel," she whispered a few moments later and touched her baby, so pale against the white sheets and with IVs in her little arms. Both relief and guilt flooded over Adella. Her baby was alive! But she was hurt because of her own mother's foolishness.

After spending some time with Angel, telling her she loved her and praying silently for her, Adella was wheeled by Derek into the waiting room, where the families greeted her even more warmly than they ever had. Her sisters had gone back because of children and work. But her daddy, Leona, the Goodsons, and Mandy were all there for the tearful reunion.

"All of us can't stay here indefinitely without sleep," Derek said. "We need to make out a schedule of who stays and for how long. The rest of you can sleep at our house, of course."

~

When they got home around noon, Adella didn't resist when Mandy urged her to eat some chicken noodle soup. Then Derek insisted she lie down for a few hours so she would feel up to seeing Angel that evening. She didn't know in which room he slept, but he looked fresher when it was time to return to the hospital.

She didn't resist either, when he said they'd go together. They were silent on the way. At the hospital they both talked to Angel, still in the coma, reassuring her of their love and that she was going to be fine. Adella knew there were things she had to get settled in her life.

"Do you know where the chapel is?" she asked quietly.

He told her it was just down the hall. She realized he undoubtedly had been there during the previous night, praying. She did not resent it this time. She was grateful. God would hear Derek's prayers.

"I'll be back in a little while," she said.

It was a small wood-paneled room, warm and inviting. A glow of light shone from behind a large wooden cross on the wall. No one else was in the room. This was just her and God. As she slowly walked down the single aisle, she felt her unsteadiness and touched the seats for balance, making her way to the cross.

She stood in front of it and looked up. "I've been mad at You for a long time," she said. "Ever since You let my mother die. And I resented my husband for loving You. I decided to do life my own way. Well, I've just made a big mess of it."

Her sobs came then, loud, heart-wrenching, and she didn't bother to cover her face. She didn't care if she looked like death warmed over, that her nose was running. She'd run too long—too long.

"In the process of running from You and trying to cover my pain by getting more and more things, I destroyed the love of the finest man in the world. I'm no good. But I don't want to be like this. Can You change me?" She fell to her knees, covered her face, and pleaded brokenly, "Can You forgive me?"

"Yes," came the answer.

"You. . ." Her head came up, and she stared at the empty cross. "What?" she whispered.

"I said yes," a voice answered, and someone knelt beside her.

"Oh, no," she wailed and covered her face again.

"I'm saying it, Adella," Derek said. "But God always says it. If you truly want forgiveness, He gives it. But I'm saying yes too. I forgive you, although it's not necessary. I knew why you married me. I just hoped you would come to love the Lord like I do and maybe learn to love me. I failed you by trying to make you happy with things money can buy. I failed to be the kind of example of God's love that I should have been."

"Oh, no, Derek. You're—"

He put his finger over her lips. "This is confession time, Adella. I followed you here because I thought we should pray for Angel together. But I know I have things in my life I need to ask forgiveness for. I was so hurt when you wouldn't love me the way I wanted you to that I buried myself in all my charitable activities. I thought I was being faithful to God's calling, but instead I was using good works to avoid dealing with your needs and my pain. Whenever we come to Jesus in repentance, wanting to change, He cleanses us and makes us more like Him."

Adella was overwhelmed with Derek's attitude. "You said. . .you forgive me?" she asked.

"Yes," he said.

"How could you even want to be around me, after what I've done to our daughter?"

"You didn't intend to hurt her, Adella. That was an accident. It could have happened anywhere."

"Will you pray for her?" she asked.

He bowed his head and prayed for them, for their marriage, for their daughter, and for forgiveness. Adella watched him as he prayed. She was overwhelmed by his unconditional love for her. She marveled at this wonderful man who loved her. She could have basked in that priceless gift for the past years instead of seeking after things money could buy.

Money could not buy her daughter's life.

After his prayer, Derek stood. "You asked why I want to be around you," he said. "You're my wife, Adella. I meant it when I vowed, 'For better or worse, richer or poorer, sickness or health, till death do us part.' I loved you then, and I love you now. But only you can decide about your own commitment to the Lord—or to me."

Chapter 16

Derek wondered if he'd done the right thing by following Adella to the chapel. He had, as he explained, meant for them to pray together for Angel. But after he was almost to the front and overheard her plea to the Lord, he couldn't just stand there and eavesdrop. What she did after he left, he didn't know. Shortly after he returned to Angel's room, their child began to come out of her coma. She would have to stay in the hospital for several days, however, for observation.

Angel steadily improved except on one level. Whenever she slept, she had nightmares about the storm, the sea, and sinking boats. Family members continued to stay with her around the clock.

During those days, Derek observed changes in Adella. He had felt it when she'd returned from the chapel, but he saw it whenever a relative would come to sit with Angel. Adella would say she must go and talk with a family whose child had been brought in that morning.

She began to talk about the children who were terminally ill cancer patients. She wanted to do something to help. "I can at least talk to the parents and pray with them. It has meant a lot to the parents that I just stop in, talk, and pray with them." She ducked her head a moment, then confessed. "They're quite poor, Derek. I gave them some money. I wanted to be helpful, but I think I got as much pleasure out of giving as they did receiving."

Derek couldn't hold back his soft laugh. "You're wonderful," he said.

"No, I'm not," she said. "I may just keep giving to make me feel good." She grinned, then grew serious again. "I think I believed money was incompatible with a strong faith in God." She shook her head. "I don't think that now. I think it's supposed to be used to help others."

"I always got joy out of giving to you," he told her.

⌒

Angel was released within the week. She talked about the accident constantly and wanted to sleep with her mother. She continued to have nightmares. A child psychologist suggested she go out on a boat again and confront her fear so she could get over it.

Adella shuddered at that suggestion. Angel was not the only person who would be facing her fears, but she knew better than to try to keep Angel from what could be a healing experience. So on a clear, sunny day, Derek, Adella, Angel, the Goodsons, and a full crew cruised out into the waterway on Irene and Judd's yacht. Angel clung to her mother going out, but upon the return trip, she relaxed and talked about the storm rocking the boat.

"We'll buy another," Derek said later that night, while sitting on the bed where Angel slept beside her mother.

"Maybe we could start up those sunset Bible studies like you used to have," Adella suggested.

Derek's heart flooded with joy. He'd always wanted his wife to share his ministry. Now hers was growing by leaps and bounds. But there was still one subject they hadn't discussed.

A couple days later, Keitha Keane visited. When she was about to leave, she said, "By the way, Ramon says he doesn't care to race in the Charleston regatta. He's had enough of the sea for awhile. He's planning to leave for Spain in a couple of days. He asked me to tell you that he hopes you and Angel are well. He is so sorry about the accident."

"Tell him I thank him for his concern," Adella said, without a trace of regret in her voice. Then she added, "You know, Keitha, the Lord works in mysterious ways. Because of that accident, I have come to renew my personal relationship with God. Just a minute." She went to the desk and returned with a couple of tracts that outlined God's plan of salvation through Jesus Christ. "Ramon might find this a comfort to help him in his time of grief over his losses."

"Well, thank you. I'll give this to him." Keitha smiled. "And you're so right. I couldn't have gotten through my time of grief without the Lord."

After she left, Adella turned to Derek, surprised. "I know she's a good person and goes to church, but I've never heard her talk like that before."

He smiled. "Maybe some of our friends just need a little encouragement to be more active and open about their faith."

She nodded, getting a new light in her eyes.

"Oh, there's something I've been meaning to do." She walked over to the mantel and took down the antique vase. She reached in and got the half jar of sand. He followed her to the kitchen, where she tossed it into the trash can, then wiped her hands as if that were the end of that.

"There's something else I want to do too," she said. "You haven't been able to go down to the mission house much lately. I know the food and clothes must be piled up, just waiting to be put on shelves. I'm going to call and see if Sarah would like to go down and help me with it."

She looked at him with a glow about her that made his heart sing.

The next day, Angel returned to preschool and handled the experience well. That night she slept in her own room without nightmares. Derek thought it time he asked his wife out on a date.

"Will you go out with me Friday night?" he asked.

Blushing, Adella agreed.

~

Derek said it was a dressy occasion but wouldn't say where he'd take her. Adella wore a long, straight black dress and a single strand of pearls. When she came down the stairs, Derek was waiting in the foyer, wearing a tux. "You look beautiful," he said. His shoulders rose in that characteristic manner of his.

"You look rather dashing yourself," she replied, realizing anew how handsome he was. How wonderful to be courted like this by her own husband. He drove her in the Bentley to the Whitehall Plantation, where he'd made reservations. They ate veal prepared by the award-winning chef, who was also the owner of the century-old plantation. They watched the sun dip into the bay, allowing the silver moon to rise.

After dinner, Derek drove down to the dock and parked, and they got out of the car. The evening was balmy. Night fell and the stars began to wink. The moon rose, and Adella's love seemed to swell with it. *What a romantic thing to do.* Derek was making this a night to remember.

He led her onto the new boat he'd purchased. She leaned back into the curve of the sunpad like she had when wearing shorts and a tank top on the first day they had gone out together. He was unusually quiet as he steered the boat away from Beaufort. He didn't speak until they were far from shore, with only a few distant lights visible. He switched off the engine and allowed the boat to gently rock like a baby's cradle beneath a silver moon making diamonds on the water, matching those in the sky.

Then Derek came over to her and knelt on one knee. Adella caught her breath. His face was serious and his eyes filled with adoration and anticipation. He reached for her hand and planted a kiss on the back of it, then rested her hand against his cheek as if it were the dearest thing in the world to him. Adella bit on her lip and tried to hold back the moisture threatening in her eyes.

"Will you marry me, Adella, and make me the happiest man alive?"

She straightened. "A–again?" she asked.

"Yes, again," he replied. "I love you, Adella Goodson. I'd like us to start over."

"Oh, Derek. After I married you for your money, I wondered why I couldn't love you for it," she said. She saw the look begin on his face that tore at her heart. Did he fear that she still didn't love him? Didn't he understand? She knew now that she had loved him all along. She had just been afraid of loving and losing. But now that she had come so close to losing, she knew how precious it was to hold love close.

"Now, I know why," she said softly. "I could never love a person for his money. I can only love you. . .because you're you."

He rose and took her hands. She stood and, rather than waiting for him to reach for her, she fell against him, longing for his loving arms to enfold her. She couldn't wait for him to make the first move. Instead she said, "I love you, Derek," against his lips. "I love you, love you," until he stopped her speaking with his kisses.

Epilogue

Five years later

It was Judson Clement Goodson's fourth birthday. The party had ended. Sarah and Broc, with their nine-year-old daughter, had been there. Meagan had stayed to spend the night with nine-year-old Angel.

Adella picked up some stray cups and joined Mandy in the kitchen for a moment.

"You just go rest now," Mandy said. "A woman in your condition can't be on her feet too long, now."

"Yes, Ma'am," Adella said playfully and put her arms around Mandy's shoulders affectionately. "I have a good life, Mandy," she said.

Mandy nodded. "The best, Honey. The best."

Adella left the kitchen but headed for the back door, where she often stood and meditated on the important things of life. She liked this house. She and Derek had turned the Goodson House into one of the historic places that tourists came to see. They used the proceeds to help build homes for needy families.

They'd built this house near Broc and Sarah's, overlooking the Beaufort River. It was modest, but big enough for their growing family. She had wanted a place where she could look out on the water, reminding her of her life as a child and the place where she'd made the most important commitment of her life—to the Lord.

She'd learned a few important things over the years about her family too. They were the ones who knew what was important after all. And she'd come to appreciate her dad. He'd retired a couple of years ago when the arthritis in his hands got so bad. He said the old boat wasn't worth anything anymore. Adella wanted it. She kept it out back as a reminder of the simple life. In particular, the simple life of a fisherman.

She was a fisherwoman now. Not for some big catch of the day, or the season, but for the catch of a lifetime. She was casting out the bait for lost souls who were floundering around aimlessly like she had done. She had become a fisher of souls. The bait was Jesus—and the message was that they could become a part of the great, eternal kingdom of God.

With a heart full of gratitude to God and a smile on her lips, Adella went into the playroom just in time to see Judson run his remote control car right into his sister's ankle, making her scream. "Uhh," Angel growled, heading for her brother with her hands in a choking motion while Meagan stifled a giggle with her hand.

Mandy was nearby to step between sister and brother. "Now, did you mean to hurt your sister?" she asked.

Judson shook his head, his lip pouting and his head bent. He dropped the remote to the floor.

Adella walked nearer and glanced at Angel, whose momentary anger turned to compassion for the little brother she adored. "It's okay," she said. "It quit hurting."

"Let's sit down for a minute," Adella said, slowly lowering herself to the couch, which wasn't easy, her being so heavy with expected twins.

Judson watched the difficult maneuver, then sat beside her. He looked up at his mother. "Will you still love me when the babies are born?"

"If you don't run your cars into them," Angel quipped.

"Hold it," Adella said. "This calls for a family conference."

"Oh, not another lecture," Angel wailed and plopped down in a chair.

Derek sat beside Adella while Mandy moved behind them to pick up wrapping paper and discarded boxes.

"I just want to make sure you children understand something," Adella said. "It's the most important lesson I ever learned. When I made the worst mistakes of my life, I went to God with them and asked Him to forgive me. He did. Do you know why?"

Angel lifted her eyes toward the ceiling. "The Bible says He will," she said blandly, as if that were the easiest question in the world to answer.

"Yes, but there's a reason. And that's because He loves us. He loved me even at my worst time. That's how I will always feel about you. I want you to do what is right. But when you make mistakes, I want you to remember: God loves you. And I love you. . .just because you're you."

As soon as Angel went to her room and Judson got down and started playing with another toy, Adella turned to Derek. "I love you," she said, "more than words can say."

His arms came around her. She gloried in the love light shining in his eyes and the grin that dimpled his cheek. Before they kissed, he asked, "Would you repeat that, please?" She eagerly complied.

Somewhere a Rainbow

Chapter 1

Brooke Haddon, driving in her compact car along Highway 278 toward the resort island of Hilton Head, recognized the depression settling over her like the gray sky over the ocean now that the sun had set. She tried to concentrate on five-year-old Ben's enthusiasm, to be as excited as her son. But all that he found so fascinating mimicked her own feelings of seven years ago. She'd been twenty then, with a model's face and figure, and as innocent and trusting as a child. Now she felt ancient—not so much in years as in experience.

She'd spent her honeymoon in blissful naïveté on this island off the coast of South Carolina. After a little more than three months of wedded bliss, her figure began to balloon out with pregnancy and the marriage began to go downhill. Politician Bruce Haddon seemingly had everything going for him—except a happy marriage. Now Bruce was dead, Brooke was a single parent, and the only thing between her and homelessness, or dependence upon her parents, was the honeymoon cottage—a reminder of shattered hopes and dreams.

A year ago when she'd walked away from Bruce's funeral, she'd known his lover was being buried on the other side of town. She'd cried and grieved over an auto accident that took two young lives, a six-year failed marriage, a son without a father, for truth that would have to be told someday, and for all she'd lost—her livelihood and her self-esteem.

"Go slow, Mom," Ben pleaded, his dark eyes so like those of his late father's. "I want to see the alligators."

Brooke again went into her discussion of the alligators being in the lagoons and not along the main roads and the danger of getting close; then she tried to divert his attention to the trees of the island, telling him about Spanish moss hanging from live oaks, pines, magnolias, palmettos, and palms. It didn't work!

"Anyway," she said resignedly, "we can't go alligator hunting tonight. I have to get to the Realtor's office and pick up the key before dark."

Brooke had called from a rest station earlier to say she'd been delayed by road work. The Realtor promised to meet her at the office, even though this was a Saturday evening. Brooke had wanted to come earlier in the week, but the Realtor said the utilities wouldn't be hooked up before late Friday afternoon.

No unsightly signs cluttered the roadways to make the island look like a commercial playground. Slowing, Brooke peered through the trees, looking for the almost-hidden signs. With a sigh of relief, she saw a long structure with a sign reading "The Mall" on the front. She turned right and felt her stomach unknot as she saw a single car parked at the real estate office.

Ben was unbuckled and ready to hop out by the time Brooke stepped out and put her hand on the back-door handle. The poor child had been exceptionally patient on the two-day trip from Indiana. Brooke had stopped only to get food and a few hours' sleep last night at a motel.

"Mrs. Haddon?" the Realtor asked, as soon as Brooke and Ben popped through the door. She would be anxious to get out of there, Brooke was sure.

Brooke nodded. "I guess you're Jessica Lawler?" They'd talked several times on the phone. Jessica, a middle-aged woman dressed casually in slacks and a cotton blouse, gave Brooke the impression she'd made a special trip to meet her at the office. "Sorry I'm so late," Brooke apologized, brushing back a strand of blond hair that had escaped her ponytail.

"It's okay," the Realtor assured her, giving a gentle push to eyeglasses that covered friendly blue eyes set in a pleasant face. "Gave me an opportunity to catch up on some picky things I always put off and rarely get—" Her words stopped in mid-sentence as she saw Ben's adorable, smiling face and his outstretched hand. She leaned over and shook his hand.

"My name's Ben," he said, his big brown eyes, fringed with dark lashes the color of his curly black hair, charming her. By the time he was two years old, little Ben had been mimicking his father this way, realizing that it attracted and pleased other people. Brooke was all too aware that she had a big job ahead, instilling in Ben the kind of inner qualities that had been neglected while his father was alive.

"Would you like to have a seat?" Jessica asked, gesturing toward the chairs.

Brooke grimaced, touching the back of her jeans. "I've been sitting in a car for two days. If you don't mind, I'll just stand."

Jessica laughed and picked up a set of keys from the desk, holding them as if reluctant to let them go. Her smile quickly turned to concern. "The electricity and water are on, like you requested. But you won't get phone service before next week." She paused. "You know, I told you we haven't been able to rent it out for a couple of years."

"You said it was damaged by a hurricane." Brooke suddenly felt a stab of concern in the pit of her stomach. "But it is habitable?"

"Well, yes, habitable," Jessica agreed, glancing away as if she couldn't quite meet Brooke's eyes. "But that's not recommended until repairs are made."

"I'll check it out," Brooke said, holding out her hand for the keys.

Jessica reluctantly laid the keys in Brooke's palm. Then she picked up an invoice. "Here's what you owe for yard work."

Brooke gulped, looking at the bill. Would the bills never stop? Never be paid off? All she'd done for the past year was try and settle bills. Bruce had a substantial insurance policy, but he'd also run up substantial bills, having lived beyond his means. She'd lost the big house and big car. After paying creditors, she'd put aside the rest for her and Ben to live on until she could begin to make a living.

With nervous fingers, she opened her purse and took out the checkbook. But she mustn't think about finances right now—just concentrate on one day at a time.

Jessica took the check and thanked her. "I can recommend some motels, if you like."

"Thanks," Brooke said with more confidence than she felt. "But if I can find at least a corner where Ben and I can lay our heads, we'll make out just fine."

Brooke put her arms around her little boy and pulled him close. He looked up at her and they shared an affectionate smile.

Jessica stared after Brooke and Ben as they left the office. When she felt sure they were out of earshot, she picked up the phone and punched some numbers.

"Jake," she said, "I thought you'd want to know. Mrs. Haddon just picked up the keys to the cottage at 26 Seabreeze Lane. She has a little boy, and that cottage is in desperate need of repairs. Nothing's been done to it since the hurricane hit. I think she's really going to need your help."

Chapter 2

This is Seabreeze Lane," Brooke commented as she read the street sign, turned the corner, and slowed the car. Seven years ago, the cottages had looked similar, but she'd had eyes only for Bruce—not for cottages. "Help me find number twenty-six."

"I think it's this one," Ben said, seeing a little white terrier running toward the road as if preparing to chase the slow-moving vehicle. "Can we keep the dog?"

Brooke glanced at the dog, now wagging its tail and barking a friendly welcome. "It's cute, but obviously belongs to someone." She didn't want to squelch his exuberance by adding that she was concerned about feeding the two of them—she certainly couldn't take on another mouth! "Anyway, the house sits farther back from the road than these."

"I like that one," Ben said. "This one's okay too."

Brooke felt a pang of guilt, knowing Ben was trying to encourage her. He'd done that ever since he'd caught her crying to her mother about the events of the past year since Bruce died. She had no job skills and an almost depleted checkbook. But, she forced a blessing-thought that at least they had the promise of a roof over their heads. Fortunately for them, the Haddons had purchased the cottage years ago, before prices skyrocketed, and had paid it off. Now, the older couple had no need of it since their many travels took them abroad.

"Oh, neat, Mom!" Ben exclaimed when Brooke turned down a short winding drive and pulled up beside the cottage, which looked much smaller than she remembered. Ben was out of his seat belt and opening the car door by the time she got the key out of the ignition.

Definitely neat, Brooke was thinking. *If you don't mind a little picket fence with half the slats missing. If you don't mind part of the roof hanging down at the left corner of the house and the banister broken off beneath it. If you don't mind a gutter sticking out precariously from the eaves, or boards in bad need of repair and paint.*

When she'd come here seven years ago, this was a honeymoon cottage. Now it felt like a last resort.

Ben ran up on the porch and plopped down in a swing hanging from a rusty chain hooked to the ceiling before she could do more than call, "Be careful,

Ben." She breathed a sigh of relief when he began to swing without its falling down, bringing the roof with it.

"Listen," Ben admonished.

Brooke smiled and nodded. "Has a real nice squeak," she said, but she wouldn't dare chance sitting on it. It was too late to mention the peeling paint and seat streaked with gritty sand.

The Realtor had reminded her more than once that the cottage needed repairs. She should have considered herself warned, nevertheless, unprepared, she reached for the screen door, yelped, and jumped back when it came loose at the top, swinging back and forth like it might topple any minute. "Don't get close," she warned Ben, who'd laughed at her yelping, then looked unconcerned and kept stretching his leg so his foot could swing that squeaky contraption.

Seeing several broken windows, Brooke wondered, *Why bother with a key?* Nevertheless, with fear and trembling, she tried the key in the lock. It turned— maybe too easily. How difficult would it be for an intruder to jiggle that lock? Then she mentally laughed at herself. With all the broken windows, an intruder wouldn't need to jiggle a lock. Cautiously opening the door, she entered precariously, allowing her eyes to adjust to the dimly lit room. Assailing her nostrils was the musty, moldy odor of something having sat in water for a long time. Now she understood why the Realtor had been unable to rent it on this resort island. This cottage was a shambles.

Ben was beside her now, pulling on her hand. "Come on, Mom. Let's go in."

"Slowly," Brooke cautioned.

She felt for and flipped a light switch. Nothing changed. "Well, the sound of the floor matches the squeak of the swing," she said with a false brightness as the floorboards creaked with her every step. Ben laughed as he found a particular spot that squeaked and creaked, and he began to rock back and forth on it.

Brooke pushed aside the drapes at the front window, recognizing them as the same ones that had hung there seven years ago. She'd stood in that very spot watching and waiting for Bruce, then feeling swept with joy when he appeared, so handsome, so confident. She'd felt so lucky, so blessed. *Why had it gone so wrong?* As soon as she asked, an answering thought threatened, and she felt the drape tear in her grasp. She let go. The fading evening light revealed a lining that was thin and worn.

Honeymoon cottage—now as changed and dilapidated as her failed marriage. At least this physical structure could be fixed up, if one had the time, the expertise, and the money. What about her broken life? How could that be fixed—especially in the house that was a constant reminder of pain, heartache, and failure?

Mentally reprimanding herself for indulging in memories best forgotten, Brooke felt her way through the shadowed house. She tried the lamp switches but saw no light! She found two light bulbs that worked—one in a bedroom and one in the kitchen. "At least it's furnished," she said, trying to be positive, but her negative self added, *Yeah, furnished with mildew, damp furniture, broken windows, and two light bulbs.*

"Ah, another light," she exclaimed with irony as Ben opened the refrigerator door to expose empty shelves. "Let's go to the store," she said, realizing that first on the agenda was food, light bulbs, and cleaning supplies. If Ben had food, he could survive the inconveniences. Maybe she could make it presentable enough for them to spend the night here. She couldn't afford to waste precious money on a motel.

"We'll leave the kitchen light on," she commented. "Might be dark when we get back."

Just as she made sure Ben was buckled up in the backseat of the car and was ready herself to jump into the driver's seat, a dark blue truck drove up. The driver leaned out the window, his muscular brown arm across the door. "Evening, Ma'am," said a deep voice with a Southern drawl.

"Evening," Brooke replied, wondering if he was a neighbor.

"Jake Randolph here," he said and hesitated. When Brooke didn't introduce herself, he continued. "I'm a carpenter and want to offer my services." He looked toward the missing corner of the house. "Looks like you could use some help. My prices are the most reasonable you'll find around here."

Before Bruce, Brooke might have been swayed by that approach, and "reasonably priced" certainly appealed to her. The man seemed pleasant enough and looked okay as far as she could make out in the dusk, but she'd learned the hard way that appearances could be deceiving. "I'm in a hurry," she said truthfully. "I'll be glad to take your card."

His grimace matched his words. "Sorry. I didn't bring one with me."

It suddenly dawned on her that she'd warned Ben about talking to strangers. She wasn't setting a very good example. "Well, thanks anyway," she said, opening her car door wider. "I plan to get estimates from local carpenters."

She jumped in and slammed her door before he could say anything more and quickly started the engine. Looking in the rearview mirror as she drove away, she saw the man looking after her. Then he moved back from his window, started his truck, and drove away in the opposite direction.

Frankly, it seemed strange that the most reasonably priced carpenter in the area just happened along as she was moving in. But he did give her his name—if it was his real one. Well, if he meant any harm, her broken windows and flimsy lock were an invitation. Thoughts of him disappeared immediately as her eye moved to the horizon. Dark clouds were blowing in, quickly changing the gray sky to black.

"Let's hurry," she encouraged Ben as she parked at the supermarket. The wind whipped her ponytail against her cheek as she held onto Ben's hand and hurried to the phone booth beneath the overhang. She made a quick collect call to her parents in Indiana, telling them they'd arrived on the island safely and would call and talk longer after her phone was hooked up.

They wished her well and said to kiss Ben for them.

Brooke led Ben into the store. After buying only the immediate necessities—light bulbs, toilet tissue, cleaning supplies, a mop, milk, cereal, and bread—she made a quick stop at a fast food restaurant to pick up their supper, a rare caloric disaster that Ben considered a treat. Oh, well, she could use a few extra pounds, after having lost about ten of them during the past year.

Brooke glanced at the sky, rolling with dark clouds, and saw the palm trees swaying in the wind. She'd remembered sunny days and cloudless skies. Maybe this was just the cloud that had followed her for the past few years. Immediately she reprimanded herself for that attitude. Those years had yielded Ben! The most wonderful blessing one could have. She smiled, remembering her mom's saying, "Good comes from the worst of things."

Full darkness had come and the wind blew strongly by the time they arrived back at the cottage. Brooke replaced a bulb in a living-room lamp, then switched it off. A light shining from that gaping hole in the corner would be an invitation for all sorts of flying creatures. After they ate in the kitchen, Ben began to yawn. For the past two nights he'd been up past his bedtime. She would let him stay up a little longer, so he wouldn't be awake before dawn. She needed her own rest too.

Ben held a chair while Brooke climbed up and changed the burned-out bulb in the bedroom. She preferred not to sleep in the bed where she and Bruce had slept. Already, she felt haunted by ghostly memories.

She stripped Ben's bed but found only moldy sheets in a closet. The blankets, stored in plastic bags, were permeated with a damp, musty odor, but at least they didn't have black spots like the sheets. They'd just have to sleep without sheets.

She didn't bother bathing Ben because the bathtub was in worse shape than a little boy who hadn't bathed in two days. He resorted to reading the books he'd brought with them on the trip, then fell into a deep sleep with a book over his face.

Brooke washed away the surface grit and grime from the kitchen table, counter top, and appliances, deciding to do deep cleaning, one room at a time, in the daylight. Finally, around midnight, she could keep her eyes open no longer. After washing off, she turned out the light, shucked out of her jeans, and climbed into bed beside Ben. While hearing the wind whistling around the eaves of the little cottage, she thought of the missing corner and broken window panes. Her last coherent thought was, *Oh, please, don't rain.*

It rained.

Chapter 3

In the middle of the night, Brooke awakened to the sound of a storm that seemed to be just on the other side of the bedroom wall. Rushing into the living room with the hall light behind her, she switched on the lamp and viewed an uncanny sight. The wind was whistling through the blinds, and the rain was blowing in through the broken front window, soaking the drapes and sprinkling the armchair.

She shoved the chair into the center of the room. A piece of cardboard box might cover the hole in the window, but she had no tape. She didn't even have a hammer or nail.

At least she found a use for the moldy sheets. After running to get them, piled in the kitchen as trash, she lay them in the corner to soak up the water running down the wall onto the carpet. So that's where the moldy, musty odor came from! That was a revelation, but what to do about it?

"Mommie? What's wrong?"

Brooke, on her hands and knees, turned to see Ben behind her, blinking his sleepy eyes. "Oh, it's just the rain blowing in." She laughed to keep from crying. She mustn't cry. The cottage was saturated with enough water already! She rose from the soggy floor. "Let's see how things are in the other rooms."

After a quick inspection, she saw that everything appeared dry, but the dark spot on the kitchen ceiling looked larger and wet, as if water were up there just waiting to find a hole, and it might even make its own. She sighed helplessly. "Let's go back to bed."

She and Ben snuggled beneath the blanket. She could pray. But she couldn't ask for anything. She'd had "everything," and it had only brought misery. *I'll count my blessings,* Brooke reminded herself, forcing her mind away from disturbing thoughts. *Thank You, Lord, that I have my son. Help me to be able to make a secure home for him—here in this "last resort" kind of place. I'm trying—but I'm scared.*

~

Brooke was out of bed before the soft morning light drifted through the cracked window, exposing the torn curtain, dirty floor, and peeling paint. Then she turned her attention to the grimy night table beside the four-poster bed where a precious little boy lay breathing easily through parted lips. A blanket twisted tightly around him except for one arm that was flung out on her side of the bed. Maybe that's what had awakened her.

Blessing, blessing, she reminded herself and smiled at her precious boy. God had let her keep the most important part of her life. She must learn how to be grateful. With that determination, she headed for the kitchen and ate a bowl of cereal while looking out upon the small back yard, filled with puddles, surrounded by pieces of a broken picket fence. Who was it who said it's better to live in a corner of an attic rather than in a mansion with a cranky woman?

Oh, yes, that was from the Bible—Proverbs, she thought.

Well, she'd try not to be cranky, but more and more she felt like the old woman who lived in a shoe with so many children she didn't know what to do. At least the old woman was able to spank her children and put them to bed. Brooke didn't have a passel of children, but still, she hardly knew what to do. She had to try, so she began by dragging the wet sheets outside and stuffing them into a metal trash can.

Ben came into the kitchen while she was washing the grime off her hands. "It's not raining in the living room anymore," he said, looking disappointed. Then he brightened. "But the floor's still squishy. It feels neat to jump on it. You wanna do it, Mom?"

Brooke laughed. *Leave it to Ben to find something positive.* "Not right now," she said. "You need to eat breakfast. We have a lot of things to do today." She poured his cereal and milk into a bowl, one of the few dishes she'd found in the cupboard.

Just then bells began to ring. The clear notes resounded and vibrated as if waking up the landscape and sending a musical message across the morning sky. It had a similar effect deep within her soul.

"What's that sound?" Ben asked, his spoon poised above his bowl.

"Church bells," Brooke said contemplatively, realizing that she hadn't heard church bells ring since she and Bruce had been on this island seven years ago. It had a nice sound, as if saying that God is alive and well. At the same time, she felt slightly guilty. She'd resolved to get Ben in church even though so many things in her own life remained unresolved. The guilt increased when he asked excitedly, "Can we go and see the bells?"

No way could they go to church. Clothes were still scrunched up in boxes in the trunk of the car. There was so much to do. "Not today," she said, and seeing his downcast countenance, she added, "But we can read a Bible story." Then she remembered the Bible, too, was packed away somewhere.

"Okay," he said. He took a big bite of cereal, then with milk running down his chin, he jumped out of his chair and ran from the room.

In an instant, he returned with one of his favorite books that her parents had given him for Christmas. "This Bible story," he said.

"Perfect," Brooke said. "Noah and the Flood." She'd read it a million times to him and he knew it by heart now, but it seemed to fit after that watery fiasco of last night. They hadn't drowned, and perhaps the church bells were a reminder that there was somewhere a rainbow. "You eat and I'll read," she said.

Finally, coming to the end, she read, "And Noah took the animals, two by two, into the ark. The birds, the butterflies, the rabbits, the dogs, the cats—"

"It didn't say alligators," he noticed for the first time.

"Well. . .no," Brooke agreed. "But alligators are like whales and fish. They live in water, so they didn't have to be put in the ark."

"Oh, okay," he said, and Brooke realized anew how much this child trusted her. She must teach him the right way. That was a huge responsibility, considering how much she herself had to learn.

Ben picked up his bowl and drank the milk. "Can we go to the lagoon and see the alligators?"

There was so much to do. She'd never get done. "Not today, Ben," she said. She heard the weariness in her voice and saw the disappointment in his eyes. What could she get done, after all? Even if the phone were hooked up, businesses weren't open. She couldn't call around for estimates on repairs. Oh, well. They made it through last night—didn't drown or get swallowed up by some wild beast or get attacked by intruders—and they were none the worse for the grime and dirt. How long would it be before she stopped saying that she didn't have time to do anything that was important to Ben?

"Let's go to the beach," she said impulsively.

"Yea!" he shrieked and ran to her, throwing his arms around her, almost knocking the chair over.

Brooke laughed. This little boy didn't need a clean cottage nearly as much as he needed a mother to spend time with him. She hugged him, then admonished, "Get your clothes on. What you wore yesterday will be fine."

"Can I go barefoot?" he called as he struck out across the kitchen.

"Put your tennis shoes on. We'll walk. It's not far."

The few blocks to the beach turned out to be a little farther than Brooke remembered; however, the crisp morning breeze and warm sunlight felt wonderful on her skin. She tried to ignore the fact that people in cars were going in the opposite direction, probably on their way to church. At least she could remind Ben that God was in nature.

"God created such a beautiful world, didn't He, Ben?" she commented as the public beach came into view.

"Yeah," he agreed. "I can't even see the end of it."

"Hey, you're right," she said, looking where the horizon should be. However, the ocean blended with the heavens. In Indiana, the eyesight would be stopped by city buildings, community houses, or a forest of trees against the sky. "It looks as if you can see forever."

"Yeah, and I never saw white sand before." He scooped up handfuls and let it sift through his fingers. Then he stood still, his eyes wide, listening.

She heard it. The sound of yelping puppies.

"Oh, Mom, c'mon!" Ben pulled on her hand, leading her down the beach toward a crowd of people.

Going closer, Brooke saw a young couple in folding chairs behind a cardboard box. Ben rushed up to join other children while adults looked on with smiling faces.

"Can I have a puppy?" Ben asked loudly, and it seemed to Brooke that everyone looked at her for the answer, as expectant as Ben. Then she saw the sign on the box: "Free Puppies."

She walked closer and peered into the box. That was a mistake, because the puppies were absolutely adorable. "What kind are they?" she asked.

"The mother is a miniature Japanese Spitz," said the young man in the folding chair as he held his hand about six inches off the ground. "We're not sure about the male."

The young woman spoke up. "The female is our dog. The male could be our neighbor's dog that got out of its fence or a black mutt that wandered into our back yard a while back. So. . ." She shrugged.

Brooke could see that the puppies were a mixture of colors. Ben picked up one that was coal black with a spot of white on the back of his neck and a streak of white beneath his mouth and down along his chest. "Oh," he exclaimed, spying another. "I want to see that one."

Brooke leaned closer and saw a coal black ball of fur curled up in the corner. It was so fuzzy she couldn't even tell where its face was. Apparently the young man couldn't either, for when he picked it up, its bushy little tail faced the group. He turned it around and set it on the ground.

The onlookers, including Brooke, gasped at the adorable puppy face surrounded with a thick mane of hair, reminding her of a lion or, she realized more accurately, a werewolf.

The puppy shook itself, lifted its tail and its head, and waddled across the sand as if it owned the world. Its tail was longer than its legs. The legs were so short, its tummy scraped across little piles of sand, making a groove. Everyone laughed, so intrigued they didn't make a move until the puppy began to scoot closer to the ocean.

"I'll get it," Ben shouted and began to run.

The puppy ran faster but Ben caught it at the ocean's edge and swept it

244

up into his arms. He brought the squirming puppy back to the group but wouldn't let go. "I saved its life, Mom. Just like Noah did."

While he was pleading, "Can I keep it? Please?" Brooke had visions of shots, visits to the vet, and dog food. At least it was male, so she wouldn't have to worry about a slew of little puppies.

"How big will he get?" she asked.

"Mitzi weighs twelve pounds," the young man said. "So, I'd say this one shouldn't get over. . .say fourteen, fifteen pounds."

It wouldn't eat much at that weight. Maybe she could cut corners elsewhere. Ben had no dad, no friends, and was without his maternal grandparents who had doted on him. This puppy could be a friend to Ben and maybe free her up to do her chores. He'd become like glue since Bruce died, as if afraid something might happen to her.

Looking at Ben and the puppy, she doubted she could pry them apart with a crowbar. "Okay," she said.

His little face simply glowed with delight, and he nuzzled the puppy's fur with his chin. Then his big brown eyes rolled up to hers. "Can I have two—like Noah?"

Brooke gasped. "That's where I draw the line!" The onlookers laughed. "Come on, young man," she admonished and they headed on down the beach, Ben hugging the little critter. He looked up. "Thanks, Mom. I really knew I couldn't have another one. I love this one. I really love him."

Brooke touched his shoulder. Yes, she'd cut corners or maybe plug that missing corner of the living room with old boards if that's what it took to make her son happy.

Chapter 4

Early Monday morning, Brooke and Ben were out back feeding the puppy a bowl of milk. "We're going to have to teach him to stay outside," Brooke told him. Last night she'd said the puppy could stay in a box in the kitchen, but the whimpering threatened to last all night, so she'd finally consented to bringing the box into the bedroom. That had satisfied both Ben and the puppy.

"You two play for awhile," she said needlessly, remembering that Ben and the dog had been content with each other for most of Sunday, while she worked on the house and even got the bathroom into decent living condition. Now, in shorts, T-shirt, and tennis shoes, she was ready to tackle that impossible cottage again.

"Pardon me, Ma'am," she heard and turned with a start toward the voice. A man came striding across the yard toward her. "I knocked but nobody answered," he explained. "The car was out front, so I thought you might be back here. I'm Jake Randolph."

That truck driver! Should she shake his hand? What did he want? Maybe he was a neighbor being friendly. No, Saturday night he drove away. "I'm. . ." She hesitated, not wanting to be impolite, yet not wanting to be too familiar. "I'm Mrs. Haddon."

"Yes, Ma'am," he said in that friendly drawl of Saturday night. Definitely a Southerner. "My friend Jessica Lawler said you'd moved in and could use some repairs."

She knew Jessica Lawler was the Realtor and nodded briefly for him to continue.

"I'm here to offer my services. I'm a carpenter."

"Thanks for stopping by," Brooke said, uncertain about this persistent man claiming to be a carpenter. He did look the part, being bronzed by the sun and with sun-bleached golden highlights through his brown hair. Also, in jeans and T-shirt, he looked to be in great physical condition and quite muscular. But if he were good at his trade, would he be running around begging for work like this? She thought not. "I plan to ask around, maybe get some estimates and then make my decision. If you want to leave a card—"

"I do have one this time," he said and laughed lightly, as if embarrassed that he hadn't had one on Saturday night. "However," he continued with a wry smile as he moved his hand to the back pocket of his jeans. "I do better than offer a card. To prove my worth, I always make at least one small repair free of charge."

Brooke's gray-green eyes locked with his warm brown ones for an instant before she quickly lowered her gaze to the card he offered. That instant was long enough to see a flush begin on his bronzed face as if he knew what she was thinking.

She stared at the card. *Puppies might be free*, she was thinking, *but not some carpenter's services! Free? Ha! He might hammer a nail in somewhere and then try to sell her vinyl siding or a new roof or new windows.*

"How did you manage during that storm Saturday night?" he asked. "I noticed your corner is missing."

Real observant, there! With a slight lift to her chin, she avoided his eyes. She'd prefer he leave before she had to demand it. "We. . .managed."

"I'm glad to hear it," he said, then walked over to Ben, who was offering the puppy a stick, then pulling it away when the puppy tried to bite it. "Hi, Buddy. I'm Jake." He stooped down.

"I'm not Buddy. I'm Ben." The two laughed together, but Brooke's motherly protective instincts surfaced seeing Ben welcome Jake as if they were long-time friends—even letting him pet his puppy.

"Look at that purple tongue. Looks like you've got a little Chow here."

"Yeah, I saved his life," Ben said proudly.

Jake, on eye-level with Ben, remarked, "Well, Son, according to an old Chinese proverb, that means you're responsible for him all his life."

Ben's eyes were big and round, basking in the man's attention. "He was going to drown in the ocean."

"That's a slight exaggeration, Ben," Brooke admonished, wondering if he got that from his politician father too.

The man grinned, like he was amused at the exaggeration. "Have you named him?"

Ben nodded, his dark eyes gazing trustingly into the eyes of the stranger. "Taz," he said.

That was the first Brooke had heard of that! Ben had simply been calling him "Puppy." She hadn't known it was a Chow either, but now that Jake mentioned it, she'd heard or read that Chows have purple tongues.

"Taz," the man mused and glanced up quickly at Brooke. "Like the cartoon character?"

"Yeah," Ben said. "He's neat."

Ben thinks the Tasmanian Devil is neat! He also seemed to think this stranger was neat. The cartoon character might look neat with those rather innocent eyes, his tongue hanging out, and that cute laugh, but inside he was an out-of-control, wild, crazy thing. This man kneeling in front of her son looked rather neat too, with that quick smile over perfect white teeth in a ruggedly-handsome tanned face with little laugh lines at his mouth and eyes, as if he laughed a lot. But who could trust what might be lurking inside that neat exterior?

She studied the card for a moment. It looked authentic. "Randolph Construction," it read. Under that was Jake's name, an address, and phone number. She was tempted to ask him to look at the corner of the house, but she'd trusted better-looking men than this—her late husband, in fact—and where did that get her? No, she simply could not take a person at face value.

"Thank you for stopping by, Mr. Randolph," she said abruptly. She couldn't stand here all day. "I'll get back to you if I need your services."

Jake immediately rose from his kneeling position near Ben and the puppy. "I understand," he said, color coming to his face. "I shouldn't have barged in. I should have explained—"

"No," she said, uncertain about the whole situation. "I just don't like people coming to my door, selling things, or making offers."

Ben came over, holding the puppy beneath its arms, exposing its belly, the only spot that wasn't covered with thick black hair. "Yeah," he said. "One time this man said he was going to give us a million dollars' worth of groceries."

"A thousand, Darling," Brooke corrected.

"Well, lots of groceries. A whole room full and Mom asked why and he said he wanted to come in and vacuum the carpets." Ben snorted and shook his head, his eyes wide. "Mom said no."

"I see," Jake said. "And your mom was right. You should never let strangers in the house, and I should never have approached you this way." His brown eyes looked truly repentant as he glanced from Ben to Brooke. "When Jessica called and said a woman and her son moved in, she told me of the damage."

Did she also tell him that she had no husband—that there wasn't a man around? "Thank you again, Mr. Randolph," Brooke said, trying not to be fooled by this now-contrite, apologetic, seemingly trustworthy, helpful man. How many of those were in the world anyway? *Something for nothing? Ha! That'll be the day!* "I will let Jessica know if I need your services."

"I realize I should have had Jessica Lawler contact you," Jake said and laughed uncomfortably. "Sorry I bothered you. Do contact Jessica, please." Brooke noticed that he was walking rather sideways then, as if afraid of her. What was this man's problem?

"Good-bye, Ben. Bye, Taz. Good-bye—" Jake hesitated, realizing she hadn't given her first name. Jessica had said the Haddons moved in. He nodded and added, "Mrs. Haddon."

"Good-bye," she said, and the word sounded final. He knew, without a doubt, there was no way this woman was going to call for his help. How did it go wrong? It never had before. It must have been his showing up Saturday night, then appearing today. Or was it that she was more distrusting than anyone else he'd ever approached? Or perhaps there was no Mr. Haddon, and she was being particularly cautious.

Whatever, she obviously wasn't accustomed to having someone come by and offer to help. Now how was he going to get himself out of this? He spread his hands and began backing away. "I'll try and approach this in a different manner."

She didn't return his smile, and her dismissing gaze plainly said, "Don't bother." He'd better get out while he could. He felt certain that if he showed up here again, she'd call the police. He didn't need that. An accusation, founded or not, could prove to be disastrous in his situation. Even something as simple as a call to the Better Business Bureau could reach his parole officer and land him right back in federal prison.

Chapter 5

Brooke tried to dismiss the incident with the man claiming to be a carpenter, but she couldn't get it off her mind as she went about the process of cleaning and throwing away. The next-door neighbors on the left, a young couple, left before eight o'clock, apparently going off to work. An older couple, on the right, came over just to introduce themselves as Mary and Frank Lee and give advice about trash pickup. Brooke asked about getting the corner of the house repaired, and they mentioned a couple of construction companies that might be able to help, but there was no mention of a Jake Randolph.

"Less expensive if you can get somebody that knows a little about carpentry," Frank informed her.

Brooke nodded. Would that be Jake Randolph?

She didn't know whether to be proud of herself for having expelled a ne'er-do-well, or whether to be ashamed that she'd turned away well-needed "free" assistance.

But no! She could not chance endangering herself or Ben.

At least the adrenaline was flowing, and that spurred her on with the cleaning. She even engaged Ben in some of it.

The air was humid, she was hot and sweaty, Ben wanted a popsicle, and she said it was too close to suppertime and decided to stop for awhile. Just as she poked her head in the refrigerator, basking in the coolness that touched her face and trying to decide what to do for supper, a knock sounded on the door.

She straightened immediately, slammed the door shut, and stiffened. *Oh, surely not that man again! Where was Ben?* "Ben?" she called.

"I'm out here," he said, his voice coming from right outside the back screen door, where he often played when she wanted him to stay nearby.

"Just stay where you are," she said and guardedly walked through the kitchen, the small foyer between the other rooms in the center of the cottage, and through the living room. If the person at the door was Jake, she would slam the front door and lock it, then run and get Ben and lock the back door. If he tried to open the front screen door, it would probably surprise him as it had her, by hanging on its lower hinge only.

Guardedly, she approached the door. A sigh of relief escaped her, and she cautioned her erratic heartbeat to calm down when she saw a pretty woman with short auburn curls, friendly brown eyes, and a light sprinkling of freckles across her nose, holding a box. Three stair-step boys stood with her, each holding something in his hands. A late model SUV was parked in the driveway.

"Hi, I'm Ginger, from a church down the way. Hope you haven't had supper."

"No," Brooke said, half laughing with relief and as surprised as when Jake had showed up, but more trusting of this woman with children from a church. Surely they weren't out to poison her. "Watch out for the screen. It might fall on you."

They stepped aside while Brooke opened the door slightly, then put her hands near the top to open it wider. "I should just take this thing off," she apologized.

"If you have children like mine, you should," Ginger agreed. "These kids broke me with buying new screens. They don't know how to push on the wooden part. Finally, I decided to quit fussin' and live with holey screens. 'Course, we do get quite a few flies."

Brooke had no idea how much of this was exaggeration, but both women laughed as Ginger and the three boys paraded through the house to the kitchen. Brooke called Ben inside.

The woman introduced herself again. "I'm Ginger Harris. This is Mike and he's ten, George, eight, and Danny, five."

"I'm five," Ben piped up. Brooke introduced herself and Ben. She'd have to question Ginger about school in the fall. But for now, Ginger had set the box on the table and was taking off a towel. "Spaghetti, anyone?" she asked.

"Yeah," Ben said, along with Ginger's children.

"Okay if we eat with you?" Ginger asked.

Brooke laughed. "Shouldn't that be my question, since it's your food?"

"Nope, it's your food. We cooked it for you."

All the children beamed as if they'd played a huge part in it—and enjoyed themselves.

"This is so thoughtful," Brooke said, feeling slightly embarrassed that all the dishes, pots, and pans were out on her counter tops. But at least the kitchen table was clean. "Are you a neighbor?"

Only the slightest pause ensued as Ginger continued taking the dishes out of the box. "Got a microwave?" she asked.

"That I do have!" Brooke replied. She put the dish of sauce in it and punched the buttons.

"Who is my neighbor?" Ginger asked, tilting her head and sort of looking toward the ceiling. Brooke recognized the phrase as something in the Bible. Maybe it was Jesus who asked, "Who is your neighbor?" and the answer was that we all should be neighbors, Good Samaritans, brothers and sisters in Christ.

Brooke nodded, seeing the gleam in Ginger's eyes, and she felt as if her spirit were communicating with this woman. Maybe she could accept friendship from her. "Okay," Brooke conceded, "we're neighbors. Now, do you live on this street?"

"No," Ginger said and avoided Brooke's eyes. "You forgot about the napkins, kids. Who wants to place them?"

"I will," George offered immediately, as Mike stuck out his hand, then withdrew it in deference to his brother. These children really wanted to be a part of this. How wonderful if she could teach this attitude to Ben. He and Danny were near the back door with the puppy, already totally accepting of one another.

Ginger's next glance at Brooke, who was watching her closely, held a note of concern, but she smiled. "We'll get to particulars later, okay?" She turned toward the boys. "Okay, wash your hands."

Brooke was glad to see that Ben put Taz in his box and ran along behind the other children to the bathroom. If he hated anything, it was to wash his hands. Ginger reached into the box and brought out a plate. Wow! She'd even brought brownies.

The microwave beeped. "Soup's on!" Ginger called.

"I thought we were having spaghetti," quipped Mike, coming into the kitchen. He and his mom exchanged an affectionate gaze, before Ginger reached over and mussed his hair.

"Okay, who wants to say the blessing?" Ginger asked after the other children gathered round.

"Me. Me. Me," came the replies in unison from Ginger's children, following by Ben's weaker "Me" that sounded like a question.

"Maybe we should let Ben say it," Ginger said, "since it's his house."

They all looked at him. He thrust out his hands, like he and Brooke were accustomed to doing together. They all held hands. Brooke wondered what he'd say. He hadn't prayed before in front of anyone but her and her parents. She watched him through her lashes.

"Mmm. God bless Mommy and my doggie and the buh-sketti." He moved his hands out of the others and spread them. "That's all."

"Amen," Brooke and Ginger said, then smiled while the children giggled until Ginger cast them a warning glance.

Everyone dug in. Brooke thought the food delicious, and the others wasted no time eating. The conversation was about children, school, the area, but nothing personal. Ginger's asking no personal questions pleased Brooke.

She was curious about Ginger, but didn't ask, lest she would have to reciprocate by revealing her own personal life. She didn't know if she wanted to do that just yet.

After they finished, Ginger said, "I'll do the dishes tonight, kids. Your turn tomorrow night."

"You always say that when we eat off paper plates," Mike said with clear affection for his mother.

"You've got to get up early in the morning to be quicker than me," Ginger said pointedly to her son. She turned to Brooke. "Where's your trash can?"

"There and there and there and there," Brooke replied, pointing at plastic grocery bags placed around the kitchen.

Ginger made eye contact with her boys. "You guys know what to do."

They each took their plates and put them into the trash. "We don't throw away our silverware," Ginger joked about the plastic forks. She filled the sink with sudsy water and put the forks in. "If you want the leftovers, you can put them in something, and I'll wash out my dishes. Now, you kids run outside."

While the two women worked together with the food and clean-up, coffee was brewing.

"Your children are so well-behaved," Brooke complimented.

"Thank the Lord," Ginger replied, and Brooke knew that was not a trite phase.

"I'm a single parent," Ginger explained. "My husband walked out on us while I was pregnant with Danny. It was hard to cope with being a single mother, and I couldn't have done it without my family and their reminding me that God can work in and change even the worst situations."

Brooke nodded. She didn't know how that might work for her. She didn't have the faith that it would—only the hope that it would. The phrase, "Oh, ye of little faith," crossed her mind, and she knew it applied to herself.

"I need to hear things like that," Brooke admitted. She asked, as if joking, "Did God send you to me?"

Ginger gazed at Brooke for a long moment. "God. . . ," she said, then added soberly, "and Jake."

Chapter 6

Brooke felt like the breath had been knocked out of her. What was going on here? "You know. . .Jake?" Maybe this was Jake's wife and children, and he was legitimate after all. She sat down in a kitchen chair.

Ginger dried her hands and sat opposite her. "I've known Jake all my life. After my husband left, I had a rough time. It's easier now, since Jake moved in with me."

Brooke regretted that her intake of breath was audible. Her immediate emotion was that this divorced woman and a man lived together—apparently with children in the house.

Oh, how judgmental! Brooke thought. This woman was being a good neighbor—regardless of her personal situation. She was obviously an excellent mother with children who adored her. She gave every indication that she was a Christian. But so had Bruce—and Brooke didn't want to think of Bruce just now, nor ever.

And who am I to judge? I am in the aftermath of a failed marriage. Perhaps my sins were not of overt commission but omission. Is that any more excusable?

Then, making Brooke's thoughts even worse, Ginger said quietly, "I'm Jake's sister."

This was unbelievable!

"Did he send you here?" Brooke asked, wondering if she should be glad or upset.

"Oh, no. He wouldn't send me out to repair any damage he's done." Ginger laughed, realizing what she'd said. "He does his own repairs—he's in that business, you know." Her expression grew serious. "But after he told me he hadn't approached you in a businesslike matter, I just didn't want you to have the wrong impression of him. And he's not begging for work, believe me."

Shaking her head, Brooke didn't know how to apologize. "He was very nice," she said. "I'm the problem. Right now, my trust-quotient with men is at an all-time low."

Ginger snorted. "Tell me about it!" she said, understanding. "When a man walks out on a wife and three kids, you never even want to look at one again." She grinned, and a wee gleam appeared in her eyes. "Well, almost never."

Brooke couldn't help but smile. She really liked Ginger. "I understand that. My husband stepped out on me during our marriage. He died a year ago. But all that's no excuse to treat your brother so rudely."

"He understands. And he really would like to repair that corner in your living room free of charge." She lifted her hand. "Oh, I know what you're thinking—nothing's free, right? But that's not the case here. And if you want, we'll come with him."

Apologetic, Brooke told her that wasn't necessary. "But I'd like for you to come."

"Great," Ginger said, smiling broadly. "If you don't mind, we will. It's good for the kids to make new friends." She looked toward the back yard. "They love that puppy."

Brooke told her how they'd acquired the puppy. "I just couldn't refuse Ben, especially after he put the Noah guilt trip on me."

Ginger laughed. "They know how to work us, but I'm not taking on an animal. They'll all be in school in a few months, and I'm looking forward to a little peace and quiet. Oh, speaking of school," she said, "Ben and Danny might be going to school together since they're the same age. There are no children Danny's age around our house. They're either older or younger or their families come here only for vacations. He and Ben have really taken to each other."

"It's helpful to me for them to play together," Brooke assured her. "I don't want to impose, but you're welcome to come over and bring the children any time."

"Great! I'll stop by and let you know when Jake can do the job."

"Okay, but supper's on me," Brooke insisted. "That is, if you don't mind sandwiches."

"A staple at our house," Ginger said.

"Any preferences?"

"Yeah," Ginger said. "We'll eat anything that doesn't bite us first." She laughed at her own joke, then screwed up her face. "Except the boys can't stand the salad type—you know, egg salad, chicken salad. They like the solid kind, like bologna or ham. Peanut butter's fine too."

"I can handle that," Brooke said confidently.

~

Although Ben was anxious to see his new friends again, Brooke was glad to have the next few days to herself, Ben, and Taz. She took Taz to the vet for his shots and then spent over an hour finding just the right collar—a bright red strip with shiny rhinestones. When they got home and she fastened the beautiful new collar, it promptly sank into the mane of thick fur around the dog's neck and was completely hidden.

She made a dent in her deep cleaning, bought new sheets and curtains for her bedroom, and discovered at night she fell into an exhausted sleep, with hardly a thought of Bruce.

Early Friday morning, Ginger stopped by to say Jake could start on the corner that evening and to confirm that supper was still on. Brooke and Ben went to the store to buy peanut butter, jelly, bread, lunch meat, lettuce, tomato, cucumbers, potato chips, a bag of chocolate chip cookies, and a bag of oatmeal raisin cookies.

Brooke dreaded seeing Jake again, wondering if she should be apologetic or what. He and his sister seemed so good and helpful, but outward appearances could be deceiving.

It was after five, with a few hours of light left, when Ginger drove up in her SUV and parked in the driveway. The blue truck pulled in behind her. While greeting Ginger and the children, Brooke's peripheral vision observed Jake getting equipment from the back of the truck.

Brooke carefully held the screen while Ginger and her brood filed in. By that time Jake was heading toward the corner of the house with a ladder. She needn't have worried about what to say. He looked her way, nodded once, and commented, "Looks like that screen could use a little fixin' too," then continued on. Before she had time to think about conversation with Jake, Ginger and the children were crowding in around her. Brooke already had the lettuce leaves separated, the tomatoes sliced, lunch meat on a plate in the refrigerator, and the paper plates and napkins on the table.

"Okay, give me your clean hands," Ginger instructed her boys, and they all held hands. Brooke and Ben completed the circle, and Ginger gave thanks for new friends and the food.

After she finished, Brooke asked, "Would your brother like to join us?"

"He wouldn't know how to sit down and eat! That guy's on the run all the time. I'll take him something."

Feeling embarrassed, Brooke insisted, "He's welcome."

"He'd rather eat while he works."

"It's really my. . ." She looked around at the children, each fixing their own sandwiches expertly and reminded herself she'd have to teach Ben to be more independent as she fixed his sandwich for him. "It's my attitude, isn't it?" she added finally.

"No. You were perfectly right. He simply hadn't thought about how his cheap and free offers might look to you."

"I want to at least invite him in," Brooke said. She handed Ben his sandwich, then headed for the front door.

She was so intent upon doing the right thing that she completely forgot the front screen, pushed on it, and nearly fell on her face, squealing as she tried to balance her feet and the door at the same time. Chagrined at her inability to even make a simple request of a man she had insulted, while at the same time telling herself she was right because he had been a stranger, she mumbled reprimands to herself.

Just as she neared the corner, a head stuck out from over the roof. Brooke jumped back. She caught herself on the swing, and it squeaked, moving back, taking her with it. She almost lost her balance again.

Jake politely stared down at the ground beneath him, but she felt sure that was a grin playing around his lips and it rather infuriated her. She straightened herself and silently reminded her feet to stay firmly planted on the porch, and after clearing her throat and swallowing, she realized she was again at a loss for words.

She couldn't very well say she was sorry she hadn't accepted a stranger upon first—or second—meeting. She still wasn't sure about him. And he didn't say a word. Was he trying to punish her for rejecting his earlier offer? Then suspicions arose again. Why would he want to come back, after she'd been what he would probably consider rude?

Finding her voice, she spoke in what she hoped was a congenial tone, but it sounded irritated to her. "Would you like to come in for a sandwich? Some sandwiches? Um, something to eat?"

"Thanks," he said, quite formally. "I want to try and finish this before dark. You might ask Ginger to wrap me up a sandwich for later."

"Sure," Brooke said, feeling a sense of relief. Something about this man unnerved her. She wasn't sure if it was him or herself. And she knew it was because she had lost her trust in many things—particularly people—after having been duped by an unfaithful husband.

She turned, hearing a movement behind her. Ginger held out a paper plate laden with food. "Here you go," she said.

Brooke took it and immediately knew that was a mistake. She was going to try and hand this up to the roof, while he would try and reach down for it. She'd surely drop it or he would topple on his head. "You want to come down?" she asked.

"Just lay it on the swing," he said. "I'll get it."

Chapter 7

Jake didn't want to chance falling on his head, but he did chance leaning over the roof and taking a look at Brooke Haddon when she'd held the plate, about to lift it up to him. She was a natural beauty without even trying, he could easily tell, although she didn't seem to wear a trace of makeup and her blond hair was pulled back in a ponytail.

Her expressive gray-green eyes, fringed with long, dark lashes, had held a touch of wariness the first two times he'd seen her. When she'd looked up at him on the roof, however, he'd sensed a trace of warmth in them, matching her thin smile, as if she might decide to give him the benefit of the doubt concerning his character. He felt a sudden emptiness in the pit of his stomach and told himself he'd better go down and devour the sandwiches and keep his mind off both his character and the pretty woman.

While he ate, alone, he did think about what Ginger had told him. Brooke Haddon was a widow whose husband had died a year ago. Having a single sister and being actively involved with the singles at church, he could understand the caution of a mother without a husband around. That would explain her wariness when he approached her about repairs.

She was even sorry if she'd treated him unkindly, Ginger had said, and she'd decided that he could repair the corner of the house. Jake had breathed a great sigh of relief at that. He didn't relish any kind of confrontation or explanation with his parole officer, who wasn't interested in excuses, just adherence to the letter of the law.

Brooke, he thought, with a sense of pleasure. It was a beautiful name, causing him to think of a gently rolling stream in a green pasture. It had a musical quality to it. *I wonder, where did you come from and where are you going, gentle Brooke?*

Jake poked the last bite of sandwich in his mouth and thrust the paper plate down on the swing. *What am I doing?* he asked himself. *I cannot afford the luxury of thinking about a woman as if I'm some young, innocent kid just looking for a companionable mate. I'm thirty-five years old, with a past that has its consequences. And I know how temptations can sneak up on a person.*

Knowing he had no excuse for thinking about Brooke Haddon, or any woman, in a way that hinted at a personal relationship, he climbed back onto the roof. How many times did he have to keep giving his personal life to the Lord? He answered that immediately. *As many times as needed!* Fighting back his instant of frustration, he pounded the nails into the wood with renewed vigor.

After finishing the corner and getting the gutter back in place, Jake began to inspect the roof for loose shingles. When he reached the back of the house, Ginger, Brooke, and the children were out there. The two women sat in kitchen chairs under a tree, watching the children give bits of bread crust to the puppy.

Jake regretted having to break up that jovial group but felt impelled to yell down, "Hey, kids. Don't feed that bread to the puppy. He'll get a tummy ache."

"What do we feed him?" Mike yelled back, squinting up toward the evening sun.

"Puppy food."

"We got some, Mom?" Ben inquired.

"No," she said, having intended to feed the dog on table scraps. "We'll get some next time I go to the store." She didn't add that she intended to continue feeding table scraps to the dog. *What people in their right mind would throw food in the garbage when you had a perfectly good animal willing to eat it?*

"Throw a stick," Ginger said. "Teach the dog to fetch."

The dog wasn't as excited about a stick as he was about the bread. If Jake's sister weren't sitting there with his little nephews, Brooke would inform the man, who apparently thought he had a right to tell her how to raise her dog, that she'd had dogs when she was a child. Every dog she'd ever known ate table scraps. They didn't go to the vet either, except to get a rabies shot. And they all lived to a ripe old age. Jake should be paying attention to the roof, not little boys playing with a dog.

As if anticipating Brooke's now-somber mood, Ginger explained, "Jake has a friend who runs an obedience school for dogs. He's learned a few things from him."

Brooke nodded. "I don't suppose I should give the poor dog a bone either."

Ginger grinned. "That's right. Jake says that's as hard on a dog's digestive system as on a human's."

Brooke couldn't imagine separating a dog from his bone. Seeing the movement of Jake standing up on the roof, she saw that he was walking over the ridge, toward the front. "If he's finished, I need to thank him and see what I owe."

Ginger stood. "We need to go too. We'll wear out our welcome."

"No way," Brooke said. "You're welcome anytime. And I mean that. But my first priority is to get this house in shape."

Ginger smiled. "I'll have you guys over to my place soon. That is, if I can make a pathway through the clutter."

Brooke laughed. "Couldn't be any worse than mine."

"Three boys?" Ginger commented with raised eyebrows, then turned toward the boys. "Okay, you guys. Time to go. Scoot your booties."

She paid no attention as they protested, asking if they could stay a little longer, if Ben could go home with them, if they could have a dog or at least a cat, that they were the only kids in the world without a pet. Finally Ginger began to count, "One—two—three—"

Off they went, running around the side of the house, with Ben and the puppy on their heels.

"You amaze me, Ginger," Brooke said. "I've never seen anyone control their children as easily as you do."

"It hasn't always been that way," she confided. "My husband couldn't discipline himself, and the boys were wild. After Jake came to live with us, he began to discipline them in a teaching way, and it makes life better for all of us. I was indulging them too, because their dad left. Jake said I was doing them no favors by letting them get by with things. They'd turn out to be as irresponsible as my ex. I began to realize he was right. Now they know that if we're going to have fun, we're going to be responsible first. Works better for all of us."

"I think I could learn a lot from you," Brooke said sincerely.

"The most important thing," Ginger said, "is teaching them about God and Jesus. I don't know how people do it without that kind of reference. What do they use as a guideline?"

Brooke nodded. "That's something we neglected 'til I moved back in with my parents. I want to get Ben into Sunday school. That's been neglected for a long time now."

"No time like the present," Ginger said, reminding Brooke of something she'd entirely forgotten. "Sunday is Easter, you know."

Chapter 8

When the alarm scared her out of her sleep, Brooke popped up like a jack-in-the-box, staring into the darkness. In an attempt to shut off the offending sound, she only succeeded in knocking the clock off the table. It hit the floor with a dull thud and continued to rattle her brain.

If she hadn't had to nearly stand on her head and roll out of bed to shut off that offending contraption, she'd simply keep her eyes shut and sleep at least until daylight.

But leave it to her trusty watchdog to begin barking and her son to come into the room asking, as if he'd been waiting for this all night, "Is it time to go, Mom?"

"Can you see to turn on the lamp?" she asked.

He did, causing her to close her eyes tightly, then open them slowly. Finally, she stared accusingly at the clock registering 5:30 A.M. That would have been bad enough, but because of daylight saving time, she'd set the clock ahead last night. To her system, the time was only 4:30 A.M.

Had she simply promised Ginger, she would call and say they couldn't make it. But Ben had been looking forward to this. And if she were going to teach her son that Easter was more than bunnies, baskets, eggs, and new clothes, then there was no time like the present to begin. With a groan, she threw back the blanket and smiled faintly at her precious boy who said, "I've never gone to a sunrise in my life, Mom. I'm real 'cited."

Pushing back her hair from her face, a faint smile was all Brooke could manage at this early moment. Yes, Ben was excited about going to church on the beach. And she felt reasonably sure it wouldn't hurt her either—if she could stay awake for it.

∽

When Brooke pulled into the church parking lot, Jake stood near the entrance. She wondered if he were the assigned parking attendant for the morning. Surely he wasn't waiting just for her. She stopped and rolled down the window.

"There are plenty of spaces back there," he said, pointing. "You'll see Ginger's van."

"Thanks," she said. She spotted the van, sitting higher than the cars. Ginger and the boys got out and reached them by the time Brooke and Ben had exited the car. She was glad Ginger had told her to wear a sweater. The early morning air was chilly. Ben and the boys didn't seem to notice.

When Jake walked up to them, Brooke figured Ginger must have stationed him at the parking lot entrance.

Ginger and Jake had flashlights, as did many others. They made their way from the parking lot, around the church, past two rows of homes, and to the beach.

While holding Ben's hand, Brooke saw people walking from all directions, many using flashlights to light their paths as they stumbled through the darkness, making their way toward the great rustic wooden cross, stark and black against a deep gray background where the sky could not be distinguished from the ocean.

Ushers were stationed along the beach to hand out programs. The people kept coming. Voices were subdued as they came onto the beach. A hush settled over the crowd as, one by one, the lights flicked off. Everyone stood together on uneven, soft beach sand. The only sound was that of the power of an ocean that could hardly be seen in the darkness. Hundreds of people, like dark silhouettes, stood beneath the cross.

How many had seen Jesus die on the cross? Brooke contemplated. *His mother? A few disciples? Several curious onlookers? Roman soldiers? Had their hopes died when Jesus died on that cross? Does Jesus know that's how I have felt? Like my feet are not on solid ground? That the light that shines on my life's path is as unnatural and single-beamed as a flashlight? Why are all these people here? Are they curiosity seekers? Are they worshipers? But more important, why am I here? To teach a religious holiday to Ben? Or—*

The gasp of hundreds of people stopped her thoughts. Brooke, too, gasped. Even Ben, knowing something spectacular was occurring, looked up at her and pointed ahead. Brooke nodded. Yes, she saw it. A golden arc of light appeared far off in the distance and seemed to rise from the ocean, as if God were separating the heavens from the water.

One voice began, then others joined in. Never had Brooke seen or heard anything so spectacular. Human voices raised in praise to the Lord as He painted a masterpiece across the sky before their very eyes. "God sent His Son," they sang while the great golden sphere dispelled the darkness and began turning the sky pink, gold, and blue. The rays glinted against the cross and cast a golden glow on the faces of those emerging from the darkness into the light.

"Because He lives, I can face tomorrow," the words rang out, stronger and stronger as light illuminated the programs. Brooke could see the words on the program. But more important, she could feel the words.

When the group, most with their hands lifted toward heaven, sang with assurance about Jesus being a risen Savior and the words rang out, "Christ

Jesus lives today. He walks with me and talks with me, along life's narrow way," Brooke saw how the sun made a pathway from the heavens, so far away the distance was unimaginable. And yet, it was right here for her to see. The rays reached across miles and miles of mighty ocean waves, making a golden, glistening pathway from the sun to the shore.

How narrow was the beam of the flashlights. Even if everyone there put their beams together, that would be as nothing compared to the light that God was bestowing on the people gathered at the cross.

Brooke's throat was too closed to sing, but the words were like a balm to her soul as they sang that Jesus is the hope of all who seek Him and the help of all who find Him.

"I was blind, but now I see," reverberated even more strongly than the sound of the mighty ocean. *Does this crowd of Christians, when bonded together in one accord, have as much power as that of the ocean?*

The preacher spoke a few words about living by faith, based on Romans 1:17. *Can I do it?* Brooke wondered. *I believe in You, Jesus. I've believed in You since I was a little girl. But how much faith do I have? Can I. . .live by faith?*

Light, almost blinding in its brightness against a blue sky, shone down upon them as the group broke up while singing about facing tomorrow, "because He lives."

Have I been stumbling around in the dark with a flashlight? Brooke wondered as they made their way back toward the church in the natural light of God's creation. She glanced at Ginger, who smiled through her tears. Brooke realized her own face was wet. A glance at Jake revealed a swipe of his hand across his cheek.

"Stay for breakfast," Ginger entreated when they reached the church.

"Yeah, let's do," Ben pleaded.

Brooke had thought they'd go home after the sunrise service, but now she didn't want to lose this wonderful feeling of peace and assurance that she hadn't felt in so many years. She wanted to be with this group of believers—and with God.

Breakfast in the fellowship hall turned out to be a feast of colored eggs, sausage and egg casserole, ham croissants, Danish and other pastries, yogurt, juice, and coffee. For so long, Brooke had wondered how it would feel to go to a singles' class after having been married. But on this day, nothing was said about why a person was single. There were so many visitors there wasn't time for more than introductions and each person telling where they were from— if they lived on Hilton Head or were visiting.

Jessica Lawler came over to speak to Brooke, introduce her husband, and ask how things were going. Brooke was able to mean it when she thanked the

Realtor for sending Jake Randolph her way.

Brooke remembered asking Ginger if God had sent her. She'd said it rather jokingly, but now she wondered if it were true. Her vision of walking into a sanctuary in a strange place had been unfounded. By the time of the worship service, she'd been introduced to so many people and had smiled so much that she felt like she belonged. Sitting on the pew next to Ginger with Ben on the other side of her helped too. Jake sat at the other end of the pew next to Mike.

When they first sat down, Brooke was aware of the long double rows of pews, the color of light oak, separated by a wide strip of royal blue carpet reaching to the steps of the raised dais, on which stood a wide lectern with white Easter lilies all across the front. Great exposed wooden beams, like dark oak, slanted high, crossed in the center, forming a cathedral ceiling. Recessed lights shone from between each beam. Behind the dais, partitioned off by a low wooden railing, sat gold velvet chairs. Above the choir loft was a round, stained-glass window of multi-colored Christian symbols such as the lamb, the dove, and the cross.

Brooke forgot about the lovely interior as soon as the choir members in white robes filed in and began to sing "Christ the Lord Is Risen Today." When the choir presented their message in song, Brooke could feel the words, "Awake my soul, and sing," and when the congregation sang, she joined in.

"We're going to my parents' house for traditional Easter dinner," Ginger said. "Come eat with us."

When Brooke began to shake her head, Ginger tempted, "Ham, melt-in-your-mouth sweet potatoes with marshmallows on top, little green peas—"

"No, really, we need to get home."

After a long look, Ginger nodded and smiled. "I understand. I'll call you soon," she said, and squeezed Brooke's arm affectionately.

Brooke had the feeling that Ginger really did know how she felt. Ginger, too, was a single mom who'd no doubt had all the same feelings Brooke was having—wanting to trust God and people, wondering how things were going to work out and if she should accept offers of kindness, wondering if it were kindness or pity?

When she arrived home, Brooke remembered that there had been a quick rain shower on Saturday, but her house was dry. Her eyes focused on the corner of the house.

I wonder, she thought, *can the corners of my life be fixed? Can I face tomorrow with faith and hope?*

～

When tomorrow came, Brooke began the day with a prayer. Then before breakfast she read a Bible verse to Ben and they prayed together. After she had him help clear the table and make his bed, he went out to play with Taz, and she set about getting rid of the grime still in most of the house. It had been good to spend Sunday as a day of worship and rest.

During the week, she tackled the house with renewed vigor, feeling more at peace with herself, her situation, the friendship that was developing with Ginger, Ben's friendship with a boy his own age, and even her changing feelings about Jake Randolph. She hadn't felt like contacting him yet about other repairs, but when Friday's forecast said rain might be expected on the weekend, she called Ginger and asked if she thought Jake could check out her roof. The dark stains on the once-white kitchen ceiling looked rather ominous.

Right after she hung up the phone, she heard a knock on the door, and her immediate thought was that Jake Randolph had ESP and had decided to come and see what she needed. However, when she answered the door, there stood Ben's Sunday school teacher, whom Brooke had met but whose name she didn't remember.

"Hi," said the petite brunette, about her own age, dressed in a pretty summer dress. "I'm Evelyn," she said. "Ben was in my class Sunday."

"Come in," Brooke said, after warning her about the precariously hanging screen door. She was grateful that several weeks of airing out the place had eliminated the mildew odor. The living room was clean, although spots were visible on the carpet and watermarks were on the upholstery on the couch and easy chair.

"I don't have everything fixed up yet," she apologized, "but everything's been cleaned, although the spots didn't come out."

"At least you have furniture," Evelyn replied, "which is more than I can say about myself. I'm a single mom too and live with my parents. That's about to change, though." She promptly sat on the big stain in the easy chair. "Is Ben here?"

Ben and Taz chose that moment to enter the room.

"Uh-uh," Brooke chastened, just as Ben got that knowing look on his face and said, "Taz, go home." The dog ran.

Brooke grinned as she sat on the couch. "The dog knows he's going to get a cookie. Well, a dog biscuit, but we call it a cookie."

Soon, Ben returned, and when Evelyn said, "Hello, Ben," he stuck out his hand. Before Brooke could ask if his hands were clean, Evelyn shook his hand. *Oh, well,* Brooke remembered. *She has a child too.*

"I have a little something for you, Ben," Evelyn said and held out a small white bag.

"Oh, neat. Look, Mom," he said. Ben pulled out a book and handed it to Brooke.

"Oops," she said, as a gold bookmark decorated with a big red apple fell out. She returned it to the book and read the title. "*Apples from God*," she said. "How nice."

"Thank yoooou!" Ben said to Evelyn, and then began to pull red apples from the bag.

"He loves books," Brooke said and then laughed lightly. "And apples too."

Evelyn smiled. "We give a bag of apples and a copy of that book to all the children in the area who visit our class."

"Can I go out and read it in the swing?" Ben asked. Brooke nodded her permission.

Evelyn gave a rundown of activities for children in the church, saying that Ben fit right in on Sunday and listened eagerly to the stories.

Brooke nodded. She knew Ben was an outgoing boy. And it was certainly her responsibility to channel his energy in the right direction. "He has a friend there already," Brooke noted. "Danny Harris."

"Yes," Evelyn said. "I saw you sitting in the sanctuary with Jake and Ginger." *She thought I was sitting with Jake?* "Ginger's been a lifesaver to me."

Evelyn nodded. "She's a wonderful example to all us single moms," she said with feeling, then stood. "Speaking of being a mom, I need to get home. My mom keeps Sara all day and cooks supper for me, so I'd better scoot."

Brooke stood too and thanked her for the visit and the gift to Ben.

"Hope to see you Sunday, Ben," Evelyn said as she left and waved goodbye to Brooke.

"And the apple fell out of the tree on the boy's head and it had a worm in it," Ben said, as if he were reading.

"What? The boy's head had a worm in it?" Brooke shrieked, and Ben laughed while kicking his feet out in glee. Brooke sat carefully on the swing with its still-rusty chain and grabbed the book. "Why, you little kidder," she said playfully. "You just said that to get me to read it to you, didn't you?"

"Yup," he replied, his big, dark eyes shining, melting her heart. *Oh,* she thought, *I must not fail to train up this precious boy in the right way.*

Chapter 9

Jake came on Saturday, although the forecast was showers. Beneath the graying sky, he was nailing away on the roof at lunch time. Brooke didn't like the idea of leaving someone at her house working while she went away, but she had an afternoon appointment to take Taz to get his rabies shot. After she and Ben ate, she thought perhaps Jake had made a special effort to work for her on Saturday, so she made him a sandwich and took it out to the swing.

She walked out into the yard until she could see him on the roof. She did not want to give the impression that just because she was a friend of Ginger's that automatically she expected Jake to be her friend. However, she could at least treat him like she would any other ordinary human being—or the dog.

Why am I having such difficulty relating to this man? she asked herself. She didn't have time to stand around and try to find an answer at the moment. Perhaps it was because he seemed always on the fringes of her activity but they'd never even had a decent conversation.

"Mr. Randolph," she called, "we have to take Taz to the vet. There's a sandwich on the swing if you want it."

He lifted his hand in a kind of salute. "Thank you, Ma'am," he said. " 'Preciate that."

She felt a drop of rain. "It's raining. You might be gone when we get back. Just send an invoice." She remembered his talking about free work, which she didn't want, and quickly added, "And for the corner."

"Yes, Ma'am," he said, and she could feel his broad smile, reminding her of what a ruggedly handsome man he was. More than that, she couldn't imagine a more appealing sight than a strong, muscular man like him with tears in his eyes at the foot of a rugged cross. Shaking away that image and annoyed with herself for her thoughts, she quickly turned and hurried Ben and Taz into the back seat of the car. The last thing she needed was to be thinking of a man! *But,* she reminded herself, as if she needed to be defended, *my thoughts about him were mainly spiritual!*

～

Mr. Randolph! Jake thought with a shake of his head, watching Brooke Haddon and her son drive away. She wouldn't call him Jake, making sure he knew to keep his distance. He could accept that. He could understand it. Once

267

your life had been turned upside down, you could never quite have that innocent kind of trust that once was a part of you.

At the same time, part of him wished he could be that happy-go-lucky kind of guy he used to be and let a girl know he was interested in her right away. In his college days he could do that, and when he'd been rejected a couple of times, he'd just shrugged it away. After all, there were plenty of others eager to accept his advances.

He wasn't like that anymore. His approach to life wasn't the same as in his younger days. He'd learned the hard way that you couldn't always take a person at face value or at their word.

Maybe after today, Brooke Haddon would realize he was not a scam artist or a lecher—just a hard-working man doing his job, and yes, hoping to favorably impress her.

He hadn't met a woman in years that sparked this kind of interest in him. Maybe it had started because she didn't trust him and he wanted to correct that impression. Maybe it was because of her physical attractiveness that a seeing man couldn't deny. But a lot of it had to do with watching her trying to get back into the mainstream of life after a devastating personal experience and beginning her efforts at a church service.

He knew how hard it was to face people when inside you felt like a tidal wave had come along and swept away everything in life that you'd thought was important.

He would never forget the day two average-looking men in business suits got out of a car in front of his shop when he opened it up.

"Jake Randolph?" one asked.

"Yes, what can I do for you?" Jake asked with a smile. He had a lot to smile about that morning. He was working on the biggest job he'd had since he and Martin Gage bought the business from Jake's dad after his heart attack. Business was booming, Jake was saving money, he and Meagan had spent a night to remember last night and were talking marriage, and the sun was shining. So what was there not to smile about?

"A Martin Gage work with you?" the talking man asked.

"We're partners," Jake said. These men definitely looked like customers. Maybe wanted a mall or business offices built. "Come on in. Martin should be here any minute now."

Jake led them to the office, offered them chairs, made a pot of coffee while they asked the usual questions that prospective clients might ask. When the coffee was done, they refused a cup. When Martin came in and was introduced, they flashed badges, read them their Miranda rights, and said they were under arrest.

"Arrest?" Jake stammered, looking from the men to Martin, whose face had turned red as a tomato.

"For refusing to pay income taxes for the past two years," the man explained.

"Give me the bill. I'll pay them," Jake said.

"Doesn't work that way," the man said bluntly. "You were given warnings and plenty of time. Let's go for a little ride."

On that ride, when Jake looked at Martin, his partner turned his head and looked the other way. Without a word from him, it was plain as day what had happened.

Martin had worked for Jake's dad for many years. After a beam fell on Martin's leg, Jake's dad brought him in as office assistant while he recuperated. After his leg healed, Martin knew his leg would never be the same and realized he was getting a little age on him, so he asked to stay on as assistant bookkeeper. He'd always been a good worker, so Jake's dad had no problem with that.

And Jake had no problem with Martin's interest in gambling. After all, Jake wasn't exactly lily-white, so who was he to spout off about it? It was Martin's business what he did with his own money. After Jake's dad decided to sell the business, Martin's big win during a trip to Vegas enabled him to come in as a partner.

That suited Jake. He liked Martin. He'd been a good employee for Randolph Construction on both outside and inside jobs. Never in a million years did he suspect Martin would be guilty of this kind of "inside job." After all, who would suspect a man would steal from his own company or not pay income tax on his own business? *Unless,* the thought hit hard, *he'd had a lot of gambling losses!*

Jake expected this would all be over in a short while. His one phone call was to his dad's attorney, who came down, and after Jake posted his own bail bond, he was free to go until he was to appear for trial.

He went immediately to Meagan. The moment he said, "I've been arrested for income tax evasion," her mouth dropped open and she looked like someone had turned her to stone.

"I didn't do it, Meagan. It's Martin. He ran the office. He kept the books. And now, he's gambled away his part of the profits and didn't pay the taxes. That's why he's been saying things like wanting to get back down to Vegas where the big bucks are. But I didn't suspect he'd do something like this."

"You're part owner, Jake," she said as if he thought her a fool for believing he hadn't known what was happening. "And you told me about all that money you've been saving." She threw up her hands. "Oh, Jake! How could you?"

That was the second shock wave of the day, and only the beginning of the personal earthquake that hit on the day of the trial. Martin had plea-bargained, pled guilty, was put on probation, and was out walking the streets.

Against the advice of the attorney, Jake refused to plead guilty to something he didn't do. Surely the jury would understand that he had principles, morals. After all, Martin had said he was guilty. But the jury adhered to what the law had to say. Jake was a partner. Ignorance was no excuse. Jake was guilty.

"Six months in federal prison!" the judge sentenced, and at the pound of the gavel, Jake felt like he'd fallen through a crack in the ground and the earth had swallowed him up.

A flash of lightning brought Jake to the realization he was not still in prison. He was on probation and on top of Brooke Haddon's roof with a hammer in his hand and raindrops falling on his head. He'd make a perfect lightning rod! With that thought he climbed down, gulped his sandwich, and did one more little chore before packing up his tools and feeling quite good about the jobs he'd done for Brooke Haddon.

Surely she would be. . .at least. . .cordially appreciative.

～

When Brooke and Ben returned, a steady rain was falling. Since Taz wasn't supposed to go beyond the kitchen, Ben ran around the house toward the back yard, with Taz racing beside him. Brooke's eyes rose to the roof, but Jake wasn't there. She sat and looked at the house a moment longer. Jake apparently did good work. The new wood needed to be painted, but then, so did the whole cottage. She sighed. The main thing was to keep the rain and the bugs out.

With that thought, she jumped out of the car and headed for the house. When she reached the porch, she saw a folded paper plate underneath the screen. Couldn't he have taken it out back to the trash can?

Oh, well! She carefully opened the screen door and gasped. It stayed in place. It was fixed. He'd put on a new hinge. Well, how nice! Or, was it? Depended upon how much it cost.

She reached down and picked up the paper plate. It was folded, and he'd written what looked like an invoice:

Roof	not finished
The corner	my "freebie"
Screen hinge	$3.98
4 screws	.20
Total due	$4.18

Was that man trying to get her attention? Well, maybe she didn't have much money and didn't know how to make repairs herself, but this was ridiculous. She didn't have to accept charity. It wasn't as if she were totally broke; it's just that the supply of money wasn't limitless and she wanted to stay with Ben this summer before he started to school.

And, Brooke thought in consternation, *no matter how charming or appealing Jake might be, I do not want to feel beholden to any man.*

Not wanting to think about Jake and how she should handle the invoice, she simply tossed the paper plate on top of the refrigerator and tried to forget it. She would go about her business and deal with that when her mind was clearer. In the meantime, she would simply wait and see if Jake Randolph tried to press her with coming around to do other repairs.

He didn't, and she told herself she was glad. Ginger didn't even mention him when she called mid-week and encouraged Brooke to take advantage of the church's "Mother's Day Out" program. Brooke said she'd take a look and see Ben's reaction.

"Cool!" he said when he saw the fenced-in children's playground, complete with sand, tunnels, slides, monkey bars, swings, and about anything a little child's active heart could desire.

She assumed "cool" was as good as "neat" when he asked, "Can I stay, Mom?" Danny's eyes also pleaded with her.

"Okay," she said, seeing there were plenty of volunteers to watch them, some of whom she had seen or met on Sunday. And Ginger's boys would be there with him.

Brooke and Ginger spent the morning shopping. Brooke was grateful Ginger knew where to get all the bargains, not only on groceries but on cleaning supplies and household items, including a sale on sheets and towels.

When they returned, Ginger showed Brooke the sunken prayer garden, a lovely spot between two buildings, surrounded by lush foliage, tall palmettos, and live oaks. She walked down the steps and onto the bricks. She could see how this place was conducive to prayer, as if she had stepped away from life for a moment into a private place to reverently commune with God.

Chapter 10

For the first time in years, Brooke felt as eager as Ben to return to church the next Sunday. It was as if her soul were starved for the Bread of Life, which was Jesus.

There were fewer people in the singles' class, and they spent a brief time getting to know each other and introducing those who hadn't met. But most of the class was spent on Bible study since the group met twice a week to interact and talk about personal needs. Brooke liked the class members, the teacher, and the warm, friendly feeling of everyone. Jake's friendly manner was the same with everyone, and he usually sat near other guys and they all listened attentively and discussed the Bible passages.

Even the sermon on Sunday morning seemed designed just for her. The pastor read from Romans 8:39 about nothing being able to separate a person from the love of God. "Death can't, life can't, the angels can't, and the demons can't," the man read. A feeling of hope and joy touched Brooke's heart when he read that our fears for today, our worries about tomorrow, and even the powers of hell could not keep God's love away.

Brooke felt both elation and guilt. *Even though my faith isn't strong,* she thought, *God hasn't abandoned me. Ben and I have our needs met, and we have each other. He even brought friends to our door, and this church is filled with caring Christians and people who understand what it's like to be broken and need help beyond what we can give ourselves.*

The song leader stood and asked them to sing "Leaning on the Everlasting Arms."

"What a joy divine. . .what a peace is mine," the people sang, and Brooke was vaguely aware of Ben and Danny rocking back and forth in time with the music.

The real meaning of the words "everlasting arms" escaped Brooke at the moment. The singing seemed to recede into the background as she gazed out over the congregation. She was reminded of how Bruce had said she looked good on his arm. He'd been happy with her until she got pregnant. Then he thought she no longer looked good on his arm. Their son was a burden to him that he hadn't been ready for.

The strands of the hymn kept tugging at her heart and mind. How she'd prayed during those six years of marriage. But the relationship had gone steadily downhill. The prayers weren't answered. She glanced toward the high beams as if to ask if there was really a caring God and if so, where He was during that time.

She quickly looked down again. She mustn't do that. She'd always known there was a God. It was just that she hadn't called upon Him until her marriage had deteriorated beyond repair. And Bruce hadn't seemed to consider God very much.

Now, as if God were speaking to her, Brooke was reminded that God had given her parents who took her in. He'd kept that little cottage tucked away on this resort island for a roof over their heads. He'd given her a wonderful son. Ben had new playmates, and she had a friend she could confide in.

Her glance inadvertently wandered over to her left, and she glimpsed Jake Randolph, whose voice and face were lifted in praise to the Lord. Despite her aversion to receiving his charity, she could even be grateful that God had sent her a much-needed handy-man.

~

"Come eat lunch with us," Ginger said, after the service ended and they were all in the parking lot. "We're having every boy's favorite."

"Pizza!" Mike shouted, and the others followed with, "Yea! Yea!"

Ginger took a deep breath and blew out through her lips as she shook her head of auburn curls and glanced at Brooke with chagrin. "We can't afford pizza for you guys with bottomless stomachs. We're having every boy's second favorite meal, cooked on the grill." She looked at Mike. "Got a clue?"

"Yeah. Barbecue chicken."

He grinned mischievously while his mother said, "You know better."

He nodded. "Grilled bread! And water to drink."

"That's exactly what you deserve," said a male voice. Jake had walked up and rested his hands on Mike's shoulders. Mike looked up at Jake with admiration in his eyes.

Brooke wondered how she could graciously get out of this. She could use a friend, but not a male one. Additional complications she'd didn't need! She was about to say she still had a house to get in shape, but Danny interrupted with a plea to his mother. "Can Ben come, Mom? And bring his puppy?"

"Yeah, yeah," the other boys chimed in, and Ben tugged on the skirt of her dress. "Oh, Mom. You should've seen how 'cited Taz was when they was at our house. He was jumping all over creation. Can we go?"

They all laughed at his childish prattle, and how " 'cited" he was over the prospect of playing with his new friends. Brooke recognized the expression of doing something "all over creation" as one her mom had inadvertently passed down to her. Now Ben was saying it. Like mother, like child?

Just as she opened her mouth to refuse, Jake spoke. "I could keep an eye on these guys for awhile and give you two a chance to get acquainted." He tousled the hair of George, who'd moved closer to him.

There was really no reason to refuse. To do so might look suspicious, as if she had started thinking about Jake as something other than a repairman. Anyway, she needed to talk to him about that carpentry bill.

"Okay, thanks," Brooke said to Ginger, avoiding looking at Jake. "But Taz?" she began.

"Oh, go get him," Ginger encouraged. "Mike can go with you and give directions to our house. It's only a couple of miles from you and easy to find. You might want to bring a bathing suit too. We have a pool."

"Bring a little dog food with you," Jake said.

For an instant, Brooke wondered if he were testing her to see if she was feeding the dog people-food. On second thought, he probably was just thinking of the puppy—as if she didn't have sense enough to know his feeding time.

George and Danny wanted to go too, and Brooke assured Ginger that would be fine. It might take four boys to hold onto a dog so " 'cited" he jumped all over creation.

Brooke exchanged her dress for jeans but didn't bother with a bathing suit because she had no intention of running around half-dressed in front of Jake. Ben changed into play clothes. He moaned that he didn't have bathing trunks.

"I have two," Danny said. "You can wear one of mine."

Mike shrugged. "You can swim in your clothes if you want to."

Just in case, Brooke picked up an extra set of play clothes for Ben.

The boys stuffed the box full of puppy on the floorboard of the back seat. That was useless! Before she could pull out of the driveway, the boys had the puppy literally climbing all over them and the car.

In spite of puppy licks and wagging tail in his face as his brother held Taz up to him, Mike was able to give simple and concise directions. "Up this street, turn there, down that road, up that street." After she'd driven about two miles, he exclaimed, "There it is!"

Brooke recognized the low country-style house as one that had appealed to her years before. She'd seen many of those, typical of the southern spacious houses that seemed ideal for large families. Steps leading to the front door separated the expansive porch that stretched the entire width of the house. The light brown banister and shutters complemented the cream-colored house, which was topped by a gray roof that blended with moss-covered oaks that seemed to offer a protective covering over the house.

A hedge of blooming azaleas—red, coral, and white—adorned the front of the house on each side of the steps and reached around the house. An immaculate green lawn lay like a lush carpet.

"They'll be out back," Mike said after Brooke parked on the white sand and shell driveway at the side of the house, facing a high, light brown wooden fence. The boys ran yelling to the back of the house by the time Brooke got the box and puppy food out of the car.

Brooke walked through the gate, left open by the boys, closed it behind her, fastened the latch, and walked around the corner of the house when she heard Ginger calling for the boys to come inside and change clothes.

"Leave the puppy out here," Brooke said, glad she'd brought the box. Ben put the puppy down, and it started to run along behind him but couldn't make it up the step. She set the box down, placed the puppy food beside the steps, scooped the puppy up, and put him in the box. His whimpering and scrambling to get out showed his displeasure.

Brooke glanced around at the back yard, understanding why the front of the house seemed to belie that three active boys lived here. The backyard was perfect as a children's playground and looked like a safe haven. The rectangular pool and surrounding concrete took up almost the entire left side of the yard. At the far end of the yard stood a swing set, on white sand, enclosed by timbers. It appeared to be any child's dream with its three swings, a long slide, and a climbing rope beside a ladder leading to a small enclosed landing. Several flowering azalea bushes lent spectacular color, and a yellow jessamine trailed up one corner and along the top of the wooden fence.

The lounge chairs and two chaises, scattered along the pool side, looked particularly inviting. Behind those on the right sat a long picnic table with attached benches. Nearer the open narrow porch, on a cobbled area, sat a large grill with a domed lid.

Smiling at the perfect picture, Brooke started out of her reverie, hearing Ginger yell, "Don't get in the pool yet," at the same time the screen door was flung open and four boys dashed across the porch, racing to the swing set. Mike got there first but let the other three boys take the swings.

"Look, Mom," Ben called. "I'm swinging up to heaven."

"I see," she said, smiling. It hadn't been too long ago that he'd learned how to push himself with his body and feet. He watched his new friend, Danny, and tried to go as high as the other five-year-old boy.

"I know you're out there somewhere, Brooke," Ginger called from a window. "Come in and make yourself useful."

Just as she turned, ready to step up onto the porch, Jake opened the screen door and stepped out. He greeted her with a nice smile and immediately turned his attention to the dog. "Okay to let Taz out?"

"Sure," she said and clamped her lips shut to keep from telling him not to let Taz fall into the pool. After closing the screen, one backward glance revealed Jake standing with his hands on his hips, chuckling, while the little puppy waddled as fast as he could toward the exuberant boys.

Jake asked himself what he'd expected of Brooke Haddon. Had he thought she'd turn cartwheels just because he repaired her corner and fixed her screen? He needed to keep everything in perspective and just hope that a word or glance from her would indicate she accepted him as a friend—or at least as a human being.

Ginger had said Brooke had had an unpleasant experience with an unfaithful husband before he died in an auto crash. He'd like to talk to her, let her know he understood the difficulties of starting over. He'd like to be her friend, and the more he saw of her, he knew he'd like to be more than a friend.

He dared not stare when Brooke and Ginger brought out food and put it on the picnic table. He had to keep his distance, pretend he wasn't interested. He lectured himself on the fact that Brooke Haddon wasn't there to hobnob with him but to engage in a friendship with his sister and allow her son to play with other children.

He knew Ginger had come to terms with her single status. Unlike some of the singles, she wasn't expecting God to bring a man into her life to make it meaningful. Why couldn't he be as accepting? Common sense told him he didn't stand a chance with a woman like Brooke Haddon, who had been married to a politician who gave her everything. She had an air about her of grace and style, something rather foreign to him.

He stabbed the hot dogs, turning them lest they burn, feeling as if a skewer had done such to his heart. Common sense told him to be realistic. And he had been, since Meagan rejected him. But he hadn't expected someone like Brooke Haddon to come on the scene and disturb his carefully controlled emotional life just by being distantly near.

Face facts, he warned himself. *This can get you nothing but heartache. You're not a teenager now, but a grown man. You're a man with a past. If Brooke Haddon distrusts you now, imagine what she would feel if you told her you were an ex-con on probation.* That had proved to be disastrous with Meagan. So, how in the world could he ever say to a woman like Brooke, "Hey, by the way, I've spent time in federal prison"?

The day was gorgeous, sporting a mild temperature, complete with a clear blue sky and a soft gentle breeze.

Brooke could be grateful that in spite of there being two mothers without husbands and four little boys without daddies, there was a good-natured man around to tell them to wash their hands and then to give thanks to God for the food.

They all held hands as Jake bowed his head and prayed. "Thank You, Lord, for the blessings of this day and those who have come to share this food with us. Thank You for the food, and may it nourish our bodies. Guide us, Lord, that we may use our lives in service to You. In Jesus' name we pray, amen."

After lunch and clean-up, Brooke and Ginger, seated in the rocking chairs on the porch, held glasses of lemonade and watched. Jake showed the boys how to coax Taz to sit and lie down, then reward him.

So that's why he wanted me to bring puppy food! She should not be so quick to think the worst of men, just because Bruce had disappointed her. Brooke was impressed with how Jake played with the boys. He was actually getting Taz to sit and get down on command. He was making a good impression on her.

She remembered that her politician husband had made a good impression too. So good, she had married him. He'd gone to church many Sundays, shook hands, and kissed babies—all for votes. But no, she was not going to be fooled by any seemingly exceptionally-caring man again.

After awhile, Jake said it was time to swim.

"I'll take care of the change," Ginger said, rising. "You just sit here and relax."

~

When Jake returned to the yard, in his bathing trunks and a towel slung over his shoulders, Ginger and the boys were nowhere in sight. Brooke still sat in the rocker on the porch, looking like she was studying the yellow jessamine at the far corner of the yard, as if she didn't see him.

It wasn't easy figuring out how to relate to her. He'd come to understand a little of how women like Ginger and some of the other single moms felt. He'd heard enough stories of men being abusive or unfaithful. He didn't know Brooke's situation, except that her husband had died a year ago and she was very wary of men—or at least of him.

He could at least talk about business, but it was Sunday and he didn't do business on Sunday. He could tell her about the singles' group, but he knew Ginger would do that—and probably had already—and Brooke was already coming to the singles' Sunday school class.

Why was he having such a hard time relating to her? He wasn't quite as outgoing as Ginger, but he certainly wasn't shy by any means. Something about this woman caught him off-guard. He was behaving like some kid with his first crush on a girl.

"Taz," he called, deciding that was the safest route to take. "Come."

The dog came running and stood in front of him, his tail shaking wildly.

Jake gave him a piece of food, then tossed his towel onto a chair, stepped to the side of the pool, and jumped in.

~

Just because Brooke wasn't interested in a man didn't mean she couldn't appreciate Jake's bronzed, athletic body as he smoothly swam several laps across the pool, while the boys were changing. The combination of his work and swimming apparently kept him in terrific shape. She needed to do something about her own body. Not that she was out of shape, but she knew the importance of aerobics and toning.

Soon, ahead of Ginger, the boys came running out, Ben in a pair of Danny's trunks. They jumped, screaming, into the pool—except Ben.

Brooke jumped up, ready to run toward him as he teetered on the edge of the pool while the boys encouraged him to jump, but he was frozen, scared to jump and scared to move away.

The boys were yelling for him to jump in. Jake immediately realized the dilemma and told the boys to be quiet. "Come down the steps," Jake encouraged. "I'll hold your hand. I won't let you go."

Jake had Ginger's boys swim away from him and Ben while he gave some basic instructions, and before long Ben was holding onto the side, kicking his feet, sticking his head under. Soon Jake had him bobbing and was giving him instructions on how to float.

"My boys are fish," Ginger said, "thanks to Jake."

"I'm afraid Ben's a rock," Brooke retorted. "The weather in Indiana is quite different than here on this mild-climate island. He never swam much and then only in shallow water. He loves water and had a great time in a plastic pool. But he's not comfortable in deep water."

"It's only three feet at this end," Ginger said.

Before long, Ben was a regular little trooper in the shallow end. When he got past the three-feet level, he'd do what Jake instructed and float or hold his breath and swim toward the side or shallow end. The other boys swam across alone or on Jake's shoulder and would dive off, head first.

Ben wouldn't. "I'll do it next time," he promised.

Brooke was impressed. "Your brother's very good with children and dogs," she said.

Ginger nodded. "I was about ready to throw up my hands and quit before Jake moved in with us. I try to keep the boys from disturbing him too much. But most of the time, he's just like a dad to those boys. We'd be in a pickle without him."

They both gazed out at the man being so patient with the little boys and seeming to love every minute of it. Brooke and Ginger laughed as Taz kept going to the edge of the pool, but the minute water splashed on his face, he'd run away.

Brooke's glance returned to Jake. "I take it he's not married," she commented.

"No, he's single," Ginger said and added quickly, giving Brooke the impression that her next words were a deliberate change of subject, "By the way, I teach water aerobics here three mornings a week from ten to eleven. There's usually about eight or ten of us. Come join us. Give you a chance to meet some other people."

That sounded wonderful to Brooke. "You're a mind reader. I was thinking about getting into some kind of regular exercise routine. But first, I have to get that house fixed up."

"Um, how long did you say it's been that way?" Ginger asked with a sly grin.

Brooke laughed. "I get your point. And I know with a boy and dog around it's never going to be shipshape. But I have to try."

Ginger wagged her finger. "All work and no play, you know."

"Okay," Brooke conceded. "Maybe you win. How much do you charge for lessons?"

"Three dollars a lesson or thirty dollars a month, whichever way you want to do it. And you can come once a week or three times a week. A couple of the single moms bring their kids. I know they'd love it if you brought Ben and Taz."

"I just might," Brooke replied, knowing it would be good for both her and Ben. She could manage the cost. "Oh, speaking of money," she said. "I need to talk to Jake about the bill for that corner. He didn't charge me for the repairs. He wrote down that it was free." She spoke somewhat apologetically, knowing she was talking to Ginger about her own brother. "Now, I could understand if the door hinge was free." She shook her head. "But not the corner of the house."

"I know exactly how you feel, Brooke," Ginger said immediately. "You think there are ulterior motives and Jake's going to make a move on you. But it's not just you. Jake does this on every job he takes. Believe me, Brooke, this isn't personal."

Well, Ginger made it pretty clear that Jake wasn't personally interested in her. But a man like him should be interested in someone! He was good-looking, had a business, was in his mid-thirties, had a great personality, was a Christian and a father-figure to little boys, a good dog-trainer, and a skilled corner-builder. *Why*, she mused, *was this seemingly extraordinary man living with his sister, not married, and not with some special woman on this fine Sunday afternoon?*

Chapter 11

Mid-morning on Monday, Jake's beeper went off. He kept his beeper on his jeans's belt-loop around his waist and the cell phone in his truck. He finished nailing the last beam in place on the house he and his crew were building, then called his answering service, who filtered his calls and let him know which ones needed immediate attention.

"A Mrs. Haddon sounded anxious to talk with you," the answering service person said.

Jake smiled at the message. Perhaps Ginger, or his job on the corner of the house, had impressed Brooke Haddon well enough for her to decide she could use his services. Yesterday, although he glimpsed her speculative gaze upon occasion, she hadn't seemed offended by him. Maybe today she'd even smile.

He was eager to have this fresh start with her after having gotten off on the wrong foot. However, unless it was an emergency, he never left his crew to finish up for the day. His regular crew all had families, and Jake wanted them to be able to get home for supper with them. At quitting time, Jake and his crew cleaned up around the property, put their equipment into their trucks, and headed for the shop.

Jake washed up while the crew dropped off their equipment. He changed shirts and ran a comb through his hair, then called Ginger to say he wouldn't be there for supper. She said she'd save him something.

Ginger had given him a standing invitation to have supper with them, and as much as he enjoyed that, he didn't feel obligated. After all, he was only an uncle to Ginger's boys—not their dad, although he felt a deep responsibility to be the kind of Christian example and male influence they needed.

A keen sense of anticipation swept over Jake as he drove along the road headed for the island of Hilton Head. He rode with the windows down. The wind cooled his face and blew his hair and rippled along his arm resting on the window ledge of the car door.

Jake thought of Brooke Haddon's cool gray gaze that morning he'd stopped by when she'd treated him like he was a potential hazard. Then he remembered how the color of her eyes had changed to gray-green when she'd looked up at him with his head hanging over the roof. The expression then had been possible repentance, thanks to the fact he had a sister who'd come to

280

his rescue. Then she'd looked down, and he'd noticed how her long brown lashes had covered her eyes, lying gently above her fair, smooth skin.

Yesterday, while he was proving to be a friend to children and animals, she'd remained cordial. What would it be like this time? Maybe a spring green look of acceptance? Did she look forward to seeing him again. *Jake!* he warned himself. *You can't do this. You cannot be interested in any woman until you're off probation, until you've fulfilled the sentence of the court. Only then will you legally have paid your debt to society. So why are you letting your emotions get in a dither?*

He shook his head as if to clear it. Of course, he knew why. He was lonely. He was a thirty-five-year-old single man, with parents he could see any time, working with a crew of spirited guys, involved in the church and particularly with singles, and living in a house where he had access to a sister and three lively boys. His life was full.

But he was lonely.

His parents had each other. His crew had their own lives. Ginger and the boys were not his family.

And you know perfectly well, Jake Randolph, he reminded himself, *there's nothing in the world you can do to change this situation. You're going to Mrs. Haddon's cottage on business. You're a man with a past. A man with a secret. God has blessed you beyond measure. You have to learn to be content with where you are and with what you have—lonely or not.*

He needn't have worried. Brooke met him on the porch, holding onto the screen door he had repaired. Serene gray eyes erased his friendly smile and turned his expression to frustration. He glanced at the corner. Had it fallen in or something? The screen door appeared intact. Her lips formed a firm line.

"Mr. Randolph," she began, holding his paper-plate invoice. "I didn't want to say anything yesterday in front of everybody, but this is ridiculous."

He relented, realizing he'd goofed again. "You're right," he agreed. "I should not have written an invoice on a paper plate. That was totally unprofessional." He sighed, mentally kicking himself in the seat of his jeans with his heavy work boots. How could he have thought that was acceptable? He'd never done such a thing before. The reason was, she'd been so concerned about getting estimates, he'd felt upbeat that his price would beat anybody's around. He wanted to impress her with that. And he wouldn't care if she didn't pay the fee of less than five dollars he'd charged. In a way, that part was a joke. The whole thing was free. But. . .it was unprofessional, and she was letting him know that.

Suddenly it dawned upon him that the reason she had called was not out of any kind of appreciation or to ask him to do further work but to complain about his lack of professionalism. That suddenly nagging fear welled up in him. If any complaint, no matter how minor, got back to the Better Business Bureau, he was sunk. That could be all it would take—one dissatisfied customer.

Jake spoke seriously. "Mrs. Haddon, I'm sorry. Believe me, I would send a legitimate receipt upon payment. I'll run to the shop and draw up a proper invoice if you like." He turned to go.

"Mr. Randolph!" she called, causing him to stop and look back at her over his shoulder. "I'm not referring to the paper plate. I wouldn't care if you wrote it on the side of the house. I'm referring to the amount."

His brows drew together. "You're complaining about the price?"

They stared at each other, both silent, as if he were speaking Chinese and she could only understand Portuguese.

Finally, Jake broke the confusing silence. "You don't need to pay me a cent, Mrs. Haddon. That small amount was sort of a joke. I thought it would make you smile. It's part of my free service. Just. . ." He gestured with his hands. "Throw away the invoice. . .um. . .the paper plate."

He grimaced at his own words. How could a businessman have been so unprofessional as to write an invoice on a paper plate? What was wrong with him? Why did he keep making a complete fool of himself? Particularly in front of the one woman he'd met in years that he'd like to favorably impress.

Brooke let the screen door slam behind her, and she held out the plate to him. "Even if you meant this as a nice gesture, it's totally unacceptable."

He didn't attempt to stop her ranting. Strangely, he was concentrated on how the late evening sun glinted in her steely gray eyes. How the color of indignation tinged the cheeks of her fair, flawless skin. How intriguing the way her soft lips moved as she spoke. Her teeth were very white and straight. There was the tiniest little dimple at one corner of her mouth as she spouted her displeasure with him.

"Maybe I've given the impression that I'm destitute and can't pay my bills," he heard in the back of his mind and forced himself to concentrate on her meaning. "Well, that's not the situation. I am not a charity case!"

So that was it! It was all he could do to keep from laughing out loud. She thought he pitied her or something. Not so. He'd done many jobs for those who couldn't pay up front, and they'd worked out a payment plan. One single mom needed a gate built across the entry to her back porch so her toddler would have a safe place to play outside without falling down the steps or wandering off. The job hadn't cost much by his standards, but with her limited income, they'd worked out a plan and she'd paid a few dollars a month, taking over a year to get it paid off.

"It wasn't charity, Mrs. Haddon."

"Just what would you call it then, Mr. Randolph?"

Her eyes dared him to have a satisfactory answer. He understood her now in plain English words and human body language. He knew she suspected he was trying to impress her for some personal reason and she was trying to convey that such attempts would be useless.

"I've given the wrong impression from the moment we met," he said, glancing toward the graying sky as if seeking help from beyond. He looked back at her then, his face serious. "It's my water-basin theory, Mrs. Haddon," he said. "If you have a few minutes, I'd like to explain it to you."

He felt her skepticism as she stared. "Water basin?" she queried, looking at him as if they'd reverted to speaking in foreign languages.

This kind of problem had never occurred before. He'd always done his work, added a free job, explained why he did a free job, and it had been accepted and appreciated. Why was this going so wrong? Maybe he should just write out a new invoice or charge her for the corner and let it go.

But that thought hit hard in his chest. He wanted this woman to believe in him, trust him, even like him. Maybe he'd wanted that too much since that morning when he'd walked into her backyard and thought there was something unidentifiably intriguing about her. Perhaps it was the mystery of her situation. Perhaps it was her instant wariness of him. Perhaps it was because, watching her, the little boy, and a dog, he felt that deep-seated loneliness, or longing for such a life—a cottage, a woman, a little boy, a dog.

Why am I fighting that man? Brooke asked herself. *I know he's in the construction business. His sister, with whom I felt instant camaraderie and want for a friend, vouched for him. His work on the corner is an excellent recommendation. He has not shown any indication of improper behavior.*

Why couldn't she just take him at face value, accept his charitable gesture, regard him as the brother of a woman who offered friendship, and just let it go?

Instead, she had to make an issue of it. She hadn't refused Ginger's food, nor had she questioned it. But a gift from a man was a different thing. She could reciprocate Ginger's hospitality, but Jake was something else.

It had been failure that set her feet on the right path. After returning to her parents' home, trying to be a good mom to Ben while settling up the bills, then becoming involved in church and depending on the Lord, she felt she had become strong. It had been time to make a move and start a life for herself and Ben without the help of her parents.

She would do it. And she would do it without charity. She'd have to be frugal, but there were definitely others who needed charity more than she. There were always her parents she could fall back on, if necessary. And she knew that if there were a great financial need for Ben, the Haddons would come through. She just didn't want to have to resort to calling upon them.

But was that any reason to be rude to a man offering nothing more than his help and kindness? This was no big deal. All she had to do was tell him in a calm way that she would pay for the repair of that corner, period.

"I need to check on Ben," she said. "He's out back."

"I'll walk around," Jake said, beginning to move as he spoke.

Brooke hurried through the house and reached the back door by the time Jake got there. Ben and Taz were playing tug-o'-war with a sock.

"Hey, Ben. Looks like you and Taz have a battle going there."

"Yeah. And I think I'm about to pull his teeth out."

Jake laughed. "I don't know about that. He'd probably let go before he hurt himself. But if you let him pull on cloth like that, he'll think it's all right to chew on cloth in the house. He wouldn't know the difference between chewing on a sock or chewing on clothes and furniture."

"He likes it," Ben said, looking at the dog pulling as hard he could on the sock, his back legs having trouble keeping his balance as he pulled back. Then Ben let go and Taz began to chew on the sock. Ben looked up at Jake with big soulful eyes. "He liked that bread you told us not to feed him, too. But boy, did he get sick. Didn't he, Mom?" He glanced at Brooke, standing on the porch, watching the exchange. "Mom was up all night cleaning Taz, and the kitchen, and herself, and—"

"Ben," Brooke said, looking away from Jake's knowing glance and small grin. "I think he gets the point. Taz had quite a time of it. From now on, it's dog food."

"An occasional snack's all right," Jake said, "but a steady diet of people food just doesn't sit well with a puppy. Hey, you want to learn to play ball with him?"

Ben's eyes got big. "Yeah."

As much as he would enjoy doing so, Jake remembered he wasn't here to entertain the child or train the dog. Mrs. Haddon had called him here to complain about the bill. "Right now, your mom wants to talk business with me." He turned questioning eyes toward Brooke.

She spread her hands. She understood what he'd said about a dog chewing up things in the house, and she'd known of dogs doing that. She couldn't keep Taz outside until they had some kind of enclosure, and she didn't want to chain him up. She shrugged. It might be good to teach the dog a few tricks. Give Ben a purpose other than pulling on one end of a sock. She relented. "If you want to show him, go ahead."

While Ben rushed inside to get a rubber ball and puppy food, Jake knelt down and gently pinched Taz's nose to make him let go of the sock, which he then threw onto the porch.

After Ben came out, Brooke sat on the top step, with her elbows on her jeaned legs and her jaw resting in the palms of her hands, watching the two do what a father and son might do.

Jake explained to Ben, "The main reward should not be the food, but love. So when he does what you tell him, say, 'Good boy.' " Jake showed Ben how to toss the ball a short way, command the puppy to fetch, then say, "Give it to me," or "Bring it here," or something like that. "Don't throw it a long way until he learns. And don't give him a treat unless he does what you say. Okay?"

"Okay," Ben said, and after watching Jake perform the exercise, he was ready to try.

"Very good," Jake said and mussed Ben's dark curls. Ben looked up at him admiringly.

What a lesson, Brooke thought, remembering all the nice things Bruce had given her when all she'd wanted was love. And little Ben responded with glowing eyes when Jake mussed his hair. Yes, that was what the world needed, love, sweet love. Puppy dogs, little boys, and grown women too. She wondered just who loved this interesting man who took time to play with a little boy and a dog.

"You practice," Jake said. "When the puppy tires of it, just stop and let him play the way he wants to. As long as he's not destructive."

While Ben and Taz tirelessly played the game, quite effectively, Jake and Brooke watched and laughed. Sometimes Taz would ignore the ball and Ben would forget and give him a piece of food anyway. "Oops, I forgot," he'd say, and Jake would reply, "That's okay. Try again."

Try again seemed to lodge in Brooke's brain. Maybe that's what she should do with Jake. Not be angry with him because he was a man or for what Bruce did to her.

Brooke could readily see that a dog would be a better pet if he were disciplined, just as children and parents had a better lifestyle with order and discipline. Watching Jake with Ben served to remind Brooke that a little boy needed guidance from a dad. She would make sure Ben's needs were met, but just as her own life would have been lacking without her father, she was aware that Ben's was lacking without a dad to spend time with him. Could Jake be a good male influence for Ben, as Ginger said he was for her boys?

"Keep on until he gets tired of it," Jake said. "I need to talk with your mom."

Chapter 12

Jake walked over to the step and stood at the side, reaching up to hold onto the banister. "Mrs. Haddon. If it would make you feel better to pay for that corner, then I'll take the money. But I would appreciate you hearing me out on that."

"The. . .water-basin thing?" she asked, trying not to appear too skeptical.

"Exactly," he said, appearing quite serious as he walked in front of her and sat beside her on the top step.

With knees spread wide, Jake folded his hands and rested his forearms on his thighs, looking out toward Ben and Taz, but Brooke thought he was looking beyond the boy and dog—even beyond the sky turning to gold and pink.

"There was a time when I lost everything and had no money. I decided to give one hundred percent to my work and offer a free service of some kind so the customers would ask why and I could witness to them, telling them that the reason is because I'm a follower of Jesus Christ, who admonishes us to do good to others, to be charitable. If the person is interested, I witness further. If they're not interested, then I've at least attempted to plant a seed, and they will remember that free gift. Jesus gave freely to us—the gift of eternal life is ours if we just receive it. Just accept it."

What a wonderful attitude, Brooke thought. And yet, she'd treated him like he was beneath contempt. But then, she hadn't known him. And some people knew how to put a spin on anything and make themselves look good. She mustn't be judgmental, but she could look at a person's fruit in order to evaluate his character.

Stealing a glance at Jake, she saw what appeared to be a sincere man, a true Christian who was serious about his commitment to the Lord. His attitude was commendable. "What about. . .the water-basin?" she asked.

He nodded and smiled, the glorious sunset reflecting a spark of gold in his warm brown eyes. "That's what gave me the idea," he said. "Our preacher talked about it one Sunday morning during the worship service. He read the Scripture where Jesus took a wash basin and towel and washed the disciples' feet. Jesus then told His disciples to do the same."

Brooke's head turned toward him. "You belong to a foot-washing group?"

He grinned. "No, but that might be good for a lot of us to do, literally.

The example was for us to serve each other. When I do at least one repair job free of charge, the customers ask me why. Then I have the opportunity to tell them that I do it because I'm a Christian. Jesus taught that we should do good to others. We should serve them. This is part of my service."

"That's commendable," Brooke said while a thought pressed in on her mind. If she were going to be interested in a man, ever again, she'd want it to be someone like Jake.

Feeling the blush in her cheeks, she looked down at the toes of her scuffed tennis shoes. "Do others give you such a hard time about it, as I did?"

He laughed. "No, but I don't generally barge in the way I did with you. Most of my customers know my company's reputation and come to me. Jessica, the Realtor, lets me know about some clients, and she recommends me to some people before I approach them. She felt your situation was an emergency and that you were planning to stay, with a child, in a house that might not be habitable."

"I'm just not trusting enough," Brooke admitted.

"I understand that," Jake said. "I have the same trouble at times. Ginger and other singles we work with find it difficult after they've lost trust in someone or something."

"It's not always fair to the other person," Brooke said.

He smiled. "I don't think you were unfair to me. Sometimes the people we trust most disappoint us. It's a fact of life that we need to be aware of and yet try to not let it get in the way of interaction, of friendship."

She nodded, knowing she mustn't let the past control her life. *I want interaction and friendship. But. . .not yet!*

"Well," she said suddenly, looking away from his questioning eyes that seemed to say that he thought she had some kind of answer, when in truth, she knew she certainly did not. "Now that I've accepted your explanation, I'll run in and get my money."

She returned with a five-dollar bill. "Keep the change," she said.

He didn't argue. Rather he simply said, "Thank you," and stuck the bill in his pocket. "I'll paint the corner of the house if you'd like."

"Yes, I want that," she said, plopping down beside him again. "I have a lot of fixing up to do around here."

He nodded. "I know there are several roof shingles to be nailed down," he commented.

"That's for sure," she agreed. "And I have a kitchen ceiling with brown splotches all over it, two leaky faucets, broken window panes, a temperamental lock on the front door, missing slats in the front banister, and a pitiful picket fence." She paused and shook her head. "That's for starters."

"Obviously, no one has lived in it for awhile," he commented.

"Well, nobody's been here since the hurricane hit. Before that, there were renters. Doesn't look like too much damage, but there are a lot of minor repairs to be done, and the whole house needs painting or wallpaper. Are those the kinds of things you do?"

"I do a little bit of everything," he said. "My crew and I work a five-day week, and I moonlight on Saturdays. Right now we're working on a half-million-dollar house on the beach. But we also have jobs like replacing a set of steps. It might be twenty steps leading to an upper deck or it might be two steps on a porch." He smiled. "I'm the owner, but I'm also my own secretary-treasurer, accountant, handy-man, and part of the clean-up crew."

"Wow! Jack-of-all-trades," Brooke said, then caught her breath. She shot him a sideways glance. "I don't mean to imply you're master of none."

He didn't laugh, just looked at her seriously. "I can't do everything. I have men on the crew who are much better than me at certain aspects of building. Tim's the best roofer you could find. Marcia can't always hammer a nail in straight, but she can paint a room without leaving a streak or an air bubble. But that's part of owning a business—employing workers with different skills. I'll tell you this, Mrs. Haddon. I give it my best. I don't scrimp anywhere. I don't get by with cheap materials. I don't put my stamp of approval on a project until I think God would approve. My crew and I have a prayer each morning before we start working. That keeps us where we ought to be."

Maybe I should have a prayer right now, Brooke thought, *to keep my mind where it ought to be. I have no business whatsoever letting a man come into my life and into the life of my boy and his dog and sit here talking like we're close or something. So we go to the same church. Big deal! He and Jessica Lawler go to the same church too. Does that mean anything personal? Apparently not, since Jessica had been at church with her husband.*

Forcing herself to look away from the interesting way the light formed a golden gleam in his warm brown eyes, she spoke quickly. "I think I should probably finish the roof or repair the windows."

Jake nodded. "I'll be glad to work up an estimate."

"I would appreciate that," Brooke said.

They sat for a moment in silence, then Jake stood. "If it's all right with you, I'll go ahead and measure the broken window panes and stop by tomorrow evening after work and bring you an estimate on those and the roof. Oh, I can paint the corner too."

Brooke nodded.

"Good night, then," he said and called good-bye to Ben.

"This is a good trick, huh, Jake?"

Brooke knew Ben was playing with a Tonka truck, filling it with sand, dumping it, making mounds that Taz pawed through, and then beginning again, but it only now dawned upon her what Ben was doing. He was hiding dog food in the mounds, and Taz was finding and eating it.

"It's a good trick if you realize that's his supper. He mustn't have too much food either. The bag tells you how much he should get," Jake told him. "Tell you what, if your mom agrees, when I stop by tomorrow, I'll help you teach Taz how to heel, so you can take him for walks without his taking you for walks."

"Neat!" Ben said. "That's okay. Right, Mom?"

"Well, we don't want to take up too much of Mr. Randolph's time."

"I did offer," Jake said, glancing at her with a broad smile.

Brooke returned the smile, then quickly glanced at Ben. "Time to come in and get cleaned up, Ben. I'll start supper."

Jake said good-bye again and disappeared around the house. Brooke suddenly realized she wasn't apprehensive about him anymore.

Only about *herself*.

~

On the drive home, Jake denounced himself for the mistakes he'd made with Brooke Haddon. No wonder she thought he had ulterior motives. Would an electrician or a telephone repairman sit down beside her on the step? Would a plumber or a painter? He thought not!

Then why in the name of Sam Hill had he done it? He'd never done that with any of his other female customers. He'd always kept a professional distance. But with her, he was going overboard—and sometimes going overboard indicated you just might sink. What had happened to his good sense?

Maybe Ginger could tell him.

After he ate the supper Ginger had kept in the fridge and then microwaved for him, Jake sat on the top step of the back porch while Ginger sat in a rocking chair and the boys played on the swing set. He told his sister he'd seen Brooke Haddon and Ben that evening.

"I'm behaving as if she's my friend, Ginger. I know you two hit it off right away, and it's not that way between me and Mrs. Haddon." He snorted. "See. She hasn't even asked me to call her by her first name. This is a business proposition, and I'm behaving like it's something personal."

"Maybe it's because you want it to be, Jake," she said. "I mean, Brooke has some emotional problems to deal with, but otherwise, she's a strong woman. She has looks, guts, maternal instinct, and faith in God."

Jake nodded. Brooke had sun-streaked, golden blond hair and eyes that changed with the color of her clothes, or the grass, or the sky. She had soft lips with a little dimple at one corner of her mouth when she smiled. She had a musical laugh and an angelic expression on her face when she looked at her son. He couldn't deny it when Ginger added, "And Jake, you're a man who hasn't met a woman who appealed to you since Meagan."

Jake gave a short laugh. "I wouldn't go that far," he said. "A lot of women appeal to me, but I've known I can't get involved. I can't even tell them the truth about myself. I know we talked about this before. When I told the truth to Meagan, she turned and ran the other way, so to speak. She didn't trust me anymore."

He picked up a stick and poked at the dirt in front of the step. "Brooke mistrusted me from the first time I pulled up in that truck and offered my services."

"That's because her emotions are in a turmoil, Jake. It's been a year since her husband's death, but the memory is still part of her life, just as Leo's will always be a part of ours. That's inescapable. Brooke shared her husband's dream. Then when she got pregnant, he wanted her to choose. She chose the unborn baby. She was no longer his dream girl. They drifted apart. His goal was ambition and power. Hers was family life and her son. Then her husband was unfaithful. Now he's dead. I think it's easier for me to be judgmental about my husband than for her. It's not considered proper to condemn a dead man."

Jake turned and gazed at his sister. "I didn't know all that."

"Of course not," Ginger replied. "We women who've been trampled by a man have to put on a front of having it all together, as if we don't need a man."

Jake thought he knew his sister. But it seemed he learned new things about her everyday. She was a strong woman—in many ways stronger than he, although she was younger. She'd grown in many ways since Leo had discarded her like an old rag. Her faith in herself had been restored. Her faith in God had grown. And yet she was admitting she would like to have a man in her life—not just an older brother. Of course she would. He'd just accepted her lifestyle and his—until now.

"She's doing a great job with Ben," he said.

Ginger nodded. "It's not easy, Jake. I'd be lost without you."

"You'd make it," he said, reaching over to pat her arm.

"Not as well without you," she said softly. "So! She's going to let you make repairs."

He grinned. "Seems that way."

"You like her, Jake. Don't deny it."

"Very much," he admitted. "But you know I'm in no position to even think about going beyond friendship with a woman."

"Jake," she said, surprised, "you told me the business was going well, and besides buying that property, you're saving and—"

"I'm not talking financially, Ginger. Living here has enabled me to save almost all my profits."

"Ha!" she exclaimed. "Your living here has been a lifesaver for me and the boys, Jake. In more ways than financially."

He laughed lightly. "Don't you think we've complimented each other enough for one day?"

Her shoulder lifted in a light shrug. "Well, I probably don't tell you enough how much I appreciate you."

"Mutual admiration society," he said and grinned, then stared into the distance. His brow furrowed.

"What is it, Jake?"

He sighed heavily. "You know I can't consider anything beyond friendship, Ginger."

"Of course you can, Jake. Someday the right woman will understand—"

He interrupted. "Meagan didn't."

"Meagan wasn't the right woman."

"I know that now," Jake said, "but at the time I thought she was. After all we'd meant to each other, it seems she didn't even know me." *But she did know me*, Jake corrected himself silently. *She knew, and she still didn't believe me.*

"Brooke is not Meagan," Ginger reminded him. "She has a lot more maturity and character than your former fiancée."

"But a lot less trust," he said. "Meagan trusted me at the beginning. Brooke's mistrust was immediate."

"You said it went well tonight."

"Yes. But I should have checked out the repairs she wanted done, assessed the needs, and suggested some of my crew or the volunteers from the church. Instead, I offered myself several nights after work and Saturday, as long as needed. I play with her boy. I train her dog. I sit beside her on the back step without invitation. I sit on the church pew with her." He sighed and shook his head like he'd committed the crime of the century.

Ginger smiled behind his back. How she'd love to see her brother get a break. And she thought Brooke would be good for Jake—and vice versa. She understood them both, the reticence of them both. "You said you're going back every night after work?"

"Yep! I committed myself."

"And she didn't tell you not to come."

He glanced around, then turned back to stare at the holes he'd made in the dirt. "Maybe I did wrong there too. I told her about my water-basin theory— my religious reasons for doing work free. Maybe I was playing on her sympathy. It's a little hard to refuse a person when he says he's doing it for the Lord."

"Oh, quit doubting yourself, Jake. I know your intentions are genuine. She will learn that. And I don't think she'd ask you to come back if she didn't believe in you, no matter what you told her."

Both were silent for awhile, watching the boys enjoy life without a care in the world except which one could swing the highest.

After a long moment, he asked the question that pressed hard on his mind. "What do you think Brooke will think of me when she learns the truth? Frankly, I wish she didn't have to know. And yet, I want her to know. What do I do?"

Usually, Ginger would advise him on almost any subject. But this time was different. "I can't answer that, Jake. It's a decision only you can make."

He nodded. He knew that. To blurt out the truth about his past would imply to Brooke that he thought there was, or could be, something personal between them. Wouldn't that be the height of presumption on his part? Shouldn't he first try to discover if there could be a personal relationship?

Knowing Ginger couldn't begin to answer his question, he muttered, "When is the right time to tell another person about your past? How much do you tell? When does withholding information become lying?"

Chapter 13

When Jake came to start on the agreed-upon repairs for the cottage, he brought Ginger's boys. Earlier on the phone, Brooke had told Ginger that would be fine, even helpful. Brooke and Ben went out to greet them. The boys immediately ran around back with Ben to play with Taz.

"Thought you might want this," Jake said, lifting a wire cage out of the truck bed. Brooke eyed the cage skeptically.

"It's a crate for Taz," he explained, realizing she wasn't pleased.

"You mean. . .lock him up?"

"A dog doesn't look at it that way," Jake explained. "It's a home, a safe haven for a dog. A place where it can feel protected. You just need to teach him to go home. Get some puppy food, and I'll show you."

Brooke went through the house to get the puppy food and took a handful out to Jake. He had placed the crate on the ground and began to demonstrate how to teach the puppy.

"Go home," he said and tossed a piece of dog food into the crate. Taz ran in, chomped on the piece of food while looking at them with big, soulful, black eyes in that werewolf face, then ran out. Jake repeated the exercise a couple more times, then addressed Ben. "Do that a few times during the day and at night when it's bedtime. He'll soon learn to go home whenever you say the words."

Brook tried to ignore the thought that came into her mind. How many times Bruce had said, "Don't run, don't yell so loud, don't track dirt in the house, no, you can't play in the rain, no, I can't play with you right now."

How different. This man was taking time to teach a little boy how to train a dog. How gratifying for a man to interact with a child instead of make demands.

But she shouldn't be comparing. That had been an entirely different lifestyle where appearances had to be a primary consideration. Bruce hadn't been abusive, just preoccupied with being an important politician. But was it any less important being a carpenter?

Her next thought startled her. Jesus had been a carpenter! Had He done work for people without pay to show His generosity? Had He been helpful like Jake? Had He stopped to speak to little children before tackling His work?

She felt He had.

An overwhelming urge to be kind to Jake swept over her. She could think of no reason whatsoever not to accept him as a friend, or at least as a friend of her son.

"Jake," she said and saw the light of surprise in his eyes before it quickly disappeared. An incredible look of pleasure settled on his face. Was that because she had called him by his first name? Perhaps. He obviously made an effort to have people like him and accept him as a Christian witness. *Do I not want the same? Didn't I spend many years feeling that I was not completely accepted by Bruce or his family, and didn't I wonder about his friends?*

She smiled. "Thanks for the crate and for teaching Taz to sit and lie down," she said. "He's really doing that for me and Ben. Watch!" Brooke reached into the bag for a few pieces of dog food. "Taz! Sit!" she commanded, holding the piece of food at his nose and moving it slightly over the puppy's head so he'd sit back.

Suddenly they all burst out laughing. Taz sat all right—right into his water bowl! And he stayed there.

Brooke gave him the dog food, patted him on the head, said, "Good boy," then turned an impish glance at Jake. She shrugged a shoulder. "Well, so now he has his own private bathtub."

~

The ice was broken. Or at least it had begun to thaw from around Brooke's heart. The cottage was becoming transformed from a broken-down, neglected honeymoon cottage to a renovated, restored home for her and Ben.

On weekday evenings after work, Jake came and finished nailing down the roof shingles, cleaned out the gutters, tightened them against the house, and applied a coat of primer to the repaired corner.

On Saturday, he arrived early to scrape, patch, and fill any holes on the outside of the house, getting it and the porches ready for a fresh coat of paint.

Ginger came by to help Brooke put up the wallpaper border in Ben's room. They stood back to survey the effect of the dogs of all types running around the center of the walls. The walls had not needed to be repainted. Brooke had simply given a basic washing to the cream-colored walls.

"Neat!" Ben exclaimed, excited about the dogs. "Taz loves it, Mom. Look!"

Taz really was loving the newspapers spotted with paint, and he began trying to chew them up.

After Ben obeyed her order to get the dog out of the room, Brooke turned to Ginger, saying proudly, "It's beginning to look like a boy's room."

Ginger shook her head, her brows making a furrow above her nose. "Not yet," she said. "You need to toss a shoe under the bed to join the dust bunnies, make sure the bed's not made, open the bureau drawers, scatter toys all over the floor, sprinkle dirt—preferably wet—in several places, scribble a little crayon on the wall, and then you'll have yourself the ideal boy's room."

By the time Ginger finished, Brooke was laughing. What a joy this woman was! She mentally thanked God for Ginger's friendship. How rejuvenating to be reminded that she and her little boy didn't have to be perfect and that she didn't have to expect such behavior from her Ben. A house to live in was much more important than a house to look at.

Ginger took Ben and Taz home with her and the boys. Brooke finished up Ben's room. She hung the blue valances, put the matching spread on the bed, topped it with two red and white pillow cushions, dragged the box of toys out of the closet, neatly stacked some toys along with books on the bookshelf, and then mopped the hardwood floor. As soon as the floor dried, she dragged in his freshly vacuumed throw rug. Perfect! A wonderful room for a little boy to live in.

Around five o'clock, when Jake had just finished replacing broken rails in the banister, Ginger returned, bearing pizza.

At Brooke's insistence, they all came in to look at Ben's room and to exclaim over the new look before going out back to eat pizza. Brooke spread a blanket on the ground for the boys to sit on while they ate, trying to keep their pizza out of the range of Taz's mouth. Finally, Ben got puppy food and ordered Taz to "go home," which he did.

Brooke, Ginger, and Jake sat in kitchen chairs on the back porch. When Jake left to clean up from his repairs and put his tools in his truck, Ginger left with her boys, saying they all had to have baths and get to bed early since tomorrow was Sunday.

When Jake was about ready to leave, Brooke went out to say good-bye.

Ben stood looking up at Jake. "You wanna teach Taz some more tricks?" he asked.

Taz was tugging on the bottom of Jake's jeans, as if he, too, didn't want Jake to leave. Brooke realized she felt a little lonely each evening when he left.

"He's been here all day, Ben," Brooke said.

"I don't mind, if you don't," Jake said.

She shook her head. "I don't."

Jake smiled broadly, as if he were in no hurry to go. He commanded Taz to sit, which he did, while looking up soulfully, waiting for his food. Jake simply patted him on the head and said, "Good boy."

Taz continued to sit, giving the impression he preferred food to a pat.

"If you have a leash, we can take him for a walk and teach him to heel," Jake told Ben, which sent the boy off like a flash.

"It might seem cruel to keep Taz on a leash," Jake said. "But it's best for him when you first begin to teach him. This is a smart dog. And he's strong-willed. Before long, he'll try to take over as the leader of the pack. If you tell him to sit and he wanders off, you've lost it. Keep him on a leash when training. He'll learn the commands and obey them after he's off the leash. Also, when you take him for a walk, keep him on the leash."

Brooke soon learned what he meant by a strong-willed puppy.

They took Taz for a walk along a nearby bicycle path that ran along through the trees. Jake was teaching her how to make him heel when they walked the dog. It wasn't too hard for Ben, since he was closer to the ground than Brooke, which meant he was closer to the dog's mouth with the food.

Jake even did all right at keeping Taz at his left heel while reaching over, behind his left leg, with an occasional piece of dog food.

When Brooke tried it, she felt awkward holding the leash with her left hand while stooping down and reaching across herself with a bite of rewarding food.

More awkward than that were Ben's words when he blurted out enthusiastically, "We look just like a family, don't we, Mom?"

Flustered, she looked away from Jake. When she did, she straightened from her cramped, sideways, leaning-over position. Her hand moved around in front of her, and Taz followed it, coming after the food. He came across the front of her legs, then ran around to the other side, wrapping the leash around her legs. Then he began to pull on the leash, tightening its hold on her.

"Oh, yes, we're like a family," Brooke spouted, trying to keep her balance. "The man and boy laugh at the woman who gets tied up by a dog! Just like a couple of men!" She struggled to get a piece of dog food in Taz's mouth so that he would stay still, hoping she could keep her balance. "Help me!" she demanded.

Jake and Ben grinned at each other, but Jake came over, stood for an instant very close, his warm twinkling eyes looking into her irate ones for a long moment. He took the leash from her hand, then unwrapped her and gave the leash to Ben.

"Food," he said, and Brooke gladly slapped her handful of food into his outstretched hand.

"I can do it," Ben said confidently.

Jake still grinned, giving her a sly glance. "Got all tied up in knots, huh?"

She gave him a warning look, then watched as Ben executed the command and reward quite well.

She was thinking, *Yes, tied in knots in more ways than one and for many reasons.* Ben said they looked like a family. Maybe someday she could put the past behind her and get her life straightened out enough to consider something like that. She wanted it to be right this time. When she thought about it or when it entered her mind unbidden, the ideal man began to look suspiciously like Jake Randolph.

~

Each evening during the following week, Jake painted the front porch and the shutters a deep gray. On Saturday he brought two crew members and a retired house painter from church who volunteered to help singles. By Saturday evening the cottage looked like a new house.

After all the men except Jake left, Brooke and Ben stood with him, surveying his handiwork.

"Cool!" Ben exclaimed.

"Oh, Jake, it is beautiful," Brooke said, looking at the soft, dove gray cottage with its darker trim and gleaming white banister. It didn't look like a broken-down honeymoon cottage anymore. It was a rejuvenated home for a mother and her son.

"I'll have to get shrubs and plant flowers below the banister," Brooke said and asked Jake if he had any suggestions.

"We're clearing land around the church where a new conference center and housing is being built. There are some azaleas that we have to take out and have permission to give away. I can bring several of those," he offered.

"That would be perfect," she said. "And I'll get some pansies. We'll just have a riot of color." She could almost see the finished product. A background of blooming azaleas, or just the green leaves, bordered by splashes of yellow, maroon, purple, blue, and white. Yes, it was beginning to shape up.

She was beginning to enjoy the present and look ahead with anticipation, instead of dwelling on the past.

Sunday at church proved that to her more strongly.

Since that first Sunday, Ginger and her boys always saved room in their pew for Brooke and Ben. Jake usually sat at the end of the pew, next to Mike. This Sunday, at the end of the worship service, the congregation took communion. The pastor related briefly the meaning of the Lord's Supper and reminded the listeners that Jesus died to take away the sins of the world.

Brooke felt that she was rededicating herself, making a new commitment to live closer to the Lord as she partook, but she had to tell Ben he couldn't participate. Her son was close to six years old. She must make as her first priority Ben's religious training. If she succeeded in every area but failed to clearly teach God's love for him and the salvation that was offered through Jesus, then she would fail totally as a parent.

With determination and a feeling of well-being, Brooke joined in with the voices and was able to hear Jake's baritone as they sang the closing song,

"Blest be the tie that binds our hearts in Christian love."

She was humming the song as she leaned over to pick up her Bible and purse from underneath the pew in front of her. She straightened up and turned toward Ben, but her glance met Jake's gaze. Their eyes held for a moment. He smiled in a way that had begun to affect her heart in unexpected ways.

How could anyone not respect him? Admire him? But. . .love?

But the song is referring to Christian love. That's entirely different from the physical love between a man and woman, isn't it? she asked herself, ignoring her rapid heartbeat. She brushed at her cheek as if to erase the warmth she felt rising to her face.

She quickly lowered her gaze to Ben. "You have all your papers?" she asked, reminding herself that other "ties that bind" had for a long time held a negative connotation in her life.

In spite of her fears, however, was her heart binding with Jake's? And much as she might try to dismiss her feelings as Christian love, if she were honest, didn't they hold something else as well?

Chapter 14

Jake had heard Ginger complain that during her last months of pregnancy, time had dragged interminably, almost stopped. That's what time seemed to be doing for him. He kept busy and looked forward to the evenings and Saturdays he could spend at Brooke's, and ever-present on his mind was that he had four months, three weeks to go until his probation was over. Then it was four months, two weeks. Four months, one week. Four months.

But the time dragged. Could he keep letting his feelings grow for Brooke without telling her the truth of his past? Shouldn't he find out if she thought there was a chance for them together? Suppose she said there was a chance and asked him to meet her parents in Indiana?

He'd have to say, "Sorry. I wouldn't be allowed to go out of state just to meet someone's parents." Now what kind of relationship could be built on that kind of information?

~

There was no denying to Brooke's mind that Jake had become, to say the least, a friend. She was not indifferent to him and could not pretend so. But a man like him deserved a woman who was as openly committed to the Lord as he. She determined to follow through with her renewed dedication to the Lord.

She decided that Ben should memorize some basic verses from the Bible. The first and most important to her was John 3:16. She had him repeat each phrase every morning, and by the end of the week, she figured it should be a part of him. To her delight, he could say it verbatim by Wednesday morning.

That's the morning she decided it was time to get her body in shape. She wasn't overweight, but she knew her body wasn't toned the way it should be. She would give water aerobics a try. She, Ben, and Taz showed up at Ginger's before ten A.M.

Ginger and the boys were delighted to see them. As soon as the children gathered at the side of the pool, Ben asked, "Hey, you guys want to hear me say John 3:16?"

"I do!" Danny said, and they all stood quietly while Ben recited it.

"For God so loved the world, that he gave his only begotten Son, that whosoever believeth in him should not perish, but have everlasting life."

Mike tousled Ben's hair like Brooke had seen Jake do. "That's really good,

Ben," he said. He looked over and grinned at his mother, who nodded her approval of him. It was beautiful how those two communicated with just a glance.

Other women began to arrive. Brooke met a middle-aged neighbor of Ginger's and her friend; a fourth-grade school teacher; two overweight women trying to get fit; a trim writer who said she needed the exercise since she sat at her computer from six A.M. until time for aerobics, pausing only for a quick breakfast; an older woman; and two single parents who shared an apartment. One worked the second shift as a nurse and the other worked as a waitress. The nurse brought her two daughters, ages six and four, and the other woman brought her daughter, age eight.

Mike drew a hopscotch outline on the concrete with sidewalk chalk, and the children began to play, except for the four-year-old girl who wanted to swing. Her six-year-old sister had to keep running over to push her little sister. The children had to be careful not to stumble over Taz, who was right on the heels of whomever's turn it was to jump. He liked to pick up the pebble and take it away too. The children enjoyed the puppy's antics.

All the women were ready to get into the pool by ten o'clock. Brooke was not surprised at Ginger's expertise. She called, "Straight-leg kick while moving the opposite arm toward the opposite leg."

The worst thing about it was seeing that the children, mimicking their mothers, did the exercises with such ease. To Brooke's relief, they soon became bored with that and returned to their own games.

While exercising, the women talked about themselves between listening to Ginger give commands. The singles talked about their difficulties, the older woman about her age, and the heavy ones about their weight.

"Fanny kick while pushing the water toward yourself. Heel kick behind and touch the heel with the opposite hand, then heel kick in front," Ginger commanded. "Leap frog" was next, and Brooke could feel her body moving in ways she hadn't imagined. But, she could tell, wet exercise was much more pleasant than dry exercise.

They ran in the water, then checked their pulses. Her heartbeat had definitely accelerated by the third round. The toning part was what she liked best, wrapping her arms around a noodle to keep herself afloat and working the leg and tummy muscles. After a cool-down of stretching and finally hugging themselves while taking deep breaths and exhaling, Brooke felt like every muscle in her body had been massaged—and it felt very good!

After an hour, the women dried off. Some slipped on T-shirts over their suits, and some left in their suits with a towel slung around their shoulders.

"Stay awhile," Ginger said to Brooke as she was drying off.

After the others left, Ginger invited Brooke and Ben to lunch, which turned out to be peanut butter and banana sandwiches. Carrot sticks again. Juice for the children. Brooke and Ginger had lemonade, then went out onto the porch with coffee.

"This is really a nice place, Ginger," Brooke complimented. She laughed. "For adults too."

Ginger nodded. "Thanks to my parents, I have it. Jake and I were raised here. My parents bought it years ago before the island was built up, so they got it for a real bargain. Then they built a new house in Bluffton and rented this out to me and Leo." She lifted her eyes and brows toward heaven. "That's my ex-husband. You wanna hear about a real skunk?"

Brooke grinned and nodded. She really did. She wanted to know how Ginger could be so warm, friendly, and well-adjusted with all her responsibilities.

"Well, it's like this," Ginger began her story. Leo Harris was raised on the golf course. In his younger days, he was a caddy to a famous golfer. He was away on the golf circuit almost all the time. He said he wanted a big family, but he must have meant he wanted her to have a big family while he traveled everywhere. Ginger had tried to understand. After all, he was their meal ticket. But it began to seem that he was away when he should have been home.

Finally, Leo claimed it wasn't fair to her and the boys for them to wait for him to come home, and the boys didn't seem to know him. Baby Danny cried when Leo came near because he didn't know his dad. Leo was a golf instructor for awhile and could have stayed with it if he'd wanted to make a living and take care of a family. But he enjoyed hobnobbing with the pros and decided he wanted to be one of them.

"He's now on the golf circuit and making good money," Ginger said. "He pays alimony and child support. That eases his conscience, and the children think it's great that he's a golf pro and sends them presents." She threw up her hands. "That's his way. Make a big splash. Be noticed. But everyday living with and caring for a family is not part of the picture."

Brooke could understand. "Bruce didn't want to be tied down either," she said. "We were very happy for three months." She felt she could confide in Ginger, and the prospect of doing so suddenly seemed freeing. She'd held back so long and hadn't even told her parents everything.

"Ours was a whirlwind romance," Brooke said. "I was in my second year of nurse's training when he returned from law school, ready to become part of a big law firm."

Brooke told about working at Haddon's Department Store and doing some modeling for them. Bruce had seen her model before, but he said she'd grown up in the past couple of years. He called her a real beauty and swept her

301

off her feet by taking her out of her ordinary life and involving her in his dreams of grandeur.

"To the public," she said, "I lived a charmed life as the wife of Bruce Haddon, handsome, young state senator." They were occasional visitors at the governor's mansion and attended political fund-raising dinners at the Haddons's. Photographs were taken and used to publicize Bruce with his model-wife impeccably dressed and made-up and his adorable young son.

"But our private life was entirely different," Brooke revealed. "He didn't want a child so soon in his career. Nor did he want a wife who refused to leave her son with a nanny and go on the campaign trail with him. When things got worse, I wanted to return to nurses' training, but he forbade it."

Tears came to Brooke's eyes as she revealed those painful years. The more public acceptance Bruce received, the worse he became in his private life. He became verbally abusive, unfaithful, controlling, and destroyed her self-esteem and ignored his son every day.

"Our marriage was over a long time ago," Brooke said. "But a little over a year ago when I walked away from Bruce's funeral, I knew his lover was being buried on the other side of town. They ran into a concrete median strip. The car flipped over, and the gasoline tank exploded. Tests proved their blood-alcohol content was above the legal limit."

She looked beyond, distantly. "I cried; I grieved for six years of a failing marriage, for a son without a father, for truth that will have to be told someday, for all I had lost—my livelihood and my self-esteem."

Ginger spoke distantly. "Jake has helped me regain some of my self-esteem," she admitted. "But I don't know if I will ever shake the feeling of failure and guilt. God is healing me, but it's not easy losing a husband and knowing your children have lost a father." She raised her voice on the next words. "Even if he was a skunk!"

"At least I have a roof over my head," Brooke said, realizing she was more blessed than many. "And Bruce's parents said to let them know if we need anything, but they seemed to blame me for the failed marriage. Somehow, I hadn't been the kind of wife I should have been. I think they expected me to live up to the image I portrayed on the runway as a model. But, Ginger, that was a youthful body, professional hair stylist, gorgeous clothes, and enough makeup to cover any blemish. That's not me at all. I'm a small-town girl with basic values."

She sighed. "At least I used to be. The more I needed God in my life, the more I pulled away from Him."

"I know exactly what you mean, Brooke. Not that the Lord causes it, but He sure can use our failures to get our attention. When you take a good long look at what's important in life, you discover it's not all those things the world can provide. Basically, the things God provides, like purpose and meaning and love, are the things that last."

Brooke nodded. "I was raised to know those things. But it was head knowledge only. I'm realizing how important family life is, and friends. You have helped me so much, Ginger, by being a friend. And Jake's attitude about serving others is admirable. I'd like to volunteer to do what I can to help some way. I know I haven't been to their nightly meetings yet, but maybe I could help with the single moms some way." She shrugged. "I can identify with them."

"Ah, perfect!" Ginger exclaimed. "We can always use help there. As a matter of fact, Evelyn just moved into her own place."

"Ben's teacher?"

"That's the one."

"Oh, she's nice," Brooke said. "I'd love to do what I can to help."

"Great. Hers is one of the older homes on the island and is in much worse shape than yours ever thought of being. Let's go tomorrow and help her clean."

Brooke threw back her head and laughed.

"What's so funny, Girl?" Ginger wanted to know.

"I was just thinking. In Indiana, I had my own housekeeper. Now, I get a kick out of thinking about going to Evelyn's and cleaning her house when mine is still under construction."

Ginger nodded. "If I waited until I had my own life straightened out before I helped another person, I'd never get anything done."

Brooke studied her for a moment, then asked seriously, "Is that what makes you so happy, Ginger? Helping others?"

"That's part of it. But it started when I decided I couldn't handle my own life and gave it to the Lord. I began to use His Word as my road map instead of making up my own. It works. And the more I try to give of myself without expecting anything in return, the blessings just come. Like with you, Brooke. I was just trying to be friendly and let you know that Jake wasn't some kind of ogre, and I'm ending up with a strong friendship between us." She looked over at Brooke and asked tentatively, "You don't still think Jake's an ogre, do you?"

"Of course not," she said. "He's a good worker and a fine Christian." She stood quickly, lest her face reveal what she felt in her heart. "Now, I'd better go and buy some sandwich makings if we're going 'foot washing' tomorrow."

～

When they arrived at Evelyn's the next day, Brooke reprimanded herself a dozen times. All went well at first, and Evelyn was so grateful for the visit, the lunch, and the offers to help. Then she began telling Ginger how great Jake was.

"Jake brought me those azaleas," she said, taking them out front to show them. "And he planted them."

Jake had told Brooke he was helping clear land at the church for a new center to be built and he'd offered to bring her some azaleas that the church didn't want.

He hasn't brought mine yet came Brooke's immediate thought, and she was shocked by what felt like a strong case of jealousy. But how could she possibly be jealous when she didn't even want a man in her life? Did she?

Maybe it was just that Evelyn seemed to be harping on the same subject. Jake had come by her place several evenings after work, and she showed them where he had torn out the bottom of the cabinet beneath the sink where pipes had leaked and rotted out the wood. He was going to replace it. And he was going to do it free of charge.

With her adrenaline flowing and trying to control her attitude, Brooke scrubbed the inside and outside of the kitchen cabinets that were in reasonable shape and would be fine for use if the shelves were covered with shelf paper. With Ginger being as much a workaholic as Jake, the kitchen took shape within a few hours while the boys and Evelyn's seven-year-old daughter played out back. The windows sparkled, the walls were stripped of old, peeling paper, and the ceiling was cleaned. Ginger talked about patching the holes in the wall so someone could either paint or paper later on.

"Jake does that kind of thing, doesn't he?" Evelyn asked.

"Yep," Ginger said. "But so do I."

Brooke got the strong impression that Evelyn would prefer Jake to do the job.

Well, what did I expect? Brooke asked herself. *Did I think I was the only recipient of Jake's water-basin principle? What's wrong with me? Where's my Christian spirit?*

Chapter 15

"D oes she ever mention me?" Jake asked in what he hoped sounded like a casual question while he sat at Ginger's kitchen table and ate his late supper. "I mean my work or anything?"

"Who?" Ginger asked, feigning innocence.

Jake gave her a hard look. "Who were we talking about?"

Ginger wrinkled her brow, as if trying to think. "Brooke and Evelyn?"

"Exactly," he said, knowing his sister was playing games with him. "You were telling me about your and Brooke's visit to Evelyn's."

"Oh, yes," she said. "She talked about you almost the whole time."

Jake kept chewing and staring at Ginger. This wasn't funny. But that silly little grin on her face indicated that she thought it was.

"Okay," she said. "Evelyn did. She praised you for bringing the azaleas, planting them, repairing the cabinets—free of charge!" Ginger lifted her eyebrows. "Brooke didn't say a word."

Jake pushed his plate away and sighed. Now, how was he supposed to handle this? How could he keep Brooke from thinking he was interested in another woman, without letting her know he was interested in her? Could he act uninterested for three more months, then tell her it was all some kind of waiting game?

"I've sure got myself in some kind of pickle," he ground out.

Ginger gently rested her hand on his arm. "Just tell her how you feel, Jake," she said softly.

He didn't have to ask if she meant Evelyn or Brooke.

～

Jake knew he couldn't "just tell her how he felt." He'd have to reveal his past first. But before doing that, he had to have some indication she could care about him in a personal way. One couldn't just blurt out, "Hey, look, I've sinned, and you need to know it. I spent time in prison where I got my life on track with God. Now I'm a practicing Christian, so accept me."

No, he knew it wasn't that easy. It hadn't been easy to admit to himself he'd been a deliberate sinner. It was much harder admitting it to a woman he cared about. But it had to be done if he expected to have any kind of close relationship with Brooke.

First, however, he'd have to have some indication she was ready for a relationship. And if so, with him!

And too, how could he expect a classy, beautiful woman like her to give him the time of day? She'd been nice to him lately, but was it because of himself, or because he was her repairman? Or because he was the brother of Ginger? She didn't have anything against him, but did that mean she had anything for him?

Didn't he have to make sure she knew him and trusted him? After all, they hadn't known each other very long. She was trying to get a handle on her life. It took Ginger a couple of years after Leo left before she could shake her bitterness and turn it over to the Lord. Even then, she had to take baby steps before she learned to walk through life with joy and confidence.

He smiled to himself. Now, Ginger was running with the kind of endurance the Good Book spoke about.

The best he could do at the time was simply let Brooke get to know him better. He took her azaleas on Saturday—and planted them. He'd like to tell her that the reason he went to Evelyn's on weekdays and Brooke's on Saturdays was because he had more hours to spend with Brooke if he went on Saturday, but he couldn't blurt that out. So he got on his hands and knees beside her in the flower beds.

He loved the way she dug her hands into the rich soil, not even mentioning the fact that the dirt got under her fingernails. She just laughed happily and said, "My in-laws' gardener did all the planting and landscaping at our house in Indiana. But I love doing this. Getting my hands in the dirt. Getting down to earth, I guess you'd call it."

Jake's heart beat fast against his chest as he looked over at her happy face so close to his. She had a little smudge of dirt on her cheek, strangely making her even more appealing. He warned himself that it was the dirt that put the joyful look on her face—not him!

So he discussed the plants. "The pansies like acid soil," he said, pushing the dirt around them. "So do azaleas. The two will thrive well together." *As we could*, he added in his mind, hoping he wouldn't blurt that out.

He liked the way she looked at him with appreciation when the beds turned out beautifully, then when he pruned off the dead and damaged leaf stalks from the trunks of the palms, giving them a tidy, healthy look.

He could easily have told her how much he enjoyed working on her household projects, asking her opinion, talking to Ben, training Taz. All that had begun to mean more to him than he could have imagined.

She was even receptive to his suggestion when he said, "You might want to consider putting a fence out back. Taz is getting mighty big, and he'll be shedding a lot of that long hair before long."

She gave him a wry glance. "He's already passed the twenty-pound mark—by six pounds." Shaking her head, she added, "That was supposed to be our little miniature puppy."

Brooke had already been finding a lot of black hair floating around. She definitely would consider a fence. Especially now that the inside of the house was getting fixed up.

It took another week and all day Saturday for him to take care of the living-room floor. When he'd looked under the moldy corner of the carpet, he not only discovered some ruined boards but that the rest of the floor was a beautiful hardwood. He suggested getting rid of the carpet and refinishing the floor. Brooke agreed.

"I'm not the greatest cook in the world," Brooke said when he began work on the floor, "but I fixed enough supper for all of us if you'd like to join us."

He sat down and ate with them beneath that dark-spotted kitchen ceiling. The conversation centered around the repairs, Ben, and Taz. Jake couldn't imagine that anyone would not love that little boy, with such winning ways, and even the werewolf-looking puppy who sat with big, black eyes looking soulfully from one to the other, hoping for people-food, which Ben couldn't resist sneaking to him.

Yes, Jake decided definitely. The time had come to find some answers for himself.

~

It was Ginger who presented the opportunity when she suggested they all go to Harbour Town on Saturday, instead of working. Telling himself not to be apprehensive about it, Jake broached the subject after he finished working on Brooke's floor Friday night.

He spoke as casually as he could. "We're all going to Harbour Town on Saturday. Ginger wanted to do some shopping, and I plan to take the boys on a boat ride to watch the dolphins. Would you and Ben like to go along?"

Brooke was glad Jake chose a time to mention it when Ben wasn't close. Otherwise, it would be hard to say no. It sounded like a wonderful outing. "We wouldn't want to impose," she said.

He smiled. "I asked you," he said. "And Ginger is going to call you. So if you want, just save your answer until Ginger calls. Good night, Brooke. I'll run around and say good-bye to Ben before I go."

"Thanks for the invitation," she said as he hastened around the corner of the house.

By the time Ginger called, Brooke had decided it would be a lovely outing for the two of them. She'd love to go shopping with Ginger. Ben would love to go out on a boat and watch the dolphins.

Early Saturday morning, Ginger picked Brooke and Ben up in her van. Jake had driven, alone, in his truck. The boys were greatly excited about the excursion. All three of Ginger's boys were filling Ben in on all they would see and that the dolphins would jump sky-high, maybe jump right into the boat. Ben was fascinated just looking at all the yachts, sailboats, and fishing charters in the harbor.

Brooke was most fascinated by the geraniums covering the entire length of a long row of shops. People sat in rocking chairs, looking out across a sea of red geraniums, while other people walked a couple of feet below, along the walkway between the shops and harbor. Amid the geraniums stood live oaks. Hanging from the awnings were baskets laden with brilliant, red geraniums.

One could move the chairs back under the shade of the awning or pull them beyond the awning into the warmth of the sunshine and look out over the red geraniums, the walkway below, out to the ships in the harbor, and the sparkling blue water beyond.

"The most famous attraction here," Ginger said, after Jake and the boys had left on the boat, "is the candy-striped lighthouse. There's a great gift shop at the top. But let's start here and work our way around, okay?"

"Okay," Brooke said, looking around at the quaint area, patterned after a Mediterranean fishing village. The two women walked along the boards beneath a yellow awning. Brooke bought a T-shirt with leaping dolphins printed on it for Ben. In one of the shops she bought him swimming trunks.

After a couple hours of shopping and sightseeing, Ginger pointed out some of the quaint restaurants, but they had all planned to eat lunch together after the guys returned. They sat in the rockers along the edge of the boards, in front of the long row of shops, where they could look out at the harbor, looking at the sailboats, yachts, pelicans, and sunshine.

"Over there's the famous Liberty Oak tree," Ginger said. "Sometimes there is live entertainment beneath it. Also, there are spectacular sunsets here."

"This is so peaceful," Brooke said. "I could sit here and rock forever. Oh," she said, looking to her right, "he has the right idea."

Ginger laughed, looking over at the sculpture of a man sitting on a timber, resting his feet on another timber. His elbows were propped on his thighs. He had a sandwich in one hand and a book in another. "The sculpture is called *Out-to-Lunch*," she said.

Brooke rocked gently with her arms on the rocker arms, basking in the warmth and beauty of this spectacular setting. "I don't think I've relaxed since I've been here," she said. "I need this."

"Yep," Ginger agreed. "We should always take time to smell the roses."

She looked over at Brooke and grinned. "Or the geraniums." Her smile faded and she grew serious. "You know, Brooke, I really value your friendship. A lot of the single moms think they can't relate to me because I'm not strapped for money. I do have a lot," she admitted. "But we live on alimony and child support and rely on my brother for repairs and plumbing and roofing. I do the water aerobics to make a little money of my own and give myself a feeling of independence and contributing."

"It looks to me like you're contributing double as a parent. Remember, I'm without a husband too."

"Right, but the world doesn't always see it our way. Anyhow, I'm planning to take computer and accounting courses after Danny starts school. When Jake moves out and all the boys are in school, the way Jake's business is booming, I can keep books for Jake and take his calls. He has an answering service now. I can do all that at home."

"Jake is moving out?" Brooke asked.

"I expect him to one of these days. He could have moved in with Mom and Dad, um, but, I. . .uh, he moved in with me to help with the kids. Anyway, I mean he will want a place of his own one of these days. You know, marriage and children and all those good things?"

Brook wondered why that so startled her heart. It suddenly dawned on her how much and how quickly Jake Randolph had invaded her and Ben's lives. And his presence was no longer unwelcome. Were he and Evelyn serious about each other? "He's. . .getting married?" she asked.

"Oh, no," Ginger said. "He doesn't have any definite plans."

"But he's going with someone?"

"Not at the moment."

"I would think a fine man like Jake would have married long ago."

Ginger shook her head. "Nope. He's never been married." She stood and gazed out over the water. "About time they returned, I think."

"Oh, are they late?" Brooke said, feeling an instant of concern.

Ginger looked at her watch. "No. It'll be thirty more minutes or so. Let's go get something to drink."

Brooke knew that Ginger had deliberately changed the subject from talking about Jake. As they walked past the shops, Ginger kept pointing out items of interest, but Brooke's mind was on Jake. Why had Ginger said he had a choice of moving in with his parents or her? Where had he lived before that? Had he lived with someone? Had he lost someone? Her curiosity was piqued. Why was Ginger so open and aboveboard about everything—except Jake?

~

The boat trip turned out to be a major success. Especially for Ben. He'd seen dolphins jump sky-high and thought they might even jump into the boat, but they didn't, and he loved his T-shirt and insisted upon putting it on right then, tag and all. He intended to sleep in it that night.

"Jake knows all about alligators," Ben reported. "He said sometime, if you let me, we can go see some."

"We'll see," Brooke answered, and Jake, taking the hint, said they needed to find some lunch for those boys.

"I have an idea," Ginger said. "Why don't we buy some sandwiches and go out for a picnic on the property?"

Brooke had no idea what the property was, but there seemed to be a challenge in Ginger's eyes as she and her brother gave each other a long look before he grinned and said, "Great idea."

As it turned out, the picnic spot was a couple of acres of oceanfront property in a section of fine homes in Sea Pines. Beneath a couple of live oaks, dripping with Spanish moss, sat a picnic table like the one in Ginger's back yard. The beautifully landscaped land, with its spectacular view of the ocean, boasted its own private walkway leading to the beach.

Brooke knew a bunch of people with four rowdy boys didn't come to places like this for an outing unless they had a friend who owned it or owned it themselves. "Whose is this?" she asked curiously, looking from Ginger to Jake, while the boys frolicked around the trees, searching for alligators.

Jake's grin said it all, while Ginger spread out the quilt she'd taken from his truck. "I've been buying it for several years," he said. "And as soon as we finish the house we're working on, I'll be close to having it paid off."

Well, she guessed Jake's business was doing all right. "It's wonderful," Brooke said, impressed.

"Thanks," he answered. "And being a builder, I think I could manage to put up a pretty good house." He added, with a grin, "At cost."

"I'll just bet you could," Brooke said, nodding and smiling. Now she could see why Ginger mentioned his moving out of her house. After it was paid for, he'd probably build. But no matter how beautiful, wouldn't he be lonely. . .alone?

Chapter 16

The following Friday evening, Jake announced that he was going to take Ginger's boys out to the lagoon on Saturday to see alligators. Now that warmer weather had come, the gators would be lying in the sun.

"Could Ben come along?" he asked.

"He's wanted to do that since before we came here when an alligator was mentioned, but frankly, that frightens me. You see how active he is. And with four boys for you to watch. . ."

Brooke heard the edge in his voice when he asked, "Don't you know I wouldn't put that boy in danger?"

She looked at him. For a long instant their gazes held. "I know," she said. "I'm just overly protective, I guess."

"That's not so bad," he said softly. "But you can trust me."

She caught her breath for a moment. She had the feeling he was not just talking about trusting him with Ben.

She nodded. "I do trust you, Jake."

His smile was warm. "Good. Then if the gators don't eat us, how about my taking you out to dinner tomorrow evening?"

Strangely, his quip about the gators eating them didn't disturb her nearly as much as his asking her out to dinner.

"Well, I guess you do deserve a good dinner after eating my cooking all week."

"The food was fine," he said. "The company exceptional."

"Well, yeah," she said, trying to hide her unexpected elation, "Ben's a great dinner companion. I assume you're inviting him too?"

"Not this time," he said. "I've already talked to Ginger. He can stay over there. After all, the boys will need to do a lot of gator talk."

Of course Brooke knew his reason for asking her out, without Ben, could be to discuss church trips or activities. There were many for children, and she'd already learned that Jake never asked about an outing in front of Ben, instead asking her discreetly when the boy wasn't right there. And too, Ginger could have mentioned to her brother Brooke's intention of getting more involved with singles. Jake could have some possible ways for her to get involved that he wanted to discuss, since he was actively involved with singles—

311

like repairing her house—and Evelyn's house.

So this wasn't necessarily personal. "Should I dress up or go casual?" she asked, hoping her voice sounded the latter.

"What about Fitzgerald's? Anything goes there. From dressy to casual."

Fitzgerald's. She and Bruce had gone there on their honeymoon. They had dressed up.

"I'd like to go casual," she said, and Jake nodded.

~

This is casual? Jake asked himself when he came to pick Brooke up. He'd brought Ben and the boys by so Brooke could see that the gators hadn't eaten her son, hadn't even bitten him, in fact. Then he'd taken them all, and Taz, to Ginger's. After he'd showered, shampooed, and dressed in slacks and a knit shirt, he'd driven the SUV to Brooke's.

He knocked on the front screen, and she was there immediately. As soon as she stepped out on the porch, he felt anything but casual. She looked anything but casual, although she wore white slacks and a sea-green silk blouse that turned her eyes the color of warm summertime, a place where one might wish to bask forever. Her eyes were fringed with long brown lashes, and her soft lips were tinted coral. Tiny gold earrings gleamed at her ears. He'd seen her dressed stylishly with her hair down to her shoulders at church, but the rest of the week she'd worn jeans or shorts and had pulled her hair back into a ponytail.

This evening, it was different. She'd dressed for him. She'd let her hair down for him. She was having dinner with him.

There was nothing casual about the two of them going out for dinner together. This was his first date in three years. For her, it was probably the first since before she married, more than seven years ago. Casual? Tonight, that word had nothing at all to do with how one dressed.

Was tonight the time for him to reveal his past? His silent prayer was for God's leadership on what to say, how to say it, and when to say it.

But for now, he wanted nothing to intrude upon this special time. Surely God wouldn't have brought this wonderful woman into his life without reason. Surely! No, God was not cruel.

They'd barely had time to begin discussing the alligator day before they arrived at Fitzgerald's, only a few minutes away.

Jake had been to the restaurant several times. He'd brought Ginger here for her birthday when his mom and dad had come up from Bluffton to stay with the boys. He'd come with a group of singles from church one time. He'd brought Meagan here when they first started going together. He knew, most likely, Brooke had been here.

312

"Have you been here before?" he asked.

She nodded. "Bruce and I came here on our honeymoon. I think we sat in the main dining room over there."

"We'd like a table by the windows, if we could," Jake said when the maitre d' came to seat them.

The maitre d' led the way down the narrow carpeted section with long narrow windows on one side and seated them at one of the many tables-for-two. On the other side, divided by a low brick wall and brick columns, were long planters filled with green ferns and vines. Green shutters were pushed aside, revealing the main dining room. The walls, carpeting, and tablecloths were in a subdued maroon and green hue. Dim light glowed from the Tiffany chandeliers, and on each table a candle glowed in a silver goblet, surrounded by a frosted globe.

Jake gave the maitre d' a grateful glance when he seated them at a table where they could look out the window into the courtyard.

"Oh, this is nice," Brooke exclaimed, looking out.

In the courtyard, groupings of small cast-iron tables, some for four, some for two, sectioned off by flowering purple and white azalea hedges, sat on fine white gravel. A cocoa palm, with its spiked branches making it as wide as it was tall, was draped gracefully with small white lights. This was flanked by tall palmettos. Surrounding the courtyard were other palmettos and large wooden planters spilling over with ferns and vines.

"This really is lovely," Brooke said, and Jake smiled.

They ordered the same thing—combination seafood platter of scallops, shrimp, and flounder. "I'll have mine fried," Brooke said, thinking she'd have to make sure and do some extra walking besides her three mornings of water aerobics.

"Same here," Jake said.

Brooke ordered the raspberry vinaigrette dressing for her green salad and Jake ordered blue cheese. They drank iced tea while Jake asked her how she liked living on the island.

Brooke looked down at her glass and ran a finger around the rim, a small reflective smile on her lips. Bruce had never asked her how she liked the island. He had been very romantic and sweet, but the focus of attention had never left himself. She realized now that was because of the way he was raised—an only son with every opportunity, expected to achieve. He hadn't been bad or mean to her—just full of himself.

Now she looked across at Jake and thought how romantic it was to have a man ask about herself, rather than try and impress her with himself. She could hardly believe she was sitting here at a small table-for-two in the light

313

of a candle, across from a handsome man, appealing to her in an even stronger way than when they worked together in the yard. This was like being on a date for the first time, and she had to remind herself that it wasn't necessarily a real date.

"I like it here very much," she said, "now that I'm beginning to understand the island. To use Ben's word, it's really 'neat' how the island is shaped like a shoe. So if someone tells me a store is located in the heel or the toes, I know what they mean."

Their laughter was soft and friendly as they propped their arms on the table, leaning toward each other as they talked. "And the sole of the shoe," Jake said, "is a twelve-mile beach."

The food came and was delicious. Brooke talked about her parents and Jake about his. When they finished eating, neither wanted dessert. Jake suggested they have coffee in the courtyard.

They sat at a small cast-iron table, surrounded by the array of azalea hedges. The hot coffee was the perfect balance to an evening with a slight chill in the air. A full silvery moon rose in the deep blue-gray sky, brushed gently by a whisk of cloud like a smudge of cotton candy.

The evening seemed so perfect. They got along so well, and she felt there wasn't a pretentious bone in his body, which appealed to her. She smiled at him. Maybe this was a real date after all. She liked the restaurant, the food, and their walking out into the courtyard. Brooke reached up to feel the texture of the moss hanging from the oaks.

"It's so graceful," she commented. "We don't have Spanish moss in Indiana. How do they get it to hang like that?"

"It isn't Spanish at all," Jake said. "And it has no roots. It's an air plant."

"Is it a parasite?"

"Nope," Jake said. "It just dangles freely, getting its nourishment from the rain and the sun. But the downside is, it attracts little red bugs called chiggers. Believe me, they itch."

Brooke jerked her hand down and grimaced.

Jake laughed but could have kicked his backside for that remark. This was to be a romantic night where they could relate on a strictly personal level, and he had to bring up the subject of chiggers. *Great going, Jake!*

He exhaled after a deep breath and suggested they walk on the beach.

They walked up the timber steps, along the concrete and oyster shell walkway, and onto the timber boardwalk leading to the beach, passing sea oats, low growing cocoa palms, and tall palmettos.

Brooke took off her sandals and spoke of the warm, white sand feeling so good on her feet and between her toes. She looked up at the full moon and spoke of the beauty of its reflection casting a silver shadow on the blue water. The night was perfect. Just cool enough that she wondered if it might seem natural for him to put his arm around her shoulders or hold her hand.

~

Jake wondered if he dared reach for her hand. Maybe he could tell her how he'd come to care for her in such a special way. Surely this night meant more than friendship to her, as it did to him. Maybe this was the time to tell her the truth about himself.

Then she began to talk about herself.

"Bruce and I came here when we were on our honeymoon," she said, which dispelled Jake's thought of holding her hand or putting his arm around her shoulder or turning her to face him and taking her in his arms.

They walked, side by side. He kept his hands in his pockets and walked where the tide had receded to keep from getting his shoes full of sand.

Just as he was thinking he should have taken her elsewhere, she turned her face toward his and spoke to the contrary. "I'm glad we came here tonight, Jake. I never really appreciated the setting. I was so young and so blinded by love. I'm sure you know what that's like."

Jake looked down at the white sand and chuckled. "To a degree," he replied. "But I sort of took all this for granted, having grown up here." He didn't elaborate further. He'd never been blindly in love, where everything faded into the background except the object of one's affection. He stole a glance at Brooke. *And now, am I not a little too old, too mature, for such feelings? Obviously not!*

Brooke shrugged. "I felt that way even in Indiana, without such perfect scenery as this. In one sense it was wonderful, being blindly in love. I can't be like that anymore. In a way, it's a loss, but in another way, it's a gain."

How they got on the topic of love, Jake wasn't sure. But the subject was here and something to be faced realistically. But they were talking about Bruce, were they not? "I suppose human love comes down to what Jesus taught when He said, 'Love your neighbor.' The very vivid lesson is that love is not just a feeling, but love is action."

Brooke nodded. "I expected action to follow and expected the same feelings could never die. There is such a sense of personal failure when marriage doesn't work out."

Brooke told him about her life with Bruce, how she had failed to be the kind of public wife he wanted, and how he had failed to be the homebody she wanted. They weren't suited for each other. They had looked at external appearances and liked what they saw. She had thought his dreams were what she wanted, but after having Ben, her priorities changed. Bruce and his goals were no longer first in her life.

"Maybe it would have been different," she said now, "if I had kept God as the center of my life."

"I know exactly what you mean, Brooke," Jake said. "My life hasn't always been exemplary. In my college days I experimented with just about everything that I shouldn't. I didn't want to be in love, so I played the field, so to speak. It wasn't until I was in my early thirties that I met Meagan when I was working on a summer house for her parents."

As they walked along the beach, Jake told about having believed he was in love with Meagan. They both were going to church, and although he was a Christian, he did not resist the temptation to engage in a physically intimate relationship, justifying it by saying they were only human, consenting adults, planning to spend their lives together.

"Those were only excuses to gratify my own desires," he admitted. He paused, looking over at Brooke. "You don't want to hear this kind of thing," he said.

"I do, Jake," she said softly. "If you want to tell me."

He didn't want to tell her. But he knew it was the only honest thing to do if their relationship was to grow. She put a lot of stock in honesty. After a long sigh, he admitted the relationship was based primarily on the physical. Or maybe it was their concentration on the physical that kept them from getting to know each other fully. "After about two years, the relationship ended."

"You must have loved her very much," Brooke said.

"I suppose I did," he said. "I've learned there are many kinds of love and many degrees. But what I felt for her at the time was what I called love."

He heard the hesitancy in her voice when she looked over at him and asked, "How does that differ from what you call love now?"

Jake wasn't sure how to answer. He knew that so-called puppy love or a crush to a young person could be as real as mature love to an older person. "I suppose it involves all the feelings I had back then, which includes the physical, the selfish, the human aspects. But the kind of love that lasts is not just based on feelings, but on action as well. My actions in my younger days did not fill all the empty spots in my life. Only since I've made God my first priority have I found the peace and purpose that had been missing in my life. I think that love of the right kind must involve the kind of commitment based on biblical principles."

Brooke agreed. "Many times I felt Bruce did not have the kind of commitment to the Lord or to me that he should have had. But I never spoke to him about it. In fact, I tried to gain his approval by trying to be the socialite he wanted." She sighed. "It didn't work. And I knew that God was missing from our lives, but I was as guilty as Bruce of omitting God. Maybe I was more guilty because I knew more about it, having been reared in a Christian home."

"Sometimes," Jake said reflectively, "the worst experiences in our lives are what bring us to our knees before God—where we should have been in the first place."

They walked back toward the boardwalk. This was not a time for taking her in his arms. They were quiet, walking together, as if they were one with the ocean, the sound of the water caressing the shore, the pale moonlight shining on them both.

Taking her in his arms would not satisfy the longing within himself. It would only perpetuate it and perhaps turn his feelings into primarily physical ones. His feelings for Brooke were physical, but he wanted more from her, wanted to give her more. He wanted their relationship to be deep and meaningful and lasting. Taking her in his arms would not convince her of that.

Was this the time to tell her more? Should he stop right now and say, "There's more"? Perhaps his hesitancy was God's way of saying wait. Or perhaps it was his own cowardice. However, the opportune moment passed.

They reached the boardwalk, and the talk turned to the sand on Brooke's feet. He showed her where a knob would bring water out of a small pipe so she could rinse the sand off.

She did so and wiped them on the grass, then slipped into her sandals while holding onto his arm for support.

But he did not take her in his arms for a moonlight kiss. He did not know the touch of her lips, the feel of her body against his, a warm breath against his cheek. He did not know and perhaps that increased his desire for it, intensified his feelings, made their relationship stronger.

He felt she had begun to trust him, just as he'd begun to distrust himself. If he took her in his arms and kissed her, he'd never want to let her go.

"Thank you," Jake said, after they were in the van, heading for Ginger's. "Thank you for making this such a special evening. I'm glad you had dinner with me."

"So am I," she said and glanced over to return his smile.

She still felt the smile in her heart after they picked up Ben, who fell asleep on the second row of seats in the van. When they arrived at the cottage, Jake took him inside, laid him on his bed, and slipped off his tennis shoes and socks.

⌒

Back in the living room, Jake said what Brooke had already observed.

"I'm real fond of that little boy," he said. "He's fit right in with Ginger's boys."

Brooke nodded. "Ginger's boys take after their momma. They're easy to relate to." She paused and then added, "And their uncle."

She saw the sudden surprise come into his eyes, followed by a look of pain that was quickly erased by the usual warmth. "Thank you," he said. "And that little boy sleeping in there takes a lot after his mother. You're a good mother, Brooke. I'm impressed."

Emotion welled up in her eyes. She couldn't think of a better compliment. Words like that meant so much more than if he'd said she was pretty or that he liked her hair, or if he'd ogled her as if he liked what he saw. "Thank you, Jake," she said softly. "You couldn't have said anything nicer."

She could have added that his actions toward Ben were more like a father's than Bruce's had ever been. Bruce had never abused Ben except by omitting the good times they might have had together.

Jake left, after no more contact than gentleness in his eyes and warmth in his voice when he said softly, "Good night, Brooke."

Later, Brooke lay in bed staring toward the moonlit window, thinking about the evening. She remembered an adage her mother had quoted upon occasion: "One rose does not a summer make."

Brooke added her own interpretation: "One date does not a relationship make."

Just what had been Jake Randolph's intentions? Was he simply being a friend, wanting to ultimately dispel any traces of mistrust she might have of him? Had he suspected she might come to care for him in a special way and wanted to let her know he was still in love with a woman who had rejected him? Had he been trying to tell her she was a fine person, a good mother, and they could be friends? Or was he implying that her spirituality had not matured to the point he wanted in a woman he could be serious about? Was Evelyn more the type of woman a dedicated Christian like him deserved?

Oh, why those doubts?

She closed her eyes against them. Of course she knew. Those years of never being good enough for Bruce had taken their toll.

But what was it Jake had said? Something about our hardest times are when we learn the most. What had she learned? The answer was as close as the question. She'd learned she could make a life for herself and her son without her husband—without a man. She did not have to depend upon a man for her happiness. Ginger was a wonderful example of that.

Brooke forced the insecurities from her mind, remembering the Scripture about God's love being sufficient. *So, Lord. If Jake Randolph is not for me, I accept that. I can handle that because I have handled losing the love of a husband who meant the world to me. You know what is best for me. I will not struggle with this relationship, but I'm giving it over to You.*

318

Right before falling into a peaceful sleep, Brooke realized another important thing. She had gone out on a date with a man, had a wonderful time, and had related well. That was something she'd thought she'd never be able to do. That was a major accomplishment.

"Thank You, Lord," she breathed, as she drifted off into dreamland feeling certain that everything was resolved within her heart and mind. She could handle whatever the situation.

However, she chided herself the following morning when she remembered that her night had been filled with dreams of a couple's walk along the beach beneath a full moon with the sound of mighty ocean waves gently caressing the shore. In her dreams, the man put his arm around the woman and drew her close.

Chapter 17

Jake knew he didn't need more dinners to determine how he felt about Brooke. A dinner date couldn't possibly tell him any more about her than he knew by seeing her in everyday life relating to her son, caring about a messy, shedding, dirty dog because her son loved him, paying rapt attention to a pastor at church, singing praises to the Lord, relating to people like Ginger and her boys, and planning for her future with determination rather than wallowing in self-pity. He admired her, respected her, and with a feeling of both joy and trepidation, he admitted to himself that he loved her. And he loved Ben, that big-eyed, mischievous, exaggerating, active little boy who was a part of Brooke.

With the way he felt about Brooke, he couldn't just put his feelings on hold for another two months, maybe not even for two days. They were growing closer. Once Ben started school and Brooke started her nurse's training, it might be easy for them to drift apart. He couldn't chance her growing away from him.

He'd been talking to Brooke about putting up fencing since Taz was growing bigger every day and had already begun to run off around the neighborhood, refusing to come until the mood struck him. Without a fence, they'd soon have to chain him up when Ben played with him outside. Otherwise they would have to keep him in the house.

"I can take you to Bluffton Saturday afternoon to look at fencing," he told Brooke. "While we're there, I'd like for us to stop in and meet my parents."

His heart skipped a beat when she readily accepted the invitation. Maybe after meeting them, she'd see he was from good stock. She would believe him honorable and serious about her.

Surely, by now, she knew he was trustworthy. She'd had a failed marriage and an unfaithful husband. She understood how things could go so wrong without anyone intending for them to, how people could even be blind to it for a while, and the emotional toll it can take. Yes, Brooke was an understanding woman. It was time to tell her about his past.

But he mustn't let her hear it from anyone else. He regretted that he must ask his parents not to mention the past, or at least not the past few years of it.

He called his parents. "Mom," he said. "I'd like to stop by tomorrow. I'm bringing Brooke Haddon. I haven't told her about the past yet, so you and Dad just don't bring it up, please."

He listened and heard the inflection in his mom's voice when she asked, sounding like a reprimand, "Jake, if you're serious about this woman, don't you think it would be a good idea to bring everything out into the open?"

"I intend to, Mom. I don't know how serious she is about me, and this is not the kind of thing I go around telling everyone."

"I understand, Son," she said. "You have to do what you think is best. I just don't like having to be careful about what I say."

He laughed lightly. She and Ginger were alike in that. They usually spoke their mind. He used to, but he had become more careful in the past few years. "Sorry to put you in this position, Mom."

"Well, Jake. If you're interested in this woman, I definitely want to meet her."

~

The afternoon sun in a Carolina blue sky spread its warmth on a beautiful day. As they sped along the William Hilton Parkway, heading toward Bluffton, Brooke rolled down the window and felt the air blow her hair. She didn't care if it were mussed. There was such a feeling of freedom. It felt good, sitting beside Jake, feeling the wind on her face and in her hair. This place was perfect for her.

Maybe she had overcome those depressing feelings of guilt, failure, loss, and the fear of raising Ben alone. She'd come to this island feeling washed up. But thanks to Ginger, her boys, and Jake, she had a new lease on life.

Particularly, she owed these feelings to Jake. She'd come to the island feeling she never wanted to be involved with a man again. But Jake had won her trust. He'd shown her what a Christian man should be like. He loved the Lord and tried to live for Him daily.

Also, he'd given her a whole new set of emotions. She'd come here hurt, disappointed, afraid. Jake made her feel like she could conquer the world. Maybe even allow a man in her life again. The past had begun to fade. She'd come to know people whose situations were far worse than hers, and she could count her blessings.

"Penny for your thoughts," Jake said.

Brooke smiled. "You were in them," she said softly.

Jake glanced over, and seeing the reflection of a warm sunny day on her face, he returned the smile, took his hand from the wheel, and held hers for a brief moment.

"I hope your parents won't feel like I'm imposing upon them," Brooke said.

"I called and told them I was bringing you. They're looking forward to meeting you," he said, hoping she wouldn't think it too forward of him to make this sound important. Her smile indicated she didn't. "They're just ordinary people," he said.

Bluffton was just across the causeway on the mainland. Jake pointed out homes and a mall he or his dad and their crews had built. Brooke was impressed with his work and the pride he took in it. Apparently, business was good, with Jake being able to buy choice property on Hilton Head.

In no time at all, he turned off the main road and drove up a long, curved, tree-lined drive to a lovely, low country home at the end of a cul-de-sac. The wraparound veranda-style front porch lent a gentle Southern flavor to the peaceful setting. As soon as they parked, a middle-aged couple who looked to be in their sixties appeared on the porch.

The woman was unmistakably related to Ginger. The family resemblance was evident, and the woman apparently kept herself in shape too. She looked to be the same size as Ginger. Her auburn curls were shorter, and there was some gray sprinkled in. The man was tall like Jake and maybe twenty pounds heavier. His hair was darker and thinner than Jake's. There was a family resemblance there too, and he must have been as handsome as Jake when he was younger.

Todd Randolph shook her hand, and Cora hugged her after Jake made the introductions. Brooke was reminded that she'd heard somewhere that Southern folks had a monopoly on hugs and hospitality. This couple seemed to prove that.

She liked the interior of the house too, from the moment she walked in and saw the cathedral ceiling, hardwood floor, and cozy fireplace. It wasn't as elegant as the home she and Bruce had owned in Indiana, but it was more plush than her parents' modest home. This one was very nice, as inviting as its owners. Cora took them directly to the large eat-in kitchen.

"She always has cookies," Jake said with a grin. "Made from scratch."

"And you've never been too old for them either," his mother said mockingly. They all laughed at that as Jake dug into the cookie jar and passed it to Brooke, who chose a big chunk full of chocolate chips.

Todd and Cora each helped themselves to a cookie too. "Come outside," Cora said, "and see where we live most of the time."

When they stepped outside, Brooke could understand why they would spend time out back. A lovely blue-bottomed pool sparkled in the sunlight, surrounded by white concrete and a low white railing. Beyond that was a tennis court. The rest of the spacious lawn was like green velvet, dotted with oaks and tall palmettos, and farther back stood a huge magnolia tree.

"Have a seat," Todd Randolph said, gesturing to the chairs beneath the awning over the white tabby patio, flanked by azalea hedges that had lost their spring blossoms several weeks ago and now boasted summer's lush green leaves.

Brooke had to look closely to see that a chain-link fence surrounded the property, for she could look out through the trees at a spectacular view of a lagoon.

"This is lovely," Brooke said.

"Thank you," Cora said. "Todd built it for us several years ago. I guess you know Ginger and Jake live in our old home place."

Brooke nodded, realizing that either Ginger or Jake must have talked to them about her.

Cora and Todd talked about having grown up on Hilton Head. Todd's dad had been an architect and had helped design many of the structures on the island. "I remember the day they turned on the electricity on Hilton Head," Todd said.

"It was in 1951," Cora said, completing his thought.

Todd nodded. "Then the building began. That was one of the most lucrative jobs to have."

"We liked Hilton Head," Cora added. "But after Todd had his heart surgery and he sold the business to Jake and—"

Coughing, she broke off her sentence, and Brooke detected a strange tension in the air. Brooke wondered what Cora had been about to say but didn't. Perhaps she was mistaken, or maybe it was simply difficult for Cora to talk about her husband's surgery.

"Anyway," Todd said, after what seemed to be a strained moment of silence, "we always talked about traveling after I retired, doing things together. I was always too busy. She was busy too, teaching those little kids in the second grade. I'd seen men younger than me end up gravely ill and then dying, so I decided that since I'd had surgery, it might be now or never that we saw the world. I could leave the business in good hands. And I did," he said. "The best."

Brooke smiled, seeing the obvious love and pride in Todd's eyes when he looked at Jake. Then Cora was saying, "Well, tell us about you, Brooke."

What could she say? "I'm from Indiana. I had two years of nurses' training, got married, and had a little boy, who's now five. Over a year ago, my husband was killed in an auto accident. His parents gave me the cottage on Hilton Head that Jake's been making repairs on. Let's see," she said, wondering what else to say. "I'm planning to resume nurses' training after Ben starts to school." She thought a moment. "Oh, and I have a dog."

They laughed as she and Jake talked about some of Taz's experiences, especially being a "miniature" who now weighed about twenty-five pounds.

"You two apparently play tennis," Brooke said, looking toward the court.

"Play?" Jake scoffed. "I don't think Ginger and I ever beat these two."

"Now, there was one time," Todd said playfully, and they all laughed. Then he looked at Brooke. "I guess you know the island's famous for its golf and tennis courts. The best women pros in the world come here to play in the Family Circle Cup every year."

Brooke had known about the golf but hadn't realized that the island was so famous for tennis.

"We could have a game right now," Todd said, standing, ready to get the rackets and balls.

Brooke couldn't help but laugh at his enthusiasm and his challenge. "Maybe another time," she said and blushed to think she assumed there would be another time. "I haven't played tennis since I was in high school."

He sat down again. "Promise! Another time."

Jake explained that they wanted to go to the home improvement store.

"And I need to get back," Brooke added. "Ben's complained about his tummy hurting the past couple of days. He might be coming down with something, so I'd better get him to bed early."

"I like them very much," Brooke could honestly say, after she and Jake were on the road.

Jake nodded and told her that his dad had built up Randolph Construction Company into a lucrative business. At a very early age Jake had wielded a hammer and saw. He'd worked for his dad for wages during high school and college, when school was out for the summer.

"I went to college on a football scholarship, and I majored in architecture and design, thinking I might become an engineer." He shook his head. "But that wasn't for me. I'm an outdoor person. I love the manual work and decided to work for Dad. Then, like he said, he retired and sold me the business."

Brooke felt that strange tension again. And again, maybe she was mistaken. His easy flow of conversation stopped only because he was turning into the parking lot in front of the home improvement store.

～

Jake could tell his parents took to Brooke and liked her immediately. They didn't have to say it. He saw it in the way they talked to her and in how his Dad found a way to ask her to come back again. He saw it in the way they both looked at him and grinned like he'd won the lottery right before he and Brooke left.

But however much he wanted it, he didn't have to have his parents' approval. He was a grown man who wanted Brooke's approval. He was happy to have her sitting beside him in the truck as if they belonged together. It seemed natural when they walked down the long aisle and she started to turn in one direction and he in another and he reached for her hand.

"This way," he said. He kept holding her hand, and she didn't try to remove it. *I want her by my side,* he thought, *always.* Surely God wouldn't have brought her into his life and given him this love for her if it wasn't right. Yes, he would have to talk to her this very night.

He was still holding her hand when it happened. He stopped dead in his tracks and stood like a statue. The couple directly in front of them did the same.

He stood eye-to-eye, face-to-face with Meagan.

Chapter 18

Brooke felt Jake's hand tighten on hers before he let go. His arms were down at his side as if he were standing at attention. She looked at the man and dark-eyed woman, straight ahead, staring at them.

After what seemed an incredible eternity, Jake spoke. The man mumbled a half-hearted greeting, the woman stared wide-eyed as if seeing a ghost, and then both hurried away, pretending to be interested in something in the store. Brooke saw a muscle in the side of Jake's jaw continue to jerk. His face was flushed. He turned to look at the fencing as if it were his enemy.

After a moment, he shook his head. "I'm sorry. I was surprised. I know that couple, and it would have been pointless to try and introduce you."

"Don't worry about it," Brooke said, sorry for the broken camaraderie that had vanished between her and Jake. She glanced over her shoulder and saw, way up the aisle, that the woman, whose black hair was pulled back into a bun, did the same. Turning back quickly, Brooke tried to focus on fencing.

She heard herself talking unnaturally fast. "Maybe chain-link would be best. I can see that Ginger wants wood since she needs privacy to teach her aerobics class. But I liked the effect of your parents' backyard, and since I have close neighbors it might be best to have a see-through fence.

"Sounds like a good idea," Jake agreed. "Ben and Taz would probably be happier with that too. If this is what you want, I can measure and see how much you need."

As they walked back through the store, Jake didn't hold her hand. He hadn't been his pleasant, natural self since seeing the couple. Brooke didn't know if she had a right to ask, but she and Jake were becoming closer. She wanted to know.

"Who was the couple?" she asked when they returned to the truck.

He didn't have to ask which couple.

Jake sighed heavily, traveled slowly down the street, and turned a corner before answering. "That was Meagan," he said, which was no surprise to Brooke. After a pause he added, "The man was Oswald Jenkins. He used to work for Dad and me. There was a time when I asked him, as a friend, to watch out for her while I had to be away." Jake paused. "He did. They're married now."

When he didn't add anything else, Brooke said, "There seemed to be a lot of tension there in the store. Are you. . .still in love with her, Jake?"

"You're right, there was tension," he said. "But not for the reasons you think. I have to talk to you about all this."

Brooke waited, but he didn't say anything more. His mood had changed. Looking ahead, she noticed a cloud had appeared on the horizon. Was that a symbol of what was to happen? She could understand if Jake were still in love. But he denied it. Was he living with regrets, as she had done so long about Bruce? Why wouldn't he confide in her? Communication was so important.

"If you want to talk to me, Jake, I'm willing to listen," she offered.

At the same time, rain began to pelt the windshield. She rolled up her window and watched the dark clouds blow across the sky and the treetops bend with the wind.

Jake rolled up his window and switched on the windshield wipers. They reminded Brooke of giant fingers shaking back and forth as if she should have known better than allow her heart to become vulnerable.

"There is something I should tell you, Brooke," Jake said, keeping his attention on the cloudburst striking the truck and the road. "I haven't known when the time is right. But I need enough time to explain things to you."

"You don't have to explain anything to me, Jake," she told him.

"Yes, I do, Brooke. Because of what you've come to mean to me. I owe it to you."

During the rest of the drive to Ginger's and then to her cottage, Jake was unusually quiet except for a few comments to Ben. His mind was obviously elsewhere.

Or, Brooke asked herself, *is it his heart that is elsewhere?*

~

Long into the night, Brooke thought about Jake's words and his mood after seeing Meagan. He indicated there was something ominous he had to tell her. She felt she could take it or accept whatever he might tell her. Jake had already revealed that he'd had a physical relationship with Meagan. But if the Lord had forgiven him, then who was she not to do so?

It couldn't be as bad as he made it seem. Whatever the situation, it was probably magnified in his mind since he was so intent upon making a good impression and being a Christian example. She could understand that, remembering how she felt that all eyes were upon her, judging her, knowing she was living a lie when her marriage was failing. Being out of God's will and the guilt that brought when you knew better placed a heavy burden on a person.

Another thought struck her. Perhaps he had an incurable disease. Could that be a reason why, at his age, he wasn't married or seeing anyone? But he was obviously perfectly healthy. And if he were dying, he wouldn't be taking her out and saying he cared for her, would he?

Brooke rolled over and punched the pillow, getting into her usual comfortable sleeping position on her stomach. She mustn't spend the night trying to figure out what she couldn't possibly know. She knew Jake. She pushed aside the thought, *But you thought you knew Bruce.*

Finally, she drifted off to sleep, praying that God would give Jake the courage to reveal whatever he wanted to reveal to her and give her the grace to accept it in a Christlike manner.

⁓

Morning came too soon. She hadn't slept enough. During breakfast she noticed the spot on the ceiling was bigger and browner. Ben wasn't feeling very well either. But her mind was set on hearing Jake out and getting this behind them. During Sunday school, Jake seemed to be his usual jovial self, talking, laughing, greeting, discussing, but Brooke had come to know him well enough to realize all that was colored with a touch of reserve. She knew he was afraid of what he had to say to her.

After church, she expected it, when they all walked to the parking lot together and Jake asked if she'd stay while he talked with her. Ginger said she'd take Ben home with her. She'd save lunch for Brooke and Jake.

Was it going to take that long?

Jake led her out to the privacy of the sunken prayer garden where they walked down the steps to a bench beneath a live oak. All signs of the storm last night had vanished in the bright sunshine of the morning. While the crowds exited the front of the sanctuary, a short distance away from the garden, Brooke walked around and touched what was likely one of the last remaining blossoms of a bygone spring.

When the sound of dispersing crowds faded, Brooke turned to see that Jake sat, leaning forward with his forearms on his thighs, his hands clasped, his head bent, and his eyes closed.

He straightened when she sat beside him, ready for whatever confession he wanted to make to her. She smiled encouragingly. After all, she'd heard that confession was good for the soul.

She was ready. Or at least she thought she was ready when Jake turned and took her hands in his. But never in a million years did she expect to hear what Jake had to say.

"I'm an ex-con, Brooke. I've spent time in federal prison. And I'm still on probation."

It didn't really register for what seemed an eternity. Slowly, slowly it dawned. An ex-con had associated with her child. An ex-con had come into her home, under false pretenses, had spoken beautiful words of love—for God, for her, for her son, for her dog.

Jake Randolph was a con-man. Like Bruce. Just like Bruce. It all came flooding in on her—feelings and emotions she thought she'd dealt with. But here she was, duped again! Her distrust of men was again confirmed.

She could be thankful for one thing. That wall of reserve had thawed but hadn't completely melted from around her heart. Hadn't she expected to be disappointed again?

But could this be a nightmare? Was Jake really a. . .a crook?

And had his crime been so bad he even feared telling her about it?

She had to get away from this. From him.

~

The instant he spoke, Jake knew he'd blurted out the news too quickly. He should have led up to it with an explanation. With sinking heart, he watched the color drain from Brooke's face. He saw the smile fade. He watched her eyes stare in horror. Her expression was what he had feared. She looked just like Meagan when he'd told her he'd been arrested, and why. Meagan wanted nothing more to do with him. Meagan hadn't even stayed around for an explanation.

And now, Brooke was going to leave too. As if in slow motion, she moved her hands out of his. She was going to bolt!

"Brooke," he said, the same as he had said to Meagan. "I wasn't guilty."

A tinge of color appeared in her cheeks. She was shaking her head. She stood, still staring at him, unable to get any words out.

He repeated, "Brooke. I wasn't guilty."

He'd thought she was about to faint and reached out for her, but she shrugged him away. Just then, the associate pastor called his name.

"Jake," he summoned. "Your sister called and said for you and Brooke to come home immediately. She said it was urgent."

~

If Jake had tried to talk to her on the way to Ginger's, Brooke wouldn't have acknowledged it. Something terrible must have happened. *Was it Ben?* She should have been with her son. *Oh, Lord. Please, please, let everything be all right.* But if everything were all right, Ginger wouldn't have called.

When Jake screeched to a halt in front of Ginger's house, a neighbor and the three boys ran out the front door and met them at the truck. *Where is Ben? He isn't there! Something terrible has happened!*

The boys looked scared to death, pale as ghosts, and the look on the neighbor lady's face indicated something dreadful had happened. Did he fall into the pool, unnoticed? Had he run out into the road and been hit by a car? Had he fallen off the swing set and hurt himself? What had happened?

"Ben? Is Ben okay?"

"Ginger drove him to the hospital," the neighbor said. "I don't know what all happened. She had Mike call me."

"His stomach hurt," Mike said.

"And he threw up," George added, while the frightened little boys nodded their agreement. Danny's lips quivered, and he started to sob. The neighbor pulled him to her and put her arms around him.

"The medical center?" Jake asked.

"Yes," the neighbor lady said. "That's where she said she'd take him."

Appendicitis! was flashing through Brooke's mind like a red danger signal. She had enough nurses' training to know what the symptoms were. Thinking back, she could see other signs. He hadn't eaten much at all yesterday, saying he wasn't very hungry. He'd had problems with constipation, but she had accredited that to his not having eaten right.

Maybe it was just a virus, she tried telling herself. But in her heart she knew better. Appendicitis was fairly common; however, if the appendix ruptured, it could turn into peritonitis. And that was much too serious for a little guy like Ben.

"Hurry," she whispered.

"Yes," Jake said, not taking his eyes from the road speeding past them.

Brooke felt as if her entire being was one desperate prayer. *Oh, God, he's so little, so young, and I'm not with him.*

Chapter 19

Ginger was waiting at the emergency room door when Brooke arrived. "His stomachache got worse, and his temperature sky-rocketed," she explained. "He threw up, and I got him here as fast as I could."

"Thanks," Brooke said hastily and rushed over to the desk. Ginger and Jake were right behind her.

The receptionist wanted all sorts of information, but Brooke wanted to see her son. Finally, a nurse came out to talk to her. "He's just fine. They're running tests and trying to bring his fever down. You'll be able to see him in just a few minutes."

Brooke nodded and relented to answering the receptionist's questions, the most pertinent being, "Who is your insurance company?"

The receptionist looked like Brooke felt when she replied, "I don't have insurance."

"Come sit down," Ginger said, taking Brooke by the shoulders. Feeling numb, Brooke followed her lead to a corner of the waiting room.

Brooke was about to say no to any suggestion like coffee or food when Jake started speaking, but his words weren't what she expected to hear. "Let's sit down and pray about this, Brooke," he said softly.

Yes, she wanted that. This was not a time to think of anything but her son.

They sat. He took her hands, bowed his head, and presented little Ben to the Lord. He lifted the young boy up and told God what had happened, as if God didn't know.

"Thank You for blessing Brooke with Ben for over five years," he prayed. "Lord, we know everything is Yours and in Your hands. We're placing our faith and trust in You, that this situation will be controlled only by You. Be with the doctors, the nurses, all the workers here, and with Brooke—that she may feel the comfort of Your presence. Thy will be done. In Jesus' name, amen."

Brooke felt it. The fear, the urge not to say, "Thy will be done," but to beg God to save Ben's life. She tried to move away, but Jake wouldn't let go of her tension-filled hands. "Lord, I have no strength," she finally began. "I know You love him more than I am capable of loving. But I want him with me, and I pray You may see fit to allow that. Thank You for the years of joy I've experienced with Ben. He was my life jacket in my sea of trouble. Lord, help me to be his life jacket now that he is in trouble. I pray that Ben's needs will be met by You—and I want his recovery—but, Lord, I'm trying to want Your will."

She wasn't even sure she could mean it wholeheartedly, but knew what she must pray. "Thy. . .will. . .be. . .done," came out in a choked whisper. "I'm trusting You, Lord. Forgive me for thinking of myself. Help me to be what Ben needs at this time."

Brooke began to sob, and feeling her hands relax, Jake released them. "Let me hold you," he said. She allowed him to come closer and hold her head against his shoulder. With the strength of his arms around her, she cried. When she felt cried out, she thanked him, then went to the restroom to splash cold water on her face.

Ginger had stayed, but Jake was gone when Brooke returned to the waiting room. She felt empty without him there. At the same time, she felt a great calm, rather like a cloud of comfort, had surrounded her, keeping her from fear and wondering and pleading. She felt covered by a blanket of God's presence and love.

Finally, the doctor talked with her. "All tests indicate appendicitis," he said, confirming her suspicions. He related that they'd performed an abdominal sonography and a blood test and that there was increased pain on the right side of Ben's abdomen. "There seems to be a slight perforation of the intestines, and we suspect an abscess," the doctor said. "We will monitor him closely for a few hours and give him antibiotic therapy to reduce any infection. That has to be done before we can consider surgery."

"Suppose it. . .ruptures?" Brooke asked, knowing that such an event could put her son in grave danger.

The doctor spoke confidently. "We are prepared for emergencies," he replied.

Shortly, a nurse came to say Brooke could go to Ben's room. She held his hot, little hand. She talked to him and told him that she loved him. She told him that God loved him and His Spirit would not leave him for a moment. She prayed aloud for his recovery.

He was a brave little tyke, but Brooke saw the concern in his feverish eyes. Soon he closed them and fell asleep.

"He's so sick," Brooke said when she returned to Ginger in the waiting room.

"I'm so sorry," Ginger said.

"It's no one's fault," Brooke said. "He had symptoms, but I didn't put them all together. I'm just grateful you got him to the hospital."

"I was scared to death," she said and quickly rose and walked over to the window. Brooke saw her shoulders shaking and knew she was crying.

Brooke went over to her and they embraced.

Ginger sniffed. "I should be helping you, not the other way around."

"You are," Brooke said. "But why don't you go home? Your boys need you."

"Jake's coming back in a little while. I'll go then."

Brooke didn't have strength enough to argue. She refused to allow anything into her mind but Ben. He was her responsibility. Yet, after Jake returned, his presence helped. She could call her parents and have them fly down, but somehow Jake's optimistic outlook was a comfort. He was someone she had come to count on during the past months. She would not send him away.

～

Hours later, Ben was taken into surgery. Brooke would not consider going home. Jake didn't even suggest it. She told him he could.

"I know that," he said. "But I'm not going to."

She bit on her lip to keep from bawling again.

"I don't want to cause you any distress," he said. "I want to be here for Ben and for you if you need me. There are no strings attached."

He didn't ask her to have a cup of coffee or listen to him. He wasn't trying to persuade her about anything. He just said, "I left to talk to the pastor. There are now around-the-clock prayer meetings going on for you and Ben. Ginger will take care of Taz."

When the flood again ran down her face, he got up, and she wondered if he was going to hold her again. If he tried, she would let him.

Instead, he said, "I'll be back," and walked out of the room.

Later he returned with a toy dog that looked a lot like Taz and had a red balloon tied to its collar.

He sat down with it. "For when he wakes up," he said.

～

After surgery, the doctor came into the waiting room, all smiles. Brooke breathed a sigh of relief when he said that surgery revealed that peritonitis had not developed and that there was no infection. Ben would have a scar about one and a half inches long.

"Oh, thank you," she said.

The doctor nodded. "You'll be notified as soon as he's out of recovery and into his own room."

Brooke turned to Jake, who held out his hands. She took them and they closed their eyes. "Thank You, God," Jake prayed.

"Thank You," Brooke added.

～

"I like this one," Ben said to Jake when he gave him the stuffed dog. "But I want Taz to come and see me."

"No way," Jake said. "That monster would eat all your Jell-O and crackers." Ben smirked. "I want pizza anyway."

"A few more days and you'll have your pizza. Now you rest, so you can get well and go home. If you're good, I'll smuggle a few boys in here to see you."

"Yeah!" Ben said and flopped his head over, pretending to go to sleep.

Brooke was full of gratitude to the Lord for Ben's successful surgery and recovery and that Jake had popped in to cheer him up. When he wasn't in Ben's room, she noticed him in other children's rooms, talking, joking, and he always prayed with them before leaving.

He might be a former criminal, but didn't Jesus say you would know what people are like by their fruits? *What are Jake's fruits?* she asked herself and could readily answer. *He helps other people. He is caring. He does good works. He serves others. He has that water-basin attitude that Jesus admonished His followers to have.*

And what are my fruits? she questioned and knew they were not nearly as obvious as Jake's. *I, too, have made mistakes. I didn't put God and His will and ways first in my life during my marriage. Maybe if I had been a dedicated Christian, I could have helped Bruce. Maybe God gave me to Bruce for that reason, and maybe I failed. I never said that I didn't want the big house, the fine car, the beautiful clothes, the attention. I did want them. And is that any different from Jake's wanting something so much he committed a criminal act to get it?*

But Jake had said he wasn't guilty.

Had she, with her judgmental attitude, condemned an innocent man?

She looked up from where she sat beside Ben's bed while he slept. Jake stood in the doorway. Seeing that Ben was asleep, he motioned her outside.

"Brooke, I heard you say you don't have insurance. I can help you—"

She shook her head before he could finish. "I appreciate that, Jake. But I have to try and do this on my own. If I'm going to have faith in God, then I have to depend on Him, not other people."

"But sometimes His way of working is through other people," Jake said.

"I know, but I have to try. Can you sit with Ben for awhile?"

"Sure," he said, looking as if she had offered him the world.

～

Brooke did the only thing she could. She withdrew her money out of savings and deposited it in her checking account. That was the money she'd put aside for her nurses' training and for her and Ben to live on.

But she had no choice. The hospital bill had to be paid.

There were only a few weeks until Ben would start to school. Maybe she could scrimp some way, then find some kind of job to see them through. Without skills, she had no idea what kind of job she could get.

When Brooke returned to pay the bill, the secretary told her the amount.

"Are you sure?" she asked.

"Pretty sure I'm sure," the woman answered. "You don't think it's right?"

"I thought it was more."

"Oh, the check we got paid part of it."

"Check?" Brooke questioned. "What check?"

"Let's see." She fumbled around on her desk. "This one," she said. "It hasn't been deposited yet."

Brooke stared, hardly able to believe it. A sizeable check that would pay a big chunk of the bill was from the church. "Who gave this to you?" she asked.

"The pastor," the woman replied. "He's here all the time to see patients." She smiled broadly. "This happens quite often."

Brooke could hardly see to write her own check. This wasn't going to take her last penny after all. *Oh, God. Forgive my little faith. I'll try to do better.*

When Ginger came later and Brooke told her about the church's gift, Ginger was not surprised. "Our church is a giving church," she said. "They do this kind of thing."

"I'll bet Jake was in on it," Brooke said.

Ginger grinned. "I think it's all confidential."

Brooke nodded. "Want to get a bite of supper with me?"

"It's about time you ate."

Brooke knew it was also about time she mentioned the situation between her and Jake. "He told me he was in prison, Ginger. That knocked me for a loop. I feel like I went into shock."

"Didn't he tell you he wasn't guilty?"

"Right before the associate pastor said you called," Brooke replied. "Since then, all I've thought about was Ben. But when Jake said he wasn't guilty, something flashed through my mind. It was a movie I saw. A prisoner was asked what he was in for. He quipped that nobody in that place was guilty, and everyone laughed, indicating they all were guilty."

"I saw a movie like that," Ginger replied bluntly. "And it seems to me the one who said that was really innocent."

Feeling reprimanded, Brooke admitted, "I don't even know what Jake's crime was."

Ginger's eyebrows lifted and she said blandly, "Income tax evasion,"

"Oh!" Brooke exclaimed. Her reaction was one of relief. Before that moment, she didn't realize that all sorts of suspicions had lurked in her mind—perversion, drugs, illegal schemes. Strangely, she felt laughter about to bubble up in her throat. It wasn't funny. It was criminal.

Ginger laughed and exclaimed impishly, "Wouldn't we all like to evade that!"

"Yes," Brooke agreed. "But we don't."

Ginger silently picked at her food.

Finally, Brooke said, "Jake said he didn't do it. I shouldn't question."

"Yes, you should, Brooke," Ginger said, looking up. "And I understand. It's so hard to trust anyone again after your heart has been trampled by a man. But if you want to know Jake's story, I think you should hear it from him. I'm the sister of the accused man, and I believe in Jake. You have to find it in your own heart to believe Jake or not—to trust him or not. And if you think he was guilty, you have to look at what kind of life Jake lives now."

Chapter 20

Brooke had been taking a look at the kind of life Jake lived for months. When he came to the hospital that night, she apologized for having doubted him.

"I don't blame you," he said. "I blurted out the fact but didn't tell you the story behind it. I'd like to tell you, if you want to hear it."

Brooke listened intently while Jake talked far into the night, leaving out nothing, blaming himself where he was wrong.

"You remember I told you that it might seem cruel or restrictive to keep Taz on a leash while training him?" Jake asked, and Brooke nodded. "Well, I feel like God had me on a leash in prison, but His instruction has been the best in my life. Before that, I was a believer. I never doubted there was a God, and I believed He was the God of the Bible. I never doubted that Jesus was His Son and that He died on the cross for the sins of the world.

"However, it wasn't really personal for me. Oh, I prayed when something went wrong. But it was always a 'gimme' type of prayer. I never had the Spirit of God leading me. I never felt the obligation to tell others that Jesus truly changes a life. That He gives peace, calm, hope, purpose, meaning."

Brooke felt as if his words echoed so much of the belief that had been in her mind for most of her life, but hadn't always been in her heart. She was so grateful that since coming to this island, meeting Jake and Ginger, getting involved in the church, she knew the difference.

"I learned that I was not in control of my life, that I needed to depend solely on the Lord. I was in a situation not of my making, and no one was able to help me," Jake said. "Not family, friends, attorneys—no one. No matter what, some people will always believe I'm guilty." His moment of sadness quickly turned to joy. "I didn't commit that sin, but I have committed others, and I needed the blood of Jesus to wash me clean. Those six months in prison became a time when I searched the Word of God, made it a lamp unto my feet, a light unto my path."

"Oh, Jake," Brooke said sincerely. "Even if you had committed that crime, I know the kind of man you are today. I've never known a person who lived his Christianity more devotedly than you."

Jake had to force back the realization that, although she complimented him, it sounded like she might still have a little doubt about his innocence. "Even if you had committed the crime," she had said. But he would try and dwell on the positive side of her words.

"Brooke," he said. "I love you. I would like to marry you and take care of you and Ben for the rest of your lives."

When she hesitated, rather than make her too uncomfortable, he added, "And Taz?"

She laughed lightly. "Oh, Jake. That's so tempting. But that's the very reason I can't consider anything like that right now. I have a money problem. I have a son to support. I was helpless after Bruce died. I need to be able to stand on my own two feet and support my son without having to depend on a man or on my parents. I think I owe that to myself and to Ben." Seeing his nod, despite the disappointment in his eyes, she added, "And Taz."

He laughed then, briefly, then said seriously, "I admire you for that, Brooke. I won't pressure you. But I'll be here, when you're ready."

~

The next morning, Jake loaded the van with the toys, flowers, balloons, and cards Ben had received in the hospital and drove Brooke and Ben home. Ginger and the boys were waiting with lunch ready when they arrived.

Brooke didn't have to cook for a week, with all the food the church people brought. The neighbors came, even the young couple who had kept to themselves and had rarely said more than "hello" before.

The visitor who offered the most interesting information, however, was Evelyn, who came one evening while Jake was painting the kitchen ceiling. He'd climbed into the attic portion and found a hole at the very tip of the roof and plugged it.

Evelyn brought a card signed by the children in Ben's Sunday school class. "You're so blessed to have a man like Jake looking after you two," she said when Brooke walked her to the door. "Makes me pine away for my guy. He's in the military, so we can only communicate through the mail or by telephone."

Brooke felt guilty about having ever felt jealous of Evelyn. She realized what she'd missed, too, by not being part of a church family for so many years. People who didn't go to church just didn't realize what they were missing in the way of love and fellowship.

And yes, she was blessed. Jake was true to his word about not pressuring her, but he was there for her and Ben. He fenced in the back yard and built a dog house. Ben helped him paint the dog house—and the grass!

But Brooke was delighted that Ben was learning to use his hands, not just for a friendly handshake, but for something more constructive.

"Come look, Mom," Ben called, and she went outside to compliment them rather than just peek out the kitchen window. "Miss Evelyn said Jesus was a cartpender," Ben said, his big eyes shining.

"She's right," Jake said.

"Well, I'm gonna grow up and be a cartpender just like Jake and Jesus."

"That's a very worthy goal, Darling," Brooke said, looking at Jake's surprised but pleased expression.

~

Many times, Brooke thought of how much easier things would be if she married Jake instead of finding a way to support herself and Ben. But if God wanted her to be a nurse, He would work that out. Fall was on the way, and she had to make her moves. She and Ginger enrolled their boys in kindergarten and were assured Ben and Danny could be in the same class.

Deciding to check out the cost of nurses' training, Brooke asked Ginger to keep Ben while she went to the university to talk to an advisor. When the advisor said she couldn't get the lower in-state tuition, Brooke knew her hopes were dashed. She couldn't afford the tuition, keep the house running, find time to work, and still spend time with Ben and have time to study. It seemed impossible, and she said as much.

The advisor pushed his dark-rimmed glasses farther up his nose and smiled. "There's a nearby hospital with a plan that might suit you," he said, peering through his lenses to find a folder in his filing cabinet. "Here it is." He returned to his seat. "The hospital will pay tuition if the student commits to work at the hospital after completing the training. Of course, if the individual decides not to work at the hospital, then that student is obligated to repay the hospital."

Brooke bit on her lip and fought back tears of relief. Her eyes automatically lifted to the ceiling, toward heaven. It was as if she could see that bright shining path of Easter morning and she was walking on it toward a clear blue sky. *I didn't even have faith things would work out this way. But I prayed. Oh, God, forgive my lack of faith. I'll try to do better.*

After checking with the hospital to confirm the possibility, she rushed back to tell Ginger. "Most of the money I had saved was for tuition," she said excitedly. "But I'm not going to have to pay tuition. I can't believe this. I don't have a lot, but I'm better off now, even with having paid Ben's hospital bill, than I was when I thought I was going to have to pay tuition."

Ginger just grinned knowingly. "The Lord works in mysterious ways."

"Yeah," Brooke agreed, and they offered a prayer of thanks.

"Where's Jake?" Brooke asked, thinking he should be off work and hoping he hadn't gone to her house needlessly.

"Not far from here," Ginger said. "He met this older couple when Ben was in the hospital. Grandparents of a child who was in for a concussion that he got from falling off his bike. He wasn't wearing a helmet. The grandpa had bypass surgery three months before. Jake found out they could use some help, so he's been over there a few times."

"I wonder," Brooke said, "if he could use a partner."

Ginger scratched her auburn curls, looking dumbfounded. Suddenly realization dawned. "By all means, go ask!" She gave directions to their house.

Brooke stopped by a bakery for rolls, then drove up to the house. The woman answered the door. "I understand Jake Randolph is here making repairs," Brooke said. The woman confirmed it and graciously invited her in, led her to the kitchen, and introduced her to her husband, who was talking to Jake while he worked.

Jake appeared shocked as Brooke gave the rolls to the woman. "I'm from a church up the way," she said. "I heard your husband recently got out of the hospital, and I wondered if there's anything I can do."

"Why, how sweet," the woman gushed, and Brooke knew she was feeling overwhelmed, the way Brooke had felt when Ginger had come to her house. "But no, I don't think we need anything. We're doing fine." She laughed and spoke ironically, saying they had trouble keeping up with her husband's medicine. "He has so much to take and forgets it half the time. When I try to help, I have no idea if he took it or not."

Soon Brooke and the woman were sitting at the kitchen table, and Brooke made out a schedule for the medicine. She made two copies. "I'll have copies run off of this, and he or you can check it off each time he takes a pill. If the doctor changes the dosage, just make the change on every copy. But he must check it off when he takes each pill."

"I'll see to that. Oh, you're a dear."

Jake packed up his tool box, and Brooke made it a point to leave at the same time as he.

Outside, walking toward their vehicles, Jake asked, "What was that all about?"

She lifted her chin saucily. "You're not the only person in the world with a water-basin mentality, Jake Randolph. You've been a wonderful example to me of Christian service, and I intend to make it a part of my lifestyle too."

He grinned. "You're a girl after my own heart."

"You're absolutely right," she replied.

Before her meaning could register, she jumped into her car and sped away.

By the time she got home with Ben, and he ran out back with Taz, Jake was on her doorstep. He stood there, holding onto the post, one foot on the step and the other on the porch. "What did you mean by that remark?"

Brooke backed up against the banister near him, on the other side of the post. She related how God had worked out her financial situation. "I can go to school without having to get another job. I can still be here for Ben and have time to study. So you see, I don't have to find a man to support me."

Jake realized he was nodding a little too vigorously and knew his smile was pasted on. Yes, it looked like Brooke had moved on. She didn't need him or any man. And that's how it should be. That's what he'd tried so hard to instill in Ginger. It had been a long, hard climb, but Ginger had come to realize that, and now Ginger had influenced Brooke. *So I'm partially responsible for this*, he thought with a sense of both pride and disappointment.

"I don't have to have a man," she reiterated, "but I want one."

"You. . .you do?" His eyes met hers.

Brooke nodded. "I do. But there are certain requirements."

"Like. . . ?"

"Well, first of all, he has to have a water-basin mentality."

Jake drew in a breath. He dared not hope she was saying what she seemed to be indicating, but there was definitely a look of mischief in her eyes. "You, um, have anyone in mind?" he asked.

"Yeah. He's handsome, strong, giving, loving—"

"Then I should leave," he said, turning as if to go.

"Oh, no," she said, reaching out to grab his arm. "That man is you, Jake Randolph. You said you loved me. If you have changed your mind. . ."

"Yes, I have," he said immediately, and Brooke jerked back like she was shot. Then he smiled that wonderful smile, and his eyes gleamed with such affection that she wasn't sure she could take it. "I changed my mind every minute of every day. I kept saying, 'Jake, you're not going to pine away your life thinking about a woman who doesn't love you. You're not going to waste another minute.' So you see, I changed my mind all day and all night long. But my heart never changed."

His hands were on her shoulders. "I love you, Brooke. I would like for us to spend the rest of our lives together." Exasperated, he shook his head. "I didn't mean to propose or anything."

"Then just what are you suggesting?"

"Brooke, you're deliberately putting me on the spot."

"Yes," she said. "I'm afraid to believe what we might be saying."

"Let's just be honest," he said.

"I love you, Jake," she said.

He reached into his pocket, and her heart beat faster, wondering if he'd been carrying around a ring. It wasn't a ring. It was a newspaper clipping. "I want you to read this, Brooke. It might help you find peace about my past and let you know that I was telling the truth."

"No." She pushed his hand away. "I believe you, Jake. I trust you."

He ignored her words. "I didn't want you to read this until you decided within your own heart what kind of guy I am. You needed to trust me on your own, Brooke, and not because I proved it."

"I'm sorry," she said.

"No, don't be. Now that you trust me, I want you to read this."

Brooke took the clipping. The headline read, "Martin Gage Commits Suicide." The article was all about Jake's partner, who had left a suicide note admitting that he alone was guilty and explaining that he had not been able to quit his gambling and he had lost everything—his self-respect, his wife and children, his home. He asked that Jake and others in the community forgive him.

"Oh, Jake."

"I feel sorry for him," he said. "But don't feel sorry for me. I was convicted of the same crime as Martin Gage because I was a partner and should have known what was going on. That was evidence enough to convict me. Then, when I was in prison, a pastor came and asked a group of us, 'If you were accused of being a Christian, would there be enough evidence to convict you?' My honest answer was no. I decided then and there that my life would be different. For the rest of my life I want there to be enough evidence to convict me of being a follower of Jesus."

"Jake," Brooke said, moving closer to him. "When I came here, I thought it would take years before I could even consider having a man in my life. You've changed my mind and my life. But," she asked, "how would you feel about your wife going to school and working as a nurse?"

"Proud," he said immediately. "Now, will you marry me?"

"Yes," she whispered. "I will."

"Then come here," he said, pulling her close. "I'm so 'cited' about this, I'm going to kiss you right in front of all creation."

Just as their lips met, a screen door slammed and a little boy's voice demanded, "Whatcha doing?"

With a great sigh, Jake dropped his hands from around Brooke, and trying not to laugh, she stepped over and sat on the swing.

"Come on over here, Son," Jake said. "We all need to have a serious talk."

Before Brooke could warn him, Jake sat beside her on the swing, something popped and creaked, the chain came out of the side where Jake sat, and they both jumped up as one side of the swing hung precariously from the rusty chain.

When Brooke finally stopped laughing, she said accusingly, "You're the one in charge of repairs."

"I guess we'll stand for this," Jake said and tested the banister before leaning back against it. He looked at Brooke. "You want to tell him?"

"You can."

"Your mother and I want to get married."

Ben's mouth fell open. "You mean, we're going to be a family?"

When Jake nodded, Ben shouted, "Cool! But first I want to show you something." He walked out onto the yard, looking up at the sky. "Over here. Over here."

Brooke and Jake walked over and finally saw it. A very faint rainbow of soft pastel colors arched across the late evening sky.

"It didn't even rain," Ben said.

"It's a reminder," Jake said.

It reminded Brooke of a verse of Scripture about God's unfailing love and how Jake had not failed her, even when she didn't trust him. But under the guidance of God's love and with His help, she, Jake, and Ben could be a family.

Just before Ben returned to the backyard and Jake led Brooke inside the living room to continue what he'd started before they were interrupted, he looked at the sky again.

"A reminder," he said, "that no matter how much rain there is in a person's life, there's somewhere a rainbow."

Southern Gentleman

Chapter 1

Heavy rain pelted the glass panes. Wind lashed the front screen, threatening to whip it from its hinges. Norah's deep green eyes, darkening with apprehension, darted toward the sound, but it was not the storm that concerned her. She'd been on edge ever since Thornton Winter's telephone call thirty minutes ago. Not only had he known her name and unlisted number, but with a deep-South deliberateness in his voice, he'd asked directions from the airport.

As soon as she hung up, she regretted having told him, then just as quickly reprimanded herself for that attitude. Apparently he felt this visit important enough that he'd flown all the way from California to Florida just to see her.

Car lights flashed across the drapes. Taking a deep breath, Norah attempted to analyze the situation calmly. The man had claimed to be Lantz's brother. Lantz was dead. He'd died yesterday, after a week in the hospital following that awful car accident. Perhaps the grief-stricken man wanted to talk about Lantz and Hillary.

Norah heard the slam of a car door, then the sound of a heavy tread on the walkway along the front of the house. She opened the door to a drenched figure, clutching desperately at his flapping trench coat. With head lowered, he stepped inside.

"This isn't the Florida I expected," came his rueful condemnation, as Norah struggled to close the door against the driving wind.

The height and breadth of the man seemed to fill the small foyer as he stood looking down to unfasten his coat.

"I haven't been here before in April, so I don't really kno-o-o-ow." Her voice wound down like a record at slow speed when he lifted his head, any other words trapped in her throat.

The light striking the left side of his face highlighted in bold relief a jagged pink scar that zigzagged down his cheek to the corner of his mouth. Another cluster of raised scars fanned out from his narrowed left eye, across his temple, and into the dark hairline. Try as she might, she could not suppress an involuntary gasp of horror.

She hadn't been curious about Thornton Winter's physical appearance, but now realized she had assumed that he would have the smooth, good looks

347

of his brother. On second thought, Lantz had many looks, depending upon the role he was playing at the time. This man was not playing a role, she reminded herself, although he did look as if he had stepped straight from the script of a movie, cast as a Gothic villain.

He disengaged his arms from the soaked trench coat and held it at arm's length. "Miss Norah Browne, I assume," he said in a deeply resonant voice in which she detected a decided Southern drawl such as she had noticed in Lantz when he hadn't been trying to rid himself of it.

"Yes, and you're obviously a very wet Thornton Winter," she replied. Forcing her eyes away from his intriguing face, she noticed he was exquisitely dressed in a dark blue suit covering broad shoulders, a white shirt that stretched across an impressively wide chest, and a conservative dark blue tie with a subdued maroon stripe, fastened by a silver-rimmed tie tack encircling what undoubtedly was a ruby stone. His expensive trousers were wet around the bottoms, above black shoes still shiny in spite of the few mud spatters.

Norah was acutely conscious of her faded jeans and dingy white shirt, its tail hanging out, and color flooded her face as she realized he was watching her give him the once-over. Her green eyes flew to his face again where rivulets of rain ran from the thick mop of hair plastered to his forehead, and down along the scar, now purple. A muscle twitched along his jawline. His eyes, glittering like live coals, stopped the apology that formed in her throat.

"Miss Browne," he began, his deep-throated words edged with irritation, "if you have completed your inspection of me, perhaps you will take my wet coat, or tell me what I might do with it."

She reached for the coat. "I'm sorry. I wasn't exactly prepared for company."

"I'm not company, Miss Browne," he said abruptly. "I'm Lantz's brother, remember?"

Lantz's brother! The thought smote Thornton like the edge of a steel blade across his heart. He'd tried. Had tried with all his might to be a responsible big brother to Lantz. Had tried to fill the void after their parents died twelve years ago, when Lantz was sixteen, and he, twenty-two. But the void hadn't been filled. Lantz had never seemed to have enough of anything—love, money, attention. He'd packed a lifetime of living in a few short years and, in so doing, had left a string of broken hearts behind him.

This was the first time, and now it would be the last, that Lantz would ever ask Thornton to pick up the pieces of a life burned by Lantz's undisciplined lifestyle.

Thornton had always believed that his brother would return to the traditional Christian faith in which they had both been reared, but he hadn't expected it to be on Lantz's deathbed, while he was still a young man with so much of life yet untasted. In a halting voice, Lantz had told Thornton what he would do differently, if he could do it all over again.

Unfortunately, it was too late. Lantz couldn't do it over again.

But Thornton was still alive and well, in spite of having been met head-on by the raging elements pounding the Florida coast, not to mention the intense scrutiny of Lantz's most recent "indiscretion."

Thornton had always known that Lantz attracted beautiful, glamorous, even older, sophisticated women, so he was not surprised by this one's face, whose features were as lovely as a magnolia blossom and whose unusually expressive eyes were as green as spring in Charleston. But he had not expected her to be so young. And at the moment, she appeared disheveled and somewhat disoriented. Well, he supposed that was to be expected under the circumstances. What caused him some pain, however, was her unabashed repulsion as she stared at his face.

"You'll like her," Lantz had said only hours before his death. "The two of you have a lot in common."

Thornton hadn't said so at the time, of course, but Lantz's leftovers weren't at all his type. Still, one so young, so apparently helpless would doubtless welcome the proposition he was about to make. But welcome it or not, of one thing he was sure—he knew what had to be done, and Miss Norah Browne wasn't about to stop him!

It was still hard for Norah to believe that this man and Lantz were brothers. Physically, she recognized little family resemblance, and their personalities were exact opposites. Lantz had exuded charm, a smile for everyone, and an easy-going magnetism that drew people to him. Lantz would have already extended his hand, at the very least, or more likely would have pulled a person to him for a friendly hug.

Not this one! So formal and aloof was he that Norah had the impression he'd rather not be here. Then why was he? Shouldn't he be seeing about his brother's affairs?

The screen door slammed against the doorcasing just as a chilling thought thudded into her brain. Surely he didn't think there was anything here for him to handle!

Suddenly, she felt the cold wetness of the coat on her arm. A shiver ran through her. Instinct warned that this man had not come for a purely social visit, nor merely to express sympathy.

Did he know about Camille? If Lantz hadn't mentioned her, then. . .

"Have a seat in the living room," Norah said lightly, making an instant decision not to provide any unsolicited information.

Winter's glance followed hers toward the living room, in plain view from the small foyer. It was dimly lighted by the glow of a TV, where players romped across the silent screen, and a lamp that flickered precariously as the wind whipped the electrical lines outside as if turning a jump rope.

Norah watched him peer inside and view the room with apparent disdain—much the way he'd looked at her. She had no choice but to find out what was on his mind. The first thing, however, was to rid herself of the dripping coat.

She walked down the hallway and glanced uncertainly over her shoulder toward the living room. Then, stealthily, she tiptoed to Camille's doorway, peeked in, observed the baby sleeping peacefully, and quietly closed the door. What Thornton Winter didn't know already, he didn't need to know.

While hanging the coat over the shower curtain rod in the bathroom, Norah admitted to herself the reason she had not been able to keep her gaze from lingering on Thornton Winter's scar. The truth was she'd always been more intrigued by a gnarled tree limb than by a perfect rosebud. Her insatiable curiosity, along with an innate sense of caring, had led her to decide upon a career that probed the innermost depths of a person.

Thornton Winter's marred face had certainly aroused her curiosity. Whatever had happened to cause such disfigurement? An accident? An act of violence?

Judging from the man's dark, brooding expression, however, he was not the type to bare his soul, and she wasn't about to ask! For just as Lantz's brother did not possess the younger man's pretty-boy features, instinct warned that he also lacked Lantz's good nature.

Turning to look in the mirror, Norah touched the thick coil of braided hair, secured with hairpins on top of her head. *It looks like a pile of orange marmalade,* she thought with a sigh of disgust. Dark circles shadowed her weary green eyes that stared out of her face, pale now except for the sprinkling of freckles across the bridge of her nose. The old joke she'd heard umpteen times—"You must have swallowed a dollar and it came out in pennies, ha ha!"—had never been a consolation. And now she could readily see that the strain of the past week had taken its toll on her. Too bad. It was too late for makeup.

A spot on her shirt caught her eye. Camille's cereal! That must have happened earlier in the evening. She hadn't noticed at the time, and a change of clothing now would only call attention to it. Since Thornton Winter's call, Norah had had time only to settle the baby after her bottle around ten o'clock. No wonder he had looked at her as if she had a contagious disease.

Hearing a movement, Norah jerked her head toward the bathroom doorway and gasped to see him standing there. What a picture she must make, with a washcloth wrapped around one finger and a wet streak down the front of her shirt. His dark eyes lingered on the spot for a moment before he raised them to meet her gaze.

"I seem to be dripping all over my suit and the carpet," he said, with a definite edge in his voice. "Could you possibly spare a towel?"

"Of course," Norah replied nervously, aware of the man staring at her and the tumultuous activity outside the bathroom window. She knew, without a doubt, which of them made her more uncomfortable.

After taking a towel from the linen closet, Norah handed it to him. He wiped his face, and for an instant the towel covered the left side of his face. *Why, he's beautiful!* came her surprising reaction as she stared at the unblemished side, smooth except for the dark shadow of a heavy beard. He didn't seem quite so foreboding now. That is, until his eye met hers. And in that moment, his glance held such contempt that she felt she had been accused and found guilty.

Turning sideways to avoid any physical contact, Norah scuttled past him and escaped up the hallway, reprimanding herself for being on the defensive. Yet, analyzing the situation, how could she be otherwise? She hadn't even known Thornton Winter existed until half an hour ago. Lantz had never talked to her about family. If he and his alleged brother were close, then why hadn't Lantz mentioned him before?

The lights blinked off, the TV gulped, and Norah almost stopped breathing. Then everything came to life again. Standing inside the doorway of the living room, Norah tried to convince herself that she was in no danger.

But sudden fear gripped her heart and her pulse raced madly when he strode up beside her, their bodies almost touching. She could feel the body heat emanating from him, strangely prickling the icy gooseflesh on her arm. And when she lifted her inquiring face to his, she was again spellbound. The scarred tissue at his eye seemed to be stitched, and it stretched the eyelid into a narrowed slit, from which a dark orb glittered ominously.

The uneasy realization dawned that she had allowed a strange man into the house. He could be anyone at all! Only her resolve to protect a helpless baby held at bay an invading sense of panic. "I would like to see your identification," she demanded, with more courage than she felt.

A glare of indignation swept his features, deepening the color of the scar to a purple streak, and she feared he would refuse. What she would do next, she had no idea.

Then, without taking his eyes from hers, he reached into his breast pocket and withdrew a thin wallet. "My calling card. Credit cards. Driver's license." He flipped from one plastic covering to another, then held it out to her. "Rarely does one resemble such photos, as you know, but the vital statistics are there."

Norah wondered whether his resentment was spawned by her impertinent request or by the photo itself. It was the image of an incredibly handsome man—stormy dark eyes, a straight nose, wide sensuous lips that curled over perfect teeth—without a trace of a scar. The wound must have been inflicted fairly recently. The dark wavy hair in the photograph was neatly brushed, while the man who stood before her, his dark curls in damp disarray, now showed touches of gray at his temples, presenting a certain air of distinction along with his villainous charisma.

"I thought you could be a reporter," Norah murmured, moistening her suddenly dry lips with the tip of her tongue. Her long lashes veiled the humiliation in her green eyes as she returned the wallet. Attempting to ease the tension with an attempt at humor, she asked coyly, "Would you like to see my identification?"

He surprised her. "I would, indeed. You see, the purpose of my visit is to see my niece."

Norah stepped back and gripped the doorjamb. He knew! It was perfectly natural, she tried telling herself, that he would leave his dead brother's side, fly to Florida late at night in the most unsightly weather of the season, just to see a baby he'd never seen. Perfectly natural! Then why was her heart battering against her chest like the wind against the windows?

"I. . .she. . .she's sleeping."

With calm deliberation, he said, "I can wait," and swept past her into the living room.

Norah reached out and grasped the sleeve of his suitcoat. "No! Wait. . . ," she tried to protest, then heaved a sigh of resignation. He was Camille's uncle. He had every right to see her.

She had to remember that they were both under tremendous strain. At least she had been forced to accept Hillary's instant death. But there was no way of knowing what Thornton Winter might have experienced during the past week, while his brother hovered between living and dying. She would be cruel to deny him his right to see Camille, if for no other reason than to set his mind at ease about her welfare. And then he would be on his way.

"Come with me." Norah retreated down the hallway, with Thornton Winter a few steps behind. She opened the door, and the sweet scent of baby powder greeted them from the nursery. A Mickey Mouse nightlight glowed near the crib.

He lifted his hand to prevent Norah's turning on the lamp atop the chest of drawers.

"It's all right," she assured him quietly, switching on the lamp, illuminating the colored balloons held aloft by a smiling clown.

"I don't think a child should be reared in silence and darkness," Norah explained softly. "As long as the noise and light are within normal limits, they don't disturb her."

He cast her a speculative glance before his gaze swept the room, taking in the Babyland decor and the pink carpet. Then he turned his attention to the white crib.

The faint glow of light revealed the baby, whose tiny pink lips parted with each quiet breath. Camille lay on her stomach, her head turned to the side, her plump little cheek facing them. A halo of golden-red ringlets curled all over her head.

Norah's heart went out to the beautiful baby, who someday would have to know the tragedy that had occurred.

"What do you call her?" Thornton Winter asked finally, his voice surprisingly tender.

"Camille," Norah replied.

"Camille," he repeated and nodded slightly, as if he approved. "Sounds like a flower, or a song."

Norah smiled as she and Mr. Winter gazed at the child.

"Lantz's child," Thornton murmured. The words caught in his throat.

A quick glance at his face revealed that he was deep in thought. Norah was suddenly aware that this was Lantz's house. Lantz's baby. Lantz's brother. Feeling a chill, Norah reached over and tucked the pink blanket closer to Camille's chin, then switched off the lamp.

They returned to the living room and stood inside the doorway. "She's adorable," Thornton acknowledged, as if he could not quite believe it.

Norah agreed, adding lightly, "Even though she's very demanding. Those middle-of-the-night snacks, you know." She laughed weakly.

She had hoped for some sign of congeniality. But he didn't laugh, not even a tiny smile, and Norah flushed beneath his poignant stare. Then his eyes traveled toward the windows, rattling their protest against the torrential wind and rain.

"Would you like coffee?" Norah asked. "Before you go back out in that?" She glanced toward the windows.

He didn't reply. Norah looked up at him. Perhaps he hadn't heard her. Then ebony eyes stared down into her face. "Yes, please."

They were sitting across from each other at the bar separating the kitchen-dining area when Thornton asked, "Are you an actress, Miss Browne?"

"Actress?" Norah repeated, staring into her milky coffee. She wasn't at all the glamorous, exciting type like Hillary. Perhaps Thornton Winter's perception had been dimmed in his grief over his brother's death. Or perhaps he thought her a bit-part actress, hanging onto her sister's skirttails. "No, I'm not an actress," she answered finally.

"How did you meet Lantz?"

"Through my sister Hillary, of course."

"Hillary Caine is your sister?" he blurted. Coffee spilled from his uplifted cup. His scar reddened.

Norah could not readily grasp his bewilderment. Apparently, Thornton Winter knew as little about her as she did about him.

"Caine was Hillary's professional name," Norah explained. "She was Hillary Browne."

"I'm sorry," he said, spreading his hands. "Had I known Hillary Caine was your sister, I would have immediately expressed my condolences."

He took a napkin from the holder on the bar and wiped up the spots of coffee. "Lantz could say very little, and when he did, it was in broken sentences. Until the end," he said, pausing, "I had no idea he had a child. Under the circumstances, I couldn't very well ask for details."

Glancing around, he found a trash can for the soggy napkin, then returned to pick up his cup and drink from it while his dark eyes probed hers from over the rim.

Norah brushed back a stray piece of red hair and fidgeted on the bar stool. *Strange,* she thought. His words expressed one sentiment, while his eyes, for some reason, seemed to convey quite another. He should be satisfied. He had seen for himself that the baby was well cared for, content.

The situation was painful for her too, but she realized the therapeutic value in sharing a crisis with another person. She recognized the element of shock after Hillary's death, then the tension of waiting to hear if Lantz would survive. "You never met my sister?"

"No, never. Of course, I've heard of Hillary Caine professionally and have seen her on the screen. She was a very beautiful, talented young woman."

The sympathy in his voice surprised Norah when he added quietly, "Your burden of grief is much greater than I realized."

Norah lowered the cup to the saucer with a trembling hand. Somehow, she had kept pretending that Lantz and Hillary were in California on assignment and would be back any day now. At the same time, she knew she would have to come to grips with losing Lantz as a friend, Hillary as a sister. Her greater concern, however, had to be for Camille.

"It's Camille that makes all this bearable," Norah said softly, "in spite of the pain that comes from losing loved ones." Norah bit her lip in an effort to hold back her tears.

It wasn't sympathy, but a note of accusation that Norah detected in

Thornton's reply. "I should think that's what a baby would mean to any married couple."

Norah drew in her breath. Maybe there was more Thornton hadn't known! But with his loss so fresh, she didn't want to risk compounding his grief. She'd have to be very gentle, make sure the time was right before explaining that Hillary and Lantz had been in love and had had a child outside of marriage. With their careers at stake, they hadn't thought public acknowledgment of the baby would be good for either of them at the present time. Hillary had been a child star and was just becoming accepted as mature talent. And Lantz was already established as one of Hollywood's most exciting celebrity bachelors.

In her own code of ethics, Norah believed that love and marriage should precede the birth of a child, but it wouldn't change anything to discuss it with Thornton Winter. It was late. She was tired. He had expressed his sympathy and had seen his niece. Perhaps he would finish his coffee and leave.

"How did you find out about me, Mr. Winter?" she asked, curious.

His expression grew pensive. "I've been with Lantz all week. Only near the end was he able to speak coherently. He seemed to be clinging to life only to tell me about his child. But he did know that Miss Caine was killed in the accident and blamed himself."

"He shouldn't have," Norah replied, looking down at her hands, clasped together on the bar.

The periodic updates on the horrible accident had played over and over on the television news. They flashed through her mind now. The late-night party. The heavy rains. The mudslide blocking the highway. Lantz hadn't seen the mud and rocks in time and had skidded down an embankment.

"It was unavoidable," Norah said finally. She saw the restrained grief in his eyes and felt an uncanny desire to reach out and put a comforting hand on his arm. However, one glance at his forbidding countenance put the skids on that impulse.

"In any event," Thornton said quietly, "Lantz had a picture of Camille in his wallet. Your name and phone number were on the back." He hesitated, then added almost kindly, "You were in his last thoughts. His last words, in fact, were about you."

That surprised Norah. "Wh–what did he say?" she stammered.

"After he asked me to take care of Camille, he said, 'Norah makes a great little mother.' "

That vote of confidence from Lantz caused Norah's eyes to mist over. "I've tried," she said in a whisper. "It takes more time than I could ever have imagined. But, Mr. Winter, the most natural impulse in the world is loving that little baby."

"You're a very, um. . .tolerant young woman," he said, "not minding that Lantz was in California with your sister, while you were clear across the country."

"If I minded, I wouldn't be here, Mr. Winter," Norah said, stating the obvious. "Their careers were very important to Lantz and Hillary."

"A career is more important than a baby?" came his scathing remark. Norah suspected that there was something other than grief eating away at Thornton Winter.

"Parents don't necessarily give up their jobs when a baby is born," Norah said tightly. "Some jobs just happen to take a parent across the country instead of downtown."

"You miss my point altogether, Miss Browne." His voice was cool and remote.

"Just what is your point, Mr. Winter?"

He downed his coffee, pushed the cup aside, and stood. "Perhaps we'd be more comfortable in the living room," he said, sounding for all the world like the bearer of bad tidings.

But what could be worse than the current situation?

Her emotions were raw—that's all, she told herself. Keeping them under control for Camille's sake had been difficult. Now to have Thornton Winter here in some unexplainable capacity gnawed at her. Determined not to break down in front of him, she quickly slipped from the stool, then tossed over her shoulder, "I'll check on Camille and be right back."

She looked in on the baby, still sleeping peacefully, and thought about Thornton Winter's words. What had he meant about Lantz asking him to take care of Camille? He obviously intended some kind of financial assistance, since he had acknowledged that Norah "made a good mother."

Norah took a deep breath, reminding herself to be wary of Thornton Winter's questions. And of her own answers. In times of emotional stress, one didn't always think rationally.

Upon entering the living room and walking across the beige carpet, her attention was immediately drawn to Thornton, already seated on the couch, at the end nearest the picture window. The contrast between the two brothers again struck her forcefully. Lantz's gaze had been touchingly transparent and open, while Thornton's eyes continually searched hers, as if he were harboring some deep secret and suspected her of one too.

Norah had barely seated herself in the overstuffed chair when he asked with slow deliberation, "What are your plans now, Miss Browne?"

"Plans?" Norah echoed, her thoughts whirling. She wished she could simply lean her head back, close her eyes, and sleep off her overwhelming exhaustion. "So much depended upon whether or not Lantz lived. But, no, I haven't made any definite plans yet. It was only yesterday that. . ."

"Yes, yes, of course," Thornton interrupted. After a moment, he asked, "Did you attend your sister's funeral?"

She could see no harm in answering that question. "My parents felt it would be adverse publicity for the reporters to find out about Camille. I don't think anyone knows about her except me, my parents," she hesitated, then added tersely, "and you."

He caught the inflection in her voice, confirming what he suspected. She resented him. But that was of no consequence. His mission here was not to establish a friendship, but to assume his responsibility. "Do you plan to take the baby to your parents?"

"They. . .travel a lot," she began, and told him that her father was a character actor who was in constant demand. Her mother had spent years in the makeup department of a major studio before she had quit her job to concentrate on reliving her acting dreams through her daughters. Hillary had gladly followed in their footsteps, but Norah had not been in the least interested.

"They've looked forward to this time in their lives when they would not be bound to any particular place." Noticing the slight narrowing of his eyes, she wondered if that sounded callous and hastened to explain. "My parents came here when Camille was born, of course, and spent several days. And we've talked on the phone since the accident. They're willing to help if necessary, but I know grandparenting is the role they want to play and should play."

The mention of grandparenting presented a memory that tugged at Norah's heart. She saw herself as a carefree child, running along the beach, startling sandpipers, secure beneath the watchful eyes and protective arms of her grandparents. They were gone now, but from them she'd learned about the frailty of human arms and the strength derived from the awesome presence of God, through His Spirit dwelling within the believer. Consequently, she'd found a kind of confidence and fulfillment in being herself that she never felt on stage, with human hands applauding her portrayal of a character.

"You said you're not an actress, Miss Browne," Thornton was saying, bringing her errant thoughts back into line. "May I ask. . ." He cleared his throat. "Just what is your line of work?"

Noticing his hesitance, Norah wondered if he were having qualms about this obvious cross-examination. On second thought, Thornton Winter did not give the impression that he was ever uncertain about anything. Probably, he was only trying to discover if she could care for Camille adequately. That would be a natural concern. Particularly for one who had been asked by his dying brother to look out for his child.

"I expect to find a job in some phase of psychological work," she went on.

"I earned my bachelor's degree in psychology last spring, worked at a health clinic in southern California during the summer, and began work on my master's in the fall."

Thornton grimaced. His brother had obviously taken advantage of this schoolgirl, had halted her career plans and gotten her pregnant, had settled her in Florida, and had then gallivanted across California with her glamorous sister. And to make matters worse, this girl didn't even seem to know she'd been wronged.

He took a deep breath rather than chance spouting some unappreciated remarks about morality. The young woman was looking at him as if she were afraid he might hit something. And well he might! This latest escapade topped anything Lantz had ever done! Her voice trembled slightly as she continued, "Then. . .I came here."

"Because of the baby, I assume," he said.

Norah's "yes" was barely out of her mouth when Thornton rushed on. "Then you have no ties or obligations to a job or persons either in California or Florida?"

"Only to Camille," Norah replied firmly.

Ah, he's convinced of my devotion, Norah thought when a trace of triumph flashed in Thornton Winter's eyes. But his very next words astounded her. Surely she had misunderstood him. No way on Florida's drenched earth would she consider doing what he was asking!

"I. . .I beg your pardon, Mr. Winter?"

Chapter 2

I'm taking you and Camille home with me," Thornton Winter repeated flatly. "To Charleston."

"You mean," Norah began guardedly, "for a visit?"

His dark eyes glittered. "What I have in mind, Miss Browne, is much more permanent than a visit, and I see no reason for delay."

Before he had completed his declaration, Norah was shaking her head vigorously. "But that's out of the question."

"It was not a question," he countered. Shadows played on his intriguing face while the lamp flickered and lightning flashed SOS signals against the windows.

"I have other plans," Norah said quickly, trying to control her inner panic.

"You just told me that you have no plans. But I do!" Before she had a chance to recover from that announcement, he shocked her speechless with his next words. "Obviously, you love your baby very much, Miss Browne."

Your baby, he had said?

My baby! she thought.

His implication struck her like the slam of the front screen against the doorfacing. Did Thornton Winter think the baby was hers instead of Hillary's? *Yes, he did,* she thought, with dawning certainty. He actually thought she had borne Lantz a child. . .out of wedlock!

"You're. . . ," she croaked, bracing her hands on the chair arms and planting her feet on the floor in the act of standing.

"Don't faint on me, Miss Browne!" he warned, rushing to assist her.

To escape the threat in his eyes, Norah slunk back into the chair, her initial shock turning to outrage. Color now leapt into cheeks that had paled considerably. Defiance and determination stung her eyes. No way would she faint and leave that helpless child in his clutches!

She flinched as his hand came up, then was aware of his fingers, surprisingly gentle, as they touched her shoulder. "Have you been eating properly, Miss Browne?"

"Eating?" Norah returned. Chagrin washed over her like the storm over the Florida landscape. Feeding herself had not been a priority in the past twenty-four hours.

"Sit still," he demanded, then moved away.

A moment later he was back, holding a glass of milk. "Here, drink this." Norah took it, her hands trembling.

Thornton returned to the couch, but she could feel his eyes on her as she drank. After the first taste, her stomach became aware of its absence of nourishment and grumbled. She finished the milk, sipping slowly while she collected her thoughts.

"Mr. Winter," she said finally, studying the glass. "I'm afraid you have some very mistaken ideas about me."

"Never mind that," he said brusquely. "You don't have to explain to me, Miss Browne. You're hardly more than a child yourself. I admire your determination, but there would be nothing wrong with your allowing me to relieve you of this responsibility."

Norah's mouth dropped open. When she finally found her voice, it rose shrilly. "I don't want to be relieved of it!" she protested. "Why would you think such a thing?"

"Well, you're young, and single, and. . . ," he paused, then had the audacity to appear slightly embarrassed before adding, "and apparently quite. . .uh, impetuous. . .to have gotten into such a predicament." He lifted his hand to halt any protest. "Never mind," he said before she could reply, "some things are better left unsaid. We must try to put aside our emotions, as difficult as that might be, and concentrate on that child in the other room."

Norah had the strange feeling that she had just been labeled "damaged goods" and consigned to the nearest garbage dump.

Just as she was about to set him straight by blurting out her true relationship to Camille, something unexpected happened. A mothering instinct surfaced, as surely as if she had given birth to that child. As Camille's aunt, she didn't stand a chance against Thornton Winter. But as her mother. . .

"What did Lantz tell you?" she asked, strangely serene. His humiliating perception of her was something she could endure if it meant protecting an innocent child. A baby needed gentleness and love more than she needed financial security from a domineering, judgmental uncle.

Thornton hesitated before answering. "A dying man's words are focused on eternity, Miss Browne, rather than on things of this world. However, after I discovered Camille's picture, with your name and number on the back, I asked him if he had married you. He shook his head 'no.' That was right before he asked me to take care of Camille." Thornton leaned forward, his disapproval evident in the frown on his face. "Did he refuse to marry you, Miss Browne? Or was that your decision?"

Norah now welcomed this misconception. It gave her the confidence to deal with this overbearing man. "I am single by choice," she replied with a defiant lift of her chin.

His glare of disdain gave her the feeling that a storm raged inside him, proportionate to the one outside. She delighted in his discomfort. It served him right!

She had a feeling that Thornton Winter had auditioned her for a role in traditional morality, and she hadn't landed the part. Well, she knew she could play the role of Camille's mother convincingly. After all, the baby's welfare was much more important than Thornton Winter's opinion of her.

He exhaled audibly and sank back against the couch. Lantz must have been hallucinating to think that this loose young woman and he had anything in common. Apparently, she was one of those star-struck groupies who fall for celebrities without giving a thought to the consequences. But what excuse had Lantz had—at age twenty-eight?

And how could his brother have believed that he would like her? He couldn't even communicate with her. All she had done so far was flash those green eyes and dart at him like a wary cat showing her claws, getting her back up at every word, when all he was trying to do was to offer her a chance at a decent life. Obviously, she hadn't an inkling as to what was good for her or the baby. For a so-called well-educated person, she hadn't a grain of common sense. She was being totally unreasonable.

Unless. . .and a thought struck him. Could she be holding out for. . .blackmail? With the help of an unscrupulous attorney, she could present that innocent child as heir to the famous Lantz Winter estate.

Thornton's determination increased. He wasn't about to let this fiery young woman out of his sight until he knew what made her tick.

Norah reminded herself that both Lantz and Hillary had entrusted the care of their child to her. This had now been confirmed by Lantz, who in his dying breath had acknowledged his approval of her. So she hoped the quivering she felt inside was not evident in her voice as she stated as firmly as she could manage, "We don't want your help, Mr. Winter. Thanks, but no thanks."

"That doesn't change a thing," he retorted. "What you want, Miss Browne, does not affect what I believe is my responsibility. My niece is going with me," he replied as calmly as if he had said, "I believe the storm is subsiding."

Norah didn't budge. "Your concern is appreciated, Mr. Winter. However, I will decide what is best for me. And for Camille."

"You're in no position to think rationally," he insisted with infuriating calm. "So I'm here to do it for you." The only indication that he felt any emotion whatsoever was the reddening of his scar.

Norah's green eyes flashed. "Really, Mr. Winter? Do you plan to resort to force?" Her voice rose to a dangerous pitch.

"I wouldn't call it force," he argued. "May I remind you, Miss Browne, that I'm not trying to take something from you. I'm making you an offer."

Norah couldn't chance it. If he discovered she was only the child's aunt, there would be no hope of keeping Camille. She shook her head. "I don't want to go to Charleston with you, Mr. Winter."

"Why are you resisting my offer?" he asked suddenly.

Why? The answer washed over her in a wave of panic. She'd lost her grand-parents. Then Roman. Now Hillary and Lantz. The fear of losing yet another close to her trembled through her veins. To cover the shaking of her hands, she set her glass on the coffee table. She mustn't think of herself. . .only Camille.

"Camille needs me, Mr. Winter. But as her uncle, you're certainly entitled to visit her occasionally." Another thought occurred to her, and she used it to fuel her argument. "After all, the child's name is Browne, not Winter."

"Be sensible, Miss Browne," he implored, leaning forward again and plac-ing his arms on his knees. "I don't want to make threats. I'm simply trying to do what is best for everyone concerned. Let's look at the facts: You have no visible means of support, you do not want to live with your parents, and you have a child to raise."

"I'll get a job."

He quirked a brow. "Enough to provide for a decent place to live? A babysitter? Even the basic necessities are costly these days."

Norah tried not to think of the few hundred dollars in her checking account, compared with the extensive list of supplies a baby would need. "What she needs most, Mr. Winter, is emotional security and love."

"Camille will have all that in Charleston—a stable home, a loving family, people who will teach her Christian values."

As if I have none! Norah thought resentfully. "And how would your wife feel about your bringing Camille and someone like. . .me. . .home with you?"

A glimmer of triumph shone in his eyes. "I have no wife."

Norah felt an unexpected surge of elation tingling through her, and she tried to ignore the images flashing across her brain and threatening to alter her heartbeat. She'd spent many years backstage, waiting for her walk-on part, while her family rehearsed. Meanwhile, she had occupied her time by reading and had become fascinated, not with the white knight on his white horse, but with the villain, brandishing his sword, his black cape flying. In her dreams, she saw someone darkly handsome coming to her rescue, someone who was not a villain at all, but her hero!

She shook off these mesmerizing thoughts. This kind of fantasy could be dangerous. Sometimes the main character turned out to be a true rogue. Right now, she should keep her mind on what was best for Camille.

Norah cleared her throat. "That presents a problem then, Mr. Winter," she began. "For Camille's sake, I must think of my reputation. Despite what you might think, you need to understand that I'm not in the habit of allowing strange men to support me."

"I had no thought of propositioning you, Miss Browne," he replied as if nothing could be further from his mind. "Frankly, I was thinking of Lantz's child."

She sighed wearily and closed her eyes. Of course he wasn't propositioning her. A man like Thornton Winter would have women falling at his feet, just as Lantz had always had. But she needn't worry about this one. He did not seem to like her at all. In fact, he was downright hostile.

She knew his patience was at an end. So was hers. She rose from the chair and walked to the picture window. Pushing aside the drapes, she looked out. The wind had quieted, and the rain was coming down in a steady drizzle.

Glancing over her shoulder, she saw that Thornton Winter was sitting calmly, his legs crossed, one hand resting against his bent knee. The scarred side of his face was toward her. She wondered what had happened. Perhaps, she thought indignantly, he had backed someone into a corner, as he was doing to her, and he—or she—had come out fighting.

In the half-light, she was conscious of the man's appearance. He was immaculately groomed and expensively attired, all the way down to his shoes and socks. His hands were large and strong, yet delicately tapered, and the nails were well cared for. His dark, tailored suit fit perfectly across the broad expanse of his shoulders and skimmed a slender waist. He had not even loosened his well-knotted tie during his entire visit. His dress and bearing were that of a Southern aristocrat, and Norah had the distinct impression that here was a man who was accustomed to having his own way.

At least, he seemed determined to take Camille. Norah knew she could do nothing legally, and she was no match for him physically. Nor had her psychology courses prepared her to tackle a personal problem of this magnitude. But one thing she knew. There was no way she would give up that baby!

She would just have to use her wits. She took a seat in a chair opposite him, thinking furiously.

"I assure you, Miss Browne," he went on quietly, "in Charleston, the baby's every need will be met. I have hired help. I will engage a nurse. . . ."

"A nurse?" Norah felt as if her voice had become a perpetual squeak. "You think a nurse can replace. . ." *Yes! She'd say it,* "a. . .a mother?"

"Obviously, you're not thinking straight, Miss—"

"Because I don't agree with you?" she snapped.

"On this issue, yes. We are going to Charleston," he insisted.

"You seem to think I have no choice in the matter."

Thornton leaned forward. There was no trace of amusement in his voice now. "Certainly you have a choice." His tone sent a chill down her spine. "I'm taking Camille to Charleston. You may come peacefully. . . ," he said, pausing for effect, "or not."

Norah winced. She could mention the authorities, but if he called her bluff, that could lead to a court fight and she couldn't risk that.

She glanced at the wall clock. It was nearing midnight. Let Thornton Winter have the last word, she was thinking. He obviously was not playing games but was determined to take Lantz's child to Charleston, whether or not she went along. She would simply have to agree. . .for now.

Norah took a ragged breath and closed her eyes. "All right, Mr. Winter," she said quietly, as if resigned to the fact, "Camille and I will go to Charleston with you."

During the ensuing silence Norah opened her eyes, aware that she was being observed. She fastened her gaze on the scuffed toes of her tennis shoes.

"Your cooperation is appreciated, Miss Browne," he said, after a long moment. "I sincerely believe you will not regret your decision."

Norah stood, hoping he could not see the fluttering of her heart. As soon as he left, she would consider what she should do. She still had the option of stealing away during the night and driving Camille to her parents' home in California. "Then it's settled, isn't it, Mr. Winter? I'll get your coat so you can leave, and we can both try for a good night's sleep."

He stood, his eyes gleaming with some kind of sinister delight as they met hers. A sardonic smile touched the corners of his lips as if he knew what she'd been thinking. "Don't bother with the coat," he drawled, his words thick and slow as molasses. "Just show me where I might sleep."

Chapter 3

Sleep?!

Norah would not be able to close her eyes with Thornton Winter laying in the darkened guest room with the door open. Norah suspected that he lay on the bed fully clothed, waiting to pounce should she make a suspicious move.

Midnight in Florida meant that it was eight o'clock in California. She could call her parents. But what would she say? Drop all your plans. . .interrupt your career. . .rescue me and Camille?

"Rescue you? From what?" they would ask.

Norah pondered what she would say. "Camille's uncle is here, intent upon taking over Lantz's responsibility for her. He's insisting we go to his home where there is financial security, loving family, Christian values. . . ."

Somehow, she couldn't imagine her parents replying, "In that case, run for your life!"

She drifted into a restless sleep, still fretting over the fact that she was helpless in the face of Thornton Winter's demands.

When her eyes opened, she focused on the gray light rimming the window. *It can't be morning!* But it was.

She had slept. Guiltily, she admitted to herself that it must have been because someone else was in the house to listen for the baby. Norah had fed Camille sometime in the wee hours of the night and then again just as the faint rays of a gloomy dawn invaded the house.

A car door slammed, soon followed by the hum of an electric razor, then the cascade of the shower—reassuring, masculine sounds. Yet Norah could not contain a shiver of apprehension at the prospect of the future this man might be planning for his niece.

"You can trust me," she promised Camille, while settling the baby in her crib. "I won't ever leave you."

When she entered the hallway, Thornton stepped out of the bathroom. He was wearing the trousers to his suit of the day before, but the white shirt looked fresh.

"We have a big day ahead of us," he said exuberantly, and Norah wondered if he were always so chipper this early in the morning. "But the first order of the day is breakfast." He rubbed his hands together in anticipation.

Norah flushed with anger. He looked perfectly rested and fresh, while she felt frazzled, bedraggled, and heavy-headed from having slept the sleep of the exhausted. Taking care of a baby was one thing, but she had no intention of becoming this man's slave too!

"There's cereal in the kitchen," she said shortly, her indignation bringing her fully awake.

Thornton gave a snort and disappeared down the hallway.

Norah showered, slipped into blue jeans, tennis shoes, and a T-shirt. She wrapped a thick towel around her dripping auburn curls and tucked the corners in at the nape of her neck. Suddenly, the most marvelous aroma assailed her nostrils. Food! Realizing she was hungry, she hurried to the kitchen.

Taking note of the two places set at the bar, Norah immediately felt a stab of guilt. She shouldn't have been so hasty in her judgment. But she quickly dismissed her concern. After all, Thornton Winter had taken it upon himself to lay claim to his brother's belongings, including his child. He might as well realize that a few other responsibilities went along with the privilege.

Norah unwrapped the towel, allowing her hair to tumble below her shoulders.

Thornton eyed the tangle of red-gold curls. "No wonder you have such a fiery temper," he observed, walking over to the bar, skillet and spatula in hand. With the dexterity born of practice, he deftly lifted an omelet onto the plate in front of her.

"It's not the hair," she informed him rather self-consciously, having detected a trace of admiration in his gaze, if not in his words. It was not uncommon to hear compliments on the glorious mane that waved naturally and hung to her waist when brushed out. But at the moment, she felt it was about as attractive as limp strands of wet spaghetti noodles.

After toweling her hair dry, Norah used her fingers to coax the ringlets away from her face. When Thornton returned to the bar with a second omelet for himself, his continued scrutiny unnerved her, and she responded automatically to his terse command. "Sit down and eat everything on your plate. We have much ahead of us, and you'll need your strength."

She grasped the fork almost as soon as the backside of her jeans made contact with the bar stool. The omelet was a simple mixture of eggs, cheese, and milk, but her green eyes narrowed as the golden-yellow concoction teased her palate and aroused a response from the pit of her stomach.

Norah was halfway through with her breakfast before she realized that she had been lost in her own thoughts and that the only sounds had been the occasional muffled noise of her chewing and the slight scrapes of butter knife against crunchy toast.

Looking up, her eyes met Thornton's across the bar. She felt certain he had been staring at her for some time. Warmth crept into her cheeks. She sat a little straighter, aware of how she must look, hovering over her plate as if she hadn't eaten in days.

"And you suggested only cereal?" he drawled, amused.

She refused to succumb to his charming grin. "I guess I was a little hungry," she confessed, finding him even more handsome and younger than he had appeared the night before. Was she warped to find a scar so intriguing?

The light caught the glint of a gold chain around his neck, nestled against his chest beneath the open collar of his shirt. She quickly averted her eyes from the mat of dark curly hair, forcing herself to remember that Thornton Winter had come to claim her treasure—baby Camille. Of course his chest would be hairy. Wasn't Bluebeard's? And dangling from that chain around his neck was probably a skull and crossbones!

Perhaps Mr. Winter seemed like pleasant company because she'd had a few hours' sleep and had eaten her first hot meal in a week.

"What kind of car do you have?" he asked, jolting her thoughts back to the stark realities of the moment.

Avoiding his eyes, which were a deep tranquil blue this morning, she described her car—a small car, standard gear shift, six years old. "It was a high school graduation present from Mom and Dad."

"I think we'd better take the rented one," he decided.

Norah bristled. "What's wrong with my car?"

His steely eyes bore into hers. "Your car would barely hold the three of us, Miss Browne," he tried to explain reasonably. "And we have your personal belongings to take, as well as Camille's."

Norah prodded the remains of her omelet with her fork. The car had represented her independence. In it, she had driven to the beach when she wanted to be alone. She had driven from California to Florida when Hillary had needed her. Now Thornton Winter was saying she would have to leave it behind.

"I–I'll need my car," Norah protested, her nerves feeling more jangled by the moment.

Obviously irritated, Thornton set down the steaming cup of coffee he had just poured. "If you need a car, you may drive one of mine until I can move yours to Charleston."

Norah had already discovered the futility of arguing with him. Besides, the little Rabbit had become more and more temperamental, often having to be coaxed into doing her bidding. But she wouldn't give in so easily. "Isn't it rather expensive to drive a rented car all the way to Charleston?" she persisted.

"When we consider the possibility of breaking down somewhere along the way, my ineptness with gears on the highway, and your having to care for an infant, I think all the comfort we can get is recommended. However. . ." He shrugged his broad shoulders, his back to her at the sink, "if you want to pay for it. . . ."

"I do not!" Norah retorted angrily. "It's your idea. I'm perfectly willing to take my own car."

A sly grin touched his lips as he turned to observe her. He slowly wiped his hands, threw the towel over his shoulder, then ambled over to the bar. With his face uncomfortably close to hers, he repeated her words, "Perfectly willing. . .to go with me, Norah?" He suspected she was not as reluctant as she pretended. Nor was she as naive. But even if she really wanted nothing for herself, surely she would not deny that baby her birthright as the child of Lantz Winter.

Before Norah could object, he continued in a deep sing-song tone, "You don't really want to fight with me, now do you, pretty Norah with the wild, curly hair?"

His words were pleasantly reminiscent of a song her grandfather used to sing, something about Jeannie with the light brown hair. . . .

Ever since their first encounter, Norah had recognized within herself the fight or flight syndrome, accompanied by the dawning realization that she really did not want to fight with Thornton Winter. Now, almost hypnotized by his disturbing nearness, her gaze lingered on the fan of scars at the corner of his eye, then moved down the streak along the side of his face.

"It. . .bothers you?" he asked, touching the purple welt with a tentative finger, then quickly added, "Never mind. Of course it does." He moved away abruptly.

"Please. . .I. . . ," she began, aware that she had offended him.

"Don't bother with apologies or explanations," he ground out. "I've heard enough of them to last a lifetime." His dark eyes were fathomless pools of shadow, and a scowl touched the lips that had come so close to hers. "Let's just say you caught me at a weak moment. But frankly, I don't know whether to shake you or console you."

Norah's heart pounded furiously. She wanted to pour out the truth to him, but he shrugged as if it were inconsequential and turned to carry the dishes to the sink. Was it possible that this self-assured man was the slightest bit vulnerable to her? Or was it just part of his ploy to further subdue and control her? And how could she ever know with this deception between them? He thought she had been his brother's lover. There would come a day when he would call her a liar. She must tell him the truth.

"Mr. Winter," she began slowly. She felt he was listening, though he did not turn from his chore. "I. . .need to tell you something."

Thornton submerged the plate in the sudsy water and scrubbed it over and over. The wetness reminded him of the liquid emotion that had threatened to scald his eyes during the night, while he stared at the dark ceiling and heard the steady rain beating against the roof. He had feared he might drown in his own grief as he replayed the memory of his dying brother and his last request. Suddenly thrust upon him was the lifelong responsibility of rearing a child. With that had also come the question of how to deal with that child's mother.

It would be simpler to say he'd tried and failed, and leave her to her own devices. But, earlier, while Norah was taking her shower, he'd gone to the nursery to look in on the baby. Camille had started to fret and, fearing Norah's recriminations, he'd picked her up.

She had stopped crying almost immediately, turning her cornflower blue gaze on him with such innocence and purity that his heart melted. She seemed to be reading his mind, extracting a silent promise from him. And in that moment he made a firm decision. He would not abandon his brother's child.

He'd even felt grateful that Miss Norah Browne had produced this miraculous little girl. Camille would never feel her daddy's arms around her again, but her uncle would do his best to make up for that.

But first, there was Norah herself!

Thornton knew he had been hard on her, and he felt a momentary twinge of remorse. But how was one expected to handle a woman who didn't know what was best for her? He had found Norah Browne to be extremely perceptive and dedicated to the welfare of her child. But she was utterly exasperating as well! Still, in her defense, he had to admit that she was very young, relatively alone in the world, and still grieving for her sister. . .and her lover. To compound the problem, she appeared frightened of what Thornton might do, and he resolved to be kinder, gentler, with her.

Now he'd gone too far in the other direction. In his attempt to blunt his own pain and the burden of his new responsibilities, he'd allowed himself to become vulnerable. Well, it was inexcusable. He simply couldn't handle any more complications right now.

Now this impossible young woman wanted to tell him something. He hoped it was not another revelation. . .that she was a jewel thief on the side! At the moment, he felt about as fragile as the plate he was washing. With the slightest jolt, it could break apart. He sighed. He'd have to hear her out. Better get it over with.

Thornton wiped his hands and walked over to the bar. "What is it now?"

Norah took in the stubborn stance, the hands folded over his chest. Basic psychology told her that this signaled a defensive posture. Nor did his dark scowl and one quizzically lifted eyebrow encourage her to continue.

Determined, she plunged in anyway. "I'd rather not begin this. . .arrangement. . .between us with dishonesty. We need to try to get along. For Camille's sake."

"I agree," he concurred.

Norah drew in a breath. She was not actress enough to pull off this deception any longer, but she couldn't find the words, so she used a diversionary tactic. "You and I need to have at least a mutual understanding that Camille's needs come first, and that we should put any animosity behind us."

Thornton, who was still stinging from his own raw emotions and his perception that she found his looks unbearable, lashed out with a tart reply. "Then maybe I'd just better leave you here and take Camille."

Norah's eyes flashed with green fire. "You try that, Mr. Winter, and I will let this story out to the press and the police and whomever else is necessary! I've taken care of that child since the day she was born, three months now. You may have more money than I, but that's all. You certainly can't be a mother to her!"

He threw back his head and laughed. "Quite a spitfire, aren't you, Miss Browne? Comes with the hair, I suppose."

She cocked her head and glared up at him. "I'm whatever I have to be."

His disarming grin caught Norah off guard, and she felt herself thawing. But it would never do for Thornton Winter to know he had her on an emotional roller coaster ride. Still, his next words made her wonder.

"In spite of your protests, Miss Browne," he said, still grinning into her eyes, "I believe you're looking forward to the prospect ahead as much as I." She held her breath when he rose from the bar stool and towered over her for a moment.

But before she could summon up a scathing rejoinder, he was issuing orders again. "But now, we've work to do. I realize you're a modern woman, Miss Browne. But since I've done the cooking and cleaning up, maybe you could do your own packing. Take only the essentials. Pack what is to be shipped later. Label everything. We have several hours' drive ahead of us, so please, let's have no further delays."

Stung by the implication that she had staged the delay, she darted him a murderous look, then twirled on the bar stool and jumped lightly to her feet. Rushing from the kitchen, she went into her bedroom to throw some things into her suitcases. Poor Camille. Why couldn't the child have a nice, kind, old uncle rather than this arrogant, overbearing tyrant?

While she packed, Thornton made some telephone calls. Snatches of his end of the conversation revealed his finesse in handling business affairs, including funeral arrangements for Lantz in Charleston. Then there were hurried references to "house, dock, weather," after which he phoned the electric and telephone companies to see about disconnecting the service. He had thought of everything. For that, she was grateful.

~

The gray late-afternoon sky pressed ominously low as Norah and Thornton left the house she had called home during the past several months. She climbed into the back seat of the rented new Buick, next to Camille's wicker car bed.

Thornton grimaced as drops of rain struck his face, then he slid under the steering wheel and started the engine. "When you need to stop, just let me know," he tossed over his shoulder.

After a curt nod, Norah glanced at Camille, who was waving her little arms and making loud cooing sounds. *Babies are so trusting,* she thought. The poor little thing had no idea where she was or where they were taking her. Didn't care, as long as she was warm and dry and her tummy was full.

Norah let out a long sigh and looked back at the house as they pulled away. Only a week ago, she had been a loving aunt, filling in for absentee parents. And then the accident had changed everything. Now a man she had never met had appeared to complicate things even further. But Thornton Winter was right. In spite of everything, she could begin to feel an inexplicable stir of adventure. What might be awaiting her in Charleston?

When Camille fell asleep, Thornton persuaded Norah to sit up front. "You'll be more comfortable," he said.

Norah doubted that but slid into the plush front seat and buckled her seat belt. "How much longer until we get to Charleston?"

"Several hours until we reach the city limits. Then we have to drive through the city, cross the Cooper River Bridge, and out to Seabreeze Island."

"Island?"

Thornton glanced at her quizzically. "Didn't Lantz tell you anything?"

Norah could reply honestly. "Nothing about his family. . .or home."

Thornton sighed and nodded. "He wanted to break free of all that. Make it on his own without help from any of us."

"Tell me about your family."

"We have a younger brother and an aunt."

"Oh!" Then it would not be just the three of them. "They live with you?" Norah asked expectantly.

He glanced over at her before turning his attention back to the road. "No. Chris is in school at the Citadel, and Aunt Tess has her own place."

Norah swallowed hard. How could Thornton Winter expect her to live in a house with him? How could he possibly think that was a better arrangement than the one Lantz and Hillary had? But that was not her worry. How to get

371

Camille away from him was the important issue. As soon as possible, she would go to her parents' home, then work toward legal adoption.

For now, she'd play the role of acquiescent mother.

"Suppose they aren't in favor of two new family members?"

He glanced at her, lifted his eyebrows, and replied blandly, "In my house, Miss Browne, I make the decisions."

Norah turned her head and looked out the side window. That's exactly what she was afraid of.

Chapter 4

Hours later, the sky yawned and the sun presented itself in the guise of a huge yellow ball, reaching out to tantalize the water with its golden rays. Norah caught her breath while Thornton drove onto a glimmering structure of burnished steel that rose high and higher, from one crisscrossed peak to another, like a giant web of strength. The intricate design lifted them and cradled them high above the ships, looking like toys, floating on the water hundreds of feet below. Awestruck, Norah watched as the bridge narrowed out ahead as if their journey was taking them straight into the sunset.

Only after they had traveled for miles and had begun their descent did the clouds clamp shut like giant jaws, swallowing the evening sun. Norah looked over her shoulder at the impressive structure, then ahead, as the world faded to muted shades of gray.

"The Cooper River Bridge," Thornton said at last, having given her time to absorb the spectacle that had been known to frighten many first-time tourists. Strangely enough, Norah did not seem in the least intimidated. Her eyes were shining!

"Seeing the strength and power of the steel bridge always reminds me of the power of God," Thornton observed with a glance in her direction. "How His strength carries us over the rough seas of life."

Norah turned to look out her window. Normally, she could appreciate such an analogy and draw courage from it. But the words struck her heart fearfully. Thornton Winter was demanding enough on his own. Suppose he decided the Lord also wanted him to bring up Camille. . .without her help? Surely God would not let that happen. He knew Camille needed a woman in her life.

With the approaching night, drivers turned on their headlights, and lamps winked on in homes as they drove through a small town. On the outskirts, Thornton followed a narrow road until he reached a private dock, drove out onto a ferry, and spoke with a uniformed security guard.

Only a few minutes later, the ferry reached the opposite shore and bumped to a stop. Thornton lifted a hand in farewell and drove the Buick onto a paved road that twisted across a bed of sand like a giant snake. On the way, the car lights raked a couple of Victorian beach cottages, planted among a copse of scraggly pines and green-brown grasses struggling for survival in the rocky soil, and spotlighted stately green-gold palms towering high above great barren stretches of sand. Norah rolled down the window to catch the cooling ocean breeze on her face and breathe in the pungent salt air.

Suddenly, Norah saw the house looming ahead. The camera was ready to roll. Soon she would have to play her part.

The road straightened, ending in front of a modern structure with bright light spilling out from glass walls and windows. Low-growing palmettos, flowering shrubs, and lush greenery surrounded the concrete drive that forked at the house, which was built on a slight incline.

The structure, built of glass and wood, gave her the impression of a bird in flight, its body stretched forth, its wings spread out on either side. The head was a balcony above the front entrance, topped with a peaked roof.

Thornton took the left curve, drove beyond the recessed front entrance, past the far wing, and into a lighted carport where he braked to a stop beside a dune buggy. As soon as he switched off the engine, a slightly stooped, gray-haired man appeared from the back of the house, joined by a white-haired woman in a light blue housedress who stepped from the doorway.

Thornton introduced the couple as Mr. and Mrs. Manchester, and Norah noticed that the man eyed Camille curiously when she was lifted from her car bed. In the next moment, he was helping Thornton remove the bags from the trunk.

"Could I take the baby?" Mrs. Manchester asked softly.

Norah placed Camille in her arms, retrieved the diaper bag and her own purse from the car, and followed the trim woman into the house and along the corridor to the second door on the right.

Mrs. Manchester crossed the ash-colored carpet to a crib and gently laid Camille on her back. The baby stirred restlessly, then popped her thumb in her mouth and went back to sleep.

"So precious," Mrs. Manchester said, turning toward Norah. "When Henry told me that Thornton asked him to have a baby crib ready, I thought he must have heard him wrong." A question formed in her eyes. "He said it was Lantz's baby. . . ."

Norah nodded and watched Mrs. Manchester's eyes grow misty. "Lantz was so special. . . ."

"Yes, and the crib is fine. Please call me Norah."

"And I'm Eloise," the older woman replied. She gestured toward Mr. Manchester, who was bringing in a couple of bags. "This is my husband, Henry. Now, you must be tired after all you've been through. Let me help you get your things unpacked. And I have grandbabies, so I know all about changing diapers too."

Norah put the diaper bag on the king-sized bed. "Have you known the Winters long?" she asked.

Eloise smiled. "The Winter boys are like my own." She explained that she had been their nursemaid when they were young, and Henry the landscaper for the estate. They were retired now, helping out when Thornton needed them. She and her husband lived in one of the Victorian cottages Norah had seen on the way to the house. "Living on this island is like living in paradise. . . thanks to Thornton," she added fondly.

Then Thornton must own the cottages too, Norah surmised. She unzipped the bag and took out a diaper, smiling at the ease with which Eloise changed Camille, turned her again on her stomach, and put the pacifier in the baby's mouth.

While Mrs. Manchester disposed of the wet diaper, Norah walked around the room, trailing a finger across the pale wood furniture, noting the white walls hung with pastel seascapes. Rose draperies could be drawn to separate the bedroom from a sitting area. Here a couch upholstered in a floral design with a matching chair and a window seat padded in pink composed an intimate grouping. Outside the windows that stretched across the entire front wall could be seen low palmetto palms bordering a grassy incline. And beyond the rolling landscape Norah glimpsed the ocean, and a familiar excitement stirred in her veins.

"Tell me what needs to be done, and I'll help," Eloise offered when Norah stepped back into the bedroom.

"Camille will need some formula," she said, casting a skeptical eye at the boxes Henry had brought into the room, "but I'll have to find it first."

"Then I'll run along and see about supper." Eloise gave her directions for finding the kitchen and slipped out, closing the door softly behind her.

Seeing that Camille was still sleeping peacefully, Norah went into the carpeted bathroom, splashed her face with cold water, and tucked in a few strands of hair that had escaped the braid coiled on top of her head. As she looked into the lighted mirror above the vanity, she was surprised to see that some of the strain of the past week had lifted.

In the next instant she had accounted for it. For the first time in weeks, she was having real conversations with other human beings. Someone else had driven her here. Another had changed Camille's diaper. She smiled, feeling as if she'd had a mini-vacation.

After finding the box of bottles and formula, Norah left the bedroom door open and headed for the kitchen. On the way, she walked through what appeared to be a game room, situated somewhere in the central part of the house.

Her attention was immediately drawn to an outside area, beyond the glass doors and windows, where light reflected off a huge swimming pool onto the wooden deck surrounding it. At the far end of the pool, shrubs and palm fronds spread out like the tail feathers of a bird.

Hearing male voices and the sound of approaching footsteps on the deck, Norah hurried past a white wicker couch set against the wall, over which two large flower prints were centered. A conversational grouping of wicker chairs with lush padding squatted at opposite ends of the glass wall. A pool table waited invitingly, balls and cue sticks arranged for play.

Separating the game room from the kitchen was a long bar flanked by six wooden stools on either side. Just beyond, the kitchen was a study in contrasts. Pristine cabinets sparkled against pale yellow walls. Gleaming white tile covered the floor, and a round table sat under exposed cedar beams.

"It's a wonderful house, Eloise," Norah said, walking into the kitchen. "Straight out of the pages of *Architectural Digest.*"

Eloise smiled and took the box of formula from her. "Oh, it's been featured there," she said proudly. "Thornton designed and built it, you know."

While Norah was trying to absorb that remark, Eloise opened the box and took out a can of formula and began reading the directions on the back. "Just add water?" she questioned.

"Boiled water," Norah replied. "Then we pour a day's supply in the little plastic bags."

"When I think of all the baby bottles I've sterilized!" Eloise said, shaking her head.

The two women had just finished preparing enough bottles of formula to last Camille through several feedings when Thornton opened the glass doors, stepped inside the game room, and walked toward the kitchen.

Norah had turned away to put the bottles in the refrigerator and, out of the corner of her eye, noticed Thornton picking up the bottle that Camille would soon be demanding.

"I had hoped for something a little more substantial, Eloise," he chided good-naturedly. "It's been hours since I've had any solid food."

What a difference a tone of voice makes, Norah thought. Had Thornton made that remark to her, it would have sounded cryptic, condemnatory.

Eloise laughed. "Now, Thornton, I'll have something for you in a few minutes."

"Good," he said. "In the meantime, I can give Norah a tour of the house."

Norah! Since when had he decided to use her given name? Norah wondered. Was it because he didn't know what else to call her since bringing Lantz's baby home? Eloise must be terribly curious.

Norah wiped her hands on a towel and followed Thornton through an archway and into the dining room. A crystal chandelier, suspended from the ceiling, illuminated the entire area. A massive wooden table, capable of seating twelve, presided over the room. Slate-gray carpeting covered the floor, and the walls were paneled in wood-stained platinum. The outside wall was entirely of glass, with the exception of a few feet of paneling ending in a ledge lined with a jungle of leafy plants.

A see-through fireplace, set into a wall of coral rock, separated the dining area and living room.

"Eloise said you designed this house. I'm impressed," Norah admitted.

He smiled in acknowledgment and walked over to one of the tomato-red couches that faced the fireplace. Inside the grouping was a low, glass-topped table resting on a silvery shag rug.

"You're an architect?" she asked, glancing around the room, spare and uncluttered, yet elegant in its concept. Heavy white drapes hung at each side of the glass walls, framing a window seat padded in red. Matching fern stands with long, graceful legs relieved the stark lines of the room.

"Something like that," Thornton replied as they reached the spacious front foyer dividing the two wings of the house. From here, a staircase wound its way to the second floor where a white railing overlooked the open foyer.

"My rooms are upstairs," Thornton said, following her gaze. "The best view of the ocean is from my deck. Feel free to make use of it any time."

Norah lifted her eyes to his for the first time since they had begun the tour. "Mr. Winter," she began, wanting him to understand that no matter how beautiful his home might be, she resented being forced to come here, nor did she intend the visit to be permanent.

"Couldn't we drop the formality?" he asked. "We're family now." A softness appeared in the deep blue eyes. "We have a little relative in common, you know."

At the same time, Norah was aware of Thornton Winter's appeal, like a rose of intricate design whose uniqueness draws and mesmerizes while disguising the thorns so near the petals' velvety folds.

Yes, they had a little relative in common, but if Thornton Winter took over, where would that leave Norah? He was willing to accept her, if necessary, but he had made it abundantly clear that any informality between them was nothing personal. Everything was done for Camille's sake. If this continued and Thornton Winter had his way, Norah fumed inwardly, she would become nothing more than a glorified babysitter.

At the moment, the name Thornton didn't come naturally to her lips. "The important thing is that Camille's needs are met," she said quietly. "That she feels safe and loved."

He prevented her turning away by grasping her shoulders with both hands. "What you've done with my little niece impresses me. . ." His touch was warm and strong as he added, "very much."

The angry redness of the scar deepened, but she knew she dare not stare. Accepting a compliment from him was difficult. She could feel it cracking the defenses she must keep intact against him. But how to do that and still behave like a decent human being, she wasn't sure. "I've done the best I could," she murmured.

"I know. But now you have others to help. You no longer have to bear the responsibility alone."

Against her will, Norah felt herself faltering, tempted by his offer of security. How she longed to be comforted, to be reassured that everything would work out. She couldn't be sure of that, however, and she mustn't allow the silent tears to surface. She was not at all sure of Thornton Winter. . . or what his offers meant.

Dropping his hands, Thornton blushed hotly, and the scar turned a livid purple. She could feel him withdrawing, and once again he was his aloof self, and his peremptory gesture toward the foyer told Norah the tour had ended.

When the doors behind them swung closed, Norah felt as if much of the tension were left behind in those coolly beautiful rooms, for stepping into the kitchen was like stepping into sunshine. Eloise's cheerful smile reflected the butter yellow of the draperies and was as welcome as the savory aromas that assaulted Norah's senses and stirred the hunger in her stomach.

Places for two were set at the small round table in the corner, and Thornton held out a chair for Norah and motioned her into it. She obeyed, then breathed a silent prayer for help as the bewildering drama continued to unfold.

Thornton took his seat across from her, spending an inordinate amount of time adjusting his napkin in his lap. In those few moments, Norah reminded herself that she had two overwhelming advantages over him. One was her unyielding love for the baby. The other was Thornton's belief that she was Camille's natural mother.

"It smells wonderful, Eloise," Norah told her when she brought over the steaming bowls of rice and shrimp creole.

"Thank you. But you need to know I'm not much of a cook. That's Hilda's department."

Before Norah could ask who Hilda was, Thornton laughed. "You're fishing for compliments, Eloise," he teased, grinning boyishly. With a wrench of her heart, Norah realized how pleasant and appealing he could be—to everyone but herself.

Eloise brought over hot biscuits and butter, then poured a glass of iced tea for each of them.

Norah savored a bite of the creole, then looked toward Eloise. "Never say you're not a cook."

Eloise laughed appreciatively. "Well, we won't tell Hilda. You just enjoy your meal, and I'll check on the baby."

"You're fortunate to have found someone so competent," Norah said sincerely after the woman had left. "Normally, I wouldn't let someone take over like that. But I think I'm just beginning to feel the strain of it all. . . ." She paused, prodding the creole with a shaky fork.

"Caring for another human being twenty-four hours a day is more than anyone should have to handle alone, Norah, even under ideal circumstances," he said sympathetically. "Now eat up. You need your strength."

Norah lifted another forkful to her mouth and gazed out toward the game room's sliding doors. Everything was dark now. Henry must have turned out the outside lights in preparation for the night. She wondered again if she, Camille, and Thornton would be the only ones occupying this house, since apparently Eloise and Henry lived in one of the cottages. And where did Hilda, the cook, fit into the picture?

"Mr. . . ," she began, after swallowing a sip of tea. His first name still wouldn't come. She began again. "Mr. Winter, your home is beautiful. And the design is perfect for the ocean setting."

"Yes?" He looked up from buttering a biscuit, obviously intent on hearing what she had to say.

She felt a little flustered. She was no expert, but she did know what she liked. "When I caught my first glimpse of this place, I thought it looked like a huge seagull, with its wings spread, ready to fly out over the sea."

He squinted in approval. "That's exactly what I had in mind when I began the design. I wanted to blend the structure with its surroundings, to capture the light, airy essence of sea and sky, and offer a sense of power, yet freedom. Not everyone sees that without the explanation first."

At his look of admiration, Norah cautioned herself about putting too much stock in this rare moment of camaraderie. It wouldn't last!

"But frankly," he went on, "I'm surprised that you would allow me to think you're pleased with anything I've done."

"I recognize superior talent when I see it," she said with a lift of her chin. "That has nothing at all to do with our present. . .uh. . .dilemma." She thought for a moment, struggling to find a way to learn more about him without prying. "I love everything about this house. But it is quite different from what I would have expected."

"And what might that have been?"

She chose her words carefully, not wishing to insult him on the brink of their first decent conversation. "I guess I expected something. . .more traditional."

Norah didn't understand the slight furrow that appeared between his brows. She watched him swallow a bite of food, then wipe his lips on the cloth napkin, his intense eyes scrutinizing her. "This is not my permanent residence, Norah," he confessed. "It's only the beach house."

Norah's eyes widened, and he continued. "The reason I didn't take you and Camille to my home is because this is the season when visitors tour the historic homes in the area. Mine is on the list. Since there are only two weeks left, I didn't think I should cancel."

"I understand," Norah assured him quickly, for he seemed so ill at ease. "Frankly, a beach setting is more appealing to me anyway."

He moaned, looking slightly amused. "Don't say that too loudly in these parts, Norah. People literally come from around the world to see these historic old homes you have so casually dismissed. Do you have any inkling of all the time, effort, and expense that goes into restoration?"

"So you renovate old homes?"

He grimaced again. "You make it sound so ordinary, but. . .yes."

It figured, Norah thought to herself. He was exactly like one of those old houses—stuffy, rigid, unyielding, standing staunchly through the years, oblivious to the changes taking place around it. "I suppose I don't really know how to appreciate history," she confessed.

"You're young enough to learn," he said matter-of-factly. "Charleston is one of our nation's oldest and most majestic cities. And—"

His lecture was interrupted by the ringing of the telephone at the end of the bar. As he walked over to answer it, Norah wondered if he planned to take on her education as well as Camille's. The audacity of the man!

Still fuming, she nibbled at her food while Thornton talked to the caller, his end of the conversation sounding fragmented and disjointed. "No, you stay with Aunt Tess. . . . Madelyn? Yes, I can pick her up. What time does her flight get in?" He paused to listen. Then, "No, I won't be home tonight. Tell Aunt Tess I'll see you both in the morning. Take care, Chris."

He hung up, then rejoined her at the table. "I don't suppose you know about Chris either?"

She shook her head.

"You and Lantz didn't talk much, did you?"

Norah choked on her tea, and her cheeks flushed scarlet.

Thornton stifled a smile of amusement and began to explain. "My younger brother is about your age—nineteen, almost twenty."

"I'm twenty-three," Norah informed him emphatically. Her announcement resulted only in the lift of a sable brow. The gesture spoke volumes.

Apparently, she was still little more than a child to him.

Refolding his napkin, he rose. "I have to leave and won't be back tonight. I'll ask Henry and Eloise to stay here, in the bedroom next to yours. You and Camille will be quite safe."

She wasn't ready to say good night, not just yet. "Thornton. . ." There, she had said it! "You've told me about everyone except Madelyn. Who is she?"

Leaning on the back of his chair, he said wearily, "Madelyn is a long-time friend of the family. She's flying in from Paris for the memorial service tomorrow." There was an imperceptible pause. "Have you decided whether you'll be attending?"

"I won't be going," she said in a small voice, expecting his disapproval. She rose and walked over to the sliding glass doors and looked out into the dark night.

He came to stand beside her. "That's probably a wise decision," he said, to her surprise. "The family doesn't know about Camille, and I need to find the right time to tell them. So, you just take tomorrow to relax. The family will come here for Sunday dinner. In the meantime, Eloise will be here with you and anything you need is as near as the telephone."

Norah studied their reflection in the glass pane of the window—the shabby girl in jeans and the distinguished-looking, mature man. A strange feeling crept over her. He'd given her a tour of the house as if she were a guest. He'd fed her at his table as if she were a friend. But in reality she wasn't even a poor relation; she was a prisoner here.

"Suppose I want to go into Charleston? Will a car be available to me as you promised in Florida?" she tested him.

She felt the tension, even before he spoke. "You're welcome to come and go as you please. There's a dune buggy in the carport and cars at the dock. Henry could bring one in for you. However. . ." Norah held her breath, feeling the blood drain from her face. She knew what he was going to say before the words were out of his mouth. "However," he repeated firmly, "Camille should stay right here."

"And suppose I tried to take her with me?" she asked, her gaze rising to meet his.

His reply was uttered slowly and distinctly so there could be no mistaking his meaning. "Don't even try. You wouldn't get very far."

"I see!" Norah snapped. "My presence here is tolerated, but not accepted. You want Camille here, but not me. You would prefer that I leave, wouldn't you, Mr. Winter?"

Thornton didn't deign to answer her question but stepped so close that he could feel the hot anger emanating from her body. He tilted her chin with one finger, forcing her eyes to meet his. "The family will be coming for Sunday dinner," he said, "and I hope by that time you will have your hair out of that ridiculous braid."

She glared at him, speechless.

Suddenly his countenance darkened, and he dropped his finger and stepped back, digging both hands into his pants pockets. "About your leaving, Norah," he began grimly, and she could hear the weariness in his voice, "please don't. Not tonight anyway. How on earth would I deal with that tiny baby in there?" He gestured toward the bedroom. "Especially now that Madelyn is coming."

Norah couldn't resist his unaccustomed tone of entreaty. She had not the faintest idea why Madelyn was so important to him, but she could understand the terrible strain he was under. And since she had no intention of abandoning her sister's child, she said firmly, "Camille and I will expect you on Sunday."

He appeared satisfied with her reply. "I'd like to say good night to Camille before I go. Do you suppose we could call a truce long enough to do that?"

Norah opened her mouth to protest, but he turned and strode toward the bedroom door without waiting for her reply. She followed him.

Eloise had emptied most of the boxes and stored the contents in drawers. As Thornton entered, she looked up from the open suitcase on the bed. "The baby is ready for her bottle now. I'll go and get it," she said and left the room.

Norah walked over to the crib, picked Camille up, and cuddled the baby in her arms.

Thornton put out his finger to the child, and she grasped it firmly, her eyes intent on his face. Norah watched as the big man took in Camille's baby antics, his expression mellowing. Could he possibly feel as Norah herself did? Sometimes, caught up in the miracle of this new little life, she could temporarily forget all about her troubles, the problems facing her.

"Do you know," he asked, incredulous, "I may need this little girl as much as she needs me." Norah could only stare into his eyes, so close to her own, as a puzzled expression settled on his face. "Now how do I get my finger back?"

"Oh!" Norah exclaimed, startled out of her reverie, and managed to help him unwind the tiny fist from his finger, whereupon Camille expressed her outrage.

Thornton stepped back, casting a skeptical glance at the baby. "Has a temper like her mother," he observed. He glanced at Norah. "I'll find Eloise and the bottle," he promised.

Why am I smiling? Norah asked herself, staring at the doorway through which Thornton Winter had disappeared. What she had felt for him in those few tender moments was far from hostility. But somehow this glimpse of his softer side was far more frightening than the overbearing tyrant. That Thornton Winter she could fight. But what defense did one have against a vulnerable man who admitted his need of a little child in his life?

Chapter 5

Sitting in the shade of several scraggly palms, Norah gazed beyond the warm sand to the white-tipped waves disappearing into the blue horizon. She had sat in this same spot yesterday, breathing in the moisture-filled air and shivering from the cool mist on her body. She had needed that time alone to collect her thoughts and begin to recover from her recent ordeal.

Yesterday, after Henry and Eloise had returned from Lantz's memorial service, Norah had raced down to the sandy beach and plunged into the icy water, allowing herself the luxury of pouring out her grief, mingling her tears with the vast ocean. The deaths of Lantz and Hillary had brought vivid reminders of her grandparents and had revived old feelings for Roman, who had met his untimely end less than a year ago.

Later, exhausted, she had lifted her face toward the overcast sky, uttering a prayerful tribute to the memory of Lantz and Hillary and renewing her own vow concerning Camille's welfare.

The clouds had disappeared overnight and now the southern sun warmed the gentle spring breezes and dried the sand. Norah's eyes fell upon her lengthening shadow. It must be four or five o'clock, just enough time to dress for dinner. With a sigh, she left the secluded stretch of beach that had become her sanctuary, her shield against the world, a world that must now be faced.

Approaching the beach house, Norah concentrated on the palms, the blooming azaleas, and other flowering shrubs coming into view. A smile touched her lips as she recalled how, in the early morning, moisture-like beads of dew, like diamonds, had glittered on fragile blossoms and outlined the spiny leaves.

Seeing a white Mercedes and a light blue Jaguar parked in front of the house, she stopped abruptly. They were early, and she couldn't afford to be seen like this! She grimaced, looking down at her swimsuit-clad body. She could scarcely cover herself with the single small towel she had carried with her to the beach. "What on earth can I do?" she said aloud.

Deciding to try to make it into the house undetected, Norah went through the carport. After sneaking to the corner, she peeked around. One quick glance revealed several figures gathered on the deck. Before she could duck out of sight, Thornton's hawk-like eyes had found her. "Norah!" he called.

Norah could only squint against the unexpected assault of late-afternoon sun. She guessed she had no choice but to walk forward and face them.

Stopping several feet away, she held the gritty towel in front of her. "I'm sorry," she murmured. With her right hand, she pushed back the stiff strands of hair that had come loose from her "ridiculous" braid. "I thought you would not be coming until later."

Thornton strode toward her. The silver streaking the jet black hair at his temples enhanced his charcoal gray suit and darker patterned tie against a stark white shirt. His scar had deepened in color, a sure sign that he was disturbed.

"Please forgive us," he said with a trace of sarcasm. "I phoned that we were on our way, but you weren't available to receive that call. I trust we haven't come at an inopportune time."

Norah felt herself flush scarlet under his penetrating gaze, painfully conscious of her scanty attire, but feeling even more emotionally exposed. A helplessness stole over her as the irony of his words brought home the fact that this was his house, and he and his family could appear at any time they pleased.

"Oh, Thornton," a well-modulated voice scolded, "do stop jesting with that lovely girl and tell us who she is."

Norah, grateful for the intrusion, saw a tall, silvery-haired woman stroll over to stand beside Thornton. She looked lovely in an elegant gray suit, a pink-patterned blouse reflecting her rosy complexion.

"This is Norah, Aunt Tess. Latessia Spearman, my father's sister," he said affectionately.

The woman smiled warmly. "Oh, don't mind him, Norah. Everyone calls me Aunt Tess."

"And this is my brother Chris," Thornton said, when a lanky young man stepped from the shade of the cedar overhead.

Taking Norah's hand, he exclaimed, "Well, if you aren't the prettiest thing to come out of that ocean in a long time!" Chris's eyes danced merrily, reminding her of Lantz.

"Thanks, Chris." She leaned toward him, confiding in a whisper, "I needed that."

Thornton urged her forward, toward a woman sitting well back in the shadows. "Madelyn McCalla, Norah Browne."

Norah held out her hand and Madelyn took it halfheartedly. Her chilling gaze traveled through Norah and beyond. "How do you do," she said in a stilted voice; then she looked down at her delicately tapered fingers, nails buffed to a high gloss.

Norah found Madelyn's appearance startling. A classically beautiful face was framed by platinum blond hair, falling softly along one side of her face and turning under below her delicately curved jawline. The other side was brushed back, exposing a diamond earring.

Madelyn's black silk dress plunged daringly low. At one side of the neckline was pinned an enormous diamond brooch. Her feet were elegantly encased in black pumps banded in gold.

Meeting people and making friends had always come easy for Norah, but Madelyn was another matter. Without another word, she retreated into some shadowy place within herself.

Thornton took Norah's arm and steered her past the glass doors and into the game room, out of sight of the others.

"Have they seen Camille?" Norah asked.

"No," he replied curtly. "The next move is yours."

"What do you mean?"

"I told them that Lantz's child is here. Anything else is up to you."

Norah felt a wash of disappointment. Was Thornton so fearful of his family's reproach that he couldn't bring himself to tell them that Lantz had not married the mother of his child? Would the acceptance that Aunt Tess and Chris had offered her initially turn to the kind of coolness Madelyn had exhibited?

"Don't look so devastated, Norah," Thornton said. "Nobody's going to hurt you. We've had our share of skeletons in the family, and they haven't always stayed in the closet. The reason I said nothing is because I felt you would resent me even more if I mentioned you in some unfavorable way. Now," he went on with an impatient frown, "would you please allow my family to see their niece? The memorial service at church this afternoon was especially trying."

Norah's eyes dropped to the gritty sand between her toes, and she breathed deeply. Lest he see the moisture in her eyes, she turned her back on him.

He grasped her bare upper arms, and Norah stiffened. Rather than some reprimand, however, his words had the ring of an apology. "I thought you didn't want to go to the service, Norah. You also told me your reasons for avoiding your sister's funeral."

"It's all right," she said, suddenly aware of his fingers, now gently stroking away particles of sand from her arm. Something about that gentle action provoked a longing to be held in strong arms, like Camille, a helpless infant who needed acceptance and security.

But she was not a baby. Soon she would either have to lie to Eloise, Aunt Tess, and Chris. . .or tell the truth and chance Thornton Winter's rejection.

Suddenly, she remembered Madelyn. Why had she excluded her from that line-up of accepting people? What was she to Thornton Winter anyway?

"I'd better dress for dinner," she murmured, moving out of his reach and heading for the bedroom.

Thornton rubbed his thumb across the tips of his fingers, feeling the sand from Norah's arm. His touch had been an involuntary effort to reach out to her. But he had not succeeded.

Strange that she seemed to have so little difficulty in relating to others. She had shown none of that belligerence with Aunt Tess and Chris, for example. She'd appeared to be a sensitive young woman, responding warmly to their overtures of friendship. Aunt Tess had obviously liked her on sight, and his aunt was a very discriminating woman.

He'd carefully watched Chris's reaction too. His brother had been sincere in his compliments, which Norah had graciously accepted.

But Thornton? In spite of the fact that she needed his help, she seemed to fear him. She was undoubtedly the most stubborn, ill-tempered girl he'd ever known. Yet she was no girl! She was a woman who had attracted the attention of a mature man, a famous film star accustomed to being idolized by beautiful women. She'd captured Lantz's heart, at least long enough to conceive a child by him.

If she could so enthrall a man like Lantz Winter, how would a boy like Chris stand a chance? Thornton flexed his jaw, determined to put a stop to it before it started.

~

For her introduction to the family, Eloise had dressed Camille in one of her prettiest blue dresses with frills at the shoulders. Ruffled panties covered her diaper. Norah's heart swelled with love as she looked at her beautiful niece, who could beguile the strongest man and hold his heart in the palm of one tiny hand.

"I hope you don't mind," Eloise apologized when Norah sailed through the door.

"Oh, you're a lifesaver, Eloise," Norah breathed gratefully. "I had no idea they would come this early."

"They usually call from the dock," Eloise explained, "but I didn't know where you were on the beach, and you couldn't have gotten here before they arrived anyway."

"We'll just have to make the best of it." Norah sighed helplessly. "Just let me wash this sand off my arms."

She returned from the bathroom, found a shirt, and slipped it on over her swimsuit, then held out her arms for Camille. "Where did you get that?" Norah asked, seeing the little blue bow tied around one of the golden-red curls.

"From a pair of her panties," Eloise confessed.

Norah laughed. "I won't tell." She buried her face in the baby's dimpled neck, inhaling the clean, sweet smell. "I love you, my sweet." And cuddling her close as she walked back into the game room, Norah renewed her promise, "You're my baby, and I'll do everything in my power to keep you with me."

Thornton stood at the glass doors. He slid the door open for Norah, his eyes dancing with tenderness as he gazed at the beautiful baby. "May I?" he asked, and she laid Camille in the crook of his arm.

Beaming like a proud father, Thornton walked over to Chris, standing against one of the cedar posts. At his brother's approach, Chris turned. A surprised gleam leapt into his eyes. Reaching out, he touched the baby's soft pink arm, and she gurgled in response.

"Hey, we communicate on the same level," he said, elated. "Welcome to the family, little one."

His glance at Norah held a barrage of questions that went unasked. She sensed his discomfort and understood it instinctively. She had witnessed it many times while working at the clinic—the age-old question of why death strikes prematurely, robbing us of loved ones. She could see that Chris was trying to deal with his loss like a man. She longed to help him.

Norah followed Thornton as he carried the child over to Aunt Tess. "Lantz's baby," she breathed, her eyes misting. "Oh, look at those big blue eyes. And that gorgeous red hair. Oh, Norah dear, she is beautiful. You must be so proud."

An uneasy silence settled over the group. Thornton was right. This family wouldn't ask embarrassing questions, but she had to tell them something. For support, Norah grasped the back of the wooden chair in front of her. She knew she couldn't accept their friendship—Aunt Tess's and Chris's—with this barrier between them, this pretense that she was Camille's mother. Strangely, she also found herself wanting Thornton to know the truth, whatever its consequences. It would have to come out soon. Best they hear it from her.

"Norah, are you all right?" Aunt Tess asked with concern in her voice.

Norah nodded and cleared her throat. "I want you all to know," she began, glancing in Chris's direction, then scanning the faces of the others. Her lips felt dry, and she licked them. "I want you to know that Hillary Caine was really Hillary Browne. She is. . .was. . .my sister."

"Oh, my dear, I'm so sorry," Aunt Tess sympathized.

Chris pulled a chair out from the table, and Norah lowered herself into it. Then he sat down nearby. Aunt Tess extended her hand and Norah placed her own in it, finding strength in the comforting warmth.

Her courage left her, however, when Thornton walked around and stood behind Aunt Tess. Madelyn sat like a still-life painting in the background, with Eloise hovering near, ready to take the baby back into the house.

Norah darted a glance at Thornton, but his steady gaze was threatening rather than reassuring. *You have the right to remain silent,* his stiff stance seemed to be conveying. *Anything you say will be held against you.*

She swallowed hard, still staring into his face. "I am not Camille's mother," she began with trepidation and watched him flinch as if he'd been struck. Why did she feel like a murderer who had just confessed? She was guilty of nothing except love for an orphaned child. "But in my heart I am her mother," she insisted with conviction.

Thornton's expression didn't alter a whit. He simply looked down at Camille, who was fussing a little, and pursed his lips to make a soft clucking sound that quieted her.

"Camille belonged to Lantz and Hillary," Norah continued, looking to Aunt Tess for the courage to go on. "They were not married, but they loved each other very much." She glanced at Chris. Neither he nor Aunt Tess appeared shocked, only interested and sympathetic.

"I've been taking care of Camille since she was born, and I couldn't love her more if she were my own. I'm sure that. . ."

Aunt Tess interrupted with gentle praise. "You are very brave to take on such a heavy responsibility, Norah. It makes all the difference in the world, having that child here. Thank you," she choked, "for sharing her with us."

Share? How ironic, Norah thought. She had had no choice. Thornton Winter had forced her here against her will. And now she had no idea what he might do. She feared his power to take legal action. Even if his family sided with her, he had made it quite clear that this was his home and he would make the final decisions.

Without a glance in her direction, he moved toward Madelyn, carrying the baby in his arms.

"Oh, Thorn! Thorn!" Madelyn wailed and wrenched aside the glass door to run into the house.

Norah was instantly at Thornton's side and took the baby from him as he ran to catch up with Madelyn. His arms enfolded her, and she cried against his chest, then lifted a beautifully chiseled profile toward him, her ice-blue eyes brimming with tears.

At that moment, he turned his head and caught Norah's eye. He shrugged his shoulders eloquently, asking for patience in a glance. Then he led Madelyn, still clinging, down the hallway toward the front of the house.

"Could I hold the baby?" Aunt Tess asked gently, coming up behind Norah, as if the disturbing scene had not taken place.

"This is her wakeful time," Norah explained, "when she's most likely to be fussy."

388

"If you'll trust us, maybe Chris and I can handle her. And Eloise is a grandmother many times over, of course. You go right ahead and get dressed if you like."

With a smile of gratitude, Norah relinquished the baby to Aunt Tess and went quickly into the house. When she reached her bedroom door, the sound of soft sobbing and a deep masculine voice attempting to console reached her ears. Apparently Madelyn and Thornton were in the living room. She shook off the multitude of questions crowding her mind and went inside, closing her door behind her.

~

Thornton was thoroughly confused. Even with Madelyn weeping pitifully in his arms, he could not forget the shocking scene he had just witnessed. What kind of mother would deny her own child? And if Norah were really Camille's aunt, she had lied to him! Who, and what, was the real Norah Browne? And how could Lantz have thought they had anything in common? But there was a more immediate problem confronting him.

"Oh, Thorn, how am I ever going to get through this?" Madelyn sobbed.

He continued to hold her close, patting her shoulder. "Time heals all wounds," he said rather distantly, grasping for anything that might sound comforting in this confusing time.

She lifted her lovely face. "All?" she whispered, seeing his scar, and a fresh torrent of tears erupted.

That wound was healing well. Another operation—some cosmetic surgery around his eye—and he might not appear so grotesque. But that was not the wound he felt so sharply. It was the inner hurts that still had not completely healed.

His arms tightened around Madelyn, but he glanced in the direction of Norah's bedroom. A lot in common, indeed!

~

Over an hour later, Norah sincerely hoped she was ready to present herself properly. After washing, drying, and brushing her coppery hair until it shone with sun-kissed highlights, she slipped into a dress she had always admired on Hillary and eyed herself critically.

Having applied makeup expertly in a manner she had learned from her mother, she knew she had maximized her best features. Her skin had deepened to a bronzed glow during the afternoon on the beach. It had been so long since she had taken time with her appearance that she had forgotten just how much she resembled her sister. At one time, Hillary had even suggested that Norah become her understudy, but Norah had refused. She had never felt comfortable on stage.

Looking at herself now, she knew Hillary would be pleased with the effect. The gold lamé tank dress came to just above her shapely knees. A crushed leather and metallic cumberbund grazed her hips, riding below her waistline and producing an easy flowing motion as she walked.

Finalizing the recreation of Hillary, she stepped into metallic high heels, slipped a brassy gold bracelet on her left arm, and completed the effect with drop earrings. Deciding against the matching jacket, she brushed her waist-length hair around her shoulders and applied a bronzed gloss to her lips. Avoiding looking into her huge green eyes that belied this attempt at confidence, she sprayed perfume on her pulses, already beating erratically.

Taking a deep steadying breath, she told herself that Hillary wouldn't have been nervous. She would have swung out onto the deck and instantly become the center of attention, causing fragile beauties like Madelyn to fade into the woodwork.

But she was not Hillary. She was Norah, and Norah had a terrible attack of stage fright. She must face Thornton Winter as Camille's aunt. Suppose he said, "We can handle things from now on, Miss Browne. You should go on about your life, without the encumbrance of a baby."

Norah closed the bedroom door behind her and stood for a moment, leaning back against it, her eyes closed.

"Just when I decided your hair was permanently knotted on your head, you prove me wrong," said an all-too-familiar voice.

Norah's eyes flew open. Thornton rose from a chair in the game room. He'd been waiting for her! The inevitable confrontation would be now. His advance reminded her of a giant wave beginning far out in the ocean, coming closer, gaining height and strength. The sand was being pulled out from under her feet, and the undertow was threatening to drag her out into deep water.

She tried to back up, but there was no place to go. She did not want to fight him. "Please," she said, desperately wishing she could make her escape. "I need to see about Camille."

"The baby is perfectly content," he assured her, blocking her way.

Norah tried to step around him, but he reached out with one big hand and encircled her arm, hauling her back. "I find you confusing, Norah Browne," he admitted. "In Florida, you were a high-spirited, indignant mother. Then, to impress my aunt and brother, you become a devoted, self-sacrificing young woman who is willing to give up her own freedom to care for her sister's child. Now, I find a glamorous Hollywood type trying to impress. . .whom, Miss Browne? Who are you, really? And what are you after?"

So he hadn't believed her when she told him she was Camille's aunt! She needn't have worried about his reaction to a lie. He didn't know the truth when he heard it. "What could I possibly be after?"

He shrugged. "Maybe the Lantz Winter estate," he said, and added mockingly, "a fortune for little Camille, of course."

Norah jerked her arm away, feeling the bedroom door against her back. "I'm not even aware there is a Winter fortune," she retorted.

"No?" he questioned. "I'd think Lantz would have told you."

"I don't know what Lantz might have told Hillary," she returned. "But he and I did not discuss such personal matters."

For a moment he almost believed her. Hillary would have been more Lantz's type—a public figure rather than a stay-at-home mother. "If you are really 'Aunt Norah,' you're every bit as convincing an actress as your sister. That mother-love act had me fooled." The smile on his lips was not pleasant.

"No, Mr. Winter," Norah contradicted. "It is you who have jumped to conclusions. You made the accusation. I simply didn't refute it."

A deadly quiet invaded the hallway. "All right," he conceded finally. "Just between you and me, who are you? Camille's aunt? Her mom?"

Norah lifted her chin. "Whomever she needs me to be," she said, her green eyes flashing.

"I'll tell you one thing," he said bluntly, "you may be a psychologist, but you need one."

"I am not yet a psychologist," she stated. "But I have been and will continue to be a mother to Camille. And I might add," she continued adamantly, "a father. I've been the only parent she's had for most of her young life."

That remark touched a sensitive chord, painfully reminding Thornton of his brother's lack of responsibility. "Just produce the birth certificate," he said wearily. "Perhaps there I will find the truth."

"No," Norah countered, "if there is any proof to be provided, Mr. Winter, it will be you who supplies it. Prove that Lantz is Camille's father."

"Everything points to that fact." He quickly named the evidence. "The house in Florida. The photos of you, your sister, Lantz, and Camille. The pictures in his wallet. The confessions of a dying man. Proof enough," he affirmed. "You and I both know it."

"Exactly," she replied. She would not go so far as to deny Lantz's paternity. "But you can't prove it."

"Blood tests," he offered.

She shook her head. "Inconclusive. That would only prove that Lantz could be the father." A great surge of confidence bolstered Norah's claim, and her green eyes narrowed with challenge. "So you see, Mr. Winter, I don't have to prove I'm Camille's mother or her aunt. It is you who must prove that you are her uncle."

"If it comes to that, I believe I could scrape up enough evidence," he assured her.

"You make one wrong move, Mr. Winter," she threatened, "and this story will make the headlines of every newspaper across the country. Is that what you want for your niece?"

"Ah-ha!" he said. "You wouldn't do very well in a court of law. You just admitted that Camille is my niece." His eyes held a triumphant expression. Then he added in a disarmingly gentle tone, "Maybe I could appreciate a devoted aunt, concerned about the welfare of her niece."

Was that possible? she wondered. Something warned her not to let down her guard. "Well, Mr. Winter, I can wonder if you are really a doting uncle or if you just prefer to keep a bevy of females around to persecute."

At that, Thornton threw back his head and laughed, then leaned forward to capture a tendril of hair between his thumb and forefinger. "With all this skepticism, Norah, I'd say you and I are on pretty equal footing, wouldn't you agree?"

She recognized the hint of amusement in his voice and saw a strange glimmer in his eyes. "No, Mr. Winter, I wouldn't say we're equal. Not financially anyway. But Camille is not into bank accounts. Nor are we equal when it comes to changing diapers, late-night feedings, or any other phase of child care."

Norah resented the condescending look on his face, as if her words were inconsequential. Perhaps they were. He could hire Eloise or others like her to do those things. She dropped her eyes to his suit coat, then lifted her face to his. "And who would play the mother role when you must leave the baby to meet. . . Madelyn. . .at the airport? Incidentally, you have a blond hair on your coat."

He looked down, picked it off, and let it float to the floor. "Be careful of that temper, Norah." He drew in a breath, looked around, then turned back and leaned closer as if sharing a secret. "You'd better be warned. Madelyn is not always as docile as she might appear."

"Really!" Norah declared in exasperation. "Are you trying to frighten me? You are very quick to make accusations about people. That is not a commendable characteristic."

His penetrating gaze left doubt as to whether he were serious. She suspected that he often deliberately provoked her. Then her eyes found the reddened scar, and she made a wild, impetuous guess. "Did. . .did she do that?"

He nodded, then his dark lashes veiled his eyes and she couldn't begin to read his expression.

"What. . .what did you do to her to cause it?" He gave a short laugh, and Norah explained, "I don't know when you're telling me the truth."

"Touché. We're equal on that score, Norah Browne, because there's a great deal I don't know about you." His eyes narrowed. "But I intend to find out."

"Is that some kind of warning?" she asked, bristling.

The wry smile left his lips and his dark eyes scanned her face. "Let's just say it's more of a promise."

His arm came up and his fingers lifted her chin. With torturous deliberation, he lowered his head and his sensitive mouth came closer. At his temples, the silver glints in his dark hair matched the glimmer in his mesmerizing eyes. For something to hold onto, Norah grasped the doorknob, aware of its coolness in her warm palm.

He galloped closer on the powerful, black stallion, his cape flying out behind him. She felt the vibration of thundering hoofbeats, heard the pounding in her ears. With a rush of force, he swept her up in his arms and bore her away. But he lost that fierceness as he gazed tenderly into her eyes, his lips so close she could feel his breath on her cheek. . . .

"Norah," he said huskily, "I want that birth certificate, and I want it now."

"You want. . .what?" she asked weakly.

"Camille's birth certificate," he replied, and with a whimper of outrage at her own foolish fantasies, she wrenched the doorknob and stumbled backwards into the room.

Thornton broke his own fall by catching hold of the doorfacing. Gaining his feet again, he waited while Norah went to one of the boxes that was yet unpacked, rummaged through a sheaf of papers, then held out an official-looking document.

He took it from her, wondering what he would find. If she were Camille's mother and was as adamantly opposed to being in his home as she pretended, then she had some scheme in mind, such as threatening a scandal. If that turned out to be the case, he'd pay her off to leave the baby and the scandal behind her.

Looking down, he scanned the facts until he found what he was looking for. Mother: Hillary Browne. Father: Unnamed.

He straightened slowly. Norah was standing in the doorway, her back to him, her long flame-colored hair spread around her shoulders like a fire.

If circumstances were different, and if he were young like Chris or charming like Lantz, he might act upon the impulse he'd felt stir in him more than once. But he wasn't. She'd correctly diagnosed him when she assessed him as history, instead of a bird in flight, soaring freely over life's choppy waves.

He came up behind her. "Shall we join the others?" His words propelled her forward, toward the game room. She walked ahead, not looking back until he spoke again. "You and I, 'Aunt Norah,' must soon come to some kind of understanding."

With a toss of her head, she retorted, "I should think that by now you would understand."

Thornton understood more than she knew. He knew how frightened Norah Browne was of losing control of that baby. She had every right to be frightened. Everything considered, the possibility was strong that he would have to ask her to leave his home—without Camille.

Chapter 6

Norah walked out onto the deck. An empty bottle sat on a table, while the contented baby sleepily surveyed her surroundings, her gaze coming to rest on Chris Winter's face as he looked down at her, making soft clicking sounds with his tongue. He had removed his suit coat, and the towel slung across his shoulder was a clue that Eloise had instructed him in the art of burping babies. At Aunt Tess's tender expression, Norah realized anew the therapeutic value of Camille's presence in this family.

Chris looked up and gave a low whistle as Norah approached.

"Time for this little girl to be in bed," she said with a smile of acknowledgment.

He rose, still cradling the child awkwardly, and walked with Norah toward the house. Glancing back and seeing Thornton's somber expression, the smile left her face. With a swift movement, her long hair swung around her shoulders and she hurried inside.

Thornton was staring at the empty doorway when he heard Aunt Tess's voice. "It's so good to have young people in the house again, isn't it, Dear?"

He turned toward her and spoke thoughtfully. "She didn't want to come, Aunt Tess."

"Oh, Thornton," Aunt Tess said, rising from her chair and joining him. "You don't think she'll leave and take that baby, do you?"

He drew her close and enfolded her in a desperate hug. "No, Aunt Tess," he said, speaking over her head. "You know how I feel about family. Camille is my brother's child. The baby stays with us."

Aunt Tess stepped back and looked up into his face. "Then Norah has decided to stay?" she asked expectantly.

"That remains to be seen," he said distantly. Aunt Tess decided not to probe and patted his arm. "Eloise said supper is ready when we are. Perhaps we shouldn't keep her waiting, Dear."

Thornton smiled down at her. With his arm around her shoulders, they headed for the house. On the way, he took time to be grateful for his aunt. She had always had a calming effect on him.

He could use some of that right about now, he decided. He was still puzzled about Norah's attitude toward him. How easily she and Chris had communicated, from the very first words exchanged. Chris had a way about him that reminded Thornton of Lantz. He tried not to be too envious as he stepped into the game room and heard the ripple of good-natured laughter from the young couple.

~

Madelyn, at Thornton's right, was the last to join them at the dinner table. Norah, seated across from her, was not surprised when Thornton said, "Let us pray." After all, this was the Bible Belt she'd heard so much about, and the proper Thornton Winter would certainly adhere to tradition.

Norah closed her eyes and listened carefully. His prayer was brief. He invoked God's blessing on the food, asked for strength in these difficult days, and expressed gratitude for the blessings recently brought into their lives.

At the close, Chris's and Aunt Tess's soft "amens" could be heard before the older woman spoke up. "That child is such a wonderful blessing, Norah."

Norah could honestly reply, "Yes, I've thanked God for her every day of her life, even prayed for her before she was born." She darted a meaningful glance at Thornton as if to let him know she had made a head start on prayer in Camille's behalf. His eyes met hers in a contemplative stare before turning his attention to his iced tea, squeezing some lemon into the glass and stirring. *As if he needed that!* she thought.

Aunt Tess patted her arm and smiled. While she and Chris unfolded their napkins, Madelyn sat motionless, gazing down into her plate. Responding woodenly to Thornton's whispered suggestion, she picked up her napkin and laid it in her lap.

Madelyn's bizarre behavior disturbed Norah. But more disturbing was Thornton Winter's earlier statement, "We must come to an understanding, Norah." The implied threat rolled around in her mind, taunting her.

Her troubled thoughts were interrupted by Eloise's appearance in the dining room, bearing a tray containing bowls of creamy broccoli soup, which she set before them.

"Delicious," Norah said after the first taste.

Aunt Tess waited until Eloise left the room before saying under her breath, "You haven't met Hilda yet."

"I've heard about her," Norah acknowledged. "But if the food gets any better, I'll end up looking like a pumpkin."

There was a spattering of light laughter. Everyone joined in except Madelyn. Then Chris said, "Speaking of looks, Norah, I'm sure you've been told that you look enough like your sister to be her twin. I've seen all her films. Was she as nice as you?"

Norah shrugged off the compliment. "I know she loved your brother very much." Had Madelyn loved him too? Norah wondered, noticing that the young woman had not taken a bite of her soup. Thornton glanced at Madelyn, then at Norah, a definite frown on his face, as if trying to convey a message.

Norah took her cue from Thornton. "I'd love to discuss Hillary with you sometime, Chris. I brought pictures with me."

Soon, Eloise was back with the main course—veal cordon bleu with mashed potatoes and rich brown gravy, tiny peas with pearl onions, and tomato aspic.

"Are you an actress too, Norah?" Aunt Tess asked.

"My dad says it has to be in your blood," Norah replied, adding, "so I suppose I missed those genes. Growing up, I was active in children's theater. Later, my big role was a lady's maid in *Henry VIII*, which my father has played in numerous community theaters for as long as I can remember. Then, there were a few bit parts in movies. But acting was never an obsession with me like it was for Hillary and Lantz."

"That sounds fascinating, Norah," Aunt Tess said.

Chris added, "I think it was in Lantz's blood."

A low moan came from Madelyn, followed by a silence that made Norah question whether she should be speaking so freely about a man who had been buried only yesterday.

"I do want to hear more about your sister, Norah, later," Aunt Tess said, with a significant glance toward Madelyn. "Suppose you tell us something more about yourself, Dear."

A disturbing thought crossed Norah's mind. She was partaking of the Winter hospitality, as if this were a perfectly natural thing to do, when in fact Thornton Winter was close to being in control of not only Camille's fate, but her own. For an instant, she felt as empty as Madelyn appeared, and for the first time, Norah could empathize with her. Is that what happened to women who came under the Winter spell? But Aunt Tess was waiting, her silvery hair cocked to one side.

Remembering her plans and goals before encountering Thornton Winter, Norah launched into a recital of her studies in psychology, as she had to Thornton that night he had appeared out of the thunderstorm. "I plan someday to earn my master's degree in psychology. I'd like to work with toddlers and adolescents."

"Such a worthy goal, Norah," Aunt Tess commended her. "Was there a particular reason why you chose that field?"

"Several. But the main reason was that, while I reject a career in acting for myself, I believe the use of drama can provide a healthy release of frustrations for children. Role playing, under the supervision of a trained psychologist, can be therapeutic in treating children with emotional disorders."

"Then that principle might apply to adults too?" Thornton asked.

"So the studies indicate," she replied, noting his genuine interest. "It doesn't mean that all actors have psychological problems, of course, but studies have shown that such problems can sometimes be understood and treated through role playing."

"You may have hit upon something that helps me understand Lantz better. Maybe he needed that escape from some of life's hard realities," he observed, thinking of their parents' unexpected deaths.

Aunt Tess nodded. "Well, Norah, will you be going back to graduate school in the fall?"

Norah hesitated. From the corner of her eye, she could see Thornton's brooding dark eyes watching her over the rim of his glass. The best thing at the moment was to reply as if she still had control over her life. "If I stay in this area, I will need to find at least a part-time job and save some money before returning to school. There will be rent to pay, as well as other expenses, and I have to consider the amount of time I will need to spend with Camille."

Aunt Tess turned to regard her more closely. "I don't mean to pry, Norah, but," she glanced at Thornton, "what do you mean by 'rent to pay'?"

Thornton's curt rejoinder was immediately forthcoming. "Norah is being a bit dramatic, Aunt Tess. She and Camille are a part of the family now. Rent, of course, is out of the question." He gave Norah a scathing look.

Her red hair, gleaming in the light of the chandelier, swung about her shoulders as she quickly turned her face toward his. "As I've said before, Mr. Winter, you may contribute whatever you like toward Camille's support. I, however, intend to take care of myself and provide for the bulk of Camille's needs. I am not a babysitter, and until I can afford a place of our own, I expect to pay rent."

"Now, Thornton," Aunt Tess said uneasily, "if this is a problem, you know I have plenty of room in my house."

Thornton's scar turned a deep purple, and Norah knew she had managed to infuriate him once more. Hoping to change the subject, she turned to Chris, who was attempting to suppress the grin tugging at his lips. "How about you, Chris? Are you in school?"

The conversation shifted to Chris's studies. He had two more years at the Citadel, where he was majoring in civil engineering.

"All Winter men have been Citadel graduates since its inception," Aunt Tess told her, continuing with a brief overview of the family. Some had taken their places in civilian life, others in the military, but each was involved in some aspect of building and design, with the exception of Lantz.

Apparently, the Winter women and those who married Winter men had not been dominated by the males, as Norah would have assumed. Many were pioneers in their fields. Thornton's mother, for example, had played an active part in her husband's construction business, which included residences and deep-sea fishing vessels. And Aunt Tess, before her retirement last year, had taught English and literature at the College of Charleston.

At that moment, Eloise came in to remove their plates and serve dessert. The cherry cheese pie consisted of a melt-in-the-mouth, creamy filling sprinkled with pecans. Madelyn picked at hers, as she had throughout the entire meal.

"I would like to give Camille a homecoming present," Thornton announced over coffee. "What would you suggest, Norah?"

He would want it to be something meaningful, something practical. Lantz and Hillary had filled her closet with baby clothes before her birth and had bought her enough toys and stuffed animals to stock a toy store.

Norah knew the perfect gift. "Swimming lessons."

He seemed surprised. "Isn't she a bit young for that?"

"She's three months older than she ought to be. Immediately after birth is the best time to begin, Mr. Winter," Norah said. "Babies are accustomed to a watery existence before birth, so water is a natural element for them. Swimming lessons have saved the lives of many toddlers. And since you have a pool and live near the ocean, it's doubly important."

Aunt Tess nodded approvingly, and Norah turned to Thornton for his opinion. He appeared quite thoughtful. "It was something Lantz wanted for Camille," Norah insisted. "I know he and Hillary talked about it even before she was born."

"Then perhaps we should consider it." Thornton wiped his lips on his napkin, indicating that the subject was closed for now.

Madelyn was fidgeting in her seat. "Excuse me," she said suddenly, pushing back her chair and hurrying from the room.

"Aunt Tess," Thornton began, "would you see about Madelyn? I'd like to talk with Norah. . .alone."

Thornton led her through the sliding glass doors to a secluded area of the deck, where they sat down in the padded redwood chairs. Glancing toward the sky, Norah saw faint pink streaks now quickly fading to gray. Feeling a chill in the air, she shivered.

"Cold?" Thornton wanted to know.

"Just cool. But I love it. Everything about the ocean is so invigorating to me." She breathed deeply of the tangy air.

"It certainly seems to agree with you," he said, eyeing her appreciatively.

"You've improved considerably over that little girl in blue jeans with a braid on top of her head."

"Well, I'm a little more rested," she said, grateful for the cover of twilight. "I must admit I've enjoyed having a little time to myself for the first time since Camille was born."

"It's not so bad, is it?" he asked. "Being here?"

"As I told my parents when I called them Saturday," Norah returned, watching his lips form a taut line, "I'm grateful that Camille has this opportunity to visit her relatives."

"Visit?" The quirk of his eyebrow said it all.

Uncomfortable, she rose and walked over to the edge of the pool. Someone had turned on the underwater lights, and the surface shimmered in jeweled tones of blue and green.

Thornton joined her. "Camille's lessons should be given here if they start right away," he said. "If you want to take her to class, then it will be best to wait until after we move into town."

Norah chose not to take issue with that declaration but gazed up at the sky, where a slice of moon had made its appearance in the darkening sky. "I'm not sure of the wisdom of your trying to make us such an integral part of your family."

Determination sounded in his reply. "I intend to do as Lantz asked and assure that his child is properly cared for. Don't you understand, Norah? Camille is all I have left of—"

He averted his eyes, but not before she saw his pain. He walked past her to the end of the deck, where he stood in the shadows, his body and shoulders taut. It was the first indication she had witnessed of how deeply Thornton Winter was feeling the death of his brother. She sensed that he was not a man who expressed his emotions easily.

Momentarily ignoring their differences, she walked up to him and touched his sleeve. "Mr. Winter," she said softly.

"Mr. Winter," he mimicked to cover his raw grief. "Even Henry, a good thirty years older than I, is called by his first name. Is it because you respect me so much or. . .that you're more comfortable with the formality?"

"Yes, I. . .suppose that's it."

"And you're uncomfortable with me," he accused. "That's why you don't want to live here. That's why you're talking about renting a place, isn't it?"

"I only meant that I expect to be responsible for the two of us."

"I know what you said. But would you object if I offered you and Camille the beach house? For just the two of you?"

Norah did not glance away in time to hide the sudden elation that sparked her eyes.

"Or," he continued, "would you object if Aunt Tess asked you to live with her? Or even Chris? No," he answered for her, "it's me you object to."

Norah stared into the darkness. Thornton Winter was right. "Yes," she admitted. "It is you."

She turned her back on him and reached out to touch a leafy shrub.

He stepped up beside her. "What are you afraid of, Norah?"

"As you said earlier," she replied uneasily, "some things cannot be expressed simply."

"Try," he urged.

Norah drew in a breath of the cool night air. What was she afraid of? The reasons were fast becoming as numerous as the brilliant stars, shimmering in the deep blue sky. "I suppose I'm afraid of your controlling our lives. You're a very insistent man, Mr. Winter," she continued with a glance at him. "My wishes seem to make no difference to you."

"I realize I tend to be overbearing sometimes," he admitted. "But I doubt that you'd let me get away with that very often." Norah smiled faintly, responding to the surprising affability of this man who had before seemed so obstinate and unyielding. "Or is it more personal, Norah? I know you are wary of me. I. . .frighten you. Are you afraid I will frighten Camille as she grows older? Is it. . .my face?"

The breath caught in her throat, painfully choking off the air. She could not speak for a moment. Finally, she looked him directly in the eye. "Your looks," she said in a whisper, "mean nothing to a child. Or to me. Actually, it is your face that has kept me from being terribly frightened of you."

He turned the scarred side from her. "I'm not seeking sympathy or some false sense of acceptance from you, Norah," he said with difficulty.

"I know," she said. "And I'm so sorry if I've given the impression that it bothers me. I know I've stared. That's only natural. Curiosity is one of my weaknesses, perhaps. Look at me, please."

He turned reluctantly.

Her voice was very gentle. "It is your face that has made me aware that you are a vulnerable, suffering human being like the rest of us, and. . .capable of being hurt."

Thornton reached for her hand and held it between his palms. "I don't want you to be frightened of me, Norah. For any reason."

"I was never frightened for myself. . .Thornton." His name fell easily from her lips.

Soft moonlight danced in his eyes, subduing the harsh contours of his handsome face. His lips formed a wide smile and she felt a breathlessness that was almost dizzying.

"I want to do the right thing," Norah heard herself saying, and the sound of her own voice surprised her. Of course she wanted to do the right thing. But how had she come to the point of giving in to Thornton Winter's wishes? Startled by her own thoughts, she lifted her eyes to his and found them to be dark and foreboding again.

"That's not always easy to know," he said. A shudder ran through her. Thornton looked toward the house, at the bird-in-flight design. He hated what he had to do, what he had to say. "Norah, you are to be commended for what you've done in caring for Camille during the past three months. This terrible tragedy has brought out your remarkable characteristics. But, no one would blame you for just being an aunt, like Aunt Tess. She's an invaluable member of our family, you know."

Thornton saw fear and frustration replacing her beginning acceptance. But the only decent thing to do was to try and make her understand. "You're not obligated to take on this responsibility. You're young, beautiful, single, and you deserve the freedom that goes with it."

Of all the options that might be open, Norah was beginning to believe that the security offered by Thornton Winter was best for Camille. *But not without me!* her heart screamed. *Oh, please, not without me!*

He saw the brave lift of her determined chin. "No one would blame you," he said, and she felt the twist of a knife with each word. "Rearing a child takes personal sacrifice."

"I know all that," she said helplessly.

"No, you don't," he retorted. "You've had three months of caring for a beautiful, perfect baby. And when it changed suddenly, drastically, irreversibly, you made an admirable decision based on loyalty to your sister, love for your niece, and personal loss."

"And what about you?" she asked desperately.

"I've faced this situation before, remember? I know what I'm getting into. I became Chris's legal guardian when he was eleven and Lantz was sixteen. But you need to think seriously before the child becomes too attached to you. I don't want you deciding later on that your personal freedom has been hampered, or that you're really not up to this. Once you take on that responsibility, Norah, nothing is ever the same."

He knew no way to say these things tactfully. "I want you to think about the situation while I'm away for a few days. You can give me your answer when I return."

She'd almost believed that Thornton Winter was a Dracula, for this man's overwhelming power to shake her confidence was uncanny. But he was not the caped vampire. She knew now that she had no reason to fear him. But she would fight for Camille, if necessary.

She squared her shoulders. "How old are you, Mr. Winter?"

"Thirty-four."

"That's not exactly ancient," she observed. "You deserve a life of your own too." Her eyes blazed. "And one more thing—just what do you know about bringing up little girls?"

His dark eyes glittered and his tone was brittle. "I seem to be having more trouble with big girls than little ones."

Norah bristled. "Camille and I are a package deal. Do you really want two extra females under your roof for the next twenty years? It seems to be getting crowded around here."

That remark seemed to hit a sensitive spot, but before he could answer, dazzling light splashed onto the deck. His marred face took on a ghostly pallor as he faced the house. Inside, a figure in black paced restlessly.

"Is Madelyn really dangerous?" Norah asked, once more aware of the cooling breeze.

"Ah, Norah," he said, watching Madelyn, "isn't every attractive woman potentially dangerous?"

With this evasive maneuver, Norah's delight in finding an equal footing with Thornton Winter turned to doubt. What had happened to the warmth and tenderness she thought had passed between them? Had she imagined it? For now he seemed far removed, as if some shadow had settled upon him.

"Let's go inside," he said abruptly and, without waiting for a reply, preceded her to the house.

Norah remained in the shadows, her eyes following the retreating figure of the man who could dispatch compliments and criticism with equal fervor. She watched him slide the door open and move inside where the woman was waiting for him. He bent his tall frame toward Madelyn, and his arm encircled her shoulders. Her blond head tilted upward and her body melted into his with an unmistakable intimacy before they moved out of sight.

Norah hugged her arms to herself. She wanted desperately to trust Thornton Winter. And she had. For one brief moment. Long enough for him to expertly manipulate the situation. She had all but admitted her acceptance of him, had called him by his first name, had tacitly accepted his hospitality without charge. But at what cost to her pride and independence? And how quickly Winter charm could turn to Winter chill!

Chapter 7

Norah let out a gasp of fright when the bang of the sliding glass doors broke her concentration. The gasp subsided to a sigh of relief when Chris walked out onto the deck and looked around.

Spotting Norah, he called out to her. "Thornton said it was getting chilly out here and asked me to bring you a sweater. I had Eloise get this for you." Strolling over to join her, Chris shrugged it around her shoulders. "You are cold. Want to go inside?"

"I'd rather stay out here for awhile," she said with a sigh.

"Mind if I join you?"

"I'd like that, Chris," she replied, and they moved toward the house where they would be sheltered from the breeze.

"Be right back," he promised. "I'll get us something warm to drink."

Norah settled back against the cushions of the chair, forcing her thoughts to the days ahead, when she and Camille would be able to enjoy this lovely setting without the unsettling presence of Thornton Winter. Perhaps then she could rid herself of the foolish thoughts that had invaded her mind tonight— that Thornton was some devious monster about to steal Camille from her. And maybe she could even bring herself to believe that he was only trying to help Madelyn, a distraught woman whose emotions lay very near the surface. Though Norah could not be sure what Madelyn's relationship with Lantz had been, she could understand something of what she must be feeling. From Norah's experience with Roman, she knew that the loss of a friend could be as heartbreaking as the loss of a relative.

This is only a bad case of nerves, she told herself. *Perfectly understandable.* In a matter of mere days, she had lost her sister and a friend, had become a surrogate mother, had encountered the enigmatic Thornton Winter, and had exchanged her simple lifestyle for one utterly foreign to her.

My imagination is working overtime, she thought. *That's all it is.* And as if to prove it, a smiling Chris emerged from the house, bearing mugs of steaming hot chocolate topped with marshmallows.

"So tell me about Hillary," Chris said as they sipped the warm beverage. "What was she like in real life?"

While the question focused on her sister, Norah had the feeling he wanted

404

to talk about his brother. Her assumption was correct, for soon he was asking questions about Lantz and his relationship with Hillary. Norah answered as honestly as she knew how. "Would you like to see those pictures now?"

When they went inside, Aunt Tess and Thornton were talking in the game room, and Madelyn was nowhere in sight. Aunt Tess hugged her. "I want you to know, Norah, that I am quite impressed with you, taking care of Camille the way you have. That shows a great deal of strength and depth of character. Now, we're here to help, Dear, so feel free to call on me any time you need me."

"Thank you so much, Aunt Tess," Norah replied, feeling a warm rush of gratitude.

"Could I stay for awhile?" asked Chris, coming up beside her.

Thornton hesitated. "If it's all right with Norah, Chris."

"Of course."

"Just don't forget there's a baby in the house," Thornton said, looking stern, "and keep down the noise."

"Oh, I'll take care of the baby, Mr. Winter," Norah said pseudo-sweetly, and lifted her accusing eyes to his. "And you have a good evening now."

Unaccountably irritated, Thornton Winter turned and stalked down the hallway. Why shouldn't he have a good evening? After all, he wasn't "ancient."

Norah brought out a picture album and sat down beside Chris on the couch. As they turned page after page, Chris began to open up, confiding in Norah the pain of losing Lantz so soon after the death of his parents. Norah cried with him, then found herself telling Chris about Roman, her young friend who had died of leukemia. "Roman was closer to God and a greater witness for Him as he was dying than most people when they are alive."

"I knew I could talk to you, Norah," Chris said, no longer trying to hide his tears.

"I'd like to be your friend, Chris." No matter how much Norah might resemble her sister, she wanted him to know the real person within.

When Chris looked up, his clear blue gaze was utterly transparent. "I hope you and Camille stick around, Norah," he said. "She makes me feel like Lantz is still with us."

She nodded and closed the book. It seemed everyone wanted her to stay—everyone, that is, except Thornton Winter.

Chris stretched and got to his feet. "I'd better be going. School starts tomorrow. But maybe I'll see you over the weekend."

"I hope so," Norah said sincerely. "Good night, Chris."

She heard him drive away, and the house grew strangely quiet. She opened the album once more and studied a photo of Lantz and Hillary taken only days before their deaths. "What would you want me to do?" she whispered to the beautiful images.

Suddenly, sensing a movement, she looked up, startled, as Thornton walked into the room. "What are you doing here?"

"I live here, remember?" he informed her and stepped nearer to view the pictures.

"Uh. . .I mean. . ." She peered around him. "Where's your friend?"

He scowled, reaching down to lift the book from her lap. "Aunt Tess is taking Madelyn home," he said shortly. "I decided I could leave from here in the morning." He sat on a stool, flipping through the pictures.

Norah slid onto the stool next to him, ready to offer explanations.

Thornton stared at a picture of Lantz and Norah, snapped by Hillary, and decided he would not mention Chris' youthful vulnerability. Once, during the evening, he had come down the stairs undetected and had overheard Chris's lament, Norah's warm consolation.

"Quite a few women found Lantz irresistible," Thornton said at last, breaking the awkward silence. "What about you?"

Norah shrugged. "There was never anything to resist. He was in love with my sister, not with me."

"And how did you feel about him?" he pressed.

She thought for a moment. "Lantz was a lot like Chris, I think, warm and open. A very decent man."

"But he. . .wasn't your type?"

She wasn't sure what he was getting at. "I liked Lantz very much. We shared a similar association with show business but took opposite views of it." She shrugged once more. "He and I just didn't have much in common."

Thornton thumbed through the pages, remembering what Lantz had said. *You and Norah have a lot in common.* For the life of him, he still couldn't figure out what that could be. A dual personality? Stubborn pride? Perhaps instead of a compliment, Lantz had intended it as a warning!

~

Thornton, in suit and tie, stood at the glass door, drinking his orange juice. His gaze was riveted on Norah and Camille at the edge of the patio where Henry was pulling weeds from a flower bed. In the wash of early-morning light, everything glistened with a luminescence that created an aura about the two bright heads. Finishing his juice, he set the glass on the nearest table and stepped outside.

Norah turned to greet him. Her hair, like a vibrant flame, swung softly against the free-flowing sundress of lemon yellow. In her arms, Camille looked adorable in a white knit sleeper, trimmed in lace.

"Good morning!" Thornton's mood was reminiscent of that morning in Florida, when he had seemed so energetic and ready for the day. Camille stared at him with eyes wide and clear as a bluebell. "And how are you this morning, little flower of my heart?" He kissed the back of her hand. "Say hello to Uncle Thorn."

They laughed together in delight as Camille gurgled happily in reply. Thornton touched the plump pink cheeks. "Picture perfect," he said, glancing up at Norah and leaving her to wonder whom he was addressing. "You slept well?"

"Probably not as well as you, after your late-night swim. I saw you pass my window, headed for the beach." That had been another glimpse of Thornton Winter, so different from his usual stiff, unyielding stance, a side of him that she'd discovered only last night was a defense against pity. The glimpse of him in his swimsuit, however, had rendered nothing surprising.

Not surprising—but disturbing. Disturbing, because she had been tempted to join him on that deserted beach beneath the silver moon, to manipulate a confrontation with Thornton Winter that would let him know how strongly she was drawn to him.

But, Norah reminded herself, she was not an actress like Hillary. She had never aspired to be Hillary's understudy, had never desired a secondary role, to stand in the wings, looking on wistfully, hoping, wishing. . . .

Besides, in this scenario there was already a leading lady—a serenely beautiful blond whose soft blue eyes constantly sought the tender glance, the protective, caring arms of Thornton Winter.

"I didn't go down to the beach for a swim," he was saying, returning her to the present. "I needed to run."

He'd needed to think too. After his run, he'd sat on the beach while the cool breeze dried the sweat that had curled his hair into damp ringlets and glistened on the dark hair of his body. He'd felt physically exhausted, but exhilarated too.

Looking toward the night sky that blanketed the white-foamed waves, he had thought of the questions Norah had raised. In another year, Chris would be twenty-one, and Thornton could consider making a life for himself in a way he hadn't been able to for the past twelve years.

Had he been too hasty? At Lantz's deathbed, he'd had the noblest of intentions. Promising to care for Camille had seemed the right decision at the time. Now, aware of Norah's fierce opposition to his good intentions, he'd had some second thoughts about his promise.

Furthermore, he had to consider what was best for all of them. He had prayed about the matter and thought the answer was clear. If he could prevent it, he would not want Camille to be denied the kind of love Norah could give her. But the decent thing to do was to offer Norah a choice.

"I'll be at the office most of the day," he said abruptly, getting to his feet. "Then I have to fly to California and Florida regarding some legal matters pertaining to Lantz's estate."

"How long will you be away?"

"It's hard to say. Several days maybe. But I won't always be this busy. Soon I'll be able to spend more time with Camille."

Norah nodded, understanding. "She sleeps most of the time right now anyway."

"Then you should take some time for yourself, Norah. You've had a very demanding schedule for three and a half months. You deserve a little time off to rest. . .and think!"

"I–I'll do that."

He glanced at her in alarm. She meant it, and the thought did not bring the satisfaction he would have expected. Suppose, when he returned, she said, "She's all yours, Mr. Winter"? He felt shaky, clear down to his black conservative shoes. Whatever her choice, Thornton's life would be irrevocably changed.

He leaned down and kissed Camille on the forehead. "Bye-bye, little one," he said gently, then searched Norah's eyes, feeling compelled to say, "Please don't try anything foolish."

The sudden defiant tilt of her chin and the ramrod-stiff spine indicated she had understood him. She still would not be permitted to leave the island with Camille. If she went, she'd go alone.

But this time, no explosive response was forthcoming. Was she beginning to trust him? Or was she resigning herself to leaving—without Camille?

Norah held the baby close and watched Thornton Winter disappear into the house. "You smell like musky aftershave," she murmured to the little girl.

The fragrance lingered. So did his words.

Nothing foolish, he'd said. Norah wasn't too sure which would be more foolish—leaving. . .or staying.

~

On Tuesday, after making an appointment for Camille with a pediatrician and learning that the hospital in Charleston would forward literature on teaching infants to swim, Norah invited Aunt Tess for lunch.

As soon as Camille was settled for her nap, the two women took a dune buggy tour of the island, only ten miles long and five miles across at its widest point. The lazy afternoon, warmed by the sun, invited an exchange of confidences, and Norah found herself wondering aloud, "Isn't it amazing that

Thornton could have built such a marvelous place on such a desolate stretch of land?"

"He's the best designer in the business, even if he is my nephew," Aunt Tess said proudly. "He designed the beach house before he finished college."

Aunt Tess parked the vehicle and got out. In a sleeveless dress and sandals, the light wind stirring her short gray hair, she looked younger than she had on Sunday. "My brother Thaddeus was Thornton's father," she said as they strolled along the beach, watching the sailboats bobbing on the water. "He was a designer and builder of ships, like his ancestors before him. But after everything passed down to Thornton, he sold the shipping business and concentrated on private homes."

Norah admitted a lack of knowledge in that area, but added, "It does seem extraordinary for one so young to have designed that beach house."

"Thaddeus was a perfectionist," Aunt Tess explained. "His stipulation for partnership was that Thornton design a house that he could approve."

"Apparently he succeeded."

"Well, Thaddeus declared that he himself would never have come up with such a design. But he admitted that he didn't have Thornton's kind of originality. Then he welcomed him into the business and told him to go ahead and build the house and furnish it—as his graduation present!"

"What a wonderful story, Aunt Tess."

"To that point, Norah," she said sadly. "Thaddeus never saw the place completed. Right after that, he and Caitlin were in a terrible boating accident and were killed instantly."

"That had to have been a terrible shock for all of you," Norah said softly.

"Particularly for the younger boys," Aunt Tess recalled. "My husband and I would have taken them, of course, but Carter wasn't well, and Thornton insisted on caring for his brothers himself and keeping them in the family home." At Norah's quick glance, Aunt Tess added, "Carter died of a heart attack four years ago."

Norah murmured her condolences, then she went on. "Do you think that was the right decision, Aunt Tess? Keeping the boys at home, I mean?"

"Well, Thornton was only twenty-four when he became their legal guardian," she admitted. "But as much as possible, he enforced the rules by which Thaddeus and Caitlin had raised him. He involved himself in his brothers' activities, managed the family business, took the boys to church every Sunday, and limited his social life drastically."

Aunt Tess gazed out over the sparkling water crested with whitecaps, like swirls of icing on a cake, before moving on down the beach. "Looking back," she continued reflectively, "I believe it was best. Carter and I were here to help when needed. But Thornton preserved a sense of family, particularly for himself and Chris. He is a brother, but he's also a father figure for Chris."

Watching the white-winged seagulls sailing so effortlessly over the sea—dipping, swooping, diving at some succulent morsel—Norah realized that Thornton's beach house was a symbol of the kind of freedom he himself had rarely known. The kind of freedom he was offering her. And by the time they returned to the house, Norah had a deeper understanding of Thornton Winter. However—and her chin went up at the thought—she did not intend to sit idly by and wait for him to deliver ultimatums and make all the decisions. She had some options of her own!

"Aunt Tess," she said, her green eyes alive with enthusiasm, "tell me more about the College of Charleston."

On Wednesday morning, Norah drove the dune buggy to the ferry, where Aunt Tess met her. Beneath a clear blue sky, they rode through the small town of Mount Pleasant, ablaze with delicate crimson, purple, and pink azalea blossoms. The intricate steel girders of the majestic Cooper River Bridge took them into Charleston and to the main campus of the College that Aunt Tess said included eighty-six buildings and extended over seven city blocks.

The campus was impressive. Mellow brick buildings nestled alongside wooden ones. Courtyards and old-fashioned lampposts gave an aura of the past, while renovated buildings offered the latest in technology.

Aunt Tess had called ahead to make an appointment, and the two women were welcomed into the dean's office, where Dr. Joshua Logan, the head of the Psychology Department, was waiting to talk with Norah and give her a tour of the campus. Dr. Logan, a big man with rust-colored hair and a thick curly beard, reminded Norah of lumberjacks she had seen in the movies.

While Aunt Tess stayed behind to talk with the dean, Dr. Logan led Norah into his office. She liked him right away. His deep, resonant voice and the spark of merriment in his dancing brown eyes gave her the impression that a class under him would never be boring.

He told her about the psychology department and of his own plans for the fall. He would be returning to the mountains of western North Carolina to take a position at the University of North Carolina. Though it would mean a cut in salary, he would be going home. "But enough about me. Let's see what we can do for you," he said. "And let's get the formalities out of the way. Call me Josh. I have an idea we're going to be good friends."

After discussing the possibility of Norah's attending classes in the fall and the prospect of her finding a job or getting financial aid, Josh said, "How about some lunch? I can offer you a cafeteria line like none other."

Aunt Tess was in her element, seeing fellow teachers with whom she had worked so many years. Several of them had invited her to join them in the cafeteria, so she waved Norah away with a smile. Over lunch, Norah briefly related her situation and discovered a kindred spirit in Josh Logan. One of his reasons for moving back home was to investigate the unsolved murder of his sister. "At the end of the summer, I'll be giving up my part-time job as youth director at my church. Would that interest you?"

Norah glanced at him with growing appreciation. There was more to this man than met the eye. "I'm afraid it would require more time than I have to give," she said, and told him about Camille.

Josh was sympathetic. "That accident was the talk of the campus for a while. I've heard of your sister, of course, but with my classes and church activities, I don't see much TV or movies. By the way," he added, smiling broadly, "you need to get involved with people, Norah. And if you haven't found a church yet, check us out. We have a fine nursery. I'd be glad to meet you there and show you around."

Norah was touched. "If Mr. Winter hasn't returned from his trip by Sunday, I just might do that."

Josh looked up from his plate. "You're talking about Thornton Winter, the builder?"

"That's the one."

Impressed, he raised his eyebrows. "I heard he was engaged to marry some woman he's known for a long time."

"Engaged?" Norah froze, completely unprepared for that revelation. How could she have been so naïve? Thornton had told her only that he didn't have a wife. But he hadn't mentioned a fiancée.

Of course. Madelyn. Madelyn was in his house. In his arms. Obviously in his heart.

And Norah was in his way. Was that his real reason for wanting her to leave? So he could get on with his life? She felt the blood drain from her face. "What do you know, Josh?" she asked. "It's of the utmost importance."

"Practically nothing, really. It was probably just a rumor anyway," he said, seeing the anguish on her face. "Hey, I've put my foot in it, and I'm sorry."

Norah lost her appetite, and Josh quickly finished his lunch and gave her the promised tour. But her mind was not on the interesting lecture or the charming lecturer, and when they got back to his office, he gave her his business card. "If you ever need a friend, Norah, call me."

"Thanks," she said weakly. "I may take you up on that."

"Good. Then I hope to see you Sunday morning."

⁓

Norah's mom and dad called on Saturday, during an afternoon rainstorm, to say that Thornton Winter had stopped by to see them. Both Nancy and Frederick Browne were obviously fascinated with him, thought him to be a most generous man, and were pleased that he had claimed Norah and Camille as part of his family.

Norah was glad to hear from them, and it confirmed what she already knew—that they were not interested in bringing up another family. She couldn't blame them. After all, they'd be in their seventies before Camille finished high school. Yes, Thornton's visit had definitely put their minds at ease about Camille's welfare—and Norah's.

Obviously, he hadn't told them the whole story—that he had asked her to consider leaving his home—without Camille.

"You're a lucky girl," Nancy said, and her singsong tone led Norah to believe her mother suspected some kind of romantic involvement. "We just might pop down there soon, but we have another tour starting next week. I'll call and give you a phone number."

"Don't worry about us, Mom," Norah assured her. "We're fine. Just have fun."

"Take lots of pictures," Nancy said. "We do want to keep up with our granddaughter."

And that's what Norah was doing when Thornton returned Sunday afternoon.

Chapter 8

While Camille napped, Norah lounged on the deck in shorts and T-shirt, reading a book Josh had given her that morning at church. Though the book, *Undivided,* by Trevor Steinborg, was a work of fiction, the story was incredibly true to life.

Hearing Camille's sleepy cry, Norah went to take her out of her crib and bring her outside, laying her on a quilt in the shade by the pool, then offering her cuddly animals to distract her. Quickly tiring of her toys, the baby became fascinated with the white clouds floating by in a sky as blue as her eyes.

Norah lay beside her, snapping picture after picture, until she heard the sliding glass doors open. She assumed it was Eloise. Couldn't be Henry, because he was asleep in a chaise lounge, his newspaper over his chest and his mouth hanging open like a flycatcher.

Not until he spoke did she realize it was Thornton. "Is this the way to greet a man when he returns to his castle after a week on the road?" he asked with mock gruffness. "Eloise is asleep in front of the TV. Henry is either snoring or pretending to be a frog. And Aunt Norah is lying on her back, taking pictures of the sky!"

Norah laughed, bringing the camera down from her eyes.

Thornton felt an overwhelming sense of well-being. The week had been difficult but had brought closure to a part of his past. Then, driving here from the airport, he had realized that spring had arrived in all its intoxicating lushness. Flowers, gardens, and fruit trees were in riotous bloom. The sun was dazzling, the sky brilliant, the air warm and fragrant.

After reaching the island, he'd felt a lightness in his spirit that was new and refreshing. "Going home" had taken on a broader significance. And now round blue eyes and oval green ones stared up at him. For the moment, he actually felt like a king.

Norah pulled herself into a sitting position, her long ponytail swinging over her shoulder. "Camille wanted me to take pictures for her memory book," she said. Her voice was light, like the breeze that stirred the air and cooled his cheek. "Look, she thinks the clouds are a new toy."

Thornton knelt beside Camille and gently moved his finger from one red-gold ringlet to another. "Hello, Beautiful. How's my little girl?"

In response, Camille began to blow bubbles and shake her fists, until one landed in her mouth.

Norah snapped the picture. Thornton looked startled and his scar turned purple. Suddenly she realized why. He was thinking of his face. Were it not for Camille, she felt he'd have grabbed the camera and flung it into the pool.

"Please don't take my picture again," he said stiffly, trying to restrain his rage for Camille's sake.

"You should be ashamed of yourself, Thornton Winter," Norah scolded as gently as possible. "You're ten times better-looking than most men with both sides of their face as smooth as a snake's belly."

At that, he burst out laughing. "You call that a compliment?"

"No," she said. "It's a fact. You need to talk about it, Thornton, and get it out of your system." He also needed to rid himself of a few other things that contributed to his gloom, Norah thought, having decided that Josh's comment about Thornton's alleged engagement was nothing more than a rumor. Or else it was a part of his past, and not a very happy part, she judged.

Thornton wondered if she realized she had called him by his first name. But he mustn't put too much stock in that, for he knew how quickly that acceptance could change to rejection. "I don't like to have my picture taken," he reiterated coolly.

"Well, that's too bad. I happen to be taking pictures for Camille's grandparents." Norah's voice grew soft. "The baby looks at you with eyes of love, you know."

He didn't reply right away, then changed the subject. "I met your parents."

"Yes, they called."

"They send their love."

Camille was staring up at him, her eyes growing heavy, and Norah sat down beside her and drew her legs up under her. "My parents think it's wonderful that Camille and I are here."

"I know," he said. "In fact, I learned quite a bit about you while I was there. For instance, I learned that you were greatly influenced by your grandparents."

Norah gazed up at the sky, looking for faces in the clouds. "I miss them so much," she said wistfully. "I always felt I had to act to gain my parents' approval. But with my grandparents. . .well. . .I could just be myself."

"Camille gives you the same feeling, doesn't she?" he asked. "That incredible feeling of being accepted and loved, just for who you are."

They smiled down at the sleeping baby between them.

Suddenly Henry snored loudly and woke himself up. Looking startled, he folded his paper abruptly and sat up on the edge of the chaise. He stared at Thornton and Norah as if they were strangers. "That baby should be in her bed," he proclaimed. "I'll send Eloise out." And he left without a backward glance.

Thornton shook his head and Norah chuckled. "Henry's teaching Camille all about plants," she said.

"He's the expert." He moved to a nearby chair when Eloise came to collect the baby.

"This may surprise you, Thornton," Norah began after the housekeeper had disappeared through the glass doors, "but I've been thinking about the options you presented."

"And what have you decided?" He waited for her answer with a considerable amount of apprehension.

"I know about your becoming a parent at a young age, so I understand your reasons for saying what you did to me. The realization is dawning that parenting is more frightening than I had thought. It's really a willingness to give up your life, if necessary, for the benefit of another, isn't it? That's pretty overwhelming."

Thornton looked toward the house, unwilling to meet her green gaze. If she'd decided to be an aunt instead of a mother, he couldn't blame her. She was not obligated.

Her voice dropped. "It really will require more of me than I had realized."

Thornton remained quiet, his mind racing. Had he overdone it? Made her feel she was inadequate? She wasn't, of course. But this was her decision.

Norah took a deep breath and faced him squarely. "I've come to understand that I don't have exclusive rights to Camille." Her chin lifted in that brave little show of defiance. "But I'm more determined than ever to keep her with me. I've bonded with that child as if she were my own. I can't leave her. You can't ask me to. And I won't try to take her away as long as I feel this is best for her. Right now," she finished quietly, "I do."

"Norah!" he exclaimed, the force of her name expressing his gratitude and relief. She wasn't going to make things difficult for him, wasn't planning to initiate a court fight. But he knew that her decision hadn't been an easy one. When losing someone dear, it was only natural to try to hold on to people—even things—very tightly. That was reflected in the position of her hands, now clasped together, her knuckles white.

"Norah," he repeated softly. "I love her too, you know."

"I know." His love for Camille was evident in his voice when he spoke to her, in his eyes when he looked at her.

"Does this make you sad, Norah?" he asked gently.

"More scared than sad," she admitted. "But as long as I feel things are working in Camille's best interests, I'm not leaving. But that doesn't mean I won't make my share of the decisions about her welfare," she added quickly.

"I understand that." Norah would share, but she would not relinquish complete control. Nor would she let down the barriers that had been raised from the moment they had met. She was wary of entrusting Camille's future to him. She was taking a chance. . .on him. It was a major breakthrough. Thornton was elated.

"I appreciate what you said about sharing, Norah. And I don't want to take anything from either of you. I want to give."

He stood and filled his lungs with the fresh spring air. He had an overwhelming urge to lift her to her feet and hug her in gratitude, to assure her that he had no ulterior motives. He wanted the best for all of them.

His eyes fell on the novel lying on the table, and he picked it up. *"Undivided.* You're reading this?"

"Yes. Josh Logan gave it to me," she said, and his head snapped around. "He said you might want to read it too."

"Josh Logan? Who's he?"

"Oh, well, you see," she began happily, "in making my decision, I also decided to be working on my life, too, not just sitting around waiting for you to make all the plans."

She had expected him to joke with her, but his countenance darkened, the scar making a vivid streak down his face. "Who is this Josh Logan?" he asked again.

"Josh? Oh, he's a psychology professor at the College of Charleston. Aunt Tess introduced us last week."

"So he gave you the book then?"

"No," she replied, finding this exchange bewildering. "He gave it to me this morning, at church."

"You went to church?"

"C-h-u-r-c-h," she spelled.

"Don't patronize me, Miss Browne," he warned. "Where did you go to church?"

"In Mount Pleasant."

He looked like a thunderstorm about to erupt, the dark clouds gathering in his eyes. "Why?" he asked stiffly, his tone giving fair warning that the storm was about to break.

"Why?" she asked, forcing her voice not to betray her confusion. "Because I'm a Christian."

He shook his head. "I mean, why that particular church?"

"What's wrong with it?" she asked, beginning to grow irritated. "Did I stumble on to some kind of cult or something?" Then, "If you must know, I felt strengthened and inspired by the sermon, and the music was a medley of old hymns that I haven't sung in a long time."

He was shaking his head. "That's not the point. I'm sure there's nothing wrong with the church. It's just that I assumed that if we were going to cooperate, you would wait until we move to my house in Charleston and go to my church there."

"You mean the one you didn't invite me to for Lantz's memorial service?"

He drew back as if she had struck him. "I've already apologized for that. It was a mistake. At the time, I thought you were an unwed mother who wouldn't want to face the crowds."

"Nevertheless," she insisted, "I would like to have been asked. I was invited to the church in Mount Pleasant." Her voice continued to rise. "That makes a difference, Mr. Winter. It's important to feel wanted. Besides, I wouldn't want to take Camille to some stuffy old historic church, as dull as dust. . . ."

"And are you in the habit of passing judgment before you've had a chance to see for yourself?" he demanded.

"No," she admitted. "It's an impression based on. . ." She hesitated, then grabbed the book he was still holding and brushed it off. "Anyway, I was impressed with the nursery facility, and that's an important part."

"I have no quarrel with the church itself," Thornton went on, striving for control. "It's just that this is the most vital area of a child's training, one that needs to be reinforced by family unity."

"I've already had my sermon for today, Mr. Winter."

"I didn't mean to preach. I take the blame for this," he said, grasping the table as if he had to hold on to something. "I asked Aunt Tess not to push you, feeling you needed this time to get adjusted."

"Well, Mr. Winter," Norah insisted, "I feel that the best adjustment one can make is to become part of a church where there are other caring Christians. Camille already notices everything around her. You saw that yourself today. I want her to grow up knowing that God is an integral part of her life."

Thornton drew himself up straighter and folded his arms across his chest. "I think part of this is your rebellion against me. If you wanted this to be a family affair, you could have attended the church my family has attended for generations."

"I'll bet you even have your own pew," she snorted derisively. When his shoulders stiffened, she knew she'd struck a nerve. "But as I said, Mr. Winter, it's important to feel wanted."

They glared at each other. Finally he spoke, "Who invited you?"

"Does it matter?"

"Unmistakably!" he replied. "Who is he?"

"Who said it's a he?"

"Your unwillingness to give a name," he retorted.

Norah shook her head stubbornly. She hadn't intended to broach the subject, but now it tumbled out. "Do you intend to fill me in on the details of your relationship with Madelyn?"

"I do not," he said firmly.

"Then don't expect me to divulge my every move. I have a right to a private life too."

"That's where you're wrong. As part of my family, I do expect you to keep everything public and aboveboard."

"But you have a private life with Madelyn," she insisted.

"Madelyn has nothing to do with this. Nor am I accustomed to discussing my private life with anyone."

"You are or were. . ." Norah rose and grasped the opposite side of the table with both hands. "Or are going to be. . .married to her. That makes her fair game since Camille and I are part of your family."

"Is that what you learned at church?" he blared.

That was not a denial, Norah knew. "You're not being honest with me, Mr. Winter. If you're planning to bring that obviously disturbed woman in to be your wife, then I have every right to know. You want me to leave, don't you? You've tried everything from threats to ultimatums, from charm to church. Church!" she snorted. "I can't believe you would stoop so low as to resort to arguing about church!"

Thornton's shoulders sagged and he leaned over, bracing his hands on the tabletop. "What we need to do is cool off, then we'll sit down and discuss the situation like two civilized adults."

"And what is that?" she hissed.

"Maybe I can depend upon my memory!" he snapped. "I used to be one!" He turned and strode toward the house.

"Oh!" Norah gasped, the color high in her cheeks. "I think you've always been one!" she yelled to his retreating figure.

He glanced over his shoulder. "Twenty years?" he called back. "Of this?" He wouldn't let her see his grin. This was more exhilarating than a run on the beach.

She stomped along behind him. "If you don't like it, you can. . .leave!"

He flung open the glass doors. Eloise was folding soft baby blankets. "Will you want supper soon?" she asked.

"Bread and water for her!" He pointed to an indignant Norah.

Norah suddenly realized he was not angry. When had it changed? The infuriating man was like a southern storm. One never knew just when it would strike, but it was inevitable.

"Well, I can cook my own," she scoffed, going along with his game. "I learned when I was six years old—seawater, sand cakes, and grass a-pair-spe-gus."

For an instant, Thornton seemed bewildered, then he threw back his head and laughed.

"And Thornton's favorite was mac-a-blony," Eloise added, joining in their laughter as she took the stack of blankets toward the bedroom.

They looked at each other. "I'm sorry," Thornton said.

Norah sank down on the couch and sighed heavily. "Since I met you, I feel as if I've been through a divorce, complete with marital discord and a custody fight, and all without the benefits of marriage."

He quirked a brow meaningfully.

"Oh, Thornton," she said suddenly, "we're never going to get along long enough to bring up a child."

"Of course we are," he countered, sitting down in a chair opposite her. "We can work at it. Remember, you promised me twenty years."

She smiled. He was trying to make up for his snide remark earlier. Then he suddenly grew serious again. "We have to talk about where we go from here. And we must consider the fact that you may someday want to marry, Norah, when you find the right man."

"That's easy," she quipped. "He would have to be as dedicated to Camille's welfare as I."

Norah caught her breath as he stared intently at her. "My experience has taught me that it is not so easy to find a mate who wants to be responsible for someone else's child. When one has a child to consider, one's social life is greatly limited."

"Limited?" She laughed, hoping to steer the conversation into less troubled waters. "Why, Thornton, this past week Camille and I watched *Sesame Street* together, read several old favorites, and went for a stroll in the fresh air nearly every day. I'd say my social life has improved considerably."

His expression grew pensive. "Do you think she's too young for Br'er Rabbit?"

"Not at all," Norah replied, hiding a grin.

"I almost wore the tar off that baby," he reminisced. "It was my favorite."

They laughed together. Then Norah sobered. "I want to start reading Bible stories to her at night, so that can be the last thing on her mind before she goes to sleep."

He nodded. "We can do that together."

"I want to expose her to all the most important things from the very beginning."

"I quite agree," Thornton said. "Including the values I mentioned to you in Florida, values I. . .erroneously. . .assumed you did not share."

Norah felt breathless. He approved of her?

"Norah," he said, his deep voice low and husky, "I know some fathers who have raised daughters without mothers, and the relationships were quite remarkably stable. It isn't ideal, of course, but it can be done. I never came close to replacing Mother in Chris's life, for example, but we had to deal with the reality as we found it. There are things I can't do for Camille as well as you, and vice versa. But I'll do my best."

"And I'll have to learn as I go along." Her eyes flashed. "But I would like to be able to make some of the decisions where she's concerned."

He arched a brow. "Decisions? Didn't you request swimming lessons for Camille, and didn't I go along with the idea?"

"Oh, I meant to tell you," she said, her voice rising with excitement. "The literature from the hospital came in the mail last week, and Camille and I have been practicing. I think we're ready now. I could call the instructor to come out anytime. What about tomorrow?"

"Fine!" he said with enthusiasm as Eloise entered the room. "I have some calls to make after dinner. Then we'll spend this evening making plans."

Thornton walked over to the sliding doors and looked out. How different this scene was from just two weeks ago. A placid pool beneath a serene sky, feathery clouds floating above. A quiet garden. The relaxing, rhythmic sound of the sea on a tranquil afternoon.

His peaceful haven would never be the same. The spotless deck was now strewn with toys, a baby blanket, a half-empty bottle. Baby cries and lullabies disturbed the utter stillness. The thought, "The Lord gives and the Lord takes away," drifted across his mind. Those he had lost could not be replaced. But his family could expand. Camille was an extension of them all, a part of himself.

Thank You, Lord, he breathed silently.

And that young woman, who had lain on her back, taking pictures of the sky! Just where did she fit into the scheme of things? *Ah, but that was the challenge.*

He realized he was smiling. It had been much too long since he had smiled or laughed. . .or argued with anyone. It felt good, invigorating.

He shook his head. Twenty years?

Then he noticed the novel lying on the table where Norah had set it aside and went outside to bring it in. A frown touched his lips. Josh Logan had given it to her. Wanted him to read it. And what did this Josh know about Thornton Winter?

Chapter 9

I 've changed my mind!" Thornton exclaimed, pausing long enough to glare at Norah as she undressed Camille down to her diaper. "I don't know how I could have let you talk me into this!"

Aunt Tess sat anxiously in a chair drawn up close to the pool, holding the soft blanket she would wrap the baby in after her first swimming lesson. Eloise and Henry, looking dubious, stood nearby with their arms around each other for support, while Thornton paced alongside the pool.

"Let's just listen to what the instructor has to say," Norah implored, refusing to admit that she felt a little uneasy herself. Willing to give it a try, however, she handed Camille to Thornton and sat on the side of the pool, dangling her feet in the water.

The instructor, a pretty young woman named Paula, reminded Norah of Liza Minnelli with her alert dark eyes and short black hair. Her tall, athletic build was proof that she was physically capable of handling not only babies but grownups as well.

Paula's vita had been mailed to Norah, along with an instruction sheet for preparing the baby for this day. She knew that Mr. Winter had checked with the hospital, confirming her credentials. However, observing the apprehensive group huddled around the pool, she restated her qualifications, which included life-saving courses, education in physical therapy, employment with the hospital for over a year, and occasional private lessons, usually with recovering patients.

No doubt Thornton was a heavy contributor to the hospital, Norah thought, *to have persuaded them to send such a well-qualified instructor to teach one small child!*

"It's really quite simple," Paula assured her doubtful audience. "You have been preparing the baby according to the instructions I sent?" she asked, turning to Norah.

Norah nodded. She had been blowing in Camille's face several times a day for the past few days, getting her to accept the exercise as a playful antic.

"Now," Paula said, going to the edge and slipping into the water, "after she comes up, praise her. Let her know she has done well."

Thornton's face clouded over. "Sounds like you're training a—a dog!" he objected. "This is my niece!"

Norah turned her face up to his. "This could save her life, Thornton, not only in the pool, but in the bathtub. And before long, she'll be out here in her walker."

"Not unattended, I can assure you!"

Paula spoke confidently. "This is not a measure to replace the vigilant supervision of children. Accidents can happen—even while you're watching."

He wasn't convinced. "She's so young and helpless."

Norah agreed. "That's exactly why it's so important," she said quietly. "Let's get started."

Thornton shrugged in resignation, and seeing that he was not going to interfere, Paula stepped forward. "Since mothers are better at this than fathers," she said to Norah, "you get into the pool."

Norah slid off the side and into the water. In spite of the reluctance and warning in his eyes, Thornton placed Camille in her arms.

Paula continued her explanation. "Now I'll blow in her face, and she will inhale sharply. That's when she should be submerged. Later, you will watch for air bubbles as she exhales. But in this beginning stage, we're only acclimating her to the water and overcoming any fear she might have. Give her to me, please."

Norah bravely handed over the baby.

Paula held Camille under her arms, facing her. The child was especially squirmy, perhaps picking up on the tension around her, and started to cry.

Before anyone could object, Paula blew into her mouth and nose. Camille gasped, halting her crying, and the entire family held its breath as Paula dunked her and held her under for a couple of seconds before bringing her up. Startled by the suddenness of the movements and the water streaming down her face, Camille cried out. Paula put her into Norah's waiting arms, and Norah comforted her, making soothing sounds.

"It's not working," Thornton declared.

"On the contrary, it worked perfectly," Paula said. "Camille will soon learn that blowing is the signal that she's going underwater. Later, she will automatically hold her breath."

Camille had quieted by now and Paula encouraged Norah, "Now you try it."

Norah took her position in the water and blew in Camille's face. The baby held her breath, and Norah dunked her and quickly brought her up. Once again, Camille sputtered in protest, but not as vigorously as before.

"That's it for today," Paula said, to the immense relief of the onlookers, who applauded and cheered this announcement.

Norah held Camille up to Thornton, and Aunt Tess bundled her in the warm blanket and crooned soothingly, praising her for her morning's work.

"I'll give her her bath." Eloise took the baby, and the little entourage disappeared inside, leaving Henry to drive Paula back to the dock after she had changed.

Norah hoisted herself to the side of the pool and cocked her head at Thornton. "Well?" she said with a triumphant grin. "What do you think? Don't you agree that I was right?"

"Absolutely!" he declared, kneeling down beside her. "Everyone should be subjected to such treatment." With that, through open lips he drew in a deep breath, expanding his chest. The wicked gleam in his eyes was unmistakable.

"You wouldn't dare!" she squealed, and to escape, she jumped into the pool, splashing him in the process.

He flinched, warding off the rain of drops. Resisting the impulse to retaliate instantly, he sat on the edge of the pool and eased his feet into the water, speaking quietly, "I can tell she's going to be a championship swimmer."

Norah bobbed in the water, dog paddling. "So, you have to admit I was right about this one!"

"You? You can't take the credit. Remember, you can't do a thing without my permission." When she opened her mouth to retort, he suddenly drew up his knees, then forced his feet into the water, making a trememdous splash.

He had intended to jump up from the side, but she was too quick. Ducking beneath the surface, she came up with her body and her arms, flinging the water at him, dousing him, and creating a stream that ran onto the deck.

Getting to his feet awkwardly, arms outstretched, he scowled at her, water dripping from his hair and down his face.

Norah chortled with glee. "You look like you did the night the hurricane blew you into Florida."

At the memory, the laughter died in her throat. That night she had been so afraid he'd take Camille from her. Now she was freely offering to share Camille with him. Had he changed so drastically? Or had she? Panic washed over her like a wave. With a thundering heart, she turned in the water and swam to the other side of the pool.

Thornton reached for a towel from a table and began drying himself. He'd seen the playful challenge in her eyes turn to doubt. Or was it fear? Was she disappointed that he hadn't risen to her challenge? Or was she afraid he might? Still, he didn't want to leave her out here alone, while the family was inside, gloating over Camille's momentous accomplishment.

"Norah," he called, when she reached the other side, "let's go in." He held out his hand toward her.

Skeptical all the way, she swam toward him. At the edge, she looked up at him. It wasn't a game anymore. She shook her head.

"Trust me."

Norah lifted herself out of the pool and hesitantly took his outstretched hand. He pulled her up and handed her a towel.

Stunned by his gallant gesture, she could only stare into his face, his lips lifted in a dazzling smile. "Thank you," she murmured.

As she was toweling off, an old saying came to mind: "The only thing we have to fear is fear itself." Surely she didn't have anything to fear from this gentle man.

Did she?

~

How could I have possibly imagined that my decision to share Camille with Thornton Winter would solve our problems? Norah wondered. Their discussions about what was best for Lantz and Hillary's child had quickly escalated to a total rehash of all the pros and cons she and Thornton had ever fought about. Only this time, it was being accompanied by the legal advice of experts—Thornton's paid experts!

Now they were sitting at the dining room table while John Grimes, the senior attorney, made notes to include in his petition to present to a judge.

"Filing for joint custody is the only way to ensure Camille's welfare," he had said, persuading her at last that it was true. And today, he went one step further as he warned, "Of course, there's always the chance that a judge might not award joint custody, but possibly will want to decide which of you should get full custody."

"But we're not divorced!" Norah protested, distressed at the prospect. "We don't want to divide Camille. We want to share her!"

"But if you two can't decide what's best," John informed her, "then there's the danger of Camille becoming a ward of the court until you can come to some kind of agreement."

That would be worse. Instead of the two of them making a decision, it would be made by an objective, unemotional third party.

"Let's try to work together," she pleaded.

"Good," John said. "Now, here's what you must do. Keep all emotions under control and think only of the baby. You must convince a judge that you're not fighting for separate custody, but that you want to share."

By Friday, John Grimes had written up the presentation he would make to a judge and, when Thornton hand-delivered a copy to Norah, she sat down and read it immediately. The document dealt only with their intentions and not with their doubts and frustrations. But John Grimes was Thornton

Winter's legal representative, paid to act in his behalf, and Norah still wasn't sure she was being fairly represented.

What other recourse do I have? she fretted silently. She did want to share Camille with Thornton Winter. She did want the security for the baby that he offered. And to fight Thornton in court would be much more painful than a few discourses in the dining room at the beach house.

"What do you think?" Thornton asked after she'd read it.

"On paper, it sounds fair," she said. "But it's not so simple. Nothing is really settled—only delayed."

"Things, and people, change, Norah. A judge will have to take that into consideration."

"I know. It's just that I'm not sure anymore what's right. I need to get away and think. I'm in your house, listening to your family, your attorneys. I need an objective opinion."

"You want another attorney?"

"Shouldn't I have my own? You pay John and his assistant to represent your best interests."

He shrugged. "That's your prerogative. Shall I suggest someone?"

"No," she said offhandedly, "I'll find someone."

"Then go ahead," he said stiffly. His eyes fell on the novel lying on the edge of the bar. He could see that the card being used as a marker was a personal business card. "You intend to call Josh, don't you?"

She shrugged. "So? What did you expect? Did you think I would open the phone book and pick a name at random over something this important?"

"All right," he said. "I have no objections."

While Norah left to make her call in the privacy of the library, Thornton picked up the book and flipped it over. On the back cover, where the critics were quoted, he read: "A penetrating, thought-provoking saga of unselfish love to rival the wisdom of King Solomon in the case of the divided child."

He looked out toward the palms, swaying in the morning breeze, and searched his memory for the familiar Bible story. Two women who had laid claim to a baby had sought the judgment of wise King Solomon. When Solomon suggested dividing the child with a sword, giving half to each woman, the real mother had spoken up in alarm. "Give the child to her!" she had cried, thus proving a real mother's love.

Thornton shook his head in denial. That plot did not fit their situation. Neither he nor Norah were trying to divide Camille. Nor did they want to fight over her. They simply wanted to share her.

Who did this Josh think he was? Some young whippersnapper who had gotten all starry-eyed over Norah and was trying to tell her how to run her life?

Thornton didn't care for outside interference in his family. And Norah was family, at least for now.

He looked up as she came back into the room. "I'd like to go out for awhile tonight, if that's all right," she said, expecting an argument.

But there was none. "Fine. I'll be with Camille. But I need to be away tomorrow afternoon and evening, possibly quite late." He regarded her silently for a moment. "I can be reached at Madelyn's."

He had hoped she might reveal her own whereabouts, but when she didn't, he said, "Come on. I'll drive you to the ferry."

~

"Why are you doing this?" she asked Thornton later as he drove onto the ferry instead of letting her out.

"Because I'm a gentleman."

"The real reason," she probed.

"You'll see when we get there," he said to her in exasperation.

"It's only Josh," she confessed on the way. "I have no other friends here."

"I suppose you've told him about the baby."

"He's the one who took me to check out the nursery at church. There he is now," she said, spotting Josh as the ferry pulled into the dock. He was leaning up against his red sports car, waiting for her.

Thornton wheeled the Mercedes into the slot beside him and killed the engine. Getting out, Norah introduced the two men, and Josh stuck out a big paw.

Thornton accepted his handshake tentatively. He had expected to find a much younger man, but Logan appeared to be around his own age, somewhere in his mid-thirties. "I want to thank you for suggesting that I read *Undivided*. Very thoughtful of you."

Josh nodded. A tense moment passed as the two men studied each other surreptitiously.

"Interesting novel," Thornton went on.

"You've read it, then?" Josh wanted to know.

"Enough to get the point. I know how it ends."

Norah looked at the two men. At Thornton's statement, Josh had appeared somewhat diminished. *Though he'd have to go a long way for that,* she thought. Like Thornton, he was a big man, and although his heavy beard and thick hair gave him a brawny look, he had the refined muscular structure of a dancer.

Feeling the tension bristling between them, she said cheerily, "Oh, Thornton, you should never read the ending first. It ruins the story."

"You're right," he agreed, "that's exactly what happened." He smiled, but his eyes were glittering strangely. "Have a good evening," he said and, without another glance, he returned to his car and drove back onto the ferry.

"I think I touched a nerve, without meaning to," Josh said after they were in the car and buckled up.

"He's just particular about the company kept by his niece's guardian," Norah explained. "He must have approved, though, or he would have escorted me right back to the island. But he's not as gruff as he appears."

"Oh, I didn't think he was gruff." Josh gave a wry laugh. "Men who own islands just speak a different language."

"I suppose so," she agreed. "And what did he communicate to you?"

"Proceed with caution."

Norah laughed uneasily, then told him a little about her dilemma. "I'm afraid of losing Camille," she confessed, "and going before a judge seems such a drastic measure. A court will decide her future."

"Do you have any recourse?" Josh asked.

"Not unless I want my parents to apply for custody. But I don't want to take Camille away from Thornton Winter. He's a fine man, Josh. Camille and he need each other. They love each other."

"I can't advise you in something this important," he said. "But since you both want to share the baby, it looks as if this is the only way, without going through a worse court battle."

"I know," she said and sighed. "But Thornton Winter has decided he will rear this child, and I have no choice but to let him, even if it means I lose control."

"You also gain some control, Norah. Being established as a legal guardian, even jointly, will give you more ammunition for what might come up later on."

"It would do the same for him," she argued.

There was a moment of silence while he contemplated the facts. "What would Camille's parents want?"

She shook her head. "Oh, Josh, they would want us both to take care of her. But even the attorney is saying a judge will probably consider the situation unstable and temporary, at best."

"And what do you think?"

"For me, it would be ideal if Camille and I could stay at the beach house, with Eloise and Henry to take care of everything, and Thornton dropping in occasionally to relate to Camille. But we have to move to town where it's convenient for him. It's scary, thinking about our living together in that house."

"Are you worried about. . .his taking advantage of you?"

"Not at all!" She laughed at the very idea. "He sees me as a female counterpart to Chris, like a sister he can parent."

Josh didn't reply that he felt Thornton Winter was more perceptive than that. "Then you might try the prayer of serenity: 'Lord, help me to change the things I can and accept the things I cannot. And give me the wisdom to know the difference.'"

"I suppose you're right," she said and they exchanged a knowing look. "I'm helpless. I have nowhere else to turn."

Unexpectedly, Josh began to sing in his baritone voice: "'I must tell Jesus all of my trials; I cannot bear my burdens alone. In my distress He kindly will help me. He ever loves and cares for His own. I must tell Jesus; I must tell Jesus. I cannot bear my burdens alone. I must tell Jesus; I must tell Jesus. Jesus can help me. Jesus alone.'"

Norah turned a radiant smile on Josh when he had finished. "Thanks. You have a way of helping me put things in perspective."

"Sometimes you can be too close to a situation to be objective, Norah. I was so bent on finding my sister's murderer that I was completely frustrated when God didn't open up a job for me in North Carolina so I could pursue the case. I couldn't see that He was answering my prayer by giving me eight years in Charleston to gain distance and perspective. Now I can return with a clear head, instead of wanting to kill somebody myself!" He shook his head. "We don't always know what's best for us, Norah, but if we seek God's will, He works out a plan for us that beats anything we could think up on our own."

"Are you saying you think a period of temporary custody would give me time to gain perspective?"

"I don't want to influence any decision you make, Norah. I can only speak from my own experience."

"Would you mind reading what the attorney will present to the judge," she asked hesitantly, then tried to make a joke of it, "since an eligible bachelor like you has nothing better to do on a beautiful spring evening?"

He grinned at her. "You're right, I don't. It's been pretty hectic for the past few years, but things are winding down now. Besides, I can't think of anyone I'd rather spend this evening with."

She flashed him a grateful smile. "I really appreciate this, Josh."

He glanced over at her as he pulled in at the Trawler, then parked and turned to face her. "If you recall, Norah, the first day we met, I offered my friendship. I knew then. . .well, you know what would settle this whole thing, don't you?"

She winced. "Only in my fantasy!" she said. "But, Josh, that's an impossible dream. About as likely as Scarlett marrying Rhett."

"Have you read the sequel?" he asked.

"No," she admitted.

"Neither have I. So, the ending is up for grabs, isn't it?" He grinned again, showing his white teeth. "Come on. Let's go in. We'll talk and eat and I'll read your papers."

After he read them, he agreed they sounded like the ideal solution for two people intent upon putting a child's best interest first, even above their own. "But that's looking at it unemotionally, Norah," he said. "I can't tell you what your ultimate decision must be. Just consider your options, pray about it, and act according to your best judgment."

Thornton left early Saturday, saying he had appointments to keep. He called late Saturday night to ask Norah if she'd like him or Aunt Tess to meet her and Camille at the dock and take them to his church. She declined.

Instead, on Sunday morning, she left Camille with Eloise and asked Henry to drive her to the ferry, where Josh met her and took her to his church. It was after church that Thornton called again. "I'll be home this afternoon," he said. "We'll have supper, and after Camille is settled for the night, I'd like to take you someplace."

"Where?" she asked, but he wouldn't say.

"Just dress casually. And wear low-heeled shoes."

Chapter 10

Casual, Thornton had said.

Norah grimaced at her reflection in the mirror. Any time she and Thornton Winter spent more than a few minutes together, it was anything but casual!

Nevertheless, she had chosen one of her own outfits instead of Hillary's—a floral print of yellow and pink roses with deep green leaves against a white background. The circle skirt fell to mid-calf; the halter top had an elasticized back and a scooped neckline. That left her shoulders bare, but her hair would cover them.

She suspected he preferred her hair loose and unconfined, so she brushed it out and let it curl freely around her face. The sun had enlivened the copper-colored spirals with a golden sheen.

She spent a little more time than usual with her makeup, enhancing her eyes with a subtle shadow and touching her lips with a dewy rose-colored gloss.

When she was done, she almost stepped into high heels before she remembered he'd specified low-heeled shoes. What, she wondered, did he have in mind? A tea rose crocheted lace flat that she sometimes wore as house-slippers would do nicely.

While fastening a gold loop earring in her earlobe and seeing the expectation in the reflection of her green eyes, she reminded herself that this was not a date. Thornton had just spent a weekend, or part of it, with Madelyn.

A kind of dread seized her. Was he going to soften her up, then present yet another demand? Sighing, she breathed a little prayer and stepped into the game room.

Waiting for her was not the aloof, formal, scowling man in a conservative business suit. Instead, Thornton was wearing a white shirt striped in blue that complemented the silver at his temples and made his eyes appear lighter. He looked incredibly young and fresh. He was sitting on the couch, reading the book Josh had given her, swinging his socked foot for Camille's amusement. The baby lay on a quilt on the floor, turning her head to follow the motion of his foot.

At Norah's approach, Thornton recovered his shoe and got to his feet, looking her over with appreciation, then glancing down. "Good, I see you're wearing sensible shoes." Then he knelt and kissed Camille's head. "Be a sweet girl for Eloise, now."

In the car on the way to the ferry, they commented on the perfect weather. The sun was a golden ball sinking into the sea. Dusk shimmered with a fiery incandescence, either from the retreating sun or the rising moon.

At the dock, there was a surprise for Norah in the garage. "My Rabbit!" she squealed, feeling as if she were seeing an old friend, one who had apparently had a facelift.

"You might want to rename it," he said playfully, holding out a set of keys. "I'm told it no longer hops, skips, and jumps, but purrs like a kitten. But we won't find out tonight. This is my treat. We go in my car."

She slid the keys into her purse and got back into the Mercedes. "Thank you, Thornton, for going to all that trouble. And as soon as you give me the bill, I'll repay you."

"Not that again!" There was an edge to his voice. "Can't you just accept a little Southern hospitality without having to feel obligated?"

She kept quiet for the entire ferry ride. It was only after they had left the ferry and had driven through Mount Pleasant, across a drawbridge, and onto the Cooper River Bridge toward the historic district, that Thornton broke the long silence.

"This place is a paradox," he said. "On one hand, it's a growing, thriving, modern city, but it's also a fascinating port that has preserved its history. Instead of just reading about it in the history books, you can walk through streets, homes, and gardens that are still virtually the same as they were in the mid-1600s."

After he parked on a side street, Thornton led her around a corner and Norah felt as if she had stepped into another world. Horse-drawn carriages rolled along cobblestone streets. Grand houses, reminiscent of the eighteenth and nineteenth centuries, adorned with piazzas and shutters, were guarded by lacy iron fences. Her eyes widened when Thornton pointed out Rainbow Row, an entire block of homes that looked like pastel dollhouses.

"I'm beginning to understand why you've found the past so enchanting," she breathed, looking about her with awe.

Yes, Thornton thought, as he led Norah along the Battery, *enchanting is the word for her.*

They stood at the seawall and looked out over the harbor. "There's Fort Sumter," he said.

"Where?" Her gaze swept the watery expanse. She felt the strong bulk of Thornton's body as he pulled her to his side, encircling her shoulders with his muscular arm.

He pointed out over the churning sea, lapping at the concrete seawall. "There," he said, as if she could see more than lights far across the water. "That's where the War Between the States began about one hundred and fifty years ago."

Her bare shoulder, cool and soft, grew warm beneath his hand, and the sea breeze lifted her hair and trailed it along his arm. They talked on about this and that, their conversation blending with the rhythmic sound of the sea.

Thornton knew the instant Norah became uncomfortable with his arm about her. Her questioning glance barely met his and she grew quiet. He moved his arm away.

They walked on through White Point Gardens. She laughed lightly when he had to dislodge a piece of lacy moss that caught in her hair as she passed under a great live oak. "Pirates once dangled from the gallows here," he said and watched her squirm.

He was enjoying introducing Norah to Charleston, his home. Seeing it through her shining eyes, he felt anew the allure of the old city. Her remarks, once so hostile toward the town he loved so much, were now filled with exclamations of delight.

On the way to the tour houses, he pointed out Catfish Row, which had inspired the opera *Porgy & Bess,* and the Four Corners of Law, an intersection with buildings representing municipal, county, federal, and God's law.

The streets were crowded with people of varying nationalities and economic levels. Some were in groups, being led by tour guides along sidewalks lighted by candles in paper bags, half-filled with sand, to denote the path.

"Oh, it's like Christmas, complete with wooden soldiers!" Norah said, referring to the uniformed guards who stood outside the homes.

"Citadel cadets," Thornton explained. "Chris might even be around here somewhere."

A young couple stood looking at a map, wondering aloud, "Where is Calhoun Mansion?"

Overhearing them, Thornton stopped to say, "That's where we're going. Why don't you just follow us?"

"Are you a tour guide?" the young man asked.

"Tonight I am," Thornton replied enigmatically, noting Norah's look of surprise. He held her hand to keep them together as a wave of sightseers surged around them and passed by.

"Incidentally," Thornton said to the young couple, as they neared Calhoun Mansion, "you'll find the gardens at the mansion particularly interesting. They've been beautifully restored."

They listened intently as Thornton sketched the history of the estate and moved over as curious passersby joined the group. "The house was built after the Civil War by the wealthy merchant and banker, George Walton Williams."

"What kind of architecture?" asked someone in the crowd.

"It's a Victorian Baronial Manor House, built in 1876, with twenty-four thousand square feet, a stairwell that rises to a seventy-five-foot domed ceiling, and a ballroom with a coved glass skylight. The ceilings are fourteen feet high, and the house boasts elaborate chandeliers and ornate plaster and wood moldings."

At his smug look, Norah cast him a sidelong glance and whispered loudly, "Is this your home, Thorn, the one you said was on the historic list?"

"Not so loud," he muttered under his breath.

"Well, you told me you owned one of these mansions," she sweetly persisted.

He scowled ominously. Those who had been following him, hanging on to every word, now peered at him with even greater interest.

As they were walking out, the young man asked, "Do you really live in one of these mansions?"

Thornton shrugged casually. "Mine's just a shack compared with the Calhoun Mansion, but it's near here. She lives out by the ocean," he said, motioning to Norah. "Now there's a different kind of experience. You can get a glimpse of the house from the beach at Seabreeze Island, and it's free!"

"Hey, thanks for telling us. We might just do that." The young man reached for his companion's hand and they slipped away.

"Which one is yours, Thornton?" Norah asked when they were outside and had joined up with a group led by a paid tour guide.

"We'll see if you can guess."

As they neared the next house on the tour, the guide began to explain. "This lovely old mansion is in the Greek Revival style and is characteristic of those built in Ansonborough after the disastrous fire of 1838."

"What was that?" Norah whispered.

"Sh," he reprimanded. "You're not interested in history, remember?"

When the group started inside, Thornton pointed out to Norah the ironwork that surrounded the house, extending to the garden in the back. An iron railing bordered the steps and the colonnaded porch, and there were second- and third-floor balconies across the entire front of the house. They slipped into the living room behind the others just as the guide began to speak again.

"The owners of this house died in a tragic accident and passed the house down to the present owner, a leading designer, builder, and renovator, the renowned Mr. Thornton T. Winter."

Thornton leaned down and spoke in a whisper, "Probably some old stuffed shirt."

Norah stifled a giggle and looked around. The entry vaunted a wide center hall and an elegant staircase that was roped off by a red velvet cord. There was an aura of grandeur and formality, enhanced by the high ceilings, long narrow windows, elegant furnishings, and gleaming antiques. Every room boasted a fireplace.

Along the right side of the house was the living room, a bedroom, and kitchen. Along the left was the parlor, library, and the dining room. "The hall extends to a back entry where stairs lead to a private garden," the guide told them. On the two floors above them, the arrangement of rooms was similar to the first.

"The current owner lives here during the off season," the guide told the crowd, and Norah was reminded that this magnificent house would soon be her new home.

When the tour ended, Thornton lagged behind, eager to learn Norah's reaction. "You don't like it," he said, unable to read her veiled expression.

"Of course I like it," she contradicted. "It's grand and beautiful, and. . . ," she wailed, "I'd be afraid to move or sit on the furniture."

His face clouded. "Norah, you sit on it just like you sit on the wicker furniture at the beach house. Or on the sand. Or the floor."

"It's no place for a baby," she said. "Have you ever seen a baby fly through a house in a walker with rollers on it?"

"You forget that I was brought up here. We didn't have walkers in my day, but I was fourteen when Chris was born, so I remember his childhood well. Haven't you heard the expression, 'If you can't keep the child away from the antique, keep the antique away from the child'?"

"In my part of the world, the word was temptation, not antique," Norah said and laughed lightly.

As they stepped outside, a voice spoke out of the darkness, "Is there a problem, Ma'am?"

Norah spun around. "Chris!" she exclaimed. "I didn't see you there."

He walked up onto the porch. "I had orders to stay out of sight until after you'd seen the house."

"Well, she hasn't seen the house yet, Chris. We're going back in," Thornton explained sternly.

"Sorry, Sir," Chris said in a military monotone. "That's not allowed after the tour has ended. You make such an attempt, and I'll have to report you to the authorities."

Norah tried to suppress her laughter, while Thornton glared.

"Those are my orders, Sir," Chris continued staunchly. "A Citadel man and a Winter man never disobeys orders, Sir."

"You don't take bribes either, do you?" Thornton asked.

"Not unless it's a white Mercedes, Sir!" Chris shouted, standing at attention.

"Suppose you don't get permission for any more weekend leaves?"

"You win, Sir," Chris returned and cut his eyes around at his brother.

"Come on," Thornton said to Norah, giving Chris a good-natured jab as he passed.

Thornton unlocked the door and they stepped into the silent house. Moonlight filtered through the long narrow windows, casting elongated shadows across the floor. Taking her hand, he led her over to the staircase and flipped a switch that lighted a chandelier suspended from the high ceiling above the stairs. He let go of her hand, unhooked the velvet cord, and turned toward her.

This was where Rhett swooped Scarlett up in his arms and raced up the stairs, Norah dreamed. A wicked gleam appeared in Thornton's eyes but died instantly, and he was once again the dignified master of the house, leading the way to the second floor.

"This floor will belong to you and Camille," he said, as he opened a door to an empty room. "The nursery here adjoins your bedroom."

They walked through the empty room and into a bedroom that looked and smelled of polished wood. Norah touched the motif of the bed's carved footposts. Seeing her interest, Thornton explained, "This is an 1800s Charleston-made rice bed."

She followed as he walked across the wool rug onto a dark hardwood floor, past gracefully curved tapestry chairs, by an antique desk, and into an elegant sitting room.

"These were Lantz's rooms," Thornton explained. "If you want anything changed before you move in, just say so. We've moved Chris to the third floor."

"Does he mind?" Norah asked quickly.

"He's delighted," Thornton replied. "The studio is on that floor where the lighting is better. He'll be working with me during the summer, along with creating his own designs."

Norah realized anew how creative this family was, how conscientious. "I wonder what Camille will be when she grows up?" she said reflectively.

"Probably Madam President. Already she exhibits characteristics of being strong-willed and intelligent, not to mention that she's a flaming-haired beauty." He laughed and led the way into the hall.

Norah laughed with him and followed him down the stairs. With each minute, each day, she gained a better understanding of why Lantz had asked Thornton to take care of his child. How selfish it would be of her to deny Camille the opportunity to grow up under the Winter influence.

"Aunt Tess has volunteered to stay here at night, if you'd feel better," he said. "She can take one of the rooms on second. Hilda comes every day and stays overnight whenever she wants. Her rooms are on the basement floor."

At the bottom of the stairs, Norah's eyes swept toward the parlor on the left, the living room on the right. "It's a lovely home."

"Thank you," he said simply. "Now, let me show you where you'll be working."

"Working?"

He grinned. "Weren't you the one who insisted on paying her own way?"

Feeling lighthearted, Norah followed him into the library, where he switched on the light. On the earlier tour, she had been impressed by the two walls of mahogany bookshelves reaching from floor to ceiling. A huge mahogany desk dominated the room, positioned in front of cabinets where Thornton kept sketching supplies. In the center of the outside wall was a brick fireplace with two chairs pulled up in front.

A silver frame on the desk caught Norah's eye. She walked over and picked it up. "What is this?" she asked, puzzled, turning it sideways, then upside down.

"A conversation piece, you might say," Thornton replied in an offhanded manner.

Norah glanced at him skeptically, then squinted. "Of course," she said, "it's a picture of the emperor's new clothes!"

Thornton's short laugh quickly subsided, and Norah noticed the guarded look that came into his eyes. He stood stiffly erect, his fingers touching the desk, some dark thought shadowing his face.

Norah lowered her gaze to the picture frame. A conversation piece, he'd said. In the silence, the part of her that sensed and responded to the deeper concerns of a hurting human being longed to reach out to him, to ask him what had caused that sudden withdrawal into himself. But how? "I don't hear any conversation," she quipped.

"You're making too much of this," Thornton said with irritation. "It's only an empty frame. I used to put sketches of a dream house in there as it developed. Then one day the dream vanished. The sketches have been. . .burned. But," he said abruptly, moving toward the door, "enough of that. Let's go." He switched off the light.

The glow from the upstairs chandelier silhouetted his tall frame in the doorway and sent a long shadow across the floor.

"Do you know when is the best time to answer a child's questions?" Norah flung across the dark gulf now separating them. When he made no response, she answered her own question, "When they ask."

"Forever the psychologist, aren't you?" he scoffed.

"You said I was family," she returned, having learned that his gruffness was a façade, a cover-up for some pain in his heart. She wanted to know—needed to know—what that was. Risking his displeasure, she walked over to the nearest chair and sat down.

Yes, he thought to himself, as Camille's blood relative, *Norah was family.* But she was also strong-willed, independent, stubborn—very much her own appealing person. Theirs was a relationship they'd have to discuss. He hadn't intended it to be tonight, but the carefree mood of earlier evening was gone. He would have to tell her his intentions for the future. And the best way might be to preface them with a brief sketch of his own past.

"I've never had a sister before," he said, turning back into the shadowed room.

"And I've never had a brother," she said, "but I guess it's sort of like having a sister."

"And how was that?"

Norah thought. "In difficult times we stuck together like glue. In good times we fought like. . ." She paused, seeing him perch on the edge of the desk, arms folded over his chest.

"Like my brothers and I," he finished. "Primarily Lantz. We were close, but he was headstrong, belligerent, wouldn't listen to anyone."

Norah suppressed a smile. Thornton could very well be describing himself. Lantz, compared with Thornton, was only a mild breeze.

He picked up the empty picture frame and stared at it. Norah waited in suspense, reminding herself that she should not feel disappointed, but elated, that he was willing to talk to her like a sister.

"Norah," he said into the dimness, "that first night, you talked about children needing more than material things. Well, so do adults." His eyes swept the room. "People from all over the world come to see this house, to admire it, maybe to wish they could live in one like it." He spoke gravely. "But for the past two years, the worst days of my life have been spent here."

Norah caught the flicker of anguish in his eyes before he quickly concealed it. "Madelyn and I were engaged," he said, staring at the frame, seeing his own life unfold. "Her parents and mine were friends. For years, she was of no particular concern of mine. I was getting out of college by the time she was entering. There were plenty of females around in those days, and Winter men are traditionally career-oriented and don't marry until we're well established in careers."

"They don't. . .fall in love?" she asked, incredulous.

He gave a wry smile. "I'm not one to think of love as something so trivial as butterflies and bells. Love, to me, involves far more than fluttery feelings. I think of love as a design that begins with a few lines on paper, then grows and develops. . .sometimes quickly, sometimes very slowly. And sometimes. . . ," he said, setting the empty frame on the desk, "the sketches don't work."

He went over to sit in the chair opposite her. "Anyway," he said, resuming his story, "the death of my parents put everything on hold for me for awhile. Later, Chris finished high school and Lantz was into his acting career. Madelyn came home from Paris, having just broken off an engagement, her third. But that didn't concern me unduly. She was in her late twenties, quite beautiful, and we seemed to have much in common."

Thornton paused, staring at Norah in the dim light, as if seeing her for the first time.

"Wh—what?" she asked uneasily.

"Just a thought," he said. Tradition, family background, financial and historic ties to Charleston—those were the common roots that bound him to Madelyn. On the other hand, despite her youth, Norah possessed many remarkable Christian virtues—deep conviction, responsibility, loyalty, self-sacrifice, a giving spirit. Had this been what Lantz meant when he'd said they had something in common?

Norah dared not move, dared not venture a question, but waited for Thornton to continue.

"We began seeing each other," he said, taking up the story. "All things considered, it seemed right that we should marry. She accepted my ring. The engagement was announced in the paper." He paused and drew a deep breath. "Lantz came home for the engagement party."

Norah closed her eyes. She could guess the rest.

"I don't know exactly when it started, but I do know the attraction was instant and. . .mutual. I tried to dismiss it. Most men would find her attractive. And women had always been drawn to Lantz."

He looked over at Norah and she met his steady gaze. *Not I*, she was thinking. He looked again into the dark gaping hole of the fireplace. "Madelyn was older than Lantz, however, and she was engaged to me. I was his brother, his guardian. I can't fault anyone for honest emotion. However, I did expect better than I received from these two people who claimed to love me."

"Are you sure. . . ?"

"Oh, yes," he interrupted before she could finish the thought. "I found out in a most dramatic way after Lantz told Madelyn it was over, that he had found someone else, whom I now know was your sister."

"You must have been heartbroken," she said.

"No," he said brusquely. "I would have been heartbroken if they had come

438

to me, confessed honestly that they were in love and wanted to break the engagement." He shook his head sadly. "But she wore my ring the entire time she was seeing Lantz. I was not heartbroken. I was. . ." He searched for a word. "Furious! Outraged!"

"Did you try to harm her?" Norah asked, her heart in her mouth.

Thornton bent his head and, for one brief moment, she suspected he was crying. Then he lifted his head and laughed. "No, it was the other way around. She almost killed me. . .in an automobile accident." He waved his hand in dismissal. "It's a long story."

He got up and walked over to the desk again, his back to her, gazing at the picture frame. "I was sketching a home for her. I felt that a house should be built around a family, instead of fitting a family into a house." Then he turned to face her. "In the hospital, Lantz asked me to forgive him."

"And did you?"

"I said the words." He looked up toward the tall ceiling. "It's not that easy, but I think I'm getting close."

"And did Madelyn ask for your forgiveness?"

"A hundred times or more," he said distantly.

Norah felt he'd entered another world. The room suddenly seemed so dark and chilly. How could they have done that to him? How could he stand it? Was he in the process of forgiving Madelyn now? Did he still love her and want her back?

Norah rose and walked to the window, where soft moonlight filtered through. Perhaps it would warm the chill she felt inside.

"Now I've spoiled our evening, haven't I?" Thornton apologized, walking over to stand beside her.

"No, I wanted to know so I could understand."

"And do you?" he asked softly.

"No." She felt the stirrings of anger as she looked into his face. "I don't understand how they could do that to you! I don't understand how any woman would choose Lantz over you!" She caught her breath, horrified at her admission.

She heard his intake of breath, saw his lips parted slightly. Didn't he know that Madelyn wasn't right for him? She'd hurt him so deeply, far deeper than a cut on the face.

"Oh, Thornton," she whispered as she brought her hand to his cheek, and before she could say more, he spoke in a warning tone, "Norah, don't," and even as she lifted her lips to his wounded face, he was saying, "Don't do this, Norah."

She didn't listen. He felt the velvet smoothness of her lips, like a healing balm, move across his cheek. Felt the soft press of her warm body against his chest, melting his frozen heart. He grasped her shoulders and held her gently away from him. Her face was turned to his, her eyes moist with caring.

"Norah," he said huskily as his head bent toward hers, drawn by the play of moonlight on her lips, "don't. . .don't let me do this."

Suddenly, caught in a powerful undertow, she felt the sand shifting beneath her feet and she was being swept away. There was no time nor space, only the impossible, wonderful feeling of Thornton Winter's arms around her, holding her close.

She swayed on the waves of emotion as his lips touched first the moonlight on her face, her eyelids, her lips—softly, gently. Her arms went around his neck and Thornton's hand wound its way through the silky strands of her hair.

"Norah, Norah. . .I didn't mean—" He stopped, turned from her, and grasped the drapes, his chest rising with his breathing.

Why did he look at her as if he didn't know who she was? Was he thinking of Madelyn? Wishing she were in his arms? Had he intended a peck on the cheek as one might kiss a baby. . .or a sister? Norah hugged her arms to herself. She'd never be able to look at him again.

Then he reached over and touched her trembling lips with his finger. "I. . .told you not to let me kiss you." His reprimand was infinitely tender.

"Well," she said, as forcefully as she could muster, with the breath driven from her body, "don't you know that you can't tell me what to do, Thornton Winter? I make my own decisions."

Lifting her chin, she turned on her heel and walked over to the chair in front of the fireplace, sinking into it. It was useless to tell her heart to be still. She felt she could understand her sister better now. How in a weak moment one could make wrong, irrevocable decisions.

Thinking of Hillary and Lantz, she spoke up. "Thornton, as I told you before, I won't submit myself to the kind of situation that my sister was in."

He turned abruptly and came to take the chair opposite her. "I wasn't suggesting that at all, Norah," he said staunchly. "Believe me. It was. . .just a kiss."

Just a kiss? Norah thought. Then it had meant nothing to him.

"Not that it wasn't wonderful, Norah. But now that you know I find you lovely and desirable, and that you respond to me, we must decide what to do about it." He rose and began to pace the floor.

Thornton knew what he had to say, regardless of his feelings. He and Norah were both vulnerable right now, could take advantage of each other and justify it on the basis of what was good for Camille. His gaze moved to the empty picture frame on the desk. He'd been fooled once. It couldn't happen

440

again. A kiss changed nothing. He did not live his life on emotion, but logic.

"Norah," he said, beginning to present the scenario, "soon we will be living here as a family. You and I will function as parents. This will be your home as well as mine. However, our commitment is to Camille and not to each other. Your reputation is to be considered, as well as my own obligations, which I cannot, in all good conscience, abandon."

Norah closed her eyes as if that would prevent his saying more. But it didn't. "Therefore, I will continue seeing Madelyn, and I suggest that you make friends and pursue a personal life of your own."

Well, what did he think? That just because he had paid her a few compliments she was ready to fall at his feet? That just because he had come to her like a hurricane, churning her emotions and turning her life upside down, she had fallen in love with him? And that just because he'd kissed her, she would forever define her life on the basis of one emotionally-packed encounter in the moonlight?

Well, if so, he was right.

Never had she expected to be grateful for all those acting lessons. If actors could learn to produce tears instantly, then perhaps they could learn to hold them back. She blinked hard and reentered the world of reality.

"Have you ever been in love, Norah?"

"Almost," she whispered breathlessly, "but he was dying with leukemia. So there was nothing physical, only regret for what could never be between us." Thornton leaned over to cover her hands with his own as she continued, "It was a kind of spiritual love, I guess, deep and good and pure. Wonderful, really. But I know that was partly because it had to end." She looked at him through misty eyes.

"Here," he said, rising to pull her to her feet, "let me comfort you. Isn't that what friends are for?" She succumbed to the security of his embrace, wishing she could stay there forever. "This is what we need to be able to do, Norah. Relate to each other without being self-conscious. I want you to know that you are special to me. I need you in my life."

Of course, he told himself, *I need her for Camille. What else?* She made him laugh, she challenged him, she complimented him when other women thought his wound such a tragedy, and even Madelyn could not look at him without crying. Yes, he needed Norah.

He needs me, Norah thought. *He needs me to care for Camille. . . .* She shrugged off the thought. She didn't care. She'd never hurt him as Madelyn had, and as long as he needed her, she would be there.

"We'd better go now," Thornton whispered. But as she turned to leave the room, he put out his hand and grasped her arm. "Wait. I think you ought to know that there will never be a repeat of what happened here tonight."

He flipped the switch that turned out the upstairs light, and they walked out into the cool, crisp night.

"And I think you ought to know," she said, as they walked to the car, "that I didn't hear any bells or feel any butterflies."

"Neither did I," he said blandly, then glanced up and smiled at the stars. They'd never looked so bright.

Chapter 11

On Monday, John Grimes called to tell them that Judge Lee wanted to see the baby before making a final decision and would expect to see Thornton and Norah in her chambers the next day.

"What if the judge rules that we can't have custody?" Norah asked fearfully. "Will Camille be made a ward of the court?"

"Don't even think it," Thornton moaned.

On Tuesday morning, feeling apprehensive, the two of them were seated in Judge Lee's office with Camille looking her best in a white knit dress trimmed in pink with matching headband and wearing her first real shoes, a pair of black patent leather Mary Janes.

The judge couldn't keep her eyes off Camille and compared her with her own two children at that age, casually dropping in references to the custody hearing. It made the proceedings much easier to take, Norah thought, though as far as she could tell, everything seemed to be going in Thornton's favor. His qualifications were impeccable since he had been his brothers' guardian for the past twelve years, and everyone knew his reputation as an upstanding businessman in the community.

When Camille became restless and began to whimper, Thornton walked around the room with her so Norah could speak with Judge Lee without interruption. She had no problem relating her feelings. She'd had plenty of practice trying to convince Thornton Winter.

The personal questioning, however, was quite blunt. Norah hoped the judge did not notice the blush she tried to hide when she was asked if she and Thornton had any romantic interest in each other. The discussion they had had the night he kissed her had put everything into perspective. Thank goodness that was settled!

"We've settled that matter," Thornton said, echoing Norah's thoughts. "Miss Browne is quite young and needs friends her own age, while I have. . .a prior commitment."

"Do either of you plan to marry in the foreseeable future?" the judge asked, her eyebrows raised over her tortoise-shell glasses. She seemed satisfied when they responded in the negative.

Judge Lee explained why custody could not be permanent. Norah was new to the area and had her own adjustments to make. She might decide that Charleston was not where she wished to make her permanent residence. They were both single. Situations could change. If that occurred, the court should be notified immediately.

"Six months joint custody," the judge ruled, tapping her gavel lightly.

Norah paled as the papers were put in front of her. Camille's future would soon be a matter of a legal transaction. But it was only temporary custody. Norah signed.

"Let me hold the baby," Judge Lee said and took her from Thornton, who stepped up to the desk and placed his signature on the document.

When he looked up, Norah saw that his eyes were misty. He reached for Norah and held her close. "Thank you," he said and she knew he'd been right. They should be able to behave as good friends, and good friends hugged each other in times of emotional stress.

After the brief embrace, they moved away. Norah's eyes, too, were wet.

"You're a lucky little girl," the judge crooned, and Camille grabbed her glasses. "Feisty too."

Norah couldn't resist a parting word as she gathered up Camille and her belongings to leave. "Takes after her uncle."

~

They began making the move into the house on Meeting Street the following day but would not complete the move until after the weekend. Norah had wanted the transition to be as smooth and natural as possible for Camille, so together they had decided that they would spend most weekends at the beach house, since the baby's swimming lessons were scheduled for Saturday.

Hilda, a tall, dark-skinned woman with a handsome face and flashing black eyes, moved into her rooms downstairs and set to work transforming the place.

Their first night in the townhouse, Hilda set a bowl in front of Norah. "Let's see how you like this," she said with a dare in her tone.

Norah dipped her soup spoon into the bowl and tasted. "Wonderful!" she proclaimed. With her second spoonful, she allowed a little to dribble down her chin, much to Hilda's delight. "I've never tasted anything like it. What is it?"

"She-crab soup," Hilda said proudly.

When she returned to the kitchen, Thornton leaned over and touched Norah's arm. "That was your initiation. I think she might let you stay."

Norah soon learned that Hilda had every right to be proud. She had more energy than three people, served delicious Southern fare that she insisted was reduced in fat and cholesterol, and kept the household running on a schedule, as much as possible with a baby in the house.

Thornton had Camille's Babyland furniture taken out of storage and shipped to the house. When Norah turned on the clown lamp, Camille stared at it curiously. She was restless that night, and Norah wondered if she might have some memory associated with the loss of her parents. So she held Camille longer than usual, even after she had finally drifted off to sleep.

Norah mentioned it to Thornton. After a thoughtful moment, he made a suggestion. "Perhaps we should have Eloise stop in a few days a week, so Camille won't feel she's lost another person she's grown close to."

Norah agreed, pleased with his sensitivity, and Aunt Tess, as busy as she was with her church work and garden club, also dropped in frequently for meals and visits. Thornton, too, rearranged his office schedule so he could spend time with Camille during her waking hours.

When he described the assistance Norah could give him in his work, she no longer doubted that it was a "real" job. He spent most of the day at his office, while she worked in the library at the house, researching, writing, editing, and recording information about homes and buildings he would renovate. Occasionally, she accompanied him on visits to potential clients. Once or twice, when they were working together, she noticed him shoving a pad of paper out of sight when she came near, as if it were something she shouldn't see. Probably one of those sketches "unfit for human eyes" when it was first started, she decided.

Norah's favorite time of day, though, was late evening, after she and Thornton had settled in the library to discuss some project or plan the next day's work. She loved hearing him talk about his plans and dreams and soon learned that renovation meant much more than a new room or a fresh coat of paint.

Thornton compared it with one's spiritual life. "It's like a rebirth, Norah," he explained, leaning back in his desk chair. "I gain satisfaction by taking something timeworn, faded, broken, and restoring its natural beauty. I love to make it useful again."

"You make renovation sound almost human," Norah mused aloud.

He smiled. "With people, the results are even more rewarding."

"Then you should feel very rewarded," she said softly.

She might have been referring to his brothers. Or Camille. But Thornton suspected that Norah was talking about herself. He knew she badly needed the security, stability, and family life that he made possible for her. It was, indeed, gratifying to know that he had enabled her life to be fulfilled in so many ways.

Still, he tried not to think of time passing so quickly. It was like Judge Lee had said—too much was temporary, changeable. And he strongly feared that someone was going to be hurt. Deeply.

But for the moment, he would enjoy this newfound happiness. It was just a matter of time until he would be able to forgive both Lantz and Madelyn.

He felt it happening. Life was too good, too busy, too full, to allow bitterness to thrive in his soul.

~

Norah had grown to love the sound of the bells of St. Michael's pealing through the city on Sunday morning, to appreciate the look of the historic old churches she had once disdained. And one Sunday after services at the Mount Pleasant church, where she was still attending with Josh, Thornton gave her a tour. Rather than stuffy, the mellow old building seemed worshipful and beautiful with its ornate carvings, chancel decorations, high pulpit, cushioned foot rests, and box pews with hinged doors.

Filled with a new awareness of God's omnipresence—past, present, and future—she knew He was here just as fully as in Josh's church, though she still felt a need for the down-to-earthness of the simple people in Mount Pleasant. It was her one activity separate and distinct from Thornton Winter's world in which she had become so enmeshed.

Surprisingly, Thornton had relented, allowing her to take Camille to the church in Mount Pleasant. He insisted upon driving them there and picking them up, however, although it was out of the way and his church was within walking distance of the house on Meeting Street.

"Make sure Josh or someone is with you, in case something happens to delay me," he warned.

It suddenly occurred to Norah that he might fear kidnapping. Camille was the child of celebrities and in the custody of a very prominent man. "Do you think it's safe?" she asked, disturbed.

"In Mount Pleasant, at that church, yes," he said, "and Josh Logan has had an impeccable reputation for the past eight years."

"You had him checked out?"

"Aunt Tess retired from the College last year, remember?" he retorted.

As it turned out, Thornton was never late. It became a weekly ritual that the Rolls, which he kept in town, would appear in the parking lot promptly at the conclusion of the service, and he'd be standing against it in his conservative suit, with his arms folded across his chest.

The first Sunday, Norah wasn't surprised to see Aunt Tess in front, but was astounded to see Madelyn sitting in the back. And when Norah climbed in with Camille, Madelyn was unusually gracious to her and entranced with the baby, who waved her arms and gurgled, apparently intrigued with the bright red color of the designer creation Madelyn was wearing.

"She's so pretty," said Madelyn in her soft Southern drawl. "May. . .I touch her?"

Norah, who had never heard the woman speak more than two words, was startled, but nodded in agreement, then watched as Madelyn extended a long, graceful finger, tipped with a perfectly polished nail. Out of the corner of her eye, Norah saw Aunt Tess turn her head to peek around the front seat.

Madelyn had barely touched the velvety skin before Camille grabbed her pearl bracelet.

"Uh-oh! We wouldn't want to get those in your mouth," Norah said gently. She unfastened the tiny hands. But Camille didn't want to be unfastened and wailed as if someone had struck her.

"Oh, I'm so sorry!" Madelyn said, shrinking back against the seat. There was a shadow in the blue eyes, and her lips trembled.

"It's not your fault," Norah said quickly. "All babies try to put things in their mouths. Here, hold up your arm."

Madelyn obeyed reluctantly.

"Now, Camille, touch the pretty bracelet, ea–sy," Norah said, guiding her hand. "Ea–sy." The wailing stopped and Camille began to enjoy the game.

Madelyn's expression softened. The look in her eyes was lovely and adoring, and Norah knew that, unless Madelyn was a schizophrenic, she was innately a very gentle person.

For an instant, Norah felt some unnamed dread, and her eyes met Thornton's in the rearview mirror. He quickly shifted his gaze to the road, and a muscle in his face twitched as his jaw tightened.

What it all meant, Norah didn't know. But the routine persisted. Each Sunday, Madelyn came home with them and stayed for Hilda's fabulous dinner and a leisurely visit afterward. And each week, within the nurturing family circle, and with the innocent baby to focus their attention upon, Madelyn opened up just a little more, blossoming like a lovely flower before their eyes.

One day soon after a particularly pleasant Sunday afternoon, Thornton said to Norah, "I think it's time you got to know Madelyn."

Norah was puzzled. "But I already know her."

"I am speaking as your employer now. The McCallas have decided to renovate. I need you to do research, make notes, take measurements, that kind of thing. We need to know the personalities of all the people in the home in order to do the job justice."

Much to Norah's surprise, she found the McCallas to be a charming couple whose heritage was as impressive as Thornton's. Their home was an antebellum plantation home, surrounded by huge old oaks. More surprising was Madelyn's overture of friendship.

"I'm sorry I behaved so badly when we first met," she confided, telling Norah that she had been in love with Thornton, then Lantz, and had been at the Winter house when Lantz broke off the relationship. She had been devastated. Thornton had returned home while the argument was taking place and had seen Madelyn run outside and jump into her car. He had followed and had managed to climb in before she roared off.

"I wanted to die," Madelyn explained in a whispery voice, "so I didn't even notice the storm or the rain-soaked roads. I just pushed the gas pedal to the floorboard. Thorn tried to stop me, but the car planed and left the road. It hit an embankment and overturned."

Madelyn put her hands over her face, and Norah had to strain to hear her next words. "The air bag protected me, but the passenger's side wasn't protected. His face. . .was full of glass and metal."

Madelyn couldn't talk any more that day, but on Norah's second visit, she learned that, after she'd seen the damage to Thornton's face, Madelyn had taken an overdose of sleeping pills and had been under a doctor's care ever since, recuperating in the home of relatives in Paris.

"Every time I look at him, I could just die," she groaned. Tears of guilt and remorse slid down her beautiful face. "Thornton has helped me with the guilt. He says he's forgiven me." There was a haunted look in the beautiful eyes. "But how can a person forgive someone for ruining his life?"

Though Norah didn't say so, she was more concerned about what Madelyn had done to his heart. And a few weeks later, she discovered that Madelyn, too, was not insensitive to that aspect of their relationship.

Madelyn's parents had dropped her off at the house with some written suggestions concerning the renovation. While she talked with Thornton in the library, Norah went upstairs to read for awhile. Later, she decided to go down and see if Thornton was ready to discuss the instructions with her.

Seeing a faint light from the living room and hearing the sound of voices, Norah paused. Madelyn must still be here. Nearing the room, Norah froze and stepped back into the shadows. Through the gap in the partially opened door, she could see the two of them standing very close together. Madelyn was gazing up into Thornton's face.

"I made a terrible mistake, Thorn," she was saying. "I'm so sorry. It's you I love. I've always loved you."

"We'll talk about it later, Madelyn," Thornton said gently. "We'll go to dinner tomorrow night and discuss it then."

Norah couldn't bear to hear any more, but turned and fled back up the stairs. She shouldn't have listened, shouldn't have watched. She didn't want to admit that Madelyn had become a very likable person—now that Thornton was restoring her.

～

Time was passing quickly. Before long, the end of the six-month period would be upon them. Norah had tried to establish a life of her own. She'd really tried. Sometimes she went to lunch with Josh, to youth outings, or an occasional dinner. Theirs was a good, solid friendship. He needed to talk about his murdered sister as much as she needed to talk about her life in the Winter household. And, without discussing it, Josh knew how she felt about Thornton Winter. She'd miss their talks when he left at the end of the summer.

It was during the weekend of July fourth, which they celebrated at the beach house, that Thornton and Norah decided to throw a party for Camille's six-month birthday during the third week in July. Norah added that she would also like to give a going-away party for Josh, who would be returning to North Carolina in August. They decided to combine the two and invite only family and a few close friends.

Norah asked the young couple who ran the church nursery. Aunt Tess invited the dean of the college. Chris brought a young couple and a pretty girl named Jennifer. Madelyn was there, of course, with her parents. But the big surprise was the young pastor of Thornton's church, who came with his wife and their two small children. Their youth and friendliness belied Norah's old conviction that historic churches must surely have equally stuffy pastors.

It was a casual afternoon affair, and no one was dressed up—except for the guest of honor. Camille was adorable in a new yellow dress, compliments of Norah, and her black Mary Janes.

There were gifts galore—a battery-run Sesame Street train set from Thornton, a five-foot inflatable dragon from Chris, and an adorable music box that played "Jesus Loves Me" from Josh, among others. But Camille wasn't about to be confined to her new walker, a gift from Aunt Tess, and insisted on being passed from one adult to another.

Norah was busy snapping pictures all afternoon—the guests, the birthday girl, the cake. She even got one of Josh leading them all in a rousing rendition of "Happy Birthday" as they gathered around the table.

It was after cake and ice cream that Mrs. McCalla asked to hold Camille. The baby loved all the attention and sat on Mrs. McCalla's lap while Mr. McCalla entertained her with a stuffed, talking Mickey Mouse. Madelyn knelt in front of them, her eyes shining. Mrs. McCalla glanced over at Thornton and said wistfully, "Oh, I've wanted grandchildren for so long."

The four of them made a touching little tableau, Norah realized, suddenly feeling out of place. She took the picture reluctantly.

Feeling her gaze on him, Thornton looked up and sensed her distress but wasn't sure of its source. Then he watched as Josh observed it too.

"Let's all pitch in and clear this mess so we can start the games. You have to have games at a party," he said loudly with a huge grin.

Soon he had everyone involved in silly relay games, laughing and completely enjoying themselves. Thornton held Camille, who chortled in delight at the scene. But the afternoon's excitment was taking its toll.

After the guests had gone, Norah got the cranky baby settled for her nap while Thornton talked to Josh about his home and family in North Carolina and his plans for the future.

Later, Josh and Norah walked down to the beach. When they returned, Eloise made a light supper, Thornton declining Norah's invitation to eat with them on the deck.

Instead, he looked in on Camille, who was sleeping peacefully. Eloise had gone to her room. With no one to talk to, he returned to the game room. All the birthday wrappings had been picked up and the new toys stacked neatly. A glance through the windows told him it was getting dark, but he decided against turning on the deck lights.

Outside, Norah and Josh sat on the unlighted deck, while Norah tried to tell him how much she valued his friendship.

"It's mutual, Norah," Josh returned. "I think God knew you needed somebody by your side, and I needed someone to talk to about my sister. Nobody mentions her anymore at home. So thank you. And remember, we're friends. That means from now on!"

He stood, took her hands and began to sing, softly at first, then filling the night air with his rich baritone.

At first, Thornton thought someone had turned on the radio. Glancing out the window, he saw Norah and Josh standing very close together, their hands entwined. When Josh finished his song, their arms went around each other, and Thornton turned away, climbed the stairs, and sat on his deck for a very long time.

He knew when they drove to the dock, and he knew when Norah returned alone a few minutes later. Coming downstairs, he met her as she was coming into the house.

"I wanted you to know that my surgery—the reconstructive surgery for my face—is scheduled for next week, Norah."

Norah gasped. He hadn't mentioned it in ages.

He touched the raised scars. "The doctors said the scars would contract. That's why the skin is pulled and tight. It's meticulous work, of course, but relatively simple. We don't expect any problems."

She knew better, even as she asked the question. "Do you want me to go with you?"

"Thank you, but that won't be necessary." He added quickly, "Madelyn will be going with me. She feels a need to be there."

Norah's heart wrenched. *And what do you think I feel?*

He stood there, running his finger over the ridges in his face. She knew he had something else on his mind. "You're taking it well," he said at last.

"Well, you just told me the operation will be relatively simple."

"I was speaking of Josh's leaving."

She nodded, feeling the loss already. "I'll miss him," she admitted. "He's leaving one day next week, but I don't think we'll see each other again. Camille and I will go to your church Sunday." She looked down. "That is, if you still want us to."

At one time, Thornton would have been overjoyed with that announcement. Now there was another pressing matter on his mind. "We'll talk tomorrow. Good night."

"Good night," Norah whispered, staring at the empty space where he had been long after he had left to go down the hallway toward his room.

He would have his surgery. Madelyn would be with him. What more was there to say?

Chapter 12

The next day there was not a breath of breeze stirring. The sun was a blazing ball in the sky, and there had been no cooling shower for over a week. Camille was especially fussy, and Norah awoke with a dull headache.

"I don't feel like going to church," she told Thornton. "And since Camille hasn't been to the nursery at your church, I'll keep her here with me."

Norah did look peaked, as if she hadn't slept well. Thornton nodded in concern. "Then get some rest. We'll be back for lunch."

Only Thornton and Madelyn came, as Aunt Tess had plans to visit a friend in the hospital. But Norah didn't feel much like joining them at the table, not with Madelyn looking cool and beautiful in white and gold, glowing like a frosty light bulb.

As the afternoon sun made its descent, the air cooled a little. But still no breeze stirred. Norah thought she and Camille might be more comfortable outside and took her to the far end of the deck, beyond the pool in the shade of the trees.

The walker was new to Camille and, for awhile, she played with the colored wooden rings along the tray. Soon she was distracted by the other toys Norah placed on the tray and made a game of tossing them on the deck for Norah to retrieve. Each time Norah bent over, however, she felt the throbbing in her head and became freshly irritated with Thornton. By the time he and Madelyn finally strolled into view from far down the island, she was thoroughly put out with him.

Leaving Madelyn under the shade of a flowering shrub in the garden, Thornton walked up to Norah. "Feeling better?"

"No."

"Anything I can do?"

"You can pick up the toys when Camille drops them. My head is splitting."

He pulled a chair close. "Norah, I'm sorry. I thought you wanted to be left alone."

"I do," she said, feeling the threat of tears. She mustn't cry.

"It's Josh, isn't it?"

A gasp raked her throat. Of course that was part of it. "Not entirely," she said. "It's just an off day. Everyone has them. It's hot, and I have a headache."

Thornton kept leaning down to pick up the toys Camille was throwing. She was fretful. She'd be crying soon. "You need some help. I'll get Eloise."

"No," Norah said. "When the baby's fussy, she needs a parent." Norah regretted the look of guilt that crossed his face at her implication. She knew she was being unfair. But she felt so miserable.

"Norah, there's something I've been needing to say to you. . . ."

She'd been expecting this. But she couldn't bear to hear it. Not now.

"Madelyn's fragile, Norah, not strong like you." Now that he'd begun, the words came quickly. "She's been so filled with guilt. She couldn't believe that God and I could forgive her. It hasn't been easy to make her believe it."

It was all she could do to endure the excitement in his eyes as he proclaimed Madelyn's virtues. "She's begun to emerge as a whole person, now that she's ridding herself of guilt. She's becoming the woman she used to be—loving, gracious. . ."

"Good for her!" snapped Norah, seeing a white vision approach from the other side of the pool. Feeling as if the top of her head were about to explode, she jumped up, rammed her toe into the walker, and half hobbled, half ran toward a cluster of trees.

Camille was making whining, engine-revving noises.

But Thornton wasn't through. It had to be now, or he could never go through with it. He followed her to the shady spot where she clung weakly to a palm. "There's more I need to say, Norah."

"I don't want to hear it," she protested. If he said another word, she'd scream.

But the scream didn't come from Norah.

The sound pierced the air like some high-pitched signal of disaster. Loud and long and frantic. Norah and Thornton turned. They saw it all in one blinding flash. They ran, but it was too late. The scene had already been set. As if in slow motion, they could see the bright-colored ball rolling into the pool, floating temptingly on the surface, Camille in hot pursuit, her red ringlets bobbing up and down, the walker picking up speed by the second, while the baby's arms and legs pumped wildly.

Eloise, seeing the impending disaster from the glass doors, could only scream helplessly and run back in to dial the emergency number.

Norah and Thornton ran, but it seemed as if their legs were weighted, as in some awful nightmare. As soon as the front wheels left the poolside, the walker tipped over, dislodging the baby and plunging her into the water head first, then toppling in on top of her.

For one horrifying moment, they lost sight of Camille. Her ball bobbed innocently nearby, reflecting the dazzling sunlight. Had she already hurtled to the bottom? Was she trapped beneath the walker?

Norah was right behind Thornton, who plunged in, shoes and all. Then they were all in the pool. Madelyn reached the screaming baby first, lifting Camille over her head, then going down with her mouth and eyes wide open in frozen terror.

Norah grabbed the baby and Thornton dove for Madelyn. Before Norah could reach the side of the pool, she realized that Camille was gurgling happily, splashing the water with her hands and feet. The baby seemed happier than she had all day, delighted with her impromptu diving lesson.

Eloise ran out and took the soggy child from Norah. "I'll check her over," she said. "I called an ambulance and the pediatrician."

Looking around, Norah saw Thornton struggling to roll a limp Madelyn over the side of the pool and swam over to help.

The sound of sirens announced the arrival of the EMTs, but Thornton had already revived Madelyn by the time they got to the pool with their stretcher. He wrapped his arm around her shoulders while she coughed and gagged and spit up water. Then unmindful of their bedraggled condition, her lovely white dress plastered against her body, Thornton held her, rocking back and forth, while she sobbed out her relief.

Feeling drippy and drained, Norah hurried inside to be with Camille, who was proclaimed none the worse for her ordeal by the pediatrician. By nightfall, however, she had a slight fever, diagnosed as a virus, and was put to bed early.

By the next day, Camille was her bright little self again. Norah, on the other hand, was ill with flu-like symptoms and felt sick enough to die. She deserved to, she knew. What if Camille had not been thrown out of the walker? What if Madelyn hadn't been there? What if. . . ?

~

On Sunday night, they moved back to the town house, and Thornton drove Madelyn back to the McCallas. On Monday he was back, along with Aunt Tess, Hilda, and Eloise. Norah could eat nothing, and when anyone looked in on her to see what she might need, she shook her head, put her hands over her face, and dissolved into fresh tears.

By Tuesday morning her fever was gone and her throat felt better, but she was reluctant to hold Camille, though she longed to cuddle her close.

"What you need is some nourishment, Miss Norah," Hilda declared, propping the pillows behind her head. "You need to get your strength back." She left to prepare her famous milk toast.

But it was Thornton who brought in the tray. Norah nervously ran her fingers through her uncombed hair. She must look awful. "Feeling better?" he asked as cheerfully as he could manage. She glanced at him, and the water-works started again.

He set the tray on the bedside table and sat on the edge of her bed. "I know," he said. "You must feel like I do." His swimming eyes overflowed.

"It's my fault," she choked out.

"No more than mine," he insisted.

"Madelyn saved her life, Thornton. I shudder to think. . ."

"Madelyn can't even swim, Norah," he said incredulously.

Norah's tears halted. "Wh–what?"

He nodded. "Her younger sister drowned in a swimming pool when Madelyn was four. She saw it happen and ran to tell her mother. It's her earliest memory and she's been deathly afraid of water ever since."

"She. . .risked her life," Norah breathed in amazement, "while I was. . . thinking about myself. Oh, Thornton. . ."

"No," he soothed, laying a comforting hand over her clenched fists. "We were both supposed to be watching Camille. You have to forgive yourself, as I have to forgive myself. We made a mistake, Norah, but we musn't punish ourselves like Madelyn has done."

Madelyn! "I must thank her," she said, struggling to sit up.

"Later." He handed her a glass of orange juice. "As terrible as this was, Norah, it's a major turning point for Madelyn. For so long she's felt completely worthless and punished herself for what she did to me."

Norah lifted the glass to her lips and sipped slowly. In the past few hours, Madelyn had made up for everything, she thought. She could never again have an unkind or jealous thought about the woman.

"Norah," he said softly when the tears again rained down her cheeks, "you're the one who thought of the swimming lessons, remember?"

Sniffing, she nodded. "And you gave your permission." She tried to smile.

"I'm having dinner with the McCallas, but Madelyn and I will stop by afterwards, Norah." He walked to the door. "I'll see you right before I leave."

Norah grasped the glass with both hands, but they were still trembling. Madelyn, not she, would help Thornton through his operation. But she mustn't think of herself. That kind of self-absorption had already proven to be disastrous.

～

They arrived shortly before seven. Norah and Aunt Tess were sitting in the parlor beneath the ceiling fan, drinking cool glasses of lemonade, when Thornton and Madelyn rushed in.

"I drove over here!" Madelyn reported excitedly. "It's the first time since the accident. I didn't think I would ever drive again, but Thornton said it was time." The adoring look she gave him chilled Norah's heart.

But she set her glass down and walked over to embrace Madelyn. "Of course you can. There isn't anything in the world you can't do now." Her voice caught and Madelyn smiled like an angel. "Thank you sounds so inadequate. . . ."

"You would have done the same," Madelyn said graciously.

"Yes," Norah agreed. "But I didn't. You did."

"I'm just glad I was there," Madelyn said, her face radiant. "May I see Camille before we leave?"

"Of course."

"I'll go up with you," said Aunt Tess and followed Madelyn toward the stairs.

"She's different," Norah told Thornton when the two women had left. "I think it's confidence."

She was also pretty sure it was love. But no matter what, Norah could no longer believe that Madelyn would not be good for Thornton. She was an extraordinary woman.

"Let's go into the library," Thornton said gently.

She turned to him in astonishment, but he was already walking toward the door. How could she face him in the room where he had kissed her? But then again, perhaps it was the most appropriate place for him to tell her of his love for another woman. If she cried, she could always blame it on her guilt over Camille's accident.

The drapes had been kept closed to block out the sun since there was still no relief from the heat. Thornton flipped a switch at the doorway, and the fan in the center of the high ceiling began to revolve. Norah was glad he hadn't turned on the light. It would be easier if the room remained dim and shadowy.

She sat down in the same chair she'd sat in that other night and held onto the arms. That was silly, she told herself, and put her hands in her lap. When a tornado strikes full force, there is really nothing much one can do. Why didn't he just go ahead and say he and Madelyn were going to be married?

Thornton stood behind the opposite chair and held onto the back, watching her carefully as he said, "After the surgery, Norah, Madelyn and I will be leaving for Paris."

He'd thought she might rage at him, condemn him for going away so soon after Camille's mishap, maybe even beg him to stay. But she made no demands, no accusation, no indication that it mattered. Regardless of his feelings, he had to do what seemed right. "If you want to leave. . .with Josh. . .I won't try to stop you." Her eyes flew to his, so he quickly added, "With Camille, of course. The two of you could make a good life for her. Josh is a good man. I've watched him. I'm convinced he would make a fine father."

Norah couldn't believe her ears. Something—the whirring of the fan or her medication—was making her senses whirl. She rubbed a hand across her forehead.

"Norah," he said with difficulty, "I mean it. You don't have to wait until the six months are up. I can't bring myself to separate you from the child you love like a mother, and I will not keep you from Josh if he's the man you love."

If she told him she didn't love Josh, would Thornton do the noble thing and not marry Madelyn? It seemed highly unlikely. And with Madelyn's act of selfless heroism, any idea of competing with her for Thornton's heart had been laid to rest forever.

"I can't believe this," Norah said, still unable to take it all in.

"Neither can I," he said. "At least I couldn't until the accident."

So that's when he had made his final decision, Norah thought, as he came around the chair and slumped into it. That's when he knew how much Madelyn meant to him. After all, she had almost died in that pool.

Thornton leaned forward, resting his forearms on his thighs, his head down, staring at the floor. "Norah, losing several people I've loved has taught me some hard lessons. We instinctively want to hold our loved ones close, guard them jealously. But the deepest kind of love means being willing to let them go, if it's for the best." He lifted his head and looked at her. "I want you to know that putting aside my own feelings in this is the hardest thing I've ever done." He glanced toward the doorway, and the light from the parlor glinted in his eyes, revealing the anguish in them.

Norah had to clasp her hands together to keep from reaching out, begging him not to do this wonderful, terrible thing. But she, too, could not listen to her own heart. If he and Madelyn could find happiness together, she mustn't interfere. Hot tears stained her face.

Thornton took another step. He seemed reluctant to go, his hand lingering on the curve of her chair back. "I'll set up a trust for Camille. We'll want to visit, of course, from time to time." Eternity passed before he could speak again. "Leave some pictures for me. . .of both of you."

She tried to speak but no words would come. All she could do was close her eyes and shake her head.

"I know it will take time for you to absorb this." She heard the starkness in his voice and her shoulders began to shake with her silent sobs. "Kiss Camille good-bye for me. I won't see her. I don't want her to sense this emptiness I already feel."

Norah sat there long after he had gone, oblivious to the whispered voices around her, the soft footsteps of people coming and going to check on her. At last she roused, her gaze falling upon the empty picture frame on the desk. It would be filled, and her heart would be empty. With an ache worse than the flu, she left the room.

~

On Wednesday morning, Norah strolled Camille along the sidewalk, speaking to neighbors and friendly strangers on the street. She went into

Thornton's silent church, regretting that she hadn't attended services there with him. "Show me the right thing to do," she prayed, and dreaded what the answer might be.

The hours she spent with Camille seemed more precious than ever. So did the house she'd been reluctant to move into. Now that she dreaded leaving, she must. Over and over, she kept reminding herself to think only of what was best for the child.

That evening, Thornton called. Norah didn't want to talk to him, so Aunt Tess took the call. "No," she said and turned away so Norah could not hear her whispered conversation. Suspecting that they were speaking about her, Norah left the room.

When she returned, Aunt Tess insisted on staying overnight. "The surgery was a long, drawn-out procedure," she reported, "but it was successful, Thornton says." She eyed Norah carefully before adding, "They'll leave for Paris tonight."

By Thursday, Norah knew she must get on with her life. There were options, she told herself. She could return to California and live with her parents until she finished school, then find a job.

And if she could believe Thornton, who had told her she was young and beautiful, she thought with a wry smile, she should be able to find a dozen men who'd fall in love with her. She could have children. Life wasn't over, she told herself, but the tears kept falling, like a southern rainstorm.

Or she might even go to North Carolina and take psychology under Josh Logan. He'd said he had a family who even took in stray cats. Josh was a friend. He could help. To a point. She could love him as a friend, but now that Thornton Winter had so invaded her life, her senses, her emotions, she knew there could never be another man who moved her so.

Maybe Thornton knew she loved him. Maybe he'd deliberately tried to influence her thinking by reminding her that when you truly love someone, you do what's best for them. Whatever his reasons, she would try and act upon what she felt was best for Camille.

Writing the letter was the hardest thing yet. "Dear Thornton," she began, then crumpled the page into a tight ball.

Taking a fresh sheet, she started over. She must forget the familiarity. She must think of him as Mr. Winter, the Southern gentleman who'd graciously taken her in, who could give Camille everything she would ever need, including his love. . .and a lovely, gentle woman for a mommy.

"But she can't love you like I do," Norah said aloud, feeling the suffocating grief. With an aching throat and hot, burning eyes, she wrote down all the things she wanted him to know, but had never dared to say. Then she threw the letter away. Some things were better left unsaid.

458

After playing with Camille for the last time, she scribbled a note:
Thornton,

I know you will take good care of Camille. If you need any papers signed, contact my parents. And please send me a picture or a note sometime. Tell her about her aunt, who will love her always. . . .

She paused, then rewrote the note, striking out the last sentence. She'd have to trust Thornton and Madelyn to tell Camille about her in their own way. She wrote a few more lines, almost adding, "Be happy," but that seemed redundant. Instead, she wrote, "God bless you all," and signed her name, "Norah Browne."

Norah called Aunt Tess, who came right over after hearing the distress in her voice. Her bags were already in the Mercedes. "I'm leaving," she said as soon as Aunt Tess stepped inside.

"Now?" Aunt Tess asked, a puzzled look on her face. "Thornton said you and Josh would be taking Camille before he returns, but I didn't know it would be this soon. I'm so sorry it had to be this way, Dear, but I understand and hope you'll bring her back to see us often."

"I'm not going with Josh, and I'm not taking Camille, Aunt Tess. I'm leaving her for Thornton and Madelyn." At Aunt Tess's bewildered look, the tears Norah had tried to suppress spilled over.

"Does Thornton know?" At the shake of Norah's head, Tess was alarmed. "Oh, Honey," she begged, "do wait till he comes back."

"I can't," Norah sobbed brokenly. "The baby's sleeping now. But if she wakes up and sees me. . .I might not be able to go through with this."

Tess patted her shoulder. "Don't worry about a thing. We'll take good care of her. But oh, how we'll miss you, my dear!"

With that, Norah fell into Aunt Tess' arms and sobbed out her pain. Then stumbling down the steps, she climbed into the car and drove away.

Tess stood watching until the Mercedes had disappeared around a corner. "I don't understand," she said, not comprehending. Then, as the truth dawned, her face lit up. "Of course I do!"

～

An hour later, Norah arrived at the dock. Henry was bending over the engine of her Rabbit with a screwdriver in his oily hand.

"Don't know what's the matter with it," he said, unwinding his tall frame and scratching his head. "Can't get it started. I've been trying to keep all the cars running, but when one of them sits here for weeks. . ."

"Let me try," she said. "It's been temperamental for years, but I thought it was fixed."

She got in and turned the ignition key, but the maneuvers she'd tried in the past failed to start the engine.

"Maybe I could jump-start it. I'll need a special kind of cable, though. I'll run home and see if I can find it. I can call you down at the house when it's ready."

She drove to the beach house to wait for Henry's call. Eloise was there. Thirty minutes later, Chris arrived.

"What are you doing here?" she asked.

"Well," he began, but before he could finish, in came Aunt Tess with Camille.

"What's going on?" she asked, bewildered.

"I talked to Thornton," Aunt Tess said. "He said to tell you not to do anything foolish, because you're not going anywhere—with or without this baby."

"Wh–what. . .did he mean?" she stammered.

"I don't know. He didn't have time to talk but said he'd be here just as soon as possible."

Norah wondered if Madelyn would be coming with him. Of course she would. She was his wife, wasn't she? Or soon would be.

⁓

Dark clouds started rolling in the following morning, and the wind picked up, bringing some relief from the blistering heat. A storm seemed imminent, a common occurrence for the last of July, Aunt Tess said, a prelude to the hurricane season when it wouldn't be sensible to stay at the beach house.

Thornton called from the airport to say he was on his way, so Eloise started supper. Norah knew she wouldn't be able to eat a bite. To help pass the time, the family engaged her in trivial conversation. The next call was from the dock. He was only minutes away.

Norah walked over to the sliding glass doors, standing like a statue, trying to convince herself that it was not her heart that was pounding so loudly, but thunder. The darkness that had enveloped the world outside those doors was but a foreshadowing of what she must endure when she'd see Madelyn hanging on his arm.

She remembered something Josh had said. When all else fails, try the Prayer of Serenity. Well, she was helpless to change the situation. She must accept it. And she had prayed for God's will to be done, not her own. Now she had to put herself aside and recommit herself to Camille's best interests. It was not best to divide that child nor to drag her through endless court battles if she could have two loving parents. If ever she had needed strength beyond her own, Norah thought, it was now.

The deck lights hadn't yet been turned on, and the sky had darkened to black. The glass doors mirrored the little group inside—Eloise puttering in the kitchen, Aunt Tess sitting on a bar stool, talking to Norah, Chris playing with Camille on a quilt in the middle of the floor.

Suddenly, the door slid aside, and Thornton burst into the room, apparently blown there by the wind that lifted his black curls above the silver at his temples. A small bandage covered the area next to his eye, but the skin was no longer taut. The eye was normal—beautiful, black, gleaming, fixed on Norah. Maybe Madelyn wouldn't cry now when she looked at him.

The scar that zigzagged down his cheek deepened in color and Norah knew he was upset with her. Why? Did he feel he had to return from a rendezvous with Madelyn—their honeymoon?—in order to take care of the baby? And where was Madelyn? Had he let her out at the front so she could come through the house?

Thornton didn't wait for Norah to comment on his face. He would be more acceptable to some people now, but he knew it had never mattered to her. Aunt Tess had read him the note Norah had pinned to her pillow. The note had stated that she was not leaving with Josh and that she would not be taking Camille. What could that mean? If she didn't love Josh, then—

Camille cried out as Thornton closed the door behind him. He hurried over to her, concerned.

"I think she wants to go swimming," Chris said, laughing. "When you came in and the wind hit her face, she held her breath."

Norah watched as Thornton picked up the baby, held her close in his arms, rocking her until she quieted while the rest of the family gathered around to comment on his surgery.

"Is Madelyn all right?" Aunt Tess asked, echoing Norah's unspoken question.

"I think she's finally convinced that she doesn't owe me her life, that she should forget the past and make a new start," Thornton said. "She had just begun to do that in Paris, before she returned here to all the memories." He paused. "That now leaves me free to make something permanent out of all this 'temporary' situation with a beautiful green-eyed redhead."

Norah's eyes met his over Camille's head, and her heart stopped. So Aunt Tess had told him about the note. "But Camille's eyes are blue," she said foolishly.

"Exactly," he said and handed the baby to Aunt Tess, who said she thought it would be a good idea if they were to check the house and make sure all the windows were closed. Eloise muttered something about supper being ruined, but better that than a couple of lives, and she left to tend to something on the stove. Chris grinned at his brother and followed the others down the hallway, pulling the string of the talking Mickey Mouse.

The wind whistled and rattled the glass doors, while the thunder clapped. Lightning flashed, revealing billowing dark clouds against a silver background.

Too long, Thornton thought, he'd been like an ocean wave, bravely approaching the shore, then losing power and timidly retreating back into the sea. He wouldn't make that mistake again. He would reach out for what he wanted so much.

In one long stride, he was facing Norah, no longer trying to hide anything from her. It was time for complete honesty. "Do you love Josh?" He had to hear it for himself.

"Only as a friend," she murmured.

"Then why do you want to leave me?" He just couldn't understand her.

"Oh, I'd never leave you if I thought you wanted me to stay. I thought you and Madelyn would be married by now. And I couldn't possibly live in the house with you and. . .a wife because. . ."

"Because?" he asked softly. Warmth and expectation sparked his eyes.

"Because I love you," she said simply. "And don't tell me not to! And this is what I think of your new face."

She moved nearer and drew his head down to hers. She kissed his scarred cheek as she had done that other night. But it was not the wound on his face she had touched and healed over the past months. It was his heart.

He felt like the seagull that had spread its wings and taken flight. "Norah," he whispered, "you began to change my life from the first moment I met you. But I'd rather give you up than have you stay with me out of a sense of obligation to Camille."

His arms came around her. The green glow of her eyes was as soft as her lips as she asked wistfully, "You love me, Thornton?"

"More than I ever thought possible. It seemed too wonderful to believe, too unreasonable, that you might love me too. I even started sketches of the kind of home you might like. You've created a storm in my life, Norah—powerful and beautiful and cleansing. I feel alive again."

"Oh, Thornton," she breathed, "I've felt so desolate, thinking I would lose both you and Camille."

He held her close. "That was your last chance, Norah. You'll never get away from me now. I want to marry you and fight with you every day for the rest of our lives."

She drew back and cocked her head. "Fight?"

He grinned. "Don't you always do the opposite of whatever I say?"

Her love for him shone through the green gaze. "I'd much rather make up."

"Delighted to oblige." He bent over her lips in a lingering kiss of promise and commitment. "It's the only gentlemanly thing to do."

A Letter to Our Readers

Dear Readers:

In order that we might better contribute to your reading enjoyment, we would appreciate your taking a few minutes to respond to the following questions. When completed, please return to the following: Fiction Editor, Barbour Publishing, Inc., P.O. Box 719, Uhrichsville, OH 44683.

1. Did you enjoy reading *South Carolina?*
   - ❑ Very much. I would like to see more books like this.
   - ❑ Moderately—I would have enjoyed it more if _____
   _____
   _____

2. What influenced your decision to purchase this book? (Check those that apply.)
   - ❑ Cover
   - ❑ Back cover copy
   - ❑ Title
   - ❑ Price
   - ❑ Friends
   - ❑ Publicity
   - ❑ Other

3. Which story was your favorite?
   - ❑ *After the Storm*
   - ❑ *Somewhere a Rainbow*
   - ❑ *Catch of a Lifetime*
   - ❑ *Southern Gentleman*

4. Please check your age range:
   - ❑ Under 18
   - ❑ 18–24
   - ❑ 25–34
   - ❑ 35–45
   - ❑ 46–55
   - ❑ Over 55

5. How many hours per week do you read? _____

Name _____

Occupation _____

Address _____

City _____ State _____ ZIP _____

$\mathcal{H}$EARTSONG ❤ PRESENTS

Love Stories
Are Rated G!

That's for godly, gratifying, and, of course, great! If you love a thrilling love story but don't appreciate the sordidness of some popular paperback romances, **Heartsong Presents** is for you. In fact, **Heartsong Presents** is the only inspirational romance book club featuring love stories where Christian faith is the primary ingredient in a marriage relationship.

Sign up today to receive your first set of four never-before-published Christian romances. Send no money now; you will receive a bill with the first shipment. You may cancel at any time without obligation, and if you aren't completely satisfied with any selection, you may return the books for an immediate refund!

Imagine. . .four new romances every four weeks—two historical, two contemporary—with men and women like you who long to meet the one God has chosen as the love of their lives. . .all for the low price of $9.97 postpaid.

To join, simply complete the coupon below and mail to the address provided. **Heartsong Presents** romances are rated G for another reason: They'll arrive Godspeed!

YES! Sign me up for Heart❤ng!

NEW MEMBERSHIPS WILL BE SHIPPED IMMEDIATELY!
Send no money now. We'll bill you only $9.97 postpaid with your first shipment of four books. Or for faster action, call toll free 1-800-847-8270.

NAME _____

ADDRESS _____

CITY _____ STATE _____ ZIP _____

MAIL TO: HEARTSONG PRESENTS, P.O. Box 719, Uhrichsville, Ohio 44683